Penguin Books
A Dark and Distant Shore

Reay Tannahill was born and brought up in Scotland, and is a graduate of
the University of Glasgow. She is the author of *Food in History* and *Sex in
History*, best-selling works of non-fiction which have been translated into
seven languages, and of two Regency detective stories written under a
pseudonym. *A Dark and Distant Shore*, her first major novel, is set in the
Highland landscape – still curiously isolated even in the last quarter of the
twentieth century – where she lived from 1974 until 1982, before moving to
Somerset.

Reay Tannahill

A Dark and Distant Shore

Penguin Books

Penguin Books Ltd, Harmondsworth, Middlesex, England
Penguin Books, 40 West 23rd Street, New York, New York 10010, U.S.A.
Penguin Books Australia Ltd, Ringwood, Victoria, Australia
Penguin Books Canada Ltd, 2801 John Street, Markham, Ontario, Canada L3R 1B4
Penguin Books (N.Z.) Ltd, 182–190 Wairau Road, Auckland 10, New Zealand

First published by Century Publishing Co. Ltd 1983
Published in Penguin Books 1984
Reprinted 1984 (twice)

Printed and bound in Great Britain by
Cox & Wyman Ltd, Reading

Set in 9/11pt Linotron Goudy by
Rowland Phototypesetting Ltd, Bury St Edmunds, Suffolk

For
Josephine and Norman Harris
with affection

Contents

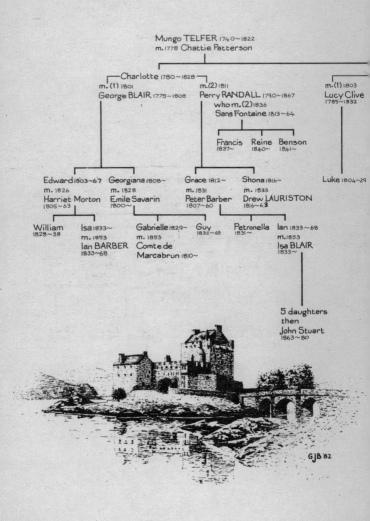

Mungo TELFER 1740~1822
m.1778 Chattie Patterson

Charlotte 1780~1828
m.(1) 1801
George BLAIR 1775~1808

m.(2) 1811
Perry RANDALL 1790~1867
who m.(2) 1836
Sara Fontaine 1813~64

Francis 1837~   Reine 1840~   Benson 1841~

m.(1) 1803
Lucy Clive 1785~1832

Edward 1803~67
m.1826
Harriet Morton 1805~63

Georgiana 1808~
m.1828
Emile Savarin 1800~

Grace 1812~
m.1831
Peter Barber 1807~60

Shona 1816~
m.1833
Drew LAURISTON 1816~63

Luke 1804~29

William 1828~38

Isa 1833~
m.1853
Ian BARBER 1833~68

Gabrielle 1829~
m.1853
Comte de Marcabrun 1810~

Guy 1832~68

Petronella 1831~

Ian 1833~68
m.1853
Isa BLAIR 1833~

5 daughters
then
John Stuart
1863~80

GJB '82

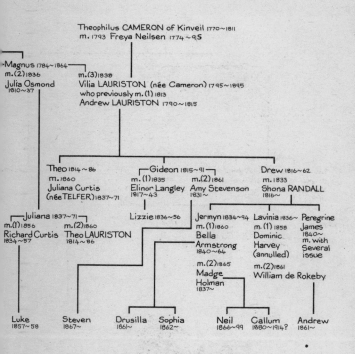

Family tree of the
TELFERS and LAURISTONS
Blairs; Randalls; Savarins and Barbers

Prologue 1803

1

When Mungo Telfer saw Kinveil for the first time, it was a brilliant day in the early summer of 1803, crisp and fresh and new-minted, with neat white clouds chasing one another from west to east across a blue, blue sky.

Even the sardonic private voice that, for all the sixty years of Mungo's life had held his imagination in commonsensical check, fell silent – for there, a thousand feet below the summit on which he sat, saddle sore and more than a little weary, was his heart's dream translated into reality. Floating above its image in the blue and silver sea lay a sturdy island castle, proud and solitary against a background of mountains that, at this season of the year, were draped majestically in velvet, in every conceivable tone of green and purple and indigo. Mungo sat and looked, the reins loose in his hands, and could have wept with happiness.

He was a small, tough man with pale eyes, a nose that sprang from his forehead like the prow of a ship, and a chin that had become alarmingly firm and not a little pugnacious during the years that had transformed him from a penniless Glasgow urchin into one of the great merchant venturers of his day. Though still plain 'Mister Telfer', he was recognized in his native city and far beyond as one of that acute, hard-headed, obstinate, and extremely rich body of men known, because of their trade with Virginia, as the Tobacco Lords. But hard-headed or not – and, as he wryly admitted, against all the laws of probability – he had contrived to cling to his own special, sentimental vision of the land that bore him. Other great merchants might be ambitious of becoming civic dignitaries, or cultural pillars of the

Sacred Music Institution or the Hodge Podge Club, or sleek country gentlemen with an interest in the new agriculture. But not Mungo Telfer. He knew what he wanted, what he had always wanted. A home steeped in five hundred years of Highland history, a castle set amid the most romantically picturesque scenery in the world. And now he was going to have it. There was no question in Mungo's mind. Whatever it cost him, he was going to have Kinveil.

His son Magnus drew rein beside him. Magnus was nineteen years old, tall, handsome, and indolent – and who he had inherited his indolence from Mungo couldn't imagine. Certainly not from him. Mungo glowered at the boy as he cast a dispassionate gaze over the magnificent panorama spread out before them and drawled, 'Devilish isolated, isn't it!'

George Blair, Mungo's son-in-law and another trial to him, was still plodding phlegmatically up the slope behind. Mungo closed his eyes for a moment, and then, opening them, exclaimed, 'Well, come on, then! Are you not in a hurry for the fine lunch the laird has waiting for us?'

The laird came as something of a surprise to Mungo, for although George Blair lived only forty miles away and was a great one for facts and figures, he was decidedly weak on insights. All he had said about Kinveil's present owner was, 'Foreign kind of fellow, head over heels in debt. His father was exiled for years after the 'Forty-five rebellion, and the present man was raised abroad somewhere.' Mungo had deduced that he shouldn't expect a tartan savage, but he had not expected quite such a cosmopolitan gentleman as Mr Theophilus Cameron turned out to be, tall, slender, elegant, and not much above thirty.

It didn't matter, of course. There wasn't a trick of the huckstering trade that Mungo didn't know, and he soon discovered that Mr Cameron had only one of them up his slightly frayed sleeve. While it seemed that he was resigned to parting with his ancestral acres, he wasn't going to swallow his *noblesse oblige* and part with them to a social inferior unless the price was very right indeed. Subtly, it was conveyed that Mr Cameron, whose pedigree stretched back into the mists of time, knew that Mr Telfer's pedigree didn't stretch anywhere at all.

Except to the bank in Glasgow.

With amusement, and quite without resentment, Mungo noted the laird's dilatory arrival at the water gate to welcome his visitors. And the lunch consisted of smoked salmon, the everyday fare of the glens, instead of fresh; salty butter that wasn't far off rancid; oatmeal bannocks that would have been the better for warming through; no French wines, but a fair whisky. Though even that was served neat instead of in the genteel form of whisky bitters. Afterwards, the condescension became more obvious. The laird summoned a groom to show Magnus and George the Home Farm, and rang for his steward to escort the prospective buyer round the castle itself.

No one had tried to put Mungo in his place for many a long day, and he rather enjoyed it. Cheerfully, he looked forward to a good, satisfying haggle.

2

What threw Mungo quite out in his reckoning was the seven-year-old daughter of the house, a waist-high bundle of fair-haired, green-eyed animosity.

They met on the open stairs leading from the central courtyard up to the sea wall.

Mungo wasn't very good at children. He beamed at her in an avuncular kind of way, and said, 'Hullo, lassie.'

The lassie, pinafored, shawled and bonneted like some old henwife, fixed him with a sizzling glare and said in a light, tight voice, 'Are you the man who wants to buy Kinveil?' There was no accent, apart from a hint of sibilance on the 's'.

'Aye.'

'Why?'

He was disconcerted. 'I like it here.'

'So do I.' Her chin came up belligerently.

Mungo stared back at her and, after a moment, tried again. 'But surely you'd like to see some big cities for a change? Glasgow, maybe. Or London.'

'No. I like it *here*.' Her lips quivered a little. 'I *love* it here.'

He took her hand and patted it, feeling the resistance. 'But that's because you don't know anywhere else,' he said reasonably. 'Just think! You might even see the king and queen.' On reflection, George III and his starchy consort were hardly such stuff as childish dreams were made

13

on. 'Beau Brummell,' he volunteered more hopefully. 'And the Prince of Wales.'

'Prince of *Whales!*' she exclaimed scornfully. 'I don't wish to be acquainted with such people.'

He gave up. 'Never mind. I'm sure your da will take you somewhere fine.'

There was calculation, he thought, in the clear green eyes. 'There's nowhere as fine as here. Come, let me show you.'

Obediently, he allowed himself to be led up to the battlements. The wall was crumbling, he noticed, and wondered what it was going to cost him to have it repaired.

His eyes followed her pointing finger.

'Look out there to the west. That's the island of Skye.' She pointed again. 'And those mountains in the south are the Five Sisters. And over there . . . Oh, look! There's a herring gull dropping a mussel on the rocks to break the shell.' She leaned over the parapet. 'And look down below here. There's a . . .'

He sensed the violent, seven-year-old push before he felt it, and was braced. His grip on the parapet scarcely even shifted.

He hesitated for a moment, and then turned to confront her. She was breathing fast, and her cheeks were pink with a combination of rage and fear.

The steward scuttled up the stairs towards them, his mouth and eyes round with horror. 'Miss Vilia! Miss Vilia!'

Mungo said conversationally, 'That's a bonny name. Is it Highland?'

The child swallowed. 'Norwegian.'

'Oh, aye?' He shook his head at her kindly. 'That's not the way, you know. You're too wee, and I'm too heavy.' He touched a finger lightly to her brow. 'You'll have to use your head to get what you want. But you'll learn. You're a spunky wee thing.' A smile tugged at the corner of his mouth, and he held out his hand. 'Pax?'

And that was a silly question, he thought. She'd not know what it meant.

She did. Hands behind her back, she gave him a wide, green, empty stare, and then turned and ran down the stone staircase. He was not to see her again for nine years – except once, from a distance.

When the steward, still mouthing profuse and incoherent apologies, took him back to Mr Cameron, who was waiting in the Long Gallery, Mungo settled for £10,000 more than he had intended to pay.

3

After seeing his visitors off at the water gate next morning, Theo Cameron returned to his study to find his daughter waiting for him. Once, when she was four years old, he had said to her, 'I do not care to see you looking like some tinker's brat. Oblige me by dressing in a more ladylike fashion.' So now, when she knew she was likely to see him, she did. Personally, she thought her one 'good' dress quite horrid. It was of crêpe, in a dusty pink colour with a flounced shoulder cape and dark blue ribbon trim, and no improvement at all on her usual homespun. But today she had more important things on her mind than her nurse's hopeless eye for colour.

Not until yesterday morning had she heard as much as a hint of her father's plan to sell Kinveil, and it hadn't been he who told her, but Meg Macleod, the nurse who had mothered her since she was born. The servants had known for weeks, as servants always did.

When he came through the door, not expecting to find her there, the breath fled from her lungs. He looked like a cat who had been at the cream. She knew with certainty that the unthinkable had happened.

The quality of his smile changed at the sight of her. 'Good morning, *ma petite*,' he said, as if this were just an ordinary day. 'To what do I owe this pleasure?'

She gulped. 'Please, papa. I wanted to know . . .' She was not very well acquainted with her father who, like the majority of civilized people, considered that the place for children was in the nursery, not the drawing-room. But he was seldom less than charming to her, and she had always assumed, without really giving the matter much thought, that he was fond of her and interested in her welfare. Now, she knew that she had been dreadfully wrong. The words came out in a rush. 'I *have* to know! You haven't sold Kinveil, have you? You haven't *really* sold it?'

He looked at her in a kind and sympathetic way, and she told herself, 'I am not going to be sick. I am *not*!'

'Come and sit over here.' When she had obeyed, he stood looking down at her, his hands loosely linked before him. 'Yes. I fear so, little one. The man who has just left, Mr Telfer, made me a very fair offer, and I agreed. I know you must be upset and, believe me, I am truly sorry. But I have come to the end here. I have reached the stage where I cannot go on any longer.'

I, I, I! she thought, her heart rising to choke her. What about *me*? 'You mean you don't *want* to go on any longer,' she blurted out. 'You don't love Kinveil at all, you hate it!'

'*That will do*, Vilia!' It came out, as it so often did when he wasn't thinking, as 'Veelia', for although he tried hard and in general successfully not to let it show, Theophilus Cameron spoke French more readily than English, and had visited the land of his fathers only once in his life before he had inherited Kinveil in 1794. Nine years had passed since then, nine years that had cost him his wife, his peace of mind, and almost every guinea he possessed. There was nothing he wanted more in the world than to turn his back on the place, and he found it ironic that the child who so passionately wanted to stay should be the living image of her mother, the only human being he had ever loved, the exquisite Nordic girl who had deployed all her considerable powers of persuasion and all her charm to make him do what he didn't want to do – return to Kinveil and take up his heritage. His own well-developed instinct for self-preservation had recommended him to sell, sell, sell! But he had given in to her and within eighteen months she was dead. Kinveil had killed her. She had been brought to bed with the child, and the nearest doctor had been fifty miles away, and winter that year had set in early and viciously. By the time the doctor arrived, smelling powerfully of whisky, Freya had been beyond his help. Theo Cameron still found it strange that he could look at Freya's daughter and feel nothing for her at all, not even hatred; he was too civilized for that. Only Freya had ever mattered to him. He had thought, more than once, how much better it would have been if he, not she, had died.

With an effort, he said, 'You must learn that what one wants, and what one may have, are not always the same thing.' Turning, looking out at the beautiful, blue, useless water, he went on, talking more to himself than the child. 'I have no resources at all. Kinveil has swallowed everything. The land and the people are a constant drain on my purse and I have no way of refilling it. If I could send timber, or venison, or kelp, or fish to the south to sell, things might be different, but as long as the roads are only bridle tracks, and as long as the sea passage depends on winds that are always in the wrong quarter, there is no profit to be made.' Rationally, he was acknowledging defeat.

Defeat, however, was something the child did not understand and could not accept. 'But, papa!' she cried. 'Real roads, proper roads, are coming, you *know* they are! The government's going to build them.' That was something else she hadn't known until yesterday. 'Surely we can last until then?'

With faint amusement on his face, he said, 'My dear child, what on earth do you know about the parliamentary roads?'

It was lucky he didn't wait for an answer, since she was by no means sure of her facts; the trouble about eavesdropping was that you couldn't ask about things you didn't understand.

'No,' he said. 'Even if the roads and canals were to be finished next year, instead of scarcely even started, it would still be too late. There has not been an April since I came here when I have not had to buy in whole cargoes of oatmeal to tide our people over the last of the winter. I have neither the cash nor the credit to do it even once more. It has come to the stage when even the *petit bourgeois* shopkeepers of Inverness will not send anything more to Kinveil until I settle what I owe them.' His lips curled at the stubborn resistance on his daughter's face. 'It is no use, my child. The people of the estate will be better off under the rich, worthy, low-born Mr Telfer than under their heredit-ary chief. It's the end of an old song.'

The end of an old song. The phrase that was always used to lament the passing of some ancient tradition. There had been Camerons at Kinveil for almost five hundred years. And now – no more.

Temporarily, Vilia was silenced. Then, after a moment, her father said with a smile of the purest amusement, 'And confess, my child! You cannot really have enjoyed living on nothing but oatmeal, and milk, and kail?'

'We have boiled mutton or pickled fish once a week,' she replied defensively.

He laughed, and with a great sigh of pleasure leaned back and stretched his arms wide above his head. 'Boiled mutton!' he repeated. 'Boiled mutton? Never again, *ma petite*. Never – ever – again!'

4

Never again. Never – ever – again. It was a refrain that haunted Vilia, waking and sleeping, for the few months that remained to her at Kinveil.

She had never, in her short life, known what it was to be really hurt, and the scale of her misery was greater than she was equipped to deal with. The days passed, and the weeks, and it was as if all her faculties were whirling in a vortex, so that she felt dizzy inside, and the only stable things were those from which she was about to be sundered.

Never again to wake in the nursery at the top of the old watchtower, with its four windows looking out to the four points of the compass, its scrubbed pine floor, its rafters black as ebony and glossy as the finest varnish from centuries of peat smoke. Never again to scramble from her own hard crib into Meg's cosy hole-in-the-wall bed, with its warm knobbly mattress stuffed with heather and chaff and felted wool, only to be dragged out again, laughing and struggling, and sponged down with icy water and tumbled into her clothes. Never to scamper down to the vaulted stone kitchen for her bowl of porridge, scalding hot and sprinkled with crunchy flakes of salt, with the cup of cool milk standing beside it so that she could dip each horn spoonful of oatmeal into it before she ate.

Never again . . . Vilia's Kinveil was not the Kinveil of her father, who had betrayed her so suddenly and shockingly. He was the laird, aloof and authoritarian, and she was only a child, if a special one. She was involved in everything, and treated, like all the children in the glen, very much as if she were a puppy. Under Meg's indulgent eye she scrambled in and out of trouble as she pleased, and Meg was always there to comfort her, and scold her, and send her off to fall into trouble all over again. Vilia knew far more about the estate and its people than her father, and because their life revolved round the progress of the seasons, there was not a moment in those last months of 1803 when she was not reminded that, next year, all the same things would be going on again – without her.

In July she went out with Archie Campbell and his son Ewen to set the lobster pots, and as she helped drop them over the side of the boat, their wickerwork seemed to creak at her, 'Never again.' In August, the women and girls came back from the shielings, the high pastures to

18

which most of them migrated every summer with the cattle and sheep and goats. Their return took the form of a great procession, with dishes, coggs, churns, blankets, butter kegs and cheeses loaded on to the crude, birch-trunk sledges that were the only form of transport in the roadless glens, and the oldest women with their spinning wheels perched on top. The uproar was indescribable, with cows mooing, sheep meh-heh-heh-ing, dogs barking, and the goats letting loose with the peculiar, gargling shriek that had more than once startled castle visitors into thinking someone was being murdered. Vilia loved the little parti-coloured sheep – the 'little, old sheep', as they were called – with their four horns and pink noses and round, surprised eyes. 'Never again,' they bleated at her as she stroked their fine, thin fleece.

She heard the same refrain in September, when Meg took her up to the top of Carn Beg to' watch the cattle swimming across, in their hundreds, from Skye to the mainland, on the first stage of their journey to the market at Falkirk, two hundred miles away to the south-east. And in October, when she helped with the reaping, she was near to hysterical tears when it looked as if she were going to be the one to cut the last sheaf, an act of dreadful ill omen.

In November, for the last time, she helped to bait the long, many-hooked lines that would catch white fish for salting and drying. In November, too, with cold wet gusts of wind, sharp with the smell of the sea, flaying through their bonnets and shawls and boots, she and Meg went for the last time to paddle through the bogs in search of buried pine knots for making into candles.

And in November, straight-backed, dry-eyed, and withdrawn, she said good-bye to everyone and everything.

They took the track south round the end of the loch, instead of rowing across, because two hundred of the men from the estate were escorting them ceremonially to Fort Augustus, where the road began and carriages and servants from the south were waiting. The cavalcade also included fifty ponies, harnessed with bog-fir ropes to sledges laden with family portraits, silver, and books, the only things from Kinveil that Theo Cameron ever wanted to see again.

The sledges smelled strongly of peats and fish, and when the clouds lifted and a watery sun came out, the ponies began to steam, and so did the sheepskins the men wore slung over their shoulders. An unmistakable miasma of mutton fat drifted over the canvas-wrapped baggage, which had been smeared with tallow to protect it against the elements.

'Phew!' said the erstwhile laird of Kinveil to his daughter. 'Take care not to breathe in, *ma petite*! I think, on the whole, that we might be forgiven for riding on ahead of this very pungent escort of ours!'

It was not slowly, therefore, but at a canter that Vilia Cameron rode away from Kinveil. It helped, a bit, for she had made up her mind that, whatever happened, she would not look back.

5

From the summit of Carn Beg, Mungo Telfer watched the long, ragged procession make its way along the shore until it disappeared at last into the defile between the mountains. He had made sure that his own ponies were tethered below the skyline, and had found himself a vantage point among some rocks where he was unlikely to be seen from the other side of the loch. He was desperately anxious that the child shouldn't think he had come to gloat.

But he hadn't been able to stay away. Kinveil would not become his, legally, until the first day of January 1804, though on any other basis today was the day on which the reign of the Camerons of Kinveil ended, and the reign of the Telfers of Kinveil began. It should have been the happiest day of his life, the crowning point of his long, distinguished, self-made career. Yet somehow it wasn't.

He knew very well that, if he hadn't bought the place, someone else would – someone who would certainly have paid less for it. Absently, he wondered how much of his £60,000 had gone on settling Cameron's debts, and hoped – without any great conviction – that it hadn't been *too* much. He knew Cameron had leased an expensive house in London, and the man had struck him as one of those over-bred, over-civilized fellows who felt they owed it to their position to live beyond their means, whatever those means might be. It wasn't an attitude Mungo had ever been able to understand. But in spite of everything he sat there feeling guilty.

Conscious of a movement beside him, he turned to find George Blair pointing his double Joe Manton at a great bird gliding smoothly, insolently, above them in the pale sky. It was one of the most beautiful things Mungo had ever seen, powerful and predatory and hooded with gold in the thin November sun.

'What is it?' he gasped.

'Vermin. Golden eagle. Don't know if I can reach it at this range, but it's worth a try.' The stolid, unimaginative finger tightened on the button.

With a sweep of his forearm, heedless of the danger, Mungo struck the barrels down.

'Not on *my* land,' he said.

Part One   *1811–1816*

Chapter One

1

Vilia had been sitting for more than an hour, pale, attentive, and monosyllabic, wishing that Mr Pilcher would come to the point. But it was beginning to seem as if he never would, and she wondered a little desperately if there were something in the rules that forbade a lawyer to say plainly what he meant. She had no experience of people like Mr Pilcher. Even his looks were non-committal – he was middle-aged, middle-sized, middle-coloured, middle-everything. It was as if even his Maker had been sitting on the fence when He created him.

'Perhaps a trifle improvident . . . but a natural reaction on being relieved of financial care . . . though only temporarily, alas . . . One would have recommended investment . . . drain on capital . . . last year's economic crisis . . . desirability of retrenchment . . .'

'Yes,' Vilia said.

'On the other hand . . .' It seemed to be one of Mr Pilcher's favourite expressions. 'Your late father could scarcely have been expected to anticipate that his – er – demise would be – er – quite so untimely.'

'No,' Vilia agreed.

'One begged him, most earnestly, to permit one to review his affairs with the object of setting them in order, but for one reason or another the moment was never opportune, and Mr Cameron, being by nature – er – sanguine, was persuaded that the question was of no great urgency. He had every hope of being able to bring himself about. But Providence, alas, decreed otherwise.' It was clear that Providence had slipped up badly.

'Yes,' Vilia said.

The lawyer placed his fingertips together and surveyed them appraisingly. 'The task of discovering the full extent of your lamented parent's obligations has been no light one. Indeed, it has presented problems of some complexity. But I believe one might sum up by saying that the state of his affairs has proved to be . . .' Vilia waited, holding her breath, while Mr Pilcher tasted his next word to make sure it wasn't poisonous. '. . . unfortunate,' he concluded.

Curbing a powerful desire to throw something at him, Vilia rose to her feet and moved to one of the tall windows overlooking Brook Street, busy as always at this time of day with bright yellow curricles, bottle green phaetons, and mulberry red barouches making their fashionable way to or from Bond Street or the Park. After eight years, the London scene was as familiar to her as her own reflection in the glass. Her mind elsewhere, she watched old Lady Watermere's landau draw up outside the house opposite, and saw her ladyship being helped solicitously up the front steps by the usual bevy of daughters and granddaughters. Three doors along, the Honourable James Prendergast emerged for his afternoon constitutional, the quarter-mile stroll that took him from home to the card room of his club. Vilia craned her neck to see who he was bowing to. The Misses Norwood, as she might have guessed, mincing along – rather young and very self-conscious – as if the October wind were only a June breeze. Vilia was reminded of her own first winter in London, when the peevish woman her father had employed to look after her had taken her, every day, for a half-hour's well-bred saunter along hard gravel paths. It had been listed in her schoolroom timetable as 'Fresh Air And Exercise'. For many long months, Vilia had wept herself to sleep for the loss of her dear Meg Macleod and all the scampering freedom of the past. Sometimes, weakly, she still did, although she was almost sixteen now and should have grown out of it.

She turned back into the drawing-room, with its Cameron family portraits staring down their collective noses at the hired furniture, and scowled at Mr Pilcher. He had risen to his feet when she did, and she thought she detected the merest trace of martyrdom in his expression. It annoyed her. Also, she was tired of behaving like a demure little miss with no more brain than a pea-goose. She was almost grown up, and had been virtually managing the house in Brook Street ever since the day, eighteen months before, when she had discovered that the butler was emptying almost as many brandy decanters as his master.

Politely, she said, 'I am not sure that I understand you, Mr Pilcher. What precisely do you mean by "unfortunate"? Did my father make no financial provision for me? Must I starve, or will the exchequer run to bread and cheese?'

With satisfaction she saw the half-closed lids fly open. For a moment, he looked almost human.

Gesticulating vaguely with the wad of papers in his hand, he said, 'Uhhh! My dear Miss Cameron! One trusts one has not conveyed the impression that you will be reduced to such – er – dire straits. Dear me, no. The situation is not as unfortunate as that.' He blinked. 'On the other hand . . .'

She sat down with a thud and fixed her eyes on him, luminous and darkly green above the uncompromising black gown. Maliciously, she refrained from waving him back to his chair and waited to see whether he would resume it of his own accord.

He didn't. After a moment, he said, 'Er, yes. That is to say, no. But one has to accept that, considering the state of your late father's affairs, one can see no alternative.'

She said tartly, 'No alternative to *what*?'

There was a twitter of remonstrance from her governess, present in the role of chaperone, but Vilia ignored it. She knew she was behaving badly, and she didn't care; in fact, she was enjoying it. For six months Mr Pilcher had been adding and subtracting and calculating and contriving, and never once had he deigned to tell her how he was getting on. If she had not insisted, he would not even have been here today, reluctantly revealing – or failing to reveal – what Fate had in store for her. Simmering, she reflected that he probably thought fifteen-year-old orphaned schoolgirls should wait meekly until it suited their trustees to enlighten them. And that they should then do, without question or comment, what the pompous old idiots told them to. If so, he was in for a shock.

She glowered at him again.

Astonishingly, he gave a snort, and then readjusted his features into what she took to be a smile. It didn't make him look any less like a walking Law Report; just like a dog-eared one.

'May I sit down?'

She surveyed him doubtfully and then, in a voice that sounded hollow in her own ears, said, 'Please do.'

'Thank you.' He was still smiling. 'You must forgive me, Miss Cameron. Your self-possession is such that I had forgotten what a very young lady you are. I am sure that, while I have been prosing on forever about your father's affairs, you are far more anxious to know what arrangements I have been able to make for your own future.'

As an olive branch, it left something to be desired, especially the 'very young' bit. Austerely, Vilia said, 'Not at all. I am grateful to you for having told me so much. It has all been extremely interesting. On the other hand . . .' It was out before she realized, and suddenly, irresistibly, she began to giggle.

He didn't see the joke at first, but then he said, a little stiffly, 'One finds it a most useful phrase, and I believe it to be preferable to some. I have, in fact, a colleague who prefaces a great many of his remarks with *audire alteram partem*, which means . . .'

'Very much the same,' she interrupted. 'I should perhaps tell you, Mr Pilcher, that although I may not be rich, I am *very* well educated. In the Highlands, where I was born, they use the Bible as a reading primer – rather as Homer and Hesiod were used in Classical Greece.' She paused for a moment to allow that piece of well-educated information to sink in, and then resumed, 'My first nurse taught me to read at the age of three, starting with chapter ten of the Book of Genesis.'

The lawyer's face was perfectly blank.

'You know!' she said kindly. 'The generations of Noah. "And Cush begat Nimrod. And Mizraim begat Ludim, and Anamim, and Lehabim, and Naphtuhim. And Canaan begat Sidon, and Heth, and the Jebusite, and the Amorite, and the Girgasite, and the . . ."'

'Gracious me! Yes, of course,' said Mr Pilcher. 'How *could* I have forgotten?'

They beamed at each other.

'Would you care for some refreshment?' Vilia asked.

'That would be delightful.'

Vilia tugged the bell-pull.

After that, the conversation went more easily. The house had been rented annually, fully furnished, when Vilia and her father had first come to London, and Theo Cameron had never troubled to look for anywhere more permanent. Vilia deduced, although Mr Pilcher was reticent about it, that after the first two or three years her father could not, in any case, have afforded to buy any house he would have been prepared to live in. Perhaps it had all turned out for the best, the lawyer said without much conviction, because it meant that Brook Street could be given up without further expense next month, when the annual agreement came up for review. 'You cannot keep the place on,' he said, 'or it would eat up every penny of your inheritance in less than three years. And it would, of course, be grossly improper for you to live here with only your governess and the servants for company.'

'I've been living here with only my governess and the servants ever since my father died,' Vilia objected.

'That was different,' the lawyer said primly. 'Now, once the house has been disposed of and the servants paid off, enough will remain to guarantee you a small annual income. One has no doubt that you will marry some day, perhaps quite soon . . .' He broke off, and then resumed in a tone not far removed from the waggish, 'though I must warn you that, as your trustee, I should feel compelled to scan – very carefully indeed! – the credentials of any young gentleman who applied to me for your hand. We cannot have you marrying just anyone, you know. Or not, at least, before you are twenty-one and able to snap your fingers at your stuffy old trustee!'

She smiled dutifully. 'And in the meantime?'

'Hah,' he said, and looked at her with the air of a man who, if he had worn spectacles, would have been peering over the top of them. 'You do realize that the responsibility rests entirely with me?'

'Yes.'

'That it is solely mine?'

'Yes.'

He sat back, crossing his black-clad knees, and sighed. 'It is a responsibility I would willingly have abrogated – most willingly! – if it had proved possible to trace any member of your family. But despite the most earnest endeavours, my agents have had no success. On your late father's side, of course, there were no close relatives, but I can only regard it as unfortunate – *most* unfortunate! – that he did not choose to keep in touch with your mother's people in Scandinavia. His own maternal relatives appear to have been – er – scattered by the – er – exigencies of the revolution in France . . .'

By which, Vilia supposed, he meant that he suspected they had gone to the guillotine.

'. . . and, of course, in the present state of Europe, it would have been of little advantage to have found them. We could scarcely export you to France, while we remain at war with Napoleon. It would never do to have you shot for a spy!'

Gritting her teeth, Vilia said, 'My French is excellent. My father made sure of that.'

Mr Pilcher ignored this caveat. 'What I have decided, therefore, is that you must make your home with some genteel family, with whom you may live until you are of an age to be your own mistress.'

'No!' Her reaction was instinctive, but, seeing the lawyer's frown, Vilia forced herself to think coherently. She couldn't understand, at first, why the idea was so repellent. It wasn't as if she disliked the human race. It was a question of being forced to become involved, perhaps. Independence had been a part of her almost since birth, and Meg Macleod had been the best nursemaid she could have had, very strong, very loving, and quite undemanding. Meg's love was of the rare kind that was complete in itself, and, because she had asked and expected nothing in return for it, Vilia had loved her far more dearly than she would have done if there had been any hint of compulsion. To give generously, even extravagantly, of one's own free will was very different from giving under coercion. In London, Vilia had soon learned that Meg was unique. As a result, she had kept her distance from the succession of nurses and governesses who had supervised her upbringing, and they, in turn, had recognized that little Miss Vilia was not to be bullied or cajoled into doing anything she didn't want to do.

But this was different. To be welcomed into the bosom of some 'genteel family' would mean being fussed over, and cared for, and persuaded to do this, or join in that. Without discourtesy, there would be no possibility of resisting. For someone who, through all the years of her short life, had been accustomed to call her mind and soul her own, it was an appalling prospect.

The nerves fluttering in her diaphragm, she stammered, 'When you said there was no alternative, was *that* what you meant?'

He nodded.

'Couldn't I – couldn't I just find some small apartment and live there with my governess?'

'When you are only fifteen years old?' Mr Pilcher was shocked. 'I would be failing utterly – utterly! – in my duty if I were to countenance such a suggestion. Most improper, *most* improper.' His voice softened a little. He had, after all, three daughters of his own; shy daughters, diffident daughters, but young and female just the same. 'I know what it is. You are afraid that I might send you to someone you dislike. Let me relieve your mind, my dear Miss Cameron. Everything is arranged, and you are to go to a charming family in St James's Square. A young couple with a small son, and admirable *ton*. Nothing could be more eligible.'

He watched her rather tentatively, wondering whether she would put her finger on the weak point in all this. Not weak, precisely; but the point from which an unsympathetic observer might be led to ask whether Mr Pilcher's professional ethics had been quite as unimpeachably pure as the Society of Gentlemen Practisers of the Law would have wished. The truth was that for the last five years Mr Pilcher had been accepting a small annual retainer from someone who wanted to be kept informed about the affairs of Mr Theophilus Cameron, formerly of Kinveil. Nothing confidential, of course. Mr Pilcher wouldn't have entertained such a suggestion for a moment. But he had seen no harm – except from the standpoint of a legal pedant – in passing on what was common knowledge. That Mr Cameron continued to live in a hired house, spent most of his time at Brooks's or White's, had no apparent intention of remarrying, appeared to be generally liked, and was dipping into the wine flask with increasing depth and frequency, although he carried it well and was never less than the gentleman. Mr Pilcher had, of course, reported Mr Cameron's demise, and had been mildly surprised to receive in return a letter asking what would happen to Mr Cameron's daughter.

Vilia said frowningly, 'St James's Square? They must be very rich. They can scarcely need to take in lodgers!'

It was true enough. St James's Square was not the kind of place inhabited by the *hoi polloi*. Mr Pilcher felt more than a little ill-used that this fragile, ethereal-looking child should have fastened so quickly on the point he would have preferred not to have to explain – or not just at the moment. He took a breath and said, 'The gentleman is the son of – er . . . You may not recall the name, but it was his father, Mr Mungo Telfer, who bought Kinveil estate from the late Mr Cameron, and . . .'

Vilia was on her feet. 'Oh, no! *No, no, no!*'

She didn't know whether to laugh or weep. To have to be *grateful* to the very people who had taken Kinveil away from her?

'I'd rather die!'

Mr Pilcher and her governess tried, in their different ways, to soothe her, but she whirled away from them and almost ran through the big folding doors into the rear part of the room, where she could be private.

It was so impossible, so completely and utterly impossible! How could she make this staid, unimaginative trustee of hers see how impossible it was? 'You must understand, Mr Pilcher, that when I was seven years old I made up my mind that I would marry Mr Magnus Telfer one day, as a means of winning Kinveil back. And, of course, I tried to push Mr *Mungo* Telfer over the sea wall and into the loch. But apart from that, I am very little acquainted with either of them!'

Whose idea had it been? The old man's, presumably, for his son scarcely knew that she existed. She had watched him, of course, during that fateful twenty-four hours at Kinveil, but he had not seen her at all as she slipped unobtrusively from spyhole to spyhole, studying the intruders. Mungo Telfer, on the other hand . . .

He had confused her. Even through her fear and hatred, she had felt an odd sense of identity with him, as if they were two of a kind. She had been too young, then, to separate the man himself from the threat he represented, but now, the threat long since fulfilled, she tried to recall him.

On the sea wall, when she had attempted to put an end to the whole thing in the only way she could think of, he had not been angry but nauseatingly understanding. He hadn't even mentioned the episode to her father. Afterwards, she had prowled aimlessly around until, frustrated beyond bearing, she had slipped up the curving staircase to the corridor outside the Long Gallery. There, with her five-year-old henchman Sorley McClure standing guard, she had climbed on a chair to eavesdrop at the Laird's Lug. This was a concealed listening tube sunk in an angle of the wall above the door, and tradition had it that former lairds of Kinveil had used it for listening in on the conversation of guests they did not trust. Vilia didn't trust either her father or the man Telfer an inch.

But she had only heard snatches of the two men's talk, because Sorley had done nothing but fidget.

'. . . my daughter, Mrs George Blair, lives not too far away . . .'

Vilia remembered Charlotte Blair, without pleasure, as a disapproving young woman who had ridden over once from Glenbraddan to pay a call, with the only too obvious intention of patronizing the little girl.

'. . . convenient to be near her. My son Magnus has had two years at Oxford, but he's not one of Nature's scholars. He'll be living in London for a while, seeing as he's . . .'

Distracted, Vilia had turned and hissed at Sorley, who was sitting on the floor at the top of the stairs, blowing vigorously at a fat black spider to make it tuck in its legs and play dead. '*Be quiet*, Sorley!'

When she turned back to the listening tube, the two men were talking about roads.

'New roads?' Her father's voice had been politely dismissive. 'Certainly it would revolutionize life in the Highlands and Islands to be properly linked to the centres of population and industry in the south, but I am told that something like a million pounds would be needed and I cannot believe the Treasury will ever be persuaded to disburse such a sum.'

'Aye, well,' the man Telfer had said. 'I wouldn't be too sure about that. The government's worried about all the folk sailing away to America, instead of staying here and starving. Every Highlander who emigrates is one less potential recruit for the Highland regiments – and if things go on at this rate it'll fairly put a crimp in His Majesty's army! They think building roads and canals would provide employment and persuade the folk to stay. I'm not so sure about that, but I doubt if it matters. What does matter is that the roads and canals would make it possible for you to market your livestock and fish and timber.'

Vilia's father said nothing, although the man Telfer sounded as if he knew what he was talking about. After a moment, he went on, 'And, you know, I've met the fellow who's in charge of the project, and I believe he's got the rumgumption to push the whole thing through. In fact, I'd wager you a sovereign to a semmit-button that, ten years from now, there'll be a network of Parliamentary roads and canals that'll bring the two hundred miles from here to Glasgow down to a mere three days. Well – four, maybe.'

Vilia's mind was racing. If what the man Telfer said was true, it would be madness to sell Kinveil. Now that her father knew salvation was so near, he *must* change his mind. Vilia thought it excessively silly of Mr Telfer to sound so positive about the roads. He was as good as inviting her father to reconsider the whole thing.

But all her father said was, 'You are more optimistic than I. I remember all too clearly that when I last made the journey it took me twelve days, and I broke my coach axle three times between Fort Augustus and Glasgow. In any case, I fear that . . .'

Vilia had never discovered what her father feared, because at that inopportune moment, Betty Fraser, the second housemaid, had rounded the bend of the stairs and let out a soft-voiced squeak of, 'Sorley McClure! Whateffer are you doing here? And Miss Vilia. Och, you wass neffer listening at the Laird's Lug, wass you? Think shame!' And that, despite Sorley's spirited attempt to defend his goddess's right to eavesdrop in her own castle any time she wanted to, had effectively put an end to Vilia's information-gathering for the day. She had finished up very little the wiser about how the man Telfer's mind worked.

The memory of that day still hurt dreadfully, even after eight years. For Mungo Telfer had been right – *damn* him! she thought, dredging up the only blasphemy she knew – and the government had put up the money for the roads. It would be a long time, still, before the Caledonian Canal was completed, and only a few of the roads were finished, but they and Mungo Telfer's money had begun to transform life on Kinveil. Every January, Vilia received a letter from Meg – a short one, because Meg's writing was large and she kept her news to a single page to save Vilia having to pay to receive a second sheet – and she knew how things were changing. If only, *if only* her father had been willing to try and survive for another few years!

It was a struggle to hold back the tears of self-pity and regret, but she managed it. She hadn't time for weeping. She couldn't, wouldn't, go to live with the Telfers. There must be something else she could do! If the worst came to the worst, she would run away. Why not? For a moment her spirits soared, but only for a moment. Only until she realized that the one place in the world she would ever run to was the one place in the world forbidden to her. Kinveil. And then the thought slipped into her mind that, if she went to live with Magnus Telfer and his wife, she might be invited to go there – legitimately.

Ten minutes later, she rejoined Mr Pilcher. 'I apologize,' she said. 'Your suggestion came as something of a shock. Are you quite sure there is no alternative?'

He was relieved to see that she had resigned herself. 'Quite sure,' he replied, prudently ignoring the reference to shock. 'There are too many advantages. You will be a guest in their house and will not be expected to make any financial contribution. Your income will be entirely at your own disposal, to use for clothes, and pin money, and to pay your personal servants, of course. The Telfers are quite prepared to take in your governess and abigail, you know, so you will not be cast into a strange house entirely on your own.'

'And Sorley McClure,' Vilia said.

'I beg you pardon?'

'Sorley McClure, my page.'

Mr Pilcher said, 'I hardly think . . . Do you really need a page-boy? I would have thought one of the Telfers' footmen could run errands for you.'

'Sorley McClure,' she repeated stubbornly. 'I made my father bring him with us from Kinveil. He is thirteen years old and it would break his heart if I abandoned him.'

She couldn't say to a man like this that it would break her heart, too. Sorley was the son of a good-for-nothing father who suffered from the strange lethargy that afflicted many Highlanders almost like a disease, although it seemed to have no physical origin. Too much whisky and too little food did nothing to cure it, but it was essentially a malaise of the spirit, as if man's fate from the moment of birth was simply to wait for the moment of death. Yet Sorley, who had never even had kail to go with his brose except when he had slipped into the castle kitchen, was brim full of all the energy his father lacked. He was skinny, ginger-haired, and amazingly freckled, with the sunniest smile it was possible to imagine. He adored Vilia unreservedly, and as long as he was with her Vilia continued, deep down inside her, to hope. Kinveil was a part of both of them, and each was a link in the chain that bound the other to it.

'Well, I suppose if he were to make himself generally useful . . . I will ask, although I can make no promises. But, on consideration, don't you think it a splendid arrangement? You will be quite one of the family, and Mrs Telfer will launch you into the *ton* and chaperone you in your first Season.'

In a colourless voice, she said, 'Would it be impertinent to ask why they are being so kind to me? I know of no reason why they should.'

Mr Pilcher took a moment or two to answer. 'You have the senior Mr Telfer to thank for it. It appears that he heard of your late father's demise, and was – er – concerned for your welfare. Most thoughtful of him. Indeed, a most generous gesture.' And one that the old Tobacco Lord could well afford, the lawyer reflected enviously, especially as it was not he, but his son and daughter-in-law who would be landed with the girl.

All Vilia said was, 'Oh.'

2

Luke Telfer was seven years old and alarmingly well brought up. So, when he was summoned to his mama's drawing-room in St James's Square one afternoon in November, he showed no surprise at finding both his parents there, looking preternaturally solemn, but bowed as he had been taught and said, 'Good afternoon, mama. Good afternoon, papa.'

'Come and sit here beside me, darling,' his mother said, patting the sofa invitingly. 'Papa and I have something very important to tell you.'

He perched himself on the edge so that he could rest his feet on the floor, which made him feel taller and more grown up, and raised innocent eyes to her face. He loved his mama dearly. She was very gentle and sweet and, he thought, very pretty with her oval face, high forehead, and silky chestnut hair, which she wore swept smoothly back over her ears instead of in the fussy ringlets that were the fashion. Her eyes always intrigued him, smiling and sad at the same time, and faintly smudged with blue in the hollows beneath. He knew that her constitution was delicate, and that she had almost died when he was born, which was why she was forbidden to exert herself and spent part of every day resting, with the curtains drawn. It had been impressed on Luke, from the moment he was old enough to understand, that he must never make a noise for fear of upsetting her. It was bad for her heart.

Until three or four months ago, it had not occurred to Luke that there was any other kind of life than the sedate, circumscribed existence of St James's Square. His mother's health was far too precarious to allow her to face the rigours of any journey longer than a dozen miles, and certainly not the six hundred to where his grandfather lived at Kinveil. Luke's papa, therefore, had always gone alone on his duty visit. Until this year, when it had been decided that Luke was old enough to go with him.

It had been a revelation, like being translated into another world. Luke had developed a vast, childish exuberance. He had run and scrambled, and paddled and climbed; yelled himself hoarse; got dirty as a tinker and wet as a tadpole. He had become semi-amphibious, and loved it. Under the aegis of the steward's eighteen-year-old son, Ewen Campbell, he had learned to ride a sheltie, a Shetland pony. He had gone bird's-nesting. And, joy of delirious joys, he had caught his first salmon in Loch an Iasgair, 'the osprey's loch'. By the sheerest good fortune, he had saved his second notable exploit for the last week of his stay. Desirous of going to sea, and having been told that all the men and boats were already out, he had purloined a large washtub from the laundry room and rolled it down, with some trouble, to the water's edge. Then, with a small plank for an oar, and a cherry-twig mast, flying his pocket handkerchief in lieu of the Jolly Roger, he had paddled off with a will in the general direction of the North Atlantic. When he was retrieved by a panic-stricken Ewen Campbell forty minutes later, he couldn't understand what all the fuss was about. Although his grandfather, a formidably shrewd and decisive old gentleman, had laughed, Luke's papa had not admired this second of his only begotten son's exploits nearly as much as the first, and for his last few days Luke had been virtually confined to barracks.

Inevitably, when they returned to London, his mother had been regaled with the episode of the washtub. She had laid a shocked hand over her heart, and Luke had been trying to make it up to her ever since.

'Now, my love,' she said. 'We know it will come as a surprise to you, but we are sure you will be pleased. You are going to have a sister.'

She might have phrased it better. Luke's eyes goggled. He knew that mothers and fathers had to do what the cattleman at Kinveil had shown him a bull and a cow doing, otherwise they couldn't become mothers and fathers at all. But to think of his own stately parents engaged on anything so undignified was beyond the range of his imagining.

Stupidly, he said, 'When?' And then, rather less stupidly, 'A *sister*?'

'On Friday,' Lucy Telfer replied, patting his hand.

He looked up at his father, standing before the fire with his hands tucked under his olive green coat tails and a benign smile on his face. Magnus Telfer was an impressive figure, just an inch under six feet tall, handsomely built, with strong brows over well-opened hazel eyes, the large family nose, full but well-shaped lips, and a nicely cultivated air of distinction. No one would ever have guessed that Magnus's own father had been born in a weaver's cottage, but neither would they ever have doubted that he had become a very warm man indeed. Two years at Oxford had put a fine, smooth polish on Magnus's manners – even if they had made little impression on his mind – and his acquaintances were accustomed to consider him a sound fellow. It was by no means unusual for ladies, especially elderly ones, to murmur to their friends, 'Such a *gentlemanly* man!' His style being lazy and a touch consequential, most people thought him several years older than he was. At this time, in fact, he was just twenty-seven.

Luke turned dazedly back to his mama, but, as she went on, his blank incomprehension gave way to a strong feeling of ill usage. 'You don't remember, of course, because it all happened before you were born. But the gentleman from whom your grandfather bought Kinveil had a little girl, who was just about your age at the time. Anyway, Mr Cameron – that was the gentleman's name – went to heaven not very long ago, and left his little girl all alone in the world.'

1811 minus 1803 made eight. Plus seven made fifteen. *Little* girl?

'So she is coming to live with us, just for a year or two until she is grown up. She must be very lonely and very sad, so you will promise to be kind to her, won't you, and treat her as if she were really your sister? But I know you will. You are such a *good* boy!'

He was a furious boy. A stranger coming to live. An intruder. Someone he would have to be polite to, and put himself out for. Someone he was going to have to share his mother with. And as if all that wasn't bad enough – a girl! Clothes and hair-styles, giggling and gossiping.

His mother looked at him anxiously, and with an enormous effort he returned her gaze. For a moment, his voice refused to obey him, but at last he managed, 'Yes, mama. Of course, mama.'

'That's fine, then,' his father intervened jovially. 'I'm sure you'll get along famously.' Then, as if Luke had suddenly become invisible, he went on to his wife, 'Though I must say I still have doubts about her upbringing. What if she turns out to be a hoyden? From all accounts, she was wild as a gipsy when she was at Kinveil. You remember what Charlotte had to say about her!'

'But that was years ago, my love. Charlotte saw her in the most uncivilized surroundings, being dragged up by servants. I am sure she will have learned London manners by now.' Lucy Telfer always thought the best of everybody. It was one of the things that made her so soothing to live with. 'After all, whatever his faults, Mr Cameron was a gentleman and knew what he owed to his position. You will be charmed to find how correct and ladylike she has become.'

'I hope so.' Magnus didn't sound convinced.

'And she is probably feeling quite crushed, poor girl. Never to have known her mother, and now to lose her father when he had scarcely passed forty. We must try very hard to make her feel at home.'

'Mmmm. I only hope we don't find ourselves wallowing in a vale of tears, that's all. Dashed depressing!'

'I will take care you are not inconvenienced, my love. You know that your comfort is always my first concern.'

He nodded absently. 'I know I have asked you before, but are you quite, quite sure it is not going to be too much of an imposition? There is still time for you to change your mind.'

She smiled. 'Indeed, no. She will be no trouble. Indeed, she will be like a sister to me, as well as to Luke.' There was a pause, and then she said with an expression that, in another woman, might have been ironical. 'And what else can we do, in any case? If your father wishes it . . .'

Entranced, Luke wriggled on his perch, which had the unfortunate effect of attracting his papa's attention. 'Ah, yes, my boy,' Magnus said. 'You needn't stay. Off you go, back to Mrs Weekes.'

Dragging his feet a little, Luke departed. But he was rewarded with another nugget of information as, slowly, he closed the door.

'. . . still don't understand *why* he wishes it! Dash it all, if Cameron has drunk and gambled his way through all the money my father paid him for Kinveil, it can hardly be laid to the Telfers' charge . . .'

'Master Luke!' said a minatory voice from the stairs.

Luke turned away from the door. 'Hullo, Weeky,' he said with a brave attempt at nonchalance. 'Did you know there was a girl coming to stay with us? We must try to be very kind to her.'

3

At noon on Friday, Magnus's town carriage drew up outside 14 St James's Square and decanted the master of the house and three females of assorted shapes and sizes. To Luke's jaundiced eye, they all appeared thoroughly shabby-genteel. However, he was primed to be gracious and perhaps a touch patronizing. He had no idea what to expect of Miss Cameron, but in view of the gipsy upbringing and the drunken father, he didn't expect much.

Magnus, looking surprisingly benevolent, led one of the females forward. She was of middling height, very pale, and as far as Luke could see under the shadow of her hood, very fair-haired. Her eyes, cast down towards the front steps, were not immediately visible.

Beside him, Luke heard his mother give a faint gasp – not, he suspected, of sympathy, but of stark horror at the girl's clothes. Unrelieved black bombazine was not the most becoming of fabrics, especially on a thin, wan, fifteen-year-old. Luke was just deciding that she looked like a crow when she raised startling green eyes and he suddenly wondered what she had done with her broomstick. She was precisely his idea of a witch. And a witch who had never shed a tear in her life, which was probably why his papa was looking so pleased with himself.

Lucy Telfer stepped forward, her arms half outstretched, but if she had thought Miss Cameron was going to rush to their shelter she was sadly mistaken. The girl's face didn't change, nor did she recoil, but her rejection couldn't have been clearer if she had put it in words.

She curtsied politely, and held out a slim, black-mittened hand. 'This is most kind, Mrs Telfer. I promise I will not be a trouble to you.'

The other two females had now been joined by a lanky, red-haired boy who had been seated on the box. He had the most astonishing collection of freckles Luke had ever seen. He was about thirteen or fourteen, and growing out of his livery – an extraordinary outfit consisting of tunic and breeches in a complicated check pattern of green and yellow on a bright scarlet ground. The narrow neckband and cuffs were faced with plain red that should have fought with his carroty hair, but didn't, because of the white lace ruffles in between. It was to be years before Luke discovered that Vilia and Sorley had designed this outfit between them.

Luke's mother said, 'Come in, my dear, out of the cold. Such an unpleasant day!'

Within minutes, one of the anonymous females had been confided into Mrs Weekes' care, the other to that of Lucy Telfer's maid, and the page-boy had been handed to the butler. The two females, whom Luke had promptly christened The Downtrodden Duo – he was rather proud of 'Duo' – were haled off, murmuring, upstairs, while the page-boy was passed like some undesirable parcel to the second footman, and vanished in the direction of the nether regions.

Luke's father, ushering the ladies into the library, said, 'You, too, Luke. Come along!'

Reluctantly, he followed. Miss Cameron was already glancing at the bookshelves, her eyes smack on a level with some elderly copies of the *Turf Remembrancer* and the *Annual Racing Calendar*. The books had been bought with the house from a gentleman whose interest in horses had been disastrously matched by his lack of skill in backing them, but Luke's father had never troubled even to have them rearranged. Although his attitude to sport was tepid, he would have admitted, if pushed, that he considered the history of Ascot a better furnishing for his shelves than the plays of Aeschylus.

Her face expressionless, the girl turned back into the room and sat down neatly in a straight-backed chair. Now that she had shed her cloak, it was possible to see what she really looked like. With her high-necked black gown, tightly folded hands, and pale unsmiling face, she was no one's idea of a merry little playmate. Even her long, white-gold hair looked serious-minded. Instead of tumbling down to her shoulders, as a girl's should, it was swept into a coil at the nape of her neck, so heavy that it seemed to tilt her head backwards. In the indoor light of a November afternoon, her eyes had lost all their colour and brilliance. To Luke she appeared stiff, drab, and unapproachable.

He paid very little attention to what was being said at first. His father, after a dutiful fifteen minutes, had made himself scarce, pleading an engagement, and his wife had seen him go with the expression of a drowning man, despairing but resigned, watching a straw being swept away on the tide. Distantly, Luke heard his mother and the girl go through all the boring details of rooms and mealtimes and servants and domestic protocol. The girl seemed to be listening carefully, and she nodded once or twice and asked an occasional question. It was a relief to discover that her voice was soft and cultured, with no accent other than a faint elongation of the 's' when it came at the end of a word. Her manners were perfectly respectable, and she didn't appear to be any more stupid than most girls. Perhaps she wasn't going to shame them after all.

'Yes,' she said in reply to a gently probing question. 'I have found it necessary over the last year or two to exercise some supervision over my father's household. His illness made him neglectful at times.'

She sounded terribly grown up and more than a little prissy.

Lucy Telfer's quick sympathy was aroused. 'You poor child! What a responsibility for such young shoulders! But you need not trouble your head about such things any longer. I know how you must be pining for your father – so sad! – but we will try what we can do to cheer you up.'

Luke could tell, and he wondered whether the girl could, too, that the first targets for cheering up would be clothes and hair-style.

'We want you to feel perfectly at home here. So, if you have no objections, my dear, I propose to call you Vilia, and I hope you will call me Lucy.' She smiled with the sweetness that was peculiarly her own.

The girl coloured very slightly, but produced no answering smile. 'You are most kind, Mrs Telfer. But I cannot think it would be proper for me to address you so familiarly.'

Lucy Telfer, seldom defeated, accepted this gracefully. 'Very well, my dear. You must do as you wish, of course. But when you feel more comfortable and at ease with us, I hope you will change your mind. Now, I have something for you, a little welcoming gift. While I go and fetch it, you and Luke can become acquainted.'

With a whisper of rose-coloured skirts she departed towards the front of the house.

There was a moment's nonplussed silence. The girl suddenly looked much younger.

Luke said stiltedly, 'My governess, Mrs Weekes, and I are accustomed to take a stroll every day in the gardens of the square here. I do not know whether you might care to accompany us?' He had been rehearsing it, sullenly, all morning.

'Thank you, but I believe I must leave that to my own governess to decide.'

He had no idea which of The Downtrodden Duo was the governess.

Neither of them had even looked capable of deciding to come in out of the rain.

He waited, but she said nothing more. She seemed prepared to go on sitting there, saying nothing, until his mother came back.

He tried again. 'I believe you used to live at Kinveil? My grandfather lives there now.' It didn't occur to him that it might sound like a gibe.

'Yes.' Her eyes dropped to the hands clasped in her lap. They were very thin, long-fingered hands with shapely, well-kept nails. On the middle finger of the right was a ring far too large and heavy for it, an amethyst seal engraved with some kind of circular design and mounted on a plain gold band.

Perseveringly, he said, 'What a handsome ring! Does the design have some meaning?'

'It was my father's. The signet of the Camerons of Kinveil. The design represents the Loch an Vele whirlpool.'

'*I* didn't see any whirlpool.'

'It only occurs under certain conditions of wind and tide. You wouldn't see it. I imagine you have only been there in the summer.'

It sounded disparaging. What was more, it didn't seem right to Luke that this girl should be flaunting a ring belonging to Kinveil. He felt quite strongly that it should have been handed over to his grandfather with the other furnishings.

Motivated by a desire to put her in her place, he said loftily, 'Oh, I know Kinveil very well. My father takes me there and we have a delightful time. I caught my first salmon when I was only six.' True. Six years, eleven months, and twenty-nine days still counted as six.

'Where?'

'Where? Oh, I see. In Loch an Ee-ahs . . . In "the osprey's loch" above Carn Mor.'

'Oh, yes. That's always full of fish.'

He was indignant. 'No, it isn't!'

The green eyes looked up in detached surprise. 'Of course it is.'

'It *isn't*!' He came very near to stamping his foot. 'I had to make several casts, and it was almost an hour before I got a bite!'

She shrugged. 'You must have been unlucky. Ospreys always choose their lochs well. They don't need rods and lines and flies, they just pounce. That's why we call the osprey "Allan-the-fisherman" in the Highlands.'

We in the Highlands, indeed! When she hadn't been near Kinveil for eight years. Very rudely indeed, Luke said, 'Pooh! What do *you* know about it, you horrid girl!'

There was a moment's appalling silence. He wouldn't have thought it possible for her face to turn paler than it already was. Her eyes expanded into great dark pools, and her lips began to quiver. Her voice, too, was shaking when she spoke, and by the time she had finished he could scarcely make out the words.

'You – you – stupid little boy! What do *I* know about it? I know everything about it. *Everything.* Far more than you ever will, if you live to be a hundred. You'll never be anything but a Sassenach. You don't even know what that means, do you! It means an Englishman, a stranger, a foreigner. But *I* know. I know because I belong there. It's my home. It's *mine!*'

Her voice broke down completely into gasping, agonized sobs that seemed to rack her whole body. Luke could see the tears pouring, like snow water, down her cheeks, and her throat muscles standing out like cords with the effort she was making to control herself. Anguish was something that had never intruded into his well-ordered life before. He had no idea what to say or do.

When his mother returned a few minutes later, bearing the pretty silk shawl she had bought for Vilia, she found the two of them still sitting where she had left them. Luke had stayed, rigid with anger and apprehension, because he felt obscurely that he ought to; Vilia because there was nowhere else she could go. She didn't even know yet where her room was.

Chapter Two

1

'I really am dreadfully afraid,' Lucy Telfer said guilelessly, 'that Luke is going out of his way to be objectionable to poor Vilia.'

Magnus, who had been succeeding tolerably well in ignoring the atmosphere in the house for the last three months, kept his eyes firmly fixed on the *Morning Chronicle*. Recognizing, however, that a reply was expected of him, he murmured, 'Not very good at it, I shouldn't think.'

'Oh, but he is, very good indeed. He seems to have a real, natural talent for it.' If Lucy had not been the sweetest and mildest of women, she might have added, 'I can't imagine who he gets it from.' Magnus, though in general a model of politeness, could take a very arbitrary tone when roused. Thoughtfully, she went on, 'I believe he regards it almost as a kind of game. Once he discovered he could break down that rather trying reserve of hers – my dear, if only she would snap, or even sulk, everything would be so much easier! – he couldn't resist going on. I don't think he wants to provoke another storm, but I do think he may be experimenting to see how far he can go, short of it. It's a new experience for him, you see, having someone of his own age group to quarrel with. Not that she quarrels back, of course. But he *will* harp on the fact that Kinveil is going to be his one day . . .'

Magnus looked up at that, and his wife smiled mischievously. 'Not for years and years and years, of course! But one can almost see her holding her tongue, and because she is so good, he is becoming quite intractable. Frustration, of course. I've told him he is being very unkind – quite cruel, in fact – but it makes no difference.'

His momentary interest dying, Magnus dropped his eyes to the newspaper again. 'Jealous,' he said briefly. 'Doesn't like having to share his parents with a stranger.'

It was something Lucy had recognized within a week of Vilia's arrival, and she was pleased that Magnus had reached the same conclusion, even if it had taken a good deal of prompting. 'How clever of you! I'm sure you're right,' she exclaimed. 'But what's to be done?'

'He'll grow out of it.'

Lucy sighed. 'Do you think so?'

Magnus turned a page. 'All this,' he said, straightening the fold noisily, 'must be tiring you dreadfully. I wish I could relieve you of some of the burden.'

His wife, perfectly capable of distinguishing between a statement of goodwill and a declaration of intent, smiled at him gratefully. 'It's not a burden, my love. How could it be? Though I confess I *should* like a rest from it all. And do you know, I think the time may have come to find a tutor for Luke, so that he would feel there is someone on whom he can rely for undivided attention.'

'A tutor? Well, we're agreed he shouldn't go to school, certainly.'

'Indeed, no. Such nasty, rough places.'

'Yes.' Magnus still remembered his years at Eton, and he'd been told that Harrow was just as bad. 'I'll make inquiries. But I don't see how we can arrange to have a rest from the pair of them. We *could* leave them here, I suppose, when we go to Ramsgate in the summer.'

He sounded doubtful, and Lucy gave his doubts a few moments to solidify before she said, delicately, 'I have been thinking. You know how much Luke enjoyed his visit to Kinveil? And Vilia loves it very much. I wondered whether we might not send them there. I'm sure it would go far towards restoring Vilia's spirits.'

Magnus, though not in general a very quick thinker, always displayed a creditable turn of speed when it came to finding reasons for saying no to any idea he hadn't thought of himself. 'I don't agree. It might well restore her spirits, but it is not her home now, and she must be encouraged to forget it. She is a charming girl, but she's not one of the family.'

'If you say so, my love,' his wife replied equably. 'I merely wondered whether visiting it again, now that she knows something of the world, might not serve to show it to her in a different light. You yourself have told me that it has little to offer an educated person who is acquainted with the richness and variety of life in London.'

Magnus shifted his ground adroitly. 'You may be right, my dear, but I am afraid she cannot go this year, and neither can Luke. They can't travel without a responsible escort, you know, and I don't intend to pay my usual visit to father this summer.'

'Not going to Kinveil? Not at all?' Lucy exclaimed, surprised. And then she realized why. 'Ah!' she said. 'Charlotte?'

Three years earlier, George Blair had stolidly ignored a chest cold and it had turned to pneumonia. 'Typical,' Magnus had said. He had never cared much for George. Everyone had assumed that the widowed Charlotte would stay at Glenbraddan with five-year-old Edward and baby Georgiana, and dwindle into a solitary middle age. But in September last year she had gone off on a visit to Edinburgh, met the Honourable Peregrine Francis Egerton Randall – who had been passing through en route for a shooting party in Perthshire – and married him, without so much as a by-your-leave, three months later.

Lucy knew that a letter had come from her father-in-law at Kinveil this morning, but not what was in it. Now it transpired that he had been making some inquiries, and had discovered that Mr Randall had been cast off by his family for being wild, irresponsible, and fatally addicted to gaming.

'Just as we suspected,' Magnus said heavily. 'Earl's son though he may be, he's a scoundrel of the worst sort. It was obvious, of course, as soon as we knew that he was ten years younger than Charlotte. One didn't have to look far to discover why he should have married her.'

Lucy sighed. 'How distressing! I always thought it a pity for Charlotte to be tied to such a tedious man as George Blair, but one wouldn't have wished her to go to the other extreme.' She looked on the bright side. 'Perhaps he isn't as bad as he is painted. After all, if he's only twenty-one, he can't really have had *time* to sink very far into depravity, can he? He may turn out to be quite charming in spite of everything.'

'One assumes he must be attractive, or Charlotte wouldn't have made such a cake of herself. Indeed, I suppose most rakes must have some such quality to recommend them or they wouldn't succeed in the role. But that has nothing to do with it. I am only grateful that my father has made sure the fellow won't have the opportunity to squander any Telfer money. He's giving Lottie an allowance, but no marriage settlement. Her dowry when she married George was swallowed up by Glenbraddan, and that's in trust for Edward, of course, but the steward seems to be making the place pay well enough – better than George ever did, by all accounts. If I'd been father, I wouldn't even have given Lottie the allowance. However, even with it, Mr Randall will find his wings clipped. More fool he,' Magnus said with satisfaction, 'not to discuss the dowry before he committed himself. But it's all of a piece! Anyway, I'm so angry about the whole thing that I don't think I could be civil. I don't want to meet the fellow, and if I go to the Highlands I can't avoid it. So I shan't go. And if I don't go,' he pointed out conclusively, 'the children can't.'

'No,' Lucy said thoughtfully. 'They can't, can they?'

2

During the next few days, even Luke noticed his mama's abstraction.
Blaming it on Vilia, he became even surlier than usual. Vilia ignored
him. On that first day he had caught her at a very low ebb indeed,
deeply depressed by her own situation, physically and mentally exhausted from supervising the disposal of her father's possessions, and
quaking with nerves at the prospect of having to come to terms with
new guardians and a new life. More than anything else in the world she
had wanted to fly to the sanctuary of Kinveil – the Kinveil of her
childhood, not of the here-and-now – and the last thing she had been
prepared for was an attack on the weakest point of her defences by a
spoilt, smug, ignorant little boy. Afterwards, she knew where the
attack was coming from and was armed. Not once in the three months
since she had come to live in St James's Square had she done more than
find release in a swift flash of temper, and even that had happened only
rarely. She had been quick to see that Luke's malice would lose its
savour if she didn't respond, although she hadn't expected it to take so
long. He was quite the most self-absorbed child she had ever encountered, and tiresomely possessive – about his mother, his father, his
grandfather, Kinveil, even the chair he liked to sit in and the books
he chose to read.

Even so, obnoxious small boys could be ignored. It was harder to
ignore the gentle, solicitous Lucy, with her relentless kindness and
sweet, unchanging smile. It had not taken Vilia long to decide that
Lucy's delicate health was a myth, and setting her down as a fraud and a
hypocrite had made it easier to reject her interference and her
weak-willed anxiety that everyone should be happy and content. The
trouble was that Lucy remained blind to her guest's determination to
keep her distance. Nothing short of downright rudeness, Vilia thought
despairingly, seemed likely to have any effect, and to be rude would
have conflicted with all Vilia's instincts, as well as the tenets according
to which she had been reared.

A state of war existed between them, but it was a ludicrously polite
war. 'Indeed, my dear,' Lucy would say. 'There can be no question of
putting off your blacks for several months yet, but I do think we might
find something less oppressive. Not even the highest stickler could
expect black bombazine of you.'

46

Vilia liked black bombazine. It suited her sense of the dramatic. If one was forced to mourn for someone for whom one hadn't cared very much, why not do it in style?

Lucy said, 'I saw a charming black cambric the other day, embroidered with silk dots. It would be perfect for you, made ankle-length rather than down to the ground, and half-high, to the base of the neck rather than up to the chin. Pray be persuaded, my dear! You will see how delightfully you look.'

Vilia did not wish to look delightfully. It was too soon after her father's death, she conveyed, for her to concern herself with such frivolities as fashion.

Regretfully, Lucy abandoned the subject of dress and turned her attention to Vilia's hair. 'That heavy knot is too old for you,' she murmured, shaking her own silken head. 'You could clasp your hair high on the crown, perhaps, and let it fall from there? When you make your come-out, of course, you will wear it in a Grecian coil on top, with one or two tiny wisps to soften the line. No, no. I don't mean those dreadful corkscrew twists. You must keep the pure, sculptured line. You have such beautiful bone structure, it will look lovely.'

No one had ever told Vilia she had beautiful bone structure before. Momentarily diverted, she peered at herself in the glass.

But when she tried clasping her hair on the crown, she reported that she thought the result commonplace.

Days afterwards, however, she discovered that Lucy was not as easily defeated as she had thought. Vilia's very own maid, brushing her hair one morning, stopped in mid-brush, the silver-gilt mane trailing gracefully from her fingers. 'How becoming it looks, just so!' she exclaimed. 'I wonder if we could persuade it to stay like that?' It took a moment for Vilia to spot the stratagem. When she did, she began to wonder if perhaps she had underestimated Lucy.

Now and then, somewhat to her annoyance, Vilia found her sense of humour tickled. Lucy was terrified that Vilia might be mistaken for a blue-stocking. *Fatal* when she came on the marriage mart! People might excuse her for not playing on the pianoforte or the harp, provided she was seen to appreciate other ladies' music. And many women of the highest rank were clumsy with their needles. It was a blessing that she could draw so elegantly, and a mark of high civilization that her French should be flawless. But Lucy had been horrified to discover that Vilia had a naturally mathematical turn of mind. Also, she was quite unacceptably well read, and in the most recondite subjects! One couldn't, after all, go around explaining to everyone that there had been no children's books in the library of the house where she had been brought up. With the greatest seriousness, Lucy told Vilia that she must never let it be known that she had a firm grasp of such things as ancient Christian heresies and the use of triglyphs in Greek architecture.

The conversation at St James's Square became more frivolous every day as Lucy tried to instil into Vilia the principles of social small talk, and it was only by exercising the sternest self control that Vilia maintained her equanimity. It was a very real relief when, in February, Lucy abandoned her gentle persecution and relapsed into an absent-minded daze. Quite against her will, Vilia was intrigued.

She was still more intrigued when Luke's new tutor arrived and Lucy promptly reverted to normal.

The tutor's name was Henry Phillpotts, and how anyone as wildly unsuitable as he had found his way into the Telfers' favour Vilia could not at first imagine. Possibly the fact of his having been recommended by the Duke of Argyll had helped to outweigh his many and obvious imperfections.

Vilia, wiser in the ways of the Highland aristocracy than her hosts, suspected that the Duke of Argyll had never set eyes on Henry, or Henry on the Duke. All Scots peers had dependants, and some felt compelled to do what they could even for distant connections of their stewards, or third cousins twice removed of their most junior footmen. The Duke of Argyll, hearing that a London neighbour was in need of a tutor for his son, might well have recommended someone like Henry, especially if the neighbour was only a nodding acquaintance and couldn't hold it against him.

When he came to St James's Square, Henry Phillpotts had been ordained for a year but had not found a parish. Nothing, he implied, would have persuaded him to accept a living from some fox-hunting squire in Leicestershire or some clothwitted manufacturer in Leeds. Oxford or London he would have considered – or even Cambridge – but how could a fine mind expand in the mud of the Shires or the weaving sheds of Leeds?

Henry's dinner-table conversation was very good value, far more amusing – if no less silly – than Lucy's small talk.

'Stimulus!' he would exclaim. 'That is what the mind requires! How otherwise to nourish that originality that is the greatest of all intellectual refinements? Even our great universities fail there, Mr Telfer, sir! In their emphasis on Classical studies, they put a higher premium on memory than originality!' Mr Phillpotts was a veritable fount of exclamation marks.

'Quite,' said Magnus after a moment, remembering his own brief excursion into Classical studies. 'Oh, quite! I'd certainly prefer that brat of mine not to be condemned to all that declining and memorizing and construing.'

Lucy, not very sure what 'construing' meant, said, 'No, indeed!' and then visibly wondered whether she oughtn't perhaps to have said, 'Yes, indeed!'

Vilia swallowed a giggle. Henry Phillpotts was a perfect fraud. He looked clever, with his piercing blue eyes, shock of badly cut black hair, and high complexion. His clothes were eccentric. Indoors, he wore a cassock of Madonna-hair brown with velvet cuffs, supplemented outdoors by a wide-brimmed, shallow-crowned hat in bright red, not unlike a cardinal's, or a kind of brimless toque that bore a perilous resemblance to the papal mitre. And his mind was the most complete ragbag, stuffed with unrelated shreds and tatters. Quotations from Dante and Paracelsus, Chaucer and Racine, Avicenna and Machiavelli, tripped from his tongue when the literary mood was on him. When he felt theologically inclined, it would be Clement of Alexandria, or St Thomas Aquinas, or John Davenant. But it always sounded as if he had been studying some eclectic dictionary of quotations rather than the originals. And he was utterly fascinated by figures from the past of whom no one else had ever heard. Not Dionysus the god, but Dionysus the Areopagite. Not St Paul of Tarsus but St Saturninus of Toulouse. Not King George of Merrie England but King George of Podiebrad.

Fortunately, he and Luke took to each other from the start. Henry was just what the boy needed to shake him out of the sullens. He was loud, he was slightly mad, but he was full of life, and it was impossible to be dull when he was around. Luke, once more the centre of someone's attention, began to improve.

It was perfectly clear to Vilia that Magnus and Lucy were congratulating themselves on having made an excellent choice of tutor. Neither of them was precisely needle-witted, and since Henry – who, though silly, wasn't a fool – took care to sound intellectual in their company, they failed to realize that his views were anything out of the common run. They decided their son was in good hands, even if they weren't very peaceful hands.

And then Vilia's comfortable sense of superiority suffered a reverse. Lucy began to wonder whether the house at Ramsgate was, after all, quite spacious enough to accommodate not only Mr and Mrs Telfer and their servants, but Luke and Vilia and Henry Phillpotts and the schoolroom staff as well. Magnus made a show of resistance, but not for long. In the end it was decided that Mr and Mrs Telfer should have two peaceful months at Ramsgate on their own while the children went to Kinveil, under the eminently responsible supervision of Luke's new tutor. Even without knowing what she later discovered – that Lucy had hinted to the Duchess of Argyll, who had passed the message on to the Duke, that the Telfers' need for a tutor was of the most vital urgency – Vilia's conviction grew that Lucy was a good deal cleverer than she had supposed. With exasperation, she also discovered that she was beginning to feel a kind of amused affection for her.

3

The journey north was a sensational success. The party travelled in a majestic berline, with servants tacked on wherever there happened to be space, and a pile of boxes and the kind of trunks known as 'imperials' loaded on the roof in such a way as to make the carriage look like a mobile mountain. Magnus had decreed that, since they were in no great hurry, they should take their own horses, which meant that they could only cover three ten-to-twelve-mile stages in the day.

With the coachman and groom on the box, and Sorley and Vilia's maid on the outside seat, it made an impressive turn-out, and one that the ostlers at the coaching houses remembered for years to come. The horses, two bays and two greys, were very sweet goers on the road; the only problem was getting them there. Three of them were merely snappish about being fitted into the traces, but the fourth, a bay known as Moonlight Flit, was in the habit of lying down in the stable yard and refusing to get up again until he had the full attention of all the ostlers, half the post-boys, and the coachman's long, curled whip.

It took three weeks to cover the six hundred miles between London and Kinveil, and the travellers – except for the governess – enjoyed every minute of it. Vilia, especially, had been transfigured from the moment the journey was decided on. In London, this had been apparent only in a kind of controlled excitement, more spring in her walk and more light in her eyes. But with every mile out of town she became more vibrant, until, by the time the coach reached Baldock, she was almost fizzing with high spirits. After the months of pale, unsmiling restraint, it was a revelation to everyone except Sorley. It was also extremely catching.

Only the governess failed to respond, sitting in petrified silence for most of the way, remonstrating faintly from time to time. It was really not *comme il faut* for a young lady to start up a chorus in the yard of a public inn, as Vilia did one day when the travellers were watching the coachman trying to rouse Moonlight Flit.

> *Here*'s to our horse and *to* his right ear,
> God send our *master* a *hap*-py New Year!

Nor did a young lady hang out of a carriage window warbling Gaelic folk songs at the top of her voice. And as for playing backgammon in the evenings – 'shaking dice boxes in a common hostelry!' – the poor woman was ready to die of shame. Vilia paid not the slightest heed.

It was a truly splendid three weeks. Admittedly, the accommodation deteriorated sadly as soon as they crossed the Border. Few people other than cattle drovers travelled much in Scotland as yet, and Luke remembered his father complaining that there wasn't an inn on the whole road fit for a gentleman. But Luke and Vilia were approaching Kinveil, and didn't mind, while Henry, who had a curiously ascetic streak, scarcely even noticed that there were no carpets on the floors, no cushions on the chairs, no curtains at the windows, and little to eat but porridge, eggs, salt fish, and barley bread.

In the evenings, they raided the brown holland book bag that travelled with them in the coach in search of something to fit their mood. They wept over *Clarissa*, yelled with laughter at *Humphry Clinker*, gasped over *Marmion*. They declaimed from Shakespeare, and never was there such a ranting as when Henry played Lear, never such a doom-struck Lady Macbeth as Vilia. Never, Luke prided himself, a more poetic Hamlet, and certainly never a younger one – not even that infant prodigy of a few years before, the famous Master Betty. Luke wondered whether the stage mightn't be his forte.

At Ballachulish ferry the boatmen had lost one of the rowlocks for the oars. The tide rushed up the strait, the oars slipped and skidded, the boatmen puffed and blew, and the coachman fell overboard and had to be fished out by the groom. When they reached the other shore, Henry paid up dutifully and gave the oarsmen their expected dram of mountain dew – not, he made it clear, in recognition of their seamanship but out of gratitude to Providence for their safe landing.

At Fort William, Moonlight Flit lost his tail. This, Vilia said, was standard procedure. Local fishermen liked horsehair for their trout lines, and any horse stabled at an inn was bound to be at risk. It didn't improve Moonlight Flit's appearance or his temper.

At Fort Augustus, Henry decided to hire a boat to row his charges up to the mouth of the river Braddan. They could just as well have gone by the new road, but Henry thought that would be insipid. Surrounded by a grinning audience of military veterans from the Fort, and canal workmen resting their barrowloads of soil and rock, he haggled like a peddler in a native bazaar with the boatman Rory Mor and his three strapping sons.

'Two shillings,' Henry said firmly.

'Och, no. I wass chust going out after the fush.'

'Fish?' said Henry. 'You're a boatman. It's your duty to carry passengers! Two-and-sixpence.'

'No, no. There iss no duty about it at aal. And the weather iss chust right for the fushing.'

'It's outrageous.' Henry tipped back his cardinal's hat. 'Three shillings.'

'Och, no. Anyway, I would neffer be getting that great big coach on my boat.'

'Of course you would. Three-and-six.'

'No, no. Come away, boys. Let uss be getting off after our fush and leave the chentleman to make other arrangements.'

Henry knew when he was beaten. The coach and horses went by road, while Rory Mor and his sons received the exorbitant sum of four shillings for rowing half a dozen passengers half a dozen miles up the loch.

Vilia enjoyed this interlude very much, being entirely on Rory Mor's side, but once they were on the road again she became progressively more silent. Luke didn't even notice at first. He was too interested in the progress the road had made in the last year. It was strange, even to a child, to see the endless grey-gravelled scar winding from one horizon to the other, from nowhere to nowhere, a raw and glaring scribble in the wild majesty of the landscape. The human vision that had brought it into being was not yet justified, for the final stretch was still incomplete. The cattle that would cross from Skye to thunder along the beautifully engineered highway, fifteen feet wide, with careful run-offs and banked-up sides, had no access to it yet; while the few humans who lived along its route continued to make their barefoot way over the soft, resilient mosses and heathers of the hills. In use, perhaps, it would begin to look as if it belonged. Unused, it was a gratuitous smack in the face of Nature. Even on a blazing June day there was something unnerving about rounding a shoulder of mountain to see ahead a great sweep of rocks and waters, tumbling on and down, into and out of narrow passes – a vista of startling greens, lichened greys, sparkling silver, sandstone reds and peaty blacks, stretching far to the horizon and the blue glitter of the distant sea. And slashed through it all the thin gravel highway, empty, bare, blind, and somehow malevolent. On Luke's previous journey, he had found nothing oppressive in this towering wilderness. Now, he was attacked by a stronger sense of isolation than ever in his life before.

They were all silent. It came as the strangest shock, rounding a bend, to see pitched in a sheltered dell by the roadside a few tents, with a handful of labourers supping their midday brose. They gazed at the travellers incuriously. The coachman's impervious London face stared straight ahead, and the groom sat as motionless as if he had been stuffed. Luke and Henry, from their lumbering cocoon, bowed in a stately way and passed on with never a word spoken. It was as unreal as a dream.

Luke glanced at Vilia. She sat absorbed in a corner seat, her bare head resting on the leather squab cushion and her eyes turned unseeingly on the bright world outside. There were deer on the hills. A pair of lapwings, large and crested, circled the carriage, shrieking to distract it from the vicinity of their nest. A male wheatear, dazzlingly elegant with his grey back, peach-gold breast, and kohl-rimmed eyes, surveyed it doubtfully from a cairn by the roadside, and then flew off with an admonitory chack-chack that was audible even over the gritty rumble of the wheels.

Vilia ignored it all. Luke glared at her. He knew she was going to spoil everything. Pessimistically, he decided that the wan, socially correct young woman of the city was the real Vilia, and that the vitality of the journey was merely a sign that she was overwrought. Now she would revert to her company manners, he thought. She was going to inspect all that his grandfather had done in his years at Kinveil – the thriving forestry development, the kelp manufacture, the stone cottages that were beginning to replace the turf houses of old, the new mortar in the castle walls, the repaired roof, the pretty stables he had built on the mainland in preparation for the day when the road should be complete, the flourishing kitchen garden. Inspect it all, and criticize – though not in words – like a returning owner inspecting the work of some conscientious but insensitive steward. For almost three weeks, Luke had succeeded in pushing his forebodings about this visit to the back of his mind. Now they returned in full force.

The sun was sparkling brilliantly on the water when they arrived, the far hills were smoky and two-dimensional like some theatre backcloth, and the fields sulphurous with new green. A lamb cried for its mother. The westerly breeze ruffled the feathery leaves of the rowan tree that guarded the end of the causeway, the tree that protected against the evil eye. Unless a witch, placing her hand on it, cursed the dwelling beyond.

Mungo Telfer was waiting for them. He had been able to see the carriage for almost five miles.

Cool, neat and contained, Vilia held out her hand to him, just as she had held it out to Lucy Telfer at St James's Square eight months before. 'This is most kind, Mr Telfer,' she said, and curtsied politely.

Mungo didn't even see Luke at first. He was much too interested in Vilia. Taking her hand in both of his, he held it, gazing into her eyes with a look of complete absorption in his own. 'Welcome home,' he said.

It was too much for Luke. With a shout of 'Grandpa!' and a wide, glad smile on his face, he ran forward and then turned to range himself beside the old man and welcome Vilia to Kinveil. He wanted to be sure she remembered that she was only a visitor, whereas he belonged there.

Chapter Three

1

The first evening was agony. Desperately, Luke wanted to rush out of doors and scuffle along the shell-strewn sands, or scramble up to some viewpoint from which he could see the long, shimmering path leading over the water to the red-gold feet of the sinking sun. It would have been enough just to lean on the castle parapet and breathe the pure, salty air, and savour the calm and the quiet, and the rose-rimmed hills in the afterglow.

It didn't occur to him that Vilia might be feeling the same as she sat there indoors making dignified and well-informed conversation with his grandfather and the other guests. To Luke's annoyance, Aunt Charlotte and her new husband had gone off on a round of visits, leaving only a skeleton staff at Glenbraddan and depositing the children, with their nurses and Edward's tutor, at Kinveil. The general opinion seemed to be that Edward would be company for Luke, while little Georgiana, coming up four, would be no trouble to anyone. Unfortunately, Edward was a pompous young bore. Luke remembered him only too well from the previous year. He didn't, in fact, say very much, but when he did it was so shatteringly commonplace that everyone else was temporarily deprived of the power of thought. Yet Vilia simply sat there, and listened, and talked, and never betrayed by as much as the flicker of an eyelash that she might have preferred to be elsewhere. Luke wasn't going to be outdone. While she stayed, he stayed.

It was better next morning. The sun was blazing in through the windows of his tower room when he awoke, highlighting the snowy linen and striking a satin glow from furniture polished with beeswax from Kinveil's own hives. Luke dashed from one window to another, dragging Henry with him to show him all the special sights.

Although Kinveil castle now ruled peaceably over an estate comprising almost a thousand square miles of mountain, loch, and river, it had been built in the thirteenth century as a watch-tower against Norse sea raiders. Whoever had chosen the site had known what he was about. The castle commanded all points of the compass. Set on the Hebridean coast of the Scottish mainland, on the angle of a long sea inlet that curled in from the west and then sharply to the south, it was protected on three sides by open stretches of water, and on the fourth – the east, to which it was linked by the causeway – by a steep rampart of mountains. Everywhere there were hills flanking the water, standing back a little along the western arm of the inlet, Loch an Vele, but rising starkly in the south to three thousand feet, their bare, salmon-red peaks riddled with white quartzite that glittered like salt crystals in the morning sun.

The slopes changed minute by minute as the sun moved round, rearranging the million-year-old scene with a fine, capricious sense of drama. It was a matter of planes and angles, Henry said unpoetically, as they watched Ben Dearg melt from something stark as an early woodcut into a soft, featureless wash of amethyst. Then, as the sun swam imperceptibly higher in the sky, everything was transformed again. The amethyst faded into emerald and jade, and they could see – etched with a miniaturist's precision – every fold of ground and every tree, every patch of heather and every frond of new bracken. Even Henry became silent after a while.

Luke almost had to be held down to eat his breakfast, the porridge that was still scalding hot, as was the way of porridge, despite its long journey from the kitchen to the top of the tower. Luke had forgotten how much he liked it, eaten not as it should be with salt and goat's milk, but with honey and warm, thin cream from the house cow, a pampered lady of indeterminate breed but unbounded generosity. Even so, he swallowed it hurriedly and then bolted downstairs to the Day Block to say good morning to his grandfather. He had his own reasons for haste, and for failing to hear his grandfather call him back as he scuttled across the causeway and took to the heather. He knew he wasn't going to be able to avoid Cousin Edward, but on this first day at least he was going to have a rattling good try.

Vilia had been awake long, long before. She had forgotten how early dawn came in June, and lay for a while smiling dreamily at the thought of all the school books that said the sun rose in the east and set in the west. Here at Kinveil, it scarcely rose or set at all in the summer, but simply dipped below the northern horizon for an hour or two. Daylight in June lasted for twenty hours; in December for less than eight. She had always thought how confusing it must be for the birds, and how exhausting in summer – especially for the dunnocks and robins, first up and last to bed.

By five o'clock she could bear it no longer, but rose and dressed and made her way a little nervously down to the kitchen, not knowing who or what she would find. But the brawny red hands wielding the spurtle and stirring a steady rain of oatmeal into the cast iron pot belonged to Jessie Graham, and the wide, innocent smile was the same as it had been when the Camerons had ridden away from Kinveil nine long years ago. There was a trace of uncertainty in it at first, as if she weren't sure what changes the years might have wrought in the child, but at Vilia's cry of, 'Jessie! Oh, Jessie!' the doubt vanished.

She drew the pot to the side of the fire. 'Haff you come to sup your parritch? Och, you are too soon. It will be twenty minutes yet before they iss ready!'

It was the characteristically Highland reference to porridge as 'they' that sent happiness surging through Vilia's whole being. This was the real homecoming, and she was hard put to it not to weep. While the porridge cooked, she plied Jessie with one eager question after another, and Jessie obliged with all the gossip of the last years. Vilia heard about Annie Bain's troublesome pregnancy, and Una Guffie's slovenly housekeeping, and how Fish Ellie had dropped a herring in the minister's teapot. And the most recent drama, of the gauger a few miles up the glen who had poked his stick in among some tree roots looking for an illicit whisky still, and found instead a wildcat's nest with kittens in it. The mother had flown out at him, a solid ten pounds of flat-eared, slit-eyed, bottle-tailed fury, so that he had missed his footing and fallen fifty feet to the rocks below. 'Near dead, he wass,' said Jessie with ill-concealed satisfaction, rising to add salt to the pot, 'when Robbie Fraser found him!' Nobody loved an excise man.

Jessie herself had been demoted from sole charge of the kitchens when Mr Telfer arrived at Kinveil, but she was perfectly philosophical about it. 'Och, I wass not bothered at aal, not at aal. I will neffer haff been anything but a good plain cook, and I haff neffer known what iss the difference between a *timbale* and a *turban*. It would not haff done, when he wass haffing guests with fancy tastes, do you see? So I am making the breakfast and the supper, and we haff a cook-housekeeper, Mrs Barrshaw – a Sassenach from Carlisle, but she iss a good soul chust the same – and she iss looking after the dinner. There is proper dinner effery day, you know? Soup and fish and entrées, and red meat and game and what she calls entry-metts. You will neffer haff seen the like!'

After the years of sitting tamely down to tea and toast, Vilia felt as if she were doing something gloriously improper by supping her porridge standing, in the traditional way, with the birchwood bowl in one hand and the horn spoon in the other. It was like a declaration of independence, and when she had finished she left Jessie to her duties and sallied forth to see old friends.

In the days that followed, she rarely set foot in the castle between breakfast and suppertime, sharing her midday meal with people who were not even names to Luke, people like Robbie Fraser the gardener, and Johnnie Meneriskay the herdsman, and Mary Matheson the gamekeeper's wife, and Becky Cameron the dairymaid, universally known as Becky Dairy. There was Nanny Macleod the henwife, who also had charge of the goat, and was permanently at loggerheads with Robbie Fraser because her dratted beast was always getting into his vegetable plot, and with Becky Dairy because both women held to it, buckle and thong, that their own animal's milk was vastly more nourishing than the other's. And, of course, there was Vilia's dear Meg Macleod, older now and heavier, but as bracing and loving as ever.

Vilia didn't ask whether Mungo Telfer was a good laird. She was, after all, a guest in his house. But she looked, and listened, and drew her own conclusions.

For days she waited for the kind of weather that would offer her an excuse to stay indoors, and at last it came. Fat dirty clouds rolled in from the west, slate grey and sullen and continuous, and the rain slanted down unceasingly on an oily sea, and the greens in the landscape were as livid as stains. And then she was able to ask Mungo, casually, if she might have permission to wander round inside the castle.

'Of course,' he said, smiling. 'Ye'll not find it's changed much.'

It was true. Vilia knew every stone of the place, and they all meant something. It was here that old Sandy Grant had slipped on the stair and given himself such a crack on the shin that he'd been able to avoid doing a hand's turn for weeks afterwards. It was there that Betty Fraser had dropped one of the Sèvres plates and set up such a wail that everyone in the place had come running to see if she was being murdered. It was along this corridor that some of Theo Cameron's guests had once raced view-hallooing after a fox that had inexplicably found its way into the castle. And this corner under the roof of the tower was where she herself had always gone to hide her heartbreak over some childish tragedy. She put her hand on the stones, almost as if she expected to find them still damp with her tears.

The tall, square tower was the oldest part of Kinveil. Over the centuries, other buildings had been added until the castle formed a rough U-shape with floors that, following the rocky substructure, had settled at a variety of levels that visitors were inclined to describe as 'interesting'. There were steps and stairs everywhere. Between the tower, which housed most of the bedrooms, and the Day Block, which was Vilia's next objective, there were four separate flights. She threw a shawl over her head against the downpour, picked up her skirts, and ran for it. That was one of the other peculiarities of Kinveil – there was no indoor access between one block and another. As each new building had been added to the old, each successive mason had come to the conclusion that there was no real need to break through twelve solid feet of stone wall merely to open up a doorway between one and the other. What was wrong with treating the central courtyard as if it were a hallway? And perhaps there *had* been nothing wrong with it in the fifteenth century, when the concept of separate rooms for separate purposes hadn't existed and everyone had lived, eaten, and slept in the Great Hall. But even Vilia was forced to admit, though never in words, that the system was scarcely ideal for nineteenth-century living. To go from the Long Gallery to the dining-room, and then to the drawing-room, and finally to bed, meant three separate forays into the courtyard – and that, more often than not, meant three separate forays into torrential rain, biting winds, and a shower of salt spray sent up by the Atlantic rollers battering against the great sea wall which closed off the fourth side of the courtyard.

Vilia turned back her shawl, shook the worst splashes from her skirt, and began to investigate the miscellaneous small rooms housed in the

Day Block. She already knew that Mungo had made himself a pleasant suite of study, living-room and bedroom, for he had told her almost apologetically that he was getting too old to have to go outdoors on a wild night when he wanted his bed. What she hadn't known was that he had also fitted up a study for Magnus and a charming drawing-room that must be intended for Lucy – *if* she ever came here. It was a far cry from the comfortable Berkshire where Lucy had grown up, and farther still from the London that was her natural habitat. Vilia had also discovered, during her months at St James's Square, that Lucy's attitude towards her father-in-law was slightly ambivalent. Certainly, it had been impressed on Luke that his grandfather was a gentleman; owning thirty thousand acres of land made him so, by definition. But the fact that it was his less than gentlemanly commercial genius that paid for everything from mediaeval castles in the Highlands to fashionable mansions in London, from Luke's own nankeen trousers to every last pin that held his mother's gleaming hair in place, was never mentioned. No one denied that the old man's fortune was extraordinarily useful, but everyone knew that it would be disastrous if society found out that it had been made in trade. Ninety-nine people out of a hundred would have felt as Lucy did, but Vilia was the hundredth. Like all the people of the glens, she was uncompromisingly egalitarian. The only human being most Highlanders looked up to was the laird, and that because he was a kind of Old Testament father figure to his people, a symbol more than a man. If ever they looked down on anyone, it was not for his station in life but for his personal failings.

With a sigh, Vilia turned back to the courtyard and scurried across to the building that housed the Great Hall and the Long Gallery above. Mungo, she could see, rarely inhabited the Great Hall, which still had its old familiar air of empty splendour. Vilia couldn't remember it ever being used, largely because the fireplace that was its only source of heat needed the better part of a tree trunk for kindling. She made straight for the spiral staircase in the corner, leading up to the Long Gallery, her own favourite room and, it seemed, Mungo Telfer's.

There was a melancholy pleasure in having it to herself. For a few precious moments it was as if the last nine years had never been. Most of the rooms in the castle were frankly chilly, for the northern sun didn't shine vigorously enough to warm the thick stone walls, and the slit windows were inadequate as a source of light, however splendid they might once have been for shooting arrows through. But some seventeenth-century Cameron had gone to the trouble of lining the Gallery with handsome oak panelling, and, deceived by the Union of the Crowns into believing that Kinveil's days as a fortress were past, had opened up a row of tall windows that gave a magnificent view westward along Loch an Vele to the islands.

His optimism had been misplaced. The windows had been shattered, time and again, in the course of the minor battles and skirmishes that had continued to plague the Highlands. The last time had been in 1745, when Vilia's grandfather, Gideon Cameron, had joined the cause of the Young Pretender in his ill-fated attempt to restore the Stewarts to their rightful throne.

It was a sadness to Vilia that she had never known her grandfather, who had loved Kinveil, she thought, with a passion as great as hers. After the disaster of Culloden, he had paused only long enough to collect a few of his worldly goods before sailing on the first tide for Europe and a life of wandering exile. He had been just eighteen years old at the time.

As far as she had been able to discover, he couldn't afford, or hadn't been invited, to accompany the defeated prince on that young man's subsequent aimless progress through Europe. Instead, young Gideon had made straight for Rome and the court of the prince's father, the throneless King James III. There, for twenty long years, he had survived as a minor functionary at the Palazzo Muti, the headquarters of the Jacobite cause in the Piazza dei San' Apostoli, sometimes even being paid a few *scudi* when the Old Pretender had made one of his formal visits to the Vatican and been rewarded with the largesse due to a son of the Church, who might one day – although the possibility receded year by year – be called to rule over Scotland and England and bring those countries back to the true faith.

But in 1766 the Old Pretender had died and there were no more Vatican subsidies. Gideon had gone to France, but his kinsmen there had made him feel like a poor relation. It had wakened his pride again, dormant for so long. He was still under forty, and his portrait showed him as tall and slim, with clear grey eyes and slightly hollow cheeks. He looked as if he had charm. Certainly, he must have had something to recommend him to the pretty and by no means penniless miladi he had married in 1768. Their son, Theophilus, had been born two years later, and had grown up in the brittle, extravagant world of Paris before the revolution.

When he was fourteen years old, the British government had decided to offer back to their exiled owners some of the Highland estates that had been declared forfeit to the Crown after the 'Forty-five, though not for nothing. The owners were expected to reimburse the government for what it had paid out during its period of caretaking. Gideon Cameron had been told he could have Kinveil back for a mere £17,326. Plus a few shillings. The government was nothing if not meticulous in its reckoning.

He had just enough, even, he estimated, the little extra that would enable him to repair the damage done by years of neglect and the depredations of the Redcoats. But his elegant French wife had taken one look at the forbidding pile, swathed in October mists, that her husband proposed living in, and had gone straight back to Paris with her relieved son clasped firmly by the hand.

Gideon had died ten years later. He had done wonders, but he was still able to bequeath to the boy only a partially restored castle, thirty thousand acres of uncultivated and largely uncultivable land, and a derisory amount of money.

Vilia didn't know, but she suspected that her father had tried to sell the place there and then. Failing, he had come to live here; and then Vilia's mother, whom he adored, had died giving her birth. After that, nothing would have persuaded him to stay. Vilia supposed he was to be pitied, but there was no space in her mind for pity. All she could think of was the betrayals – of herself, who loved it so much, and of his own father, who had also loved it so much that he had stripped himself of everything for its sake.

Vilia stared at the ring of old weapons, the dirks and the claymores, that still hung in formal array on the wall above the fireplace, and wept a little, for her grandfather, and for herself.

2

She was not yet aware of Mungo's consuming interest in her. He had been taken aback at first to find her so different from the passionate child he remembered. She was too pale, and too thin, and the fire in her eyes had been quenched. But because he knew what there had been, he refused to believe that this prim and correct young lady, with her conventional manners and almost oppressive politeness, could be all that was left. So he kept his distance to give her time to settle down, and was rewarded as day by day her complexion gained a little colour, and she began to come running up to the Gallery at suppertime with her hair very slightly ruffled and her company smile tinged with breathlessness and an afterglow of happiness.

Although five o'clock dinner was the main meal of the day at Kinveil, in summer it was informal. Those who chose to come indoors for it washed and tidied but didn't change, because the sun was up for another four or five hours and life continued in the open unless it was very wet. But Mungo insisted that everyone sit down to supper at nine thirty.

'Everyone' consisted of Mungo, Vilia and Luke; Henry Phillpotts; Vilia's governess, who spent her days like a lost spirit, wondering where her pupil had gone; and Edward and his tutor, an incorrigibly dull young man from somewhere around Aberdeen, whose accent no one but Edward could understand. Even everyday phrases came out like abbreviated hiccoughs. Luke amused himself one day trying to transliterate some of them, and the nearest he could get to 'What do you want?' was 'Fitchy*wah*hnt?' Fairly soon, everyone became so tired of saying, 'I beg your pardon?' and the tutor of repeating himself two or three times, that he gave up altogether and relaxed into a Trappist silence.

Supper was brought up on trays. Jessie Graham knew that Mr Telfer liked something plain at this hour, and she had been brought up to believe that folk who had been out in the open all day needed to go to bed with something substantial in their stomachs. So there was a central dish of mutton cutlets, flanked by smaller dishes of mashed potatoes, minced collops, rumbled eggs, and the vegetable purée known as 'bashed neeps' – mashed turnips flavoured with chopped onion tops, pepper, and a hearty amount of butter. To follow, there would be some kind of fruit pie or pastry. Mungo unfailingly welcomed this collation with what he knew Jessie wanted to hear. 'Nothing I like better than a good mutton chop. And a three-year-old Blackface ewe beats all the others to flinders.'

When Vilia, one evening, spooning a single best-end cutlet onto her plate, remarked, 'I'm surprised you haven't turned over to Cheviots, even so,' he was privately much cheered. It was the first time she had volunteered an opinion, and he set himself to draw her out. 'Aye, well,' he said. 'I might if I were going into the business, but I'm not moving folk to clachans on the shore just to make room for a wheen o' sheep. There's little enough good land hereabouts, and folk need it more than beasts do. No, I'll stick to my wee flock of Linton Blackfaces. They're enough to give us a bit mutton for ourselves and wool for the women's spinning.'

'But grandfather,' said Edward in his pursed-up little voice. 'Don't you think sheep make better use of the land than people?'

Edward was a disappointment to his grandfather. He was George Blair all over again. 'Aye, maybe they do. But what's that got to do with it? There isn't room for both.'

Henry, in insatiable pursuit of new material to add to the ragbag of his mind, inquired, 'But, Mr Telfer, sir, is there no alternative to clachans on the shore? Could the people not emigrate?' He waved his arm spaciously, and Vilia's governess, who was seated next to him, flinched. 'America or Canada, perhaps? All those wide acres! The land of opportunity! What might they not achieve in the New World?'

Mungo surveyed him dourly. 'It's well seen you're a stranger here! Their own wee corner of their own landscape matters more to a Highlander than someone like you could ever imagine.' Henry, who always claimed that imagination was his speciality, looked as if he were about to argue the toss, but Mungo forestalled him. 'I grant you a good many thousands of folk sailed to America from hereabouts not very long ago, but that was because they weren't given any choice.'

Vilia looked up. 'The people from Glengarry, you mean?'

'Just so.' Mungo snorted. 'That tup-heided tartan tooralorum that calls himself Alistair Ranaldson Macdonell of Glengarry . . .' He was delighted to hear Vilia choke on a giggle, but went on witheringly, 'Yon one! He'd geld a flea to make a farthing's profit! He moved them all out of their cottages, told them where they were to live in future, and was so indignant when they refused that he even used force to try and stop them from sailing. In my own view, if they had to move, they were right to move properly. It's a fine place, America; I served my own apprenticeship there. And looking back, the folk from Glengarry were lucky, too. It's not so easy to emigrate these days. The landlords have seen to that!'

Henry, frowning, said, 'But if they don't want the people on their land, sir, why should they interfere?'

Mungo had no great opinion of Henry, but at least he was showing an intelligent interest. Resignedly, he put his knife and fork down and said, 'They do want the people. It's just that they don't want them cluttering up the decent land Edward here thinks would be better for sheep.' Edward gulped, and stared fixedly at his plate. 'No, you have to understand. In these parts, there's no such thing as good arable land. You can graze sheep and a few cattle, and they don't need many people to look after them. But some things do need people, and a lot of them. You can't afford to be short of labour if you're cultivating timber, or barrelling fish, or making kelp . . .'

Henry said, 'Kelp?'

'Seaweed ash. It's used for making soap and glass and bleaching powder; a kind of alkali, I'm told. But it takes a lot of seaweed to make just a wee bit kelp, and that means a lot of folk to gather it. If you want to know what I mean, take Master Luke along the coast a bit tomorrow. The season's in full swing.' He fixed Henry with a glare, and then popped a forkful of rapidly congealing mutton in his mouth, saying, not very distinctly, 'My supper's getting cold with all this talk. I'm sure Miss Vilia can tell you as much as I can.' His pale eyes resting on her expressionlessly, he went on, 'Why don't you satisfy Mr Phillpotts' curiosity about how the lairds have put a stopper on emigration?'

After a moment, Vilia transferred her slightly pensive gaze back to Henry. 'You won't have heard of the Passenger Vessels Act of 1803?'

Mungo grinned to himself.

'It was sharp practice, nothing less. Conditions on the emigrant ships used to be terrible, and the Highland landowners prompted the government to pass an Act forcing them to improve their standards. It all sounded very fine, but the shipowners couldn't meet the new regulations without doubling their fares. It used to cost £3 or £4 from Fort William to Nova Scotia. Now it's nearer' – she looked at Mungo questioningly – 'nearer £10.' He nodded. 'And that's the kind of sum no Highlander can raise, especially if he has a wife and children as well. It's still a barter economy here, you know.'

Luke was feeling very much out of things. 'Couldn't they sell their furniture or something?' He had no idea whether there even was any furniture in the little turf or stone cottages the local people lived in. He'd never seen inside one.

'Don't be daft, laddie,' said his grandfather briskly. 'I doubt there's a cottage in the Highlands with furniture worth a couple of pounds, all in.'

Luke subsided into a sulky silence. His grandfather was looking at Vilia in a serious, approving kind of way, and she was looking seriously back at him. It was painfully clear that they were the only two people in the room who knew what they were talking about. Luke resented it deeply.

3

Next day, Luke insisted that Henry take him to see the kelping. It proved to be a splendid idea, not least because Edward explained in a very superior way that he had seen it all before, and besides, Georgiana might get dirty. So, if Luke didn't mind, they wouldn't accompany him.

Mind? Luke had been racking his brains for two weeks, wondering how to escape from the pair of them. If it had been Edward on his own, things wouldn't have been so bad, but he always insisted on bringing the baby along. Dear little Georgiana! Luke could have strangled her. All their expeditions were circumscribed by her infant needs and whims, because she couldn't run, or climb, or scramble, and a couple of hundred yards was as far as she could walk without becoming wobbly at the knees. The adults all nodded and smiled, and said how delightful it was to see two small boys taking such care of the little girl, but it was to be quite a while before Luke ceased to regard her with loathing and began to recognize her for the enterprising and engaging brat she was.

This unexpected respite from his cousins sent Luke off to watch the kelping in an unusually cheerful mood, and by the time he and Henry, inexpert oarsmen, had splashed their way up to the kelping beach – instead of doing the sensible thing, and walking – he was in a state bordering on hilarity. The beach was a hive of activity, and when the dinghy hit bottom Luke leapt out with a squawk of excitement, recognizing, among the crowd of unknown faces, that of Ewen Campbell, his mentor of the year before. He was crouching over a long, low stone kiln that appeared to be stoked with peat, and barely took time to throw Luke a smile before he turned his attention back to the fire again.

Luke watched avidly, though what he was supposed to be watching he had no idea. After a moment Ewen raised his hand and said something in Gaelic, and a woman in a short jacket and heavy striped skirt stepped forward and gradually tipped the contents of her creel on to the peats. Then Ewen said something else in Gaelic, and she stopped. Ewen had a ten-foot pole in his hand, tipped with a three-foot iron hook, and he used it to spread the seaweed carefully all over the surface of the fire; like spreading butter on bread, Luke thought, and making sure it was smooth and even, and went all the way to the crust. After a while, Ewen said, 'Aye, that should do,' and turned to Luke with a grin. 'The temperature iss ferry important, so it iss. Haff you come to giff us a hand, then?'

'Can I?' Luke demanded eagerly.

'Well, you could maybe start filling some of the creels from the slype over there.'

'Slype?'

'That sledge thing with the box on top.'

There was a crowd of local women and children round the slype with its load of wind-dried seaweed, and Luke approached them with some trepidation, noticing how their laughter and chatter died, to be replaced with shy smiles and silence. It didn't occur to him that none of them had the English, just as he didn't have the Gaelic, and he was very much relieved when, after an hour of exchanging beams with anyone who happened to catch his eye, in a mute attempt to convey goodwill, he saw Ewen beckoning him over to show him what was happening in the kilns.

'There you are,' Ewen said. 'That iss kelp.' The seaweed ashes had begun to accumulate in a kind of glowing, molten mass. 'When it cools down it will be aal brittle and blue-coloured. You will see if you stay with us long enough.'

By midday Luke had been promoted to the post of assistant seaweed-spreader, and was blissfully engaged when he glanced up and saw that Vilia had arrived. She was looking at him with her eyebrows raised – no doubt because he was as filthy as a chimney boy. The ten-foot clatt, or poker, hadn't been designed for someone his size, and the air round his kiln was thick with the black snowflakes he had succeeded in stirring up. But at least he was doing something useful.

No one was so unkind as to disabuse him of the idea. Vilia had come down from the castle kitchen with Jessie Graham and Sorley McClure, bringing the kelpers' midday meal, and within minutes they had been absorbed into the cheerful group round the slype, who had gone back to their chattering again. Luke's high spirits plummeted. It wasn't fair.

After a while, Vilia came over to where he was sitting munching oatmeal bannocks and crowdie and feeling left out. She plumped down beside him.

'Are you enjoying yourself?'

'Yes, thank you.' He swallowed a mouthful of buttermilk.

'You'll have to learn the Gaelic, you know.'

'I don't see why. My grandfather gets on perfectly well without it.'

'He speaks it a little.'

Luke hadn't known that. 'Only a little, though,' he risked.

'Well, he has an excuse. You can't expect a man of seventy to be fluent in a strange language. Everyone appreciates that.' She looked at him in exasperation. 'But the people here will expect *you* to learn, if you're going to be the laird some day.'

'Pooh!'

'Luke!' she exclaimed. 'I am trying to *help* you! Why must you be so sulky?'

He didn't answer, but made a great show of masticating his bannock.

Just at that moment, Sorley came over, juggling with some hot baked potatoes. They were pot black, and Luke wrinkled his nose disgustedly. Sorley grinned and tossed him one. 'Peats iss good for cooking other things as well as kelp.'

Vilia said, 'Sorley! How do you always manage to read my mind? I was just remembering how good baked potatoes were when we were children!'

'Aye, and I remembered something else, too.' Triumphantly, he produced a twist of cotton from his pocket, and opened it to reveal some salt.

Vilia laughed. '*Clever* Sorley!'

It was the first time Luke had seen Sorley since their arrival at Kinveil. He had abandoned his dashing London livery and was wearing a plain shirt and breeches, and his carrotty head was topped with one of the pom-pommed woollen tams known locally as 'toories'. Luke hadn't made up his mind about Sorley. He was only a servant, and Vilia's servant at that – two considerations that should have damned him wholly in Luke's eyes. But he didn't behave like a servant, though he was never forward or impertinent; more like a respectful equal. And there was no denying that he was likeable. He had the sunniest smile Luke had ever seen.

Luke surveyed his potato. 'What am I supposed to do with this?'

'You could try eating it,' Vilia said. 'I'll show you.' With her fingers she stripped away part of the skin, and then squashed the potato a little so that it popped open. 'Now, salt. And – Sorley, don't tell me you haven't brought a spoon?' He rummaged in his shirt pocket. 'Thank you. Now scoop some of the buttery lumps out of your buttermilk, and drop them in the middle. That's right.'

It was the best potato Luke had ever tasted. Through it, he mumbled, 'What were you all laughing at?' It didn't sound like an apology, but it was.

Vilia smiled. 'Just one of the latest dramas.'

'What was it?'

'There's a man called Willie Macrae who lives at Dunbarchan, very fond of his dram. Well, he was coming home one night, rather bosky, with a bottle of barm – that's yeast, you know? – in his back pocket for his wife to make some bread. He had to pass through the Howe of the Elms, which is a pretty eerie place even in daylight, and this was midnight. Well, he was getting more and more nervous when all of a sudden there was a faint hissing noise, just by his ear. It got louder, and louder, and louder, and eventually he panicked and began to run for all he was worth. But it didn't do any good, because suddenly there was a tremendous bang, and he felt a violent blow between his shoulder-blades.'

She giggled. Henry had flopped down beside them to listen – revealing that, under his cassock, he wore a serviceable pair of dark grey trousers.

'Well, as Henry knows,' Vilia said, with a mischievous glance at him, 'there are more things in heaven and earth, etcetera. When

Willie reached home he was more dead than alive. "What ails ye, man?" his wife said. And Willie said . . .'

She giggled again. 'Sorley, you tell them. You can do it better than I can.'

Sorley grinned, and declaimed, 'Och, I am done! I am done! Forgiff me, Lord, for my sins. Och, Guid save me. Guid save me. I am dead, woman! I am elf-shot. As I came through the Howe, the devil took me. See the blood pouring down my back. It iss a terrible thing, surely! I am dead, I am dead.' He clapped his hand over his chest and fell to the ground.

Luke couldn't begin to imagine what was so funny about this rather sinister tale. 'What happened?' he gasped.

Vilia showed signs of relapsing. 'I'll spare you the detail. When Donella got him inside, he wasn't covered with blood, but he *was* very wet. What had happened was that his nervousness – and the whisky – had made him rather warm, and the heat of his body had started the yeast working and *that* had forced the cork right out of the bottle. "It must haff given a great pop, do you see?" Donella said. "But it wass not an elf-shot at aal. Not at aal!"'

Henry gave an unclerical hoot, and after a moment Luke began to laugh, too. It really was very funny. Amusement grew like a bubble inside him, and soon he and Henry and Vilia and Sorley were all puffing and chuckling in companionable unison. Suddenly, Luke realized that here, in the peat-reeking heat of a June midday, surrounded by people with whom he had nothing in common, whose language was a closed book to him, he was happier than he had ever been in his life before. Except when he'd caught the salmon, of course.

And then Vilia spoiled it completely. 'It sounds much better in the Gaelic,' she said. 'You really *will* have to learn, you know!'

He tossed his head pettishly. 'I've no intention of doing any such thing. And you needn't sound so governessy about it, either!'

4

It was Mungo's birthday not long before they were due to leave, and he decided to make an occasion of it. There was to be a family dinner party first in the Great Hall, and then everyone on the estate was invited to a *ceilidh*, which, Mungo told his grandson, was a portmanteau word for anything ranging from a neighbourly cup of tea to a full-scale riot.

Dinner was at five, and the table was handsomely set with damask and crystal and silver, and there was a great bowl of red roses in the centre. Everyone was dressed to kill. There hadn't been any occasion for the visitors to wear their best clothes since they arrived, so Chrissie Fraser, the laundrymaid, had been working like a beaver all day. A faint miasma of hot irons and pressing cloths hung round the table. Mungo, whose everyday garb was an iron-grey shooting jacket – a concession to what he called his lairdliness, for he had never shot anything in his life – was smartly turned out in his best blue swallowtail coat, with gilt buttons, a buff waistcoat, and black trousers instead of his usual breeches. Round his neck were several soft white muslin neckerchiefs, and there was an impressive display of pleated shirt ruffles cascading from the front of his waistcoat. Luke and Edward were both clad in long pantaloons whose waists rested somewhere around their armpits, with short jackets and soft shirts to complete the ensemble. Luke could hardly wait for the day when his mama decided he was old enough to have a properly tailored coat.

But Vilia dumbfounded them all. She had condescended for once to abandon her bombazines, now a little rusty and salt-stained, and was wearing an exceedingly pretty half-mourning gown of pale grey muslin. The amethyst and gold filigree necklace was the first jewellery, other than the Kinveil ring, that Luke had ever seen her wear.

There was a strong atmosphere of best behaviour, although Luke's virtuous resolutions took a tumble when he discovered that Vilia had been seated at the opposite end of the table from his grandfather, as if she were the hostess rather than a mere guest.

It wasn't a very vivacious gathering, although everyone was pleased enough to be indoors. It had been an overcast day, not cold, but grey and depressing. The Great Hall looked surprisingly welcoming with a huge log fire, candles lit in their wall sconces, and the most enticing meal Luke had ever seen set out on the table. Although he would have died rather than admit it, it was his very first grown-up dinner party, and for one accustomed to nursery rules about eating what one was given, and no nonsense, the choice was stupendous. Mrs Barrshaw had obviously been as busy in the kitchen as Chrissie Fraser in the laundry.

There were two steaming tureens on the table, one full of chicken soup and the other of a delectable cream of barley and carrots.

'Potage d'orge perlée à la Crécy,' said Robert Fraser the butler with the greatest aplomb, just as if he weren't the gardener's son and the laundrymaid's brother. There seemed to Luke to be an impossible number of Frasers, and most of them employed in the castle.

The soups were removed with grilled trout and lobster cutlets, but it was the entrées that betrayed Luke into a childish gasp of sheer gluttony. Mrs Barrshaw had excelled herself. Afterwards, Luke particularly remembered the suprêmes of wild rabbit, the timbale of macaroni, some salmon steaks with a beautiful green sauce, and the sweetbreads. He scarcely even glanced at the pièces de résistance when they were brought in, since no boy of taste could be interested in a mere roast of veal and a boiled leg of mutton. Instead he persevered with the entrées, but when the entremets arrived, he wished he hadn't. For here were devilled kidneys, braised lettuces, potatoes in Hollandaise sauce, scrambled eggs with the first chanterelles of the season, and pastries, and caramel custards, and Genoese cake with a heavenly coffee-flavoured filling, and early raspberries. No one was expected to try even a mouthful of all of them, but Luke did his best.

He was much too busy to pay attention to the conversation which, in any case, was the usual duologue between his grandfather and Vilia, with occasional intrusions from Henry. Luke knew that, if he were to match Vilia's knowledge of Kinveil, he ought to be listening. But the Genoese cake was more appealing than modern forestry techniques, and the chanterelles a revelation beside which the saga of Macdonell's war against the Caledonian Canal Commissioners paled into insignificance.

In the end, blissfully full, he sat back and began to take notice.

His grandfather was saying, with a sly twinkle, 'I've passed then, have I?'

Vilia didn't answer directly. In her pale gown, and with her hair a bright aureole in the candlelight, she looked fragile, almost ethereal. Her eyes were like green opals. She said slowly, 'I was very excited to be coming back, and then I was afraid. I thought you might have changed everything, so that I wouldn't recognize Kinveil any more.'

Luke congratulated himself on having made an accurate analysis of her changes of mood on the journey. Well, almost accurate. Fear wasn't precisely the emotion he had credited her with.

'I thought you might have bought thousands of sheep, and demolished all the houses, or cut down all the trees. You might have added a modern extension to the castle, or panelled all the walls, or painted them. You might have brought in glossy new furniture, and neo-Classical paintings, and fashionable knick-knacks. That would have been dreadful.'

Luke raised a replete eyebrow. He had thought, as they sat down to dinner, that the Great Hall would be much the better for a coat or two of lime wash, and some decent pictures and up-to-date furniture.

Mungo said placidly, 'Aye, well. I might have done, I suppose. But I bought Kinveil because I admired it and wanted to stop it falling to bits. I wanted to preserve it, not change it.' He grinned. 'And you'll admit that, other considerations apart, it's not just the kind of place that lends itself to being converted into something modern and cosy!'

She smiled, but said nothing.

Mungo consulted his watch and then rose, glass in hand. Everyone else followed his example, even, with some officious assistance from Edward, little Georgiana, who needed both hands to clasp her tumblerful of water, faintly pink from the teaspoon of claret she had clamoured to have added to it.

'Now,' Mungo said decisively. 'My birthday was only an excuse. This party is really for Miss Vilia. As long as I'm alive, she'll always be welcome here.' Everybody smiled and beamed at Vilia, who was suddenly looking a little less than her usual composed self. Everybody but Luke, busy repressing a chanterelle-and-coffee-flavoured burp. 'And I'd like you all to join me in a toast – though not to the lady, because that would be bad form, wouldn't it?'

He grinned, and there was a moment's inexplicable pause. Then Luke saw his grandfather's eyes go past his shoulder, and there was a flurry of air which meant that the courtyard door had opened. The candle flames swerved wildly, and then steadied. The door must have closed again. Vilia's eyes were enormous, and – lethargically – Luke wondered why.

His grandfather resumed. 'The toast I give you is Kinveil! May its walls never crumble!'

Luke thought they were going to.

From behind him, quite without warning, came the most blood-curdling noise he had ever heard, a kind of breathy wail on a deep, single, interminable, and incredibly piercing note that gradually intensified, and then multiplied itself, until it became a ferocious, deafening, cacophonous, gargling discord loud enough to wake the dead. And then it stopped. Bang. Just like that.

Luke stared at the other people round the table, his mouth open and his eyes almost popping out of his head. His grandfather's face was expressionless. Georgiana was bouncing happily up and down, being held in some kind of check by her unmistakably bored brother. The tutor wore his usual slightly vacuous expression. But Vilia – thank God! – had obviously heard the noise, too. For a moment, Luke had thought he was going mad.

The silence lasted for only a few seconds. Then, right at Luke's back, and – inconceivably – at even greater volume than before, all cater-wauling hell broke loose. It was far, far worse than anything he could have imagined. It was like massed choirs of banshees, screaming hordes of Valkyries, a prehistoric plain-chant of tone-deaf dinosaurs. And all of them screeching in unison. Luke turned, very slowly indeed.

It was a man playing the bagpipes.

Weakly, Luke subsided into his chair while the noise, in which he was now able to discern something that might have been a tune, rolled round and round the Great Hall, rattling the glasses and the cutlery, shaking the candles in their sconces so that the flames shuddered and the wax dripped onto the floor, roaring from wall to wall and bouncing from echoing flagstones to resounding roof and back again. It was indescribable. Luke sat and shook, and waited for his eardrums to burst.

The governess was white as a winding sheet, but Henry was watching with the liveliest interest and an appreciative smile as the man strode up and down the length of the room, kilt swinging, eyes closed, cheeks puffed out, one long black tube between his lips, another in his fingers, and what appeared to be a whole fan of them over his shoulders. 'Good old Henry!' Luke thought faintly.

Then he glanced beyond Henry to Vilia. She wasn't looking ethereal any more. In fact, she was scarlet in the face, and her mouth was opening and closing as if she were saying something. Although she was only about five feet away, she might have been shrieking treason, murder, rape, and arson, for all Luke could tell. Then suddenly, and quite uncontrollably, she began to giggle as if it had all become too much for her. She had her hand flat against the base of her throat as if she were trying to hold back the pressure of her laughter, and he could see her drawing great gasping breaths. And in the end she collapsed completely, reduced to utter helplessness and clutching at both sides of her waist as if her ribs were aching. Her eyes were brimming with tears.

Luke's grandfather was watching her with the suspicion of a frown on his brow and an expression that was a little puzzled, perhaps even disappointed.

Silence fell. Crash. It was the first time Luke had ever understood the meaning of the expression. He had never thought of silence as such a positive thing.

No one said anything. It was as if all life and breath had been suspended. Everyone just sat.

Then, after a few blissful moments, Mungo said in a very polite, quiet, and controlled voice, 'Do you not like the pipes either?'

Vilia stared at him, and then, breathlessly, said, 'Not indoors. Never indoors!'

Mungo was surprised. 'They play them indoors in Glasgow.'

She turned to the piper, standing there waiting for his encore. Luke wasn't surprised to discover that she knew him.

'Dougal Mackinnon!' she said. 'I'm ashamed of you!'

'But I *told* him, Miss Vilia,' the piper replied, injured. 'I swear to God, I did! He chust would not lissen. He said you would be pleased!'

She turned back to Mungo. 'It was a lovely thought. But no matter what they do in Glasgow, it's different here.'

His beetling white brows lifted a little.

'The pipes are military instruments,' she explained, almost as if she were apologizing. 'They're meant to call the clans to arms and cheer them on in battle. They're no more intended for indoors than a battery of guns. I shouldn't think you'll ever meet a Highlander who truthfully likes the pipes in his ear any more than he likes standing under a gun emplacement.' She looked at him, her eyes wide. 'Truly. They're much better at a distance!'

Edward made his contribution. 'They sound best from across the water,' he said helpfully.

Mungo's smile was rueful. 'Aye, well. You know better than I do. So much for my surprise!' He pursed his lips. 'And what are we going to do tonight, then? Dougal here's supposed to be playing for the dancing.'

Vilia looked as if she were about to have a relapse. She turned to the piper. 'In the courtyard, with the doors open?'

'It's aawful near, Miss Vilia,' Dougal objected. 'But you'll maybe chust be able to stand it, I suppose.'

Luke saw that his grandfather was watching Vilia with amusement, admiration, and something very like affection. 'Whatever you say,' the old man agreed.

So Dougal stood out in the courtyard to play for the reels and jigs in the Great Hall that evening. The pipes did sound better from a distance. But Luke had the feeling that Edward was right about them being best across the water. Preferably the Atlantic.

Chapter Four

1

Magnus and Lucy, much refreshed by two self-indulgent months in Ramsgate, viewed the imminent return of the Kinveil pilgrims with an optimism that, in the event, proved to be sadly unjustified. When the lumbering berline rolled into St James's Square in September, it was at once apparent that, whatever their Highland sojourn might have done for the travellers' health, it had done nothing for their spirits. Even the horses looked despondent. Henry Phillpotts reported that two months of fat living and no exercise had turned them into the merest plodders, and Moonlight Flit had given up lying down in every stable yard because he knew he would be put to all the trouble of getting up again.

Lucy sighed and resigned herself. Her son, it appeared, disliked Vilia even more than before, and Vilia was as withdrawn as she had ever been. Her governess had re-entered the portals of St James's Square only to leave them again forthwith – Lucy had no idea why – but Vilia refused to employ another. Instead, she took on the role of companion to Lucy, shopping for her, arranging the flowers, consulting with the housekeeper, dealing with correspondence in her neat, legible hand, and keeping everyone at arm's length. It was as if they had never been away. The only one to derive any satisfaction from the situation was Magnus, who was able to say, 'I told you so.'

Then, in the downstairs parlour just before dinner one cold, raw evening in November, when Vilia and Magnus were conducting a desultory conversation before the fire, with Henry Phillpotts fidgetting in the background, and Luke, who had only just been promoted to dining with the grown-ups, standing by the window minding his P's and Q's, the air was rent by a faint shriek, accompanied by some rattling noises, and followed by a succession of bumps. Then there was silence. After a frozen moment, Luke, who was nearest, bolted through the intervening arch and doorway to the staircase hall.

There, he stopped dead, so that Vilia, close on his heels, collided with him. The scene that met their eyes was surprising enough, for there sat Lucy on the second stair from the bottom, knees wide, ankles showing, and an expression of extreme outrage on her face.

The butler and the first footman were already on their way to her when Magnus pushed past the two youngsters with a cry of 'No!' Reaching his wife's side, he knelt and took her hand. 'What happened, my dear? Are you all right?'

She didn't even look at him. Her gaze was fixed on her son, and she was clearly – and for the first time in anyone's experience – in a twenty-four carat rage. Jehovah confronting the legions of the damned could scarcely have invested his voice with a more ominous significance. 'Luke!' she said.

'Me, mama?'

'Yes, you. *Marbles!*'

All eyes swivelled towards him, and he turned a dusky red. 'I . . . I . . . I don't know anything about any marbles!'

She raised her hand and pointed. The marbles were not easy to see, because some were white china with cinnamon or ginger hairlines that merged almost invisibly into the *antico rosso* marble floor, while others were clear glass that picked up colour from their background. Luke's favourite shooter, a big black beauty, had come to rest at the foot of one of the pillars. It had always brought him luck. But not this time.

'Then how do you explain,' asked his mama, 'the fact that I – have – just – trodden – on – some?'

He couldn't. He had left Sorley McClure to dispose of the evidence. The game of marbles, much in favour with street urchins, was strictly *non grata* in polite society, and Luke and Sorley, who would have given themselves away if they had gone around chalking circles on the floor, had been inspired to use the stairs, whose inlaid pattern might have been made for the purpose. They had even invented special rules about the penalties to be imposed if one player sent his opponent's 'bool' over the edge of the tread. But today, they had heard someone coming, and Luke had cravenly taken to his heels. Sorley could hardly be raked down for being found in possession of marbles; he was only a servant. But it was different for Luke, whose papa held the strongest possible views on what gentlemen's sons did, and did not, do.

Looking a picture of guilt, Luke opened his mouth and then closed it again. His father advanced on him sternly. 'Have you been playing marbles, Luke? Answer me!'

The boy gulped. He knew only too well that he wasn't very popular with anyone. If he put the blame where it belonged, no one would believe him. *Everyone* liked Sorley.

The butler and footmen had tactfully evaporated, and Vilia was nowhere in sight. Henry was hovering uselessly, and Luke's mama showed no sign of moving from her stair, where she sat with one hand laid absent-mindedly over her heart. His father said again, 'Have you been playing marbles, Luke? Answer me!' And then, because the boy seemed to have lost his tongue, he took him by the shoulders and shook him until his teeth rattled. It was the first time anyone had laid hands on Luke in anger since his infancy, and on that occasion the offending nurserymaid had been dismissed without a character. Even through his mounting hysteria, Luke thought it silly that his father should be so angry about him *playing* marbles. What really mattered, surely, was that someone had left the beastly things where they could cause an accident. If his mother hadn't fallen backwards rather than forwards, she might have been killed. It was a very hard floor.

He gulped again and shook his head violently. From the corner of his eye he could see Vilia leaning against the archway to the front hall, her eyes closed and both hands pressed against the jamb.

'*Luke!*' his father bellowed.

And then Vilia's clear, silvery voice broke in. She was back at Lucy's side. 'Mr Telfer,' she said. 'I have sent a servant for the doctor, and asked the housekeeper to come up. I believe the most urgent thing is to see whether Mrs Telfer has sustained any injury.' Reminded, Lucy clutched at her heart and looked as if she were about to swoon.

Magnus loosed his son so abruptly that he almost fell. There was the briefest pause, and then he said, 'Thank you, my dear. You have done just as you should.'

Between them, they persuaded Lucy to her feet. No serious damage had been done except to a well-cushioned part of Lucy's anatomy that nothing in the world would have induced her to mention. It did cause her to groan a little as she was helped upstairs by Vilia and the housekeeper, clucking sympathetically. Magnus brought up the rear. Luke noticed that he didn't volunteer to carry her.

Apprehensively, Luke wondered whether he should join the procession, but all his instincts said no, and so did Henry. That young man grasped his charge firmly by the arm and sent him off to the schoolroom, recommending the backstairs route and a policy of least-in-sight for the next day or two. 'I'll see that someone brings you something to eat,' he said. Watching the boy scamper off, he decided that perhaps he, too, would be wise to make himself scarce.

2

It was almost two hours before Vilia was able to leave Lucy, suffering from slightly delayed shock, and make her way to her own room. She had just enough strength to close the door before her knees began to give way. Dispassionately, she wondered whether she would even be able to reach a chair.

Ten minutes later, she was still shivering completely and ungovernably, as if every nerve in her body were separately sheathed in ice. However tightly she clenched her teeth, however closely she drew her limbs together, compressing herself into the smallest possible compass like some wild animal preparing for hibernation, she couldn't stop it. When there came a quiet tap at the door, she had to summon up all her reserves to reply.

Her maid took one look at her and ran to the drawer that held the shawls. They didn't really help, but Vilia, through chattering teeth, thanked her just the same. 'And Berthe . . . F-fetch me a cup of hot w-water, if you p-please!'

With a hasty curtsey, the girl disappeared leaving her still in the half-dark. She stared at herself in the glass, her face ghostly above the garish plaid that hadn't been worn since her father died. In the weak glimmer of the single vigil candle, all the planes were softened and blurred – the high, slanting cheekbones, straight nose, the neat, firm chin and the arched brows over eyes that appeared huge and almost black. It was a face that didn't *look* wicked or evil, only ill. But she knew she wasn't ill. This was a *crise des nerfs* of a kind that had attacked her twice in her life before; once when she was seven years old and her father had told her they were to leave Kinveil forever; and once just a year ago, on her first day at St James's Square, when Luke Telfer had pushed her beyond the bounds of her endurance.

This time, she had no one to blame but herself.

She had found, at Kinveil, an unexpected kinship with Mungo Telfer. Her first uncomplicated joy at the prospect of going back – going home – had almost at once been alloyed by more and subtler emotions than she had been able to identify. There had been fear of change, of course; and resentment of Mungo Telfer. But when she found that Kinveil hadn't changed, and that Mungo Telfer had restored it and cared for it with insight and a loving discrimination, it had neither relieved her mind nor diminished her desire. Seeing it at its best, as in her dreams she had always done, had only made her exile more brutal. Better that the man himself had been vulgar and insensitive, and Kinveil transformed into a parody of what it should have been. She would have hated that, but it would have forced her to recognize that the past was irrevocably dead. Instead, her need was greater than ever.

One effect of the visit had been to change the focus of her resentment. She could accept Mungo at Kinveil now, but the thought of Magnus and Lucy inheriting it was quite unacceptable. Pleasant, indolent Magnus, who in the last analysis cared for nothing but his own comfort and convenience – and perhaps, a very little, for Lucy – would never stir himself to cherish Kinveil as his father had done. He didn't like the country much, and the Highlands even less. Left to himself, he would be a disaster as laird. Left to himself . . .

When Lucy had fallen on the stairs, the thought had flashed into Vilia's mind that it would have solved everything if she had broken her neck. Vilia's long-ago, forgotten dream of returning to Kinveil as Mrs Magnus Telfer had sprung up again, fully armed, from the darkest recesses of her soul. For what Magnus could not, or would not do for Kinveil, *she* could. She was appalled at herself.

A despairing, cataclysmic shudder racked her just as she became aware of a subdued bustle outside her door. '*Non, reste ici!*' her maid's voice hissed, sharp with annoyance, and a stubborn whisper, unmistakably Sorley's, replied, 'That I will not!' There was a faint scuffle, and then the door opened to allow the pair of them to shoulder their way in.

Berthe was carrying a tray with a cup on it and a vast, steaming silver pot, and Sorley bore a warming-pan and several flannel-wrapped hot bricks. His narrow hazel eyes flew to her worriedly and she contrived, somehow, to summon up a smile for him. While Berthe turned down the bed and Sorley ran the warming-pan between the sheets, she sat with her hands gratefully clasped round the hot cup, and sipped, and sipped again. Sorley, duty done, paused on his way to the door.

'Are you aal right?'

She nodded, and tried to smile again, but ruined the effect with another uncontrollable spasm of shuddering.

He stared at her for no more than a moment, and then turned and went. Even through her misery, the expression on his face puzzled her; anxiety, frustration – and something that looked remarkably like annoyance. She almost welcomed the problem, because it took her mind off the thing she didn't want to think about. Why should he be annoyed? He was the most contented human being she had ever known. Nothing ever worried him except when he knew that she was unhappy. She had sometimes thought that her well-being was the sole criterion by which he judged what was right and what was wrong, and that frightened her a little. She wondered whether he might be annoyed with Luke for causing the trouble that, indirectly, had upset her. Or was it possible that he himself had left the marbles where they shouldn't be? There was no one else in the house Luke could have been playing with. But no. Luke would never have taken the blame for Sorley's misdemeanour. And what did it matter, anyway?

By the time she was settled in bed, surrounded by the hot bricks, the shivering had begun to grow less, and she was no longer able to postpone the confrontation with her own horror and self-disgust. She felt physically sick as she remembered the moment when, leaning against the hall archway after she had sent for the doctor, she had suddenly realized what it might have meant to her if Lucy, instead of sitting ludicrously on the stairs glaring at Luke and his marbles, had been lying dead on the floor. Kind, generous, considerate Lucy, who might be a fraud in some ways, but didn't deserve *that*. Vilia would not have believed herself capable of feeling as she had felt in that moment of revelation. It was wicked, evil! And all because of Kinveil. She had always known that her obsession with Kinveil was dangerous, that it was distorting her life, although she had tried – God knew she had tried! – to break the bond. But she couldn't. As long as she was with people who couldn't help but remind her of it, she *could not*.

Her mind, arrested, remained in suspension for several moments, and then, laboriously, she went over it again. As long as she was with people who couldn't help but remind her of it . . .

The shivering had almost stopped. She put the cup down and gazed straight ahead through the pretty, sprigged curtains framing the foot of the bed. There was an old-fashioned mezzotint on the wall – 'The Farewell', or something of the sort. She had scarcely even looked at it before.

When Berthe entered quietly half an hour later, carrying a bowl of broth and a glass of negus, Vilia was exhaustedly asleep.

3

Lucy Telfer kept to her bed for a week after the accident, and looked on her son with reproach for a week more. Magnus, in the comfortable knowledge that no real damage had been done, spent most of his time shuttling between his clubs, although he spared half an hour to deliver an unpleasantly fluent lecture to Luke and his tutor. Luke meditated the possibility of giving Sorley a good hiding, but since Sorley was almost a foot taller and six years older than he was, decided against it. Vilia turned over a new leaf.

Lucy accepted the transformation with devout gratitude and no questions, even if a sentimental tear came to her eye when Vilia first called her 'Lucy' instead of 'Mrs Telfer'. She couldn't think what had brought the change about until, several weeks later, a letter came from Magnus's sister Charlotte, who had a flatteringly persuasive explanation. It wasn't Charlotte's custom to flatter, which made Lucy think that her remarriage must have something to commend it after all. '. . . and I know,' Charlotte wrote,

'that you will do your best to persuade my brother that I am happier than I could have believed possible with my *dearest* Perry! I cannot tell you with what feelings of joy we look forward to the arrival of the new baby. We *both* hope it will be a *girl*, and a girl with a nature as sweet and loving as yours, my dear Lucy! For I am convinced that Miss Cameron must have been *shocked* by your accident – which might so easily have proved fatal! – into realizing that you had found a place in *her* heart, as in the heart of everyone who knows you. Your goodness could not fail to touch even such a reserved girl as you tell me she has become – although only *you* could persuade me that she has changed so much from the hoyden I remember! But depend upon it, this is what has happened. And now that she has truly come to love you, she will certainly bow to your wishes and follow your advice on the course she should pursue.'

It was a pity that Charlotte, even in such a mood of Christian benevolence, still couldn't refrain from carping.

'Yet, my dearest Lucy, do you *truly* think she should make her come-out so soon? I collect she will be only just past her seventeenth birthday when the Season begins, which seems to me to be very much too young!'

But Vilia wouldn't hear of postponing her come-out until the spring of 1814, when she would be eighteen and, as she said, 'quite on the shelf'. Lucy wasn't sufficiently convinced that her present mood of amiable cooperation would last to run the risk of arguing, so it was settled.

In fact, Lucy was rather looking forward to the whole thing. Awe-struck, Luke listened to his mother – who should have been worn to a thread at the very thought of launching Vilia into society – blithely talking of all the pleasures in store as if she had never suffered a day's illness in her life. Balls, routs, assemblies, masques, balloon ascensions, military reviews, Venetian breakfasts, Turkish suppers . . . No one was tactless enough to ask whether her heart would stand the strain.

The weeks between what Luke thought of as The Great Decision and the beginning of the Season were a period of trial and tribulation for the males in the household. Before very long, Magnus began to lead an unusually active social life; there was scarcely an evening when he dined at home, so that Lucy and Vilia were able to discuss fashion to their hearts' content, while Luke and Henry sat in dejected silence.

Very occasionally, Henry would make an effort. 'Pomona green lutestring, did you say? What an interesting conjunction of words! Pomona was the goddess of fruits, of course. Under-ripe in this case, one must suppose!' Lucy failed to see his little joke, and Vilia, who had seen it coming from the moment he opened his mouth, accorded it no more than the faintest smile. 'And lutestring is what?'

'A fine corded silk.'

Luke gave his tutor a hearty kick on the ankle; anything to stop him embarking on a lecture on the relationship between dress fabrics and stringed instruments!

Morning dresses and walking dresses and riding dresses. Dresses for quiet parties and dinner parties and fashionable balls. Spencers, pelisses, cloaks, shawls, tippets, and Wellington mantles. Shoes, and half boots, and sandals, and satin slippers. Victoria hats, and caps à la russe, and bonnet caps, and gipsy hats, and cottage bonnets. Stockings, gloves, reticules . . .

The list was endless. Luke dropped his eyes to his plate. His mother and Vilia had been boring on for days about a pelisse with couched borders that was almost, but not quite the shade of Vilia's pale, silky hair. Cream-coloured. Moodily, Luke pushed his plate of cream pudding away.

4

When the Season began, it seemed as if the knocker at St James's Square was never still. The card rack was always full, and the number of hopeful young gentlemen who favoured Mrs Telfer with morning calls was prodigious. It was scarcely possible to enter or leave the house without running into somebody. Vilia was out most of the time, walking, riding, driving in the Park, going on picnics to Richmond or visits to the Botanical Gardens, and there was hardly an evening when she and Lucy were at home. Luke and Henry couldn't decide whether to feel left out or relieved that they didn't have to listen to any more talk of fashion.

Magnus was the only one who complained, and only at first. Lucy had told him soothingly that he must not put himself out for them, but he couldn't – he said – be expected to let his wife and ward venture unescorted to such perilous places as Almack's or Lady Sefton's. However, when he had been complimented a few times on his wife's protégée – a beauty, and quite out of the common run! – his grumbles became less convincing.

Over the matter of Vilia's wardrobe, Lucy had been forced to resort to a little mild deception. Twice, Vilia had rejected, regretfully but firmly, gowns that while not precisely cheap were so flattering that Lucy maintained they could not be considered an extravagance. But Vilia was adamant. She knew what she could afford. Lucy contemplated talking it over with Magnus, but he wasn't a natural conspirator and, besides, he had the fixed conviction that Telfer money should be kept in the Telfer family. So she sent off an urgent private letter to her father-in-law. As soon as she received his reply – which took the form of a messenger from his London attorney's, bearing a fat packageful of banknotes – she exchanged some confidential words with the various modistes who enjoyed her custom. After that, anything which particularly suited Miss Cameron turned out to be providentially reasonable in price.

Unfortunately, with the best will in the world, neither Lucy nor her father-in-law could think of any private way of increasing Vilia's distressingly meagre dowry, and no parent, however well-to-do, could be expected to approve a son's allying himself with a penniless bride, whatever her breeding and charm. But in the event, Lucy's fears proved groundless. Vilia was the success of the Season, and Lucy derived the greatest satisfaction from the envious glances thrown at her by other chaperones who had expected *their* charges to lead the field.

The only thing that worried Lucy now was the quality of Vilia's suitors. Among the most assiduous was young Merricks, heir to a substantial patrimony and worth, it was generally believed, not a penny less than £20,000 a year; it was a pity he was so volatile. Lord Shawe was another, though his estates were said to be somewhat encumbered by debt. And there was Sir Gethin John, a personable boy but rather too malleable; he was only nineteen, though, and might improve. Vilia seemed to have no particular preference. It was singularly unfortunate, Lucy considered, that this Season's young men should all be so immature – lightweight was the word that sprang to her mind. The only really adult ones were army or navy officers on leave, and they were not at all what Lucy had in mind for Vilia. Apart from anything else, most of them were younger sons. Heirs to substantial properties were seldom allowed to go to war and put their lives at risk. But there was no denying that even quite young officers had an air of authority and experience that could not help but be attractive to a girl like Vilia, who had an assurance far beyond her years. There was one in particular, a pleasant but reticent captain from the Peninsula, who was doing his best to monopolize her, and though Vilia was far too well-bred to permit him to do so, Lucy was apprehensive.

'But what is he *doing* in London?' she asked a little fretfully one evening on the way home from the Opera. He had been there, as he had been at every party they had attended of late. 'I understood that Lord Wellington was quite strongly opposed to his officers going on leave!'

Vilia laughed. 'Oh, yes. He hates them coming home, because it sets such a bad example to the men. But Captain Lauriston just happened to choose the right moment to ask. When Wellington took up winter quarters in Portugal last November, it seems that all his young gentlemen took one look at Frenada and promptly put in applications for urgent home leave. Captain Lauriston says it's a horrid place – a filthy village, with mouldering houses and rutted streets and a church bell that never stops tolling. Anyway, Old Hookey was so . . .'

'Vilia!'

'I assure you! That's what they call him. Oh, very well. His lordship was so annoyed that he turned them all down flat. When Captain Lauriston applied two or three weeks later, Wellington was still in such a good humour at having put so many of his "idle young gentlemen" in their places at one blow, so to speak, that he granted his request with scarcely a murmur!'

Magnus looked down his high-bridged nose, so like Wellington's own. 'Doing it rather too brown, Vilia! I don't believe the field-marshal can be quite as childish as that.'

Vilia twinkled at him. 'I have it on the best authority, I assure you! But I think the truth probably is that Captain Lauriston is very conscientious, and what they call "a good fighting officer". Brrrr!' She shuddered expressively. 'And he had been in the Peninsula without a break since 1809, so even Lord Wellington might have thought he deserved a few weeks' leave. He is in London now because he was told to come here when his leave was up and await further orders, which haven't yet materialized. So all he has to do is report daily at the Horse Guards and spend the rest of his time going to parties. He doesn't lack invitations, as you may have noticed.' Lucy glanced suspiciously at her, but her expression was quite artless. 'Hostesses are always happy to have dashing young officers on their guest lists.'

'Surely he must be recalled soon?' Lucy asked hopefully.

'No doubt. But not before the ball!' This time there was no question in Lucy's mind but that Vilia was being provocative. She shook her head reproachfully.

The ball she was giving for Vilia was imminent, and she was determined that it should be a triumphant success. For a week beforehand the house was in turmoil, and the day itself saw as much coming and going as if three thousand guests, rather than three hundred, were expected. Tradesmen and errand boys and delivery men thronged St James's Square and the mews behind. Magnus had said, in a magisterial way, that all such persons should enter through the mews, but this soon proved not only impractical but very upsetting to the horses. By the time fifty or sixty gilded chairs had been manhandled through the stables, the head groom was at his wits' end and the housekeeper almost in tears over the straw and manure that were being tracked into the house, sheeted floors notwithstanding.

By midday, a good deal of intemperate language was also coming from the Square, as lads bearing unwieldy trays from Gunter's and baskets of fruit from Covent Garden cannoned into the men who were erecting the awning over the flagway, or trod mud on the clean red carpet that was being unrolled down the front steps. The crossing sweeper was beginning to feel as if he hadn't sat down for a week. Indoors, the staff and extra help were here, there, and everywhere, laden with great boxes of candles for the dining-room and ballroom, or tottering piles of table linen, or potted plants, or curtains for draping over the front of the musicians' platform. There was an occasional nightmare crash as a tray of wine glasses met its doom, and at one point there drifted upstairs the unmistakable sound of a kitchen-maid having hysterics.

Lucy spent most of the day laid on her bed, while Magnus did what the harassed butler had been hinting he should do for a week, and took himself down to the cellar to select the champagne. Vilia was left to deal with all the problems that arose above stairs, and did so as capably as if she had been supervising such affairs for years.

Luke and Henry, having been tripped over and bumped into by almost everyone, took themselves off to Mr Bullock's Museum, just round the corner in Piccadilly. It was a restful place, full of stuffed elephants and zebras and boars, and visitors so overcome by the atmosphere of dust and scholarship that they, too, might have been products of the taxidermist's art. Even the attendants looked as if they hadn't moved for years.

Long before the last of the guests had arrived, it was clear that the ball was going to be a great success. It was an impeccably *ton*-ish company that trooped upstairs. Debutantes in pale satins and muslins, with gold or silver nets on their hair and a few ringlets clinging to one cheek. Their elders in stomacher bodices and trains and diamonds, with Moorish turbans or small, plumed satin hats. Most of the men were in tail-coats and black satin knee breeches, but there was a sprinkling of military and naval dress uniforms.

Lucy's smile became a trifle fixed when she found Captain Lauriston bowing to her in the receiving line at the head of the stairs. His uniform gave him an unfair advantage – doubly unfair when he had a figure that would have been striking even in civilian clothes. His face was no more than conventionally handsome, and customarily wore a rather stern expression, but his considerable height and muscular build gave him an air of splendour with which few other young men could compete. Magnus, beside her, was also studying the captain. No need for his tailor to pad out the shoulders of *his* coats, or cut his waistcoats to conceal an incipient bow window. Then a new group of guests came smiling up the stairs, and Captain Lauriston was released to go in search of Vilia.

Another man, freed from the Telfers' dismaying scrutiny, might have allowed his relief to show, but not Andrew Lauriston. At the age of ten, overgrown and awkward, he had been sent to a school for young gentlemen that was prepared to admit the son of a minor Scots ironmaster only because its finances were so unstable that even an ironmaster's money was better than none. Andrew hadn't expected to enjoy the experience, because he had known he would be jeered at for his inferior birth, but what he hadn't foreseen was that his fellow pupils would find the contrast between his eager, anxious nature and his

Herculean size hilariously incongruous. It had taken him a good deal of time, and a good deal of heartache, to develop a manner to match his physique, but by the time he left school for the army no one would ever have known that his impassivity hadn't been part of him from birth. And by the sheerest fluke, it had been reinforced when he found himself appointed temporary aide-de-camp to Lord Wellington. His lordship's regular staff included such men as Sir Alexander Gordon and Lord Fitzroy Somerset, who were kin to some of the greatest peers in the land and showed it in an easy self-assurance with which Andrew couldn't compete. All he could do was cultivate his habit of reticence. It proved an acceptable substitute.

Otherwise, he had learned never to put a foot wrong. Even the highest social stickler could find nothing in him to complain of – except, perhaps, a certain lack of sparkle – and no one doubted either his breeding or his dependability. The only trouble was that, deep inside, he was as eager and anxious as he had ever been. It was his misfortune – almost his tragedy – that he had reached a stage, not where he *wouldn't* show it, but where he couldn't.

Not even to Vilia Cameron, who had haunted his dreams, day and night, for weeks, and who belonged to the world that wasn't, despite all appearances, his. But for once in his life, he didn't care. He was obsessed to a point where he would allow no consideration to stand in his way.

He moved across the upper hall towards the series of large and elegant chambers that served the house as a ballroom. Everywhere was splendidly decorated in white and gold, and lit by huge crystal chandeliers whose lustres had taken the second footman, the pantry boy, and Sorley McClure two days to wash and polish. On pedestals between the long windows that looked out over the square were great urns of early summer flowers, crimson and pink, and the orchestra was banked into a green and leafy bower. The whole effect was charming.

The captain found Vilia at once, surrounded by a throng of gallants who had besieged her as soon as she came off the floor.

'. . . quite radiant!' one of them was saying.

'Thank you.'

'And how fortunate,' interposed another comically, 'to be able to match your gown to the decorations!'

Vilia, watching a girl in an unhappy shade of puce move hurriedly out of range of the roses, gurgled delightfully and agreed. 'One of the undoubted advantages of living here.'

Radiant was the word, the captain thought besottedly. Most debutantes wore insipid whites, or jonquils, or powder blues, but Vilia's ball gown was of the finest, silkiest Indian muslin, woven of smoky green crossed with pale rose threads so that it changed colour as the light caught it. The style was the very latest, a tunic overdress falling to about a foot above the ground, revealing a straight, clinging slip below. The neckline was low and round, but Vilia hadn't made the mistake of filling it with vulgarly glittering stones. Her only adornments were a delicate string of pearls and a single pink rose in the Grecian coil of her silver-blonde hair. Lucy had feared that this toilette was altogether too *à la mode* for a girl in her first Season, but it was so ravishing that she hadn't had the heart to say no.

Andrew Lauriston bowed over Vilia's hand and wished her good evening. But before he could say more, she told him demurely, 'My friends are all so determined to do their duty this evening that every dance is bespoke, Captain Lauriston!'

She had been going to tease him a little, but relented almost at once. He was not the kind of person who understood teasing. 'However, I have saved the third waltz for you. If, that is, you *wish* to dance with me?'

Her smile melted his bones. He stammered, 'Oh, Miss Cameron, as if I . . . And perhaps you will permit me to take you down to supper?'

She hesitated. Lucy would disapprove. And then, 'That would be delightful,' she said.

The captain had come only to see Vilia, and for almost an hour stood just inside the door, oblivious to the dagger glances cast him by chaperones of the partnerless young ladies sitting on their gilt chairs, chattering vivaciously with one another. Expressionlessly, he watched Vilia go down a country dance with that unreliable puppy Merricks. Then she stood up with Julian Lewis, spineless young cub. Then with Thornton of the Life Guards, a smooth fellow with a vicious streak. Captain Lauriston disliked him intensely.

Lucy, entering the ballroom on her husband's arm, observed the direction of the captain's gaze and was not slow to interpret its meaning. What a provoking young man he was, standing there as if he were on sentry duty and ready to murder anyone who stumbled over the password!

'Captain Lauriston,' she said sweetly. 'Do allow me to present you to Miss Delavalle. I am sure she would be pleased to stand up for the cotillion with you!' Inexorably, she bore him across the room and introduced him to a blushing damsel who accepted his hand with real gratitude, subsequently a little dimmed by the discovery that her partner was paying more attention to Miss Cameron than to the intricacies of the figure.

The supper interval did nothing to console the captain. It would have been too much to hope that he would have been left alone with Vilia, but their table at once became the scene of a convivial party, so that he had to devote more time to ensuring supplies of lobster patties and champagne than to advancing his interest with her. By the time it was over he had come to a decision.

When he claimed Vilia's hand for the promised waltz, he was as wrought up as he had ever been in battle. The situation didn't seem to him very different. It was a question of win or lose, and nothing in between. All his experience of soldiering taught him that it was folly to wait for ideal conditions that might never come, and that action, once decided on, should follow before delay had time to drain the stiffness from one's spine. After they had circled the floor only twice, therefore, he swung Vilia towards one of the long windows, open to the mild air, and out on to the rail-enclosed ledge that the house-builder had dignified with the name of balcony.

There was no real impropriety, as they were still in full view of the ballroom, but Vilia was annoyed. The captain's attentions had been altogether too particular, and although she had nothing but contempt for jealous tongues, she saw no purpose in stimulating them unnecessarily. She looked up at him, her eyes wide and startled, but he forestalled her.

'It's wrong, I know,' he said, 'but it is torture to me never to have you alone. It is like living in a glasshouse, not just this evening, but every evening, every day. You are always surrounded by people.' He paused, and gathered his courage together. 'My time is running short. With Wellington on the move again, I will be recalled very soon. And there is something I must say to you.'

Her heart sank to the level of her pink satin slippers. She had known for days that something was coming, but she hadn't expected it tonight and certainly not in full view of three hundred people. How *very* unhelpful of him, she thought. No taking her hand, or clasping her in his arms, or going down on one knee to her, as young Gethin John had done only a week ago. She had handled that situation with perfect sang-froid, because he was only a boy and she had felt sorry for him. But Andrew Lauriston was different, although he was only five or six years older. He was undoubtedly a man, and a determined one. She didn't know how she felt about him, and thought that perhaps a kiss or an embrace might have told her. Perhaps! A quiver of fear or excitement, she didn't know which, ran through her as she realized for the first time how very inexperienced she was.

He was standing as rigidly as if he were on parade, and to Vilia it seemed as if everyone in the ballroom must be watching them. A little helplessly she turned to face out on to the square, which forced the captain also to turn his back on the company.

Politely, she repeated, 'Something you must say to me?'

He took a deep breath. 'I am no hand at pretty speeches, I fear, and I can't offer you a title, or great estates, or a fortune. I have only a modest competence. But you know my situation.' He turned his eyes to hers, and her heart began pounding erratically in her breast.

'I have little to offer you now, compared with your other suitors, although if you gave me your love I know I could achieve great things. But no one – *no one* – could offer you more devotion or deeper adoration than I.' He stopped, as if to regain control over his voice. 'Miss Cameron. Vilia! I love you so much. If you will not marry me, I . . .' Leaving his words hanging in the air, he turned his face away from her again.

To her own surprise, she felt a sudden desire to stretch out her hand to him. Instead, she said softly, 'I understand.' It would have been maidenly to blush and ask for time to consider, but she felt that, somehow, that would be insulting. They weren't adolescents playing adolescent games.

She had made up her mind that, whatever happened, she would find a husband before the summer, because only marriage could release her from the orbit of the Telfers – and Kinveil. She could more readily imagine marrying Andrew Lauriston than any other of her suitors. She didn't think she was in love with him, but love matches were rare in the property-conscious world of the *haut ton*, and most girls married the husbands their parents chose for them. Vilia, at least, could choose for herself. And if she refused Andrew Lauriston, who else was there? Although she had smiled at Lucy's animadversions on this Season's crop of eligible males, Lucy had been right. Nothing but unformed, pleasant boys still tied to their parents' or their trustees' apron strings. That would mean a long period of engagement. It would mean living in a mother-in-law's shadow, even – impossible thought! – in a mother-in-law's house. Whereas if she married Andrew, whose mother was dead and whose father lived four hundred miles away, she would have her own life and her own home. She would have privacy, too, for it was in the nature of a soldier's calling to be much abroad. The French wars had begun before Vilia was born, and she couldn't envisage a world where the army was on anything other than a war footing. In most ways, marriage to Andrew Lauriston would suit her very well. It was just that . . . But perhaps, she thought, encouraged by the music and lights and laughter in the ballroom, she might in time be able to persuade him to take life a little less earnestly.

The silence had lasted too long. She glanced at him obliquely. He was as still as if he had been cast in bronze, his eyes resting unseeingly on the first of the departing carriages. Somehow, his very stillness made up her mind for her. Since she was seven years old, she had always felt alone, but now, uncharacteristically, she had a sudden desire to be like all those other women in the ballroom – bound by ordinary family ties to flesh-and-blood people. She wanted to be loved and protected, to have someone to lean on, and if Andrew Lauriston was the strong, reliable man she believed him to be, she would try very hard to love him in return.

She said, 'Captain Lauriston,' and he stirred. 'You must speak to my trustee, because it is not for me to give you an answer. But for my part, I will be most – happy – to be your wife.'

5

By the time two days had passed, Luke Telfer was almost frantic with curiosity. Although the ball had been a *succès fou*, his mother looked as if she were about to dissolve into tears at any moment, his father was distinctly grumpy, and Vilia appeared to be holding her breath most of the time. No one would tell Luke anything, including Henry, but he suspected Henry didn't know anything anyway. The only thing to do appeared to be to embark on a rigorous programme of eavesdropping.

Not until the Friday, when he was almost ready to give up, did he hear anything worth hearing. Late in the afternoon, he was lurking assiduously in the hall when the knocker went.

'Captain Lauriston to see Mr Telfer,' said a faintly Scots voice.

'Yes, sir,' replied the footman. 'You are expected.'

The two sets of footsteps marched past and faded in the direction of the library, the footman's muffled like those of all good servants, and the captain's clicking with military precision. When the footman had returned to his post in the hall and everything was quiet, Luke picked up a copy of the *Morning Chronicle* for an alibi, and made his stealthy way towards the library.

There was a figure already standing outside the door, with its ear glued to the crack. Luke poked it in the ribs with his newspaper and mouthed, 'Sorley McClure! What are you doing here?' But Sorley only grinned and reapplied his ear to the door. Luke hesitated, feeling it was beneath his dignity to join him, but curiosity won.

'. . . not her guardian,' his father was saying. 'The late Mr Cameron's man of business was appointed to that office. It is to him that you should address yourself.' He sounded thoroughly starched-up.

'I understand that, sir, but it appeared to Miss Cameron and myself that it would be the gravest breach of courtesy if I did not first apply to you. You have been kindness personified to a young lady who has no claim on you. Miss Cameron assures me that you have been as considerate to her as a – as a brother.'

Andrew Lauriston was an honest young man and found it difficult to dissemble. What Miss Cameron had actually said was that Magnus, although not yet thirty, had a knack of behaving to her like a great-great-grandfather.

'Ha! Harrumph!' Magnus responded, vaguely flattered, and went on a little less stiffly. 'There is no doubt, of course, that Pilcher will attend to what I say. On the other hand, I am by no means convinced that you are a suitable match for her.' In actual fact, the captain could have married Vilia tomorrow, with Magnus's goodwill, but Lucy had forced him into a corner. 'It is not,' he resumed, 'up to me to inquire about your prospects, or what you have to offer a young lady who has been accustomed to live in the most genteel circumstances.'

It might not be up to him to inquire but, by Jupiter, Andrew thought, he was going to be piqued if he wasn't told. 'I appreciate your scruples, sir,' he said. 'But I could not expect you to put in a word for me with Miss Cameron's trustee without knowing more about me than you do. I have been with Wellington in the Peninsula since 1809, when I was nineteen years of age, and if the war continues I hope soon to have my promotion. The field-marshal gives me to understand that he finds me a satisfactory officer.'

'Even so, you can scarcely set up on a captain's, or even a major's, pay!'

'No, indeed, sir. My father makes me an allowance, and I expect he would increase it if I were to marry. I believe I might be able to rent a small house in the better part of town. Somewhere like Half Moon Street, we thought.'

Outside, Luke and Sorley nodded at each other approvingly. That sounded all right; small but tasteful, and quite suitable for a pair of newly-weds, especially if the captain wasn't going to be cluttering the place up all the time. Luke had succeeded in placing him now, a curly-haired fellow of godlike proportions, in one of the Highland regiments. Henry said the 42nd, but since Henry always said things authoritatively even when he had no idea what he was talking about, Luke couldn't be sure. But for Vilia to be thinking of marrying him – well, well!

'Do you have brothers or sisters?'

'No. I am the only child. My father, like yours, I believe, has devoted most of his life to business . . .'

Luke almost spoiled everything then by giggling at Sorley, who was tearing his hair in anguished dumb-show. The captain had made a serious mistake, and Luke hoped it wasn't going to scupper his chances for good and all.

But Andrew had noted Magnus's reaction to the vulgar mention of business, and was quick to change his tack. '. . . but he succeeded early enough to ensure that I had a good education. A tutor, of course, and then public school. I would have gone on to Oxford, except that nothing would do for me but to have my father buy me a pair of colours!'

Magnus, to whom such an ambition appeared the height of absurdity, smiled perfunctorily. 'And – uh – what precisely is your father's business?'

'He's an ironmaster. The foundry is near Falkirk, not far from Edinburgh.'

Magnus wasn't impressed. Ironmastering was a dirty, manual kind of work. At least Mungo Telfer had kept his hands clean. He harrumphed again, and then said, 'Plenty of business for him with war materials, I suppose? Any – uh – prospect of a title, or anything like that?'

Andrew was startled. 'I shouldn't think so. My father has no political involvement.'

'Pity. Have you consulted him about the marriage?'

'I have written to say I hope to have the felicity of receiving Miss Cameron's hand, but there hasn't yet been time to receive a reply.' He wasn't, in fact, looking forward to the reply. The old man wasn't going to be pleased.

'Yes, well,' Magnus said. 'You are aware that Miss Cameron's dowry is not large. A matter of a few hundred a year – barely enough to pay for her gowns.'

'That makes no difference to me, sir. I have no need to marry Miss Cameron for pecuniary reasons!'

Magnus was not a small man, but when the captain pokered up he felt like one. Hastily, he said, 'Quite, quite! Well, I suppose we should have her in.'

Sorley recognized the significance of Magnus's footsteps before Luke did. Miming the tug of a bell-pull, he took the younger boy by the shoulder and hurried him off at a fast tiptoe back towards the parlour where, with one of his blinding smiles, he left him.

A few minutes later, Luke heard the tap of Vilia's sandals making for the library, and then his mother's more languid step. After that, it was the butler with the refreshment tray. Too much traffic, he thought gloomily, and with the greatest reluctance turned his attention to the *Morning Chronicle*. Jesu, but it was dull!

6

Vilia's mind was made up, and nothing Lucy could say would shift her. The wedding took place two weeks later at St George's, Hanover Square, with Lucy acting as matron of honour, and a monosyllabic fellow officer of Andrew's filling the role of groom's man. The only other guests were Magnus, Luke, Mr Pilcher, and Andrew's father, an even larger man than his son, and with manners anything but conciliating.

'Goodness,' Lucy murmured to Vilia, who was looking subdued and colourless. 'What a disagreeable person!'

'He is, isn't he? Thank heavens he lives at a safe distance. I should be frightened to death otherwise.'

The wedding breakfast at St James's Square was not prolonged. Luke thought the groom a very dull dog. Even though he was grateful to him – Lord, *how* grateful! – for taking Vilia off the family's hands, he wondered what on earth she had seen in him. But perhaps soldiers were always beef-witted on their wedding day. Vilia wasn't at her best, either. The white poplin gown with blonde lace flounces and the pink-trimmed yeoman's hat seemed to emphasize her pallor and thinness. All through the meal, there was a small, cheerful voice in Luke's head warbling, 'Good-bye! Good-bye!' He smiled and waved with what his mother later told him was unbecoming enthusiasm when the happy couple drove away to Grillon's hotel, where they were to stay until their house was ready.

They had been at Grillon's for two weeks, and in the house in Half Moon Street for two days, when Andrew was recalled to join the Peninsular army at Santander.

Vilia wept when he had gone, but not from regret. She had thought she knew what she was doing in marrying him. She had thought she was prepared for the physical side of marriage. Her country childhood had taught her what happened, and Lucy, with real heroism, had told her more, in blushing and somewhat convoluted terms, on the night before the wedding. 'That side' of the relationship, she had said, appeared to afford pleasure to one's husband, but one should not oneself expect anything from it other than the pleasure of giving one's husband pleasure. 'Oh, dear! Am I making myself clear? However,' she had gone on, 'I am perfectly sure that Captain Lauriston must be aware of this, and will be as gentlemanly about it as dear Magnus is. You have only to express your disinclination, you know, if you feel that you are not quite up to it on any occasion. The merest word is enough.'

It was a week before it occurred to Vilia that Lucy's 'merest word' carried all the weight of years of delicate health and a reputedly weak heart. And perhaps Magnus was less – less *hungry* than Andrew. She had married him hoping to gain privacy for her mind, and instead was being forced to surrender the privacy of her body, totally and completely, again and again and again, insatiably. It was as if Andrew could not look at her without wanting her, and no word from her could stop him when he was in need. His only concession was to say, 'Please! Why not? I love you so much!' without for a moment hesitating in the urgent ritual that left him gasping with ecstasy, and her weary, aching, and filled with shame. Just so, she imagined, did a man treat his whore. As she lay under his heavy, invading body, morning after morning, time after time throughout each night, the only thought in her head was, 'What have I done? Oh, God, *what have I done?*'

She wept with relief when he left for Santander. At least, for a while, her body was her own again. Or so she thought, until she found herself – she, who had never been ill – racked at the beginning of each day with a nausea that was its own diagnosis.

Chapter Five

1

It was Vilia's attempt to cut Kinveil out of her life that led to Luke Telfer's real discovery of it.

It was a discovery that began in June 1814 when he had been separated from his parents for almost a year. The part Lucy had manifestly played in Vilia's introduction to society had provoked Mungo Telfer to an ultimatum. Her first visit to Kinveil, he wrote, which had been postponed year after year because of her health, would now doubtless appear as no more than a minor fatigue after the exertions she had undergone, apparently without ill effect, in London.

He would therefore expect his daughter-in-law, his son, and his grandson at Kinveil during the latter part of July. If that was convenient.

With a sigh, Lucy had bowed to the inevitable. Accompanied by three maids, four footmen, one valet, one tutor, and the most imposing collection of baggage the ostler at the Green Man at Barnet ever remembered seeing, a family cavalcade set out for the Highlands three weeks after Vilia's wedding. When it returned in September, Luke and Henry Phillpotts were no longer with it. By sheer force of personality, and without so much as a mention of who controlled the family purse strings, Mungo had carried his point that it was time for the boy to learn something about the estate he would inherit some day and the world that encompassed it. Luke was to attend Inverness Academy during term and spend his holidays at Kinveil. Only for a year, Lucy had said pleadingly, and Mungo, who had no opinion at all of Henry Phillpotts and a high opinion of Inverness Academy, had replied mendaciously, 'Aye, well. We'll see.'

Looking at the weary and woebegone ten-year-old who returned to Kinveil after his first year at the Academy, he wondered whether he had been wrong. The school had been founded by voluntary subscription in 1791, and its governors made sure that the subscribers were given value for their money. Education was what they had paid for, and no one could doubt that the boys were educated to within an inch of their lives. English and trigonometry, Latin and navigation, Greek and natural philosophy – Luke's mind had reeled at the very sight of the curriculum. There was no slacking even on Sundays, and holidays consisted of two weeks over Christmas and the New Year, and a magnanimous five weeks in the summer that Luke thought must have been granted by some kind of oversight.

He had never been so exhausted in his life, and his grandfather, with a sigh, conceded that he could stay at Kinveil until he recovered his strength, even if it took five months rather than the five weeks allowed by the school calendar. Like the majority of belligerently healthy people, Mungo was terrified of illness.

It was a summer that Luke was always to remember, one of those periods of pure, unshadowed happiness that rarely last for more than a few days. This one lasted for twelve idyllic weeks.

2

It began one night in the latter part of June. Mungo, taking advantage of the season, when there were only a couple of hours of darkness, had driven over to Glenbraddan to see Charlotte and the children, who now included eighteen-month-old Grace. Henry Phillpotts was away, too, because his mother had died and Mungo had given him permission to go and settle her affairs. Luke couldn't imagine what kind of woman had borne and reared Henry, whom he had always thought of as springing fully-cassocked from between the pages of some volume entitled *Great Windbags of History*.

Luke should have been in bed, but he found it difficult to sleep during the light nights and eleven o'clock found him leaning on the sill of his tower window, gazing south for a sight of his grandfather's carriage returning. True visibility was only about fifty yards, but it was possible to see much further when there was something moving against the background of the water. All, however, was silent and empty. Restlessly, he strayed to the opposite window, wondering whether anyone was still awake in the village. Not a gleam of light showed from the little cluster of cottages a mile away up the beach.

It was a few moments before he became aware that there was something going on much nearer at hand. Highland nights were full of rustlings and creakings and shufflings, especially in June, when even the wildlife seldom slept and the chaffinches did their best to ensure that no one else did either. Luke could have throttled the voluble little male whose territorial round included his bedroom window-sill, for he began his song at three each morning and didn't give up until just before midnight. Unless he was seriously disturbed. Luke became aware that he hadn't heard him for a while.

Firmly suppressing thoughts of ghosties and ghoulies and long-leggity beasties and things that went bump in the night, he hitched himself up on the sill and turned over on his stomach to wriggle forward into a position from which he could see what was going on at the base of the tower. It wasn't easy to look out of the window when the wall was twelve feet thick. Peering downward, he was dimly able to make out a scene of intense, and extremely stealthy, activity. There seemed to be a great many people engaged on something productive of faint squeaks, subdued thumps, and occasional muffled exclamations in Gaelic.

Luke, though inquisitive, was also extremely lazy. He backed into the room again and tugged the bell. One of the servants, he thought, would know what was going on. No one came. He tugged again, and waited. In the end, curiosity won. Tucking his shirt into his pantaloons and lighting a candle, he set off on the long eerie journey down the windowless staircase to the courtyard. As he reached it, his candle died in a puff of wind and he stopped, his heart in his mouth.

It was a few moments before his eyes adjusted themselves. Then he tiptoed quietly up the stairs to the sea wall and sidled round the corner of the ramparts until he could see what was going on. There were almost thirty men on the beach, and there was also something floating in the little bay that he hadn't seen from above because it was so close in to the castle wall. A boat. An ordinary fishing smack by the look of it. He had been out in one, once. It had a single cabin aft, and most of the space below deck consisted of a hold ballasted with stones when it wasn't full of fish. There was much coming and going between the boat and the beach, although the faint sough of the wind helped to smother the sound of feet splashing through the water.

All at once, Luke heard a pleasant English voice murmur quizzically, 'Fine, Ewen. But what next? That's the question.' The voice came from a tall, lithe figure in shirt, waistcoat and breeches, and it sounded vaguely familiar. But Luke was temporarily diverted by realizing just what all the activity meant.

Smuggling in the Highlands wasn't an illegal occupation for the few, but a casual labour for the many. No one was remotely interested in the laws against it. People who would run a mile after a stranger to restore a shilling he had dropped would break the smuggling laws without a thought. Everyone, lawyers and ministers of the kirk included, either made, bought, sold, or drank illicit liquor. Even excise men, however dedicated in the early days of their careers, usually gave up after a while, so that it was sometimes necessary for the smugglers to bury a cask where it couldn't help but be found. Rumour had it that this often meant putting it in the excise man's own peatstack. The newspapers were then able to puff off a 'seizure of illicit spirits', thus restoring the gauger to the favour of his superiors and saving the local people from having to put up with an enthusiastic new broom. The sad truth was that illicit whisky was vastly superior to the legal product, and considerably cheaper besides. But it was inevitable that people who ignored the rules about whisky were apt to ignore them in the case of other kinds of liquor, too – French brandy, for example. All this Luke knew; he had heard his law-abiding grandfather complaining about it scores of times.

He was still gazing open-mouthed at the ankers of spirits – dozens of them! – that the men had already carried from the boat to the beach, when he heard Ewen Campbell hiss, 'He iss risking it! He iss coming in!'

It was only then that Luke saw the other boat, nosing its way carefully in through the narrows of Loch an Vele. It was still two or three miles away, he supposed, and it had no more than a shred of sail hoisted, but it was a sleek ship with fast lines. With a shiver of excitement, he realized that it must be a revenue cutter.

'Damn!' said the shirt-sleeved voice cheerfully. 'Have we time to reach the caves?'

'Neffer. They are too far, and he iss sure to be seeing the movement on the hill.'

'How long before he hoists out the boat, do you think?'

Ewen breathed out gustily. 'Half a mile, a mile maybe. He iss sure to send a dozen men at least, and it iss a long way to be rowing.'

An aged retainer hobbled up to the two men, who were standing slightly apart from the centre of activity. It was George Macleod, the Kinveil orraman or jack-of-all-trades, who was joiner, butcher, weaver, lint-dresser, wool-comber, dyer, and a good many other things besides. Including, it now appeared, smuggling foreman. He mumbled something in Gaelic and Ewen said, 'Thank the Lord! Tell Peter Fraser to get hiss men back on board and take the *Bride* down to Inverbeg. He will find shelter there. Tell him chust to leave the cargo to us.'

Within minutes, the entire crew was in a rowing boat towing the fishing smack quietly and smoothly through the water. The skipper was at the wheel, no sail was showing, and they kept close inshore where the mountains cast a dark shadow on the choppy water. In no time at all, they had merged into the scenery.

'Right then, Ewen!' said the Englishman gaily. 'Let's go. If we keep to the top of the beach we should be invisible against the rocks. We must stay clear of the sand and the roadway.'

'Aye,' Ewen agreed a touch sourly. 'But where are we going *to*? They will be searching effery corner, so they will, and a dozen excise men will be going through the clachan and the byres like a dose of salts.'

Perhaps because Luke knew less of the countryside than the men on the beach, the answer seemed glaringly obvious. There was only one place nearby where the casks could be hidden. He tried an 'Oi!' but they didn't hear, so he attempted instead one of those low, penetrating, sibilant whistles produced by curving the upper lip and teeth over the lower, and blowing. Even to him, the resultant 'wheep' sounded like a gust of wind finding its way through a door that didn't fit very well. He hissed again, with no better result. Then, with one eye on the cutter and the other on the beach, he risked a subdued 'Hey!'

'What the deffle!' Ewen's head jerked round.

'Up here,' the boy squeaked excitedly.

Both faces looked up, white masks in the shadows.

'Ye gods!' said the Honourable Peregrine Randall in mock despair. 'We are undone. Flee, Ewen! All is discovered!'

Luke had met his Aunt Charlotte's new husband only twice, once just after Christmas and once the previous summer during his parents' stay. Mungo Telfer had developed a reluctant liking for the young man, but Magnus had refused to budge from his opinion that the fellow was a gazetted fortune-hunter, a scoundrel, and probably a libertine as well. It would have taken a saint to convince him otherwise, and whatever Perry Randall was, he was not a saint. Their first meeting had been very stiff indeed, and both men had gone out of their way to avoid a second. Luke, on the other hand, had been desperately impressed. Perry Randall was the very model of what he would have liked to be – tall, elegant, stylish, with darkly waving hair, amused grey eyes, and a long, smiling mouth. He badly wanted Perry to take notice of him.

Unable to think of a witty riposte, he ignored his uncle's frivolity and said breathlessly, 'What about the kilns where they burn the kelp?'

There was a moment's silence, and then Perry Randall slapped Ewen triumphantly on the back. 'That's it! Of course. The boy's got it in one. Can we get the stuff there?'

'Maybe. Yess. But we need the slypes and the peat barrows.'

Luke, perched on top of the parapet, was gratified. Then it occurred to him that, although he wasn't strong enough to carry an anker of spirits, there was something he *could* do. It didn't strike him as noteworthy that he should want to do anything at all, nor did he realize that, if Perry Randall hadn't been there, he probably wouldn't even have raised his voice in the first place. 'Shall I go up to the village and get someone to bring them? I could ride up on the sheltie.'

'The hoofs,' Ewen objected. 'They would hear them across the water.' He threw a glance towards the cutter, still creeping along slowly but perceptibly nearer than it had been ten minutes before. The night was by now almost as dark as it was going to be.

'Don't be such a killjoy,' Perry said. There was a smile in his voice. 'Do you have your dirk?'

Ewen removed the little dagger from the top of his stocking and handed it over.

Perry was stripping off his waistcoat. 'And we'll need strings, laces, or something of the sort.' He began tearing the garment apart at the seams. Wordlessly, Ewen picked up some strands of rope from the beach. 'Fine,' Perry said. 'Come on, boy! Down to the stables as fast as you can!'

On winged feet Luke ran back through the courtyard, through the Great Hall, then outdoors again and over the causeway. When he reached the stables, his uncle was already there, swaddling the pony's hoofs in sections of his waistcoat and tying them in place with pieces of rope.

With a laugh, he hoisted the boy up on to the willing little beast, saying, 'Bareback along the top of the beach. Can you do it?'

The boy felt he could do anything. He laughed back. 'Of course! Try me!'

'Send the sledges to meet us, then. We'll be on the way!' He gave the pony a slap on the rump and they were off.

The sheltie made nothing of the difficulties. It was as if he, too, were infected by Luke's exhilaration. The boy sank his fingers in the pony's mane and the pair of them went hell-for-leather along the beach in the direction of the village. Not until they were level with the fourth house did Luke manage to convey to him that this was as far as they went. Reluctantly but amiably, the pony pattered to a halt and Luke slid off and made for the nearest front door.

He tapped as quietly as he could. Too quietly. There was utter silence. He tried again and this time heard the faintest shuffle of movement inside. The door opened a crack on darkness, but he was able to distinguish a rheumy eye, with part of a woollen night-cap above and a shawl beneath.

'Michty!' quavered this apparition. 'What for are you chapping on my door at this hour of the night?'

'We need the slypes and the peat barrows in a hurry, mistress,' Luke gasped. 'The revenue cutter is coming in.'

'Michty!' said the apparition again, a good deal more decisively. The door opened fully, a muscular arm reached out, and Luke, without a moment's warning, was seized by the scruff of the neck and yanked inside. He had never been more surprised in his life.

It seemed that he had established his credentials. He found himself confronting a sturdy, elderly woman, fully clothed despite the night-cap, and as brisk and businesslike as if it were full day. Her face was vaguely familiar.

'Wass you knowing Meg Macleod's house? No? Well, I will be going there while you tell Mairi Campbell next door that her man wants the slypes. Go on with you, laddie!'

'What about the sheltie?'

'I will be seeing to him. He can be going in the byre.'

Within a few minutes, every woman in the place was out and the first of the slypes was gliding smoothly round the top of the beach towards the castle. Luke found himself sharing the ropes with a remarkably pretty girl of about eighteen. Her name was Kirsty. Puffing, he said, 'Why wasn't everything ready and waiting? We're never going to do it in time, are we?'

'We wass not expecting anything,' she said. She had a soft, seductive voice. 'Peter Fraser wass supposed to be going over to Portree, do you see, but the revenue cutter must haff seen him and chased him in here. The men chust went down to see what it was aal about, and it must haff seemed that the most urchent thing wass to unload the smack and send it clear.'

Over the loch they could hear the sound of the cutter's lead being cast, and the voice of the leadsman telling off the depth of water under the bow. The skipper, unlike Peter Fraser – not *another* Fraser! Luke thought – was unfamiliar with Loch an Vele and taking no chances. Even so, by the time the two smuggling parties met, the cutter was only a mile away.

As the men who had been humping the casks eased their burdens on to the sledges and barrows, they heard a sharp rattle of orders and looked up, momentarily frozen. Against the open water, lighter than inshore, they could see the longboat being hoisted out and the dark figures swarming down into it. Scores of them, to Luke's inexperienced eyes.

Ewen Campbell's low voice said, 'Hurry!'

'Move, young Luke!' murmured another voice at Luke's side, breathless but vivid. There was a mischievous grin on his uncle's face as he turned to the girl. 'And Kirsty Macintyre, by all that's wonderful! What a pity I can't stay and pass the time of – er – day with you, but I have things to attend to.' With a carefree wave of his hand he was off, pursued by an almost inaudible chuckle from Kirsty. Luke stared at her. There was a smile at the corners of her lips. He stored it away for future reference.

By the time the sledges had been loaded, turned, and dragged back towards the kilns, Ewen and Perry and half a dozen of the other men had almost finished what they were doing. Usually, at the end of the day, the kelp was removed from the kilns and the fires 'smoored', or half-smothered, by drawing the ashes over the embers to keep them alive for next morning. The men had been shovelling out the ashes and dousing the embers with water, a regrettable but necessary precaution, since a few ankers of overheated spirits would have produced a blaze to put the Northern Lights to shame.

Although they could hear the cutter's longboat, they could no longer see it, for it was now in dark water. Very stealthily indeed, they placed the ankers of spirit in the kilns, covered them with fresh peat, and then with great shovelfuls of ash. The boat was very near. It seemed to be making not for the beach, but for a point slightly north of the village.

'The deffle,' Ewen breathed. 'If they get there before we do and find all the cots iss empty . . .'

Perry murmured, 'There's only one thing to be done. Get all the people from the village back there right now. The castle folk can stay a few minutes longer. Luke and I will see that everything is done that needs to be done.' There was a flash of white teeth in Luke's direction, and he felt ready to burst with pride and happiness.

Ewen's hesitation lasted only a moment. 'You are right,' he said. Almost at once the beach began to empty itself. There were no giveaway sounds of clacking heels or nailed boots as the villagers fled back to their homes, for at Kinveil, as everywhere else in the Highlands, people went barefoot in summer, and often in winter too.

Those who were left – who included Robert Fraser the butler, a couple of maids, and Jessie-Graham-the-good-plain-cook – swiftly cleared up the evidence. The slypes and barrows were lined up innocently side by side, the kilns were inspected to make sure that not even a gleam of wood was visible under the ashes and peats, and the sand was stirred up to hide where the dousing water had been spilled. When they heard the longboat scrape to a landing on the beach further up, Perry sent the servants back to the castle while he himself remained for a last careful survey of the scene. Luke was almost dancing with impatience before, with another flash of teeth, his uncle tapped him lightly on the shoulder and the two of them sped back along the beach in the direction of home. Somewhere behind them they could hear the disciplined tramp of feet along the road.

Luke was trying to gather enough breath to gasp, 'We've done it!' when his uncle's hand dragged him to a slithering halt. The gravel was crunching ahead of them as well as behind. None too gently, Perry pushed his nephew into the shadow of the causeway. 'A carriage!' he whispered.

It was then that Luke remembered his grandfather.

After a stunned moment, Perry subsided helplessly onto a rock, doubled up in silent laughter. Honest, law-abiding Mungo Telfer! The only man within a hundred miles who virtuously paid duty on his champagne, claret, port, and Madeira! 'I thought he was safe in bed, sleeping the sleep of the just!'

'No, he's been to see Aunt Charlotte and the children. He'll meet the excise men! Jesu!' Luke shook his afflicted uncle by the shoulder. 'Come on! We've time to get indoors before him. They won't see us if we bend low over the causeway!'

The carriage rolled past. Mungo, it seemed, was on his way to investigate the activity up the road. They heard a rumble of voices, and then Mungo's, crisp and clear. '*Such* nonsense! I never heard the like!'

'They won't see *you*, you mean,' Perry whispered. 'I'm not here at all. I'm twenty miles up in the hills, inspecting the sawmill at Monadh!'

Luke hesitated. It hadn't occurred to him to wonder why Perry Randall had been here to be caught up in the smuggling operation.

They heard Mungo say, 'Do you mean to tell me you're waking up the whole clachan? Getting respectable folks out of their bed in the middle of the night because you *think* there *might* be some smuggled goods about? We'll soon see about that! Just you take me to whoever's in charge, and I'll put a stop to it. *Such* goings-on!'

The sounds began to fade.

'Well done, the old man!' Perry said. 'Now's your chance, Luke. Off with you, and I'll see you again in a day or two!' As the boy moved away, his uncle's soft voice followed him. 'And well done you, too!'

Bent low, Luke scuttled across the causeway, into the castle, and up to his room. Half an hour later, as the sky was beginning to lighten, he witnessed the rout of the enemy as the excise men, empty-handed, retired to their boat and rowed off again to the cutter waiting in the bay.

3

News travelled fast in the glens, and the official version of the night's events reached Kinveil the very next day. The revenue men, it appeared, had been pursuing an innocent fishing boat which, owing to some of its crew being asleep and the others a trifle well to live, had failed to respond when the cutter ordered it to stand to for a routine search. The skipper had subsequently explained this lapse to an irritable but unsurprised revenue officer, who knew enough about the fishing fraternity's drinking habits to see nothing out of the ordinary in it. Peter Fraser had been deeply apologetic.

Mungo, still simmering three days later, pounced delightedly on Perry Randall when he rode over to make his excuses for having been absent when Mungo called at Glenbraddan. It was Perry's custom to keep an unobtrusive eye on his wife's grieve, or steward, who, though an admirable fellow, needed supervision, and this meant that he sometimes had to spend a night away from home, up at the shielings, perhaps, or at one of the little sawmills just below the tree line, powered by the mountain streams.

'Aye, well,' said Mungo, who wasn't listening. 'I was sorry to miss you. But it was my own fault for not having let you know I was coming.'

Perry gave such a sympathetic hearing to Mungo's views on having honest citizens rootled out of their beds by jumped-up jacks-in-office who wanted to turn the country into a police state – as if that wasn't what we'd just finished fighting a war to prevent! – that when the young man raised the second purpose of his visit, Mungo agreed without a murmur. Knowing that Henry Phillpotts was away, Perry said, it had occurred to him that Luke might like to bear him company on days when Glenbraddan business brought him within reach of Kinveil.

Turning to his grandson, Mungo said, 'What do you think, laddie? Would you like that?'

'Yes, please!'

'And we might,' Perry went on, 'teach you to handle a gun. It's about time you learned.'

'Yes, *please!*' Luke said again.

'Fine. That's settled, then. We'll have a splendid time, the pair of us.'

Mungo blinked. 'The pair of you? What about young Edward?'

Perry was standing with his back to the window and his expression was unreadable. But there was no mistaking the sardonic note in his voice when he said, 'You must have noticed, sir, that my stepson regards me as a frippery fellow. Some day, no doubt, we will call a truce, but in the meantime I am still a very inadequate substitute for his father. I understand they had a good deal in common.'

Mungo grinned. 'Aye, you could say that!'

'In any case, Edward knows the countryside as well as I do. Better, perhaps. There's little I can teach him. Whereas in the case of young Luke here . . .'

'I want to know *everything*,' Luke said, with all the emphasis at his command.

During the next few weeks, his education began in earnest. He learned about birds and plants and rocks and rivers. He visited the shielings and the sawmills. He discovered how the local people lived and what they worked at. He became quite a good shot with his little gun, a single-barrelled muzzle loader that weighed no more than four pounds. Although the game season hadn't begun, there was plenty of vermin to practise on. His first great triumph came one day when a hoodie crow sat on a post and sneered at him from what it thought was a safe distance. When the smoke of the black powder cleared, there it lay on the ground with its toes turned up, dead as a dodo. Luke was jubilant.

Sometimes they went fishing, although Luke considered fly-fishing poor sport compared with the mass slaughter that could be achieved with a seine net in the bay. One day they played truant and set off on an excursion to the islands in a fishing smack not unlike the *Bride* of joyful memory. And on another occasion, this time with permission, they stayed out all night climbing to the 3,000-foot top of Ben Guisachan to see the dawn break. It was September by this time, and there was a touch of frost in the clear air. The whole firmament glittered. Even what seemed at first to be empty spaces revealed, when Luke's vision became adjusted, a teeming mass of pinpoint sparkles – stars, stars, and more stars.

They slept under them for four hours and then climbed the last few yards and waited for day. Gradually the dusk began to fade to a clear, pale green, and then to silver, and then the sun edged over the horizon, turning the little streamers of mist from grey, to coral, and then to white, while the whole eastern horizon shimmered in rose and flame, and the rivers and lochs glistened darkly, and the shadows began to appear, long and black. Soon, they could see for twenty miles in all directions. To the west, the sun tipped the Red Hills of Skye with a dazzling pale pink, outlining them against the dark serrated ramparts of the Cuillins behind. The islands drifted on a colourless sea, and beyond them, stretching from end to end of the far horizon, there was a wide, rich band of apricot and gold.

Suddenly, it was day. They lit a campfire and made coffee, and ate oatcakes and cheese, and laughed and shivered in the clean, crisp air. It was like being in at the creation of the world.

And Perry was Luke's god, though Perry didn't realize it at first, noticing only, with amusement, that the boy was trying to copy some of his mannerisms. It seemed harmless enough. The unfortunate brat had been starved of normal human company, deprived of natural outlets for his youthful exuberance. It had been Perry's impression, to begin with, that the boy had been ruined by the combined efforts of his parents and tutor. He had been sullen, tongue-tied, and lackadaisical. But the smuggling episode had suggested that there was still hope for him, and Perry, carelessly kind, had decided to take him in hand. He himself, God knew, needed something to distract his mind from problems that grew daily more acute.

Luke, suffering from a bad case of hero-worship, had neither the desire nor the perception to separate the man from the idol. Spoilt, possessive, and incurably self-centred, he judged other people entirely from his own standpoint, and noticed only what affected himself. In general, he liked people who treated him well, and disliked those who did not. In Perry, he had met for the first time someone who gave him, without reservation, something he had not known he needed – a sense of excitement, adventure, a humorous vitality that acted on him like a tonic.

He tried very hard to model himself on his hero. A returned Henry Phillpotts, sulky over his exclusion from the boy's expeditions with his uncle, caught him more than once seated before the glass practising the art of raising one eyebrow, or crinkling his face in the attempt to produce a smile that touched his eyes alone. He clocked up a good many miles striving after a lazy grace of movement, brushed his hair with unheard-of vigour until a single, waving lock began to droop over his left eye, and ruined so many neck-cloths that Chrissie Fraser, the laundry-maid, was brought almost to the point of revolt. He failed dismally with what he most wanted to achieve, Perry's vivid, heart-warming grin. But he went on trying. With rare wisdom, Henry Phillpotts said nothing.

The idyll came to an end with the summer. In the middle of September, the equinoctial gales began to blow, and when they died and the hills reappeared out of the clouds, their peaks were thick with snow. Winter was on the way.

And so was Vilia. She wrote from Marchfield House, near Edinburgh, where she was on a visit to her father-in-law, Duncan Lauriston. She hoped that Mr Telfer would forgive her for inviting herself, and at only three days' notice.

Mungo was delighted.

Chapter Six

1

The air was scorching and sulphurous and red, but somewhere on the margins of Vilia's sight dusk was falling, and a heavy, sooty rain. All round were noises of sizzling and crackling, and the thud of engines, and a roaring of fire, and from somewhere in one of the buildings that surrounded the yard came the ring of helve hammers, regular and relentless as the heartbeat of some mechanical mammoth. Overriding everything, making it impossible to think, rose the splitting, shrieking whistle of air driving through the blast pipes into the furnaces.

'What did you say?' It wasn't that she had failed to hear, for her father-in-law's voice had been pitched to a level audible through the din. But somehow the sense had failed to reach her.

Sourly, he repeated it. 'This is the coking yard, where we turn raw coal into coke for the furnaces. And what I said was that I had a letter from Andrew this forenoon, and the answer is no!'

She didn't reply at once, too busy fighting the physical onslaught of smoke and smell and heat and unendurable noise. It was like being transported into the pages of some mediaeval painting showing the tortures of the damned. All round burned the fires of hell, live volcanoes, white-red, cracked and misshapen, tended by filthy, sweating demons who shovelled as if Satan himself stood over them with his pitchfork. Satellite goblins, grimy dwarves with downcast eyes, flitted in and out of the shadows behind, burdened with ore baskets or trundling barrows of fuel, while the air shimmered with hot currents, flakes of falling ash, and the stench of toiling humanity.

Duncan Lauriston turned away, his oversized spectacles reflecting, like twin mirrors, the building he was making for, the one with conical projections on its roof from which great sheaves of flame darted sixty feet into the sky to lick at the curdled clouds. She had never seen him wear spectacles before.

She followed him in and the atmosphere hit her like a blow in the face. If the coking yard had been purgatory, this was a living inferno. She was almost blinded at first.

'The blast furnaces,' he said. The temperature was fearsome, and the roar and shriek of the huge bellows was something she could never even have imagined.

The men were running off molten iron from the furnaces into long troughs, or pigs, where it lay scummy and scalding, setting up swirls and surges in the air above. 'Pig iron,' Duncan Lauriston said laconically. 'Furnace temperature six hundred degrees. The blast air's fed through the pipes by a 38-inch cylinder steam engine.'

It was clear that he hadn't the slightest interest in whether she understood or not. She had only asked to see the foundry out of politeness, which she now recognized to have been misplaced. It hadn't softened his mood at all, but had given him the opportunity to add a touch of sadism to the contempt with which he ordinarily treated her. He had no time for women, and especially no time for his son's wife.

'What do you mean, the answer is no?' She could scarcely make herself heard amid the clamour. 'No, what?'

He was bending over the pigs, seemingly oblivious to the heat. A big, muscular man, with a harsh, impervious face. His skin was pitted with the scars of smallpox, and his complexion had the purplish-red tinge that spoke of heart disease, but his eyes were like Andrew's, green with amber flecks, set wide and straight under heavy brows. He was just over fifty, and his brown hair was beginning to turn grey although it was still plentiful. He was wearing what she took to be his working coat and clumsy knee boots, as if to suggest, not very subtly, that her visit was an unwelcome interruption of the working day. Outside the foundry, he was usually well enough dressed, if not precisely modish.

He didn't trouble to turn his head but, ignoring the furnace keepers busy around them, as if they were so many pieces of furniture, he said, 'I mean I'll not have him idling his time away in London like all those dandies and perverts and fornicators you're so fond of.'

She gasped. It was such an extraordinary remark that, in other circumstances, she might have laughed. But one of the furnace keepers, a brawny fellow, half naked, whose open shirt revealed a mat of moist, black, curling hair, dashed a huge hand over his eyes to brush away the sweat, and gazed at her over his master's head with an almost animal speculation. Another, younger and fairer, slid her a sideways glance, his mouth half open over broken teeth and a jeer twisting the corners of his lips. She looked round. All the men were staring at her as if they had never seen a woman before. Abruptly, she was grateful for the thick veil she had thrown over her satin straw bonnet. Duncan Lauriston's housekeeper had warned her to wear something to protect her from the dirt and soot and ashes, and since it had been wet and cold when Vilia left Marchfield House earlier in the afternoon, the veil and heavy grey travelling pelisse had seemed a practical solution. The housekeeper hadn't mentioned the heat.

Vilia could feel the perspiration starting on her forehead under the smothering gauze. 'That's not true!' she exclaimed. 'We're not even acquainted with such people!'

As if it had broken some spell, all the men returned to their labours, pushing the molten iron down the feeding channels, smoothing and levelling what was already in the pigs. Duncan Lauriston rose to his feet. 'Fine!' he said. 'Then you'll not miss them when you come to live at Marchfield with me. There's room enough.' He strode off to the door facing the one by which they had entered.

Vilia took a moment to pick up her skirts and devoted more care than she would otherwise have done to circumventing the obstacles strewn about the vibrating floor of the furnace shed. Her mind refused to recognize what her father-in-law had said. As a prospect, it was unthinkable.

He was in the store yard outside. He pointed. 'Low-sulphur coal for coke making. Some of it comes from Rothes, some of it from Sheriff-hall in Midlothian. Owned by his gracious lordship, the Duke of Buccleuch. Friend of yours, no doubt.'

She said nothing. She had never met anyone who loathed rank and distinction as he did. Good breeding to him was synonymous with luxury and privilege, which he condemned with an Old Testament virulence that smelled strongly of envy. Vilia supposed that her own birth and breeding were largely accountable for the fact that she had failed so badly with him, for although she had disliked him on sight she had tried to overcome it, and had been as charming and pleasant as she knew how. But even on the day of her wedding she had heard him say to Andrew, without troubling to lower his voice, 'Highty-tighty! You'll have trouble with that one, you mark my words!' And during this last week, when at Andrew's insistence she had brought the baby to visit him, she had come to suspect that he not only disapproved of her but hated her. It was a dreadful feeling. She had never been aware of anyone hating her before, except, in a very juvenile way, a small boy called Luke Telfer.

Duncan Lauriston pointed again at other heaps piled about the yard. 'Iron ores. Red one's haematite, very rich. Yellow-brown one's ordinary grade, very hard. The violet-grey stuff comes from Dunbar, on the sea coast the other side of Edinburgh.'

The noise was fractionally less, here. She cleared her throat and said, 'Live with *you*?'

'You'll not be able to afford to live anywhere else if my son leaves the army. If you'd brought him a dowry, that might be a different story.'

So that rankled? He must have hoped that Andrew would marry money.

'But you thought *he* had enough blunt to pay for your high living and fancy gowns. Well . . .'

It suddenly seemed very important to say, 'I pay for my gowns from the small income my father left me!'

But he gave no sign of having heard. 'I tell you now, if he gets out of the army he'll not have a penny except what I give him. And I'll give him *nothing*' – he put a venomous emphasis on the word – 'unless he comes to live here and learn about the business.'

He was stumping ahead again in his clumsy boots, and Vilia ran to keep up. 'I gave in when he was so desperate to join the army, and he was doing me credit. I looked to see him a colonel at least, before he was finished. But it doesn't suit you, does it? I know your kind.' As he disappeared through another doorway, his words were snatched away by hammer thuds and the roaring and reverberation of the furnaces inside. But, incredulously, she thought she heard him say '. . . vain and sinful.'

Her legs were trembling, and she had no idea how to deal with him. Andrew had said, 'Go and stay with my father, and I'll write to him so that my letter arrives when you are there. He hates the thought of money being wasted, but *you* can turn him up sweet, my darling!' How blind was it possible to be?

She straightened her shoulders and followed him. Here, the furnace doors were open and there were men before them, guarding their eyes with one hand while, with a long tool in the other, they raked and stirred and spread in the very heart of the fire. 'Puddlers,' said Duncan Lauriston briefly. 'The pig iron's melted and puddled – that means raked – to make it fit for forging. The hammers are beating the melted stuff into blooms – lumps – and then it's squeezed into bars by these rollers here.'

He turned to her before she had time to recoil, so that his spectacles were only inches from her face. She understood the purpose of them now. 'Are you not interested?' he said.

'What? Yes, of course. It's just that it's difficult to take it all in at once, especially with the noise and the heat.' The hammers were clanging through her head and the furnaces blazing in her face. She could scarcely remember what it was like to be quiet and cool. Unbidden, a vision of Kinveil in the snow came to her mind.

'Aye, you like your comfort. Well, you'd best recognize that the money that keeps you isn't comfortably made. You never think of that when you go flittering off to parties and balls, night after night, leaving the bairn to some gin-sodden wet nurse! Well, you'll find things a bit different at Marchfield. We don't go in for dissipation, and Andrew'll be a sight too weary to squire you about, anyway. You'll just have to stay at home and look after the boy.'

He never called the baby by his name, which was Theophilus – Theo for short – after her father. It had had to be that, or Duncan, and Duncan she couldn't have borne.

'And you can comfort yourself,' he added with a sneering smile, 'with the thought that you've only yourself to blame. I've no doubt it's you wants my son out of the army . . .'

Vilia found her voice and the strength to make herself heard. 'Stop! *Please* stop! It's not I who want him out of the army. The French wars are over now, and Napoleon is in Elba, and Wellington has turned diplomat. The army will soon be on peacetime strength, and Andrew believes the prospects for advancement will be very few indeed. It's *he* who sees no purpose in going on. It's *he* who wants to resign his commission!' But there was only disbelief in Duncan Lauriston's face.

He turned away. They were off on their travels again. Somewhere in an unrelated corner of her mind she was grateful she had decided to wear comfortable shoes.

He said, 'I'll believe you. Thousands wouldn't. But I'll not believe you had no hand at all in his decision.'

She could have wept. Not once, during the sixteen months of their married life, had Andrew ever asked her opinion about anything. Not once – when he had been there to forestall her – had he allowed her to make a decision, even on her own behalf. He didn't want her worrying her beautiful head. She had come to the conclusion that it was the only way he knew of expressing his love, except in bed.

She said again, 'No. The decision was his own.'

Her father-in-law threw open a heavy door, its padlock hanging loose. 'The workshop.'

It was a haven of quiet, full of cast-iron stoves and grates and kitchen ranges, kettles and pots, spades and hoes, hinges and bolts. There was no machinery working, and the place was empty of people. She remained just inside the door.

'Times are bad,' he said. It wasn't a complaint, just a statement of fact. 'We'll do no more casting until we've sold this stuff. We're under-capitalized, always have been. Skilled labour, high costs, dear transport, it all adds up. Welsh iron's cheaper, you see, and we weren't like Carron at Falkirk, with big war orders.' He took his spectacles off, and his eyes gleamed inimically in the reflected glow from the furnaces across the yard. 'We've no reserves, but we've no partners either. It's all mine – and Andrew's, and the boy's. D'you understand me?'

'I think so.'

'If he sells out of the army he won't even get the full price for his commission. The Horse Guards'll keep some back for the reserve fund, *if* they agree to him selling out at all. He's supposed to have twenty years' service before they'll even consider it.'

Vilia said, 'He thinks that, with the war over, they may be more flexible.'

'Aye, maybe. But maybe, with the war over, no one will want to buy his commission. He might not even get back what I paid to make him an ensign in the first place. And, by God, I could have done with that money these last years! No!' His voice was blunt and final. 'I've had enough of all this. Even if I could spare it, I wouldn't increase his allowance. I won't even maintain it. The Bible has things to say about wasting one's substance on sin and loose living, so you can reap your whirlwind, my girl! You'll come to Marchfield and learn to be a good wife to my son and a mother to his bairns.'

His bairns. Theo, who was seven months old, and whom, after the first shock, she had wanted and welcomed, because she thought a child might transform her match with Andrew into a real marriage. And the second child, already on the way. The first pregnancy had given her a

117

respite from her husband's passion during his all too frequent visits home; Wellington had been using him as some kind of courier for dispatches to London, and he had been back and forth across the Channel like a homing pigeon. But this time he had said, 'The fellows tell me I don't have to stop. It's just a question of' – and he had turned a fiery red – 'of not doing *everything*.' More than ever she had felt like a whore, and when he had left for France three weeks ago the relief had been so intense it was almost an anguish.

She looked at the hateful man towering over her, and suddenly she was furiously angry. She didn't realize how many generations of well-bred ice were in her voice when she said, 'Mr Lauriston! You do neither yourself nor your son any credit by speaking to me in this way. I am aware that you disapprove of me, but I must tell you that I married Andrew in perfect good faith, and that I have conducted myself with perfect propriety ever since. I would not dream of doing otherwise. Only blind prejudice could make you speak to me as you have.' She had thrown up her veil, and her eyes were glittering.

There was a disastrous silence. Duncan Lauriston's face was frozen, but his amber-flecked eyes seemed to grow and grow, intent and greedy. He moved a step nearer, but her back was to the door jamb and she couldn't retreat. Her heart was pounding like one of the hammers in the foundry furnace. A breeze from outside sent a hot, fetid smell into her nostrils.

Then his hands clamped down on her shoulders, and he said viciously, 'Blind prejudice, is it?' She could see every pore and vein and scar on his face, hideously magnified, and his lips, which must once have been as well-shaped as Andrew's, were moist and slightly parted. He was breathing heavily. 'Don't you dare take that tone with me, you bitch. You Jezebel! As God is my witness, I'll make you pay for it!'

The world was spinning round her head, and she knew suddenly that she was deathly afraid of him in a way she had never dreamed of when she had said carelessly to Lucy, on her wedding day, that he frightened her. She knew that she was very near to fainting, but every nerve in her body screamed at her not to. With a tremendous effort of will, she brought her reeling senses under control, and even managed to cast disdainful eyes down on his bruising hands.

For an eternity, they stood there immobile, and then Duncan Lauriston dropped his hands and moved back a step or two. He said nothing at first, but simply went on staring at her so that, although superficially she had won, she had no sense of victory or even of relief. Then, 'It's all settled, is it?' he asked flatly.

'That is for Andrew to decide.' Her voice sounded almost normal.

'How long will it take to make the arrangements?' He turned away and began studying a hinge he had taken from one of the shelves, looked at it as if he had detected a flaw in the moulding.

'It depends on the army authorities, and of course on the continuation of peace. A few months, perhaps.'

He didn't offer to escort her home from the foundry. He didn't even see her to the carriage, which was just as well, because Sorley had come with her and the sight of him acted on Duncan Lauriston like a red rag to a bull. The idea of her having a personal footman wasn't the only irritant; he appeared to sense that Sorley, wooden and impersonal on the surface as any other well-trained footman, wasn't quite an ordinary servant. And Duncan Lauriston, being the kind of man he was, also found it disgusting that a well set up young fellow should spend his life dancing attendance on a supercilious little chit of a girl. 'Why don't you find some *man's* work?' he had exclaimed the other day.

When they arrived back at Marchfield House, Vilia went straight to the nursery. The baby was awake, a solemn infant with observant eyes and fair, downy hair. She sent the nurse away and stood at the window with the child in her arms, gazing out into the dark garden with its high, prison-like walls, lit here and there by dim lanterns. After a while, the baby began to whimper, and she put him down in his cot, which had once belonged to Andrew, and went downstairs to write to Mungo Telfer.

2

She set out two days later, taking her maid and Sorley McClure with her, but leaving the baby and his nurse at Marchfield. Duncan Lauriston was furious, and it gave her great satisfaction to reflect that, on this occasion, she had given him valid cause for complaint. Let him bluster, she thought. She was going home, where she belonged.

Mungo's welcome was so warm and genuine that the tears sprang to her eyes. He gripped both her hands crushingly, and smiled at her, and said, 'Welcome, my dear. I told you before. You don't *have* to ask! Just come, whenever you need to.' The strange thing was that the constraint between them, which had still lingered even at the end of her visit two years ago, seemed to have evaporated completely in the interim. It wasn't only Kinveil she was coming home to, but Mungo as well. She gripped his hands in return, and said, 'I know. And thank you!'

Even Luke, greatly changed in the months since she had last seen him, greeted her with a quizzical grin. He wasn't very good at it, and she was surprised into a watery giggle that made them all laugh as they went, arm in arm, across the causeway and into the dear, familiar indoors.

Now that Luke felt himself in possession of Kinveil, as he had never felt before, he was able to see her more dispassionately, although he watched her as avidly as ever. Her green eyes, lustrous and a little strained, no longer made him think of a witch but of a mermaid. He noted also that, this time, she didn't fly to her childhood friends as she had done before. Instead, in an old grey gown and a voluminous plaid cloak, she walked from dawn until dusk, or sometimes, if the day was calm, sat on the hill behind the castle, gazing for hours at the restless autumn sea, and the hills in their livery of gold and scarlet and snow-streaked ebony. One day, he took her cloak from her when she came in, and the hand that brushed against his was cold as frost rime at dawn.

Mungo was troubled. What was wrong, he had no idea, but he knew that there was something serious. And then, slowly, the mists began to lift and the tension to relax. When, twice in the same day, she twinkled at him mischievously, he knew it was all right, and risked suggesting an idea that had occurred to him as soon as he knew she was coming.

Mid-October was the time of the Northern Meeting in Inverness, the Highlands' answer to the London Season. There was no real comparison between the two, but for an annual week in October all the Highland gentry succeeded in persuading themselves that Inverness was the hub of the Polite World. All the lairds competed to bring the largest possible party of southern guests to the little capital of the north, and for five days the place was thronged with people of fashion and distinction. There were grand dinners or balls every evening, where everyone who was anyone within a hundred miles was able to make new acquaintances, revive old ones, and catch up with any tiny item of gossip that, by some extraordinary oversight, they might have missed during the last twelve months. No society on earth knew more about its neighbours' affairs than that of the Highlands.

Perry Randall had taken Charlotte up for the whole week, and Mungo had bought tickets for most of the affairs without intending to use them. But it occurred to him that Vilia might like to go. When he first raised the matter, she looked so downcast that he immediately said, 'What am I thinking of? Of course you don't want to go. You want to be here at Kinveil. Dinna fash! I should not have mentioned it.'

At once she was repentant. 'No. Please let's go. I had quite forgotten about it, that was all.'

'No, no. I don't doubt you go to enough parties in London to last you all year.'

'But . . .'

It was showing all the signs of developing into one of those polite arguments that went on for ever. Bored, Luke said, 'Couldn't you just go to *one* of the balls?'

They both looked at him as if he had sprouted wings.

Mungo slapped his knee happily. 'Why not? Why did I not think of that? What about the one on Friday? It's the great occasion of the week.'

Vilia smiled charmingly. 'Why not, indeed?'

As a reward, Luke was taken along too. Children were not usually welcome at such events, but he was a well-grown, if weedy, ten, and anyone who didn't look too closely might have taken him for several years older, especially if he followed his grandfather's stern advice to stand up straight, keep his hands out of his pockets, and speak only when spoken to, and preferably not then. His childish treble would fool no one. He wasn't to dance, nor even to glance into the card room, in fact he was not to do anything but stand mumchance by the old man's side. Luke didn't mind. He was dying to go to a grown-up ball, and felt very superior about the whole affair, especially when his grandfather refused to take Henry along. An orthodox cleric he might have countenanced, but a tutor in skirts went quite beyond the line. Henry, as usual, was offended.

They set off early on the Friday. Mungo had arranged that they should put up with his man of business, Mr Norman Cooper, at his house in Church Street, spending the night there, and returning to Kinveil in the morning. It was a pleasant drive, for the weather was bright and unseasonably mild, and the foliage was in the full glory of its autumn colours and Loch Ness a clear, thirty-mile sheet of dappled grey. There was no snow on the hills here, for the loch, deep and cold though it was, had some special climatic effect that held winter at bay even when all the country around was frozen hard.

Mungo had also sent ahead to ensure that Mr Urquhart, whose emporium was the great fashion centre of Inverness, would have time to dress Vilia's hair. Luke, better acquainted with Vilia than his grandfather, maliciously observed her bite back a protest when this considerate arrangement was mentioned, and also noticed that the signs of Mr Urquhart's genius – only too apparent when she returned from his shop – had more or less vanished by the time she was ready for the ball.

Vilia's gown was in a style that neither Mungo nor Luke had ever seen before, which made them think it must be the *dernier cri* in London. It was an elegant thing in blonde lace over deep cream silk, buttoned down the front with pearl clusters, and it skimmed her figure instead of clinging to it, giving her a willowy look that suited her very well. Mungo, who had never seen her fashionably gowned before, gasped at the sight, and even Luke couldn't help but admire. It didn't occur to either of them that the gown had been designed to disguise the fact that she was almost four months pregnant with her second child.

Vilia mounted the broad, handsome stairs of the assembly room on Mungo's arm, with Luke trailing meekly behind. The noise, the blaze of lights, and the press of humanity were almost overwhelming, and at first glance he couldn't imagine how or where anyone could possibly find space to dance. Nor could he imagine how they were ever going to find anyone they knew. Yet scarcely were they inside the ballroom than his grandfather was exchanging civilities with one of the smaller Ross-shire lairds, who introduced them to his wife; to his sisters, and her sisters, and their husbands; to an assortment of cousins; and to a small and ugly colonel with his equally small and scarcely less ugly wife. They had just returned from India, and she was dripping with diamonds, to prove it.

Vilia was whisked away almost at once by a good-natured rattle of a man who claimed to have known her in the cradle. Swallowing this patent untruth with the most sweetly incredulous of smiles, she allowed him to lead her into a country dance that was forming. Next time Luke saw her, she was being partnered by Lord Huntly. Then she was drawn into a cotillion with Sir Francis Mackenzie of Gairloch, and then into a reel with Mackenzie of Applecross. He, it was said, was the matrimonial catch of the northern counties, but Luke thought him a poor figure of a fellow, and he was certainly no dancer.

Mungo seemed to be acquainted with at least half the people in the room, and Luke's ears resounded not only with the fiddles, but with knowledgeable discussions about forestry, sheep, kelp, fish, canals, roads, deer, and cattle prices. What else! he thought resignedly. Gradually, he began to find it all rather flat, and when he finally caught sight of Perry, dancing with one of the Misses Duff, he waited only until the music ended before burrowing a way through the throng towards him.

'Luke!' exclaimed his Aunt Charlotte in tones that were less than welcoming. 'What on earth are you doing here?'

She had a knack of seeming to criticize, even when she wasn't. Luke said belligerently, 'I'm here with my grandfather and Vil – Mrs Lauriston.'

'Good heavens! I wonder what father can be thinking of!'

Perry said amiably, 'Why shouldn't the boy be here, Charlotte? It's time he learned something about how the world goes round. We should have brought Edward as well, now I come to think of it.' He winked brazenly from behind his wife's back, and Luke almost burst with the effort of trying not to laugh.

'Vilia Cameron,' said his aunt thoughtfully. 'How interesting. She was only five or six years old when I saw her last.' She turned to Perry. 'The wildest little girl, quite *farouche*, but Lucy tells me she has improved. Where is she, Luke? Point her out to me.'

Every other lady in the room was by now faintly dishevelled, but Vilia remained cool, and perfect. There was a smile on her lips as she addressed her partner, and her eyes were astonishingly green. The coronet of silver-blonde hair gleamed like raw silk in the candlelight.

'Oh,' said Charlotte, raising the quizzing glass she had lately begun to affect. She herself was held to be a good-looking woman, with clean-cut features, a heart-shaped face, and a neat figure. She wore her brown hair in smooth bands, and she was dressed tonight in a gown of lilac crêpe whose modest decolletage was filled in with a handsome but heavy gold collar set with shell cameos. Luke wished she had left off the matching tiara and earrings. They made her look armour-plated.

Perry was studying Vilia, too, a little absently. 'Is that Mrs Lauriston?' he said after a moment. 'Yes, I wondered who she was.'

Charlotte turned to her nephew. 'You may bring her over and introduce her when this dance has finished, Luke.'

'Yes, Aunt Charlotte.'

He intercepted Vilia just as she was coming off the floor. 'Aunt Charlotte wants to see you,' he announced, raising a sardonic eyebrow. He was getting quite good at that, and amusement leapt to her eyes. 'Royal command!'

Perhaps Charlotte misinterpreted the half-smile that lingered on Vilia's face, but whatever the reason, the temperature dropped several degrees. She said, 'So delightful to meet you again after all these years, Miss . . . Dear me, of course! It's Mrs Lauriston now, is it not? Pray sit down beside me and let us have an agreeable chat.'

Perry was bowing over Vilia's hand. 'My husband,' Charlotte said cursorily.

Vilia inclined her head. 'Yes, it *is* a long time since we met, Mrs Blair. Oh, no. I'm so sorry. It's Mrs Randall now, isn't it?'

Touché, Luke thought. Definitely *touché*.

It had been so elegantly done that Charlotte didn't even notice. She said, 'Yes, Mr Randall and I have been married for three years now. What a pity we have not yet had the pleasure of entertaining you at Glenbraddan.'

Luke hoped Vilia wasn't going to be fool enough to agree that it *was* a pity. She might find herself landed with two or three days of unadulterated Aunt Charlotte, and Luke wouldn't have wished that on anyone, even Vilia.

Wisely, Vilia smiled and said nothing, neither did she sit down. Charlotte waved her fan towards the empty chair at her side, and said again, 'Pray do sit down.'

'If you will forgive me, I think I should not. I am engaged for the next country dance, and it would be impolite to disappoint my partner.'

Charlotte took it as a personal affront. 'You are very much in demand,' she said with a honey-sweet smile. 'But I wonder if I might venture to put you on your guard. Having been away from the Highlands for so long, you can't, I imagine, be acquainted with all the gentlemen who have been besieging you. You will forgive me, I know, but I must say, as someone longer accustomed to society than yourself, that it is not quite the thing for you to dance with gentlemen who are perfect strangers to you.'

Vilia was listening with an arrested expression, but her voice was no more than politely interested when she said, 'Indeed?'

'Well, Inverness is not precisely London, you know, and it is quite fatal to set people's backs up. In a place where most people have known each other forever, they are inclined to be critical of outsiders. And I know you would not wish to be thought *fast!*'

Luke held his breath. It wasn't the 'fast', it was the 'outsider'. He risked a glance at Perry Randall, but his uncle's face was impassive. He didn't know Vilia, of course.

But all Vilia said was, 'Indeed, no! But don't you think I might be acquitted of that charge, since my family and that of everyone else in the Highlands has been acquainted for at least a dozen generations?'

Not for a moment did Luke think that Vilia had been comparing the length of her own descent with Charlotte's, but Charlotte was sensitive on the subject. 'Hardly,' she replied, the sweetness turning a little sour. 'Even the oldest and most respected families include rackety young men with whom a gently bred girl would hesitate to associate. You would be well advised, I believe, to dance only with gentlemen to whom you have been introduced by some older lady who is a little more – how shall I put it? – up to snuff.'

Vilia was looking at her meditatively. 'Only with gentlemen to whom I have been introduced by an older lady?'

'Undoubtedly.'

'How kind of you to warn me, Mrs Randall.' Luke glanced at her sharply, but her face was perfectly innocent. 'Out of common courtesy, I must fulfil my engagement for this next reel. After that, I promise I will follow your advice to the letter.' She turned her head slightly. 'I see my partner approaching, so perhaps you will excuse me?'

She curtsied gracefully to Charlotte and inclined her head to Perry, then, flicking open her fan, turned towards the striking figure bearing down on her, middle-sized, handsome, high-nosed, and kilted and plaided to within an inch of his life. It was the best-known of all the

Highland chiefs – Alistair Ranaldson Macdonell, laird of Glengarry, chief of the Glengarry Highland games, popularizer of the Glengarry bonnet, colonel of the now-disbanded Glengarry Fencibles, evicter of thousands of the Glengarry population, and avaricious thorn in the side of the Caledonian Canal Commissioners. The man Mungo Telfer described as 'that tup-heided tartan tooralorum'.

With a grunt that might have meant anything, Glengarry looked down his nose at Charlotte, bobbed his head at Perry, and then, beaming widely, led a demure Vilia off towards the floor.

Charlotte's face was a bright pink. Luke caught a significant glance from his uncle and tactfully removed himself.

The next time he saw Vilia, she was waltzing with Perry. They danced beautifully together.

The time after that, she was in a quadrille with Perry as her partner.

It wasn't until the third time he saw them together that the glorious truth dawned. Undoubtedly, Vilia had been introduced to Perry, and by an older lady.

Aunt Charlotte, Luke thought gleefully, must be absolutely furious.

3

Charlotte Randall wasn't furious, but frightened. There was a tightness at the base of her throat under the expensive cameo collar her father had given her, and a raw feeling behind her eyes as, helplessly jealous, she watched her husband dancing with the Cameron girl. It was a long time since she had seen his face lit by that peculiarly brilliant smile, the smile she didn't believe any woman capable of resisting.

Under her no-nonsense manner and discreet lilac gown, Charlotte was still as infatuated with the Honourable Peregrine Francis Egerton Randall as she had been when she first set eyes on him in Edinburgh three years before. He had been so different from George, her late, sedate, and not much lamented first husband. Estimable George Blair, square and sturdy in his homespun shooting jacket and serviceable gaiters, with his double Joe Manton always under one arm, and the air of stolid hauteur he affected when she offended against his fuzzy but hard-held code of ethics. She had never succeeded in penetrating its mysteries, although she still found herself clinging to some of its tenets as if they were gospel.

She had been so anxious to marry a 'real' gentleman, and George had been available, and prepared, in a superior way, to overlook her non-existent pedigree in favour of her substantial dowry. Not as substantial as it would have been if Mungo Telfer had formed a higher opinion of him, but George had never known that. He thought himself a sound, sensible, plain man, and she had taken him at his own valuation and worked hard to make herself worthy, though with little reward. When he had deigned to comment on the excellence of her housekeeping, he had made her feel like one of the upper servants, and when he had come to her room, as he did but seldom, he had appeared to derive little more pleasure from the performance of his marital duties than she did. After two or three years she had begun to recognize that she was becoming finicky and censorious, and less and less able to find anything to laugh about. More than once, it had occurred to her that, if she were able to make her choice over again, she would make it differently.

And then, miraculously, the opportunity had come and she had grasped it, blind to reason. Rebelling against a widowhood as dull as her marriage had been, she had lost her heart, like some green girl, to Peregrine Randall, a man with nothing to recommend him but looks and charm, which he had in impossible profusion. He was not only the most attractive man she had ever met, but the most attractive man she could ever have imagined.

He had been perfectly frank about his situation. As the penniless third son of an impoverished earl, he had taken to gaming in the hope of improving his situation, and had failed. 'Dismally!' he had said, with the smile that turned her knees to water. He had no idea how he was going to extricate himself from his current predicament. Indeed, he suspected that his case was hopeless.

Utterly bewitched, she felt as if she couldn't live, couldn't breathe without having him near. Quaking, trying to convince herself that what she was doing was for his sake more than hers, stumbling awkwardly over her words, she offered him an orthodox business relationship – for him, release from his embarrassments; for her, congenial companionship. The awkwardness of the situation was enough to account for her nervousness, which was fortunate, because she thought – with unusual perception – that it might frighten him away if he knew how she felt about him. Afterwards, in the privacy of her room, she had wept tears of mingled gratitude and fear. For the second time, she had bought a husband, but this time less honestly. Glenbraddan, held in trust for her son Edward, was almost all she had; she would have to use what she had saved from the income of it to pay Perry's debts, although she had implied to him that fulfilling that essential part of the bargain presented no difficulties at all.

Her father had refused to help her out, although she thought afterwards that perhaps she hadn't really conveyed to him the depth and completeness of her need for Peregrine Randall. Mungo, censuring in his own children, as he so often did, what he would have tolerated in others, took exception to her remarrying without consulting him. He regretted that there would be no decent interval between decision and deed, no time for second thoughts. He disapproved strongly of the difference in age. And, a careful man himself, he was scandalized by Perry's gaming. Not one penny, he said forcefully, would he put in the way of a young man whose first instinct would be to squander it on cards and horses. Even when he began to revise his opinion of his new son-in-law, on that point he remained adamant. He was generous enough with gifts, but none that could be unobtrusively translated into cash.

Yet despite the disapproval of her family, the resentment of her children, and the feeling that friends, neighbours and tenants were all smiling quietly behind their hands, for more than a year Charlotte had been truly content. Settling back into her familiar household routine, she hadn't given much thought to how Perry would pass his days. Vaguely, she had always assumed that English gentlemen, as a breed, were accustomed to shoot, fish, ride to hounds, attend to correspondence, and keep abreast of public affairs, and it was her joy to think that by continuing to shoulder all the responsibilities of the estate, as she had learned to do during her widowhood, she was leaving Perry free to lead just such a life, even if riding to hounds had to be omitted from the schedule because of the unsuitability of the landscape.

The grieve managed the land and the tenants. The head shepherd provided meat and milk, fleece, hides and horn. The gamekeepers kept the table supplied with red deer and roe deer, hare, grouse, pheasant, partridge, trout and salmon, pike and char. Charlotte herself was endlessly busy supervising the drying, smoking, salting, pickling, and candying of substantial quantities of food for the store rooms, the making of jams and wines, the spinning, the carding, and weaving, and candle-making that all went to make Glenbraddan almost self-sufficient. Although night after night she went to bed too exhausted to keep her eyes open, she had learned to be proud of the fact that nothing had to be brought in except some groceries, some wheat flour, and a few ankers of French wine and brandy.

There was no need for Perry to stir himself, no need for him even to take a gun out unless he wished. She had been surprised to discover that, though an excellent shot, he derived no pleasure from killing things, except sometimes predators like foxes, wildcats, and hoodie crows. He had suggested that perhaps he might ride round the estate occasionally and talk to the tenants, and although Charlotte had seen no purpose in it she had been touched, and almost tearfully proud when, suspicious though they were of the 'Sassenach chentleman', they had all succumbed to his charm.

To her, as to everyone, he was considerate, kind, and unfailingly cheerful. If he hadn't bargained for the isolation and careful economy of Glenbraddan, so different from the hospitable country houses he knew in the south, he showed no sign of disappointment and never uttered a word of reproach. And yet, gradually, she had begun to feel he was slipping away from her, though not in any way she could identify. She had said nothing, because there was nothing she knew how to say. Inwardly, she fretted, wondering if the fault were hers, and being the kind of person she was, she had become prickly and defensive, taking his most casual comments as criticisms. More and more, she had become conscious of the differences in their age and background. It had come to the stage when even a 'Good morning' had become fraught with hidden dangers. She had been trying, these last months, to curb her tongue, to appear a little less busy and harassed, to play the lady rather than the housewife. But it had been an effort, and it showed.

And now, seeing Perry Randall and Vilia Cameron together at the Northern Meeting ball, she knew it had all been in vain.

It was more than six months before the crisis came, six months during which Charlotte had privately succeeded in transforming Vilia, the mischievous but unwitting symbol of her misery, into its wilful cause.

On a torrential day in April, when the hills were lost in thick banks of cloud and the great grey sheets of rain swept in relentless progression from west to east along the glen, she went into her drawing-room and was surprised to find Perry there, gazing idly out of the window.

Mungo Telfer, when he had first seen Glenbraddan House, hadn't been much impressed. With a scornful glance at the '1614' chiselled on one of the stones in the chimney stack, he had condemned it as too bland and modern. No romance. No memories of Viking raids. No eldritch screeches from the ghosts of Covenanting warriors. And the fact that Bonnie Prince Charlie had spent a week in hiding among the corries further up the glen didn't alter Mungo's view. The 'Forty-five was something he was just old enough to remember for himself, and he knew the troubles it had brought to Scotland, then and after. 'And forbye,' he had remarked to his daughter in the manner of one who had studied Nature's design and found it wanting, 'there isn't enough water about. Nothing but a douce wee river, when what these hills need is a proper loch or a bit of sea.' It had been a very dry autumn that year; the douce wee river Braddan was ordinarily nearer a torrent.

Charlotte knew that her father's real objection to Glenbraddan was that it was too neat and civilized. The original Glenbraddan House had consisted of a fortified tower and a round peaked turret. Then, some time in the eighteenth century, George Blair's grandfather had added new buildings to extend it into the customary U-shape. The eighteenth century had been an urbane period for building, and Glenbraddan's floors were all on the same level, and most of its rooms pleasantly proportioned and gracious in size. Except in the original tower and on the top two floors, all the walls were either panelled or plastered.

Charlotte, despite her father, was proud of Glenbraddan, indoors and out. She had made a charming garden, with an old dovecote, and alcoves in the kitchen garden walls to contain beehives. Glenbraddan's heather honey was excellent; even Mungo admitted that. Never for long, though. The sight of her drawing-room was always enough to set him off again, complaining in the half-jocular tones he reserved for what he considered her sillier pretensions, that he felt like Gulliver in Lilliput threading his way among the spindly tables covered with fragile knick-knacks. Duck-shaped soup tureens, even if they were made of Chinese porcelain, and teapots painted with pictures of half-naked women, even if they came from Meissen or Vincennes, were not what he admired and certainly not what he would have chosen to display in a drawing-room. Sitting down with exaggerated care, he would add, 'And these chairs are a sight too dainty. Would you not like me to get you something a bit more comfortable?' But his eyes would be twinkling, and she would know, irritably, that he was teasing her.

It was a pretty room, which always made her feel like the lady she so much wished she had been born. She wasn't used to finding her husband in it, however, and now she felt the little catch of breath that always afflicted her when she came on him unexpectedly. Biting back an automatic, 'What are you doing here!' which she realized just in time would sound ungracious, she said, 'What a dreadful day. It feels as if spring would never come. If only the wind would move round to the east, we might have drier weather.'

'Yes.'

She had come in only to collect a list, but she hesitated, and after a moment he turned away from the window and began to trace a path towards the fire, hands behind his back and eyes focused on his booted feet as he placed them, with concentrated deliberation, one before the other. It struck her as an oddly boyish trick, and she watched him indulgently, wondering at the same time what was in his mind. He was wearing a dark green cloth coat with brass buttons, and his breeches were of buff leather and his hessians slightly mud-stained. In his cravat, she noticed, was the pin her father had given him for his twenty-fifth birthday last month, a coiled serpent in gold, with opal eyes. Its intrinsic value was negligible, but it was an elegant little thing, and he seemed to have taken a fancy to it.

He looked up. 'Have you a moment to talk?'

His expression was perfectly neutral, but she was assailed by a sudden sense of danger. 'Of course,' she said, and then added, as if it were some kind of protection, 'though if I am away for very long the Mackie girl will certainly knit up little Grace's shawl quite wrongly. She has no

131

more idea of pattern than a speck of dust in a storm.' She smiled nervously.

'Always busy. You should rest sometimes, Charlotte. You do too much.'

It was a familiar comment, and she bridled. 'I should like to know how you imagine this household would go on if I didn't supervise everything! If I . . .'

Her husband stopped her, raising his hand in a weary gesture of surrender. 'Please, Charlotte! I apologize. I spoke out of turn. It's just that I see so little of you.'

The tone was matter-of-fact, but the words soothed her a little. She said, 'Of course I have time to talk. What is it about?'

He didn't reply at once. There was a violent rattle of rain against the windows, as if some errant gust had scooped up a shovelful of pebbles and tossed them against the glass. Half startled, Charlotte turned her head. There was a pied wagtail marching oblivious about the lawn in his black-and-white livery, self-important as some civic dignitary at a banquet. Charlotte had always thought that a Highland raindrop must fall on a bird with much the same impact as a brick falling on a human being, but the wagtail didn't even notice.

Perry said, 'I think I must go to London.'

Charlotte's head snapped round. Regardless of sense or logic, London meant nothing to her nowadays but Vilia Cameron. 'May I ask why?'

'My investments, if such they can be called. You must know how Napoleon's escape from Elba has thrown the markets into a state of flux. Shares are going down, and everyone is dreading the prospect of Europe being plunged into war again. You also know that the only capital I possess is invested in government funds. Well, my man of business wants me to sell.'

'Surely he can deal with it? What is the purpose of having a man of business if he can't? Why should you have to make the journey?'

His expression was strained. 'I don't know whether I can make you see how I feel. If I sell now, it must be at a loss, and God knows I'm near enough a pauper already. I have to discover whether his fears are well grounded, and at this distance I can't weigh the risk for myself.' He turned away restlessly. 'Somehow, through thick and thin, I have managed to hold on to those shares, and I *will* not give them up without being absolutely convinced of the necessity. The choice is between selling them now, at a loss, and holding on in the hope that the market recovers.'

'A gamble, in fact?'

It was unkind. His jaw tightened, but all he said was, 'Of course. If I hold on and Napoleon plunges us back into war, I may lose everything. But if he doesn't – if Wellington, say, meets him in battle and defeats him fully and finally – I might even make a modest profit.'

'Then why not hold on? Even if you lose, it would scarcely be a major disaster. The interest can't be much, and I am sure we could manage perfectly well without it.' She had meant to be reassuring, but as soon as the words were out she knew that, somehow, she had made a calamitous mistake.

He drew a ragged breath. 'Oh, certainly! *We* can manage without it. But I'm not sure whether *I* can.'

She didn't understand. Floundering, she said, 'But you have very few needs! Glenbraddan would be in a sorry way if it couldn't contrive to pay your tailor and your gunsmith. Especially when you do so much to help the estate run smoothly.'

He sank down into one of the gilt and ormolu chairs and buried his face in his hands. It gave his voice a hollow sound when he said, after a few moments, 'I deserve my wages, you mean?'

It was, she supposed, precisely what she had meant.

She could only just hear him as he went on, 'How can I explain? It's foolish, of course, but I don't enjoy being beholden to you. While I have some money of my own, however little, I am still my own man. If I lose it, I lose my self-respect as well.'

'But why? I don't see *why*! All I have is yours as much as mine, and not only because the law says so.' She hesitated, torn between her wish to give him everything he desired, and resentment at the discovery that he didn't want her to. Her voice grated a little. 'I want you to have it because I love you.'

It was out, for the very first time, the truth she had never before put into words. And he didn't even notice.

As if she had not spoken, he sat back in his chair and said, 'Don't think I have anything against earning a wage, my dear. But if my accounts were to be set against those of the estate, I think young Edward and I would find ourselves in agreement for the first time in our acquaintance. Make no mistake about it, Charlotte, I don't earn my keep. The estate would go on just as well without me, better, perhaps. There's nothing for me to do except suggest ideas for your grieve to turn down.'

'That's unfair!' On several occasions during the last three years Perry had proposed ways of making Glenbraddan more efficient and more productive, but the grieve, James Osgood, was naturally conservative and had always succeeded in finding sound reasons for saying no. Charlotte hadn't thought Perry had been very much concerned. She said earnestly, 'Glenbraddan is Edward's, and until he comes of age I have no *choice* but to follow the advice of someone who is properly qualified. You know very well it would be wrong of me to listen to you rather than Osgood!'

'Perhaps.' He shrugged. 'But I spend my days going from here to there, and back again, smiling and chatting like some royal consort, and everyone defers to me, and everyone knows what a sham it all is.'

She found that, hurt and defensive though she was, she couldn't bear the bleak finality in his voice, as if there were no more to be said, ever. It had sounded like an epitaph. Through the ache in her throat, she said, 'It needn't be a sham! If I had only known . . . I am *sure* we can find something useful for you to do, if you really want it!' But all she was doing was making things worse.

His mouth curved into a humourless half smile. He had a beautiful mouth, crisply muscled at the corners, with a long, spare, well-shaped upper lip, and a lower lip that was a little fuller but still straight and firmly chiselled.

Drearily she struggled on, self-pitying tears beginning to well under her eyelids. 'I thought this was the kind of life you wanted, without care or responsibility. Without anyone making demands on you. I thought you were settled. I thought' – it came out almost as a wail – 'I thought we were happy!'

The grey eyes widened. 'Did you, Charlotte?'

As always when she found something too difficult for her, her mind recoiled from it and took refuge in the easy safety of platitude. If, indeed, there was doubt about whether they were happy or not, there was only one explanation she was prepared to confront, the explanation in which, perversely, she had found a kind of comfort over the last months. 'It's that girl, isn't it! You don't love me, you never have. It's Vilia Cameron you want!'

Her eyes were too full of tears to see the blank astonishment on his face or the exhaustion that followed it. Nor had she any idea of how she looked herself, her neat features disfigured by misery and spite. 'Don't trouble to deny it! Every soul in the Northern Meeting rooms last October saw the look on your faces when you were dancing together. She's why you want to go to London! It has nothing to do with all that nonsense about the Funds, that's only an excuse. I'm too old for you, and too commonplace, and too – too stupid! You think you can go to London, and make love to her, and . . .' Her voice broke completely.

He rose, his face drawn and his movements oddly graceless, and laid his hands on her shoulders. He said, 'Charlotte, don't – please don't – upset yourself so. You are quite wrong. I meant just what I said. I want to go to London on business that is of the greatest importance to me, whether you understand it or not. That is my only purpose, and I'll come back to you as soon as it's settled, richer or' – a gleam of tired self-derision lit his eyes for a moment – 'or poorer. Forgive me, but this is something that matters to me very deeply.' She wouldn't meet his eyes, and after a moment he released her and stepped back. 'As for Mrs Lauriston, I think it most unlikely that I will even see her except by the purest accident. You're quite wrong about that, you know.'

She was past the stage of listening. Nothing less than an impassioned embrace would have lightened her misery, and Perry, hopelessly honest – except sometimes with himself – neither could nor would resort to it.

'I don't believe you,' she choked. 'I believe you'll come back. Oh, yes. You can't afford not to. But if you go, I'll know you've gone to her and I won't *have* you back! Do you hear me? *I will not have you back.*' Even as she said it, she knew deep down that she was killing any feeling he might ever have had for her, but she couldn't help it. Furiously, she dashed a hand across her streaming eyes, and then fumbled for a handkerchief. She couldn't find one, and it seemed like the last dismal, degrading, unbearable straw. Turning, she blundered from the room.

A Chinese vase rocked slightly as the door, flung back, glanced against the table on which it stood, but Perry didn't even notice. He remained where he was, motionless and absorbed, for several minutes, and then at last addressed the empty air. 'But I am going, just the same,' he said softly. 'Tomorrow.'

Chapter Seven

1

'But I am going tomorrow,' Andrew Lauriston complained sulkily.

Vilia, drawing on her gloves, smiled at him. 'And will be so deeply occupied for the whole of today that you won't even notice my absence.'

It was true enough, but he would have preferred her to stay at home, just in case. Anyway, it wasn't right that she should be setting off to enjoy herself at Ascot when he had just received orders to leave at first light tomorrow, with dispatches for Wellington at Brussels.

He said again, for the fifth time in as many minutes, 'I still don't understand why you are so determined.'

'Because it's Thursday the eighth of June, my dear! Gold Cup day! And I have been *so* looking forward to it.' She was dressed as charmingly as always, in a habit of grey-green levantine, with her blonde hair coiled away under a matching, softly draped turban affair, worn rakishly to one side and ornamented with a prince's plume. He knew that when she came back that evening after a round journey of sixty miles, she would look as perfectly groomed as she did now. 'Just think,' she went on. 'This will be my first visit to Ascot since my father took me there when I was eleven, the very year the Gold Cup was first run.'

She could see that the idea didn't excite him, and the sparkle died from her eyes. 'In any case,' she added, with a final look in the glass, 'it would be most impolite to cry off at this late hour, when my host's carriage is almost at the door.'

'It's only the Telfers,' he objected.

'*Only* the Telfers? You mean courtesy doesn't matter with people one knows well?' She cocked her elegant head at the sound of a carriage. 'That must be them now. Never fear, I will be home by eight at latest, so that we can have a quiet supper together.' She surveyed his discontented face ruefully. 'Be honest, my dear. You will be busy till then, whatever happens!'

He wouldn't admit it, so she kissed him lightly on the cheek and, with a shrug and another smile, went swiftly from the room.

The barouche was brand new and quite magnificent. As Magnus handed her up to join Lucy, Vilia said in a rallying tone, 'Fine as fivepence! Now I see why you have broken your rule about attending race meetings. Nothing less than the Gold Cup would do for such a splendid turnout!'

Magnus had very little sense of humour, and none at all of the ridiculous. 'I'm glad you think so,' he said. 'It seemed to me that today's journey is just what is needed to loosen up the springs. We'll change horses at Staines, of course. I've sent a team of rather nice blacks ahead to wait for us.'

She smothered a smile. The carriage was a beautiful bright yellow, picked out in black, and the mountings and trappings were of brass. Black horses were the obvious choice, but in her own view the four nicely matched, dappled greys already harnessed to it were much more subtle. 'How splendid!' she said dutifully.

To Lucy, whom she had not seen for several weeks, she remarked severely, 'And how is this, Mrs Telfer? I was never more shocked in my life than to hear that you were proposing to expose yourself to the view of the scaff and raff on Ascot Heath. You must be all about in your head!'

Lucy was sufficiently well acquainted with Vilia to know when she was quizzing her, but her answering smile was tinged with apprehension. Casting a hasty glance at her husband – occupied in giving the coachman directions about a route which that worthy knew a good deal better than his master – she whispered, 'Pray, my dear, do put a guard on your tongue today. Magnus is really not himself at all, quite fretful. Such doings at Glenbraddan, I cannot tell you. Well, I can, but not at this precise moment. Later, perhaps. Hush, now!' Turning, she smiled at Magnus in an apologetic way that made Vilia long to shake her.

One hour and ten miles later, Magnus was in a fidget. They were no further than Hounslow, and while the horses were being watered he stood with his watch in his hand and his toe tapping, muttering, 'One o'clock when the royal party reaches the course! I should not like to be late for that, you know!'

Lucy said, 'But my dear, we have only another twenty miles to go, and almost three hours still. Surely there can't be any doubt that we will arrive in time?'

'No doubt?' replied her spouse with something approaching a snort. 'Just wait until we are within reach of Windsor. There will be dozens – *hundreds* of vehicles of all kinds. Tilburies, carts, gigs, chaises, one-horse waggons with upwards of eight or nine people in them. Mark my words, there will be more traffic between Windsor and Ascot than you have ever seen in London, my dear!'

Discreetly, Vilia held her tongue. For once, Magnus was probably right. And indeed, by the time they reached Windsor they had been reduced to a snail's pace and Magnus was scarlet in the face. Not all the beauty of the countryside served to divert his mind, though it was rural England at its most perfect. The trees were in full leaf, the elder bushes in scented bloom, and many of the houses were clothed in china roses, clambering twenty feet to the eaves and bursting on the senses in a cascade of blush-pink fragrance. But all that concerned Magnus was whether they would arrive in time, and whether his groom – sent off before dawn with the somewhat antiquated town carriage – had managed to find, and keep, a place beside the rails. It was the greatest relief to discover that the groom had, in fact, succeeded in keeping a place, although backing the town carriage out of it so that the barouche could move in – for Magnus had no intention of allowing himself to be seen either by the plebs or by the royal party, if they should happen to be looking, in anything else – presented several unforeseen problems, notably in the form of other spectators, who showed a reprehensible tendency to edge into the vacant space as soon as the town carriage began to edge out. For the first time that she could remember, Vilia saw Magnus on his mettle, and had to admit that he was impressive.

Even so, he deeply resented having to exert himself, and when it transpired that the royal party consisted only of the Duke of York and a princess or two, he took it as a personal insult. The Regent, it seemed, had returned to London on Tuesday to be on hand for when war broke out again with Napoleon. 'As if it mattered a penny piece whether he's here or there,' Magnus fumed. Although by no means a party man, he had Whiggish tendencies. 'I should think the last thing they need at the Horse Guards is to have Prinny poking his nose in!' Lucy's mild remonstrance – for she had felt a childish *tendre* for the Prince Regent in his salad days – failed to move him.

Not until the luncheon interval after the first race, when he was able to assure himself that the claret had not been too badly shaken up by the journey, did he begin to recover his equanimity, so that the ladies were free to look about them. The crowd was considerable, lines of carriages four or five deep edging the inside of the track for almost a mile. Strung along the outside was a motley assortment of wooden shelters, with the Royal Stand near the winning post and, just across from the Telfer carriage, the much larger betting stand erected some years earlier by an enterprising builder called Slingsby. Everywhere else was a vast concourse of tents and booths, selling all kinds of refreshments or offering the usual fairground entertainment. There were jugglers and ballad singers and glee singers, ladies who danced on stilts, a man who could balance a coach wheel on his chin, thimblerig men who fleeced the yokels by taking bets on which thimble hid the pea, and confidence men of all descriptions.

Vilia revelled in it. The life, the noise, the colour, the sheer stimulus of seeing so many people enjoying themselves, acted on her like a tonic. She felt as if she had been released from prison, for although Andrew had been prepared to attend all kinds of social gatherings when he had been trying to fix his interest with her, she had discovered that, his conquest made, he preferred to stay at home. Despite his apparent ease, it seemed that *ton* parties reminded him of his origins, and made him ceaselessly aware that this was a world to which he did not belong. He wouldn't have cared for Ascot, either, Vilia thought, for the vulgar and vociferous throng would have reminded him of his origins in a different but no more acceptable way. She, who had learned in her childhood to be equally at home in cottage and castle, found his prickliness hard to sympathize with.

When, for the dozenth time, she felt Lucy's soft fingers grasp her arm, she wondered with amusement what in the world could still be left to intrigue her. Lucy, protected all her life from contact with the common herd, had been gazing on the scene with saucer-eyed fascination, applying to Magnus or Vilia at frequent intervals to have this or that explained to her. But on this occasion her grip was vice-like, and her face full of suppressed alarm. Meaningfully, she drew Vilia with her as she leaned across to Magnus, who was occupying the seat facing them, and it was patent that she wanted help in diverting his attention from something she was anxious he shouldn't see. With a strong effort of will, Vilia restrained herself from looking round.

'Magnus, my dear,' Lucy said brightly. 'Vilia and I would so much like to be daring, and place a small wager. What do you think?'

'Ummm.'

'I don't see – do you? – that it could be considered improper, provided the horse was a *respectable* horse, of course!'

Vilia giggled, and Lucy cast her a reproachful glance.

Magnus said, 'In the Gold Cup, you mean?'

'Do I? Oh, yes. I would think so, wouldn't you?'

'Which horse?'

'*Which* horse? I've no idea! What about – does the royal family have a favourite?'

If she went on like this, Vilia thought, Lucy's race would be run. Coming to the rescue, she said, 'The Duke of York has entered Aladdin. He's a five-year-old, and he should do well over two-and-a-half miles. I am prepared to stake a whole sovereign on him!'

Lucy gazed at her admiringly. 'Are you, Vilia? Oh, I'm sure you are right. What do you think, Magnus? Is it a nice horse?'

'Good-looking enough,' he replied, unerringly diagnosing what his wife meant by 'nice'. He shrugged. 'He wasn't even placed in the Derby in '13, mind you.'

'Oh, dear. Is that bad? But it – I mean, he – might be better now. It – he – must have had a lot of practice since then.'

Just in time, Vilia suppressed another giggle.

Magnus said resignedly, 'Very well. But you won't make much even if he wins. He's five-to-two on.'

'What does that mean?'

'Means if you put five shillings on and he wins, you only get seven shillings back.'

Lucy was undaunted. 'Then that's all right, surely? There can't be anything improper in winning only a *little* money!'

Vilia glanced unobtrusively over her shoulder, but could see nothing to account for Lucy's lapse into twittering idiocy. Turning back, she began to fish in her reticule. 'Will you send your groom?' she asked Magnus.

'I suppose so.'

'Then here is my sovereign.'

'And you will,' Lucy added anxiously, 'give Williams a sovereign to wager for me, too? Pray tell him now, my dear. I should so much dislike it if he were not able to – what's the expression? – lay the bet in time.'

Grumbling, though quite good-naturedly, Magnus descended from the barouche and strolled off to find his groom, while Lucy, hand to heart, subsided weakly into her seat and gasped, 'My goodness, what a relief!' She was looking very pink.

'What in the world was *that* all about?' Vilia demanded. 'I am dying of curiosity!'

Lucy's reply swept the amusement from her fair, elegant face. 'Peregrine Randall! Charlotte's husband! I saw him walking up the course with another gentleman. Thank heavens he didn't see *us*. My dear, I haven't had the opportunity to tell you, but he has left Charlotte. Actually left her!'

'Left her?'

Lucy was too busy fanning herself to notice Vilia's sudden pallor. 'He wanted to come to London. Something to do with his gambling, Charlotte says. And she told him that if he gave way to his baser instincts – for he was really a dreadful gamester before they were married, though she thought she had quite cured him! – she would cast him off, and refuse to have him back. But he paid no attention. My dear, he simply walked out the next morning, without so much as a by-your-leave. Well, not walked out precisely, for he had to take a horse, of course. And he did,' she added fairly, 'arrange for it to be sent back to Glenbraddan afterwards, so he can't have been lost to *all* sense of propriety.'

'When was this?'

'Oh, several weeks ago. In April, some time. But Charlotte wrote to us only the other day. I have been wondering why she took so long, and strictly between ourselves I believe she may have hoped he would go back to her, and that Magnus would never find out. Then we had another letter from my papa-in-law this morning, saying that he thinks Charlotte may have been in some degree at fault. Magnus is furious. I have never seen him so angry.' She paused. 'Pleased, too, in the most lowering way. He has written to Charlotte to say he always knew how it would be, and that she has brought it all on her own head. He was quite severe with her, and of course it is perfectly true that he considered the marriage doomed from the start, and disliked Mr Randall quite amazingly. But I fear that his letter wasn't such as to endear him to Charlotte. So tiresome to have people remind one that something is quite one's own fault!'

'He hasn't come to call on you, I take it? Mr Randall, I mean.'

'Gracious, no!' Lucy sounded faintly regretful. 'Of course, I *have* only met him once, but I thought him a charming young man. I imagine he must be quite embarrassed, and far too well-bred to embarrass *us* by calling on us.'

'Yes.' Vilia's voice was as drained of colour as her face. Since October the previous year, she had succeeded in banishing Perry Randall from her waking thoughts, but not from her dreams. The laughing grey eyes and long, humorous mouth sprang alive, so often, behind her closed lids, and the tall, limber body brushed against hers as it had done when they danced together on that sweet-sour evening at the Northern Meeting ball. Once or twice she had woken in the dark, to feel her own body melting in a way she had never known before, in a sensation that was half anguish and wholly delight. She had lain waiting, her breathing shallow, her stomach muscles taut and trembling, her legs limp as the stalks in a wilting daisy chain, and her mind adrift on some powerful and mysterious current. But the excitement had died, unfulfilled, because the man sleeping beside her was Andrew Lauriston, the husband to whom she had given her vows and borne two sons.

By the time the second race had been run, she had recovered her countenance. Then it was time for the course to be cleared of the spectators who flocked onto it the minute the horses had passed the post – sometimes before – so that the great event of the day could take place, the race for the 'Gold Cup of 100 guineas value' for three-year-olds and over, mares and entire horses only, to start at the Cup Post and race once round the course.

Lucy was ridiculously pleased when the Duke of York's Aladdin, carrying 124 pounds of purple-clad jockey, reached the winning post nicely ahead of the field. With a cry of delight, she threw her arms round Vilia, exclaiming in a carrying tone, 'Oh, *Vilia*! Hurrah! How *clever* of you to know that it would win!'

Vilia, smiling faintly, withdrew her gaze from the winning post and, with a shock that drove the breath from her lungs, found herself looking full into the arrested grey eyes of Perry Randall.

Afterwards, she realized that he had probably been pushed off the course with the other promenaders at the beginning of the race, into the space between the carriages and the rails, and that he must have heard Lucy's voice even through the commotion. But at the time, it seemed like a miracle. Their eyes locked, and she knew then that she had inhabited *his* dreams, too. A wild, glorious happiness flooded through her veins.

Then there came an explosive, 'Good God!' from Magnus, and it was too late to do anything but let events take their course. Courteously, Perry fought his way through the press of people who separated them, until he was standing beside the carriage making his bow to an appalled Lucy and her fair, self-possessed companion.

Magnus, as much put out by the fellow's effrontery in approaching them as by his presence at the races at all, spluttered a forbidding 'Good day', and then retreated into thin-lipped silence, but Lucy was made of sterner stuff.

'How delightful, Mr Randall,' she said. 'I hope you are well? Was it not splendid that the Duke's horse should win? Mrs Lauriston and I . . . Oh, you *do* know Mrs Lauriston? But of course you do! We were quite daring – it being a royal horse, you understand? – and I believe we will find ourselves richer now. Though I am not sure by how much. We staked only a sovereign, you know. I do hope you backed it – him – too?'

Perry smiled into the soft, anxious brown eyes. 'Not my kind of odds, Mrs Telfer! I favour nothing less than twenty-to-one against.'

It was hardly the wisest thing to say under the circumstances, but Vilia knew he had spoken without thinking. Lucy's expression was a study, and Magnus ostentatiously turned his head away and allowed his eyes to survey the course as if he wished to be counted out of this conversation. If Vilia could have thought of something to ease the tension, she might have spoken. But she had lost all power of thought and speech, and knew only an overwhelming need for the man who lit up every corner of her soul.

After a moment, he raised his high-crowned beaver and brushed the dark hair back from his forehead. Then, and it seemed to her almost against his will, he turned towards her. His smile was as engaging as ever, but there were lines of strain at the corners of his eyes, and a new sharpness to the creases that bracketed his mouth. In these last months he had known what it was to be unhappy, and she wondered whether he could sense the rush of tenderness that possessed her as she recognized the signs.

It felt like an eternity, but it was no more than a second or two before he said, 'I trust Major Lauriston is in health?'

She nodded, her eyes in the sunshine as green and translucent as young leaves against the sky. With an effort, he went on, 'I thought I might call on him, unless you have any objection? It would help me greatly to know at first hand something of the situation in Belgium. I have some shares which give me concern.' He faltered a little under the clear, consuming gaze of her eyes – a wood-nymph's eyes, he thought suddenly – and then rallied again. 'My military acquaintances seem all to have vanished in the direction of Ghent and points south, but I heard the other day that the major was still in town.' Her eyes clung to his, draining him of sense and sanity.

In a small, detached corner of her mind she remembered that she hadn't told the Telfers Andrew was leaving tomorrow, which made it easier. But nothing in the whole wide world would have stopped her from finding an excuse for seeing Perry Randall again. She said, 'I'm sure he would be happy to be of help. But you mustn't delay more than a day or two, for he expects to be ordered to Brussels very soon now.'

There was a surge of movement among the spectators, and he was caught in the current making for the nearest gap in the rail. Just before he was swallowed up by the crowd, he called back, laughing, to Lucy. 'Pray give my compliments to young Luke, Mrs Telfer!'

'Really, Vilia!' Magnus began, and then stopped. One didn't, after all, broadcast one's sister's misfortunes to all and sundry, not even to someone as close to the family as Vilia. She would find out soon enough, he thought gloomily; Lucy would tell her if no one else did. But it was all damnably unfortunate. He felt a renewed surge of irritation. He couldn't conceive what the girl was about, inviting that fellow to her house. 'I don't imagine Lauriston will thank you for wishing that ramshackle fellow on him!' he resumed, a touch sourly.

'You should have sent him about his business. No bread-and-butter of yours if he's worried about his shares!'

Vilia was searching in her reticule, her face invisible. 'Lucy, do *you* have the betting vouchers? Oh, no. I have mine here after all.' Her expression when she raised her head again was perfectly innocent, though she could scarcely believe that Magnus couldn't hear the anthems resounding in her heart. 'I'm sure you are right, Magnus. But how could I be so uncivil to your sister's husband? His request was perfectly unexceptionable!'

Lucy came to her aid. 'Of course it was, Magnus. At home, one always has the servants to turn people away, but it is not so easy to do it oneself. Besides, Vilia, if he does call and you would prefer not to receive him, you have only to tell your butler to say you are not at home!'

Vilia laughed, as if she hadn't quite enough breath to laugh with, and then said quizzingly, 'Such genius, Lucy! I should *never* have thought of that!'

Magnus, outmanoeuvred, abandoned the subject. 'Well, well!' he said with unaccustomed vigour. 'That's the Gold Cup over. We've seen what we came for. No point in staying longer, do you think, and if we leave now we'll miss the rush.'

As the smart barouche picked its careful way through the throng, its occupants caught one more glimpse of Perry Randall, standing by the entrance to a tent marked 'E O'.

'E O?' Lucy asked.

Her husband, directing a glassy stare in the opposite direction, said, 'A kind of roulette. Gambling – what else! Just as one would expect. It's all of a piece, all of a piece!'

2

When the carriage deposited Vilia at Half Moon Street soon after seven o'clock, Blackwood, the butler, informed her that the major had not yet returned. He was still not back when, having visited the nursery, washed, and changed, she descended to the little parlour by the dining-room. At nine o'clock, she emerged from her dreams long enough to decide that it was unfair to ask Mrs Blackwood, the housekeeper, to put supper back again, and sat down to dine in solitary state and with no consciousness at all of what she was eating. Then she went back to the parlour and picked up a book.

It was eleven before she heard the bustle that meant Andrew had come in, and another ten minutes before Sorley appeared with a tray of decanters and glasses. 'The major iss gone to tidy himself, Mistress,' he said expressionlessly. 'He says will I tell you he will be choining you in a few moments.' She looked at him blankly. Andrew always came straight to her the moment he entered the front door, however tired or dusty he was. Sorley sighed and shook his head a little. 'Aye,' he said, and then turned like a good footman and left.

She recognized the warning, but didn't take it very seriously until Andrew walked into the room soon after. Then, the sympathetic smile died on her lips at sight of him, clean, controlled, and hostile. In her own elation, she had almost forgotten how resentful he had been that morning, and it seemed the day had done nothing to soften his mood. Indeed, his 'Good evening', spoken in the tone he might have used to some distant acquaintance, was like a douche of ice water.

He poured himself a glass of brandy and then crossed to the table that held the latest periodicals. 'I hope you had a pleasant day?' he said.

Through all the hours of that same, interminable day, while he had been receiving his final orders at the Horse Guards, making arrangements for the journey, instructing his servant as to what should be packed, he had been unable to banish Vilia's disloyalty from his mind. Always before, when he had been disturbed by her contempt for convention, her levity, her occasional dismissiveness, he had succumbed to the first glimmer of her smile. He knew it was weak of him. He knew his father was right when he wrote, as he frequently did, that 'the girl' needed to be ridden on a tight rein. But he loved her too much. And that, perhaps, was why it was different this time, why her carelessness, her selfishness – for he saw it as nothing less – had hurt him so. Tomorrow, he might be leaving to go to his death, for if it came to a battle between Wellington and Boney, he, Andrew, would be in the thick of it. Yet she had gone gaily off to Ascot as if it were all a matter of no consequence. For the first time, he had found himself wondering whether she loved him at all. But she *must* love him. She was his wife.

'Very pleasant, thank you. The Telfers sent you their kindness, and were sorry you couldn't join us.'

'Were they?' Unseeing, he flipped over the pages of the *St James's Chronicle*. 'Didn't they think it strange that you should have chosen to go with them to the races, instead of staying here in case I needed you?'

She sighed heavily. 'Oh, Andrew! Surely you can't still be brooding about that? Be honest – did you or didn't you go out immediately after I did this morning? And did you or didn't you come back after I did this evening?'

'I did.'

'Very well, then. Where is your grievance? Was there anything *at all* I could have done if I had stayed at home all day?'

His hands clammy and shaking a little, he turned to face her. 'There might have been. And I might, for all you know to the contrary, have stayed away so long because I knew you wouldn't be here if I hurried back.' Seeing her lips curl in amused scepticism, his pose of cool displeasure began to slip. His voice was raw as he said, 'After all, it will be weeks, perhaps months, before we see each other again. It *might* be never.'

She tilted her head a little and, with the tolerant half-smile she bestowed on the children when they misbehaved, said, 'Andrew! Such dramatics! You have gone off on military duty, how many times – half a dozen? – since we have been married, and have always come back safe. The Lauriston luck, my dear. Why should it be different this time? I regard you as quite indestructible.'

He had a sudden vision of the battles he had been in, and the skirmishes. Of men he knew, stretched on the blood-muddied ground with arms or legs torn off, or their guts spilling out, or their faces shot away. Of himself, possessed by frenzy and fear, urging his Highlanders on to mad charges and madder assaults, while the air was livid with cries and screams and the thunder of artillery and the clash of arms and the whinnying of horses, and, close and private, quite separate from all the other sounds, the hoarse, laboured breathing of the men at his shoulder, and the rattle in his own throat as he tried to summon the voice to yell, 'Forward!' And again – and again – 'Forward!' He was always dully surprised at the end of the day to find himself relatively whole, and counted his escapes with the nervous care of a cat keeping tally of its nine lives. In the moment's lull before the beginning of each new engagement, he would stand preparing his mind for the end that, this time, must inevitably come – praying to be spared, not the end itself, but the agony that went before. Praying to the harsh, righteous, punishing God of the Old Testament whom he had learned to fear even before he was old enough to walk. The God of his father, Duncan Lauriston, and very like him.

It didn't occur to Andrew that, desperate for his wife to believe she had married a fine, upstanding fellow who didn't know what it was to be afraid, he had never told her what war was like, or how he felt about it. Neither did it occur to him, who thought only cowards knew the meaning of fear, that Vilia might suspect it was only fools who didn't.

'You don't know what you're talking about,' he burst out. 'No one is indestructible! And the battle we're facing now will be the bloodiest any of us has ever fought!'

'But the Allies will win, surely?'

It wasn't the point at issue, and she knew it as well as he did, but he answered just the same. 'Perhaps. Probably. Although it will be the first time Wellington has ever taken the field against Boney in person. Neither of them can afford to lose. They'll be bound to go on fighting until there's not a man left to fight or stand. And the Duke always throws the Highland regiments in where the fighting is hottest!'

A little, a very little of his dread found its way through to her. Since they had been married, she had never once thought about what he had been going *to*, when he left her. Her sense of release had always been so great that, after the agonized heart-searching that had followed his first departure, she had tried deliberately not to think about him at all when he was out of her sight. But now, when it was much too late, when today's encounter at Ascot had turned the whole focus of her being on one man alone, a quirk of insight told her something about her husband she had never known before. It was as if, looking over the abyss today had dug between them, she could see him more clearly.

He was wearing civilian clothes this evening, but tomorrow he would ride off, splendid in his blue-faced scarlet coat, with the famous red-and-white plumes of the 42nd's grenadiers waving in his hat, and enough gold coins, special passes, and authorizations to ensure that he would be accorded priority over all other travellers. He might be afraid of the battle that lay ahead, but he wasn't going to be late for it. She rose and took a step towards him. 'My dear, I don't know what to say. I hadn't realized . . . Forgive me? I must have seemed very thoughtless.'

But his resentment was not to be so easily assuaged. Indeed, it was fanned by her tacit admission that he had been in the right. Fanned, too, by the knowledge that he had given himself away. 'Thoughtless?' he repeated. 'More than that. I asked you not to go, but you went. It shouldn't even have been necessary for me to ask. My father is right . . .'

Her face stiffened and she moved away.

'My father is right when he says you have no idea how a wife should behave. Two years of marriage, a household to run, two sons – and none of it has changed you. You think you can go on just as *you* see fit. But marriage isn't like that!' Angrily, he struggled to put it all into words. 'There are some things that are morally right, and some things that are morally wrong. Things one simply doesn't question! It's *my* moral duty to provide for you and the children, and *your* moral duty to – to do as a wife should, without even being asked. It's like the army. I know my orders. It would never occur to me to disobey them.'

Her tone lightly ironic, she said, 'And do you propose to court-martial me for disobeying mine?'

Looking back afterwards, she was to realize that they were both being ridden by their private devils that night, she by her passion for freedom, he by his Calvinist upbringing. They were like two people trying to communicate the most complex thoughts and instincts without knowing each other's language.

She had never seen him really angry before. His neck muscles hardened into ropes, and a vivid red flush sprang to his cheekbones. 'Take care what you say, Vilia! Until now I have let you have your head, but it doesn't mean that my patience is inexhaustible. I had hoped that, as you grew older, you would lose this unbecoming habit of levity . . .'

'Not levity,' she flashed, as angry as he. 'Vivacity, I believe, was the word you used when you were so anxious for me to marry you!'

'Be silent!' He spoke in the bark he would have employed towards an erring subaltern, and his voice, as he went on, was loud and hectoring. 'It's time you realized that *I* am the master in this house. When I return, things will be done differently, I assure you! Come what may, we . . .'

His head snapped round. 'Yes!' he rapped. 'What is it?'

Sorley McClure stood in the doorway, his freckled face wooden, his arms hanging straight at his sides. 'It iss midnight, sir,' he said. 'Do I haff your permission to lock up, or will you be going out again?'

'Lock up. But see the doors are opened promptly in the morning. I will be leaving at five.'

'Yess, sir. Goodnight, madam. Goodnight, sir.'

Sorley closed the door behind him. Subtly, the pressure had eased. Vilia said, without expression, 'You should go upstairs, or you will have no sleep.'

Andrew's high colour had gone, and his voice had relaxed a little. 'We shouldn't be coming to cuffs like this on my last night. I won't say anything more than this – if I survive these next weeks, I *will* sell out of the army, come what may, and we will go and live with my father. When we see more of each other, we may learn to understand each other better than we do now.' He hesitated. 'But I mean what I say about being master in my own house. You pushed me too far today, Vilia, and I have no intention of letting it happen again. However,' his tongue flickered over his lips, 'let us cry quits for the moment, and forget about it.' He moved towards her.

She was standing by the far window, and couldn't retreat any further. She couldn't mistake the look on his face, the indefinable slackening of the muscles, and the breathless laxity about his mouth. His hands felt warm and clammy on her bare arms, and his words came out in a rush. 'You go on up, and I'll come to you soon.'

3

She had learned endurance in the last two years. She had learned, somehow, to detach her body and even her mind from what was going on, until all she was conscious of was a mixture of distaste and boredom as her husband's handsome, muscular body went through its fixed ritual. She had discovered that he didn't expect her, or even want her to participate, as if, by taking all the labour on himself, he was giving the fullest proof of his love. It was like a worshipper making his devotions to the statue of a goddess. On one occasion, with a touch of hysteria, she had wondered if every army officer behaved as Andrew did in bed, whether there was some official series of manoeuvres to which all His Majesty's officers were required to conform?

Never had he succeeded in touching any spring of pleasure within her, as with busy hands, probing tongue, and industrious loins he proceeded urgently, night after night, through his private drill manual. So she had learned to lie under the strong, smothering body and cut herself off from its thrusting assault on every corner of her being.

But tonight, emotionally stripped, her defences failed her. Andrew, she soon realized, must have been drinking steadily for hours before he came home, and the reek of brandy sickened her. As she felt the clumsy hands and invading tongue go to work, her nerves began to quiver as if they had been exposed, raw and sensitive, to some cold, salt wind from the sea. She screamed deep inside, and screamed again, and then continuously, though not a sound escaped her. He must finish soon, she prayed, must hurry on to those last convulsive moments which brought him to ecstasy and her to deliverance, must recognize his own need for rest before the days ahead. But, dear God, he did not. And did not.

He stayed with her until it was time for him to rise and dress, and was touched by the tears that racked her towards the end. Just before he left, he bent over her to stroke the white-gold hair that lay tangled on the pillow. 'Don't cry, my dearest,' he murmured. 'Don't fear for me. I'll come back safe. I promise I will!'

4

On the Sunday, she received a letter from her husband, dated from Ramsgate on the evening of the day he had left her, June ninth, 1815.

My dearest wife – I have time to write you only a few words before I leave our shores. We sail almost at once and hope to be in Flanders in thirteen hours or less, for there is a good fresh breeze, I am told. I could wish I were not prey to that vilest of maladies, sea-sickness, although I have learned by now to bear it with tolerable equanimity! We arrived here, saddle-weary but in good heart, soon after midday. I believe I did not mention to you that I was travelling in company for the first part of the way, at least, with Mr Gordon, a sub-lieutenant of my own regiment, and two surgeons, who have not so far shown any sign of that distressing propensity medical men so often have, of exchanging reminiscences of their experiences. One of them, Surgeon Storey, seems a very good fellow.

How strange it is that no more than a few hours have passed since I bade you farewell. Never before, I think, have you wept to see me go! Be assured, the memory of those loving tears will give me strength to face whatever may be to come.

Ramsgate is very empty of company. There are only a few parties of private soldiers who will embark with us. The Duke has been complaining that, although he has a small and (he swears) ruinous army of no more than 90,000 men, he has generals and staff enough to command ten times that number, so perhaps he will be glad to see even these few! But it has always been in Old Hookey's nature to complain, and to tell the truth, I shall be much surprised if he and Blücher cannot, after all, contrive to put the Little Corporal to rout. So do not fear, my dearest, for the wellbeing of – Your most loving husband, Andrew Lauriston (Maj.)

Postscriptum: If I should have the fortune to encounter a courier returning to England, I will take the opportunity to write to you again, even if no more than a note in haste. – Yrs &c, A.L. (Maj.)

Vilia was young and resilient, and three days and two nights without Andrew had done much to restore her to herself. She was able to read his letter with a trace, even, of amusement. Who but Andrew could think to reassure his wife with talk of sea-sickness, and surgeons, and Wellington's disgust with the army on which the fate of Europe, and of Andrew himself, depended?

She had asked the messenger who brought the note whether there was any news. He had been a very junior subaltern, his uniform caked with dried mud and sweat, and his face white with tiredness. He had come straight on from the Horse Guards after travelling from Ostend. 'No, ma'am,' he had said. 'Nothing. Boney was still in Paris on the morning of the tenth, according to reports.'

'The tenth? Yesterday?'

His bloodshot eyes had been hazy. 'Was it? Yes,' I suppose it must have been. My apologies, ma'am. I seem to have lost sense of time. Now, if you will forgive me . . . Your servant, ma'am.' And he had saluted and gone, refusing her offer of refreshment. He had looked younger than she was herself.

On Sunday evenings, no one came calling and the house was quiet. Even the servants were out – or most of them. The Blackwoods, who acted as butler and cook-housekeeper; little Maggie, the maidservant; Jenny the nurserymaid; and Vilia's personal maid, Rachelle. Andrew had disapproved of the servants being given a night off every week, but

Vilia had insisted, and gradually he had become reconciled. She took pleasure in having the house to herself – except for the babies, and Nurse, and Ellen the second maidservant, and Sorley, God bless him! – and was accustomed to dine sparingly on cold meats and salads and a glass of wine, served on a tray in the drawing-room, her own private sanctum.

The house was tall and narrow and inconvenient, and didn't lend itself to a satisfactory arrangement of rooms. The kitchens, store rooms, servants' quarters, and night nursery were distributed between the basement and the attics, while the day nursery occupied the back of the top floor, with Andrew's bedroom and dressing-room at the front. On the ground floor, of necessity, were the dining-room and Andrew's study, and there was a snug parlour where she and Andrew sat of an evening. It would have been more orthodox for them to retire to the drawing-room, on the middle of the three main floors, but somehow they had never fallen into the habit of it. Somehow? Behind the drawing-room lay Vilia's own bedchamber and dressing-room, too close – much too close – for comfort. It was only when Andrew was away that she felt at ease in the drawing-room. But then it was her favourite room.

For almost three days, her tormented mind had fretted ceaselessly at her problems, seeking solutions that it discarded as soon as they suggested themselves. She wouldn't even contemplate the thought – the intolerable thought – of living with Andrew in his father's house. The old man hated her, and she knew that he and Andrew would bring out the worst in each other as they competed to bring her to heel. If she could persuade Andrew – but how? – to stay in the army! If it hadn't been for the babies, she could have left him altogether and gone gipsying. The discomforts of such a life seemed to her a small price to pay for the unimaginable treasure of freedom for her mind and body. But with the babies, if she left him she would have to find some genteel way of earning a living for the three of them.

When she found herself giggling aloud at the thought of setting up as a modiste or milliner – she, who would never thread a needle if she could possibly avoid it – she knew that the darkest shadows lay behind her. There was no way out of her troubles that she could see, nothing positive she could do. She could only resign herself and let Fate take its course. It was a restful sensation. She felt suddenly quite tranquil, as if her emotions, scrubbed and scoured and beaten and rinsed, had been laid out peacefully on the heather, under a mild, warm sun. The kind of sun that, at Kinveil, sometimes shone out of a pale sky on bland spring days set like jewels in the cold heart of winter.

Insensibly, the thought of Kinveil led her to thoughts of Perry Randall. The wild elation she had felt on Thursday afternoon had been bludgeoned to death on Thursday night. She knew she had been mad to invite him to Half Moon Street, but still couldn't regret it. She settled back in her chair, and the tiny black kitten in her lap stirred, and purred voluptuously. With a gentle forefinger, Vilia stroked between its ears and it opened its golden eyes a little, and gazed at her as if heaven could hold no greater bliss. She smiled at it. Andrew had bought it for the nursery, but within hours it had fled from the clutch of infant hands and attached itself to her like some familiar spirit.

Perry Randall had not come. She thought, now, that he wouldn't. Driving back from Ascot, she had justified her madness to herself with the argument that all she wanted to do was see him again, and talk to him. There couldn't be any harm in that. She had made it sound quite reasonable, but now she smiled at her own self-delusion. Reason had nothing to do with the alchemy between them, and he, wiser than she, must have recognized the danger.

All that remained was to teach herself, once again, to banish him from her mind. If, by some mischance, they were to meet, she must be capable of decent self-control. She was, after all, not some giddy schoolroom miss, but nineteen years old, a wife, and twice a mother.

With the faintest of sighs, she scooped up a sleepily indignant kitten and crossed to the bookshelves. Something light, or something difficult to concentrate her mind? The new novel by the author of *Sense and Sensibility*, or Ricardo on *The High Price of Bullion*?

She was still staring blindly at the shelves when she heard the thick, metallic, rat-tat-tat of the front door knocker.

Chapter Eight

1

'The major iss not at home, sir.' Even after twelve years in London, Sorley still hadn't lost his Highland sibilance.

Perry hesitated. 'Has he gone out of town?'

'Yess, sir.'

'Very well. Thank you.' He smiled. 'You must be McClure?'

'Yess, sir. Kind of you to remember, sir.'

He was turning away when the footman's voice halted him. 'With your permission, sir? Mistress Vilia is at home, and I am sure she would be blithe to see you. Would you be wishing me to tell her you are here?'

Before he could answer, Vilia's voice came from the staircase. 'Who is it, Sorley? Oh, Mr Randall. How kind of you to call.' Descending a step or two, seeming almost to drift in her simple muslin gown, she said, 'Please stay a moment and relieve my tedium. My husband has been called away, but I pride myself on being as well informed about affairs at Brussels as any gentleman at the Horse Guards. Perhaps I can tell you what you want to know.'

He tried to withstand her. 'I mustn't disturb you, Mrs Lauriston. Indeed, I apologize for calling at such an hour, but I found myself in Piccadilly and thought the major might not object. Forgive me. I won't trouble you.'

She couldn't read his face, or his feelings. All she could see was the tall, lithe figure outlined against the dusk. She said, 'Napoleon was still in Paris yesterday. Did you know?'

There was an infinitesimal pause. 'No, I didn't know.'

'Does it help you, knowing?' She was behaving like a shameless hussy, and she didn't care.

After a moment, he glanced down at the gloves and cane in his hand, and then, stepping across the threshold, handed them to Sorley, with his hat. He looked up, and smiled. 'As you see, Mrs Lauriston, my consideration for your comfort crumbles at a touch. If it wouldn't incommode you, I should indeed be grateful for anything you can tell me.'

'Will I bring the tea tray up, madam?'

'Yes, Sorley, if you please.' She turned. 'Unless Mr Randall would prefer something else?'

'Thank you, no. Tea will be admirable.'

Their conversation at first was extraordinarily banal. The weather. The convenience of Half Moon Street as an address, and the inconvenience of its style of architecture. The form shown the other day by the runners at Ascot. Nothing that could be remotely construed as personal. They might have been discussing Paracelsian medicine, the Hindu scriptures, or the Baltic herring trade, and Vilia would have been equally content. All she wanted of him was his presence, and the sound of his light, warm, humorous voice. She sat, and sipped tea, and smiled serenely, and said very little.

Sorley came to remove the tray even before she had rung, which surprised her a little, and when he departed, the kitten, its eyes on the cream jug and its tail in the air, pranced out at his side. The door closed, and they were alone without prospect of interruption, and Perry Randall said with a rueful grin, 'How delightful to have desires that are so easily satisfied. Does it have a name?'

'She. My maid has christened her the Duchess, because she is so supercilious with the servants.'

He laughed a little. They were sitting facing each other across the fireplace, which was screened off, the evening being warm, with a great vase of greenery. The room had a fresh, outdoor charm, with pale woodwork, upholstery that was the green of young leaves, and sprigged curtains that blew in the light breeze from the open windows. He thought how well it all suited her.

It was, he supposed, the peculiar fragility of her looks that made the incisive style of her mind so disconcerting at first. All the fair beauties he had ever known had been shallow and vapid. But with Vilia Cameron the mind's quality was there to be observed in the candid eyes, the chiselled features, the soft but resolute lips . . .

He said abruptly, 'The news from Brussels. I believe you have heard something?' Then, before she could answer, he collected himself and went on, 'I should, in all courtesy, explain my interest. I am not a rich man, but I have some investments in government stock which, in the present situation, are losing value daily. The jobbers, in fact, closed their books some time ago, although my man of business tells me that private dealing is still going on. The essence is that, if I sell – as I am advised to do before the situation deteriorates further – I must make a loss, which I can ill afford. And matters *will* deteriorate further if

156

Napoleon is restored to his former glory, for then all Europe will be at war again and British government stock could become almost worthless. It wouldn't just be a question of panic in Change Alley, but a general failure of public confidence.'

'And if Napoleon isn't restored?'

'If Wellington were to defeat him, the Funds would revert to their normal level. They might even go higher, though not at once. And I would find myself back to where I was before the crisis.'

'Would that satisfy you?' The words were softly spoken and quite uncritical, but he looked at her sharply.

He said, 'Of course.'

'I have no means of knowing what rumour says. Does the City think Napoleon might win?'

'Yes.'

After a brief silence, 'Do you remember last year,' she asked reflectively, 'when Lord Cochrane and his friends made – how much was it? thousands and thousands of pounds – by spreading a premature rumour that Napoleon had been deposed? The value of their stocks shot up, and they sold at an enormous profit. I had never realized until then how *quickly* great profits or losses could be made. It can't have been more than a day or two before the news came that he hadn't been deposed at all.'

Their minds were beautifully attuned. With the purest amusement in his eyes, he said, 'But Cochrane was a distinguished naval officer and a Knight of the Bath. I can't think that I, a very minor and quite unbelligerent Honourable, could convince the City single-handed that Boney had been defeated finally and forever!'

She wrinkled her nose, dissatisfied. 'No, I suppose not. What a pity! It would have been by far the simplest solution. For you really need to make a vast sum of money so that you needn't be beholden to Charlotte.' The silence told her what she had said.

'You know, then?' His long, capable fingers were tightly intertwined.

'Only that you have – parted. Something to do with gaming, I believe.'

She wasn't asking a question, and he could sense that she didn't think it important, but he felt compelled to answer. 'In a way. My wife doesn't enter into my feelings about the importance of my investments, and of course she's perfectly right. As far as Glenbraddan is concerned, they are of no account at all. It's just that they matter to me.'

'Then why take any risk, if they are so important? If you sell now, you will lose – what? – ten or twenty per cent? If you wait, you *might* lose sixty or seventy. If your savings are a kind of lifeline to you . . .' She *did* understand. '. . . you have to maintain them. Lose a little, gain a little, the lifeline is still there. But lose a lot, and it's gone. Or am I wrong?'

His laugh was a travesty. 'Not wrong. If I were a sane, rational human being you would be perfectly right. But, unfortunately, after I had been speaking to some of Wellington's more devoted admirers, I had an inspiration. It occurred to me that the intelligent thing to do would be to buy, not sell. The object, as you will readily appreciate, being to unload the new stock when Wellington defeats Bonaparte, and so make a neat and satisfying profit.'

'That sounds perfectly reasonable to me.'

'Thank you. The only flaw was that, having no ready cash to buy with, I resorted to gaming with the object of raising some. I was going to buy the stock with my winnings, you understand.'

'But you lost.' Her voice was perfectly matter-of-fact.

'Of course. Almost to the full extent of my holdings at their pre-crisis value. I now owe more than I could possibly recoup by selling at today's price, and far, far more than I could recoup if Napoleon were to defeat the Duke. On the other hand, if the Duke won, I might still find myself with a few pence change on the transaction. Enough, I should think, to allow me to go on buying my own cravats.' His face was empty. 'So, you see, any news from Brussels is of interest to me.'

Her heart ached for him, and yet it all seemed so unimportant. No, she corrected herself, not unimportant. Irrelevant. With something of an effort, she said, 'All I can tell you is that Wellington and Blücher command an unsatisfactory and inexperienced army consisting of half the nationalities of Europe, but that generals and men alike hate Napoleon bitterly. Victory matters to them more than anything else in the world. It matters to Napoleon, too, of course, but perhaps not so much to his men. The thing to be feared, I am told, is that he still has that unpredictable genius that carried him through for so long.' She tried to lighten the atmosphere. 'You might say that the odds are much the same as Aladdin carried in the Gold Cup!'

'Five-to-two on Wellington?' A reluctant smile flickered round the corners of his mouth. 'And I told Mrs Telfer that nothing less than twenty-to-one against would do for me! I can't tell you what a fool I feel!'

'I don't know,' she said thoughtfully. 'You gamble with money. Others gamble with people's feelings or people's lives. I wouldn't like to have to sit in judgement.'

'You are very kind.' There didn't seem much else to say; nothing, certainly, that he dared to say. 'I can't imagine why I should have bothered you with my troubles in this way.' It was a lie. He had been trying, against all his instincts, to shift the burden of his desire by making her think him a fool, so that it would be she who broke the deadly, dangerous current of attraction that flowed so strongly between them. Against all his instincts. Desperately, he didn't want the current to be broken.

There was a silver branch of candles behind her, but the light in the rest of the room was muted, so that he saw her eyes only as twin pools of shadow. She was sitting perfectly calm and relaxed, but it suddenly came to him that she was waiting.

He rose to his feet, almost stumbling in his haste. 'I must go,' he said without preliminary. 'It has been unforgivable of me to trespass on your courtesy for so long. You must be wishing me at Jericho!'

After the space of a heartbeat, she said, with more composure than he, 'I will see you out.'

Despite its dimensions, it was a very small room when one walked from a chair by the fireside to a door one didn't want to reach. When one's mind was seething with the attempt to find some admissible way of saying, 'I can't bear you to go. I can't bear the thought that I might never see you again.'

But as she stretched out her hand to the reeded brass knob, the problem was resolved for her. Briefly, he stood so close behind her that she could feel the warmth of his skin, and then his long-fingered hands came to rest, steady and firm and final, about her waist.

She could have stopped it all, even then. Killed the joy opening like a day-lily in her heart. Closed her eyes to the jewel-bright gate because she feared the long, dark vista beyond. She had only to ignore his

159

hands, and open the door, and walk ahead of him down the narrow staircase with its portraits of Camerons dead and gone, until they came to the front door, its fanlight silhouetted against the faint glow from the street outside. And then good night, Mr Randall. And good-bye. And with every step she would have died a little.

They stood motionless for a very long time, and she was aware of nothing in the world but the weight of his hands and her own passionate thankfulness, as if all her life had been a preparation for this moment. Then his lips brushed her hair and he turned her gently towards him, and looked at her with eyes that were wide, grey, and lucent. As his mouth came down on hers, she made a faint, inarticulate sound in her throat, and then her lids closed and darkness swirled around her, swaying and lapping like some fronded current parting to embrace the unresisting dead. Drowning, dissolving, lost, she opened her lips to his, and with an uneven gasp he drew her tight against him so that the whole length of their bodies melted together and she could feel the hard muscles of his thighs against hers.

At last he withdrew from the kiss and raised his head a little, his breathing light and quick. Her face, below his, was calm and smooth, the lips vulnerable, the sweep of dark gold lashes fringing closed eyelids as slanting and mysterious as those of some Romanesque saint. In the candlelight a trace of tears gleamed on her cheeks, and the coils of her hair, loosened by his embrace, fell in a pale cascade against the dark cloth of his sleeve. He touched his lips to the tears, and then stretched out a hand to turn the key.

There was no need for them to speak, no question that needed to be asked or answered, for this was a day that had been written in their stars since they were born. Nothing could change it. Nothing could touch them, neither past nor future, nor any awareness of the present beyond the enchanted circle that enclosed them. As his lips became more demanding and his hands more eloquent, they moved only towards an end that was never in doubt.

He carried her, after a time, to the curtained bed that lay beyond the other door, and set her down softly among the heaped pillows under the tasselled canopy. And there, she who had never before experienced either beauty or pleasure in love – who, in her innocence, had even doubted their existence – there she discovered what it was to be swept into a realm where torture and delight were one, where her whole being strained towards the fulfilment of a desire she did not yet recognize, a fulfilment that was promised and withheld, and promised again, and then with a wild, unimagined thrill, granted to her at last.

An hour, a month, a year later, she opened her eyes to see his face poised over hers, mysterious in the shadows. As if he were finishing a speech long begun, he murmured, 'Always, and forever.' He was leaning on one elbow, his free hand resting lightly in the curve of her waist, and, dreaming still, she raised a finger and ran it slowly down the taut skin of his side. With a laugh that was half a groan, he stopped her, and then caressed her lips gently with his and drew away.

She was surprised to discover, as she coiled her hair before the glass, that it was not quite midnight. There was a reproachful kitten sitting on the landing, and she gathered it up and stroked it as she accompanied Mr Randall to the door. 'I hope,' she said politely, as she bade him good night, 'that your stocks recover. I will send to let you know if I should hear further from Brussels.'

'You are most kind, Mrs Lauriston.'

She watched his tall figure stride away in the direction of Piccadilly, and then turned back into the house. Sorley was just emerging from the service door under the stairs. 'You may lock up now,' she said, smiling. 'And good night, Sorley.'

He watched her mount the stairs again, the purring kitten held against the curve of her shoulder, and his face was alight with happiness for her.

2

In the days that followed, they couldn't bear to be apart. Restored to some kind of sanity, Perry would not come to the house again, but they met, sometimes for an hour, once for a whole, idyllic afternoon, in the Green Park, where Vilia had always found refuge since she had come to London as a child. At first, they scarcely spoke. It was as if they were still suspended in a dream of space and time, seeing the real world through a frosted glass. It was enough to be together, and touch hands occasionally, and watch each others' faces.

But on the Friday, as she stood invisible as a chameleon in her pale green gown against the curtain of a weeping willow, she saw him coming before he was aware of her, and was shocked and alarmed by the strain on his face. It vanished when he saw her, and they clasped hands briefly and then turned to walk along the leafy path, with its scattering of other strollers. 'What is it?' she said at last. 'You looked so ill!'

His eyes clung to hers. 'Did I? I'm sorry. I don't know what I would do if you weren't here to give me strength.' He turned his head away, and went on, 'It was just that I heard a rumour that Napoleon joined his army on Tuesday, and I was oppressed by the thought that not only Europe's fate, but my own, has come a seven-league step nearer.'

She didn't want to think about it. Brightly, she said, 'Oh, ye of little faith! Have you no trust in the great, the glorious, the invincible Duke of Wellington?'

'A general is invincible only until the first time he is defeated. I don't know, my darling! I don't know anything any more. But if it hadn't been for you, I think I would have weakened and sold my stocks by now.'

'If it hadn't been for me?' she repeated, frightened. 'But I haven't tried to persuade you!'

He stopped and faced her, ignoring the passers-by, and his voice was almost impatient. 'But don't you see? I *must* gamble now. If I gamble and win, there might – somehow, some time – be hope for us. But if I lose, the extent of my losses scarcely matters. It will be the end.'

'Why? Why should it? Your losses can't be so great?'

'Can't they? I need £10,000 to make them good.'

The sum was astronomical. A hundred years' wages for a French cook, Vilia's ridiculous, mathematical mind told her helplessly. The kind of sum that, at three per cent, would keep a country family in comfort forever, with the capital still intact. Enough to pay the rent at Half Moon Street for forty years or so. How was it *possible* to lose so much at the gaming table? Her father could probably have told her.

'You fool,' she said quietly. 'You fool.' But it sounded almost like an endearment.

He turned and began to walk again. 'At their value earlier this year, I had stocks worth £10,000. During these last weeks I have gambled and lost to much the same tune. My creditors have agreed to wait, but not for long. If I sell at a loss, I will have to dishonour at least £3,000 of those debts, perhaps as much as £6,000 or £7,000 if Wellington is defeated. In neither case will I have any future. In neither case will *we* have any future. Only if I have the courage to hold on, and only if Wellington wins, is there any possibility of my escaping a debtors' prison. Will you come and visit me in the Fleet?'

She found she resented being tumbled off her rose-tinted cloud. 'The Fleet? Pooh!' she said with a brittle laugh. 'If the worst comes to the worst, you can always take sanctuary in Edinburgh.'

He didn't understand.

'Didn't you know? Ever since the time of King David I there's been a right of sanctuary at Holyrood. I believe the precise area stretches from the foot of the Canongate to Duddingston Loch, and includes the whole of the King's Park and Arthur's Seat. You pay two guineas to the Hereditary Keeper, and then you can stay in the district free from harassment. There are lodgings at a few shillings a week, and on Sundays you may even venture outside the sanctuary bounds. There are supposed to be about a hundred insolvents and levanters living there now, beyond the reach of the law.' She laughed again. 'But this information can't be new to you? I understood that all dedicated gamblers learned it at their mother's knee.'

She could see how much it hurt but, for the moment, wouldn't spare him.

He had no excuse, not even the excuse that gaming was in his blood. He enjoyed the challenge of cards; enjoyed trying to assess the quality of a horse. But the dice box held no magnetic attraction for him, and he felt no compulsion to go on betting when the odds were stacked against him. It was his own judgement, not the dice, that had failed him again and again. Yet he had persisted, regardless of reason, urged on by a kind of desperate, inexorable hope. He had chosen to go on betting – *chosen*, dear God! – and had lost all the way along the line.

After a time, he said, 'Not dedicated, only desperate.'

They had reached a small clearing which, for a marvel, was empty. Knowing all they needed to know about each other, they still knew very little about each others' lives. Now, laying a hand on Perry's arm, Vilia forced him down on to a picturesque iron bench. 'Why!' she said. 'Tell me why.'

And then it all poured out. Charlotte, a young widow in holiday mood, glowing under his careless attentions. His own weariness of being dunned by his tailor and his bootmaker, of being put to the most complex shifts to pay his debts. His feeling that, if he could start again with a clean slate, far from the cards and clubs and racecourses that had been his life – and his downfall – since he was sixteen, he might do better. The leisurely attractions of a country estate, with a pretty, lively wife, and no financial worries. None of it had been cold-bloodedly planned. Somehow, it had all just come about, and he had been content to drift with the tide.

But nothing had turned out as he had hoped. Nothing ever happened at Glenbraddan. He had no responsibilities, no occupation, no friends. When he had invited some acquaintances for a week's sport, Charlotte had been ill at ease and fertile with reasons why he shouldn't invite anyone again. Nor had he wanted to. Once home, Charlotte had lost her vivacity and become a bustling, preoccupied housewife. He had allowed his exasperation to show a little, and it had made things worse. He had tried, then, to spend most of his days outdoors, which meant that the early dark of winter had sometimes caught him far from home, and forced him to seek a bed for the night in some estate worker's cottage. And sometimes – he hesitated and then plunged – sometimes he had been driven to seek comfort from a – a kind-hearted local girl. He had . . .

Vilia gave a strangled gasp. 'Not Kirsty Macintyre?' Then, at the sight of his face, she surrendered to helpless laughter. When she spoke again, her words were almost indistinguishable. 'Oh, my dearest love!' she wailed. 'What a *dreadful* time you must have had! And sharing her with Magnus, too!'

He couldn't believe his ears, but even the mention of Magnus wasn't enough to divert him. 'You don't mind? You're not hurt? Or jealous?'

She struggled to control herself as a small group of people strolled into sight, a young woman with a nursemaid and two children so well-behaved that they looked as if they had been starched and pressed. The young woman looked at her disapprovingly.

When they had gone, Vilia turned and said, with the slanting smile that stopped his heart, 'Jealous? Why should I be? Why should I be jealous of what happened before we knew each other?' The smile faltered a little. 'It's only the future I'm jealous of.'

This time, neither of them saw the people sauntering by. He, who had been so bitter with himself, so deeply ashamed, suddenly felt as he supposed the devout must feel when granted absolution. It seemed to him, now, as if there was nothing she would not understand and forgive.

And because of that he went on, almost without realizing, into deeper and far more dangerous waters. Smiling back at her, ruefully, he said, 'Of all the mistakes of my life, marrying Charlotte was the worst and least forgivable. I chose an irresponsible way out of my irresponsible troubles, and I can't break out of the trap except by wounding my daughter, and my stepchildren, and Charlotte herself. Perhaps mortally.' His eyes, focused on a patch of shrubs on the other side of the clearing, were full of pain. 'For, however little I deserve it, Charlotte loves me very much.'

It was his own need, perhaps, that made Perry think that Vilia had more wisdom than she did, in fact, possess, for she was not very experienced in human relationships, nor very perceptive. She couldn't believe that Charlotte would be much hurt, except in her vanity. She remembered the condescending woman of the Northern Meeting ball, and the much younger Charlotte who had come to visit the little girl at Kinveil. She had talked of sending some children's books over, the kind with bright red marbled bindings and columns of nice, big, black print, and stories about Puss in Boots, and Blue Beard, and Cinderella. Vilia, offended, had refused, and had come off very much the victor of the encounter by saying that she had her grandfather Gideon's library to draw on, and had just finished studying Mr Wood's *Views of Palmyra* and the Duke of Buckingham's *Short Discourse upon the reasonableness of men's having a religion*, and was about to embark on William Lithgow's *Rare Adventures and Painefull Peregrinations in Europe, Asia, and Affrica*.

'A mésalliance,' Perry went on morosely. 'And I have no idea what to do about it. For, if I stay with her, it will be a living death.'

It was a long time before Vilia was able to force the words out. 'If you stay with her?'

Almost savagely, he turned to her. 'I swore I would go back, and I meant it. I said I didn't expect to see you – and I meant that, too.'

Her mind wasn't capable of absorbing it. 'See *me*?'

'Oh, yes! After the Northern Meeting ball, Charlotte was convinced that you were at the root of all our troubles. But I told her I was only concerned with my investments. I thought I was speaking the truth. And she said, "But we can manage without them!" and of course

165

we can. All it would mean would be that I should be wholly dependent on my wife.'

Her mind was reeling and spinning, like a leaf trapped on the edge of a whirlpool. She hadn't thought about the future at all. She had refused to think about it, because all she wanted to think about was herself and Perry, and the joy of lying in his arms. She looked down at the silk-sheathed handle of her parasol, grasped in slender, suddenly rigid hands. 'But . . .'

'Even if I win, and pay off my debts, what can I do?' She thought that, if they had been alone, he would have shaken her. 'Forget about honour and chivalry and all the spiritual virtues. Forget even about decent, civilized behaviour. *Tell me, what can I do?* I'm a gentleman. That means I'm fit for nothing. Nothing but to live on my capital – which doesn't exist – or on someone's charity. On my wife's charity. I have thought, and thought, and thought, in these last days. If I win, there might just possibly be some hope for us, but if I lose there is nothing in the whole wide world I can do but go to Mungo Telfer and beg him to save me. And after that, I must live out the rest of my life as my wife's pensioner.'

'And if Mr Telfer won't save you?' she asked through dry lips.

He sank his face in his hands. 'How do I know? Flee to America, perhaps.'

'You think that might be a more congenial place for an unemployable gentleman? What would you do there?'

Flinching a little, he said, 'Survive, no more. But at least I wouldn't be hag-ridden by all the rules and customs about what a gentleman may, and may not do.'

She couldn't see his face, but her eyes scanned the supple muscles of shoulder and thigh outlined under the dark blue coat and pale, glove-soft leather breeches, and she felt a strong, subversive quiver run through her. Mind and body wholly at odds, she said dully, 'I see I have no place in your plans for the future.'

His head came up at that, eyes flaming. 'My darling, *why* am I holding on? *Why* haven't I resigned myself to my own unforgivable, inconceivable stupidity? *Why* haven't I gone trailing home already, like a cur brought to heel?'

Even in childhood, she had learned that the human race could be divided into two kinds of people, the invincible pessimists who, always expecting the worst, failed to recognize the best when it came, and those others in whom hope sprang eternal. The safe and responsible; the reckless and the vital. It was only the optimists, dangerous though they were, who could light up a room with their presence, or melt one's soul with the warmth of their spirit. There were so few of them.

'You were born out of your time,' she said unexpectedly. 'You should have been an adventurer, a corsair, a Crusader.'

'Perhaps. Every generation, I suppose, gambles in its own way. It's my misfortune that, in ours, one gambles with one's money rather than one's life.'

She gave a choke of overwrought laughter. 'You sound more like a highwayman than a corsair!'

'Have a care, madam! I may yet be reduced to holding up your coach on Hounslow Heath!'

'And that would be a great waste of time, sir!' Her laugh was more natural. 'For I have no money or jewels, and I should be very much surprised if my coach would hold together if you waved a pistol at it!'

'Perhaps it's as well, then, that it would be you I wanted, not your money or your jewels or your coach.'

The tone in which it was said brought a warm colour to her cheeks, and the glow back to her eyes. Her voice trembled a little as she said, not without difficulty, 'We have – we have no idea what will happen tomorrow, or next week, or next month. Must I go on my knees to you?'

He was sitting forward, forearms resting on his thighs and the knuckles of his clasped hands white with stress, but he refused to help her.

She struggled on. 'Can't we live while we have the chance?'

It was wrong, all wrong. Last Sunday had been unplanned, their passion ungovernable. There could be no such excuse, Perry thought, if he were to take her in his arms again. That would be a real, deliberate betrayal of trust, of Charlotte's love for him, and Andrew's for Vilia. He had given Charlotte his word – and his word meant something to Perry who, despite all his faults, tried to live according to the code of honour he had learned in his father's house. And then, with bitter

167

self-mockery, he recognized that he was deceiving himself. There had been no excuse at all for last Sunday, and what right did he have now, in any case, to invoke a gentleman's code of honour? If he stubbornly refused to do what he so consumingly wanted to do, it would only be another betrayal – this time, of Vilia.

She had been watching him, her eyes huge and vulnerable, but when he turned it was with a suddenness that startled her. And then it was all right, because he was smiling at her with the heart-stopping brilliance that was all his own. He lifted her hand lightly and kissed it, and although an onlooker would have seen only a courtly gesture, a little old-fashioned, his lips burned against her skin. 'Why not?' he murmured. 'Why not?'

3

She wouldn't have believed that the joy could be greater, or the ecstasy more complete. But this time they had all afternoon, and part of the evening; and this time, too, she knew where she was going, the pattern of her journey and the rapture of its end.

On the previous Sunday, he had led her slowly and with infinite self-control along the paths of beguilement, but today her desire was as urgent as his and even the haste of their first passion was beautifully, magically perfect. Swiftly, unerringly, he took them both straight to the heights, and held them there, quivering, glorying in it, for just so long as they could bear it. They were together all the way, and together, blindly and wonderfully, at the end.

When they had lain in drowsy enchantment for a little, he raised himself to one elbow and looked at her. With the slim figure exposed, her hair loosened and silver-blonde on the pillow, and her fine skin warmed by the wildfire that had consumed them, her allure was breathtaking. Whatever happened, he knew that for the rest of his life he would never be complete without her. Absorbed, almost unthinking, he murmured, 'If ever any beauty I did see, which I desir'd, and got, 'twas but a dreame of thee.'

The green eyes opened, crinkling a little with laughter, and she said, 'I beg your pardon?'

He smiled back. 'John Donne.'

She chuckled, and a tremor of renewed desire ran, swift and commanding, through his body. 'I know,' she murmured, and he sank his lips on hers again, and set his hands wandering, tender and tantalizing, over her flesh. 'I am *very* well educated.'

It was not just her body he loved, although it was the most exquisite thing he had ever seen. Nor was it her mind, whose quality he recognized. It was something far more elusive. It was the knowledge, perhaps, that in every single way they belonged together. It was as if they were inseparably part of each other, obverse and reverse of the same coin, the warp and weft of the fabric of life, the fuel and the flame of love and desire and every other aspect of being. Made for each other, and incomplete without each other.

His voice roughening, he murmured, 'I love you. I love you. *How* I love you!'

She brought her palms to his temples, fingers meshed in the darkly waving hair, and her voice, too, throbbed as she replied, 'And I you. So much, so very much.' And then the cadence of her breathing changed as he began to move within her again, and she cried out softly in delirium.

At some time during the long, joy-filled hours of that summer Sunday, she realized that all his concentration was on her, and on her pleasure. 'Teach me,' she whispered, 'teach me how I can make love to you, too!' But all he would do was smile at her, and touch his lips to her breast, and run his hands, light as thistledown, over her tingling skin, and set himself pulsing inside her again, ravishing her senses, until she was reduced once more to moaning, mindless ecstasy. 'Some other time,' he murmured, lips to her lips. 'Some other time, my darling.' And then he, too, began to drown in the torrent that engulfed them.

When the light outdoors failed at last, she stirred in his arms. Although the house was still wrapped in Sunday quiet, faint sounds of activity were floating up from the windows of the kitchen, two floors below. When he had arrived, early in the afternoon, Vilia had opened the door to him herself, her face a picture of guilt and mischief, and a finger laid warningly to her lips. The door didn't creak, nor the stairs as they walked lightly up, and when they reached the drawing-room she had looked at the expression on his face and laughed delightedly. 'No, surely not! My darling, you look quite scandalized! As if there were something more improper in arranging to be private than in – than in . . .' Her voice had trailed off because she was, after all, a gently bred girl and didn't know the words to use.

'Than in making love,' he said, and took her in his arms.

'Not scandalized,' he resumed, a few breathless minutes later. 'Only sad that we have to meet in this clandestine fashion.'

'Clandestine? What a stuffy word!' She was laughing and defensive, like an over-excited child. 'Especially when I have been so clever. My darling, there isn't a soul in the house but us! Apart from Sorley, of course, and the second maid. And I wouldn't care to guess how *they* will choose to occupy their afternoon!'

Aware that his mouth was open, he closed it again. 'Dear God, Vilia! I hope you don't make that kind of remark to anyone but me!'

But his eyes were smiling, and she fluttered her eyelashes at him. 'Of course not. I am, in general, a very model of respectability. Quite mealy-mouthed, in fact. But what matters, my dearest, is that we can be together and private for hours. *Hours!* The Blackwoods always go to her father's on Sunday and spend the night there. The first maid and the nurserymaid sleep out, too; I have no idea where, and I don't ask as long as they're back by six on Monday morning. And my crowning stroke of genius was to grant Nurse's dearest wish and allow her to take the babies to visit her sister in Kensington. I've told Sorley that I don't wish to be disturbed before nine, as I have serious things to think about. But I did say that a certain Mr Randall might, just possibly *might*, call in at about that time, and that I might, just possibly *might*, invite him to join me at supper. Was I not born to be a conspirator?'

She raised her hands, and with the most delicate concentration began to remove the pin from his cravat. An elegant thing, she noticed, a coiled gold serpent with opal eyes.

His voice husky, he said, 'I won't pass judgement about that. But born to be a witch, and a wanton, and my only love . . .'

They supped at nine, half-formally, in the dining-room. Sorley, who was acknowledged by Mrs Blackwood to have the lightest hand with an omelette she had ever encountered, stayed only to clear away his chef d'oeuvre and lay out the cold cuts, the salads, and the cheese, and then they were alone again.

They were still at table when the knocker sounded. It was followed by a low-voiced conversation and then Sorley entered again, bearing the butler's silver tray and on it, somewhat creased and grimy, a letter. 'From the major, madam,' he said. 'I thought you would be wanting to haff it at once. The messenger would not wait, but I asked him if there wass any news and he said there wass none.'

'Thank you.' She weighed the letter in her hand until Sorley had left the room, and then, with a flicker of some expression Perry could not identify, picked up a knife and slid it under the seal.

He sat, gently twirling the stem of his wineglass, and tried not to watch the play of feeling on her face as she read it. It didn't take very long. Afterwards, she passed it to him. 'I think you should read this.'

He didn't want to, but he took it. The handwriting was large, and lacking in character, but very clear. Only the fact that Andrew had crossed his lines so as to keep what he wanted to say within the limits of a single sheet made it difficult, here and there, to decipher.

It had been written in instalments, the first of them from Ghent on June eleventh, exactly a week ago.

'My dearest wife,' it began.

After a somewhat tiresome journey, with a very rough crossing to Flanders and an unconscionable time disembarking the baggage and horses, I have made good time here by way of Bruges, a pretty place that I think you would admire, although I found it too irregular and picturesque for my taste. Approaching Ghent, I was strongly reminded of Oxford, which will make you think me very insular! The city itself is full of bustle and confusion, and the narrow and winding streets are crammed with French royalist officers hung about with more orders and medals than one would think had ever been minted, as well as some newly formed Belgian infantry – a skimble-skamble lot who, it must be hoped, will make up in numbers for what they lack in belligerency. I leave almost at once for Ninove. The Duke, it seems, waits only for the Austrians and Russians to arrive on the French frontier before commencing operations.

The second instalment had been written at Brussels on the fifteenth, and Perry's stomach lurched with apprehension as he read it.

I must be quick. Boney has moved with all his old unexpectedness, and today broke the Prussian line at Charleroi. The news is just in that Blücher is falling back, and the Duke has put all of us in Brussels under arms. I do not know where we will be tomorrow, but I put my trust in God.

He had to turn the sheet sideways to read the third and last instalment. It was headed from Quatre-Bras on the sixteenth, Friday. Two days ago.

Today we were engaged, and held our ground only with the greatest difficulty and heavy losses. My Highlanders were badly mauled, but I, though tired and tattered, sustained scarcely a scratch. The Prussians were worsted again at a place called Ligny. I do not know what the Duke has in mind, but I think we must fall back to match the Prussian withdrawal. There is a place called Mont St-Jean, a kind of ridge where the Brussels road passes through a wood, with a village called Waterloo close by. I must stop now, for there is a messenger going to Brussels, and I hope this letter may be sent on to you. I do not know how long it will take to reach you, but pray for me, my dearest wife. You are always in my thoughts – Your loving husband, A.L.

Perry couldn't at first bear to look up from the almost illegible scrawl of the last two lines, which had put his own fears into a new and painful perspective. He knew almost nothing about Andrew Lauriston, not even how Vilia felt about him. He and Andrew, he had suddenly realized, must be very nearly the same age, and in a way he envied the other man, who had at least done something with his life.

Vilia's face was drawn, and he recognized that, whatever she felt for Andrew, he was still her husband, that she had lived with him for two years, and slept with him, and borne him two sons. Just as Charlotte was still his wife. He had no idea at all how he would feel if he heard, suddenly, that Charlotte was in danger. With a raw ache in his heart, he said, 'It doesn't sound good.'

'No.'

'Do you fear for him?'

She cast him a puzzled, almost angry glance. 'Of course.'

'Because you care for him?'

She sighed, and ran one forefinger round the rim of her glass. 'In a way. Is it possible not to care – even a little – about someone you know so well?' After a moment, her eyes, green and intent, came up to his. 'Don't mistake me. To compare what I feel, or ever felt, for him with what I feel for you – there *is* no comparison. I belong to you. Before you came, I belonged only to myself, never to him. But I still have to say, yes, I care what happens to him. We had a hideous, awful quarrel the night before he left, and the fault was mine, though I blamed him for it, and hated him for it. He said things my pride couldn't accept. But he was so righteous, so inflexible! He thinks he owns me.' She grimaced a little. 'Strange, isn't it? I said a moment ago that I belonged to you, and I do. But that doesn't make *you* think you own me, does it?'

He shook his head, wordlessly.

After a moment, she stretched out her hand to him. 'It doesn't sound hopeful, does it? But we must win, surely!'

He didn't know which 'we' or which battle she meant. His eyes on the slim fingers, with the narrow wedding band and the single pearl that guarded it, he said slowly, 'I'd already heard that Blücher had fallen back after Charleroi, although the rumour was said to be unfounded. But it didn't stop the panic in the City. Sell, sell, sell. Tomorrow, they'll hear of these affairs at Quatre-Bras and Ligny, and then the fat will be properly in the fire. I don't know what to think.' He sighed. Nothing settled, nothing solved, nothing clear except his passion for her. The smile didn't reach his eyes, when he said again, 'I don't know what to think.'

4

She didn't hear from him at all next day, but a note was delivered by hand on Tuesday afternoon.

My very dearest – I have gone. I hope you will forget me, but pray that you will not.

When I returned to my lodgings on Sunday evening, I was met with an ultimatum from one of my creditors demanding settlement within twenty-four hours. I went to see him, but he wouldn't listen and pretended to believe that I had promised to settle more than a week ago. So I have had to sell, after all, to silence him, and have told my man of business to settle with as many other of my creditors as he can.

This means that everything is over. Ashes to ashes . . . There is, I suppose, a kind of melancholy justice in the fact that the gentleman who chose to press me is a close friend of my disapproving brother-in-law, Magnus Telfer. Malice, revenge? I don't know. I only know that I deserve it, but that you don't.

Don't think too harshly of me, my very dearest. I have to leave within a few minutes. I don't know where I shall go, or what I shall do, but my heart is in your keeping. I love you always – Perry.

That same evening, there was wild cheering in Piccadilly as the whole of London turned out, singing, dancing, shouting, to escort the postchaise that bore the three captured Eagle standards, symbols of Wellington's great and glorious victory over Napoleon at a place called Waterloo, on Sunday, June eighteenth.

5

A few days later, Vilia was officially informed that Major Andrew Lauriston of the 42nd Highland Regiment had died on the afternoon of Sunday, June eighteenth, from wounds sustained during the victorious engagement at Waterloo. And a few weeks after that, she realized, without a shadow of doubt, that she was pregnant again.

Chapter Nine

1

It was late, and Perry Randall was tired and hungry as he spurred his borrowed horse along the last wet, winding miles to Kinveil. The many-caped greatcoat over his shoulders, relic of better days, was heavy with rain. It smelt sour, too, for it had been bedding and blanket as well as coat to him during these last months in the gaunt, grimy Edinburgh tenement that had housed – it sometimes seemed to him – almost as many humans as vermin. He hoped he had succeeded in ridding himself of fleas and lice on the journey, but couldn't be sure, although he had bathed compulsively in every icy river and loch along the way.

They had told him at Glenbraddan, with soft, careful politeness and no trace of curiosity, that Mistress Randall and the children had gone to spend a few days with Mr Telfer at Kinveil, and his code of honour, battered and bruised though it might be, had forbidden him to make free of his wife's house without her knowledge. So he had ridden on like an automaton, without pausing for rest or refreshment.

It came as a shock, when he approached the castle causeway, to see the glow of many candles behind the slit windows of the Great Hall, and to hear, over the water, the sound of fiddles and many voices raised in conversation. He hesitated for a moment, and might even have turned back except that there was nowhere else he could go. Nowhere except to Kirsty Macintyre, warm, open-hearted, uncritical Kirsty, with her comforting arms and cheerful ways. He closed his weary mind to the thought of her.

The youngest Fraser boy came running from the stables as he dismounted at the end of the causeway, and Perry said, with an obstinate attempt at normality, 'It looks as if you're busy tonight!'

A beam of pleasure came to the lad's rain-spangled face. 'Aye, Mr Randall, sir! There iss dozens of people, so there iss. I will neffer haff seen so many!' He ducked his head a little, and then looked up, slantwise and shyly polite. 'Welcome back, sir. Wass you wanting me to bed the mare down for the night?' As Perry hesitated, the boy shifted his gaze self-consciously to the horse, and was surprised into an exclamation. 'Och! It iss Archie Lamont's old Knock-kneed Jenny, so it iss!'

Perry laughed for the first time for months. 'Is that her name? How very appropriate!' Somehow, the decision had been made. 'Yes, bed her down, please – Ian, is it?' Then he turned and set his foot on the shallow stone bridge over the water.

The butler, who was also Ian's eldest brother, greeted him with stately calm, his large, pallid face showing no trace of any expression other than a trusted servant's proper pleasure at welcoming back a member of the family who had been absent too long. Neither the heavy eyelids nor the wide nostrils so much as quivered as he accepted the malodorous greatcoat, the sodden beaver, and stained gloves. He said, 'Himself hass house guests for the shooting, sir, and some other ladies and chentlemen who iss staying only for tonight. Wass you wishing to choin them in the Great Hall? If you wass to prefer, I can inform Himself privately that you are here.'

To the best of Perry's knowledge, Robert Fraser had never in his life been further south than Fort William, but no London butler could have handled the situation with greater aplomb. He smiled faintly. 'Thank you, Robert. I'll wait in the dungeon.' It seemed apt that Mungo should have chosen to turn the old torture chamber into an anteroom.

Within a few minutes, Robert was back with a tray. 'Himself will be down as soon as he can manage, sir. May I pour you a dram while you are waiting?'

All his senses craved the comfort of whisky. He couldn't have survived in Edinburgh without it, cheap, rough, and plentiful. For twelve long weeks he had never been quite sober. It was whisky that had cushioned him against the noise, and the sweating heat, and the smells, and his fellow lodgers – people, rats, fleas, and lice. It was whisky that had helped him swallow the endless thin porridge, the oatcakes and palate-scraping cheese, and the pickled herring, too long in brine but cheap now that the new season's catch was on sale to anyone with the extra pennies to pay for it. Whisky that had helped him to forget all the things he needed to forget if he were to keep his sanity. In a whisky daze, he had arrived at certain conclusions and known what he must do, and had at last left the house in the Canongate during the Sunday truce, with just enough money left to see him home – if 'home' was what it was. Somehow the release from prison-sanctuary had given him back enough will-power to make at least one resolution and stick to it.

'No, thank you,' he said. 'I find that spirits don't agree with me these days.'

Mungo bustled in at last, small, sturdy, and wary. 'Oh, aye,' he said. 'You're back, are you?' His eyes took in the ill-pressed dark blue coat, the dull, mud-caked boots, and the elegantly tied but far from snowy neck-cloth. Though at least the laddie hadn't pawned the cravat pin Mungo had given him, which was something.

Braced for he didn't know what, Perry was completely taken aback by this matter-of-fact reception. He knew precisely what he intended to say to his father-in-law when they settled down to talk seriously – if he were allowed to say anything at all – but the preliminaries were suddenly beyond him. Involuntarily, his hands came away from his sides to display the palms, open and defeated, to Mungo's gaze. After a moment, he said inadequately, 'I . . . Yes, I suppose so.'

Mungo compressed his lips and muttered a non-committal, 'Aye, mphmmm.' He could see the laddie had had a bad time, and he was torn between pity and exasperation, and the desire that was afflicting him more and more with the passing years, not to be bothered with other folks' troubles. He supposed he would have to do his best to sort things out between the boy and Charlotte, and how he was going to manage it he didn't know, because Charlotte was behaving like the worst kind of hysterical female over the business. It would be too much to hope that they'd succeed in sorting things out for themselves. Then a thought came to him, and he realized with grim amusement that they were going to have to try.

He said, 'You're not fit to be seen. I'll send Jeannie Grant up with something for you to eat, for I jalouse you'll be hungry. But I've no time to talk now. I've got a houseful of guests for the shooting, and I must get back to them.' Deliberately bracing, he went on, 'You'll know Charlotte's here? Well, unless you want to sleep in the byre, you'll have to share her bed. There's not another room in the place.' He couldn't put a finger on the change in Perry's expression, but it irritated him. 'D'ye not want to see your wife after all these months? Aye, well, then. Ye'll do as you're bid, and I'll have a word to say to you in the morning. It's the Yellow Room on the second floor.' He turned and walked out.

Charlotte was in full control of herself when she walked into the Yellow Room, without knocking, just before midnight. Her maid didn't appear, and Charlotte showed no sign of emotion whatever – no excitement, no relief, certainly no pleasure. Her eyes were cold and waiting, and her mouth turned down at the corners. Unconsciously echoing her father, she said, 'You're back, then?' and at once disappeared behind the screen to change into her night attire, as if he had been away for no more than a day or two, on an errand she didn't approve of.

After the civilized supper that had simultaneously revived and sickened him, he had discovered that the Yellow Room had no dressing-room attached, and that there wasn't even a truckle bed hidden under the fourposter. There was no retreat, nothing he could say or do without provoking a confrontation for which he was not prepared. He had no choice but to lie down on the side of the high bed she so ostentatiously left for him.

Like a pair of tomb figures they lay, silent and immobile. Then, somewhere in the middle of the night, he drifted out of a half sleep to the knowledge that she was weeping, inside herself but not quite soundlessly. He remained as still as he could, but she soon sensed that he was awake, and it was enough. Clumsily she turned towards him and laid a shaking hand on his chest. His chest; how like her, he thought bleakly, to choose the least responsive, least intimate part of him she could reach. He didn't move at first, but then the dam broke and words and tears came tumbling out in an unintelligible flood. Her distress was painful, brutal, and only someone who actively hated her could have ignored it. At last, he realized that what she was saying, over and over again, was, 'I've missed you so much, my darling. Hold me, *please* hold me. I've missed you so much. Please, *please!*'

And because he felt drained, and guilty, and haplessly sorry for her, and because he didn't know what else to do, he turned and comforted her.

2

Chrissie Fraser pressed Perry's coat and breeches in the morning, and laundered his neck-cloth, while Mungo's valet removed his boots with deep distaste and returned them cleaned, polished, and newly soled and heeled by the orraman, old George Macleod.

At eleven, Perry went down to confront Mungo in his study. He hesitated for a moment before the wide iron-bound door and waited for his heart to stop thudding. It was like those long-ago days when, as a boy, he had prepared himself to face his father's wrath over some juvenile misdemeanour. Then he knocked and heard the brisk, homely voice bid him enter. The day, unlike yesterday, was bright and sunny, but it was dim indoors, even though Mungo's own sanctum was neither slate-floored nor stone-walled, but cheerfully carpeted, and panelled in light pine. To comfort his ageing bones, he said.

From where Perry stood in the doorway, the old man's face was no more than a mask etched in with shadows. 'Good morning, sir,' he said without much conviction.

'Morning, laddie.' Mungo's voice held a hint of some expression that might almost have been amusement. 'Shut the door and sit ye down.'

A disembodied hand waved towards the chair on the far side of the desk, a massive piece of furniture veneered in zebra wood, of which Mungo, though no one else, was inordinately fond. Perry closed the door, and a wisp of breeze fluttered the papers on the desk. The slap of Mungo's hand on them ricocheted from striped desk top to door, to walls, to window embrasures, and then to ceiling, before it died, suffocated, in the hand-knotted Axminster on the floor.

Mungo grinned, and it was infectious, but by the time Perry had seated himself the grin had gone. There was a brief silence, the suspended silence of indoors in the Highlands. A lapwing shrieked in the distance, and there was a gentle plash of water against the rocks. One of the servants said something, laughing, under the window, and then her voice was abruptly stilled. Everyone, Perry thought, must know that Himself was engaged on bringing his erring son-in-law to book.

'Aye, well,' Mungo said, clearing his throat. 'You'd better tell me about it, hadn't you?'

It was some time before Perry reached the end of his careful narrative, and afterwards Mungo sat chewing his lip for a while. He'd never believed all Charlotte's nonsense about Perry and Vilia. Even if they'd been attracted at that dratted ball, they certainly hadn't met again in the six months or so before Perry had left Glenbraddan for London. It was then the boy had told Charlotte about the Funds, and Mungo didn't think Perry was a liar, even if, like most folk, he could sometimes be sparing with the truth. No, the sad tale of the Funds, and the gambling, and the forced sale just when a few more hours would have seen everything right, sounded to Mungo like the real thing. He knew a good deal about stocks, and Perry hadn't put a foot wrong in the telling. There was no reason to doubt him.

Not that lack of doubt was the same as approval. Unhelpfully, Mungo said, 'And what now?' He assumed the laddie was going to ask him to settle his debts. There was no other solution. And he supposed he'd have to, otherwise as soon as the news got around that Mr Randall was back in the district that jeely-piece of a sheriff-substitute would be down on them, with his limp, sugary smile and smirking apologies for putting a member of such a distinguished landowner's family under lock and key. Mungo wondered absently whether the boy had made his peace with Charlotte last night, and felt momentarily guilty at having forced them to face up to things without decent warning. He said again, 'What now? You want me to settle your debts, I suppose?' It was a lot of money, he reflected irritably.

Perry's eyes were on his fingers, steepled before him. 'That's for you to decide,' he said slowly. 'I have been God's own fool, and I deserve nothing from you, certainly nothing as generous as that. In fact, I wasn't going to ask it of you.'

Mungo's brows drew together. 'Well, *someone*'s going to have to settle them! You've not struck gold in the Cluanie hills, I take it? And you're not thinking of setting up for life in the Canongate!'

'No,' Perry said.

The thick old eyebrows bristled at him thoughtfully. 'Well, then?'

'America.'

'Running away?'

'There wouldn't be anything new about that, would there? I've run away from responsibility all my life.'

Mungo didn't contradict him. His lips folded, he said, 'Are you trying to tell me that, this time, you're running *to* something?'

'Perhaps.'

'What, for example?'

'To having to stand on my own feet.'

Although it wasn't altogether intentional, there was nothing he could have said that would have pleased Mungo more. He liked his son-in-law, and thought he had been ruined by his upbringing. Maybe there was some gumption in him after all. America might be the making of him, if it wasn't the final breaking.

Without realizing it, he was staring at Perry with the shrewd, calculating expression that, years ago, had reduced his competitors to blancmange. Perry could almost see the thoughts ticking over in his head. 'You'd let the debts go hang?'

Perry sighed. 'They should be paid, of course. Debts of honour, and all that. But I've done a lot of thinking in these last weeks, and I can't see that gambling debts are a matter of great importance. Moral rights and wrongs hardly come into it. The gambler who loses is merely paying for his foolishness, and the one who wins is making profit out of the fact that his luck isn't as bad as the other man's. I'd like to pay them, yes. But if I can't, I can't, and that's all there is to it.'

The argument seemed to Mungo a little specious, but he let it go for the moment. 'Ye'll not take Charlotte with you?'

'No.' Perry's voice was flat and final. 'The kind of life led by a penniless immigrant is no life for her.'

'What's she to do, then?'

'She'll be better off without me, once she becomes used to the idea.'

It wasn't easy to explain without hurting the old fellow, and Perry phrased his reply with care. 'You know – as I do – that people have the ability to change themselves, and their outlook on life, only so much, and no more. We've both tried, and failed. I should never have asked Charlotte to marry me, especially since I knew that she cared for me more than was wise, however she tried to hide it. The fault was entirely mine, and you can't possibly blame me more than I blame myself.'

Mungo's face was unreadable.

Perry went on, 'She has tried and I have tried. Genuinely. But it can never work. We're too different. All we ever do is bring each other unhappiness.' He was talking in fits and starts, as if he were reasoning things out as he went along. 'I won't pretend I'm being wholly disinterested. I'm not. My own life matters to me. But if I thought that, by staying, there was any possibility of making Charlotte happy, I would stay. These months of isolation have taught me something about myself, though. I realize now that, if I did stay, I'd lose all the qualities – this may sound foolish, or vain, I don't know! – that attracted Charlotte to me in the first place. Do you know what I mean?'

Mungo knew very well. The humour, charm, and vitality that were the essence of the man. He pursed his lips again and said nothing.

'Anyway, that's how I see it. And there's something else. If I go now, all the fault will be seen to be mine. Everyone will say good riddance to a bad lot, and Charlotte will be accorded universal sympathy.' He smiled wryly.

'Does she have nothing to say in this?' Mungo's paternal instincts were not strong, and he was having a struggle to remember whose side he was supposed to be on. He wondered how Chattie would have dealt with the situation, sensible, comfortable, practical Chattie, who had died almost twenty years ago and whom he still thought of – more often than he would have expected – with a sense of loss. They had never been what the books called 'in love', which would have been foreign to their natures. But there had always been a kind of conspiratorial relationship between them, as if they were the only two adults in a juvenile world. He'd had the same feeling with Vilia Cameron, which, considering her age, was just ridiculous.

He had missed Perry's reply. 'What?' he said.

'No, Charlotte has nothing to say to it.'

'You mean she can argue the pair of you blue in the face, but it won't

181

make a pennyworth of difference? In other words, *your* mind is made up.'

'Yes.'

'Let me get something clear. You don't want me to settle your debts. You won't stay. You want to go to America. And you're not even prepared to talk to Charlotte. Then why are we being honoured with your company?'

'I came to say good-bye. I thought I owed you that much at least. And though I don't ask you to settle my debts, I would like to beg something from you.'

'Money?'

'Money. Not £10,000. Just £10 or perhaps a little more.'

'Your fare on the emigrant ship to Nova Scotia?'

Perry smiled. 'What else? If you have any hesitations, I won't ask it of you. As it happens, I still have a little money of my own.' The familiar, irresistible grin broke through the strain on his face. 'I have, to be precise, £6.11s.5d. It may not sound much to Mr Telfer of Kinveil, but to Mr Randall of Nowhere it sounds a good deal. Somehow, perhaps, I can raise the extra few pounds I need.'

'Havers, laddie!' Mungo exclaimed, his face scarlet. 'I'll let you have what you need, and a wee bit more forbye. There's one condition, though. Ye'll stay here as long as the shooting party lasts – another week or so – and see if you and Charlotte can't patch up your differences after all. If you can, well and good. If you can't . . .' Uncharacteristically, he shrugged. 'Away ye go, now. You're respectable enough to meet my guests, and I'll thank ye to help me with the entertaining of them. I only invited them so as to take Charlotte's mind off her troubles, which means they're as much your responsibility as mine!'

3

There was a brig sailing from Fort William three weeks later, and Mungo, for diverse and vaguely sentimental reasons of his own, decided that he and Luke would go to see Perry off. Charlotte had flounced back to Glenbraddan with the children ten days before, her face set, and her manner – Mungo had been sorry to see – vindictively self-righteous. Her father had been relieved to see her go, for although he had no real idea of the depth of torture to which his stipulation had subjected Perry, he had been worried stiff by the change in his son-in-law. Perry had been numb when he arrived at Kinveil, but in the days that followed it was as if he were dying by inches.

The journey to Fort William wasn't enjoyable, because the two adults' conversation rang hollow, however much they tried to sound at ease, while Luke swung like a weathercock between laments over the departure of his idol, and envy at the excitements he thought Perry had in store for him.

To Mungo, everything seemed unreal. Even the countryside was at odds with itself. Below the thousand-foot level, the trees were still full of sap, and the leaves hanging on past their usual season, some still green, others in the full splendour of crimson and copper, gold and amber, while the berries and bracken and dying heather displayed every colour in the spectrum from acid yellow to purple. But there had been three or four days of biting east winds that had brought snow to the higher ground, and the rioting colour stopped dead and perfectly straight at the snow-line, separated from the bright blue sky by a wide stripe of black-and-white slashed mountain tops. It was all as improbable as a theatre backdrop by some artist who had never set foot outside a city. Even the sunset was pure melodrama. When they came at last to Fort William, the sun was dropping behind the hills of Ardgour, and the whole vault of the sky for as far as they could see was a violent blood red, streaked with long black-purple clouds whose feathered edges were ablaze with purest flame. The high snows of Ben Nevis were alight, and the silhouettes of the western hills fringed in fire. It was awe-inspiring, savage, and magnificent.

The sky sat like a Chinese lacquer lid over Fort William's single mean and narrow street which, like the surrounding fields, was full of people due to sail next day on the brig *Rapido*. Mungo hoped the name was justified, but doubted it. Not a wall or patch of scrub, not a doorway that didn't shelter some emigrant, or someone who had come to see a dear one off. Mungo assumed it would be mostly the young ones who were going. Some of the bundles they clasped contained not clothes, or food, or necessities for the journey, but babies whose disconsolate howls made a kind of litany all the way along the street, as the carriage struggled through to the inn where Mungo had bespoken accommodation.

It was both better and worse the next morning when they walked the few yards to the shore and found a place a little apart from the crowd. Luke, who hadn't yet learned humanity, wrinkled his nose disgustedly and said, 'Phoo! I don't envy you your travelling companions, Uncle Perry!'

'Hold your wheesht!' his grandfather told him sharply. 'Och, the poor folk! The poor folk!'

Three hundred people were to sail on the brig, and for most of them – perhaps all – it would be a last farewell to the land that had borne them. Months and years of scrimping and saving had been needed to bring this day about, and it should have been one of triumph. Instead, there was undisguised heartbreak in the pinched faces that thronged the beach, as if the realization of a hope they had never really believed in was the cruellest blow they had ever been called upon to bear. It seemed to Mungo as if they were thinking of today not as the first day of the rest of their lives, but as a kind of death sentence.

Trying for the light touch, he muttered to Perry, 'Och, it's a shame, isn't it! Who'd want to leave the Highlands on a fine, sunny day like this? If Fort William had only produced its usual downpour, they'd be glad enough to get away!' But there was a dampness about his eyes.

The scene would have moved a harder man than Mungo. Ceaseless, unregarded tears streamed down the faces of men and women alike as they tried to smile through their last embraces. The older folk, who had trudged forty or fifty miles to see the young ones sail, refused at first to prolong the misery, pushing their children away from them towards the boat. But the younger women seemed unable to break the last physical contact and, time after time, as the calloused old hands with the swollen knuckles deliberately set them loose, flew back again into their parents' arms and clung to them fiercely, until their husbands, in little better case, had to drag them away to the boats that were waiting to carry them out to the brig. One girl, her baby in a knotted shawl on her back, flung herself face down on the shore, sinking her clawed fingers into the rough sand in a passion of grief until at last two of the sailors brushed her man aside and, oddly gentle, pried her hands loose and carried her bodily to the boat.

Perry was one of the last to embark, because the families had to be settled first in the cramped hold with its makeshift bunks and great piles of boxes, bags, and chests taking up all the space that remained. Mungo was unashamedly weeping by now, and Luke, though trying hard to be manful, wasn't succeeding very well. But Perry himself showed not a trace of emotion, although there was perhaps a touch of sadness in the handsome, exhausted face as he shook them both by the hand. If he held his clasp a little longer than usual, it was scarcely perceptible.

All he said was, 'Tell Charlotte that, however little she may believe it now, it is for the best. And try, if you will, not to let her bring little Grace up to hate her father. God bless you both.'

The brig's boats were hauled in, and the crowd on the beach managed somehow to raise a cheer, although the answering cheer from the brig sounded more like a dirge. When there was no more possibility of words being exchanged between brig and shore, the piper on board inflated his bag and sent the wild, haunting notes of 'MacCrimmon's Lament', the finest and saddest of all pibroch tunes, into the clear air. *Cha till mi tuille* – 'I will return no more.'

It was too much for most of the folk on the beach, but Luke had sufficiently recovered to say with a watery grin, 'The pipes do sound better over the water, don't they!' He was old enough, too, to be able to interpret the wry, approving smile that twisted the corners of his grandfather's lips. Mungo clapped a hand on the boy's shoulder, and they stood watching the brig tack south down Loch Linnhe until she was almost out of sight, still listing heavily to port with the weight of all her passengers seeking a last, desperate sight of the place and people they would never see again. At last, Mungo blew his nose resoundingly and said, 'Well, that's the end, laddie. Time to go home.'

They were almost halfway back to Kinveil when it struck Mungo that he had never brought Perry up to date on all the things that had been happening to family and friends while he had been shut up in his sanctuary in the Canongate. Not that there had been much, except about Andrew Lauriston being killed at Waterloo. He thought about it for a moment, and then decided that since Perry had scarcely known Vilia, and Andrew not at all, it wouldn't have been of more than passing interest. Funny he should have forgotten to mention it, though. If 'forgotten' was the right word.

4

It was on a Tuesday in March of the following year that Mungo encountered Iain Mor the Post, plodding across the sleet-swept causeway with his home-made leather pouch over his shoulder and his shaggy woollen toorie pulled down to his eyebrows, so that he looked like a wildcat glowering out of a gorse bush. The postie's round was a long one, almost seventy miles, and was accomplished entirely on foot twice or three times a week. It was Mungo's humane custom to press a good strong dram on him to help him on his way, although this generosity wasn't wholly disinterested. Iain Mor, in the right mood, was a fount of local gossip, and besides, it gave Mungo an innocent pleasure to see the man's usually truculent expression melt into genial satisfaction as the whisky did its work. A full tumbler, a straight wrist, and the neat spirits disappeared down his throat in a smooth and single gulp.

'Aye, aye,' he said on this occasion, passing the back of his hand genteelly across his lips. 'It iss a poor return for your hospitality right enough, but I am afraid I will haff to lift seffenpence off you. All your letters but the one iss franked. I see it iss from young Sorley McClure, and he would not be able to get a frank, being only a footman. But iss it not a fine thing that he iss able to write, and a fair hand, too? He will be telling you how Mistress Vilia iss getting on at Marchfield. I would be ferry obliged – if it iss not inconvenient, mind you! – if you would be sending her my kindest regards. Och, well. Thank you, Mr Telfer, sir, and good day to you. I will be getting on my way.'

With a grimace of foreboding, Mungo broke the seal. Sorley wouldn't have landed him with the postal charge without good and urgent reason. The letter was short.

Dear Mr Telfer, sir – I trust you will pardon the libberty I take in writing to you and without a frank but I could not get one. You know that Mistress Vilia has been staying here with Mr Lauriston (Sen.) since the Major was killt. She is not happy and very unwell. The baby is due any day and I am fritened for her. She needs a friend and not just me. This is why I am being so bold to write tho I know it is not my place to. If it is not convenient I am sorry for troubling you and please will you accept my apollogies. Yours truly – S. McClure.

Mungo, who didn't approve of swearing, swore furiously for several minutes and then began to make his arrangements.

5

In the last days of August 1815, too sick in mind and body to go on resisting the pressures that were being exerted on her, Vilia had given up the house in Half Moon Street that Duncan Lauriston now refused to pay for, dismissed most of the servants, and with the babies, their nurse, her maid, Sorley, and the kitten to keep her company, had left London for her father-in-law's house at Marchfield. She didn't know, as her coach rolled into Edinburgh, that she was passing within a few hundred yards of where Perry Randall lay in sanctuary.

Languidly, she noticed the splendid new buildings that had been finished since her last visit the year before, hotels like palaces backing onto the narrow, fetid wynds of the Old Town, and the mansions of the New Town across the Nor' Loch, clean and supercilious still despite the encroaching smoke. Summer or not, Auld Reekie went on reeking, the dwellings so piled up on one another round the Castle Hill that none of the smells or smuts were wasted on the desert air before the inhabitants had been able to derive the fullest benefit from them.

'Mercy me!' Nurse exclaimed. 'You could smoke bacon just by hanging it out of the window!'

The air was clearer out to the west as they drove the last sixteen miles to Clarkstoun village, but the countryside had no pastures and few hedges or dykes, only crop lands where the harvest was being taken in by men and women with no spring in their movements. It was flat and open, and there was a damp wind from the Firth. Even to the adults it was dull and enervating, and baby Gideon, normally a placid child, woke up and began to whine miserably. Theo, eighteen months old and never demonstrative, wriggled when Nurse put a hand on his shoulder and jerked away pettishly. He didn't like being coddled.

Clarkstoun was pretty enough in a white-washed, old-fashioned way. The houses had thick walls, and small windows set in wide stone surrounds, smooth against the rough harling. The steeply gabled roofs were crow-stepped, although it was seagulls, not crows, that perched on the ridged copings. Many of the houses still had outside staircases giving access to the upper floors. But the east wind from the Firth raked through the narrow streets, overlaying the farmyard smells of unswept cobbles with an odour of salt and fish, and it was a relief to turn inland for the last mile to Marchfield House.

While she lived, Duncan Lauriston's wife Mary had been in sole charge of domestic affairs, and it was she who had chosen and furnished Marchfield. Everything about it spoke of her worldly ambition, the same ambition that had ensured a gentleman's education for Andrew. The house was not to Vilia's taste, but at least it was relatively civilized. It was about fifty years old, built originally for some sprig of the minor gentry, and took the form of a square, symmetrical block with a hipped roof and handsome pediment. Over a sunken basement there was a central forestair leading to the front door, which was in the first of the two main floors. The house sat on the edge of a semicircle of gravel and turf, whose straight side was closed off by a high stone wall. At one end of the wall was the coach house, and at the other the stables. The house was trimly painted, the gravel and lawns impeccably kept. It was a very respectable, rather dull dwelling.

Vilia's father-in-law, determined though he was to oversee the upbringing of his grandsons – his *three* grandsons, for he was sure it was another boy on the way – was not minded to have them spoil his comfort. He had therefore resigned the whole of the upper floor to Vilia and the children, and had grudgingly allocated rooms in the attic to Sorley and the other servants. All he insisted on was that Vilia sup with him in the evenings, and then sit with him until it was time to retire.

Things could have been worse, but Sorley, observing, thought they couldn't have been much worse. If Vilia had been in normal health, she could have stood up to her father-in-law. If she had been in normal health, she would never have come to Marchfield House at all. But where her previous pregnancies had been uncomplicated, this one was not. Nausea racked her almost unceasingly, and her nerves were raw as torn flesh. Then her ankles began to swell, and she was constantly dizzy, and had a headache that never left her and a paralysing fatigue that settled round her like a blanket. Day after day she would lie half-fainting on the sofa in her dressing-room, only to drag herself up when evening came so that she could appear at supper to suffer her father-in-law's brutality.

It was all pride, Sorley thought, gritting his teeth. Stupid, idiotic, heart-breaking Cameron pride.

'Aye, you're a poor thing, aren't you?' Duncan Lauriston would sneer, wolfing down a mouthful of the stuffed cod's head whose very smell made Vilia's stomach turn over. 'And you were supposed to be a lassie with spirit! I can mind you even having the brass neck to bandy words with me in my own foundry. What's the matter? Are ye no' weel?'

'I'm all right.'

'I'm all right,' he would mimic, pursing his lips and tightening his vowels so that it came out like a parody. 'Then what are ye looking so perjink about? Have I offended your ladyship?'

There was nothing she could say.

'You've months to go yet! So what ails you? D'ye not know that childbearing's a natural process for women – all you're fit for, most of you! There's drabs in my packing shed that're back at work the very day after they've had their brats. Aye, and they've been there until the day before, too. And here you are, looking like a drookit lily when you're only four months gone. Och, you make me sick! It's time you had something to do, so you can start keeping an eye on the kitchen. And you can tell that McKirdy woman I don't want to see any more of this kind of rubbish served up at my table!'

She would drag herself upstairs again after such exchanges, shivering in every limb, despairing and terrified. But she didn't go to bed until Rachelle, her maid, was also ready to lie down on the truckle that was drawn out every night and placed – not for any reason that had ever been put into words – across the doorway just inside Vilia's bed-chamber. Neither of them knew that Sorley spent most of the hours of darkness dozing in an alcove across the hall.

She couldn't even weep. It was as if her heart had congealed, and she was dully grateful until she had a letter from Lucy Telfer at the end of October that broke the spell. The pain was almost beyond bearing. Embedded in Lucy's cheerful catalogue of gossip were two sentences that stood out in letters of flame. *'Magnus had a letter from Kinveil the other day, and – my dear, you won't believe it! – but Mr Randall has turned up again after being missing for weeks, no one knows where. Although my papa-in-law does not say, I imagine Charlotte must be vastly relieved; so unflattering to have one's husband run away like that!'*

Sorley, keeping as close an eye on his mistress as he was able, went into her dressing-room next day to find her sitting, still and soulless,

189

with a foot-long kitchen skewer in her hand. He took it from her as gently as he could, and threatened Rachelle with unimaginable tortures if ever she left her mistress alone again.

There was another crisis in January, also precipitated by a letter from Lucy. This time her letter said, '*and, my dear, such news! Charlotte is in an interesting condition! Very distressing for her, really quite embarrassing, especially as everyone seems to know that Mr Randall has been sent off, utterly in disgrace, on one of those dreadful emigrant ships to Canada. I know it is very wrong of me, but I feel quite sad to know that we will never see him again.*'

After that, Vilia sank into a blind, deaf, insentient apathy that not even Sorley could penetrate. For weeks, day and night, he fretted his brain for some solution, and then one evening, when Duncan Lauriston's venom had passed all bounds, it came to him that there was only one person in the world who might be able to help.

Sorley wrote to Mungo Telfer.

6

Months before, Mungo had made it his business to find out what he could about Duncan Lauriston, for Vilia had said nothing about him. A hard man, he had been told by acquaintances who had dealt with him, with his own rigid ideas of right and wrong. Accordingly, Mungo sent no message asking if it would be convenient for him to call, and took the precaution of reserving rooms for himself, Luke, and Henry Phillpotts, at the Clarkstoun Inn before he set off, with the other two as protective colouring, to see Vilia.

It was eight o'clock and black dark when they arrived, the carriage lanterns casting a weak glow on grass and gravel as they rolled up to the poorly lit front door.

Mr Lauriston and Mrs Andrew were at dinner, the butler said. Perhaps the gentleman would wish to return at some more convenient hour?

The gentleman eyed him thoughtfully, and after a moment the butler, a shifty-looking fellow, added, 'Unless, of course, you prefer to wait in the parlour. Mr Lauriston does not care to be disturbed at his meal.'

Mungo said, 'We'll wait.'

It was fully half an hour before the master of the house entered with his daughter-in-law trailing listlessly behind. Mungo's face froze when he saw her. The child was due any day now, but though her body was gross under the black gown, her face and arms were bleached and attenuated, almost transparent. Even her eyes had lost their colour. She smiled at him with a weak, fibreless affection that cut him to the heart, and he sprang forward, ignoring his host, to help her lower herself into a chair.

'Telfer, is it?' Duncan Lauriston said in his thick, harsh voice.

Mungo released his crushing grip on Vilia's hand, and bowed slightly. 'Mr Lauriston.'

They stood there measuring each other, like terrier and mastiff, Luke thought, and then Mungo said, 'May I make my grandson known to you, and his tutor, Mr Phillpotts?'

'Oh, aye?' Lauriston's glance was an insult. Taking in Henry's cassock, he said, 'Papist, are you?'

Sharply, Mungo said, 'Mr Phillpotts, as it happens, is not of the Catholic faith, nor have his religious beliefs anything to do with his abilities as a tutor of Latin and Greek.' Then, regaining command of his temper, he went on, 'You have no objection to my visit, I hope? I found myself in the district on business, quite unexpectedly, and thought I would take the opportunity to call and assure myself that Mrs Lauriston was in health. But you look peaky, my dear. Quite unlike yourself!'

The other man snorted. 'Women's cantrips! Nothing the matter with her that a good dose of will-power wouldn't cure.'

Mungo, swallowing his anger, said, 'I have known Mrs Lauriston since she was a child, and she has never been lacking in *that* quality. Have you had medical advice, my dear?'

Vilia opened her mouth hesitantly, but her father-in-law spoke first. 'It's not a doctor she needs. Leeches they're called, and leeches they are. Money-grubbing scum. I'll not have them set foot over my threshold.'

Mungo's mind was racing. How, without being dangerously offensive, did one convey to an unsuccessful, miserly, and probably purse-pinched bully that one would pay anything – anything at all – from one's own purse to prevent harm coming to this girl? 'Aye, well,' he said at last. 'I've been a kind of guardian to her for years now, and I don't think it would do any damage if I were to bring someone to see her. It would set my own mind at rest, and maybe make her feel better, too.' Then he caught Lauriston's expression, and his hold over his temper began to slip again.

No one had asked them to sit down. Luke was standing as far away from their host as he could manage, his dilated eyes fixed on him as if he were a man-eating tiger who might at any moment decide he fancied a snack, while Henry had his hands sunk in his sleeves like some monk on the way to vespers, and was breathing audibly through his nose.

'You'll not bring a doctor to this house,' Lauriston said with crude finality.

Mungo stared at him. He had always known instinctively that Vilia was out of sympathy with her father-in-law, but had put it down to youthful ignorance of the world. One didn't climb the ladder from common labourer to ironmaster without shedding a good many of the gentler attributes on the way. It simply hadn't occurred to Mungo, who knew all there was to know about the kind of struggle Lauriston must have had, that the man was anything other than a normal human being with an abnormally tough and opportunist streak. But now, observing the brutal reality of him, he saw that he hadn't understood the half of it. He had met the type before – a mind barren of tolerance, a heart riddled with envy, a soul ignorant of the Christian charity the tongue so loudly professed, and no motivating force other than the desire to possess or to destroy what could not be possessed. A violent man, and a dangerous one. Bitterly, Mungo reproached himself for leaving fastidious, sensitive, over-bred Vilia in such a man's care. He wondered whether Lauriston knew enough about his, Mungo's, commercial success to be able to contrast it with his own. It might help to account for the element of personal dislike he sensed in the man.

It seemed to Mungo that the only thing he could do was take Vilia away with him now, but when he looked at her he knew he didn't dare. The Clarkstoun Inn was no refuge for her, especially when the bairn must already be overdue. And there were the two boys as well, drat it! He'd have to take them when he took Vilia, or Lauriston might well find some legal way of holding onto them. He made up his mind.

Tomorrow. Tomorrow morning he would find a doctor and bring him here, and the moment the doctor said yes, he'd carry her off to the nearest decent hostelry – the Hawes Inn at South Queensferry, maybe, or the place at Cramond if she were strong enough to travel a few extra miles – and then they could decide what to do next.

It had been a long silence. Mungo didn't even look at Lauriston as he said, with all the authority of his years and achievement, 'I'll be here the morn, lassie, and bring the best man I can find to see you.' He smiled reassuringly.

Her weak, responding smile was overlaid with a kind of distraction, as if there were something she ought to say, if only she could think of it. She opened her mouth, but again Duncan Lauriston's thick voice forestalled her.

Surprisingly, he seemed to be giving in. With a curl of his lip, he said, 'If you must, you must. They say there's no fool like an old fool, and maybe you don't mind throwing your money away. But you'll be wanting to get back to wherever you're racking up for the night. There's going to be a heavy frost, and if you leave it any later, your cattle will be skiting around all over the road. Forbye, the woman wants her bed. She's tired out after her hard day lying on the couch!'

Having carried his point, Mungo thought it would be wise to go, despite a lingering uneasiness. He smiled again at Vilia, sitting there vaguely detached from it all, and said, 'We'll have a good talk tomorrow, lassie, never fret.' Half-embarrassed, because it wasn't his habit to make a display of affection, he went over and dropped a kiss on her forehead, then, with the still silent Luke and Henry at his back, gave the merest nod to Lauriston and walked out of the house.

When he returned next morning with the doctor, he was told that Mr Lauriston and Mrs Andrew had gone.

7

Duncan Lauriston didn't want her dying on his hands, though he thought the possibility remote, but neither was he going to spare her on this day of all days. So he allowed her to stay in the carriage for the first few hours after they reached Edinburgh, and only went to fetch her when, above the clamour of every church bell in the city, he heard the distant cheering take on a more purposeful note. He was a big, powerful man, and despite the press of people had little difficulty shouldering through to the front again, dragging Vilia by one arm while Sorley McClure slithered along, eel-like, on her other side. Duncan Lauriston glanced at him contemptuously, making a great show of protecting her from all the folk who were jumping up and down for a view, knees and elbows going like badly handled puppets. The scourings of every alley and gutter, he thought, and pushed the girl to where he estimated the front row would be when the rabble had been cleared off the roadway.

Here, up at the West Bow, the crowd was particularly thick, for despite the projecting, rickety bulk of the Weigh-house, there was a kind of open space that, earlier on, had drawn people from the crush further down in search of more room. There was none of that now, with the great moment approaching. The great moment when the men of the 42nd Highland Regiment, nine months to the date after the battle of Waterloo, in which they had served so gloriously, were coming home to a vociferous welcome from the massed citizens of Scotland's capital.

It had seemed for a while as if they would never get here. It was almost three o'clock now, and they should have arrived long since at Edinburgh Castle, the terminus of their ceremonial march. But rumour had reported in the morning that there were so many people, horses, and carriages on the road from Musselburgh that the regiment had been brought almost to a standstill. Much later, it had been said to be passing through Portobello. And now, by the sound of things, it was at the palace of Holyroodhouse and about to enter the mile-long main highway up the Canongate, the High Street, and the Lawnmarket, that would bring it to the West Bow and then, finally, to the esplanade of the Castle, perched high on its rock above the city.

Not a window along the route that wasn't packed with watchers, not a rooftop that wasn't creaking under its load. Every dwelling and workshop in the city seemed to have emptied its inhabitants into the Royal Mile. From the elevation of the West Bow and with his own advantage of height, Duncan Lauriston commanded a view right down to the Canongate. The perspective was acute, narrowed not only by distance but by the reducing width of the street, whose sides huddled closer and closer under the jutting upper storeys of houses two hundred years old and more, erratically tiered like some upside-down bride's-cake. The people were as packed and yet as fluid as grains of sand on a river bed, spreading where space permitted, round the Tolbooth; swirling out and then in again round the market-stall island of the Luckenbooths; funnelling closer and, impossibly, closer where the highway abruptly narrowed just by the house that was said to have been John Knox's. And from every wynd and close along the route, more and more people were trying to fight their noisy way in. As if, Duncan Lauriston thought savagely, it were some vulgar saturnalia. All should have been still and silent, in reverence for those who had laid down their lives on the field of Waterloo.

Down in the mouth of the Canongate, a new turbulence became apparent, and the head of the procession struggled into view, a cheering, dancing throng of citizens, old and young, tall and short, fat and thin – the unofficial, wildly ecstatic vanguard of the heroes of the day. The crowd rippled back before them, fanning sideways into the serried ranks of people who already lined the street and were now forced to retreat into the arcaded fronts of the older buildings, or back into the closes and wynds, or up the already bulging outside staircases of the tenements, desecrating the bright carpets that adorned them, treading on the ribbons and bunting that draped them, crushing the well-dressed ladies who had thought themselves safe from contact with the common herd. Folk who had no place to retreat to now joined the procession willy-nilly, so that the vanguard multiplied by the minute, and the regiment was reduced to a funereally slow march. The ripple of movement spread and spread until it was lapping against the crowd that crammed the street at the West Bow. Some of the old Town Guard, in their ancient cocked hats and muddy-red coats and breeches, had been brought out of retirement for the occasion, and with gnarled hands and the hafts of their Lochaber axes tried un-availingly to clear a space for the approaching hordes.

Duncan Lauriston could see, now, that the regiment's band and pipers had been forced to lay up their instruments since there wasn't enough room for them to play, while nothing was visible of the soldiers except their bonnets and feathers. Lieutenant-Colonel Dick, the regiment's commander, who was supposed to be leading the column with Major-General Hope and Colonel Stewart of Garth, was nowhere to be seen. With a snort of amusement, Duncan Lauriston observed the plight of some of the better-dressed spectators, who, having succeeded in removing their hats and waving them, were now quite unable to lower their arms sufficiently to put the hats back on their heads again.

The advancing throng, a long fat snake compressed by the buildings and pushed by thousands upon thousands of folk behind, was now beginning to buffet the crowd at the West Bow. The press and the noise were indescribable, and the smells almost beyond belief.

Suddenly, Duncan Lauriston felt his arm taken in a grasp like a tourniquet, and impatiently dragged his gaze from the procession in which his only son should have held so proud a place.

It was Sorley McClure, the girl half fainting against his shoulder. 'It iss too much for her, sir. You must let me take her back to the carriage!'

'What!' he roared. 'Don't tell *me* what to do, you scum! We are here to pay honour to my son, and she will stay – *by God she will stay!* – until we have done so.'

Vilia, almost beyond feeling, could still feel Sorley controlling his breath.

He said politely, 'Then perhaps we could move a bit, sir. It iss the smells that are the worst.' He gestured towards the Weigh-house.

The air reeked, if one stopped to think about it, not only with sweating humanity but with the sour tang and cloying thickness of the tons of cheese and butter that were weighed out there day after day, week after week. And the street hadn't been swept this morning to clear it of the libations sloshed out from hundreds of chamber pots at last night's curfew, emptied down from high windows on to the cobbles with the arbitrary warning cry of 'Gardy loo!' Every surge of the crowd's movement seemed to gather up all the smells into a single noisome, insalubrious blast and fling it full in one's face. Most of the bystanders were too engrossed to notice, but even Duncan Lauriston was aware that pregnant women were more likely than most to be overtaken by queasiness. Trust that arrogant bitch to choose her moment! He hesitated.

Sorley said, 'Higher up the Castle Hill, perhaps, sir? Towards Blair's Close? The people seem to haff moved down from there to get a better view.'

It was true. The last narrow enclave that led to the Castle esplanade was by no means empty, but it wasn't full, either, though it would be soon, as the procession entered the final stretch. It was now or never. Besides, from there it would be possible to see the soldiers better, perhaps even get close enough to grip one by the arm and ask, 'Did you know my son? My son the major.'

Without a word, he grabbed his daughter-in-law by the arm and began to push again. The crowd wasn't pleased, but managed somehow to make way for such a big man, and one who looked as if he would have no hesitation about loosing a clout on the ear of anyone who resisted him. Only one woman, a rough-looking harridan in a fishwife's apron, thumped him on the back with her fist as he passed, and shrieked, 'Ye big sumph! Yon lassie shouldny be oot in yon state, so she shouldny! Huv ye nae feelings? Och, the puir lassie!' But the man beside her pulled her fist down and growled, 'Haud yer wheesht, wumman! She's maybe lost her man in the wars. Let the folk be.'

The relief of getting out of the press was almost unbelievable, although it didn't last for long and Vilia was almost past awareness of it. All it did was allow her to hold on to the last, teased-out strands of consciousness. When the procession, after aeons of waiting, at last began to draw level, she could sense the soldiers through their blurred cocoon of civilians only as a wavering thread of colour, hazy and undefined, swelling and receding, a nightmare of scarlet jackets, and black-and-green kilts, and braided loops, and bright red plumes, and scuffling feet. Far and faint on the very edge of her perception there was a sound of cheering and yelling and shouting – a sound that merged in her head into screams and groans and the clash of swords and bayonets. She could hear horses neighing in terror, and the muffled crump of artillery, and the sharp crack of hand guns. And then a searing, murderous pain ripped through her, and she screamed, too, and folded her body almost double, her hands splayed wide and taut over her swollen stomach.

She screamed again, and again, and then two brutal hands seized her by the shoulders and hauled her upright, and a face glared into hers and a voice shouted, 'I'll not have it! I'll not have it! Stand up straight and look! *Look!* He should be there, too! *He* should be there!' And it was Andrew's face, and Andrew's voice, and he was going on shouting. On and on. 'You killed me! You killed me! And while I was dying, you were in bed with another man, and he was getting a child on you. *His* son . . . My son . . . You killed me! *You killed me!*'

And she screamed again, this time in words. 'No! No, no, no, *no, no!*' Her voice rang out on a pitch far above that of the crowd, and the last soldier in the procession turned to look at her, startled, just as, with all the force she possessed, she pushed away the figure that was looming over her, torturing her mind without mercy while the pains of childbirth tortured her body.

8

Mungo Telfer, thrusting his way frantically along the rearguard with the doctor hanging on to his coat, saw the great figure of Duncan Lauriston stagger backwards. Then, even as Sorley McClure, with one arm still round Vilia, lunged forward to save him, he lost his balance and toppled like a felled tree straight in the path of the wild tumultuous mob that – propelled into the last narrow funnel leading up to the Castle by the irresistible force of the thousands of others behind – could not halt, or hesitate, or even step over him. Could do nothing in the whole wide world but trample on him.

9

The child was born, incontinently, in one of the houses in Blair's Close before they had even succeeded in retrieving what remained of Duncan Lauriston from the cobbles outside.

It was a boy, and the two Misses Webster who lived in the house cooed over him and said how beautiful, how perfect he was, and that Mr Telfer mustn't think of moving Mistress Lauriston until she had recovered from her dreadful ordeal, poor young lady. They didn't even hesitate when the doctor, who had consented to accompany Mungo only because he had been promised the fattest fee in medical history, pursed his lips and gave it as his opinion that it would be a week at least before the lady was able to raise her head.

It was ten days before they could move her, and another three before she began to recover from the journey back to Marchfield House.

Then, on the morning of the first of April, when Mungo was ushered, pink and self-conscious, into her bedchamber for his ritual visit, he found her sitting up smiling, and holding out her hand to him.

'April Fool!' she said, her eyes unnaturally brilliant, and he had to swallow hard before he was able to reply, 'It's the best trick anyone's ever played on me!'

For almost five minutes, he simply sat and held her hand, beaming foolishly at her and murmuring sentimental, meaningless phrases like, 'That's a good girl!' and 'That's better!' and 'That's more like yourself!' And because she was, indeed, more like herself, she understood and said nothing.

During these anxious days he had talked to Sorley, persuading him with matter-of-fact kindliness that a footman, even one who had attained the mature age of eighteen, wasn't expected always to behave like the three wise monkeys rolled into one. The thin, freckled face under the ginger thatch had run through every single nuance of doubt and distress, and at last Sorley had given way to the relief of tears. Mungo had learned a good deal, although he was sure Sorley hadn't told him everything, and there were one or two things he still found puzzling. He wouldn't have thought that Vilia had loved Andrew enough to be thrown into quite such a state by his death; and what was more, an intelligent girl who married a soldier must always be half prepared for such an outcome. But he supposed that the tragedy, and the difficult pregnancy, and all that trauchle with Duncan Lauriston would have been enough to throw anyone into a fit of the dismals. For a sensitive lassie like Vilia, they had all added up into something that was too much for her to bear. And all alone, too. That was what he could not forgive himself, and never would. He had been terrified that, even when she recovered her strength – as the doctor said she would – she might never recover the spirit that had made her the child of his heart. It was a mawkish phrase, and he shuddered at it, but it was the truth. He loved her far more than he loved the children of his body.

But it looked, now, as if her mind had been freed from its burden of shadows at the same time as her body had been freed from the weight of the child she was carrying. Smiling inwardly at this notion, he said tentatively, 'And he's a fine wee boy, too.'

She had refused to see the child since she had recovered consciousness, and maybe it was understandable. But Mungo hoped that, now she was better, she might begin to give the bairn a bit of motherly attention. Wet nurses were all very well, but . . .

All she said at first was, 'Yes.' But then, forcing the words out, she added, 'I'm glad my foolishness over these last months hasn't done him any damage. There was a time when – when I didn't want him.'

Mungo pursed his lips and shook his head at her reprovingly. He knew she didn't mean it.

She looked away then, and concluded, 'I'll call him Andrew, of course.'

It had all been said in a colourless tone, but it had been said, and that was what mattered. Mungo decided not to press it. 'Aye, well,' he sighed, and then became brisk. 'Now! I'm feart we're going to have to talk about business. Are you fit for it?'

She nodded, but stopped him just as he was about to launch forth. 'One thing. I haven't said thank you. Sorley is a marvel, but I can't think what might have happened if you hadn't turned up when you did.'

'Turned up?' he responded humorously. 'Well, that's one way of putting it! I'd have been there a deal sooner if that sleekit butler fellow hadn't refused to tell me where you'd gone. It took me the better part of an hour to get it out of him. I didn't even know about the regimental welcome home, you see? And when I'd got that information out of him, I still had to winkle out where you were supposed to be watching from. I tell you, I was gey near to giving him a good skelp on the lug by the time I was done – and he could see it, too!' He almost added, 'I'd get rid of him, if I were you,' and then stopped himself. All in due course.

'Anyway,' he said, 'by the time we were done it was so late that the roads were jammed. We came round the back, of course, and left the carriage down off the South Bridge, and came the rest of the way by Shanks's pony. But I tell you, I've never been more relieved in my life than when I caught sight of Lauriston's head towering above the crowd. I could see him a hundred yards off. Aye,' he reflected without much enthusiasm, 'if we'd got there sooner, he might be alive today instead of snibbed in a mortsafe in the kirk yard.' It was Mungo's un-Christian but practical opinion that men like Duncan Lauriston were better off underground, for everyone's sake.

She said, 'Tell me one thing. I don't remember what happened. That day is almost nothing but a blur. But I think I pushed him.' She was looking at Mungo very seriously. 'Did I?'

In face of that gaze, he couldn't lie. 'You'll have to know some time.

Yes, you did. But you mustn't blame yourself for what happened.' He took her hand in a sustaining grip. 'A push from you, in your condition, couldn't have moved a man that size more than an inch. No. The inquiry came up with the right verdict, that I'm sure of. All you did was give him a surprise, so that he stepped back a pace. Maybe his foot skited on the cobbles – they were slippery enough, for guidsakes! – or maybe someone's stick caught him at the back of the knees. Who's to tell? The bailies had been expecting dozens of folk to be crushed or trampled when they saw the crowds that turned out, and I'd be telling a lie if I didn't say they were gey relieved that there was only one fatality at the end of the day. So – *don't blame yourself!*'

She nodded. 'Thank you.' It was true that she remembered almost nothing about that day. Nothing but the pain, and the fear, and the supernatural strength she had put into – she *thought* she had put into – that push. She smiled. 'It's forgotten. Now tell me what you wanted to talk to me about.'

'Plans!' he said expansively. 'You don't know about Duncan Lauriston's dispositions yet, do you? Aye, well. He's left everything he possessed to the boys, except for the house, which is yours.'

An expression of the most complete astonishment came to her face. 'Never! It must be a mistake. Are you sure?'

'Quite sure. He was maybe a wee bit soft in the head the day he made his Will . . .'

She giggled, and his heart soared with relief. He grinned. 'I mean it! It wasn't only the house. He left the ironworks to "my three grandsons". We'd have been in a fine legal fankle if wee Andrew had turned out to be a lassie! Now, the thing is that since he didn't expect to die for a long time yet, he didn't make any provision for how the ironworks was to be run until the boys come of age.' Mungo shook his head gloomily. 'No wonder he never made a success of his business. No foresight. But I'm not sure yet where it leaves you. The lawyers might insist that you put a manager in, but if I were you I'd try and persuade them to sell and be done with it. They might listen. I've no doubt they've got clients or friends or family who'd be pleased to buy a nice wee foundry at a competitive price.'

'Mungo!' she exclaimed on a note of mock reproval. 'You're an old cynic!'

He gazed at her speechlessly for a moment. It was the first time she had ever called him 'Mungo'. He wouldn't have expected it to give him quite such a sharp delight.

She was too preoccupied to notice. 'But why sell?' There was an intent frown on her brow. 'I know I hated Duncan Lauriston – and hate isn't too strong a word – but I can't think it would be right to throw away all his years of struggle, just like that. It wouldn't be fair to him. Or to the boys. Just think, Mungo dear! Ironmastering might run in their veins!'

He eyed her suspiciously. 'Aye, you *are* getting better, aren't you! But just you be quiet and listen to me, miss, because I've been thinking. I want you to come to Kinveil with the children for as long as you like, and get better in your own time. And while you're there, you can make up your mind about the future. I'll tell you now – what I'd like is for you to come and stay with me permanently.' He said it brusquely, because he had no idea what her reaction would be.

She was tired now and lying perfectly still, her hands loose on the coverlet. But her eyes had become luminous, and her light, silvery voice was unsteady when she said, after a few moments, 'I think you are the kindest man I have ever known. I'll come to Kinveil with – with gratitude, the deepest gratitude, when I'm well enough to travel. But I don't think I have the right to remain more than a few weeks.' He didn't know what it cost her to say that, although he thought he did. 'Some day, you know, it will belong to Magnus, and I wouldn't wish to be his . . .' She hesitated, '. . . his pensioner.' There was a faint smile in her eyes now. 'Indeed, I don't dare to think what he and Lucy would say if they found they were inheriting me as well as Kinveil! If I stayed with you, you know, it would only postpone the day of decision. And the decision more or less makes itself, anyway. We'll keep the foundry, and have a manager, but I'll run things myself. That being so, the sooner I start the better, don't you think?' His mouth was slightly ajar, but before he could give vent to his feelings she added, 'But thank you. *Really* thank you.'

He scarcely even heard. 'A woman run a foundry!' he gasped. 'You must be demented, lassie! Never in my life . . . I've never heard the like of it!'

Vilia had slipped down so that she was almost flat on the pillows. She turned her head towards him, looking so fragile that it nearly broke his heart. 'Never heard the like? Then you haven't been listening,

Mungo dear. Someone must have told you about the ladies of Coalbrookdale, the Darbies. Deborah, Sarah, and Rebecca, they were called. They carried on the family foundry for years and years, between them, until young Edmund Darby grew up. Not so very long ago, either. And they were English, and Quakers. Surely a Scotswoman, and a Presbyterian, can do at least as well?'

She smiled sleepily. 'And it will give me an interest, won't it? Say it will, Mungo dear!'

Part Two   *1816–1822*

Chapter One

1

'Ambition,' Mungo said, 'is a fine thing if you know what you're doing. But if you don't, it's lethal.'

Vilia's own intelligence would have told her as much, though whether she would have taken it so seriously without Mungo's dire warnings was another matter. She thought probably not. There were some things it was quite easy to forget. Some things . . .

She had wanted to pay just one visit to the foundry before Mungo whisked her off to Kinveil to recuperate, but he wouldn't hear of it. 'Have some sense, my dear!' he had exclaimed, exasperated. 'Setting aside the fact your legs are so dwaibly you'd be hard put to it even to walk across the coking yard, what effect do you think it would have on the men? New owners need to look impressive! It's bad enough that you're a female – and I grant you, there's not much we can do about that! – but there's no call for you to emphasize it by turning up looking as if the first puff of hot air from the furnace would blow you away! You want to be in full possession of all your faculties, right from the start.'

He was right, she supposed. 'But . . .'

'But, nothing! I'll talk to Moultrie, and tell him to keep things ticking over for the next few weeks. He and Richards – that's the accounting clerk – are perfectly capable, even if they don't look it. I've a suspicion that they were both so feart of Duncan Lauriston that they didn't dare waggle their little fingers without he told them to. Now he's stopped breathing down their necks, they'll have a chance to prove their worth. I'll tell them that, when you're recovered, you'll look forward to sitting round a table with them and hearing their views. How's that?'

Vilia surveyed him quizzically. 'You seem to have been busy while I've been lying here idle.'

'You'd have been in a right pickle if they'd let all the furnaces go out just because Lauriston was dead and you were in no state to issue orders!'

'Let the furnaces go out? Really, Mungo! You don't let furnaces *go out!*'

'Oh? What do you do, then?'

'Blow them out, of course, or put them out of blast. Everyone knows that!'

He grinned. 'Aye, well. I'm glad to hear *you* do. Because the first thing you'll need to learn is how to talk their language. Seriously! If you're set on going ahead, you have to start on the right foot.'

He said no more then, or during her first weeks at Kinveil. But one afternoon in May he took up the refrain again.

It was a perfect day. Under the clear blue arch of the sky, landscape and seascape shimmered with the bright, deceptive innocence of the Highland spring. Sun today was no guarantee of sun tomorrow. Rain was more likely, and snow still possible. One learned to take the weather as it came, but the beauty of spring days was balm to the soul, even when one knew it was as transient as breath.

Today, the rowan tree, bare less than a week before, had turned to sage lace, and the birches into clouds of airy green. The wild cherries had begun to unfurl their thin, bronze leaves, translucent against the sky, and the acid fronds of new bracken to stain the brown-purple hills. Primroses jostled like crowds in a city street. New lambs, curly and engaging, butted their mothers for milk, tails twirling like clock hands in a frenzy. The faint, sweet, resinous smell of bog myrtle drifted down from the hills in counterpoint to the salt tang of seaweed from the shore. The peace was almost tangible.

They were sitting on the wide stone terrace abutting the sea wall, and Vilia had thought Mungo was asleep. It was the kind of day when it would have been perfectly reasonable for a man who was well beyond the Biblical span of years to drop off into a doze, lulled by a good lunch, a cushioned chair, and the smiling sun.

'Start as you mean to go on,' he said suddenly.

She had been gazing dreamily out over the sea to the islands, slate and violet and indigo, floating on an invisible horizon where blue merged softly into blue. Sapphire air into hyacinth sea? Or robin's egg blue into aquamarine? She couldn't decide. She didn't want to think about the foundry.

Reluctantly, she said, 'Yes', and wondered what had prompted the remark. It wasn't like Mungo to be insensitive. During these last weeks, her feeling of release had been so acute that she had given herself up to unthinking contentment. Once or twice she had tried to force herself to consider the future, but her mind had slipped wilfully away, sideways, towards pleasanter things. It was as if she had lost her power of concentration, or perhaps just the will to concentrate. She didn't want to face up to tomorrow. She smiled faintly, remembering the Englishman who had once said to Willie Meikle, 'You Highlanders are like the Spanish for putting things off. Mañana, always mañana!' And Willie, who had fought in the Peninsula, had considered for a moment and then said, 'Mañana? Och, no. There iss no word in the Gaelic, I am thinking, that conveys quite the same sense of urgency.' It was true. There was a certain lotus-eating quality in the glens. But how could one think about ironfounding on such a day as this? Was Mungo, she suddenly wondered, slyly reminding her that she didn't belong to the foundry but here, where he wanted her to stay. Where *she* wanted to stay – dear God, so much!

'You'll have to make it clear, straight off, that you've strength and determination and a brain. I know you've got them. You know you've got them.' He stopped, his eyes still closed, but she felt that he was waiting, testing her. When she didn't answer, he went on, 'The question is, how to prove it to folk who don't know you? If you were a man, you'd find the situation sticky enough. As a woman – and a chit of a girl, at that – it'll be near impossible unless you've a good, sound plan of campaign. And more besides.'

'They'll resent me, you mean?' There was a seal drifting around, looking for somewhere to bask.

'More than that. They'll do everything they can to make your life impossible. I probably would myself, if you weren't you.'

She turned her head slowly. 'But it's so silly. It must be in their interest as much as mine to see the foundry flourishing.'

'You might think so. But they'll argue that it never *will* flourish under you, and that if they get the better of you, you'll be forced to stand aside in favour of a man. You can see their reasoning. A man's more likely to understand the physical difficulties they have to contend with, for one thing. And for another, they don't have to mind their language in front of a man. Believe me, they'll have all sorts of reasons, some of them quite good ones. I'll tell you what will happen. The knowledge-able ones will talk down to you. Folk like Moultrie and Richards will try to blind you with science, so that you'll have no choice but to let them run the place as they see fit. If you produce any ideas of your own, they'll smile politely and pityingly, and explain that whatever you have in mind is technically not possible. There'll be questions of melting points and steam stresses and phosphorus content that you can't be expected to understand. And that will be that. As far as the labourers are concerned, I imagine you can look forward to a good deal of veiled insolence, because they'll be sure you won't have the courage to sack them for it. A young woman who hasn't a man to protect her isn't in a happy position. If she's treated with what you might call undue familiarity, most folk are liable to think that she's asked for it.'

'We'll soon see about *that!*' Her tone was brisk, and Mungo smiled to himself.

The seal was flippering purposefully towards a low, flat rock. It heaved itself up in a flurry of drips, swayed a little, and then subsided.

Vilia's gaze returned to Mungo. 'I see. I have to show them I know what I'm talking about. But I don't! And how do I find out except by experience? Without, of course, letting Moultrie and Richards find *me* out in the meantime!'

Mungo opened his eyes. 'There are things called books.'

'About iron founding? I suppose there must be, but surely not for the complete ignoramus? They'd be for advanced apprentices.'

'They are. But it just happens I can help you. I've a wee present I've been saving for you until you were well enough.'

She looked at him speculatively. 'I remember the model soldiers you had five years ago, so that you could work out what the local volunteers ought to do in the way of manoeuvres if there was a French in-vasion . . .'

'Aye, they were grand, weren't they?' He grinned reminiscently. 'I've often regretted the Frogs didn't come after all. Those wee models fairly gave me a taste for soldiering!'

'Mmmm. And if the volunteers had been half as smart, and a quarter as well armed as the models, they'd have frightened Boney's cohorts right back into the sea, and not a shot fired! Mungo, you haven't – you *haven't* – had a model foundry made for me to play with?'

'I wish I'd thought of it,' he said with a trace of regret. 'No. But I've every book James Thin's could supply. You're right, they're all a bit advanced for you, so I wrote to a man who owes me a favour or two. He's got a wee foundry of his own at Glenbuck in Ayrshire, and he's written down everything you need to know to make a start. All nice and simple, so that after you've mastered it you'll understand what the books are talking about. And while I was at it . . .' He looked a little uncomfortable. 'I didn't tell him why I wanted it all, mind! I suppose it would rank as unfair competition. While I was at it I got him to write down all about the state of the market, why prices are dropping and foundries going out of business. We can't have that happening to you. I thought it might all come in handy, like.'

She had slipped out of her chair and was kneeling on the warm flagstones beside him. She took his hands in her own thin clasp, and said with a catch in her voice, 'You are such a *dear*.'

'Aye, well. If you're really, truly set on it . . .' It was a question, and the last time the question would be asked.

She said, 'Yes.'

After that, there was no going back. They both had their pride.

2

For a month, she read and absorbed, and every day Mungo questioned her – 'like an old dominie', he remarked wryly. What had she learned? About coal and coke and iron ore; about pig iron, and forge iron; about ordinary furnaces and blast engines and puddling furnaces. About raw material costs; and production costs; and selling prices.

'Over-production,' he would say. 'Too much iron chasing too few customers. What do you do?'

'Sell cheaper than anyone else.'

'Which depends on . . . ?'

'Cutting production costs, or accepting a lower profit margin.'

'And if the profit margin's too low?'

'We're as much out of business as if we hadn't cut the margin in the first place.'

'Right. What could you do instead?'

She hesitated. 'Produce better quality than anyone else?'

He made what was unquestionably a rude noise. 'There's not many folk care about quality these days. Try again.'

'Make something no one else is making?'

'Such as what? There isn't anything but pig iron and wrought iron – sorry, forge iron – is there? Except steel, and that would mean an impossible capital investment.'

She said, 'I didn't mean that. You know Lauriston's makes simple cast-iron things like pipes, and plates, and beams. We could expand that side of the business and make more kinds of manufactured product.'

'You'd need capital for the moulds, then.'

She sighed. 'Oh, Mungo! You're really not being very encouraging.'

'Try again,' he said inexorably.

Her chin resting childishly on her hands, and her elbows on his zebra wood desk, she exclaimed, 'Pooh! All right, then. Improve our sales of the things we make already and wouldn't need new moulds for.'

'And how would you do that?'

She wrinkled her nose thoughtfully. 'Lots of people are still using wood for things cast iron could do better, and others are using forge or wrought iron for what cast iron could do just as well, and much more cheaply. I know we make forge iron, but it's an expensive process and it uses up a great deal of pig iron that we might be able to use more profitably in castings. We could try and sell castings to people who haven't thought of using them before.'

He smiled in satisfaction. 'That's better. What kind of people?'

She had no idea.

Mungo said, 'I can think of someone not a hundred miles from here.'

A hundred miles from Kinveil? There wasn't a potential customer as near as that, surely? There wasn't a proper town or city within twice that distance. She looked at him, frowning.

'Come on, lassie!' he said impatiently.

And then she had it. 'The Caledonian Canal?'

'Of course. They're working on the middle stretch now, round Fort Augustus. Lock gates, lassie! Lock gates!'

He could see her mind begin working, and it cheered him though he was still worried about her. Her health was almost completely restored, and after the weeks of fresh air and freedom her complexion had begun to take on the clear warmth he always associated with young folk in the Highlands – the lovely smooth, faintly golden skin with the rose-amber glow on the cheekbones. It looked, even to down-to-earth Mungo, startlingly exotic against the blonde hair, streaked by the weather into every shade from cream through citrine to buttermilk. He could still, in his mind's eye, see her five years ago, a pale wisp of a thing in the heavy, melodramatic mourning she had worn for her father. Then, she had been making a youthful parade of something that hadn't been a hundred per cent sorrow. Now, she knew how to draw the line between theatricality and stylishness. Her ribbed poplin gown, new in the spring of last year and hurriedly dyed after Waterloo, was worn over a pure white, lace-ruffed habit shirt, and became her extraordinarily well. Though her figure was still too slender for Mungo's taste, there was no doubt that she was well on the road to physical recovery.

But although she had recovered her spirits enough to look at him, now and then, with the glint of mischief that had always bewitched him, there was a withdrawn quality that hadn't been there before, a reserve that seemed to him different in essence from the reserve she had affected during her early dealings with the Telfers. That had been defensive, an adolescent armour deliberately donned. This might be defensive, too, but it sprang from within. She had always been self-sufficient – though less so, Mungo thought, than she had appeared – not really needing other people. Now, it was as if she didn't want them. Except, perhaps, for him. He hoped.

He had tried to persuade her to renew her bonds with the folk on the estate, and she had done so; he had noticed, with interest, that those who didn't know her well enough to call her 'Mistress Vilia' all called her 'Mistress Cameron', following the old Scots custom by which a married woman retained her maiden name. But he hadn't been able to coax her into venturing beyond the boundaries of Kinveil. It was as if her strength depended on the place itself. She wouldn't go with him to Inverness, or to pay a call on that kilted pea-goose, Glengarry, or even consent to drive along Loch Ness to see how the Canal was getting on. Nor would she consider going with him to Glenbraddan to see

Charlotte. That had disappointed him. The silly prejudice Charlotte had developed against her at the Northern Meeting ball had grown stronger over the last year, and nothing Mungo could say had any effect. He had thought that if the two women could meet under everyday circumstances Charlotte might see Vilia for what she was, not a *femme fatale*, but a tired, charming, not very strong young widow. It had seemed to him that now was as good a time as any, with Vilia just having given birth to a new baby, and Charlotte expecting hers any day now. In his experience, there was something about babies that always seemed to bring women together, and he wanted the two women he loved most in the world to get on with each other. But Vilia wouldn't hear of it, although she had phrased her refusal more tactfully than that. Maybe, Mungo thought, she sensed that she wouldn't be welcome at Glenbraddan; maybe she felt that meeting someone she didn't know very well would still be too much for her; or maybe it was her new resistance to people in general. There were no other reasons that Mungo could think of, or none that he was prepared to contemplate.

'Yes,' she said. 'Lock gates.'

He wriggled down more comfortably in his chair. 'Let's get back to something else for a minute. Cutting production costs. You should go into that when you get back.'

'Oh, I will. But I imagine my father-in-law must have pared those to the bone already. He had that kind of mind.'

'Maybe aye, maybe no. Ore prices and wages, no doubt, but experts often have their blind spots. There was one thing that certainly struck me when I saw round the foundry.' He waited expectantly.

'I know what struck *me*,' she replied simply. 'The noise and the heat. The heat? Is that what you mean? Oh-h-h-h. All that heat blasting out of the furnace doors into the empty air? But . . .'

'But, nothing. Think of Count Rumford.'

She giggled. 'Honestly, Mungo – the way your mind works! No wonder you made all that money when you were in business. You're like a grasshopper. I shouldn't suppose any of your competitors ever came within shouting distance of you. Count Rumford – the cooking stove man? I don't see your point.'

'Drat it, you know how the Rumford range works, surely!'

After a moment, she said resignedly. 'Yes. The heat from a single fire is led off in all directions to heat goodness knows how many different ovens and hotplates and things. Yes, indeed. You win! You think we could do the same with the heat from the furnaces? It's an idea. If we could work out *how*, it would make an enormous saving on fuel.' She looked at him. 'Mungo dear, are you an inventor *manqué*, or has someone else done it already?'

'I've no idea, but I shouldn't think so. It's the kind of notion that strikes economical folk like me more than geniuses. Anyway, you could take it up with Moultrie.'

'I will. Have you any other brilliant ideas up your sleeve?'

'Not a one. Have you?'

She said nothing at first. They were sitting in the comfortable, wood-panelled Gallery waiting for Jessie Graham to come in with the supper. Although it was early June, it had been the kind of day that might have strayed from November or March. Dirty, sullen clouds still swept across the sky, and the rain was lashing against the rooflights and the sea roaring on the rocks below. But indoors it was warm and companionable, with the fire blazing, and enough candles burning to remind Vilia that there wasn't a hive within twenty miles that couldn't be tapped for wax. At her feet, the Duchess stretched comprehensively and produced an enormous yawn. She was no longer a kitten, but she still hated to be separated from Vilia; fortunately, she had taken to coach travel as to the manner born.

Vilia said tentatively, 'I have an idea, yes. But it brings us back to the problem of capital for moulds. I'm sure you're right about lock gates, but I'm sure *I'm* right, too, in thinking there's a market for making large quantities of things in cast iron that are usually made, in small quantities, in wrought iron. Stop me if I'm wrong, but as I understand it the price war comes from too many foundries producing raw materials – pig and forge – and fighting to sell them to the people who make the finished product. Now if we made the finished product ourselves, we'd be out of that war, wouldn't we?'

'And into another one with the manufacturers.'

'Yes, but we would have the advantage over them because our finished products wouldn't have to take two lots of profit into account, and some of the overheads, like transport, would be halved.' She looked at him doubtfully. 'Wouldn't they?'

Mungo let out a long puff of breath, and shook his head. 'Don't think for a moment it's going to be as easy as that! Quite apart from anything else, you're probably making far more pig than you can use yourselves, and to reduce your capacity might well make the whole thing uneconomic. Never mind. Go on, tell me what this market is you're so keen on. I can see you're not just talking in general terms. You've one special market in mind, haven't you?'

'Yes, I have. Don't laugh at me, but in the south of England – and to some extent in Edinburgh and Glasgow, too, I should think – the amount of new building that's going on is almost unbelievable, and I'm sure the pace must have accelerated now that the wars are over. And all the houses that are going up at the moment – and I mean *all*, Mungo, or very nearly – have railings and balconies and canopies. Very pretty, really *very* pretty. And what I'd like to do is specialize in architectural ironmongery.'

'Do you know if anyone else is doing it?'

'I'd have to find out. My impression is that it's mostly wrought iron, because that kind of thing used always to go on quite expensive houses where only the finest finish would do. But all these books tell me that, although cast iron is more brittle, and doesn't look quite as smooth, it's possible to produce a perfectly satisfactory finish merely by remelting the pig in the foundry furnace before one moulds it.' She giggled irresistibly. 'There! Didn't that sound impressive? I wish I knew whether I was talking sense or nonsense!'

He grinned back at her. 'And?'

'*And* we could do it more cheaply *and*, as I said, there's a huge market. Besides which, you must admit that I have an eye for design and a tendency to be a perfectionist, and I'm sure I could sell much more convincingly to house builders than any rough old run-of-the-mill ironmaster could!' A little wistfully, she added, 'And it would be pleasant to produce a few attractive things, as well as cooking pots and lock gates and building beams and plates, wouldn't it?'

He was as delighted as a hen with a new brood of chicks at seeing her enthusiasm, but too old in the wiles of commerce to let his feelings run away with him. 'It's an idea,' he said cautiously, 'but you'd have to sound the market out very carefully indeed, and you'll still need the capital for the moulds.'

She sighed. 'I know. I'll have to run the foundry on the old lines until I can afford to embark on something I *know* will be profitable – if it still is, by that time! Isn't it frustrating? And I don't suppose any builder will be persuaded to pay in advance!'

He permitted himself a small smile. 'Why not start off by seeing what new applications you can think of for the pipes and beams and things you make already. You can investigate the prospects for your balconies and canopies at the same time. You'd certainly be better employed on that than peering into pigs and furnaces and whatnot. And when you've got it all worked out . . .' He paused significantly. He'd been trying for years to think of a way of using his own money to smooth her path for her, and had failed. To offer it openly would have been insulting, and even if she had chosen not to be insulted by it, it would have been bound to spoil their relationship. But now the opportunity had come, and there need be no taint of charity attached. 'The day you come to me and tell me you've got a real, live buyer for your architectural ironmongery, I'll put up the capital for the mould-making. But mind you! I'll want four per cent. My merchanting instincts aren't dead yet, not by a long chalk.'

When Jessie Graham entered the room a moment later, balancing two steaming trays and a nice saucer of liver for the Duchess, she was taken aback to find Mistress Vilia with her arms flung excitedly round the neck of a blushing Mr Telfer.

3

Mungo waved Vilia good-bye on a sunny, gusty day in the middle of the month, when the wind was whipping the loch into white caps, and small clouds streaked across the sky with tails spun out behind them like woolly fireworks.

She had made up her mind suddenly, and within forty-eight hours she was gone. He would have liked to go with her, but she thought there was no need and, besides, he was feeling his age a little. It would have been silly for an old man like him to go poking his nose into foundries and such, about which he knew less, now, than she did. It was her future, not his. She was still only twenty years old and had all her life ahead of her, whereas his was nearing its end. Listening to her make plans, watching the intent gleam in the rekindled green eyes, he had developed a sudden awareness of mortality. He was deeply depressed as he watched the two carriages bowl away into the blue distance at the far end of the loch.

Mungo had always been proud of taking things as they came, of not being a worrier. But now he was subject to the most complex feeling of unease. It bothered him that, when the carriages left, Vilia was in one and the children in the other. It bothered him that the laddies were going to be brought up with no father, and a mother whose mind was on something else, for he knew Vilia well enough by now to recognize that the challenge of the foundry would absorb all her energies for as long as was necessary. He was bothered about Vilia herself, ignorant of the realities of industrial life, unfamiliar with the disciplines of earning a living, desperately ill-equipped to deal with the coarse, rough type of men who would surround her every day. She would manage, he knew. She wasn't the kind of lassie to give up. But it would be hard for her, and he didn't know quite what kind of effect it would have. The foundry would be bad for her health, too. Even in London, she had always been able to spend part of the day outdoors. He'd have to make quite sure that she came to Kinveil as often as humanly possible, for the sake of both body and spirit. Sighing, Mungo recognized that he'd just have to wait and see, but in the meantime Iain Mor the Post had never been more assured of his welcome.

'I have sacked the butler,' Vilia wrote,

and am much relieved to see the last of his shifty countenance. I am sure he was constantly at the port, although the port deserved no better. My late father-in-law's wine cellar, while surprisingly extensive, was as acidulated as its owner. So I called Sorley in, and told him that, since his palate is perfectly capable of distinguishing the whisky from every illicit still on Kinveil and Glenbraddan – Mungo dear, do you *know* how many there are? – it was time he put this talent to use in learning about claret and burgundy. I am *not* being extravagant! I said he was first to sell what was already in the cellar, and use *that* money to buy a smaller quantity of something better, which I think was commendably businesslike of me. Anyway, Sorley's smile quite lit up the room, whether because he fancies himself as a connoisseur of wine, or simply because he was pleased to hear me sounding decisive again, I don't know. Fortunately, he has no ambitions to be a butler – he wouldn't be a very good one – so I have employed the housekeeper's husband, Angus McKirdy. I suspect that when you come to visit me you will take to him as instantly as I did. A very shy but handsome man, with bright blue Highland eyes, and the loveliest smile – almost as dazzling as Sorley's. I have also rearranged the entire house. Thrown things out, moved the furniture, put up my own family portraits, brought my books out of the packing chests in which they have reposed for the last year. You won't believe it, but there wasn't a bookcase in the house. The gardener, however, turns out to be a genius with wood and chisel, and is now engaged on remedying the deficiency. The babies send their love – or would, if they were old enough to think in such terms. Theo is turning into a real chatterbox, I may say. You remember that he was formulating whole sentences – even using the first person – at the ripe old age of one year and ten months. Well, he has now discovered that that was really rather clever of him, and refuses to let us forget it. He only found out because Nurse let it out when she was talking about Gideon, who at fifteen months is now expressing himself in phrases rather than just single words. Theo doesn't like the competition, I'm afraid! As for the baby, he's still just a baby, though a handsome one, you must agree. But Nurse says he actually chuckled the other day, though I don't remember either of the others doing so at under four months. Oh, well! Perhaps he has a forthcoming disposition!

No mention of the foundry. Mungo fretted for almost ten days before the next letter arrived.

Well, I have done it! You would have laughed to see me prepare myself. After what you said about the men at Lauriston's expecting a frail female, wilting under the load of her bereavements, I decided to take the wind out of their sails. I have had two riding habits dyed black, which, with white shirts, look very severe, especially since I have drawn my hair tight back and wear no jewellery other than my wedding band and a rather intimidating mourning ring I found among Duncan Lauriston's belongings. Every morning I stand before the glass and glare at myself, fixing an austere expression firmly enough on my face to be sure that it stays all day. I may say that I leave home at eight in the morning and return at seven at night, so I am not shirking. I drive to the foundry in an antiquated maroon carriage with a pair of ill-matched bays and a coachman whose entire vocabulary seems to consist of, 'Aye, Mistress,' 'No, Mistress,' 'Giddyup!' and 'Whoa!'

But you will have to possess your soul in patience, Mungo dear, because I am not going to tell you about the foundry until I have had a few more days to take in all the overtones and undercurrents. The overtones, unfortunately, include a strong whiff of attar of roses from Walter Richards, the accountant, and something much less sweet from James Moultrie. Would it be too pointed, do you think, to instal baths at the foundry?

She wrote again, a week or two later, but still told him almost nothing of what he wanted to know. This time, she filled her letter with a frivolous account of how she had decided to stop using Duncan Lauriston's old office, which was no more than a cubby-hole where she felt suffocated, and move into an unused loft over the storeroom.

You would be astonished to see what a difference two coats of limewash, some pictures, a carpet, curtains, and the pantry shelves from Marchfield have made to it. So now I can breathe again, as long as I stay to leeward of Messieurs Moultrie and Richards. I will have to find some kind of stove for the winter, as there is no chimney, but sufficient unto the day. Besides, I can always go and warm myself at one of the furnaces, can't I!

The children are well, thank you. Theo still hates being hugged, Gideon is as placid as ever, and baby Drew almost effervesces with self-assurance. Strange are the ways of Nature!

4

She knew the letters sounded brittle, but not even to herself would she admit that all she wanted to say was, 'I hate it! I hate it! I want to come back to Kinveil!'

She hated the dirt and the noise and the seediness. Her nerves were tensed into knots, day after day, as with incredible fluency she trotted out all the jargon of the trade as if she had learned it with her ABC. She waited for someone to catch her out, but no one did. This was partly, she thought, because Duncan Lauriston had trained his employees never to speak out of turn, never to say a word that didn't accord with his own opinions. Sometimes, she wished he hadn't been so successful. It was disconcerting to have Moultrie twitch every time she spoke to him, as if he expected her to bite him. And Richards's smile was as fixed as if it had been incorporated into the fabric of his face. It was only when the smile was accompanied by an almost curtsey-like bob that it meant anything positive.

The two men were chalk and cheese, and she couldn't decide which was more difficult to deal with. Neither of them would express an opinion unless his back was practically nailed to the wall, and extracting information was like drawing teeth – a succession of tugs, jerks, and stoic silences.

After the initial conferences, when she succeeded in convincing them that she was serious, business-like, and knew, roughly, what she was talking about – and during which she modelled herself on an elderly and thoroughly starched-up dowager of her acquaintance – she began, with care, to tread the path she had mapped out with Mungo.

From behind the wide table, laden now with piles of papers and dog-eared specifications that helped to hide the dents and scratches on its surface, she watched Walter Richards bowl into the office. Although he had crossed the yard in a drizzle and mounted the outside staircase that was the only means of access to her loft, there was not a flake of ash on him, nor even a raindrop. He was pink, and plump, and looked as if he had been polished from top to toe with a soft cloth and a great deal of elbow grease. Vilia found it difficult to understand how her father-in-law had managed to put up with him for almost five years, for he was certainly not Duncan Lauriston's kind of man. She hoped it had been because he was a good accountant.

Simple things first, Mungo had said. She waved Richards to the chair on the other side of the desk.

'Would you enlighten me,' she said calmly, 'about basic costs? I know that over-production is a serious problem in the iron – in *our* industry, and that every iron foundry is trying to undercut every other iron foundry. But I would like you to be more specific, please. There are some figures that don't appear in the material you gave me, possibly because they are such common knowledge that you felt no need to write them down.' Her hands were folded on the table before her, as if the thought of having to make notes hadn't even crossed her mind. Only the ignorant needed to make notes – she hoped. 'The standard price for pig is how much?'

Mr Richards's curly lips pouted, and he nodded his head in a considering way, as if that was answer enough.

After a moment, Vilia repeated, 'The standard price for pig iron, please?'

His brows arched in surprise. 'Oh! We-e-ell, it depends on the grade.'

'No doubt. Perhaps you would give me an example.'

'Ummm. If you were talking about Number One Super . . . Would that do?'

'I am sure it would.'

'If you were talking about Number One Super, let's say £9.5s. a ton. Give or take a few coppers.'

219

'Give or take how many coppers?'

'Oh. Well, for the purposes of calculation, you could ignore the coppers. Just say . . .' He puffed his lips out and gave a little pop of exhaled breath. 'Just say a round £9.5s.'

'Thank you, I will. Now, what does it take us to produce?'

Silence. 'How much does it cost to make, do you mean?'

'Yes.'

'Oh. Say £9?' He smiled cooperatively, as if she didn't need to say £9 if she'd rather not.

Vilia reminded herself that she could make it sound quite funny when she wrote to Mungo. She knew from Mrs McKirdy that Walter Richards was a bachelor and lived at home with his doting mother, who was presumably very saintly or very stupid, as it seemed that Wally could do no wrong in the old lady's eyes. He was probably a model of cooperation at home, too. Would he like sausages or kippers for his tea? 'Either would be splendid, Mama. Sausages, perhaps? Or kippers if they would be less trouble? Whichever suits you. I really don't have any preference.'

With a muted sigh, she said, 'That means five shillings profit on a ton of – er – Number One Super Pig. Could we balance the books on less?'

'And cut prices below everyone else's £9.5s?' Mr Richards sucked in his lips vigorously, but it was some time before Vilia was able to establish that the foundry would be left with no latitude to speak of if she tried it. 'Very little latitude. Ooooh, *very* little latitude!' She had the impression that only the spectre of Duncan Lauriston prevented him from coming out with an unequivocal, 'I couldn't recommend it!'

Thoughtfully, she watched him depart, the smile still on his face.

Moultrie was a different problem. She had the feeling that just one radical suggestion would frighten him into treating all subsequent suggestions, however innocuous, with the deepest suspicion. And she didn't dare frighten or alienate him, because if he were irritable, slovenly, or uninterested, the whole foundry would suffer. Delicately, she worked round to the question of castings.

'Aye,' he said. 'Mr Lauriston wasn't very enamoured of casting. Och, he made a few locks and cooking pots and wee things like that, just for the local folk, you know. But he was a foundry man at heart. He had a real appreciation of a nice iron bar.'

Vilia permitted herself a twitch of the lips. 'And are you a foundry man at heart, too, Mr Moultrie? I hope so, for the "nice iron bars" will be all your responsibility.'

She had said the right thing.

'I'll not deny I'm pleased to hear it.' He had an unusually wide mouth, and spoke out of the side of it so that one cheek bulged as if there were a toffee lump sticking to his back teeth. His voice, too, sounded as if he were talking through an obstruction. 'Furnace work's what I'm best at. I had a good training under Mr Lauriston, that I did.'

He had been apprenticed to Duncan Lauriston when he was a boy, over twenty-five years ago, and Vilia could imagine the two getting on rather well. Moultrie's stolidity must have acted as a baffle against her father-in-law, cutting off any flying sparks. The contrast between Moultrie and Richards was so extreme as to be ridiculous. If Richards was Humpty Dumpty, Moultrie was Mr Punch, long and lean and bony, with liquid brown eyes, and a nose and chin that seemed to have been hewn from the same half-circle and were utterly dedicated to reunification, curving sharply towards each other and only just failing to meet. She wished he was as fond of soap and water as he was of nice iron bars.

It eased his mind when she made it clear to him, tactfully, that she wasn't asking him what he thought Lauriston's should do, but what it could do. On that basis, he was prepared to admit that the foundry had already made cast-iron pipes for the blast furnaces, and plates and beams for the furnace-stoking bridge. He was even prepared to concede that they could make the same kind of thing for outside customers. People like the Caledonian Canal Commissioners.

Vilia said, 'Jonathan Wells, at the Inverness New Foundry, is clearing at least £100 a month on rails and castings for the lock gates, you know. And I'm told that Outram's Butterley Works in Derbyshire must have made a good £15,000 out of cast-iron rails and framing for the locks since building began.'

Moultrie ran his hand through the long pepper-and-salt hair that sprang back from his forehead like a field of grain in a high wind. 'Aye, well. Money, now. That's Mr Richards's department, you know. I wouldn't like to express an opinion about that.'

'I quite understand.' Moultrie earned a princely £450 a year as works manager compared with Richards's £150, so it had to be canniness rather than protocol that made him guard his tongue. She said, 'There is, however, not much canal work remaining to be tendered for, so if we want to supply we must enter into negotiations soon. I am prepared to try and sell our products. It was simply that I wanted to be sure we could, in fact, produce what I will be offering.'

He shook his long head lugubriously. 'Aye, well. It would mean taking men from other work.'

There was one item that, for no particular reason, had stuck in her mind. 'I see that making the working gears for a Boulton and Watts forge-hammer engine takes one man a whole month, and yet we can't charge more than two guineas for them. How much work could that man do on simpler things like beams and plates?'

It was a home question, and Moultrie's teeth appeared to stick for a moment before he replied. 'Aye, well. I'd have to think about that.' It was a concession – or something that might be developed into one.

Her first victory. She didn't tell him that, after the canal work, she hoped to tender for some of the iron bridges that were being planned on the lines of the ones recently put up at Bonar and Craigellachie. Nor did she mention Count Rumford's stove and the possibility of using waste furnace heat to drive the boilers and blast engines. Least of all did she talk about architectural ironmongery. One thing at a time.

5

Writing to Mungo helped her to keep it all in some kind of perspective. She even began to assess the things that were preying on her mind according to the difficulty she had in treating them lightly. She didn't know, although she suspected, how anxiously Mungo awaited her letters. She did know what a lifeline his were for her. Although Kinveil was only two hundred miles away, she felt as much of an exile as some empire-builder on the other side of the globe, and a hundred times more of an exile than she had felt in London.

This puzzled her for a while. And then she realized that, when she had been in London, her hands had always been tied. Whether living with Magnus and Lucy, or married to Andrew, the initiative had never been hers. By saying yes to Andrew she had deliberately, and she had thought irrevocably, cut herself off from Kinveil. But this time nothing was irrevocable. She had made her choice, and chosen the foundry, but she could abandon it just as easily. Indeed, assaulted by the everyday realities of it, she couldn't imagine what had possessed her to embark on it. It was only pride that kept her here. Forlornly, she recognized that the sense of exile was stronger and harder to bear because she *could* go to Kinveil if she wanted to, but that, for everyone's sake, she mustn't. Although for Mungo's sake she couldn't stay away entirely. She was trying, still honestly trying, to break free, but no one was helping her.

Mungo's letters were like some drug, which she depended on while trying to reject. There was nothing he could say in them that didn't set her either dreaming or despairing. There were days when, sitting at her desk, her eyes would look right through some wretched drawing for a sugar mill that had come in from the West Indies, and see instead Ewen and Robbie and Johnnie hauling in the seine nets. Days when Wally Richards's attar of roses dissolved into the sharper scents of seaweed and peat smoke. Days when the shriek of the blast pipes was blunted into the roar of a September gale, wet and powerful and bracing.

Sometimes he wrote about things that all her senses rebelled at. In July, he reported that Charlotte's baby had arrived, 'a bonny wee girl who's to be called Shona. Charlotte's recovering well enough, but she's got no warmth for the bairn.' Vilia found she couldn't read the words that came next. The pain, it seemed now, would never leave her. The pain of the betrayal and, more, of the year of silence that had followed. Not a word. For all she knew, he might be dead.

It was half an hour before she brought her eyes into focus again.

'I can't think,' Mungo wrote,

that Charlotte's attitude can be good for the other bairns, though Edward hasn't even noticed, maybe. I've never come across anyone so insensitive before. A real wet blanket. Luke calls him The Wastepipe, because he says that after an hour in Edward's company he feels as if someone has pulled the plug out of his big toe, so that all his life essence has drained away with a horrible whoosh. From which you'll gather that Luke's growing up. The two girls are an unlikely pair. Georgiana – she's eight now, or nine, I never remember – is a bright wee thing, full of fun and gig, while Grace is as earnest and bossy as you could well imagine. Wants to take all the ills of the world on her shoulders. And if she's like that already, God knows what she'll be like when she grows up! Sometimes I find it hard to remember that it's she who's Perry Randall's child, and Georgiana who's a Blair. It ought to be the other way round.

Och, well, that's enough about Glenbraddan. The weather here's terrible, if that cheers you! I need one of your letters to brighten me up.

He wrote again at the beginning of September, urging her to do what she wanted to do more than anything in the world.

Are you not going to be able to come to Kinveil for a wee break? Luke and I would be blithe to see you. He came back last month – after being in London since I sent him off there so hurriedly in March – with Henry Phillpotts still in tow, drat it! Magnus came too for a fortnight, and maybe it's a sign of age, but these duty visits fairly rile me. One of these days, I'm going to have to put my foot down and insist that he and Lucy come here permanently. That way, at least, I'll be able to set him on the right track with the estate. If he doesn't come till I'm dead, God knows what kind of mess he'll make of things. Don't worry, though. I'm not feeling ill, just looking ahead.

I was delighted to hear that you've seen James Hope and he's giving you a trial for the lock gates on the Canal. I remember him as a very clever fellow, though I aye had to be careful not to talk politics with him, me being a Whig while he's a red-hot Tory. Anyway, I'm glad my introduction came in useful to cushion the shock when V. Lauriston, ironmaster, was ushered in and turned out to be a lady. We should be ashamed of ourselves, misleading the poor fellow like that!

Vilia could almost hear him chuckle. But she wrote back to say she couldn't leave the foundry when she was just getting to grips with things. Maybe at the New Year. But at the New Year the roads were impassable.

The weeks passed, and the months, and it became clear to Mungo that he was going to have to provide her with a real reason for coming, not just an excuse. Craftily, he began bombarding her with information about the latest developments on the Caledonian Canal. There was a new kind of dredging machine being tried out; if it worked, there'd be a demand from elsewhere for something of the sort. It was the kind of machine Lauriston's could make – 'no bother!' That didn't bring her. Then an old bridge near Invergarry collapsed to let a postchaise – 'horses, occupants, and all' – fall into the water, though none of them was much damaged. 'But a wee cast-iron bridge would be just what the doctor ordered.' That didn't bring her either.

Not until the spring of 1818 did she come, while the snow was still lying. It was a bridge that brought her, after all, this time the one near Glenbraddan that had been put up when the Skye road was being built. It was made of wood, and had looked solid enough to stand for a hundred years. But the winter of 1817–18 was unusually severe, and Charlotte's grieve, who had been busy with the forests, had piled up four thousand birch logs on the river bank, ready to be floated down when the weather improved on the first stage of their journey to the north-east, to be used for making staves for herring barrels. The floods in January were tremendous, and on one wild night all the logs had been swept into the torrent. There was a log jam of impossible dimensions, and it was the bridge that lost the battle. For the people who used the road from Skye to Loch Ness it was a disaster, and a temporary replacement had to be flung up in haste. Something more substantial was needed, in stone or cast iron.

Vilia was competent, and rather impressive. She knew now how to study a site, assess what was required, and give a general estimate – on the spot – of time and costs. The local Roads superintendent wouldn't have hesitated about recommending Lauriston's to his superiors, if only she had been a man. As it was, he muttered, and dithered, and procrastinated.

She stayed with Mungo for a week. She hadn't brought the children, and she looked tired and preoccupied, and took all of two days to stop being brisk. But although she didn't laugh at all, and smiled only seldom, she talked a good deal and Mungo was reassured. When the superintendent finally gave in and decided to forward her estimate to the appropriate quarter, Mungo was so proud of her he was almost speechless.

6

There were things Mungo didn't tell Vilia, though he would have been hard put to it to explain why. There was no real reason why he shouldn't have mentioned that he'd heard from Perry Randall, even if he kept it from Charlotte – who was better off not knowing – and from Magnus, who would have started carping about 'that fellow' all over again. He did tell Luke, though he didn't show him the letters and swore him to secrecy.

But Vilia and Perry had met only twice, once at that dratted ball, and once, according to Magnus, at Ascot. Why load his letters, long enough already, with information about someone she scarcely knew?

The first note came in the summer of 1818, brought from Canada to Liverpool in the baggage of an acquaintance, and posted on from there. It was brief. The voyage, Perry said, had been trying, and by the time the brig had made its landfall, forty passengers had been dead of typhus and a dozen others of acute dysentery. The *Rapido* had not lived up to its name.

Nova Scotia is not unlike the Highlands, but I don't think I was made to break virgin soil. I moved over to Montreal after the first winter, but am finding it difficult to make progress. Everything is in the hands of the early-established settlers, who form a kind of aristocracy and grant favours only to those and such as those. It is, you must agree, a neat irony that I, with my background, should for the first time be on the receiving end of this kind of condescension. The biter bit, in effect. I wish I had been here a few years ago, when smuggling from Canada to the United States was quite *de rigueur*. As it is, I have been trading in furs from the west, but that will almost at once come to an end, for it looks as if free Canadian access to that part of the fur country is to be forbidden, and besides, a new convention has at last decided where the western boundary between Canada and the States should lie – along the 49th parallel, if you care! – which will take all the spice out of life. Undelineated borders have their uses.

Mungo sniffed to himself, a little disapprovingly, and it was almost as if Perry had anticipated his reaction.

So it will, no doubt, please you to know that I am about to decamp for New York, where I hope to find some more congenial, respectable, and perhaps even rewarding occupation. I must only add that I will never cease to be grateful for your kindness and understanding during my last weeks in the old country. When opportunity offers, I will write again. Please give my kindest wishes to anyone who will find them acceptable!

It was more than two years before the next letter arrived. Mungo hadn't replied to the first, because there had been no return address, though that wasn't surprising.

It may amuse you to know that I have become a drummer. No, not that kind! A drummer here is a kind of salesman, and most of them inhabit the narrow and – in more senses than one – exceedingly crooked thoroughfare known as Pearl Street, New York, which is where importers and store keepers from all over the country do their buying and selling. The store keepers come into town every year, or every few years, to do their stocking up, and are recognizable from a mile away by their well cared for but exceedingly antiquated Sunday-go-to-meeting clothes and their cowhide boots, which are cut to a pattern that compromises between right foot and left foot, so that one may pull on whichever boot comes to hand first. Convenient, you must admit, if not precisely elegant. I have decided that I like America.

Anyway, to cut a long story short, I discovered that this country has no equivalent of the commercial travellers with whom we are so familiar at home, those rubicund old gentlemen in their top hats and brass-buttoned coats, with samples in their saddlebags and whips in their hands, who had begun to penetrate even into the glens by the time I left. It seemed to me that the American backwoods might welcome a travelling 'drummer', and since the only saleable objects of which I have any worthwhile knowledge happen to be guns, I have become a gun salesman. Everyone here, outside the cities, needs a gun, if only to fill the pot, and most appear to be made by local blacksmiths. Even so, there are some fine gunsmiths, and I have an arrangement with a man in Pennsylvania for selling his Kentucky rifles, which, like Ezekiel Baker's, are based on the old German jaeger. I hope soon to be able to offer a new kind of hand gun, too, a version of the pistol made by a man named Collier, with a revolving cylinder that fires five shots before it needs reloading. The future, I think, is promising, though my profits are still very small.

Mungo was pleased. It sounded as if the laddie was settled into something at last, and even if it didn't sound over-respectable at the moment, what did that matter? Charlotte would have a fit at the thought of her husband becoming a commercial traveller!

How much I would like to have news of you! But I move from inn to inn around the country, sleeping on the floor to avoid the bedbugs – which are omnipresent – and jouncing along in my buggy over roads surfaced with cross-laid tree trunks so that they resemble corduroy to the eye, if not to the base of one's spine. I have no settled address to give you. Nor are the store keepers who act as postmasters very enthusiastic about holding letters for a recipient who may not turn up for a year or so to claim his mail and pay the postal dues!

Pray give my kindest remembrances to Luke, and also to Charlotte, if you think they will be acceptable. I find it difficult to credit that little Grace must be eight years old by now. Strange to think that my only child is growing up half a world away. Strange and sad. Knowing that so much of the fault was mine doesn't make it easier, however much I try to think of the past as water under the bridge. The present, however, has its own interest and challenge, so I don't repine too much. My warmest regards to yourself, of course.

Mungo sighed. Such a waste! He was past his eightieth birthday now and thought that probably he'd never see Perry Randall again, which was a pity, as he'd a soft spot for the boy. It was a pity, too, that there

227

was no way to write and tell him he had *two* daughters growing up half a world away. Or perhaps it wasn't. Perhaps it was better for him not to know.

Chapter Two

1

His Majesty was no fool, and it was clear to Vilia that he had a shrewd idea of what that old harridan, Lady Saltoun, was cackling about. Her ladyship, hearing that he had appeared at his Edinburgh levée in the full glory of a kilt, had remarked that, 'since his stay will be so short, the more we see of him the better.' She had been repeating this sally to everyone she met ever since – including, a few moments ago, young Mrs Lauriston, who had heard it before. As also, to judge by the look in the royal eye, had HM King George IV.

The king smiled charmingly at Lady Saltoun and then transferred the smile to Vilia. 'Mistress Lauriston?' he said. 'Our lady ironmaster? I find it hard to believe. There are other ladies present whom I could much more readily envisage in that role.' His eyes didn't even flicker.

Vilia dropped into a straight-backed curtsey. Not even when she was having to swallow a giggle at this stout and engaging roué would she bend her neck to a member of the House of Hanover, which had usurped the throne of the Stewarts. 'You Majesty is too kind,' she murmured formally.

He drew her a little aside, and his entourage moved tactfully out of earshot. Everyone knew that he was susceptible to a pretty woman, especially a fair-haired one. His voice, however, was more serious than anything else when he said, 'How charmingly you look! Perhaps I may ask *you* what I have been meaning to ask my friend Scott. Why do more ladies not wear the tartan? You are the only one, and with all the gentlemen so splendidly clad, it seems a pity.' He smiled again, disarmingly. 'You mustn't think that because I choose to wear civilian clothes this evening, I don't admire the kilt! But a monarch is supposed to be easily seen in the crowd, and what can he do, when all his subjects are so gaily dressed that they quite take the shine out of him, but go to the other extreme? Though I confess to feeling like a crow in an assemblage of peacocks!'

He was really very appealing. Vilia knew that he relied on charm of personality to compensate for his flaws of character, but the charm was real enough. She twinkled at him. 'You may be sure, Sire, that most of the gentlemen here tonight are wishing they had been sensible enough to follow your example.'

'No! Do you mean that?'

'Of course. I imagine they're all feeling the draught quite dreadfully.' It was a slightly daring thing to say, but she didn't think His Majesty would be offended.

He wasn't. 'Since the whole of Edinburgh seems to know that I wore flesh-coloured tights under my kilt last week,' he said with a chuckle, 'I am hardly in a position to comment, am I? But I thought these people wore the kilt all the time. Has Scott – Walter Scott, you know – been misleading me?'

Vilia couldn't very well say that this was precisely what Scott had been doing. With the aid of General David Stewart of Garth, Sir Walter had been largely responsible for designing the ceremonial for this 1822 royal visit to Edinburgh. Not a monarch had been near the place for a hundred and fifty years, and no one had the remotest idea what to do when the newly crowned king announced his intention of remedying the situation. The provost and bailies, in a panic, had gone running to Scott, thinking that he – the still 'anonymous' author of those highly successful antiquarian romances, the *Waverley* novels – probably knew more than anyone about the intricacies of Scottish history and tradition. They had been right, in a sense. It was just that Scott's view of the past was rather highly coloured. When the programme for the visit was made public, there was a great deal of muttering among the Lowland gentry. All those bagpipes and kilts and tartans! The douce folk of Edinburgh and Glasgow, with justice on their side, had pointed out that these were things that belonged to the Highlands, which represented a diminishing and increasingly unimportant section of the nation. But almost at once a strange chemical change had taken place, so that even the unemotional Lowland breast had begun to swell in contemplation of the picturesqueness of it all.

Scott's house on Castle Street was besieged not only by the bailies, but by Highland chiefs as proud of their bloodline as any Bourbon and a good deal readier to defend it. It had fallen to Scott to mediate in the struggle to decide which of them was to have precedence in the royal escort from Leith to the Canongate. With bated breath, Edinburgh's citizens waited to discover which wild cateran was to march nearest to the king's majesty. The chiefs had already agreed that their position vis-à-vis His present Majesty should be based on the positions held by their clans at the battle of Bannockburn five hundred years earlier, when a previous Majesty had been well trounced and sent back to England with his tail between his legs. It wasn't the most tactful yardstick, perhaps, but none of the protagonists cared for that. The trouble was that there was only clan tradition to say which clan had been where on that fateful day in 1314, and the battle came near to being fought all over again in Castle Street as the chiefs tried to establish their own claims to glory. If it hadn't been for Scott, no one would have wagered a groat on a peaceful settlement.

It was all very entertaining. So were Garth's manoeuvres with the Celtic Club, a society of young civilians bent on rehabilitating the kilt, which had been banned for half a century after the 'Forty-five and was no longer much worn, even in the Highlands. Edinburgh's citizens gaped while the general drilled his plaided platoons in magnificent style, and began to think there might be something to be said for ancient splendours.

The net result was that the tartan weavers of Killin and Stirling and Tillicoultry, accustomed to keeping their looms going on orders from the Highland regiments, had been swamped. It scarcely mattered that the tally sticks recording the traditional setts had, in most cases, been destroyed long ago. Tartans the people of Edinburgh wanted, and tartans – however uncanonical – they were determined to have, and by the mile. Even Scott himself, who had to go back to a great-grandmother to justify his right to wear it, began to appear in the blue, green and black of the Campbells.

The king, blinded all the way from Leith to Holyroodhouse, had come to the understandable conclusion that tartans and kilts were the national dress, and no one had disabused him of the idea. He had always had a weakness for the exotic. He had been deeply disappointed, therefore, to find all the ladies as conventionally clad in lace and satin, plumes and pearls, as if he had still been at home in

London. Except for the decorative Mrs Lauriston. He wasn't to know quite how deliberate that was.

Vilia raised her voice above the strathspey. 'I imagine Sir Walter wanted you to see Scotland at its most colourful. But, you know, the kilt and the plaid are really outdoor garments. You can adjust them in all kinds of ways, depending on whether you want to keep your shoulders warm, or your head dry, or to protect something you're carrying. Even so, in my own part of the Highlands the men prefer to wear trews for fishing, and there's no reason why a city merchant should wear the kilt and plaid at all.'

He took her point. 'Yes, I see. But the tartan is very attractive. Why don't the ladies wear it? I haven't seen more than an occasional sash over gowns that might have been made in London, except for your own. Most striking!'

2

It had certainly struck Lucy Telfer speechless earlier that evening. Lucy had almost forgotten Vilia's attitude towards fashion.

Long before anyone had known of the royal visit, Magnus had hired a house in Edinburgh for the whole of August. He and Lucy had been living with Mungo at Kinveil for almost two years, but Luke was going up to Oxford, and Lucy – always delighted for an excuse to leave the Highlands – had persuaded her husband and father-in-law that it was necessary, quite essential, in fact, for the boy to be taken somewhere civilized to do some final cramming, see his tailor, and have a last, mild schoolboy fling. She would have preferred London, of course, but one simply couldn't be seen in town in August, and besides, the St James's Square house, now rarely used, had been rented for three years to a French diplomat.

'Truly providential!' she exclaimed to Vilia. 'For if Magnus had not been so beforehand with the world – as one must confess he always is – it would have been quite impossible to find a lodging. I don't believe there can be a garret in the city that isn't overflowing with people come to see the king. No, don't sit down, my dear – stand back and let me look at you. How very provoking you are! You are still as slim as you were when you first came to live with us – how many years ago? – eleven, I suppose. While *I* – well, *plump* is the only word for it!'

'Fair of flesh,' Vilia laughed. 'And there would be no justice in the world if you didn't pay *some* penalty for your sweet tooth! But it suits you, so why complain? Indeed, you are looking very well, as if the Highland air agrees with you.'

Lucy's eyes dilated. 'Highland air? If only there weren't so much of it!'

'At least you can't say it's dull. Think how boring it would be if the weather just sat around doing nothing all the time.'

'But I enjoy being dull. Why do you think I visit so many of my friends in the south, if not to get away from all that energetic blowing and raining and shining and sleeting? My only regret is that we always seem to have been away when you've had time to snatch a few days at Kinveil. Such bad luck! But, Vilia, do sit down and talk to me while Sibbald finishes my hair, and tell me all the things you haven't put in your letters.'

Obediently, Vilia sat down on the edge of a chaise longue and embarked on a highly edited version of her recent career at the foundry, perfectly aware that Lucy had asked out of the generosity of her heart rather than from any real desire to know. Lucy would never understand – just as Vilia herself couldn't – the strange pull the place had come to exert on her, so that at the same time she could hate it and yet still have a fierce sense of pride in its achievements. It had taken her six years of struggle to establish everything on a sound footing, against odds that, at first, had seemed impossible. Young, ignorant, inexperienced, she had found herself managing a business brutally hard hit by the post-war depression that was sending many other businesses to the wall, and the ironworks had staggered from crisis to crisis from 1816 until just last year, when things had begun gradually to improve. That Lauriston's had managed to survive was due almost entirely to Vilia's decision to expand the production of beams, plates, and pipes and other simple castings for bridges and heavy machinery. If the foundry had remained wedded to 'nice iron bars', it would have gone under, for competition in that market had become cut-throat. But now Lauriston's had its own small reputation for accurate casting, quality iron, and reliable delivery, and Vilia knew that most of it had been her doing. She was, justifiably, pleased with herself, even if she felt sometimes as if she had been building the Colossus of Rhodes, single-handed.

Lucy, a smile on her face and appreciative exclamations tripping from her tongue as occasion seemed to require, watched the younger woman covertly in the glass. Unbelievably, it was seven years since they had met, seven years since Vilia had left London in the August after Waterloo and Andrew Lauriston's death. Lucy had thought, then, how strange it was that she should have driven out of their lives looking as pale, exhausted, and black-clad as when she had driven in. The pretty, frivolous interregnum of the Season, and the brief marriage which had given her a touchingly youthful maturity, were almost as if they had never been.

She was very different now, exquisite, self-contained, and at twenty-six approaching the height of her beauty. Yet, watching the play of expression on the fine features, Lucy felt there was something lacking. Suddenly, she remembered the day at Ascot when they had both put some money on the royal horse – whatever its name was – and it had won, and Vilia had been so excited that it was almost as if she had been lit up inside. She was talking vivaciously now, and smiling, and making her management of the foundry sound really quite amusing, but the spontaneous warmth had gone. Lucy sighed to herself. Vilia wasn't holding her at arm's length as she had done during those first months at St James's Square eleven years ago, but Lucy was still reminded of the curious impression she had had then, as if Vilia were some detached observer from another planet.

'. . . and so I coaxed contracts out of Tom Cubitt for some of his houses in Bloomsbury, and from James Burton for St Leonard's-on-Sea – which he is hoping to transfigure – and your father-in-law invested in the moulds, and we have now begun casting area and balcony rails. The canopies, I fear, are beyond us.'

'How splendid,' Lucy said. 'But how on earth do you find time for anything else? What about the boys?'

'I see them before I leave in the mornings, and they are old enough now to stay up until I come home in the evening. On Sundays, we have all afternoon together.' Catching Lucy's expression, she added, 'They see as much of me as most children do of their parents – a good deal more than I ever saw of my father! Besides, they enjoy Sorley's company much more than mine. He is very good with them, and takes charge of them a good deal of the time. I assure you, Lucy, they are doing very well!'

'Are they downstairs? Then they'll have met the other children by now.'

'The other children?'

'Oh, yes! Charlotte's girls were so anxious to see His Majesty that I could scarcely do other than bring them, especially as the house is so spacious. Even with you and the boys, there's still room to spare. But thank heavens Edward decided not to come! *Such* a stuffy boy. Charlotte hasn't been well, and he felt it his duty to stay with her. Very commendable, of course.' Lucy's voice was hollow, and Vilia laughed. 'Though just between ourselves, I should have thought she would feel better for a rest from him. What could I say, though? He *is* nineteen, and one can hardly order him about like a child. So we have Luke – and Henry Phillpotts, of course – and the three girls, and their governess. Dreadful woman! I can't imagine why Charlotte employs her. Georgiana and Grace suffer her reasonably well, but poor little Shona – such a sensitive child – is quite miserable.'

'Shona?'

'Poor little lamb, she's so much the odd child out. I hate to say it, but' – Lucy's voice dropped – 'Charlotte does treat her so distantly, and it's distressing because the unfortunate mite very badly wants to be loved. You'll see what I mean when we go downstairs.'

When Vilia entered the parlour an hour later, its only occupants were the children, lined up – tallest to smallest – in a row against the wall, measuring themselves and quarrelling amicably the while. Luke, eighteen and no longer a child, had cloudy brown hair and sleepy eyes, and the stringy build of a boy who had grown too quickly. He overtopped fourteen-year-old Georgiana by a foot. Mungo had said once that Georgy should have been Perry Randall's child, and Grace George Blair's, and Vilia could see what he had meant. Georgiana had bright, brown impertinent eyes and looked as if she might be something of a handful, whereas Grace's neat features and compressed rosebud lips suggested that she was a very proper young lady indeed.

Next to Grace were Vilia's three boys, as neatly stepped as if some architect had measured them out. Theo, eight, Gideon seven, and Drew six – all born in March, all of them slender and fair and self-possessed, although Drew was darker than his brothers and his hazel eyes had more sparkle. His nature, too, was more vivid, more demanding, asking always for the love Vilia hesitated to give, and perfectly sure that all he needed to do was find the right way to ask.

With a deliberate effort of will, Vilia transferred her gaze from Drew to little Shona Randall, the last in the line. Vilia smiled at her, and she smiled shyly back, pretty and brown-haired and unremarkable, and resembling Drew not at all.

Laughing, Vilia said, 'Hello, children. No tutor, or governess, no Aunt Lucy? I wonder they dare leave you alone!'

They were all a little drunk on fresh air and excitement after watching the king review his troops earlier in the day, and eager to tell her about it. Their voices came tumbling over one another as they competed for her attention. 'We watched from the Mound, just as you told us, Mama,' said Theo, his eyes wide and virtuous, and Georgiana chimed in belligerently, 'We saw it from the esplanade, and we watched them marching off afterwards, from the hill at the West Bow, just where they've demolished the old Weigh-house.' She stopped. Mrs Lauriston's beautiful green eyes, which had been surveying her amusedly, had suddenly gone out of focus. Then little Drew rushed across to grasp his mother's hand possessively. Gazing up at her in admiration, he piped, 'Oh, Mama! How pretty you look. Prettier than anyone!' After a long moment, she blinked and then smiled faintly. Ruffling his hair, she said, 'Thank you, darling. Now, isn't it time you younger ones were thinking of supper and bed?'

Just then, the door opened to admit Lucy, with Henry Phillpotts and a woman whom Vilia assumed to be the Glenbraddan governess in her wake.

'Vilia!' Lucy gasped.

Vilia was aware that she made a striking figure. Indeed, she had designed her gown for the Peers' ball with precisely that object in mind, for she was unblushingly determined to make an impression on a monarch famous not only for his philandering, but for his taste in architecture and active promotion of a number of highly ambitious building projects. She was a businesswoman, and royal favour was valuable in business. It seemed to her that they ought to get on very well together, His Majesty being notoriously short of money, and Lauriston's new line in architectural cast ironwork being not only as stylish as the ordinary kind, but a good deal cheaper as well. Before she

235

could enrol him as an ally, however, it was necessary to attract his attention, and she thought that might not be easy at a ball attended by the flower of Scotland. She could rely on Glengarry to present her, if necessary – for Glengarry, by sheer force of personality, had made the most profound impression on any number of impressionable people – but there had to be something to lead on from there.

The answer had been obvious enough once the style of the celebrations had been made public. Vilia knew that every lady at the ball, terrified of being thought provincial, would be gowned in modish tulle or lace or satin, in pink or violet, jonquil or blue, milk chocolate or London smoke, and dripping with pearls or rubies or garnets. So she had looked long and consideringly at a portrait of one of her ancestors, painted two hundred years before, and had decided that, as a model, it would do very well.

The final version was cut on the simplest lines, with a low, round neck, the waist at natural level, and the skirt slender and gracefully draped. The sleeves were long, close-fitting, and deeply cuffed, and made of fine, almost transparent muslin to give a touch of evening formality to what might otherwise have been regarded as an insufficiently *grande toilette*. There were no scallops, no slashings, no braids, no rouleaux to spoil the perfect simplicity of the ensemble, which depended entirely for its effect on the fabric, which, of course, was in the Cameron tartan – a bright clear red, with narrow quadruple overchecks of myrtle green, and a fine yellow thread running through at wide intervals; the muslin of the sleeves was of plain scarlet. Vilia's crowning inspiration had been the wide belt that clasped her waist. Correctly, it should have been of leather, studded with silver ornaments, but she had recently installed a small melting-chamber at the foundry for some experiments with steel, and it had given her a good deal of amusement to set the steel man the problem of producing her an elegant belt. It was constructed of two-inch square panels with cut-out designs based on old Celtic forms, linked together with tiny interlocking rings. The result was light and delicate, and very handsome indeed, and the drop earrings, on a smaller scale, pleased Vilia no less.

Lucy said again, '*Vilia!*'

'Do you like it?' She twirled round gracefully. 'I really think it is quite successful.'

'It's certainly very – er – it's very . . .'

236

'Thank you, Lucy,' Vilia said melodiously. 'I knew you would feel just as you should.' Then, a little dubiously, she glanced at her reticule, a simple scarlet pouch gathered into a polished steel frame. 'But do you think . . . ? I am really not sure about this. I wonder if I shouldn't, after all, have had it made in the form of a small sporran?' But the sight of Lucy's face was too much for her, and she went off into a peal of laughter. 'Oh, Lucy! When will you learn not to take me so seriously? But admit it – the gown *is* becoming, isn't it?'

'Oh, my goodness, *of course* it is. You look superb. But – you don't think perhaps a little dashing? It's not that I wish to criticize, dearest, but it's hardly the kind of quiet good style one expects of a lady of breeding.'

'I should hope not! I don't wish to be quiet, I wish to be memorable!'

After five minutes' conversation with His Majesty, she knew that he would remember her. He had little real power in the world of affairs, although he was quite able to block legislation that offended him, but his influence on taste was considerable. As reel followed strathspey, and country dance followed reel, he remained at her side, delighted to find a pretty woman who could carry on an intelligent and well-informed conversation about things that interested him. When, at last, one of his retinue murmured a reminder in his ear about the others still waiting for the favour of his gracious attention, he smiled at Vilia and drew a plump forefinger conspiratorially down the side of his nose.

'I – uh – will shortly be having some repairs put in hand at Royal Lodge – at Windsor, you know? I would enjoy knowing that the ironwork had been supplied by such a charming lady. I'll talk to Wyatt about it.' He paused, thinking. 'There's my little menagerie at Sandpit Gate, too. Nothing dangerous, just a few wapitis and gazelles and chamois. Railings for the animals not beneath you, I hope? Dear little things, they are. Well, I won't make any promises. You might not think so, but kings aren't always their own masters, any more than commoners. But we'll see, we'll see.'

She curtsied to him, the lovely green eyes sparkling mischievously, and he bowed, his Cumberland corset creaking a little, and moved off. He'd done a good deal for her already, singling her out for attention in full view of most of Scotland's leading citizens, and Vilia knew – as did His Majesty – that such royal interest would almost certainly bring

Lauriston's a rush of orders. Exultantly, she blessed the gown that had started it all.

3

The gown had started something else, too, although it was to be years before Vilia discovered it.

Luke Telfer, to his own extreme astonishment, had taken a single look at her when she walked into the parlour of the house in Edinburgh and had fallen head over heels in love.

He recognized, on reflection, that it wasn't perhaps quite as surprising as it seemed to him at first. Everything during his childhood and adolescence had conspired to make him dislike her. There had been the awkward, unbridgeable gap of eight years' difference in age. There had been Luke's own jealousy of the intruder, and what he had always seen as Vilia's arrogance – her resistance to his mother's early attempts at friendship, her dramatization of mourning, her claim to emotional rights over Kinveil. And during her Season, when she had been brilliant, admired, and adult, he had still been a child. After that, he had seen very little of her, except for those few days in October 1814 and again, eighteen months later in Duncan Lauriston's house, when she had been a wan, spiritless, heavily pregnant widow, dressed once more in the funereal black that so ill became her. The day after that particular encounter, his grandfather had sent him briskly off to London, saying that he had enough to worry about without having Luke under his feet, and in London he had stayed for most of the time since then, even, for the sake of his education, after his parents had taken up residence at Kinveil. His visits to Kinveil had never coincided with Vilia's, and he had the uneasy feeling that this was by his grandfather's design. The old man wanted Vilia to himself. In the eyes of someone as possessive as Luke, this had been another sin to set down to Vilia's account.

But in the six years since they had met, the age gulf had suddenly been bridged. Whereas the difference between twelve and twenty had been great, the difference between eighteen and twenty-six seemed nothing at all. It was, he thought, a matter no longer of years but only of self-assurance. And that was something that could be rectified.

His jealousy of her was forgotten almost as if it had never been.

He had just sufficient sense to recognize that he was at a peculiarly susceptible age, but he would have defied any man – he who had seldom considered her more than averagely pretty – to withstand Vilia when she walked into the room on the evening of the Peers' ball, looking, in her scarlet-sleeved gown, like some mediaeval portrait come dazzlingly to life. She was beautiful, vital, breathtaking, and it was only after ten stupefied minutes that Luke realized, with horror, that for her the gulf was still there and that she still thought of him as one of the children.

Next morning, after a night during which he had slept scarcely at all but dreamed without cease, he set about putting things to rights. By lying in wait on the stairs, he was able to catch her alone. Even in her simple, olive-green carriage dress she was still radiant, and it was obvious that everything had gone well at the ball.

She smiled at him. 'You're very dashing, Luke! What height are you now? A good deal taller than when we last met!' It was precisely what every adult always said to a growing boy.

He treated her to his carefully cultivated, nonchalant grin and, consciously deepening his voice, drawled, 'Tall enough to hold my own at Oxford.' Then he allowed his eyelids to droop in a man-of-the-world way, and said, 'It has been a long time, hasn't it?'

She twinkled at him, and he hoped her amusement was only at what he hadn't quite said. 'And we are both older, and wiser, and more tolerant now? Yes. Perhaps we should start again.'

He was annoyed to feel himself flushing. 'Why not? Will we see more of you while we are in Edinburgh?'

'I doubt it. Your mother and I are just leaving for Marchfield House now. I assume you know she is having a sabbatical and staying with me until Monday? But after that . . . No one ever does me the favour of believing it, but I do go to my office every day like any other hardworked manufacturer, and not even His Majesty offers a sufficiently compelling reason for me to abandon my desk for more than forty-eight hours.'

His heart in his boots, he said, 'What a pity. But perhaps – might the official opening of the Caledonian Canal qualify as a compelling reason? It's on the twenty-somethingth of October.'

She laughed. 'It might, though I don't expect to be asked. I imagine

239

the Commissioners will invite only landed proprietors to sail on the opening voyage.'

'My grandfather will be invited, but he says he's too old to spend two days *voluntarily* being rained on, so he's sending me instead.'

'You? Not your father?'

Luke's shout of laughter had already begun to echo round the stair-well before he realized how juvenile it sounded. Swiftly recovering himself, he said in a very superior tone, 'My dear Vilia, can you see papa feeling at home among all those local worthies? It wouldn't be his kind of occasion at all. In fact, he has already made a whole string of engagements in London for the end of October, just to be sure the risk doesn't arise.'

A little drily, she asked, 'And you? Can Oxford manage without you?'

'Who cares? Do come, Vilia. Grandfather has promised we'll make a real occasion of it!'

But she wouldn't commit herself. She didn't know how desperate her need of Kinveil was going to be by then.

Chapter Three

1

Vilia was still glowing with a kind of amused self-satisfaction when she swept Lucy off that afternoon to spend the weekend at Marchfield House, a prospect which Lucy viewed almost with beatitude, although she took good care to conceal it from Magnus and the children. Lucy quite enjoyed children in small numbers and small doses, but a house full of them for a month was too much. Hurriedly, she fished in her reticule for a handkerchief, and found it just in time to trap a small, refined, but unmistakable sneeze.

Vilia, glancing at her, said, 'Bless you!'

Lucy didn't think Magnus would miss her much. Tonight he was attending the dinner given by the provost and corporation, and tomorrow he thought he might look in at St Giles, where His Majesty was to attend divine service. The children wouldn't miss her, either, as

Vilia had left the boys to become better acquainted with their honorary cousins. Lucy sighed. The only one who had found fault with this admirable arrangement had been Grace, who knew how her mother felt about Mrs Lauriston and made it clear to Aunt Lucy that she thought it morally wrong of her to permit the two families to be thrown together, which would greatly upset Mama when she heard of it. Regretfully, Lucy had to admit that she did not care very much for Grace. Pretty cool, for a ten-year-old girl to criticize her aunt! For a moment, Lucy felt all of her thirty-seven years, but then, catching Vilia's mood, gave a mental shrug of the shoulders and an airy, 'Pooh!' which merged almost at once into another and more definitive 'Atchoo!'

'Have you caught cold?' Vilia asked concernedly.

'Oh, no. No! It's just this dreary weather. Atchoo!'

The rain had gone off by the time they reached Marchfield House, and Lucy's sneezes had temporarily abated. Descending from the smart green barouche, she looked round with interest. 'But you led me to believe the house was quite dowdy! My dear, it's nothing of the sort. So simple and stylish.'

'It looks better than it did. I've had a few things done these last eighteen months since the foundry began to show a profit. The stables and coach house used to be separate from the main block, but those new walls linking them to the main house make everything look more of a piece. The doors and windows in the walls are *trompe l'oeil*, of course. Come along and see the inside. It's quite civilized.'

She stopped as they heard a faint scuffling noise, and then smiled as a neatly built, sleek little black cat came streaking across the grass, uttering sounds that made Lucy think of a rusty hinge, and evincing the clearest intention of scrambling up its mistress's corded olive-green skirts. Vilia said 'No!' very firmly, and the cat sat down with a thump at her feet and fixed her with a look of injured innocence.

'Heavens!' Lucy exclaimed. 'Whoever heard of a cat doing what it's told?'

Vilia smiled again. 'It's a confidence trick, though who is playing the confidence trick on whom I have never been able to decide.' She picked the little animal up, dusted off its paws, and then tucked it, purring vigorously, in the crook of her elbow.

The butler had the front door open, waiting. His bright blue eyes scanned his mistress's face, and then passed on to her friend, sweet-faced, brown-haired, and fashionably attired in tints of azure and gold, with a fetching hat perched over her forehead that made her look like a plump little blue tit.

'There iss a chentleman waiting to see you, mistress,' he said.

'Gracious me! On a Saturday? Who is it?'

'He would not giff me his name, mistress, but he says you will be knowing him.'

Her eyebrows rose. 'How very mysterious! Quite Gothic, in fact. Where is he, Angus? Has he been waiting long?'

'Ferry near an hour. I put him in the parlour.'

Vilia turned. 'You don't mind, Lucy? I had better see who it is.'

Lucy shook her head and blinked, trying to suppress a resurrected sneeze.

Vilia moved towards the parlour, her gloved hand still teasing the nape of the Duchess's neck, but she had scarcely taken three steps when the door was opened from within and the figure of a man, tall and athletically built, appeared on the threshold.

Vilia stopped as suddenly as if she had walked into a sheet of glass.

For a moment, Lucy's watering eyes could see the man only as a silhouette, and then her vision cleared and she said, 'Oh!' She herself had no idea whether it was amazement or horror that was dominant.

The silence held for what seemed an eternity, and then Vilia and Perry Randall both spoke at once.

'I hope you . . .' he began.

'Why, Mr Randall!' Vilia said on a descending note. 'What a surprise.'

She wasn't smiling, and neither was Perry Randall. He had always been handsome, and he still was, but there, as far as Lucy could see, the resemblance ended. She remembered him as graceful and humorous, in a careless way, and very *approachable*. But now . . . If she hadn't been so concerned about her cold, Lucy thought she might well have succumbed to a spasm. This new Perry Randall was sinewy-looking, taut, and deeply tanned, and the sardonic lines that bracketed his mouth looked as if they had been cut with a chisel. His tailoring was certainly not English. In fact, he looked quite *foreign*, and there was a hard resilience about him that Lucy found little short of alarming.

He bowed slightly. 'Mrs Lauriston. And Mrs Telfer. I hope you will forgive me for not standing on ceremony, but I am in Scotland only for a few days and thought you might not mind my plaguing you for news of old friends.'

The cat wriggled suddenly in Vilia's arms, as if in protest, and made to clamber up on her shoulder, but she disentangled its claws and set it gently down on the floor. It scampered off towards the stairs, sat down, glared, and then settled to an urgent wash and brush up. Perry Randall watched it thoughtfully, but said nothing.

A trifle absently, Vilia smoothed down the threads of the *gros de Naples* where the cat's claws had caught them, and then said, 'I will be happy to tell you anything I can. You are fortunate that Mrs Telfer is staying with me until Monday. Her news from – from Glenbraddan and Kinveil is more recent than mine. But perhaps, having waited an hour, you would wait a little longer while we rid ourselves of the dust of travel? Angus, I assume you have already offered Mr Randall some refreshment, but Mrs Telfer and I would like tea in half an hour. Mr Randall?'

'Please. After seven years of coffee and rum, I can't tell you what a pleasure it is to be offered tea again.'

Vilia's smile didn't reach her eyes.

Somewhat more than half an hour later, having taken as long as she decently could, Lucy entered the parlour to find Mr Randall still in solitary possession. She could scarcely retreat, so, sitting down and making a great play of arranging her soft blue skirts, she said politely, 'We had quite given you up, Mr Randall.' Her voice sounded dreadfully gummy, and her mind and stomach were both churning; colds in the head always had the most unfortunate effect on her digestion. Almost at random, she went on, 'Is Nova Scotia quite uncivilized, as one hears?' and then blushed hotly. That was always the trouble when one spoke without thinking. She hoped it hadn't sounded too much like a criticism of his appearance.

He was as tall as Magnus, and she wished that he would sit down, too. But he was looking puzzled rather than offended, as if she had posed him some vastly intricate problem. After a moment he said, 'As a matter of fact, I left Nova Scotia several years ago and went on to Montreal, and then to New York. I have been out on the fringes of the new territories since then.' Suddenly he smiled at her, with all the old, blinding charm. 'The postal system there isn't very good.'

'Isn't it?'

'There are twenty-four states, and they all have different systems. And none of them likes cooperating with the others.'

'Dear me! Almost as if they were different countries?' He nodded. She could feel another sneeze coming on, but managed to say, 'How inconvenient!' before it overtook her.

Perry had forgotten what a very nice person she was. He smiled again, and began to say something, but the door opened just then to admit a maid with a tray, followed by the butler. Vilia entered on their heels.

'I apologize for taking so long,' she said coolly. 'A slight crisis in the kitchen.'

Lucy noticed, reproachfully, that she had taken time to change into a figured morning dress that was much more modish than anything Lucy possessed. And one that hadn't been precisely cheap, either.

'So,' Vilia said, dispensing tea. 'You've been in Canada, have you, Mr Randall?'

Again, the puzzlement shadowed his brow. 'Not for some time. I removed to America a few years ago, and have just been explaining to Mrs Telfer how unreliable the postal system is there.'

'Indeed!'

Lucy cast her a startled glance.

Perry Randall's jaw tightened. 'And, of course, I am travelling all the time – I sell guns, you see – and I have no settled address where mail can be sure of reaching me.'

'*Sell* guns?' Vilia said. 'Do you find it a profitable occupation?' Her eyes flickered over Mr Randall's tailoring in a way that was nothing short of insulting.

Lucy snatched for her handkerchief. She would never have believed that Vilia could be so rude.

In the hall, Lucy had been stunned to realize that, whatever there had been between Vilia and Perry Randall in the past, it hadn't been simple acquaintance. There had flashed into her clogged mind, like a pencil of sunlight bursting through a bank of cloud, the thought that Charlotte had been right after all. But now she was not so sure. From the way they were talking to each other, it sounded more like acute dislike than love. And yet even acute dislike couldn't have developed – could it? – over a mere two or three casual encounters. What *would*

Charlotte say if she knew he was here! And Magnus! Lucy closed her eyes and wished the world would end. She sneezed violently.

'Are you cold, Lucy?'

She opened her eyes again. 'Dho! I beanh dho!'

'Oh, Lucy!' Vilia exclaimed with a forced laugh. 'What you mean is, you mean no! I don't believe you. I'll have the fire lit at once, and as soon as you have swallowed your tea I think you should retire to bed.'

Lucy shook her head, and said, 'Dho! I'm berfectly all right, dank you.'

She couldn't concentrate on Perry Randall talking about his experiences in the backwoods of America – he couldn't be a *commercial traveller*, surely! – while in another corner of her mind Magnus's voice was saying, with a good deal of asperity, 'But you should have walked out of the house! If Vilia Cameron is prepared to entertain him, that's her concern. I won't have you exposed to such a fellow!'

If only Magnus hadn't disliked Mr Randall so much, right from the start. There had been every justification, of course, even before he had crowned his follies by running away from Charlotte. But Lucy had never felt it altogether right of Magnus to have encouraged that rather unpleasant friend of his to demand his dues from the poor young man quite so brutally, so that he had been ruined and had to flee, giving Charlotte another child – of all the mortifying things to happen! – on the way. Though it was, Lucy supposed dismally, perfectly reasonable that Magnus should side with his sister. Lucy had even found it difficult to persuade Magnus that Vilia hadn't been involved in the affair at all, and had succeeded only because her father-in-law had said the same thing, rather more bluntly and a good deal more forcibly. Had they both been wrong?

Tactlessly, she remembered something. 'Is it safe for you to be in this country?' She could have bitten her tongue out.

Fortunately, he didn't seem to mind. 'My debts, you mean? As it happens, I came back to pay them. My business hasn't been entirely unprofitable.' The ironic grey eyes rested on Vilia for a moment. 'But I discovered they had already been settled by Mungo Telfer. He must have done it soon after I sailed, if not before. I've tried to repay him, but he won't have it. He says starving in a garret is all very well, but it's never struck him as the way to build up a good, sound business. To quote, "A wee bit capital's what you need. You can pay me back in your own good time, when you see your way clearer." He's a kind man, and he's been a good friend to me.'

'You've *seen* Mungo?' Vilia's voice was sharp.

'I'm sorry to say, no. I couldn't go to Kinveil without going to Glenbraddan, and the old man thought that would be a mistake. He's probably right. He says his daughter's peace of mind must be his first concern and, besides, he's getting too old to put up with any more family tantrums. From his letter, he seems sorry we won't be able to meet, and so am I. I'm fond of him, and I fear he'll be gone by the time I'm able to make another trip over here.'

She said flatly, 'So you are only on a visit?'

'Yes. I must leave for New York again within the week.' Lucy began to feel brighter. 'Apart from the matter of my debts, I came only to see what London's gunsmiths are doing about the new revolving pistol – whether the future lies with hand-operated or spring-operated cylinders. I have to decide whether to go on as I am, or whether to think of expansion. My plans are fluid.'

Lucy said, with what in another woman might have been a touch of spite, 'My goodness! You are as bad as Vilia. You both make me feel very useless. Did you know, Mr Randall, that Vilia actually runs her late father-in-law's ironworks? We all thought she was out of her senses at first, but she has made *such* a success of it! The king himself talked to her for quite thirty minutes at the Peers' ball yesterday evening, all about the – er – the architectural ironmongery she is producing for those sweet little houses everyone is building nowadays, the kind with balconies and railings, you know? In places like Brighton and London and – St Leonard's, was it, Vilia? And Cheltenham, and so on.' On an afterthought, she added, 'Or don't you have that kind of house in America?' And then her voice trailed off into a suppressed sniffle.

Vilia's smile was weary, but she said nothing.

Perry Randall cleared his throat. 'I only discovered a few months ago that Major Lauriston had lost his life at Waterloo. By the purest chance, I encountered an emigrant who had served with his regiment. Pray accept my condolences, Mrs Lauriston.'

'Thank you.' Her voice, throughout the conversation, had been oddly clipped, as if she were holding herself on a tight, but impatient rein. 'It is very difficult for us to understand how cut off you have been from news of all your friends and acquaintances. America must be an extraordinary place.'

'It is. However . . .'

Lucy couldn't remember ever having sat through such a – such a *sticky* conversation, but she was determined to go on sitting through it to the very end. Obscurely, she felt it was her duty to protect Vilia.

'It seems,' Perry Randall was saying, 'that you have been not unfortunate in your inheritance. I hope the boys are well?'

Vilia had been turning to place her cup on the tray, and the spoon slipped. 'Thank you, yes,' she said, as she retrieved it from the floor.

Lucy was suddenly aware that his gaze had transferred to her, and said hastily, 'Oh, we are all very well, too. Magnus and I live at Kinveil now with my father-in-law . . .'

'Is he in health?'

Magnus or Mungo, Lucy wondered, but only for a moment. 'Oh, quite remarkable. He's eighty-two now, you know, but he shows not the slightest sign of failing, even if he tires more readily than he used to.' The curious thing was that Lucy and her father-in-law, despite what Lucy always thought of as their early 'misunderstandings', got on like a house on fire. He wasn't a gentleman in her sense of the word – in fact there were times when he could be just a little uncouth – and he was opinionated, and not very considerate, and went out of his way to annoy Magnus. She would have been perfectly justified in thinking of his age as a promise of release, but she didn't. She would be genuinely upset when he went.

'And what about – please don't answer if it embarrasses you – my wife?' His attention was focused wholly on her, as if Vilia weren't even in the room.

She was possessed by an inane need to chatter. 'Charlotte? Oh, well enough, in general, though she has some tedious infection at the moment and is confined to bed. But the children are so good with her, especially the girls, which is just what one would expect, of course, isn't it? They all seem to be growing up very quickly. And Edward, of course, is nineteen, though you may find it difficult to believe.' Vilia was looking at her a little oddly, but Lucy had the feeling she was too concerned with her own thoughts to see all the problems that loomed so hideously large and near in Lucy's mind, fuzzy though it might be at this particular moment. Anything to prevent Perry Randall from finding out that the children were only a few miles away! He might insist on seeing them, and Magnus would never forgive her. And Charlotte! She could scarcely bear to contemplate what Charlotte would say, or how frequently she would say it. If the man had really cared about his daughters it might have been different, but he hadn't sent word for seven years, and even now hadn't left himself time to go to Glenbraddan. But of course, father-in-law had said he shouldn't! How complicated it all was. And then, suddenly realizing that Mr Randall probably didn't even know Shona existed, Lucy began to feel a strong desire to faint and have done with it. She couldn't even fall back on Luke with any safety, because she would have to say he was in Edinburgh, and Mr Randall might suggest dropping in on him. And then he might run into Magnus! It was too much for her. She took refuge in a paroxysm of sneezing.

The next hour seemed interminable. Vilia said very little, and Lucy not much more. When pushed, she meandered on about the weather, and the fishing, and the forestry, about which she knew very little, and about the splendid raspberries that old Robbie Fraser grew in the walled garden on the mainland, about which she was better informed. Anything but the children. When she touched on them it was always *en bloc*. She went quite cold when Mr Randall asked specifically about Grace, but he didn't pursue the subject and she was grateful. She decided he must still have some gentlemanly instincts left beneath his uncivilized exterior.

It was a wonderful relief when Perry Randall rose to his feet and said, 'Mrs Lauriston, I have trespassed on your time too long. It was generous of you to receive me. Your servant, Mrs Telfer. I leave Edinburgh on Monday, so we will not meet again. Perhaps you will give my regards to your father-in-law, if you feel they would be kindly received.'

Vilia's hand was on the bell. 'Must you go?' she asked politely, and gave it a decisive tug.

For the first time, laughter flashed into his eyes. 'I must,' he said. 'Thank you again for seeing me.' And then he was gone.

2

Lucy's cold had almost disappeared by the time Magnus arrived to reclaim her on Monday, just before noon, bringing the Lauriston boys and Sorley McClure home with him. She had been grateful, in more ways than one, for her Sunday in bed. It had relieved her of the need to make conversation. Acutely uneasy in mind, she didn't dare talk about Mr Randall, and yet knew that, if she didn't, it would look odd. All she had said to Vilia, and that with some difficulty, had been, 'I don't know what you think, but I would prefer not to mention Mr Randall's visit to anyone. There seems no purpose in reopening old wounds, especially as he appears to have no intention of coming back to this country permanently.' And Vilia had said, with a remote smile, 'I am sure you're right.'

Magnus had to be shown the house and grounds, and persuaded, somewhat against his inclination, to partake of a morsel of luncheon before Vilia was at last able to wave them good-bye. Seeing Magnus again after a gap of years, Vilia was absently surprised to discover how much less middle-aged he appeared. There was only a dozen years' difference in their ages, but it had always felt more. Perhaps it was just that the high-nosed stateliness and bland self-satisfaction that had sat a little incongruously on a man of twenty-seven seemed more natural now that he was only two years away from his fortieth birthday. The years had given him distinction in place of self-consequence, and taken from him some of the fussiness. Though not all of it, for when Lucy displayed a tendency to linger he reminded her testily that they were going to the Caledonian Hunt ball that night and must have an hour or two's rest beforehand.

When they had gone, Vilia set off for the foundry where she spent the afternoon making decisions, swiftly and concisely, that Moultrie or Richards could just as easily have made during her absence. She knew now that she was unlikely ever to bring them to the pitch of accepting responsibility, or to break them of the belief that there was something mysteriously and impenetrably feminine about her own perfectly logical cast of thought. Sometimes it irritated her, but today she could not care.

By the time she arrived home she was unbearably tired, and would have gone straight to bed after her usual hour with the boys except that it would have set the servants wondering. Even the effort of preparing for bed seemed beyond her, in any case, and it was easier just to go on sitting and to ask Mrs McKirdy to bring her something on a tray. She didn't want it, but Mrs McKirdy was determined. 'A vol-au-vent and salad, then,' Vilia said. 'Nothing more.' Mrs McKirdy sighed and went to roll out some of the pastry she mixed fresh every morning and kept in the larder. It was beautiful pastry, for she had the Lowland housewife's light hand with it, but she worried about her mistress eating so little.

Just before nine, Vilia heard a horse coming up the drive and its rider dismounting at the front door. She frowned a little when the knocker clanked. A neighbour? If so, it couldn't be anyone important, for the local notables had all gone to the Caledonian Hunt ball.

After a moment, there was a tap on the drawing-room door and Sorley entered. His narrow eyes were almost apprehensive, and he hesitated, uncharacteristically, before he spoke. 'It iss Mr Randall,' he said, his voice rising as if he couldn't believe it himself. 'He says, will you see him if it iss not too late?'

Sorley didn't know, of course, that Perry Randall had been here on Saturday, but Vilia was too paralysed to remember that. She stared at him, her face as white as the shasta daisies in the vase behind her, and said, 'I . . . I . . . Yes. Ask him to come up, Sorley, please.'

Perry Randall took no more than two steps inside the room while he waited for Sorley to close the door, then he moved back and leaned against it.

'I couldn't just go,' he said, his voice low and uneven. 'Not like that.'

No social courtesies. No polite bows. No artificial apologies. No inquiries after other people's health and welfare. This time it was just the two of them. This time it was real.

'No,' she said expressionlessly. She didn't move from her chair by the fire. As so often in August, the evening was damp and chill, and the fire gave an illusion of warmth and normality. But her blood ran like ice water in her veins.

He couldn't tell what she was thinking or feeling as he stood there gazing at her, all passion and longing ruthlessly excluded from his face in case it should give him away. He had no idea whether her hostility on Saturday had been genuine, or whether it had been a performance for Lucy Telfer's benefit. Seven years ago he would have known, but

250

now he didn't. He only knew that as a performance it had been convincing, and he was afraid.

Her eyes were wide and clear under their long lids, the eyes that had haunted him, waking and sleeping, for seven years. She was more beautiful than he had remembered. Trapped in his memory had been something frail and evanescent, an incorporeal vision of silver-gold hair and pale skin and water-green eyes; and a character that was at once strong and yet desperately vulnerable. The reality was richer and more positive. Her skin looked warmer than it had been, her hair more golden, and her eyes darker and more lustrous. He didn't know whether to set the differences down to a fault of memory or the passage of time. Her face was framed by the white ruffle of the shirt she wore under a gown cut as severely as a riding habit, a gown of the same subtle grey-green as she had worn on that fateful day at Ascot. There was a flush of colour on her cheekbones, and she was looking at him as if he were not welcome.

When the silence had reached its uttermost limit he moved forward and sat down, unbidden, on the chair facing her, his legs crossed and hands loosely clasped on his knee. If she had been on her feet he would have settled everything – he would have *hoped* to settle everything – by taking her forcibly into his arms, but her chair was as effective as a barricade. And perhaps it wouldn't have solved anything very much, anyway.

He would have given all he possessed to feel her body against his, but when he spoke, all that he said, in level tones, was, 'How are you?'

Her delicate brows rose. 'Well enough, thank you.'

'Happy?'

A faint smile flickered across her face. 'What a sweeping question! I have the boys, the foundry, an occasional evening's relaxation, a visit to Kinveil now and then. My life is satisfying enough.'

'That wasn't what I asked.'

'I know it wasn't.'

It seemed she had no intention of making it easy for him. There was a kind of fatality in the air, as if everything had already gone wrong and could never be put right.

He closed his mind to it, and, brushing the familiar, straying lock of dark hair back from his brow, said, 'I owe you a great many apologies.' It wasn't how he would have chosen to begin. If she still loved him, the apologies weren't important; if she didn't, they were irrelevant.

She shook her head.

'But I do, surely?'

She looked away from him and into the heart of the fire. 'I have no patience with apologies. No apology can repair damage that – damage that should not have been done in the first place.' Her voice was cool and empty.

He didn't understand her at first, because it was so unexpected, but then he gave a laugh that might as easily have been a groan. 'You mean that if one behaves decently and properly, no need for apology will ever arise? And if one behaves badly, no apology can rectify it? Well, that's true enough, God knows! But it's a Spartan creed, Vilia. It doesn't leave much space for ordinary human weakness, and none for forgiveness, either.'

She frowned a little. 'I suppose it doesn't. But apologies and excuses have never seemed to me to be anything but a secular substitute for the confessional. Say you're sorry, and your sins will be forgiven you. It's too easy.'

'There are penances.'

'And what help are penances, except to the sinner? They can't bring the dead back to life. They can't put together again the ruins of someone's heart and soul.' She sounded as clinical as if they were engaged on an academic debate.

The chill settled deeper into his bones. He didn't know what he had expected, but it wasn't this deeply rooted, emotionless resistance. It didn't seem possible that someone as loving and vital as the girl of seven years ago should have changed so completely, but if it hadn't been for the animation he had glimpsed on Saturday, before her face had closed down at the sight of him, he might have believed it. Her hostility then, and this evening's flat and total detachment . . . What in God's name had happened in these last seven years? What could have happened to bring about such a transformation? He had come to believe, during that single week in London, that he knew all he needed to know about her – how her mind worked, and the shape of her emotions. He could still read her, he thought, given the materials. He could still judge how she would react to things – if he knew what the 'things' were. But he didn't know the history of these last years, and that made her a mystery to him.

It had been the devil's own luck that Lucy Telfer, of all people, should have been here, plunging them into a maze of deceptions and unspoken lies that contaminated everything, even the truth. If Vilia had been alone, he would have pulled her into his arms and made love to her with all the passion that was in him, and her response would have told him all he needed to know. The very surprise would have ruled out everything but honesty. He wouldn't have given her time to think of all that had gone wrong, but would have reminded her only of all that had been joyously, wondrously right between them. Perry didn't subscribe to the idea that physical love was all-important, but he did believe that love was for the heart, and explanations for the mind, and that the heart could often accept what the mind alone would not. Because of that, he had hoped first to touch her heart. And then, he had thought – sure that a love such as theirs couldn't die – and then would come the time for explanations, apologies, even the deepest self-abasement.

But nothing had gone right. As effectively as if she had intended it, Lucy had displayed him to Vilia in the worst possible light. He had been dropped back, as neatly as a round peg, into a series of round holes. Erring husband and uncaring father. A gambler who levanted from his debts of honour. A liar, and a poor one, who couldn't even sound convincing about the problems of communication between New York and Scotland. And an unsuccessful entrepreneur in a cheap and shabby business. It didn't help that Perry himself, all his mind on Vilia, had talked more openly than was wise about these matters. But there had seemed to be no possible subject for conversation that wasn't alive with dangers. Except the raspberry beds and the fishing at Kinveil. And even Kinveil was dangerous, given Vilia's obsession with it.

There was something else, too. Until Saturday, he had thought that the experiences of the last seven years had stripped him of every last remnant of pride, but he had been wrong. It had been bitter as gall to match Vilia's achievements against his own. She had started with more, much more, but that didn't matter. He knew that, through her eyes, he must seem to have failed again, as he had failed before.

'Very well,' he said. 'No apologies. But I must give you some explanations.' He didn't allow her time to speak. He had to get it over with, even though he already felt that nothing would convince her. 'You know why I left when I did. Magnus Telfer put pressure on his friend Wendell to demand immediate settlement of what I owed him. Another day, and all would have been well. My life – our lives . . .' He glanced up from his locked hands, but her eyes were still fixed on the heart of the fire. 'Yes. Well, it's hardly profitable to speculate, is it? I fled, as I assume you know by now, to sanctuary in Edinburgh, where I drank most of the little money I had. I decided, there, that I could never go back to Charlotte, but the irony was that the only person from whom I thought I might borrow enough money to go to America was Charlotte's father.'

He stopped and sat back, flexing his shoulder muscles a little. He was trying to be cold and factual. No excuses. Nothing of the agony of mind. Nothing of the self-disgust, the exhausted desire for oblivion.

Vilia said, 'The refreshment tray is on the table over there, if you would like something to drink.'

He looked at her sharply, but she didn't seem to have meant anything by it. 'Thank you, no.' Even though he was feeling the strain. Confession wasn't as easy as she pretended. 'Mungo Telfer was very kind to me. Once he was persuaded that there was no possibility of Charlotte and myself being reconciled, he gave me my fare and a hundred pounds to tide me over when I arrived in Nova Scotia. I won't bore you with the expedients I was reduced to during those first years. They weren't very prepossessing. But I survived, even though I still have nowhere I can call home. On the other hand, I have some good friends now, and a business that looks promising. No more than that.'

There was a note of finality in his voice, although he had stopped only because he needed to find the right words for what he wanted to say next, on a subject of overriding importance. He had been watching her profile intently, but it had told him nothing. The soft glimmer of the flames, warming her skin, illuminated only the same calm detachment, as if nothing he had said had made any impression. He knew now that her mind had erected an insuperable barrier against him, and that there was no route by which he could scale it unaided.

Vilia completely mistook his silence. She had discovered on Saturday that seven years of deadly separation had only served, week by week, month by month, year by year, to burn her need for him deeper and deeper into her soul. Most of the time she had been able to ignore it by losing herself in the rigorous schedule of her days, but it seemed the passion had not grown less, and neither had the pain. On Saturday, because of Lucy, there had been no possibility of expressing the passion, and for the last two days, believing he had gone, she had been ruled only by the pain.

She had been angry at first, over his sudden, unceremonious arrival after all the years of silence, but it hadn't been an irrevocable anger, and it had been exorcized by the coolness Lucy's presence had forced her to assume. And then he had said he was leaving again almost at once. It was hours before the agony of that really reached her. She had never known whether her reaction to great sorrows and great joys was unique to her, or perfectly commonplace, but it was as if her brain accepted and noted the message, and then scanned every tiny detail for proof of validity before passing it on to her heart. She had learned, now, to use the interval to advantage. This time, the hurt had been on a scale too great to contemplate, so that she had pushed it away, deliberately deadening herself to it and retreating into a kind of emotional limbo. It seemed the only way she could defend her sanity.

But her success wasn't complete. When Perry Randall walked into the room, there had been two Vilia Camerons waiting for him, one numb and quiescent, the other superstitiously terrified of inviting new suffering, and at the same time consumed by love and need for this man who was so like, and yet so unlike, the Perry Randall of seven years ago.

It was the neutral Vilia who, thinking he had finished what he wanted to say, asked, 'Is that all? Is that the "explanation" you owe me? It leaves a great deal out, don't you think?'

Diverted from his purpose, he snapped, 'What do you want me to say? I thought I'd said it! I was weak, spineless, irresponsible, and I ran away. As far as I knew, you were safe and cared for. Don't ask me whether I wanted you to forget me, or to wear the willow for me, because I don't know.' He stopped. 'Hell and the devil confound it! Of course I know. But I also know that if I had been confined in a debtors' prison, everything would have been over for us, for ever.'

'And isn't it?'

Frustration exploded within him, and he leapt to his feet and strode the length of the room and back again, before coming to a halt before her, his arms folded tightly over his chest. 'What do you think I have been *doing* these last years? I have been trying – under God knows what difficulties and handicaps – to build up something I can ask you, some day, to share with me!'

She understood the words, but the censor in her mind needed time to consider them. She studied his handsome, furious face carefully. 'Perhaps you should have written and told me.' The long silence had hurt more – or almost more – than anything. It had been the proof that he hadn't really cared at all, or that he had forgotten her. The one fault, among all his faults, that persuaded her not to listen to him now.

'God damn it, Vilia! How could I write? The minute I set foot in Nova Scotia I began to think of ways and means. I can scarcely bear to remember what I went through!'

He threw his head back, and his next words were forced out through clenched teeth. 'How many times – *how many times* did I put pen to paper and then throw it away? As far as I knew, Andrew was still alive and back with you, now that the wars were over.' His eyes, grey and compelling, returned to hers again, as if he could will her to understand. 'For your sake, I didn't dare write. Then, at last, I thought to hell with Andrew and I did write. And nothing happened. I gave you a string of addresses where, with luck, a reply might reach me. But I heard nothing. And nothing. *And* nothing.'

He swung round savagely. 'So then I wrote to Mungo Telfer. I thought you might have moved, so that you hadn't received my letters. I prayed that was what had happened. And I thought that Mungo might at least pass on the message that I was alive and reasonably well, because I knew you would never lose touch with Kinveil. But I gather from what Lucy Telfer said that he told no one. Is that true?'

Her eyes were narrowed and half-believing under frowning brows. 'He told *me* nothing. When did you write?'

'About four years ago, I think it was, and again a year or two later.'

'He said nothing about it.'

Perry flung himself down in his chair again. 'I couldn't have foreseen that. But you do understand, don't you? After those first months when I feared to write, I didn't know where you were, and I couldn't find out. I could have asked Mungo to write to me, at some friends' in New York, and tell me. But I didn't know whether he would be prepared to. It would have been asking a good deal, considering I was the man who had deserted his daughter, and it could so easily have wrecked your life. *You do understand?*'

It was all so simple. Such a reasonable explanation of something that had come near to breaking her heart. She dropped her eyes. 'Yes, I understand.'

If he hadn't thought her mind was shuttered against him, he might have stopped, perhaps, to give her time, but he went on. 'And then I heard that Andrew was dead, and from that moment I began to gather together every penny I could, so that I could come and find you.' However uselessly, it had to be said.

If only she had said nothing, or even 'I don't believe you', everything might have turned out differently. But it was too important and too dangerous a subject for her at that moment, and instead she asked, 'And how *did* you find me?'

To Perry, it sounded like rejection. 'From the people who manage the house in Half Moon Street. They told me in person what a few months ago they refused to tell me by letter. And so I came here.'

Her mind running along quite different lines, she said, 'I would have expected you . . . You should have gone to Glenbraddan.'

Of all things, he didn't want to talk about Glenbraddan. 'No,' he said.

The bluntness of it jarred her back to the present. With a calm that astonished her, she opened up a topic that her voice was just capable of discussing. The worst betrayal of all, the betrayal that had almost killed her. She said reasonably, 'But you must understand, I have to ask. You and Charlotte . . .'

'We can never be reconciled. I have no feeling for her, nor she for me. She made it clear before I left that she felt nothing for me but distaste.' He hurried through it, as if by dismissing the question that hung in the air he could efface it for ever.

Vilia said, 'Surely not.'

It stopped him dead. For a moment he floundered, and then he said, 'If I had gone back prepared to beg for mercy, things might have been different. But as soon as she realized I was determined to leave, it was the end.'

He was treating it all very casually, she thought, as if he were talking of some meaningless encounter with a woman of the streets. Suddenly, at long last, her temper began to rise.

'Hardly the end,' she said sharply.

He raised his head. 'What do you mean?'

'I mean the child, of course! That poor, unfortunate child whose mother can *still* scarcely bear to look at her. Little Shona!'

His response baffled her at first, for his face went perfectly blank. Then a slow, stark horror began to dawn on it. 'Oh, no,' he said on a falling note. 'No. Oh, my God!' He buried his face in his hands.

She stared at him. 'Are you seriously trying to tell me that you didn't know?'

He ran the long, capable fingers through his hair, but didn't look up. Then she heard him take a deep, ragged breath and, slowly, he shook his head. 'I didn't know.'

She was diverted, for the moment, from the real point at issue between the two of them. Thinking back, she remembered that he had been at Kinveil for only three or four weeks in the autumn of 1815 before he sailed, so he wouldn't have known then. And he had received no news at all from home in these last seven years. But he had said on Saturday that he had exchanged letters with Mungo since he had been back here. Why hadn't Mungo told him about the child? For the same reasons he had given for advising Perry not to visit Kinveil and Glenbraddan? And, perhaps, because he didn't want to add to Perry's burden of guilt? That would be like him.

She rose to her feet and went to pour a glass of whisky, Johnnie Meneriskay's twelve-year-old best. She would have put it in Perry's hand, except that she didn't trust herself to touch him. There was nothing more she wanted in the world than to have this dark tormented stranger, this lost lover, take her in his arms and make her forget all the fear and misery and heartbreak that held her back from him. But she mustn't give in. *She must not give in.* It was too dangerous and she was too afraid. She couldn't live through such agony again, and wouldn't believe that, this time, the need might not arise. So she merely set the glass down on the little table at his side, and said, 'You need a drink.'

He picked the glass up and drained it, shuddering violently as it began to bite on its way down. 'I didn't know,' he said again. But he did know, now, something of what had happened to change Vilia during their separation, and he had no idea how to fight it. He could remember, still, his own anguish as he had driven himself to fulfil his part of the bargain with Mungo, sharing Charlotte's bed, caressing Charlotte's body as if that might, somehow, bring them together again. In trying to be honest with Mungo, he had been dishonest with Charlotte, and himself, and Vilia. It had been a dreadful charade, that ever since, in retrospect, had sickened him. He had believed, he had hoped, that Vilia would never find out, but she had, and in the most irrefutable way. He looked at her, his eyes full of pain, and said, 'How you must have hated me.'

'Hated you? No. That, perhaps, would have been easier. But I was – unwell – at the time, and I . . .' She allowed her words to tail away. Somehow, during the empty years, it had never occurred to her that there might be things he didn't know. About his daughter, Shona. And about . . .

And about his son, Drew. Sometimes, even now, she tried to convince herself that Drew was Andrew's son, but she knew he wasn't. Not because of any magic awareness of the kind of union that brought forth a child. She would have distrusted any such romantic notion, especially after these last years when she had seen haggard factory wives bring a dozen children into the world, and bury half of them, without ever knowing a moment's joy in their procreation. Sex, for them, was nothing other than a brutal, drunken imposition. No. After Gideon's birth, following so soon after Theo's, Vilia had talked to the midwife and the wet nurse. 'A little bit o' sponge,' they had said. 'Soak it in oil and tie a scrap o' ribbon round it. Put it in before you goes to bed, and you'll be all right, missus. Don't always work, but it's better than nothing. Fifty-fifty chance, or a bit better, they say, the people wot knows.' After that, she had used it when Andrew was home, and he hadn't even noticed. But with Perry . . . The first time, she hadn't expected to need it, and the second, she had been so happy, so full of wild anticipation, that she hadn't even thought of it.

She listened as, stumblingly, Perry tried to explain what had happened at Kinveil when Shona was conceived. She should have stopped him, she knew, because all it did was bring everything back to her, so that her fear grew and grew. If only he hadn't lied to her. Just a few minutes ago he had tried to pretend that he and Charlotte had been estranged throughout the weeks when he had been at Kinveil. She could understand why, but that wasn't enough. Real love, she believed, would have kept him from Charlotte. Real love would have forced him to confess, honestly, to her. Real love would have found a way – some way – to break the seven years' disastrous silence.

Never in her life before had she felt so confused. With part of her mind she sensed that she could anchor him to her side forever, simply by telling him about Drew, but she didn't want him to come to her in that way, from duty as much as desire. She wanted too much, perhaps, for she wanted the whole, all-pervading love of mind and body and being that she had once thought – mistakenly, it seemed – was theirs, the love he had betrayed by going to Charlotte, and by his silence, and now by lying to her. But the tears rose to her eyes, and lingered, and then brimmed over, because she knew that, despite everything, the current of attraction that flowed between them was as strong – stronger, perhaps – than it had ever been. She loved him too much, and that way madness lay.

It was her tears that wrecked his decent restraint, his careful, civilized attempt to put right everything that had gone wrong. Things had gone far past the stage when words could mend them. Defying the sense of doom that hung in the air about them, thick and cloying as a London fog, he forgot everything but his need for her and, pulling her to him, sank his lips roughly on hers. There was none of the graceful circumspection of that first kiss, so many years ago. This time it was the desperate culmination of a lifetime of loneliness, an end to starvation, a slaking of thirst in the desert. She quivered convulsively at his first touch, and then, moaning under his lips, gave herself up to him with an abandon that sent a wild paean of thankfulness thrilling through his veins. It was a kiss that lasted forever, the melting of two separate beings into one, muscles without fibre, bones without marrow, flesh without substance.

It was all she wanted, to have him hold her like this, mind suspended, body oblivious to everything but his presence, heart slowly coming to life again like a stunned bird opening its eyes and waiting, patiently, before it dared to fly again.

But then, his lips still clinging to hers as if, by this one contact, he could wipe out all the lost years, he freed his fingers from her fair, silken hair and, directed not by mind or will or anything but awareness of their devouring, inexorable need for each other, brought his hand blindly round to pull at the fastenings of her gown.

It was too soon.

The spell was shattered. With a raw intake of breath, she tore away from him and found refuge behind a table. For a moment they confronted each other, breathing heavily as if they had run a long, tiring race. In Perry's eyes was the bitter knowledge of defeat; in hers only fear and anger and, if he had been able to see it, the ghost of love betrayed.

Then she gasped, 'Oh, no, my friend! You walked away from me before, and stayed away for seven years, without a word. And now you come back and – and expect me to fall in your arms for an hour or two before you disappear again. For another seven years? No. If that is your idea of love, it isn't mine.'

Weary and drained, he wondered how it was possible for every imaginable thing to go wrong between two people who belonged together, as they did. During their separation, he had never lost hope because he had never forgotten the wisdom and understanding he had felt in her. Had he expected too much? His only fear, after he heard of Andrew's death, was that she might have remarried, but the London agents had told him her name was still Lauriston. So he had journeyed north, buoyed up with dreams, thinking of her as a young widow living in genteel poverty or on her father-in-law's charity. 'Come away with me,' he would say to her. 'Come back with me to America. Here, I am not free to marry, but there we can live as man and wife and be happy. I don't have much to offer now, only love, but there are great opportunities. Come away with me – today.'

The dream had been wrecked, the moment he saw her, on the shoals of her own success. She was more beautiful, more desirable than ever, and richer than he by far. She had been hostile on Saturday, distant today, and perhaps her response to his kiss had been no more than a matter of chemistry. He knew now what had happened to damage her feeling for him in the years they had been apart, but the knowledge had come too suddenly and too shockingly for him to be able to assess it. And perhaps there was more, still, that he didn't know. But there wasn't time to find out; there wasn't time to plead, or persuade, or bring her back to him by any means he could think of. Unless he left tonight, he would miss his sailing, and he couldn't afford to wait several weeks for the next. Especially as he couldn't conceive that what he had to offer her – so patently mistress of her own destiny – would be enough.

So doubt and pride held him silent, and prevented him from saying the one thing that would have convinced her of his full and final commitment, the one thing that would have persuaded her to forgive everything he had done, and everything he had failed to do.

All he said was, 'Won't you believe that I *do* love you, more than life itself?'

'How can I?' she replied. *'How can I?'*

It wasn't a question he could answer. He had played what he thought was his only card, and had lost.

After he had gone, she wept as she had not wept for many long, forlorn years. If he had loved her, truly loved her, he would have said, 'Come away with me!' And she would have gone with him gladly.

Chapter Four

1

Lucy's drawing-room at Kinveil had once been some kind of guard-room, watching over the loch to south and west through tall slit windows set in floor-to-ceiling arches, and it had taken all Lucy's ingenuity to transform it from real Gothic into the make-believe Gothick that her instinct for fashion told her would soon become all the rage. It hadn't been precisely easy to tack 'ancient' timbers on to the rough whinstone ceiling, or crocketed wooden frames round window arches and doors, but the orraman had managed it somehow and Lucy was pleased with the result. She thought it 'amusing', and it was. Fortunately for comfort, her mock mediaevalism had stopped short after the crossed swords above the fireplace and the portrait so dulled with age and peat smoke that it was impossible to decide, not only whether the sitter had been male or female, but whether his/her complexion had been black, white, yellow, or tartan. The rest of the room was very civilized, with a thick Turkish carpet on the floor, a pair of handsome landscapes by young Mr Constable on the walls, and a few light and elegant little tables situated at strategic points, all bearing dishes of bonbons. The chairs and sofas were brightly upholstered and deeply cushioned.

On the evening of October 22, 1822, Lucy was in London with Magnus, and it was Vilia and Luke who sat in her drawing-room. It was late, and Mungo had gone to bed. Luke, indolent by nature and more tired than he would readily have admitted after his ten days' journey from Oxford, was only half awake, lounging in a chair with a glass of whisky bitters in his hand and his heavy-lidded eyes resting on Vilia. The radiance that had captivated him in Edinburgh had gone, but he thought that perhaps she, too, was tired. It was scarcely invigorating weather. The rain had been falling without cease for days, and he had heard that Loch Oich, in Glengarry's territory, had risen seven feet in the last seventy hours, and was now almost five feet above danger level. Sleepily, he thought that, unless the weather changed, tomorrow's Caledonian Canal opening was likely to prove something of a fiasco.

He could hear the thud of the tide on the rocks below, and the erratic rustle of the wind, and the spurts of rain that rattled on the windows like petrified rosebuds strewn by some Bacchante of the passing dark, or pebbles tossed by some spectral wayfarer seeking asylum for the night. He blinked. That was the trouble with Oxford. Too many poetry classes by half.

Yet it was at times like these that he understood why Highlanders remained prey to so many ancestral ghosts. An hour before, he and Vilia had gone outside for a breath of air. It had been black as the pit of hell, but seething with activity as if all the elements were diligently engaged on some secret, malevolent business of their own. Within minutes, he had been overtaken by a sensation of sheer, primeval panic, and it had taken all the will-power he possessed to walk negligently back to the courtyard door again. If Vilia hadn't been there, he would have slammed it hurriedly behind him and probably taken a long time to recover his nerve. But Vilia *had* been there and, pagan that she was, had revelled in it, though the sparkle in her eyes had died almost at once.

Tomorrow, Mr Charles Grant, representing the Canal Commissioners, was to set sail – if that was the word – in one of the new steam yachts, accompanied by half the landowners of three counties, to make the first full voyage from the eastern to the western sea, from the Muirtown locks at Inverness all the way to Fort William. It was assumed that every inlet and promontory along the sixty-mile route would be thick with people, pouring out of the hills and glens to cheer the vessel as it puffed along with its military band dispensing cacophonous echoes across the valley, and its oversized pop-gun firing off salutes to the chiefs. Since it was going to have to stop every few miles to pick up some distinguished resident or other – Mr Grand of

Redcastle, the Reverend Mr Smith of Urquhart, the other Mr Grant from Corriemony, Mr Telfer (junior) of Kinveil, Macdonell of Glengarry – it had been decided that the voyage should take two days, and that the first night would be spent at Fort Augustus.

Mungo had said, 'Start from Inverness with them if ye want, but I wouldn't choose to, myself. Just think of having to listen to that dratted band for all of two days! If you've any sense, what ye'll do is come with Vilia and me to stay at Glengarry's place on Wednesday night, and then go with him to join the boat on Thursday morning. He means to ride up to Fort Augustus and go aboard there, so that he'll be with them before the point where the Canal runs across his land. He's got some legal ploy afoot, but I don't rightly know the details.'

It had sounded like a sensible idea. Luke had no desire to ride all the way up to Inverness just for the doubtful pleasure of sailing all the way back again. Thank God, it meant he could have a restful day tomorrow, with nothing to face but the four-hour drive from Kinveil to Invergarry.

His eyes on the slender figure opposite, he said absently, 'What time does grandfather want us to set out tomorrow?'

She had looked as if she were miles away, but just as he spoke she sat up sharply, almost violently, startling him into wakefulness. He wondered what on earth there had been in his question to provoke such a response, and then saw that she hadn't even heard him. Her face had gone quite white, and her eyes looked huge and dark. The cat, lying on the carpet with its head resting comfortably on the toe of her slipper, bounded to its feet at the same moment and pressed itself against her leg, back arched, tail stiff and quivering, golden gaze wide. There was utter silence. Even the rain had gone off, and the wind had dropped.

An icy breath played round the back of Luke's neck. Very carefully indeed, he set down his glass and rose to his feet. 'What is it?' he asked, and wondered why he was whispering. She raised a tense fist for silence, and he saw that her knuckles were bone-white, the Kinveil ring in stark relief against them. Her lips were curled inwards, caught between her teeth.

Obediently he remained still, though every nerve was tingling.

After a few seconds, she murmured in a voice that was scarcely audible, 'Do you hear it?'

'Hear what?' He had been listening, as she had, but there was nothing. He couldn't remember whether it was high notes or low notes that cats could hear better than humans, so he had tried both, but still, nothing.

She whispered again, imperatively, 'Do you hear it?'

He shook his head and then, because she wasn't looking at him, said, 'No.'

A shudder ran through her. 'Oh, God!' And then, as if she were terrified, she breathed, 'Come here,' and held out her hand to him. 'Touch me.'

It wasn't an invitation, he knew, and she wasn't asking to be comforted.

He laid his fingers over hers, and she said, 'Now, listen. Do you hear anything?'

It was the most extraordinary thing. The moment his hand touched hers, he did hear something. It was like opening the door of a concert hall in the middle of a concerto. Nothing – and then something. Something that was already going on.

His face slack with puzzlement, he said, 'Yes, I hear it.' It wasn't much. It wasn't anything, really. Just water dripping slowly somewhere outside. Though it didn't sound quite as if it were outside, or inside, either. It scarcely seemed to warrant all this high drama, he thought, and said quite audibly, 'It's only water dripping.'

She shook her head angrily. *'Listen!'*

It did sound a bit odd, regular, and hollow, and – and what? Leaden.

He took his hand away from hers and it stopped. His voice grating, he remarked, 'With all the rain we've been having, the water ought to be cascading down, not just dripping!'

She fluttered her fingers peremptorily, and he clasped them again. And he could hear the drips again. For almost ten minutes they stayed there, hands touching, and listened.

Then the sounds stopped. The cat subsided to the carpet as if it were exhausted, and Vilia freed her hand from Luke's and sank back in her chair again.

In some ways, Luke was like his father. Perplexity made him irritable. 'What the devil was that all about?' he asked and, turning, picked up his glass and drained it at a gulp.

'The dead-drap,' Vilia replied tiredly. 'The death drip. Oh, Luke!

265

Have you learned nothing about the Highlands in all these years? It's an omen. Someone in this house is going to – to die. Soon.'

He laughed uncomfortably. 'Really, Vilia! Second sight? Omens? You don't believe all that nonsense, do you? Damn it, in this climate, if someone died every time there was a drip from the eaves the country would be completely depopulated by now!'

'There are more things in heaven and earth, Horatio . . . No. Laugh if you must, Luke, but don't scorn the second sight. I don't know what it is – some kind of nervous vibrations, perhaps – but it doesn't matter. Have you ever heard rain sound like that before?'

'Well, no. But there could be any number of explanations. It might just have been hitting the gutters at an odd angle.'

'And how do you explain that you couldn't hear anything except when you were touching me?'

He couldn't but he tried. 'A freak of sound? So that I could catch it only when I was near you?'

She smiled without humour, and then closed her eyes with a spread forefinger and thumb. 'One person hears the dead-drap, others only if they have hold of the one who hears. That's why the Duchess heard it as soon as I did, because her head was against my foot. That's why you heard it only when you were clasping my hand.'

After a few minutes he became conscious of the sea on the rocks again, and the wind gusting, and the rain lashing against the glass.

Stoutly, he said, 'I hope your watery omen isn't as apt as it sounds. Just think! If the steam yacht goes down on Thursday, half the estates in the Highlands will be looking for new owners!'

2

But it was Mungo who died.

He was perfectly well during the drive from Kinveil to Glengarry's house overlooking Loch Oich. He even enjoyed himself in the evening, when Mac-mhic-Alistair laid himself out to be a jovial host. Mungo had never seen him in this mood before – 'so normal', as he muttered to Vilia – and began, very slightly, to revise his opinion of him. Not that he thought much of the things Glengarry set such store by. The monument at the Well of the Heads, for example. They had to listen to the familiar story, told at great length, of the vengeance taken on the orders of an earlier Glengarry on seven clansmen who had murdered their local chief. With what Mungo considered an indecent regard for the niceties, the avenger had rinsed the severed heads of the offenders in the well before delivering them up to Himself. If it had been Mungo, he'd have had the well disinfected in case anyone drank from it, but Glengarry instead had raised a monument bearing a lengthy inscription in Gaelic, English, French, and Latin, and topped with a sculpture that depicted a hand holding not only a dagger but, with a certain amount of difficulty, seven severed heads as well. There was no accounting for tastes, and the sculptor, Mungo noted sadly, had been no Chantrey.

Nor could he believe in the vast key that hung on the chimney breast of the room where they dined. According to Glengarry, it belonged to the ancestral ruin that had been gutted by the Redcoats during the 'Forty-five, but its size and ornamentation and, above all, the number of wards, made Mungo very suspicious indeed. It didn't look like seventeenth-century workmanship to him.

But never mind, it was interesting. He was wryly amused, and not in the least offended, that it had taken Glengarry almost twenty years to invite him to his house, and knew that even so he had been invited only because of Vilia. Glengarry, following Highland tradition, still insisted on calling her 'Mistress Cameron'. Mungo himself, in the view of Mac-mhic-Alistair, belonged among the townsfolk, tradesmen, and merchants whom he was accustomed to damn up hill and down dale, in their hearing as well as out of it.

Cannily, Mungo held his tongue and left the conversation to Vilia and Luke, who seemed to have the knack of handling the fellow. It was only to be expected of Vilia, but he was pleased to see that Luke was getting on with Glengarry's heir, a boy of his own age who was magnificently turned out, as was Glengarry himself, in the full glory of The Dress, plaid and kilt and sporran. Mungo thought that it was a wee bit incongruous, maybe, that the boy's belt sheath held his knife and fork as well as his dirk. However . . .

Not surprisingly, most of the conversation had to do with the Canal. Glengarry's opinions were typically inconsistent. 'We shipped one and a half million birch staves out of this district in 1820, when the northern stretch of the Canal was opened,' he said proudly. 'And there are people in Fort Augustus who can burn coal in their fireplaces now, because it's so cheap to bring in. Did ye know that?'

'Aye, mphmmm,' said Mungo, carrying a piece of his host's excellent venison to his mouth. The folk who were burning coal were burning it because Glengarry wouldn't let them have so much as a twig of kindling that he could sell at a thumping profit elsewhere. Another few years and there wouldn't be a birch tree left on all Glengarry's vast acres.

'On the other hand,' Glengarry went on. 'I and my fellow landowners are losing a great deal by having the Canal go through our land.'

'Oh, aye?' Mungo said, and took another bite. A few years ago, Glengarry had squeezed £10,000 out of the Canal Commissioners for the privilege of cutting a short stretch of it through his land. Mungo estimated that had been about three times what the privilege was worth.

'Of course, we haven't yet agreed the compensation for disturbing the fish, and the Canal people will have to pay for permission to navigate Loch Oich. And, assuming that's settled, they'll have to give me assurances that those filthy passenger boats and smoking steam vessels will keep to the far shore of the loch, well away from this house.'

'Oh, aye?' Mungo said again. There didn't seem much point in saying anything else, but he hoped one of the others would ask the question he was dying to.

Vilia did. 'But if you let the steam yacht through Loch Oich tomorrow, won't that undermine your claim to control the navigation rights?'

Glengarry beamed at her with a vast self-satisfaction. 'Ha! Ha!' he barked. 'I'm too old a hand at litigation to make that kind of mistake. No! If I join the yacht at Fort Augustus, I'll be aboard before it enters Loch Oich, and will therefore be in the position of acting as host through my own waters. What do you think of that, eh? So it won't undermine my position at all.'

Mungo had to admit that it was ingenious.

But it was to be a case of the best-laid schemes of mice and men. This one went agley at half-past seven the next morning, in the middle of breakfast. No one except Glengarry was very talkative, and even he had to stop occasionally to swallow, since he was anxious to get off in good time to board the yacht at the Fort.

He had just masticated a mouthful of cold roast beef and was raising his tumbler of whisky bitters to wash it down when his eyes suddenly started out of his head. Loud and clear, and more than a little off key, there wafted across the loch the unmistakable strains of a military band playing the ancestral anthem of the Macdonells. It was punctuated by a succession of shots from what sounded like an overgrown pop-gun.

With an explosive oath in the Gaelic, Glengarry shot to his feet and rushed to the window, where he was rewarded by the sight of the steam yacht, well over an hour early, just about to draw level with the house, its passengers cheering and waving with extravagant enthusiasm. His pale eyes fairly popping with rage, Glengarry let out another bellow to one of the plaided servants standing dumbfounded by the serving buffet and then made a beeline for the door, followed after a moment by a bewildered Luke.

Repressing a tactless desire to sit and laugh themselves silly, Mungo and Vilia followed Glengarry's wife and children to the window in time to see the chief, pursued by his panting retinue – including bard and piper – making for the loch side at a record-breaking sprint, kilts and plaids flying in the breeze.

Just at that moment, a distraught figure burst through the breakfast-room door, having entered the house, it seemed, from another direction. 'Och, dearie me! Dearie me!' this apparition intoned between gasps for breath. 'There wass no way I could be getting here in time, so there wassn't! They were feart Himself would stop the boat from entering Loch Oich at aal, do you see, so they set off from the Fort at the first glisk of daylight. Och, dearie me, dearie me! Himself will be furious. And I ran aal the way, too. Och, mistress! He will neffer forgiff me, so he won't!'

Rebecca Macdonell looked at him sadly. 'I fear you may be right, Angus Mor,' she said. 'In fact, if I were you, I wouldn't show my face for quite a while. Have you not got a daughter a good long way away that you could go and visit?'

The erring clansman gave this a moment's thought. 'There iss Jinty in Stornoway, Mistress?'

She nodded. 'That would be best, I should think.' She turned her eyes back to her husband's diminishing figure. 'Och, just look at him, the poor man, having to run all that way, and him not even finished his breakfast. And Jamie will have to row him out. It's not dignified at all. And he will be so upset at having his lovely plan all spoilt!'

'Yon woman,' said Mungo a few hours later, when he and Vilia were on the way back to Kinveil, 'has a real nice nature. Tell me honestly, do you know any other wifey who would still be capable of calling Glengarry "poor man" after being married to him for twenty years?'

There was a faint twinkle in her eye as she said, 'Lucy?'

He gave a snort of laughter. 'Aye, you're maybe right.' He was glad to see the farce at breakfast had cheered her up. She'd been desperately depressed when she arrived at Kinveil, and it had taken him almost a week to coax a smile out of her. And just when he'd thought she was on the way to recovering from whatever ailed her, she had come downstairs – was it only yesterday morning? – looking as if the world had come to an end. She and Luke had been behaving with a kind of bright artificiality ever since, but he didn't think it was because Luke had made some silly mistake like trying to kiss her, though he looked as if he'd like to. What a fankle!

Luke would be spending tonight at Fort William, and tomorrow night at Glenbraddan on his way home. With the darkness drawing in, the journey was too long to do in a day. Mungo was pleased that he was going to have Vilia to himself, because there were one or two things that, at long last, he'd decided to say to her. Although he had admitted it to no one, he was always tired these days, and he suspected that he mightn't be here next time she came to visit the place where she'd been born, which he'd taken from her, and which he had tried over these last years to give back to her a little.

But they weren't even half way home when it happened.

3

Willie Aird, the coachman, knew the road so well that he was driving like an automaton when he was startled out of his trance by a violent tugging on the check cord.

It was Mistress Cameron, face and voice full of despair. 'Pull up, Willie! It's Himself. I don't know what's wrong. Mungo! Can you tell me? Do you feel pain?'

She had known. She had known. Because the warning had come to her, who was so close to him, she had known it must be Mungo.

He was struggling harshly, agonizingly, for breath, his body arching with the effort, and his face was so contorted that all the blood had fled from it. She thought at first that he didn't hear her, but his hands began to flap weakly and aimlessly in front of his chest, as if somehow he could ease the terrible pressure and through stiff, gasping lips he managed a sound that might have been 'Yes'. But then all his concentration focused again on the need to draw air into his body. She tore the neck-cloth away from his throat and opened the shirt beneath.

Once before, Willie Aird had seen a man in such straits, and the doctor had said afterwards that his heart had failed him. He said, 'We'll have to take him to Glenbraddan, Mistress Cameron. There's nowhere else.'

She was half cradling him with one arm round his shoulders, the other hand pressing against his diaphragm as if to force heart and lungs back to their normal rhythms. 'Yes,' she said. 'As smoothly as you can, and as fast as you can. If we see anyone on the road, you must stop them and get them to send to Fort Augustus for the doctor. Oh, why couldn't it have happened when we were nearer there? Hurry, Willie. Please hurry.'

The road was empty, and the finely engineered surface still firm. The coach itself was one of the new ones, with elliptical springs and a low centre of gravity. Willie Aird flicked his whip round the horses' ears and set them to a full gallop, and within a couple of minutes they were going flat out and the coach was flying over the ground. Willie scarcely drew rein when he saw Mr Edward cantering towards them. At the full power of his lungs, he yelled, 'We need the doctor for Mr Telfer! Can you fetch him?' and then laid his whip to the horses again and concentrated on keeping them to their matched stride as the road bore left and then right again, following the line of the river. Vilia had a momentary glimpse of Edward as they flashed past him, his mouth a little open but his shoulders already turning as if, for once, he were going to act without first taking an hour to meditate. 'Hurry, Edward. Hurry,' she prayed.

The last narrow, winding mile off the main road was a protracted torture, but although Mungo had lost consciousness he was still alive when the carriage lurched to a standstill at Glenbraddan. For an incredulous moment, Vilia thought Charlotte was going to refuse to allow her to cross the doorstep, but the sight of her father's face drove everything but concern for him from Charlotte's mind.

She dithered. God, how she dithered! It was as much as Vilia could do not to start issuing orders. But at last Mungo was laid on a soft feather bed, his outdoor clothes removed and replaced with a night-shirt from his baggage. Then the butler and Willie Aird, inexperienced but kindly valets, were dismissed, and Charlotte and Vilia sat down to wait for the doctor.

It was three hours before he came, riding well ahead of Edward, whose horse had gone lame just outside Fort Augustus. By then, Mungo lay conscious on his pillows, his lips blue and his eye sockets deep and dark as if they had been excavated from his skull. His struggles for breath had subsided a little, but it was not a bettering.

Vilia and Charlotte waited outside while the doctor examined him, Charlotte dull-eyed and resentful, and Vilia as insensate as a sleep-walker, moving or standing still as occasion required, aware, some-where deep down, that the moment of waking must come.

At one stage, Grace came tiptoeing downstairs, her neat little features determined. 'Mama,' she whispered. 'You will make yourself ill again. I've been watching you from the schoolroom landing. You must sit down, and I'll ask Mrs Lamont to bring you some tea.'

Charlotte's expression under the frilled muslin cap, with its improbably skittish bows, softened a little. 'How like you to think of it, my dear. But, no. I don't require any tea. Go back to the schoolroom, please.'

But the child turned to Vilia. Hospitality had its rules, however unwelcome the guest, and she said, 'Perhaps you would care for some refreshment, Mrs Lauriston?' She didn't seem to hear at first so, obstinately, Grace repeated the question. This time, she received the ghost of a smile and a nod of refusal. Worriedly, she made her way upstairs again, where Georgiana said with a kind of morbid satisfac-tion, 'I told you so.'

The door of Mungo's room opened at last, and Dr Gordon came out, rolling down his sleeves. He wasn't a very good doctor, and Vilia suspected that he drank more than was good for him, but he was the only medical man in the district, and he had a kind heart.

He shook his head when Charlotte started forward and asked, 'How is he?'

'He's an old man, Mistress Randall, and he's had a full life. It's coming to its end now, so you'd better prepare yourself.' Again, he shook his head. 'No, dinna fret about him. He's ready enough. He knows all he has to do is to put up wi' a few more hours of it, and then he'll have peace.'

It was the wrong thing to say to Charlotte, for whom there were conventions in death as in life. Stoicism, she thought, was something that grew out of long, lingering illnesses. Her father's dying would be short and she couldn't believe that he was prepared. She worried about it. 'If only the minister would come.'

Vilia looked at her curiously. But she supposed that people who found comfort in religion were bound to assume that others did, too. She herself had never been much impressed by the narrow-minded and not very intelligent men whose mission it was to trot out panaceas dreamed up two thousand years before to meet the needs of an illiterate tribal people. It wasn't that she didn't believe in God, just that she didn't think much of His earthly spokesmen. Mungo was a wise man, and a good man, who didn't need any minister. What he needed were love and understanding and friendship to bolster his own strength during the last ordeal.

Charlotte said, 'I must go in,' but the doctor stopped her.

'Not now. He wants to see Mistress Cameron.'

'No!' The reaction was crude and unequivocal. 'I'm his daughter. It's my right!'

The doctor looked at her. 'I can't stop ye, of course. But will ye not respect his wishes?' Then, more soothingly, he went on, 'Calm yourself, Mistress Randall. He's got a few hours to go yet. Come on, sit ye down. Ye're not well yourself yet, after that illness. I'll come and keep you company, and maybe that housekeeper of yours will bring us a drop of tea. I'm fair parched. Then, when your father's had his word with Mistress Cameron, ye can go in yourself. But only if you promise to sit quiet, though. No tears and no laments.' He turned to Vilia. 'And that means you, too, Mistress Cameron.'

She didn't need the warning, and he knew it. He had said it only for Charlotte's sake. She nodded her head, twice, and then set her hand to the doorknob.

It was not a large room, and the bed seemed to fill it, heavily curtained in a cloth that had probably once been red but now, after many washes, had faded to an uneven pink. The walls were darkly panelled and hung with a few old-fashioned prints in dull gold frames. Outside the small, deeply embrasured windows, the sky was dark, and there was a faint soughing of wind in the trees. The doctor had pulled an embroidered fire screen alongside the bed to shield Mungo's eyes from the candles. A peat fire burned slowly in the grate, but the room smelled cool and damp. Vilia shivered a little.

He was propped up on the pillows, his eyes sunk in deep pits of shadow, and his face, under the broken veins that patched the cheekbones, wearing the cold, waxen look that Vilia had seen only once in her life before, when her own father had lain on his death-bed. But that had been different. He had resented the pain, and the fear, and the knowledge of dying. Mungo didn't.

There was a glimmer of something that might have been a smile round his mouth, and he had just enough strength to turn his hand, palm upwards, on the counterpane. She went to him, treading lightly on the worn carpet, and knelt beside the bed in a soft rustle of skirts.

She had thought all her faculties were in suspension, and that she could manage. But his first words, slurred and yet vehement as he launched them separately on each outgoing breath, nearly broke her.

'I'm – loathe – to go. You – need me. Too late for me to – ask you – what's wrong.'

She made as if to speak, but he shook his head a little. 'No. Let *me*. My investment in the foundry – that's yours. And a – bit more. Magnus won't miss it.' The shadow of a frown constricted his brow. 'Wish I – could have left you – Kinveil – too.'

She dropped her forehead on their clasped hands, unable to look at him.

'If I'd been able – to see ahead – when I – bought it . . . If! If! But it's a – funny thing – life.'

His hand moved in hers, and she raised her head again.

'The boys are – all you have now. *You need them.* Remember that.'

There was a long, long pause, then his eyes flickered away from hers. 'I've aye wondered . . . You and Perry Randall – at that ball – years ago.'

The breath fled from her lungs.

'I thought – made for each other. But Charlotte's my child.' His voice was almost pleading. The next intake of breath racked him, and she held his hand tightly until the gasping subsided.

Then he whispered, 'Oh, lassie! It's worried me for so long. Do you love him?'

He trusted her not to lie to him, and because he had said, 'Do you?' and not 'Did you?' she was able to cling to her newborn illusions. She said, 'No.'

After a while, he said, 'I'm glad. I know where he is – where he's been – all these years. I could have told you – but I didn't – because of Charlotte. It was a question of – who would be hurt – you see? But if you don't – love him – then it didn't matter after all – did it?'

'No,' she said. 'It didn't matter.'

'Och, I'm glad. I'll go to the Lord with a – clear conscience about – that, anyway.' He turned his head so that his darkening eyes looked deep into hers, and the words came out in a rush. 'But you were – made for each other, just the same.' After another long pause, he added, 'It's as well, though. Unless he's changed, you're – too strong – for him.'

The effort was intense, now. His tongue came out, agonizingly slowly, to moisten dry lips. 'You'll have to be strong for – yourself. But lassie, not too strong, not hard. Drat it!' There was a weak, frustrated rage in the whisper that was all he could manage. 'If I could only – give you back – Kinveil. Then everything would be – all right. But it has to go to Magnus. You see that?'

She raised his hand, cold and heavy, to her lips. 'I see that, Mungo, have you said what you want to say?'

His hand tightened a little in her grasp.

'It's my turn, then. You have been dearer to me than anyone I've ever known. No faults. No demands. No – betrayals. Only kindness and support such as I wouldn't have believed could exist. There have been times when, if it hadn't been for you, I couldn't have gone on. No, don't frown, my dear. Let me finish. I'll mourn you for the rest of my life. I'll weep for you, out of love and out of selfishness.' Her voice faltered. 'If I could come with you, I would.'

In her desolation and loneliness, she meant it. With Mungo's death, a part of her – another part of her – would die, and she didn't think she could afford it. It was as if, one by one, the chambers of her heart were being sealed off, each a separate coffin with its plaque commemorating warmth, happiness, kindness, love. Coffins never to be opened again, no prey for the resurrection men.

She was becoming morbid, or maudlin, she didn't know which. Gathering her voice together again, she went on, 'But since I can't come with you, I will go on, and I promise you I'll try to be strong, and try, if I can, not to be hard. Though that won't be easy, Mungo dear, without you. But I promise you, *I will try.*'

His smile was almost successful, and she smiled back through the tears standing in her eyes.

They were still sitting motionless, in a silence punctuated only by Mungo's gasping breath, when the door opened and the doctor's head appeared. With a single glance he took in Mungo's closed eyes and the shallow movement of his chest. 'I think Mistress Randall should see him now,' he said.

After a moment, she replied, 'Yes,' and, rising, bent over Mungo and dropped a light, evanescent kiss on his forehead. His lashes fluttered, but his eyes remained closed. Gently, she laid his hand on the coverlet, and murmured in a voice she hoped he was still able to hear, 'Good-bye, Mungo, my dear. Go in peace, and with love.'

4

Late the following afternoon, riding carefully because his head was still splitting and his stomach queasy from the forty-three toasts he had drunk at Fort William the evening before, Luke Telfer arrived at Glenbraddan and was lethargically puzzled to see that every door and window in the house was wide open to the grey drizzle outside. Not until he stepped inside the unattended front door, shaking off his dripping greatcoat and sodden beaver, and noticed that the mirror was covered with a cloth and that the clock had been stopped, did he realize that there had been a death in the house and that the windows were open to let the departing spirit fly free. When the butler made a belated appearance, all Luke said was, 'Who?' He felt cold all the way through, remembering that eerie little scene at Kinveil on Tuesday evening. If that had meant anything, it could only be one of two people.

Edward took him to see his grandfather, already laid out in the bedchamber, clothed in a ruffled shirt, and with his hands crossed over his breast. A white sheet covered him, and there were white napkins pinned over the chair cushions, the chest of drawers, and the pictures on the wall. Aunt Charlotte sat near the bedhead, watching over him, and there were two little tables, one set with wine and seedcake, the other with bread, cheese and whisky, to be offered to visitors according to their station in life. It all looked as a decent Highland death chamber was supposed to look, but almost at once Luke discovered that the peace was deceptive.

Aunt Charlotte, it seemed, was determined that her father should be laid to rest in the little cemetery near Glenbraddan, but Vilia, shocked out of what Luke realized must have been a deliberate self-effacement, had said that Kinveil was where he belonged. As far as Luke could discover, they had only been waiting for him to arrive to settle the matter, because in the absence of his father he was head of the family. He wouldn't have been equipped for it even if his mind had been in a fit state, and his precarious maturity slipped badly, especially during the course of a highly charged interview with Aunt Charlotte. When he went into the drawing-room to face Vilia, he was white and shaking. He was grateful when she said that Mungo's man of business, Norman Cooper, had already been summoned from Inverness, and that they would probably find Mungo had left instructions in his Will.

'Oh, God, Vilia! Do you think so? Aunt Charlotte always reduces me to a jelly. And it's damned unfair. I was fond of the old man, too, you know!'

'Yes. But you must make allowances for her, Luke. It's partly my fault. I should have held my tongue. In a way, I suppose we were both trying to take our minds off what has happened. But he's gone, and his spirit with him. I doubt whether it really matters very much where his body is laid to rest.'

Norman Cooper arrived not long afterwards, short, fat, red-haired, and wilfully quaint. But Mungo would not have employed him if he hadn't been very capable indeed, and Luke didn't know what he would have done without him in the days that followed. He suspected his father would have relied on the man as heavily as he did, if he had been there, but there was no possibility of Magnus reaching Kinveil until long after the funeral.

After the ceremony of the *kistan* – laying the body in an open coffin –

Mungo was taken quietly home to Kinveil in a carriage, without any of the antique ostentation Charlotte's soul craved; if it had been left to her, there would have been a long, slow march, with bearers numbered in the hundreds. But once back at Kinveil, tradition could not be ignored. It was necessary for the coffin to lie in the Great Hall for at least two days and nights, so that friends, neighbours and tenants could pay their last respects. Luke was astonished to discover how many people there were in the district who came to do just that, many of them walking twenty miles or more, dressed in their Sunday best, to doff their bonnets to the man they referred to as Himself. He lost count of the number of times he heard them murmur 'a fine man', 'a good man', 'a kind-hearted gentleman'. And through it all, wake had to be held. Edward Blair, Norman Cooper, Luke himself, and Sorley McClure took it in turns, and there were always half a dozen men from among the servants and tenants to keep them company. Luke didn't think it proper that Sorley should be involved, but Mungo, it seemed, had made a point of it.

Privately, Mr Cooper told Vilia that 'the late Mr Telfer', knowing that it would not be possible for Mistress Cameron to take part in the ceremonies, had expressed a wish to have Sorley represent her. 'And, indeed, it iss a blessing that you were both here, Mistress Cameron, for Mr Telfer said more than once that you were like a daughter to him, and he would go more peacefully if he had you beside him at the last.' He looked at the young lady's averted head, and added, a little clumsily, 'There now! There now, Mistress. It comes to us all, and to die quickly iss what most of us would want. It iss chust a bit hard for those who iss left behind.'

Then, at last, the coffin lid was screwed down, and the coffin lifted from its trestles, and the trestles overturned, and the first bearers set out on the two-mile journey to the kirkyard. It was an impressive procession, with Dougal Mackinnon in the lead, black streamers flying from his pipes, and the mournful notes of Cha till mi tuille – 'I will return no more' – echoing weirdly from the mountains across the loch. Luke was reminded of the last time he had heard it, when Perry Randall had sailed away down Loch Linnhe bound for the New World. He wondered whether that had been in his grandfather's mind when he had asked for it to be played.

Behind the piper came the coffin, with its eight bearers and others marching in slow step beside them, ready to slide the coffin on to their own shoulders when the first half mile had been covered. 'Half a mile?' Luke had said. 'That's not very much. Must the bearers change so often?' And Norman Cooper had replied, 'It iss well seen you haff neffer had to carry a coffin, Mr Luke!' Luke himself walked in solitary splendour behind, his stomach churning with nerves and lack of sleep, and the sheer physical strain of the slow march. He felt horribly conscious of his dignity, and preternaturally aware of the mile-long tail of honoured guests and tenants and neighbours stretching behind him. It was a relief to arrive at the kirkyard, rank with frost-browned nettles and yellowing grass, because to cut them would have shown disrespect for the dead, and to see the coffin lowered into the ground at last. The Reverend Mr Swinton, tall, shy, and well-meaning, was there to utter a short prayer at the graveside, although the Presbyterian Church had no burial service and it was not required of him.

And still it wasn't over. Before the procession left Kinveil, food and drink had been served to mourners with no claim to rank or precedence, but afterwards there had to be the funeral feast for the elect. Luke presided, nervous as a cat. He was grateful that the journey to the kirkyard had gone off soberly, for, like everyone else, he had heard tell of longer journeys when the bearers, pausing to refresh themselves, had set the coffin down and failed to notice, until several miles further on, that they had omitted to pick it up again. Funeral feasts were no less notorious. It was the rule rather than the exception for guests to progress from respectful sadness, to relaxation, and then to mirth, and finally to total incapacity. Luke had always thought this highly improper, but today he felt a glimmer of understanding. In his own relief from tension, he could easily have drunk far more than he should. But this funeral feast was perfectly sedate, he supposed because most of the guests were staid incomers from the south, rather than imaginative and emotional Highlanders. Gradually but irrevocably, all the great estates were passing into the hands of men who could afford to own them. Theophilus Cameron hadn't been the first, and by no means the last, to surrender his centuries-old inheritance to the new rich.

The guests left next day, and then it was really over. Luke had never felt so alone. He wished, agonizingly, that Vilia had stayed. But women were, by custom, excluded from Highland funerals, so she had stood for a while at a high window in the tower watching the cortège wind away along the loch side, and listening to the piper's lament. Then, when Sorley returned from the kirkyard, his duty as bearer done, she had walked downstairs, and through the Great Hall, and across the causeway, and had driven off back to her own life.

Part Three   1822–1829

Chapter One

1

When Mungo Telfer died, Kinveil suddenly became empty. As Luke waited for his parents to arrive, he could feel that everyone in the castle and on the estate knew that the rudder had gone. Mungo had carried a sense of purpose round him like an aura. It wasn't that he had been committed to doing things, and certainly not to innovation. His primary concern had been to preserve Kinveil as an oasis in a troubled world, but he had tried to preserve it at its best, so that the people who fished for a living fished more successfully, and the people who farmed their little patches for food farmed them more effectively. And that, Luke now recognized for the first time, had probably been a far more challenging task than sweeping the land clear of awkward, contrary humans and starting again with sheep and trees. Mungo had been tough, kindly, and unselfish, a rare combination in a Highland laird, and the people of Kinveil had responded by accepting him much more quickly than they usually accepted newcomers. Luke remembered his grandfather telling him, with a chuckle, what one of the local people had said about a family whose land marched with Kinveil's. 'Och, but they are chust incomers!' Mungo, wondering whether he'd heard aright, had said, 'The Grants? But surely . . . They've been here about three hundred years, haven't they?' And the local had said, 'Aye, it would be about that.'

Mungo, after the first few years of feeling his way, had managed the estate himself, with a little help from a man who was dignified by the name of grieve, but given no latitude whatever. Mungo had strong views about grieves. 'They're no more nor a buffer between the laird

281

and his people, and while I grant you the laird's often happier for a buffer, the folk are anything but.'

When Magnus arrived, he had a grieve in tow. He wasn't even a Scotsman. 'Splendid fellow!' Magnus exclaimed to his disapproving son. 'Heard about him from a man at White's, and thought it would be worth breaking the journey to look him over. And when I saw he was an obliging sort and seemed to know something about this kind of country – he comes from the Yorkshire dales, you know! – I engaged him on the spot.' He stopped and harrumphed. 'Sorry you were left to handle the funeral, by the way, but I'm sure you managed very well.' Luke stared at him. From the tone, it sounded as if that was the last his father intended to say about the old man's death; and it was. 'Anyway,' Magnus resumed, 'you don't have to set off for Oxford yet awhile, do you, my boy? Henry Phillpotts will keep your seat warm for you, won't he? Take down lecture notes and all that rubbish. You can take another week or two to show Bannister round the estate. Better equipped than I am, and younger, too!'

With difficulty, Luke banished the disbelieving expression that was trying to take over his face. 'Yes, Father,' he said drily.

He didn't take to Jonathan Bannister, a slight man several inches shorter than himself, with smooth black hair, quick brown eyes, and an eager and over-helpful manner that Luke distrusted. He had no reason for thinking the man dishonest or artificial, but he knew very well that his manner wouldn't recommend him to the quiet, reserved folk whose lives he'd be meddling in. It didn't.

After the first few introductions, Luke found he was tying himself in knots trying to convey that Bannister wasn't his choice, and after a few more, gave up and retired into a kind of aloof courtesy, hoping he'd be able to sort everything out later. As a result, Jonathan Bannister set him down as an arrogant young puppy, and Ewen Campbell thought regretfully that young Master Luke was giving himself airs, now that he was next in line to inherit the estate.

It wasn't easy for Luke to accept that he could no longer shuffle off responsibility for things he didn't like, but after a few days he nerved himself to approach his father.

In a voice not quite his own, he said, 'Now that I'm heir to Kinveil, I'd like to feel myself involved in the managing of it. I mean . . .' He looked at his father's astonished eyebrows and stumbled on. 'I mean it would be – er – proper, wouldn't it, for us to discuss together what's to be done about things. Future plans and – er – things.'

Magnus's 'Ye-e-ess?' was a masterpiece of incredulity.

'I mean I ought to know about it, since it'll be mine some day.'

'But not,' his father pointed out, 'for a – very – long – time.'

'No, no, of course not! I only meant . . .' He rushed his fences. 'I mean Bannister's quite the wrong man for grieve, you know! You can see with half an eye that the tenants will never accept him!'

He groaned inside. His father's expression was one of outraged dignity, as if someone had planted the sole of a boot on the seat of his spotless buckskin breeches.

Afterwards, his mother shook her head at him. 'Not the way to go about it, darling. You should have asked me first. Your papa is really feeling quite unsettled at the moment, not himself at all. You can't expect him to like you telling him he's in the wrong.'

So, teeth clenched and mind resentful, he went on showing Bannister round the estate, watching him mentally measure out the tracts of land suitable for new timber, and the raw hillsides that would be just the thing for the new breeds of sheep.

Seeing the sense of his mother's warning, he tried not to offend his father again, but it was a near thing one day when his Aunt Charlotte came over on a visit and, by the most awkward mischance, he found himself an unwilling audience of one at an acrimonious disagreement.

'Did that woman, or did she not,' Charlotte almost screeched, 'contradict me in my own house on the very day I lost my father? Did she, or did she not, try to tell me what to do?'

Luke was her only witness to Vilia's iniquities, and he quailed at the glare she fixed on him. Aunt Charlotte had always been his idea of a Tartar. He knew she disapproved of him, and, unused to being disapproved of, he didn't like it in the least.

'Yes, but . . .' he said weakly.

'It was *not her place* to say where papa should be buried!'

'But grandfather wanted . . .'

'That has nothing to do with it. Of course it was necessary to respect papa's wishes once we knew what they were. But until Cooper arrived, we didn't know them. And yet she – that woman! – tried to tell *me* where *my* father should be buried!'

Magnus, bored, said, 'Really, Charlotte, I can't imagine why you are making all this fuss. Vilia Cameron was very attached to father, and you must admit she seems to have guessed his wishes better than you did.'

She said again, 'That has nothing to do with it. Do I have to remind you, Magnus, that I am your sister, and you owe me a certain consideration? In view of her past behav . . .' She bit the word off, and after a forbidding glance at Luke, went on, 'In view of the past, as well as her intolerable impertinence last month, I don't wish ever to see her again.'

Magnus shrugged. 'No one asks you to.'

But Charlotte hadn't finished, not by any means. 'Papa allowed her to run tame at Kinveil, through some misplaced belief that he owed it to her, but you have no such excuse. And I warn you that, if you invite her here, it will place a very serious strain on our relationship.'

Christ! Luke thought, aware that panic must be written all over his face. But fortunately, neither of his elders was looking at him.

His father's mouth was slightly ajar, and it was a moment before he spluttered, 'Are you trying to dictate to me? Really, Charlotte! I thought you would have had more sense of what is fitting!'

'I am your sister, Magnus. Your *elder* sister. You owe me a duty.'

'Oh, do I! It would be wise for you to mind what you say. Remember, I'm the head of the family now . . .'

Charlotte wasn't impressed, and her eyes met his, glare for glare. Then, after a brief, tense silence, Magnus thought of a clincher. Smiling superciliously, he said, 'And I may not be disposed to open my purse to you as readily as Father did.'

Christ! Luke thought again, on a different note, and cast a swift look round the Gallery to be sure there weren't any blunt instruments within reach.

But Charlotte only sneered. 'How like you, Magnus! Empty threats. I need no money from Kinveil's coffers.'

Magnus's colour was considerably heightened, for as soon as the words were out he had recognized what a very vulgar thing it was to have said. He wouldn't apologize, but compromised by drawing a long-suffering breath and saying, 'I'll be damned if I'll – oh, sorry, sorry! – I'm dashed if I'll tell her straight out that she's not welcome here. But I'll go so far as not to invite her, if that will satisfy you. Lucy won't like it, mind you.'

'I do Lucy the justice to believe that she will understand how I feel.'

Luke was feeling physically sick. 'But *Father*!' he exclaimed, and was irritably waved to silence.

'Anyway,' Magnus went on, with the air of a man who expected to be on the winning side whatever happened, 'from what I know of Vilia Cameron, she's as likely to invite herself as wait to be asked. And I tell you, Charlotte, if she does I won't be so uncivil as to turn her away.'

There was a small, chill smile on Charlotte Randall's face. 'Thank you, Magnus. I'm pleased to know that we will remain on good terms. I imagine Mrs Lauriston will think twice before inviting herself, now that Kinveil is yours.' The spite in her voice was unmistakable when she added, 'And *that* will teach her!'

Later, Luke said in the airiest tone he could muster, 'But Father, it'll be damned hard on Vilia. You know how she loves the place. I do think Aunt Charlotte is being unreasonable.'

As always, it was a mistake. Magnus said, 'You will oblige me by refraining from criticizing your aunt. It is presumptuous and unbecoming. At eighteen, you know nothing of the world.'

'Dash it! You were only nineteen when you were *married*!'

'Mind your tongue!' There was a pause while Magnus regarded his son's heated countenance. 'That was different. But I will overlook your insolence this time. Let us hope that Oxford will help to mend your manners.'

Disregarding, with some difficulty, the injustice of this remark, Luke said, 'Yes, Father. But what about Vilia?' If she didn't come to Kinveil, and he had no opportunity of going to Edinburgh, he might not see her for years. And if he didn't see her, he didn't think he could go on living.

Magnus was tired of the subject, and consistency was never his strong point. 'Yes, well,' he said. 'Your aunt's got no sense of proportion where Vilia Cameron's concerned. You know what women are. She'll cool down eventually, I suppose, and then we can all go back to behaving like civilized human beings again.'

2

But Charlotte didn't cool down and Vilia wasn't invited to Kinveil. Neither did she invite herself.

Foolishly, Luke had a word with his mother during his first vacation from Oxford, and Lucy, who had been racking her brains for a way of reconciling Charlotte and Vilia, promptly gave up the struggle. Fond though she was of Vilia she didn't want Luke falling in love with her, and from the expression in his eye she could see there was a danger of it. Assuming he would grow out of it, she contented herself with writing to Vilia in her vaguest style, and always when she was able to say, 'We are off next week on a round of visits', or 'We leave for London in ten days, for the Season', or 'Isn't it just like the thing that, when we are at last settled at Kinveil for a few weeks, the roads should be blocked and impassable for everyone except Iain Mor the Post, who manages to struggle through, whatever the weather.'

More than he would have believed possible, Luke thirsted for Vilia's presence, but for a long time couldn't think what to do. He couldn't tell whether she knew she wasn't welcome at Kinveil any more, or whether she resented it, or whether she even cared. Unable to get her out of his mind, he tried desperately to think of some way of bringing about a meeting that would appear natural, casual, accidental. His dreams were filled with chance encounters, during which he did her some great service that led her to look at him with adoration in those incredible green eyes. His awakenings were bitter. As the months passed, Oxford came to know Luke Telfer as the tall, good-looking fellow with the caustic tongue.

Then, very suddenly indeed, he developed an interest in steam navigation. His mother thought it very *avant-garde* of him, and his fellow scholars, who had no time for the proletarian sciences, very peculiar. It occurred to no one that his interest was entirely purposeful.

Travelling from Oxford to Kinveil by road would have involved a detour of more than a hundred miles to take in Marchfield House, but the London and Edinburgh Steam Packet Company had recently introduced regular sailings between London and the port of Leith. It wasn't always faster than going by road, but it was much more interesting, more comfortable, and more invigorating. Or so said Luke. It was also cheaper, if he'd cared about that. What really mattered was the rest of the journey. After disembarking from the *City of Edinburgh* or the *James Watt*, Luke had to drive from Leith to Falkirk to catch a Forth and Clyde Canal barge for Glasgow, where he joined the *Comet*, which took him close to home by way of the Caledonian Canal. And just off that convenient stretch of road between Leith and Falkirk lay the village of Clarkstoun, and Marchfield House. It would have been grossly impolite not to drop in on Vilia.

The first time, he arrived unannounced, but when it became a habit he was absorbed into the household like some brother or cousin, whose visits weren't anxiously awaited but welcome enough when they occurred.

It wasn't what Luke wanted, but it was better than nothing. He began to live through college terms, and tutorials, and studying, and examinations, and undergraduate junketings, only for those few hours every few months when he could see Vilia. She was a creature more of visions than flesh and blood. In fact, he scarcely even thought of her in physical terms. His sexual needs were perfectly well catered for at Oxford, and even at Kinveil, although Kirsty Macintyre – dear, pretty Kirsty with her agreeable ways, who had taught him most of what he needed to know about his body – had retired a year or two since; to marry and settle down, she had said ingenuously. Her successor, Jinty Macleod, was very different. There was black Irish in her somewhere. Raven hair, deep blue eyes, a pert and vivid face, and a figure that even through all the layers of Highland clothing was blatantly voluptuous. Jinty, though she was livelier in bed, wasn't always as kind as Kirsty had been, and she was always nagging about the fact that, since Magnus had become laird, he had taken his custom elsewhere. Luke had spent a good deal of expensive time explaining that his father probably thought it was beneath his dignity for all his tenants to know what he was up to, but all Jinty would say was, 'If Mistress Telfer will not giff him what he needs, she must know that he hass to go to someone else! What does it matter if other folk know too?' Luke, remembering the effect it had had on his own fifteen-year-old virility when Kirsty had first let it slip that his father was one of her most valued customers, had decided it was time to change the subject.

No, he had no compelling physical need of Vilia. All he really wanted to do was look at her, listen to her, touch her hand, and perhaps – the summit of his ambitions – imprint a chaste, delicate kiss

287

on her lips. It was mawkish, he knew, but there was nothing he could do about it except take good care that he didn't allow it to show. He suspected that, if he did, he would instantly be given his *congé*.

In many ways, she was a stranger to him. Older and a little wiser than he had been, he gradually came to understand that he had no idea of what the essential Vilia was like. Although they had been acquainted for a dozen years, he had scarcely known her except when she was under some kind of stress, whether of bereavement, or elation, or even that special mood that had possessed her in his grandfather's company, a lifting of the heart, a mischief, a kind of spiritual ease. Now, she was prey to none of these, and what struck him most was her air of complete self-containment. That, and the fact that her tongue had developed a cutting edge.

She seemed quite to enjoy his visits. The two of them, after all, were of the same world and spoke the same language. He was quite successful at amusing her, he thought, in an astringent way, for he had worked hard at developing an elegant, engaging style, and was still retrospectively grateful to Perry Randall for teaching him the rudiments of it all those years ago. Sometimes he even wondered how his uncle was faring in America as a – what was it he had called himself in that last letter to Mungo? – as a 'drummer'. Not too well presumably, or he would have been home on a visit before now.

They didn't talk about Kinveil very much at first, because Luke was terrified that Vilia might come straight to the point and ask why she was no longer invited. It wasn't his fault, of course, but that wouldn't make it any less embarrassing. And then one evening in 1824, just before the start of a new term, an idea occurred to him. He wasn't, in general, sensitive to other people's moods, not even Vilia's, but on this occasion it seemed to him that, even though she made all the right responses and appeared to be listening to his every word, she was really somewhere else.

'Back to the mausoleum,' he had groaned. 'Oxford has to be lived in to be believed. There's scarcely a don in the place who wouldn't cross to the other side of the street to avoid coming face-to-face with a new idea! You know the theologians claim that God created the world in 4004 BC?'

'Yes.'

'Well, there's a professor called Buckland who's dated some fossils at four thousand years older than that.'

'How very inconsiderate of him.'

'Yes, but no one's in the least worried! Deacon Keble merely says that, obviously, God created the fossils at the same time as He created everything else! Can you believe it!'

She laughed. 'I like that. At least it has the merit of consistency.'

There was a tap on the door and the second footman entered with the tea-tray.

'No Sorley?' Luke asked.

'His evening off.'

'How is he?' It was a struggle to ask, although Luke didn't dislike Sorley. No one did. It was just that, where Vilia was, Sorley was seldom far away, tall, thin, and sandy, with the same freckles, the same narrow hazel eyes, and the smile that could still light up the landscape. He seemed to have no other ambition than to serve her as footman, manservant, and slave. Luke knew that it was utterly illogical, but he was jealous of Sorley, jealous because he and Vilia shared so much of a past and present from which Luke himself was excluded. He hated the thought of any other man, even a servant, being closer to Vilia than he was. He was prickly about Sorley, resentful of the hordes of unknown admirers he was sure she must have in Edinburgh, sullen at the memory of her rapport with Mungo, and he hated – God, how he hated! – the memory of Andrew Lauriston. Ludicrously, he was even jealous of her sons.

They were growing up into nice lads, handsome, intelligent, and well-mannered. Luke had been surprised to discover that they called their mother Vilia. She had shrugged and said, 'It makes me feel like a real person, rather than an assortment of attributes. To the servants I'm "the mistress". At the foundry I'm "the ironmaster". To most of my acquaintances I'm "Andrew Lauriston's widow". It would be altogether too much to be "mother" as well. I have to preserve my – my sense of identity *somehow*.' Luke, who had never had any problems with his identity, hadn't really understood what she meant.

He had certain reservations about Theo, the oldest of the boys, who was slender and fair and just a little difficult to handle. It had made Luke feel quite mature at first, when he realized that Theo was developing the same kind of passionate admiration for him as he had felt for Perry Randall when he was ten years old. And then he had begun to wonder if it *was* quite the same. A few terms at an all-male college had taught him more than Greek literature and Latin commentaries and how to deal with dons steeped in port and privilege. Everyone knew that Theo didn't like being cuddled or cosseted – 'pawed', as he put it – but Luke found it disconcerting, when he gave the boy a friendly slap on the back, to have him look up with an excited gleam in his bright, impenetrable eyes. After that, Luke learned to keep his hands to himself, but he remained the recipient of Theo's confidences and an object of the greatest interest to him. A damned inquisitive brat, if the truth were told, but Luke had a certain sympathy with him, there. He'd been the same himself as a child, and he knew how frustrating it was when no one would satisfy one's curiosity. So, though his motives might be muddled, he did his best to appear interested in Theo's current ambition – the oddest one Luke had ever heard – to be at once the best ironmaster and the best poet the world had ever seen.

'Listen to this,' Theo would say. 'I don't think I've got it quite right, do you?'

> . . . and thine the thews that gleam in furnace glare,
> And thine the labour that my love will share,
> While molten metal trickles from the flame
> And blast pipes shriek the echo of thy name.

Luke hadn't been able to think of a thing to say, other than a feeble, 'Yes, well. It sounds very grown up. Scans, too. Keep at it, Theo. We'll all be proud of you some day.'

But the boy wasn't satisfied. '"Blast pipes" is *wrong*, isn't it!'

'Well, it's not exactly poetic, I admit. You don't think flowers and trees and things would be easier – just until you get the hang of it, I mean?'

'Pooh!' the boy had said, his mobile mouth curling. 'They're too *soft*!'

With Gideon and Drew it was easier, although Gideon had an elusive quality. He was quite the most reasonable child Luke had ever encountered, but while he wasn't negative, he wasn't positive, either; more like a bundle of unrelated threads waiting to be woven into a pattern. Drew was the opposite, bright, forthcoming, and appallingly opinionated. Luke had been taken aback at first to find the boy looking at him calculatingly, as if he didn't measure up to some obscure but absolute yardstick. It had been months before he discovered that Drew's yardstick was Andrew Lauriston, the father he had never known, who had died a hero's death at Waterloo.

Vilia said, 'Sorley? He's well enough, I think.' She handed Luke his teacup. 'He's very adaptable.'

And then for no reason at all, Luke suddenly realized – his mind flashing back through half a dozen visits and a score of guarded conversations – that the only times he had ever been sure of Vilia's scrupulous and complete attention had been when he was talking of Kinveil, or something or someone associated with it. He had been too taken up with himself to notice before, which hadn't been very bright of him. He knew how she felt about the place. He wondered if he could manoeuvre her into inviting herself. Magnus had said, if that happened, he wouldn't turn her away.

He said, 'You mean he misses Kinveil. As you do?'

She smiled non-committally.

He said, 'It's changed since grandfather died. Oh, not in any way you could put your finger on, but there's something in the atmosphere. You know its moods as well as I do.' He was careful not to say 'better than I do', which would have been the truth; he wanted to persuade her, without quite saying so, that he loved it, too, and wasn't the ignoramus he had been once. 'When the weather's fine, it's just like a pretty toy in a rainbow landscape, and in winter, when the mountains look like ghosts in trailing robes, it's no more than a huddle of dark shadows among other shadows. But last time I went home it was one of those calm days that look like a painting in *grisaille*, with the whole world drowning in mist. Except the castle. There it was, looming through the murk, rugged and four-square, and very much a force to be reckoned with.' He paused. 'And then I crossed the causeway and walked slam into the most complete and cosy domesticity. I was repelled – really repelled! I don't think I'd ever quite understood before what you and grandfather felt about Kinveil. I always thought you were being over-sentimental about the past. But that day I was cured. Curtains and carpets and pretty knick-knacks. Flowers in tubs along the sea wall. It was wrong, wrong, wrong! Like harnessing a lion to a governess cart, and tying ribbons in its mane.'

He was pitching it a bit high, in the attempt to impress her, but he *had* felt something.

Ignoring what he had considered to be some rather fine descriptive prose, she said, 'Yes, your grandfather had a kind of decision and purposefulness that suited Kinveil. Even though he looked the comfortable Glasgow merchant he was, he knew what Kinveil needed. He matched the place.'

'And my parents don't.' She didn't contradict him. 'My father's never going to live up to the old man. Only two things interest him, his comfort and his self-esteem.'

'No, you're being unfair. If Mungo had been less shrewd, less powerful, your father might well have developed differently. But he couldn't compete. Even so, he has managed to stay a personality in his own right. He may have his quirks, as we all have, but he's civil, well-mannered, and really quite kindly. Don't underestimate him.'

'No. You're right, I suppose. It's just that there has never been any spark of human contact between us. He defeats me. I can't tell how his mind works.'

'Or even *if* it works?' Her smile was quizzical.

He laughed. 'Sometimes I wonder! Frankly, if I hadn't been due to leave the other day, they'd have had to summon up the Bedlam wagon for me. Father has suddenly decided that, although Bannister does all the work, he ought to take an intelligent interest. Even in things he doesn't understand. It was almost too much for me when he began to explain to me – very kindly! – how kelp is made!'

'Whereas even I can remember you, black as a tinker, wielding the kelping clatt with your own hand when you were only eight. Poor Luke! It must have been very frustrating.' She frowned a little. 'I'm surprised you're still making kelp. I thought the government was going to abolish the protective tariffs, and if that happens the market will certainly collapse.'

Luke shrugged. 'Bannister doesn't seem to be worried.' Bannister, in fact, had raised the matter, but Magnus had said, 'Everyone's used to kelping and we don't want to change things too much, you know!' So the grieve, the brightness of his brown eyes scarcely dimmed by two friendless years, had said, 'Dear me, no, sir. We could still compete with the imported alkalis if we improved the quality. Tangle from below the low-tide mark, and more care with the burning . . .' He was a cooperative little man. Magnus had said, 'Splendid! Splendid!' and gone back to the cloth samples that had just arrived from his tailor.

Showing off, Luke said, 'The price has dropped a pound a ton in the last year, though, and if the tariffs come off, you're right and it will be a disaster. Kelp isn't much of a substitute for the best alkalis. Canada's had fifteen hundred ships transporting pearl ash across the Atlantic lately, and when Mediterranean barilla can come in freely, *and* when the new artificial chemical manufactories really get into their stride with making alkalis from salt, the bottom's bound to fall out of the market.'

'Very impressive,' she said drily, and he coloured. 'Does your father know all this?'

'I've no idea, and it would be a waste of breath telling him. But, you know,' he went on earnestly, 'I had rather he didn't know. Because if Bannister gives up kelp, he's sure to start covering the estate with sheep or trees or both. And we don't want that, do we?'

3

Impossibly, he became more and more obsessed by Vilia, although her attitude to him changed scarcely at all. As the time for each visit drew near, he promised himself that this time he would do something about it. And then, at sight of her – cool, assured, detached – his courage would fail him and he would think, 'Not this time. Next time.'

Meanwhile, it gave him a dismal pleasure to distress her, as if he were exacting recompense for his own unhappiness. Just talking about Kinveil hadn't been enough. Now, he deliberately began to foster her uneasiness about the place, persuading himself that concern for it was something they truly shared. If he could worry her enough, she would be compelled to go and see for herself. It was not until the end of 1825, when he was on his way home from Oxford for the last time, that he discovered what a dangerous game he had been playing, for he had observed none of the subtle signs that might have warned a more sensitive, or less self-centred lover, to tread with care.

It was a Saturday evening and Vilia had come back late from the foundry. She didn't show any sign of being tired, and was even drily entertaining about her afternoon discussing the accounts with Wally

293

Richards, pink and plump and well-polished as ever, although he had abandoned his attar of roses for a more sophisticated blend of cloves and orris root. 'I had always thought,' Vilia said, 'that he used some kind of liquid soap to keep his hair in place, because there seemed no other explanation for the scent being so tenacious. He's as fragrant at seven in the evening as at seven in the morning. But I discovered the other day that he keeps a silver washball slung over the hanger where he puts his coat when he is working alone in his office. So the scent comes not only from his morning baptism but from the coat as well, which is quite *permeated* with it. I should so like to keep him standing out in the rain some day, to see if his coat works up an independent lather!'

Unfortunately, the subject of soap led straight to the subject of alkalis, and Luke, even more unfortunately, took no trouble to disguise his satisfaction when he said, 'Kelp dropped another pound a ton this year, but Bannister's still trying to improve the product.' He laughed.

It startled him out of his skin when Vilia came as near to snapping his nose off as she had done since she was fifteen. 'Luke!' she exclaimed. 'Don't you even *begin* to realize that it isn't just a matter of you feeling superior to your father? I assume he's continued Mungo's system of dividing the profits with the kelpers, which was an excellent system when the stuff was in demand. But the people who make kelp haven't time to cultivate their own food crops, and they rely on their profits for that. If there aren't any profits, how are they going to eat? I don't suppose either you or your father has even thought of that!'

They hadn't. Luke said sulkily, 'Well, it's not easy. At least kelp gives them the *chance* of making money. It's a gamble, but so is growing oats and barley! Look at last year – "the year of the short corn", they're calling it. Even in quite good agricultural country – and Kinveil isn't *that*! – the harvest was a disaster. If we give up kelp, then it has to be black cattle, and their price is only half what it was ten years ago. Or fishing, and the herring are moving away from inshore. Or something else. What do you want us to do? Go in for sheep after all? Well, we might. Father says we'll wait and see how Edward gets on at Glenbraddan, but if he gets on well, sheep it could easily be. So don't say I didn't warn you.'

He wasn't being quite as ingenuous as he sounded. Oxford was over. Three years gone, and he had scarcely noticed because his mind had all been on Vilia. This was the last time he could turn up at Marchfield as if it were some posting inn. From now on, he would have to stay at Kinveil, doing all the things his father couldn't be bothered doing. Journeys wouldn't be casual any more, and if he wanted to visit Vilia he would have to write first and ask if it was convenient. And it might not be. It was his last chance to worry Vilia into inviting herself to Kinveil.

'And how *is* Edward getting on?'

He shrugged, still sulky at being criticized. Edward had come of age in 1824 and, solemnly and ceremoniously, had taken the management of Glenbraddan into his own hands, keeping the grieve on to do the dirty work – like telling the tenants Edward wanted their holdings for his sheep. Not that Edward liked doing it, but he didn't let it stop him.

Luke had pointed out that there were thousands of acres of empty land, and it didn't seem necessary to shift the people, but Edward, his round eyes fixed and earnest, had said it wasn't economic to keep a flock of less than two thousand, and that meant he needed the high pastures that were the best and richest of the spring and summer grazing. And there was something else. 'You know the tenants have a few so-called sheep of their own?'

'Yes, of course. The "little old sheep" they keep for their milk.'

'Just so. Useless beasts. One gets practically no mutton from them, the fleeces are too thin to sell, and they're impossible to herd. Cheviots bunch together into flocks, but the "little old sheep" scatter to the winds at the first sight of a sheepdog. No. If one is going into sheep farming, one doesn't want those hairy little brutes grazing the same land as one's expensive Cheviots. Just think of the risk of cross-breeding! A decent flock has to be pure, you know!'

The conversation had been brought to a summary conclusion by thirteen-year-old Grace, who had Views on almost everything. 'Well,' she had said severely, 'I believe it to be quite improper to put poor people out of their homes just so that you can make a profit!'

Her brother's prim mouth had tightened. 'Don't be impertinent!' he said, and added in his most damping tone, 'Unless I make a profit somehow, you and mother and Georgiana and Shona will regret it as much as I. It should not be necessary for me to remind you that you all rely for your comfort on *my* generosity.'

And Edward couldn't understand why nobody loved him!

Vilia said again, sharply, 'How *is* Edward getting on?'

Luke shrugged again and said, 'Well enough, I suppose. He's only just started.'

'Has he moved the people out yet?'

'That was the first thing he did, or tried to. He's split some of the old joint farms into separate crofts for them, and fenced them off. Doesn't want their plebeian "little old sheep" fraternizing – if that's the word – with his genteel Cheviots.'

Vilia didn't even smile. 'How are the people taking it?'

'Not very well. Some of them are refusing to move, which only makes Edward more determined, of course. Unless somebody backs down, there's going to be trouble one of these days, and it won't be Edward who backs down. Did I tell you? No, I don't believe I did. Just after the flocks arrived there was a good deal of sheep stealing, and none of Edward's well-publicized threats had the least effect. So when the mutton-fancier was caught, nothing would do for Edward but to hand him over to the law. He was tried at the August circuit in Inverness, and hanged.'

Vilia could remember being taken as a child to watch a hanging at the Longman, because it was thought to be a salutary experience for children. Even today, she could still see the procession from the jail to the gallows two miles away on the shore. Soldiers first, and then the town officials in their red coats, and then the magistrates and council. Then the culprit with the noose already round his neck, and the hangman holding the free end of the rope. And all the way, the sound of someone praying – one of the clergymen, or the condemned man himself. And the man's family crouched weeping at the foot of the scaffold.

'Who was it?' she asked.

'Someone called Wat Gillespie. I didn't know him.'

She drew in a violent breath. 'I did.' Rising abruptly to her feet, she took a few hasty paces round the room, hands gripping her folded elbows. It was a pleasant room with a comfortable elegance about it, but no particular character, as if Vilia had never taken the time to set her seal on it. She turned. 'Couldn't you have stopped it?' Her voice was peremptory. 'Couldn't you have shown Edward what a fool he was? Wattie Gillespie probably didn't even know he was doing anything wrong. He never had as much sense as you could put in a thimble. And to hang him!' She turned away again sharply. 'God! It's incredible! How could you let Edward *do* it!'

'Damn it all, Vilia! Don't blame me! What could I have done? Tell me!'

She whirled round. 'Tell you? Tell you? If you don't know, what *can* I tell you? You didn't care enough. If you had cared, you could have stopped it!'

'I did care. I did! But Edward wouldn't listen.'

It didn't occur to Luke that Vilia was venting her own feelings rather than apportioning blame, and he took her criticism far harder and more personally than it was intended. He was hurt, angry, and defensive, and all his careful nonchalance dissolved into a juvenile sarcasm. 'He would have listened to *you*, no doubt! We all know that Mistress Cameron only has to speak to be obeyed! But I'm only a cousin, and younger than he is, and I don't have a mother and three sisters depending on me. In fact, as Edward so obligingly pointed out, I have no experience of responsibility and might think differently if I had. He might be right, too. Perhaps I *would* take a different moral stance if the sheep that had been stolen were mine. If one criminal escapes unhung, other criminals multiply!'

'Don't be childish. Did Edward import shepherds as well as sheep?'

'Of course.'

'What do you mean, "of course"? I can understand that the solution mightn't have occurred to Edward, whose intellect is scarcely profound, but you have no excuse. If Edward had simply employed local people their pride would have been involved, and they would have taken good care that there was no poaching.'

Luke's colour was high. 'Don't patronize me, Vilia,' he said hardily. 'I'm not one of your unfortunate employees. For which I thank God!'

She stared at him. She could see that it had taken every ounce of his will-power to stand up to her, and wondered why. His jaw, partly hidden by the shallow white shirtpoints projecting above his fashionable black cravat, was lax, and his lips when he spoke had not been altogether under control.

'So do I!' she snapped.

His resistance collapsed. 'Damn it all, Vilia,' he almost whined. 'It wasn't my fault.'

Would he never grow up, she wondered. He had all his mother's anxious desire for universal harmony, but with him selfishness was at its root. What he wanted was the flattery of general approval, and he was still immature enough to believe that such a thing existed. To Vilia, he seemed younger even than eleven-year-old Theo.

Whatever her failings as a mother, Vilia had at least succeeded in inculcating into her sons a spirit of self-reliance – a truer self-reliance by far than the kind she had thought she herself possessed until that dreadful year of 1822, the year when Mungo had died just when she needed him most. She hadn't known how heavily she had leaned on him. The pain of his death had been worse than the pain of Perry Randall's second desertion, and worse even than the banishment from Kinveil that had followed, although that was a pain that grew now with every passing month, perhaps because she knew it must end soon. Deep inside, she was possessed by a sense of expectancy, as if all her instincts were holding their breath.

She knew now what a farce they had been, all those years of trying to cut Kinveil out of her heart. Not only farce, but fiasco. Of her three loves, it alone remained. Since Mungo's death, when she had learned her last salutary lesson and begun, with care and deliberation, to hold back from the human relationships that brought nothing but hurt in their wake, she had discovered the true extent of her need for Kinveil. She could manage without people, she felt, provided she was not cut off from that mystic corner of the Highland landscape. Her mind, cool and analytical, assessed her feelings and found them absurd. But reason had nothing to do with it. Acknowledging the truth of what her mind told her, she was still, and increasingly, driven by the intuition that she would never again be happy anywhere except at Kinveil.

Her eyes, green as opals in the candlelight, returned to the present. Exasperation still in her voice, she said, 'Oh, for goodness' sake, sit down, Luke!' and herself sank back into her chair.

She was silent for a moment longer, turning the heavy Kinveil ring absently on her finger, then she said more calmly, 'I apologize. Why should I read you a lecture, when you didn't even know poor Wattie?' There was the hint of a smile on her lips. 'My temper isn't altogether reliable these days. I don't know whether you've heard that there is a serious financial crisis on the horizon – too many years of extravagant speculation, and now the banks are beginning to take fright and call in their loans. The foundry won't be directly affected, but half-built houses are being left unfinished, and Edinburgh is full of unemployed masons and bricklayers, and I am having to give serious thought to the problem of our architectural materials.'

It was, on the whole, a very generous apology, but Luke's reply made no acknowledgement. 'Indeed?' he said, his voice stiff and expressionless. 'That must be worrying for you.'

There had been a light throb in her head all day, and it was becoming stronger and more insistent. Suddenly, the effort of appeasing him was beyond her, and she didn't care very much, anyway. He was only a boy, who didn't know anything, and didn't want to know. So she smiled again and said, 'Yes. But let's talk about something more interesting. Tell me about your plans for the future.'

4

How had it all flared up? Afterwards, Luke didn't even know. But she had criticized him, made him feel inadequate, spoken to him as if he were still a child. When he rode away from Marchfield House next day, he knew she was glad to see him go. Still in the grip of a sick resentment, he had no idea when he would see her again, or even whether he wanted to. He tried to convince himself that everything was over between them, but there had never *been* anything between them. And that, perhaps, rankled more than anything.

Chapter Two

1

Luke Telfer stepped out onto his balcony and, leaning his elbows carefully on the crumbling balustrade, looked out over the towers and domes of Venice, 'Queen of the Adriatic', now tinted a dusky rose in the light of the setting sun. It still surprised him how pink Italian sunsets were, how insipidly pretty compared with the fiery splendours of nightfall at Kinveil. But tonight, for the first time, it also struck him that the air tasted stale, flat, and unwholesome, and that the eternal lapping of muddy water against steps and buildings and the hulls of gondolas was beginning to prey on his nerves.

The city's ramshackle grandeur, its atmosphere of long and leisured decadence, had pleased him at first, although the hordes of sightseers had not. So, with the new assurance born of a year of European travel, he had suggested to Henry that they abandon the modest comforts of the Hotel Gran Bretagna in favour of one of the apartments that were to let in the palazzi along the Grand Canal. They had inspected several, and the Palazzo Solari had looked, from the outside, no more inviting than the rest, a damp-stained edifice painted – though not recently – in salmon and white, with a kind of boardwalk balanced over the front stairs so that it was necessary to scramble, rather than step, out of the gondola. Luke and Henry had groped their way through a pitch dark hall in the wake of a voluble gentleman who interrupted his discourse to warn them, first, to beware of the *cane*, and then, a moment later, of the *scimmia*. A dog seemed reasonable enough, but a monkey? Within seconds, something had landed neatly and talkatively on Luke's shoulder, where it stayed until they reached their objective on the second floor. Then it took off with a flying leap and swarmed up the peacock blue damask curtains to settle, with a chatter of self-satisfaction, in one of the hammock-like swags at the top.

Luke had grinned back at it, and then turned his attention to his surroundings. They were faintly raffish, but also spacious, striking, and very palatial indeed. The saloon in which he stood was all of eighty feet long, and there was scarcely an inch of wall or ceiling that wasn't covered with paintings or frescoes. Turkish carpets argued vociferously with the patterned marble floor, and the furniture was so extravagantly carved and gilded that it verged on the preposterous. Luke didn't even have to ask Henry what he thought of it; he knew his tutor's tastes only too well by now. At seventy-five guineas a month, the apartment wasn't expensive by Venetian standards, and they moved in next day.

Now, six weeks later, Luke wondered whether he wasn't becoming *blasé*. He was tired of admiring buildings and pictures, tired of his daily ride near the Lido, tired of the food sent in by the local trattoria, tired of the fashionable little casinos behind the Piazza San Marco where everyone who was sufficiently anyone to be invited was expected to while away the nights with coffee, conversation, and cards before trailing home to bed after dawn.

He tapped his mother's letter thoughtfully against his teeth. Her bulletins had run like a thread of counterpoint through the major theme of his European travels. He could even remember where and when each one had arrived, crisp and crackling, with its neat superscription and lavender wafer. The first had been waiting for him in Paris in May of last year, when he had returned from an expedition to the châteaux of the Loire.

I so much hope you are yourself again! Your father and I were quite distressed to see you so unhappy during those months after your return from Oxford. Indeed, it seems to us now that we should have suggested the Grand Tour a good deal sooner than we did. But never mind. How I wish I could be with you. So exciting! Our excitements here seem quite pale by comparison. Edward's marriage to Harriet Morton went off very well, and they are admirably suited. And you may interpret that remark in whichever way you choose! She is, I fear, somewhat plain, with hair verging on the mouse and an expression of piety that reminds one dreadfully of all one's own imperfections. But she has a very methodical nature and likes everything to be just so, which, as you may imagine, has put Edward in such a glow that he is almost human. Your Aunt Charlotte, who has been unwell again, is pleased to have her, since Georgiana is not to be relied on. I cannot imagine who that young lady inherits her disposition from, for she is perfectly giddy – there is no other word for it. Your father says she must be a throwback, but I can't think to whom. From all I have ever heard, both the Telfer and Blair ancestors were uniformly, and quite tediously, respectable. Gracious – don't misunderstand me! I don't for a moment mean that dear Georgy is not respectable!

Luke wouldn't have cared to bet on it. During that morose year at Kinveil, he had tried to lighten his depression by getting up a mild flirtation with dear Georgy, but half-way through the first non-cousinly encounter he had sheered off hurriedly, pointing out to a frustrated Georgy that it was he, not she, whom Edward would be after with a shotgun. She had shrugged. 'Pooh!' she said. 'I wouldn't marry you anyway. I have no intention of drowsing the rest of my life away at Kinveil. Dear me, no!'

The second letter had come when he was at Cologne in August, just about to set sail on the Rhine. He had been to see the cathedral, and his head was full of flying buttresses and mullions and quatrefoils and cusps. The slender, soaring beauty of the cathedral choir had made him

301

think of Vilia, but his mother's letter spoke only of Georgiana, with her retroussé nose, dusky curls, and diminutive figure. More like a dissenting chapel, he had thought, pursuing the analogy, and had grinned to think how incensed Georgy would have been if she'd known.

Georgy, it seemed, had fallen passionately in love with a French gentleman who had come to admire the Highlands and stayed to admire Miss Blair. 'Extraordinarily handsome, in a luxuriant kind of way,' Luke's mother wrote, 'as well as being extremely charming, with that rather baroque French charm.' Georgy said she would die if she were not allowed to marry him, but Edward was determined to make some inquiries about the gentleman first, in case he turned out not to be a gentleman at all.

By the time the third letter arrived, it was November, and Luke had finished with the Rhine, where he had admired the castles but not the wines, and travelled on to Salzburg by a roundabout route that had allowed him to spend time in Vienna. There, he had ignored the architecture, enjoyed the music, continued to dislike the wine, and eaten his way round every warm, sugar-and-spice-scented konditorei in the city. He had also put on weight. He hoped the Alps would take it off again. But although his mother's letter was full of dutifully maternal laments about his absence at the festive season, he had still felt no longing for home. Florence seemed to him a much more appealing place to spend Christmas. And after Florence, Rome. Disappointingly, Henry's cassock and cardinal's hat failed to raise even an eyebrow in the Eternal City, but Luke had no time to dwell on it, since Henry had enrolled them both for an antiquarian course designed to ensure that they saw every church, palace, villa and ruin that was held to be worth seeing – and all within the space of six weeks.

Lucy's February letter had arrived in the middle of it. Edward's bride, it appeared, was now in an interesting condition, and Georgiana was to be married to M. Savarin later in the year.

'Dear Georgy!' his mother exclaimed charitably.

She is so very happy! But another piece of quite different news. My dear, you won't believe it, but Glengarry has gone to his ancestors! In the most ludicrous way, and *perfectly* characteristic. He was on his way to Glasgow on the *Stirling Castle* when it was driven aground in a storm near Fort William. Glengarry – of course! – could not wait to be rescued, but jumped impatiently ashore, lost his footing, and was killed on the rocks. It remains only to add that the other passengers were landed without the least difficulty and in perfect safety. I am told the funeral was something quite out of the ordinary. There was a tremendous thunderstorm, which was quite appropriate, you must agree. His blind bard keened over the coffin, having composed a special lament for the occasion – 'Blessed the corpse that the rain falls on'. What a lot of blessed corpses we must have in this part of the world! His heir seems to have been left nothing but law suits and debts, and talks only of declarators, advocations, issues, answers, and avizandums. No, *don't* ask me! I have no idea what an avizandum may be!

Luke was sorry about Glengarry, tiresome poseur though he had been, with his passion for 'old' customs whose antiquity wasn't merely doubtful, but certifiably bogus. But he had been likeable in his way. Luke had shrugged and gone back to his ruins.

And now it was April, and he was in Venice, and he was weary of it. And he knew why.

He didn't need to reread *this* letter, even if there had been light enough. Thoughtfully, from the balcony bowered in climbing greenery and decked with tubs of bay and orange, he watched the tapers start to glimmer under the awnings, and the lanterns of the gondolas turn their wakes to oily flame. Far to his left, a brightly lit barge full of musicians drifted to a halt, its raised sweeps gleaming, before one of the palazzi, and played a serenade before the oars were dipped again and it glided off into the darkness. A nearby gondolier caught the melody and took it up, and was answered by others, further away, whose voices echoed under the bridges, plaintive and soulful.

It was the purest romance, but Luke's thoughts were on another bridge, not far from Glenbraddan, built from cast iron supplied by a certain foundry near Edinburgh. Because of administrative delays, it had taken almost ten years to complete, but it was to be opened officially at the beginning of October.

And Vilia was to be there. It was the first news he had had of her for more than two years, although he had written to her twice, casual, conversational notes that didn't seem to need a reply unless one read very carefully between the lines.

'It will be such a joy to see her again,' Lucy Telfer had written.

Your father and I agreed that now, if ever, was the time to try and bring about a reconciliation between Vilia and your Aunt Charlotte, so I spoke very seriously

303

to your aunt and the long and the short of it was that she agreed to let bygones be bygones. I think that, even now, she might not have given in if she had been her usual self, but I must tell you that she is suffering from a malady that gives her a great deal of pain, which can only be controlled by opiates. Indeed, I fear she has not many years to live. So sad. I had more trouble with Edward than with his mother, though *really* it is no concern of his! And I had just succeeded in bringing him round when Georgy very nearly ruined everything by exclaiming that Vilia must be invited to the wedding, too, which takes place three weeks before the bridge opening. With the most provoking want of tact, she said she wanted Emile to see that we had 'at least one truly stylish person among us'. *I ask you!* Even *I* was a little offended, though I knew what she meant. Anyway, the important thing is that Vilia is to come to us at Kinveil in the first week of September, and stay until the bridge is opened in October. It *will* be delightful!

The long siesta of the Venetian day was over and the city waking to life again. But, Luke thought, remembering what Socrates had said of Athens, Venice was *melior meretrix quam uxor*, a better mistress than wife; a fine place for a few weeks, but not for a lifetime.

Light sprang up in the chamber behind him as a servant came in, as always at this hour, to bring refreshments and set a taper to the candles. Luke sighed, and turned back into the room. His charming mistress, black-haired, voluptuous, and drowsy, still lay among the disordered sheets of the vast, velvet-hung four-poster, smiling at him invitingly. But he crossed first to the buffet cupboard and poured out two cool glasses of Turin vermouth. Then, clasping her lax fingers round the stem of one of them with his own curled palm, he sat on the bed beside her and teasingly stroked his free hand down the rich, warm contours of her body. Involuntarily, her muscles tightened, but he laughed and stood up. Then, raising his glass, he said with a smile she couldn't quite interpret, 'To us. But you will have to find someone else now.'

This was a lover she would be sorry to lose, attractive, amusing, and – for an Englishman – surprisingly expert. She was a little, a very little, in love with him. With sultry, carefully calculated mischief, she stretched out a hand and turned back the skirt of his barbaric silk dressing-gown. Her brows raised in mock disbelief, she murmured, 'Can it be that I bore you?'

He chuckled. But as he set down his glass preparatory to proving that she didn't bore him in the least, he said, 'Never that. It is just that it's time for me to go home.'

2

It was several moments before the people round the fire became aware of Luke's presence. Once, it would have made him nervous to know that, as soon as he stepped forward, a dozen pairs of eyes would swivel his way, but such things no longer troubled him. Instead, he took his time and looked the company over.

Blindfold, he would have known that he was back at Glenbraddan. All houses had their own particular smell, and Glenbraddan's was compounded of beeswax and peat smoke, good housewifery, and the special sweet-scented candles his aunt made from the bog myrtle that flourished on the moors. Here, in the Painted Chamber, there was an extra tang of woodsmoke. Only logs were burned, to preserve the tempera ceiling that gave the room its name; tucked in between the beams were long, thin panels depicting long, thin prophets and patriarchs, with their attributes. Luke, as a child, had always been deeply worried about Moses, who was illustrated with the burning bush under his feet and several very substantial-looking tablets of the law just above his head, and seemed in perpetual danger of being either toasted or concussed, or both.

The room was cool. Gathered round the hearth at the far end of it were eleven people including Henry Phillpotts, who could change his clothes faster than anyone else of Luke's acquaintance. Aunt Charlotte was closest to the fire at one side, shockingly thin and haggard, and still in a warm, high-necked day dress, with Luke's mother beside her, wearing the soft wide-eyed smile that told her son she was putting up bravely with discomforts to which she was not accustomed. Then there was an unfamiliar, nondescript young woman, *plein comme un oeuf* – clearly Edward's wife, Harriet – and then young Grace, two years older and two years more earnest than when Luke had seen her last. Directly in front of the fire, though further from it than at least one of the group would have wished, were Edward, who was pontificating about something; Henry, who looked to be half asleep; and Magnus Telfer, who was making no attempt to hide his boredom or disguise the fact that he thought it high time someone put a glass in his hand.

But it was the group on the other side of the fire who held Luke's gaze. Their attention was concentrated on a young man whose waving chestnut hair and extravagantly Gallic gestures proclaimed him to be

Emile Savarin, tomorrow's bridegroom. Standing at his side was another stranger, a slender, dark young man of about twenty, moderately good-looking, with a high forehead, thin-boned nose, and meditative expression. Georgiana was seated, gazing up at them with a smile that only just fell short of roguish in her deceptively candid dark eyes. Her natural curls had been tortured into a style that was unmistakably the latest fashion, puffed out on the temples and raised on the crown into an Apollo knot of three plaited loops, perched like basket handles on an arrangement that reminded Luke irresistibly of a cottage loaf. Her gown was of celestial blue, with outrageously wide sleeves and a bodice tapering from a shoulder line that wouldn't have disgraced a strong man in a circus down to a waist that measured scarcely a handspan. She was *à la modality* personified.

Luke had to make a deliberate effort to turn his eyes towards the last person in the group, who had already seen him and was watching him with eyebrows slightly raised.

Vilia's attention had been wandering, and she had caught the movement at the far end of the room as he entered. But it would have been discourteous to interrupt M. Savarin's display of histrionics, so she waited until he was diverted by a self-conscious witticism from Georgy before she allowed herself to turn. Even from forty feet, she could see that there had been a radical change in Luke Telfer. Somewhere along the highways of Europe he had shed the languor and suppressed nervousness that had always irritated her and replaced them with an air of assurance and controlled vigour. The change showed in his straight shoulders, the poise of his head, and the relaxed and peaceful way his hands hung at his sides. She watched his sleepy brown eyes survey the company and noticed his amusement at Magnus's patent discontent, and the swiftly suppressed laughter when the full glory of Georgiana's toilette burst upon him. Then, at last, his gaze met hers and lingered for an arrested moment before he smiled, firmly and vividly, and stepped forward.

She smiled back at him, with the enigmatic smile he had recognized more than once among the sculptures of Mozac and Chartres, and then turned to touch Georgiana lightly on the arm and say, 'Your cousin is here.'

And then it all deteriorated into an ordinary family occasion, and Luke had to make his bows, and apologize to everyone for being three days late because the carriage spring had broken at Fochabers, and be introduced to tomorrow's bridegroom. Aunt Charlotte had opened up the formal dining-room for the occasion, a place designed in more spacious times to accommodate some fifty persons without crowding, so that at dinner a good three yards of table separated each cover from the next, which imposed its own strains on the conversation. Aunt Charlotte herself didn't help. She nagged at Georgiana, made it clear that she thought Luke had been permitted far too much licence on his travels – causing Luke to wonder what she would have said if she had been vouchsafed the full, unexpurgated version – and directed barbed comment after barbed comment at an infinitely patient Vilia. As far as Luke could judge, the only time she drew blood was when she said, 'I imagine, Mistress Lauriston, that it will not be long before *your* eldest son will be setting off on his Grand Tour?'

Before Vilia could speak, Magnus surged to her rescue. 'Nonsense, Charlotte! The boy's no more than a child. Hasn't even left school yet!'

But Vilia, her eyes suddenly dancing, said, 'Oh, but he has! He is just preparing to go to university!' And then, neatly putting Charlotte in her place, turned to Savarin and said, 'Though I should, perhaps, tell you that in Scotland fourteen is the age for going to university, not seventeen or eighteen, as in England.'

Luke wasn't impressed by Savarin, who seemed to his jaundiced eye to be playing the caricature Parisian, and was also paying a damned sight too much attention to Vilia, on whom he blandly relied for translations of all the words he didn't know in French or English. At one point, the fellow remarked, 'How should I have understood all this so enlightening conversation without you, madame? How comes it that you are so fluent in my language, if I may ask?'

Vilia looked very slightly nettled, as if he had cast a slur on her education and upbringing. 'My father lived in Paris for most of his early life,' she said, 'and spoke to me as often in French as he did in English. As a child, I learned the two languages almost simultaneously.'

Luke had forgotten what a cosmopolitan gentleman Theophilus Cameron had been, and suddenly realized how much it helped to explain about Vilia.

All the way home, by Milan and Geneva and Liège and Rotterdam, he had been haunted by uncertainties. It was almost three years now since he had ridden away from Marchfield House in a haze of resentment, a resentment that had persisted during the misanthropic months at Kinveil that had finally driven his parents to send him off on the Grand Tour, not for the sake of his education, but to give themselves a rest from him. When the excitement of travel had at last begun to shake him out of the sullens, he had been surprised – for he knew he was inclined to harbour grudges – to find that he was forgetting his resentment, but not forgetting Vilia. He had tried. In the climate of European society, it was easy enough for a good-looking young man with plenty of money to find charming and complaisant ladies to divert him. And not professional ladybirds of the kind Luke had known before, but fashionable, experienced young widows and pretty, neglected wives. They had taught him a great deal, and he had enjoyed his lessons prodigiously, but just the promise of seeing Vilia again had been enough to make him cut short a delightful liaison in Venice and set out on the journey home. At Milan, he had dreamed of the glow that would light her eyes when she saw him and knew how much she had missed him. At Geneva, he visualized himself taking her hand masterfully in his and telling her how he felt, and had always felt, about her. But by Liège he was remembering that she had never so much as set foot across the Channel in her whole life. By Rotterdam, he had begun to suspect that when he saw her again he would find her no more than a pretty, provincial woman who couldn't hold a candle to the glorious creatures he had enjoyed in the most civilized cities in Europe. And by Aberdeen he had succeeded in convincing himself that, in another few days, he would be cured of her for ever.

And he had been quite, quite wrong. He had forgotten what an air she had. Forgotten the length and thickness of her eye-lashes and the way her hair shone like raw silk. Forgotten how exotic her colouring. Forgotten her agile mind. Forgotten, above all, that strangely positive quality that had nothing to do with beauty.

After their first exchange of glances, he had dragged his wandering wits together and recognized that he must prove to her, and at once, that he had at last achieved maturity. Slowly, over the last three years, it had been borne in on him that he must have seemed very gauche to her during his Oxford days, always on edge, always deferring, too preoccupied with the image he was presenting to her to be able to behave naturally. Never in either of their lives, or so he had thought one despondent evening in Maastricht, had she seen him at his best. Now he was a grown man, urbane, amusing, more than capable – or so he had been assured – of holding his own in any company, and it was necessary to let her know it.

The problem was how to go about it. For what remained of that evening, and throughout the next day, Luke was so preoccupied with showing himself in his best light that he noticed very little of what was said, or what was going on, except as it related to himself. Only occasionally was his attention attracted by some remark or other that offered him the opportunity to display his superior taste or knowledge. There was a certain irony in the fact that he made his greatest impression with a nugget or two of information he had gleaned from his grandfather.

The older members of the company had retired to bed, and Georgiana collapsed back into her chair with a sigh of relief. 'Poof!' she exclaimed. 'Why is it that all one's nearest and dearest are so staid and stuffy?' Ignoring Grace's instant protest, she went on, 'If *only* my stepfather hadn't had the good taste to run away all those years ago! How I wish you had met him, Emile! The most elegant man, and with such style!' Impulsively, she turned to Vilia. 'You knew him, didn't you, Mrs Lauriston? He *was* charming, wasn't he? I was still quite young when he left, and perhaps not a very good judge, but it has always seemed to me that he was quite out of the common run.'

There was the briefest of pauses. It seemed to Luke that Vilia was searching her memory, trying to conjure up an image of the man she had met so briefly almost fifteen years ago. Even Luke who had been closer to Perry Randall than anyone else in his whole life – except Henry, which was rather different – found it hard to recall his uncle's features in any detail. What he remembered, mainly, was the sense of life and warmth and adventure he had generated in a lonely, unhappy, ten-year-old. The withdrawn, defeated man who had sailed for America at the end of 1815 had no more place in his recollection than an insubstantial, irrelevant ghost.

Vilia said, 'I met him only twice, you know, the second time for no more than a few minutes at Ascot. But yes, I seem to remember that he had a – an unusually attractive way with him. Dark hair, I think?' She turned to Luke. 'And about your height? I was told he went to America. Did you ever hear what became of him?'

'Oh, yes,' Luke said omnisciently. 'He went into business. Guns, I believe. Grandfather had one or two letters from him . . .'

'*What?*' Georgy squeaked, round-eyed.

'. . . although since he was out in the least civilized parts of the country, mail was dreadfully unreliable. I believe he had a difficult and dangerous time in the early days, but grandfather thought there was hope for him. Very pleased he was, too, because he had a fondness for Uncle Perry.'

'When was this?' Vilia asked, with polite interest.

Luke couldn't remember at first. 'Oh, in about '20 or '21, I suppose.'

'And he never told anyone!' Georgy exclaimed. 'Well, I do think that was unfair of him.'

Grace, with sad reasonableness, said, 'It would have upset Mama. But I confess I should have liked to know that my father was safe and well. Have you heard nothing since, Luke?'

It rather spoiled the effect to have to confess, 'No, not a word.' But it occurred to him for the first time that perhaps something might have happened to his uncle. Seven years was a long silence.

Vilia was looking thoughtful, and Grace showed signs of wishing to pursue the subject, but M. Savarin had more urgent matters on his mind than the errant Mr Randall, and Luke retired again into abstraction while Georgiana embarked, for what didn't sound like the first time, on a detailed description of everything the groom and his groomsman, the silent Peter Barber – who was apparently a student of philosophy – needed to know about the next day's ceremonies.

Even so, the two young men had clearly not been prepared to find the bridal route lined with crofters and tenants liberally endowed with black eyes and make-shift bandages – evidence of the impromptu game of shinty, a murderous kind of hockey, with which they had whiled away the waiting time. Nor had they expected the volley that greeted them on their emergence from the kirk, which came from as motley a collection of firearms as Luke ever hoped to see. There were pocket pistols, carriage pistols, a blunderbuss of heroic proportions, and something that looked uncommonly like a musket, as well as shotguns old, new, and prehistoric. Luke didn't altogether blame Savarin for flinching. And after that there was the public wedding breakfast in the great stone barn, complete with a whole ox and several sheep roasted on the spit in true mediaeval style. The cooks weren't used to it, and the results were uneven. It was M. Savarin's misfortune that his plate happened to be piled with the carbonized bits. 'Mon dieu!' he breathed, surveying it reverently.

Luke watched it all, without really being part of it, concentrated wholly on himself and Vilia, as if they were at two ends of a telescope and everything else was peripheral to his vision. He was waiting for some sign from her, a sign that she had recognized the change in him.

But when the sign came, it wasn't like that at all. Without being conscious of any particular feeling, he had watched her progress through reels, flings and strathspeys, country dances and quadrilles and cotillions, with everyone from his father, through a variety of Grants and Frasers and Macraes and Macleods, to Glengarry's debt-ridden young successor, Aeneas Macdonell, nervous and stiff and wearing an eagle's feather in his cap. And then she stood up with Sorley.

Luke had never seen her so vivid, so carefree, so sparkling, and his stomach contracted violently with jealousy. Sorley led her to her place in the reel, and Vilia, laughing, held her mouth up to him for the smacking kiss that, among Highlanders and among friends, was the natural preliminary to the dance. Sorley hesitated for a moment and, then, with his blinding smile, planted his lips on hers before standing back to take up his position. For Luke, suddenly, the world turned upside down.

He stood and watched them. They scarcely spoke during the dance, for they had no breath to spare, and since a Highland reel always sounded like war in heaven they could scarcely have made themselves heard, anyway. But it made no difference. Luke could see that they were in perfect accord, sharing something he was unable to identify, something deeper and more intimate than the simple pleasure of the moment. What he couldn't know was that they were both remembering the ceilidhs of their childhood, in the warm friendly kitchen of Kinveil, once a vaulted dungeon but by then a wonderful place lit by pungent tallow candles and reeking of the clean, eye-stinging smoke of the peats and the appetizing odours of toasting oatmeal and stewing mutton. Not since Vilia was seven and Sorley five had they hopped together to a fiddler's tune. Kinveil, then, had been their whole world. They had loved it blindly and devotedly and had believed such days would never end.

When Sorley led Vilia, laughing and exhilarated and absurdly youthful, off the floor, Luke was waiting, every muscle under control, and his eyes glinting with the private, humorous smile that experience had taught him was the surest way to any woman's heart. But the control was precarious and the humour false. For six years he had worshipped Vilia from a distance, as if she were some lady of courtly love. Even last night, even today, his preoccupation with her had remained romantic, only fleetingly touched by the physical. Until he had seen Sorley kiss her, when everything had changed.

3

Not for another three weeks was Luke able to catch Vilia quite alone, and even then it was difficult.

A few days after Georgiana's wedding the equinoctial gales had begun to blow, so that the islands had disappeared into thick banks of cloud that parted only briefly to show the Cuillins, black and menacing, swept by great grey sheets of advancing rain. The wet, gusty wind blew with bewildering velocity and strength, and the noise outdoors was stupefying, for the howl of the gale and the separate shrieks that punctuated it were backed by the unceasing roar of the Atlantic, surging along Loch an Vele in great rollers twenty feet high, leaden grey, with long plumes of spray at the crests. As they hit the curve of the land they broke into colossal, tumbling confusion, curling over and then thundering down on the rocks and bursting into pillars of white foam, before the undertow caught them and swept them into a huge vortex, the whirlpool that gave the loch its name.

At last had come a morning of seeming calm, as if the winds had blown themselves out, and Luke's mother suggested that Shona, who had been a guest at Kinveil for the last ten days, must be anxious to go home and see Harriet's new baby. Shona hadn't been very enthusiastic, and Luke could understand it. By all the laws of probability, the child was bound to resemble either Edward or Harriet or – gruesome thought – both of them. On the other hand, Luke had been finding Shona's adolescent passion for Vilia more than a little trying.

Seeing Shona at Glenbraddan had reawakened a dull ache in Vilia's heart, and it was this, she later thought, that had drawn the child to her, for Shona, though pretty, and sweet, and shy, received scant kindness from her mother and governess, and was treated with no more than careless tolerance by Edward and Georgiana. Only Grace paid any attention to her, ruling her with all the tyranny of good intentions. But, somehow, Shona had sensed that Vilia was not indifferent, and Vilia, fighting her own private battle against the past and aware that the child was its innocent victim, had been touched by her timid advances and could not help but be kind.

Luke couldn't understand why Vilia was so patient and gentle with her. He had found it impossible to prise the child from her goddess's side. With admirable promptitude, therefore, he had volunteered to drive Shona back to Glenbraddan that very day, adding in an undertone to his mother, 'I believe she might consent to go more readily if Vilia were to accompany us.' It would be a squeeze in the curricle, but he didn't care.

Lucy, who enjoyed children only in limited doses, had exclaimed, 'How clever of you! I will suggest it at once!'

But they were very nearly back at Kinveil again, without Shona, and it was beginning to appear as if Luke's resourcefulness had been wasted after all. The calm, sunny morning had proved to be deceptive, and the wind was working up to gale force once more, thrashing the trees that had somehow retained a foothold in the inhospitable soil, and filling the narrow passes between the mountains with a roar that assaulted the ear as unremittingly as a torrent in spate. It was scarcely the weather for romance, but Luke was desperate by now. Even so, he had almost given up when, on his right, he saw a smooth patch of turf scooped out of the mountain just at a point where the road curved round preparatory to plunging straight back into the teeth of the wind. It looked as if it might be sheltered, and it was now or never. Sharply, he reined in his horses and drew the curricle on to the grass.

Vilia looked at him in surprise, her colour whipped high and curling tendrils of silver-blonde hair escaping from the scarf rakishly tied over the tam o' shanter that had moved Lucy to shocked protest. 'But only *peasants* wear such things!' She looked as if she were enjoying herself, and was for once less than perfectly groomed.

Luke wound the reins round his right forearm and turned to her, saying in mock sorrowing tones, 'A week at Glenbraddan and almost two weeks at Kinveil, and we haven't had the opportunity for a private

313

talk in all that time. Tell me, my dear. How are you? What's been happening since we last met?'

Her smile was quizzical, and a little measuring. He wondered whether he had overdone it with that slightly superior 'my dear'. And then he was diverted for a moment, because the horses were restive. When he had calmed them, he turned back to her. Even in shelter, the wind was still loud enough to drown the intimate tones he should have used, echoing from the rocks in a way that made him think of distant thunder. But he was keyed up and wouldn't be diverted now. Possessing himself of her hands, he held them hard, and in a voice robbed of careful nuance, said in a rush, 'Vilia! I love you! I've loved you so long. You *can't* be indifferent to me!'

He couldn't quite read her expression. She stared at him for a moment, and then, her eyes wide and dark in the shadows thrown by the mountains and the scudding clouds, swallowed and said something he didn't quite hear.

'What?' It came out as a muted shout, and she swallowed again and shrieked back, 'I said, "Oh!"'

It was scarcely encouraging, but he went on somehow. 'I know I must always have seemed very young, very immature to you, but these last months . . .' He realized that the wind was whisking his voice away, and went on more loudly, '. . . have taught me a great deal. I thought they might have cured me of you, but they haven't. I love you – *I love you* – far more than I ever thought possible.'

She was gazing at him, almost as if stunned, her eyes open on his and the delicate brows a little raised, and suddenly he was overcome by a wave of desire, the pent-up dreams of six long years. Madness to wait for an answer, he thought, when words could never express what he felt for her. Casting a swift glance up and down the empty road, he pulled her roughly into his arms and sealed her lips with his. For a delirious moment he felt the soft mouth yield under his, but then, even as joy flooded into his heart, she gave an inarticulate sound and began to push him away. All his senses rebelled. He wouldn't, couldn't, accept a rebuff – not now – and with a smothered groan he exerted his strength to draw her back to him.

But just as his lips were about to descend on hers again, he realized that her face was alive with amusement and that she was trying, unavailingly, to tell him something.

Uncertainly, he raised his head. And this time she was able to wail, loudly enough for him to distinguish, 'Luke! You niddicock! Stop!' And then, 'Can't you *hear*?'

Suddenly, he did hear, and released her with such unflattering alacrity that she fell back against the side of the curricle, gasping with helpless laughter.

The distant thunder, now, wasn't distant at all, but just round the shoulder of the mountain and approaching fast. '*Christ!*' Luke exploded, and with a surge of fury struck the heel of his palm against his forehead. 'The Skye cattle market!'

Then his horses began to plunge, claiming all his attention as there swept into sight, travelling at breakneck speed, the vanguard of what sounded like an enormous herd of cattle, flanked right and left by a dozen sheepdogs, their stomachs low to the ground and tongues lolling out of their mouths. They were far too intent on keeping the wild-eyed shorthorns in line to spare any attention for the curricle as they raced past, but Luke was just getting his horses under something approximating to control when a skinny, badly dressed little man with a hooked nose and ferret eyes came into view, riding a wiry pony and flicking his whip over the heads of the beasts nearest to him to keep them to the road. Seeing Luke, he dragged the pony round on to the grass and reined it in so sharply that it bucked and reared, and started Luke's horses plunging all over again.

'Damn you, Jamie Lowson!' Luke yelled in response to the little man's grin. 'How the hell did you get your animals away from the market so soon? I thought it only started yesterday!'

Jamie was beaming at Vilia, who, clinging to the side of the swaying vehicle, wore an expression that was perfectly seraphic. 'Aye, weel!' he bellowed in a voice of astonishing power. 'Ah thought Ah'd pay a shulling or two above the odds this time, to save higgling, and since Ah knew jist whit Ah was wanting – only stots, and nae coos – Ah went roon' yon market like a flea in a lodging-hoose. If I can get the beasts frae here tae the Fa'kirk Tryst aheed of a' the ithers, Ah can sell high enough to cover the extra Ah paid for them, and mair besides.'

Luke nodded at the steers thundering past, and shouted, 'If you keep them going at this rate, you'll be at Falkirk before any of the other drovers has even left Skye!'

'Canny dae that!' Jamie said regretfully. 'It's jist a wee trick o' the trade. You keep them going like the hammers to begin wi', tae lick them intae trail shape, but then you huv tae slow doon. There'd be nae flesh left on them itherwise.'

Vilia, with more foresight than her harassed swain, shrieked, 'How many have you bought this year, Jamie?' and when he replied, 'A thoosand heid o' cattle, and there's five thoosand sheep as weel,' dissolved into an uncontrollable fit of giggling.

Jamie, eyeing her percipiently, turned to an appalled Luke and yelled, 'Ye'll no get home till the morn's morn if ye dinny spring your horses the meenit this lot's past. The sheep're behind, but they're no sae easy tae drive, so you'll maybe make Kinveil before they get there!'

'Thank you!' Luke exclaimed bitterly. 'I didn't know you two knew each other.'

'Och, aye. Mistress Vilia was jist a wee bit lassie when Ah startit working fur the big drovers . . .'

Vilia interrupted. 'Don't you dare say how long ago, Jamie Lowson, you old blether!'

'Ah wusny going to,' he replied, injured. 'All Ah was going to say was, before Ah went intae business for mysel'.' He grinned. 'Aye, weel. Ah'd better be getting on. Johnnie Soutar and Wee Hamish are back there a bit, near the tail o' the herd. Ah'd advise you tae huv thae horses rarin' to go the meenit they've passed.'

With a valedictory grin and a salute with his whip he was gone, but it was well over twenty minutes before the tail of the herd rounded the bend, to the accompaniment of a great many Glasgow oaths from black-avised Johnnie Soutar and the grubby, ginger-haired urchin known as Wee Hamish, who looked as if he were having the time of his life. His face split into a wide, gap-toothed grin when he saw Luke, but he just had time to yelp, 'The sheep's three mile back, if yoose want tae beat them hame!' before he disappeared into the cloud of dust that, despite the recent rains, the herd had succeeded in kicking up.

When she was able to make herself heard again, Vilia said happily, 'Whit a stoor!' and Luke cast her a glance with more exasperation than amusement in it. 'One would think,' he said, 'that you had been associating with the lower classes. Anyway, stoor or no stoor, we'd better move. For God's sake, wrap your scarf round your mouth so that you don't inhale too much of it.' He slapped the reins on his horses' rumps, clicked his tongue imperatively, and said, 'Let's go! And devil take the hindmost!'

4

As declarations of love went, it hadn't been the most successful of all time, and what worried Luke was that, afterwards, Vilia seemed to be avoiding his eyes, although he couldn't tell whether it was deliberate or not. And then, next morning, his mother, with a pleased murmur of 'Alone at last!' – which provoked Vilia into a gurgle of laughter – swept her off to the drawing-room to catch up with half a dozen years' gossip, recommending her son to go and join his father and Henry Phillpotts, who were engaged on trying to settle Henry's future. Gloomily, Luke did as he was told. There didn't seem to be much alternative.

At twenty-four, Luke couldn't, even by the most optimistic stretch of the imagination – and Henry's imagination was nothing if not optimistic – be said to need a tutor any longer, but the openings for a forty-year-old eccentric were limited, even though Rome had given Henry a distaste for cassocks and he now dressed rather more conventionally. If one regarded claret broadcloth and purple velvet as conventional. Luke was very tired of Henry.

His father said, 'Well! Haven't you any suggestions?'

Henry's only real talent, as far as Luke had ever been able to discover, was that he had an unusual affinity with birds and animals, but he couldn't very well suggest that Henry apply for a position at His Majesty's little menagerie at Windsor. 'Something literary,' he replied hurriedly. 'His spelling's quite good, and you know how fond he is of books, and how many he's read. Down in the village, they call him the Mobile Library.'

For an unguarded moment, Henry allowed a look of pleased surprise to cross his face. Then he remembered that he had no opinion of the Kinveil yokels and, clearing his throat, said with a frown, 'A librarian, do you think? But there are very few gentlemen who employ private librarians these days.'

Luke had more important things to think about than wading through Debrett's *Peerage* in search of potential employers, which he could see would be the next stage. He had a thought. Gazing solemnly at his father, he said, 'You know, I believe Henry could be of the greatest assistance in relieving you of some of the burdens of the estate. All those papers you have to deal with, I mean. All that wearisome correspondence and administration!'

With malicious enjoyment, he saw that his father was swallowing it, hook, line and sinker, though if he spent more than an hour a day on administration, Luke would have been surprised.

Magnus nodded his head, much struck, while Henry bent an intent regard on his erstwhile pupil.

'You mean . . . ?' Magnus said.

'I mean that you'd find a secretary uncommonly useful, wouldn't you?'

Henry had not, clearly, been thinking of anything quite so lowly, but Magnus said thoughtfully, 'I've often considered . . . Indeed, I suppose I owe it to my position.'

Luke wondered whether his mother and Vilia had finished yet. 'And if you wished,' he said, with a minatory glance at Henry, 'I'm sure Henry would also be happy to relieve you of reading the Bible to the tenants on Sundays. *Wouldn't you, Henry?*' The minister of the united parishes of Kinveil and Glenbraddan had so much territory to cover that he preached at the various kirks in rotation. As a result, Magnus had to rise from his bed early on three Sundays out of four to fulfil his lairdly duties. Fond though he was of the sound of his own voice, he considered it a heavy imposition, especially since the service also included a number of lugubrious psalms and at least two interminable prayers, delivered extempore and in Gaelic by certain of the more devout members of the congregation. It made Sunday a very trying day for everyone.

Henry said, 'Well . . .'

'He could even preach a sermon,' Magnus said thoughtfully. 'And one or two rather short prayers, perhaps. That would certainly speed things up.'

Henry said, 'But . . .'

Luke silenced him with a glare. The conflict between Henry's High Church beliefs and the dour Presbyterianism of the glens was something that could be resolved later. Perhaps.

'No,' Magnus said. But Luke and Henry both knew that Magnus would come round, in a day or two, to thinking it had all been his own idea, and then it would be settled without further need for discussion.

'And I assume you'd like it to be settled?' Luke inquired acidly of his mentor, when that gentleman showed a continuing tendency to grumble. 'Acting as secretary to my father is the nearest thing to a sinecure you're ever likely to be offered!'

And Henry, while resenting most of the implications of this forthright remark, found himself compelled to agree.

Two minutes later, Luke strolled into his mother's drawing-room. The weather had cleared, and already on his lips was the casual suggestion that Vilia might care to join him in a walk on the hill. But his mother was alone with her embroidery, and Vilia had already gone.

5

All Vilia had wanted to do for more than three long weeks had been to escape to the hill and savour the knowledge of being back at Kinveil, where she belonged. Mungo would have understood, and would have shown he understood by making himself invisible, so that there was no need for excuses or explanations, or anything at all but to go in perfect freedom when she wanted to. But now she was only a guest, and had been forced to smile and chat and look regretfully out at the rain, as a civilized person was expected to do, and ask Magnus – in a helpless and feminine way – one or other of the questions about Catholic emancipation that ignorant ladies were asking well-informed gentlemen this year.

Then today, at last, opportunity had offered and she had fled, straight for the little hollow that had been her private eyrie in those long-ago days when the boundaries of the estate had been the boundaries of her world, the place where on warm August days she had lain half asleep in the heather, tattooed like an American Indian with bilberry juice, hummed around by insects as somnolent as herself, and relying on her own stillness and the sprig of elder tucked in her collar to ward off the midges that were the bane of the Highland summer. She remembered watching the buzzards planing and mewing over the hills, teaching their young where the best hunting grounds were. She saw again the people from the clachan working on their stacks, black or gold, depending on whether they were storing peats for the fire, or fodder for the beasts. Was reminded of the slow transition from day to dusk, with the landscape melting gently from green to smoky black, until the mountains turned to shavings of ebony, rimmed with peach against a sage-leaf sky. And then the moon would appear, a thread of worn silver, waking her to the realization that she was hungry and should have been home long since. And she would scamper down over the hummocks, and skip across the burns, and run laughing into the kitchen to be hugged and scolded and have a toasted bannock and a glass of goat's milk thrust into her eager hands.

It was strange how dancing with Sorley at the Glenbraddan wedding had brought those childhood days back so sharply. She had gone barefoot in homespun, then, but there were sandals on her feet now, and the simplicity of her gown had nothing to do with poverty. She was thirty-four years old; had been married, and widowed, and borne three sons; had proved herself, as few women had done, in a man's world. Had wept, and wanted to die. Yet nothing had changed at all. The boundaries of Kinveil were still the boundaries of her heart's world.

For more years now than she could remember, when she had dreamed of Kinveil she had dreamed of it with Mungo there. She had been happy to share it with him, for he had the same deep, uncritical, committed love for it as she, and belonged to it as she did. More, in a way, because she had been born to it, whereas he – rich enough, after a full and successful life, to have bought something much grander – had *chosen* it. She wondered whether Mungo's continuing presence in the dreams stemmed from the fact that she hadn't been back at Kinveil since he died, although she had been near to inviting herself a dozen – a hundred – times. Perhaps this visit would break the pattern. Perhaps now, her dreams would come to recognize, as her conscious mind had done long since, that the time of sharing had gone and the love was all her own again.

She sat in her eyrie on a patch of thick, mossy turf and gazed out, dreaming, over the water. The gales had really died now, and two weeks' rain had already drained away into ground parched by the six preceding weeks of drought. The mountains were capped with snow, but there was no breeze to carry the chill of it to where Vilia sat in the early October sun. Tonight, she thought, there was going to be a magnificent sunset, one of the golden ones that poured its antique riches over the polished sea and turned the slender halo of cloud above the islands into a burnished crown. Later in the month, the sun was more likely to go down in purple and flame, and in November the sky would be so overcast that it wouldn't go down at all. But after that, if the snows came early, there would be a few majestic moments of turquoise and apricot and slate before the darkening. And in January . . .

She stopped herself. Those were sunsets she wouldn't see, just as she wouldn't see the wheatears return in spring, or hear the wild geese pass overhead, calling, or the whooper swans with their eerie bugle note. She wouldn't be here – unless she were invited – when the irises and orchids and gentians, smaller than dewdrops, opened on the hills, or when the infant birds flew the nest and thrush-babies lurked squeaking in the undergrowth, their beaks opening and closing like excitable buttercups. She wouldn't lie, without moving, in the shelter of a rock and watch roe deer fawns playing, the loveliest things in Nature, slim, dappled and graceful. Or, when the harsh weather came again, see a sparrow-hawk doubling through the bare branches to trap a pretty, silly dunnock, too innocent to dive for cover. So many things she wouldn't see, except in the eye of mind and memory.

Her vision was suddenly blurred, and she shook her head a little. Madness, all madness, her mind told her. If love were currency, Kinveil should be hers, but she had no right to it in any other terms, and never could have.

Unless.

There was one way she knew of.

She lay back on the soft carpet of turf and then, after a moment, turned over and rested her forehead on her hands, eyelids fluttering over unseeing eyes. Long ago, during the weeks after her father had sold Kinveil, she had cast around despairingly in her seven-year-old mind for some way of winning it back, not for her father but for herself. Childishly arrogant, she had made up her mind that, one day when she was old enough, she would marry Magnus Telfer. It had seemed the easiest, and the only, way of doing it. Then Magnus had married Lucy, and Vilia, brought face to face with reality, had abandoned a plan that had been doomed since its inception, remembering it only once, when Lucy had slipped on the stairs and might have been killed.

She had never thought of Luke as a substitute for his father. But he was the heir, now.

Raising her head a little, she propped her chin on crossed wrists. The germ of the idea had been planted in her mind when she saw what Luke's travels had made of him; when she saw, too, that this new, adult Luke was very much aware of her. She had been in the mood for noticing. Effervescent with the delight of coming home after so long, she had felt ten years younger – and probably looked it, too. There had been a bubble of irrepressible happiness trapped inside her like a bead of rosewater in the scented oil she used on her skin. She smiled wryly at the comparison. Nowadays, she had begun to pamper her complexion, although her mirror told her she had lost none of her looks. She wasn't vain of them, but neither was she foolish enough to despise them. They gave her an almost impersonal pleasure, and she would be sad when time began to flaw them, just as she was sad when a flower began to fade.

Quick to sense Luke's appreciation, she had been ready enough to find release for her high spirits in being feminine and frivolous and a little flirtatious with him in these last weeks. He had, after all, turned into an unusually attractive young man. She hadn't troubled to think beyond that. And then, yesterday, he had told her that he loved her, and seemed to mean it. Had talked of loving her 'for so long'.

How long? He hadn't loved her when he was a child, certainly. She could never forget how he had competed with her for emotional possession of Kinveil, although she had always thought that for him it hadn't been Kinveil, but possession, that had been the key to the equation. Later, when he was adolescent, they had scarcely met. And that left the Oxford years, those years when he had turned up so regularly, and sometimes so inconveniently, at Marchfield House, nervous as the overgrown schoolboy he was but trying very hard to appear adult. He had been more than a little tiresome, and it had been difficult not to be impatient with him when the foundry was absorbing all her energies. It had sometimes been too much for her to come home drained after a day poring over the accounts with Wally Richard, or puzzling over some illiterate drawings in the moulding shed, to find Luke waiting for her, at once jaunty and diffident. If she hadn't had an obsession about manners and hospitality, she would have been hard put to it to welcome him with even the appearance of complaisance. But only once, as far as she could remember, had she weakened to the point of snapping at him, and that had been when he had told her – as he so frequently did – something about the glens that he must have known was bound to upset her. Every time he had come to see her, he had harped on the changes in the glens, as if to emphasize that there was nothing she could do about them, because Kinveil was his father's now, and would some day be his.

But the jealous, selfish, possessive boy had changed in the last three years, or seemed to have changed. Had he? He had said he loved her, but how deep, she wondered, did it go?

She twisted round again and sat up. Did it matter? Dear God, *did it matter*? He swore he was in love with her, and that was enough.

The sun was sinking now, and the castle lay below her like some rare and precious trinket from Croesus' treasure chest, lapped around with gold and chrysoprase. The sheer beauty of it lacerated her heart, and tears sprang to her eyes as, steepled fingers pressed tight against her lips, she tried to control the emotions warring within her. Love, and need, and a bitter self-disgust.

To set out, coldly and with calculation, to make use of another human being for her own private ends . . . She had done it once before, when she married Andrew, promising herself to make it up to him so that he would never know he had been cheated, never know that he was only a pawn in the game she was playing in her own destiny. Innocently, she had thought that good intentions would be enough. And then Perry Randall had entered her life and she had found out her mistake.

The tears were pouring down her cheeks now, and she could do nothing to stop them. The memory of Perry, repressed so resolutely and for so long, flooded through every nerve and muscle in her starved body – the memory, not of the irresolute man who had loved and failed her, but of the man *she* had loved and in whose arms she had found a joy that was almost beyond bearing. She had tried to make herself recognize that she would never, could never, know such a perfect relationship again, and because of that – or in spite of it – had rejected, with a light and absent smile, the advances of several worthy, and a few less worthy, suitors. They had called her heartless, but had not given up their pursuit, and she had finally become almost a recluse because she could not bear the kisses, clumsy or practised, of any man who was not Perry Randall.

She dropped her face into her hands, and it was as if all the torments of the years, all her complex needs and desires, concentrated themselves into one soundless cry of longing, deep in her heart.

6

Afterwards, she tried to persuade herself that what happened wouldn't have happened except for a trick of the failing light. She became aware that she was no longer alone, and slowly, because there seemed no help for it, she raised her head. There was a man standing watching her from a dozen feet away, his tall, lithe figure outlined against the sky. She could scarcely see his face, but his hair was dark, and a single, waving lock of it drooped over one eye. He seemed to hesitate for a moment, as if unsure of his welcome, and then he smiled, with a flash of teeth that lent the smile a familiarly engaging quality. Her own face was pitilessly exposed in the glow of the setting sun, and she didn't realize until much too late what a light had sprung into her drowned green eyes in that brief moment when she thought she saw the only man in the whole wide world she wanted to see.

Her face was the face of a woman welcoming her lover, and it told Luke Telfer more than he would ever have dared to ask. With a passionate relief in his heart, he flung himself down on the turf beside her and gathered her into his arms.

She was too stunned, at first, to make any response at all. Even as, slowly, almost voluptuously, she struggled back to the hillside, and the golden evening, and the words of love and desire Luke was murmuring against her lips, she didn't believe any of it. It was as if her limbs, and her consciousness, remained trapped in the clinging web of dreams. A small voice, somewhere, whispered, stop him; you must stop him. And the second voice said, *but not quite yet.* Resist him, you must resist him. And the second voice said, *but not too strongly.* He must have seen the invitation printed on your face. Don't let him suspect it was for another man. *Wait for the right moment, and then stop him.* Gently. But she couldn't think how.

And even as her brain debated the issue, her body resolved it, responding with forgotten sweetness to the hands drifting over her flesh as seductively, as potently, as those other hands, the mouth that ravaged hers as gently, as demandingly, as that other mouth. There was no wild lifting of her heart, but she had been starved for too long to withstand the caresses, adroit and felicitous, that Luke Telfer had learned from lovers far more experienced than she. Warm, heavy with the pleasure of it, she lay in his arms and didn't resist him, or help him or stop him.

Because he had dreamed but never carried his dreams so far, and because she had dreamed without hope of fulfilment, they met and matched and came together like musician and instrument, the one at the height of his powers, and the other perfectly tuned and waiting for his touch. It was swift, and beautiful, and almost mystical. And afterwards they lay hand in hand, together, until the sun dropped below the horizon and a chill wind sprang up with the afterglow.

Just before they turned back down the hill to the castle, he took her in his arms and, resting his lips on the heavy, silken hair, murmured, 'I love you, I love you, I love you! May I come to you – *please* may I come to you – tonight?'

He could feel her hesitating, and then she said, 'No. We mustn't.'

Knowing that she would be bound to say that, like any other gently-bred woman, he took her shoulders in a crushing grip and stared down into her eyes. 'Why not? We love each other so much. Why not? It *can't* be wrong!'

But she dropped her lashes, and a little smile began to quiver at the corners of her mouth. 'The age-old cry of illicit lovers! No, my dearest, not tonight. Give me time, please. Not tonight.'

Chapter Three

1

It rained ferociously the next day, and again the day after.

Lucy and Vilia, from their closed carriage, watched a sodden Lord Colchester snip a sodden tape and declare the Bridge of Braddan officially open, although through the drumming of rain on the roof they could scarcely hear the dutiful hurrahs raised by the crofters and tenants huddled round its approaches.

'Oh, Vilia!' Lucy exclaimed distressfully. 'It should have been a *beautiful* day, with hundreds of people cheering, and you out there with the others receiving congratulations. For everyone says the bridge is a triumph for you, and a vindication of all your efforts at the foundry!'

Vilia's smile was mechanical. It was almost as if she weren't interested, but Lucy knew it couldn't be that. Perhaps it was just the weather, which was enough to depress anyone. Shivering a little, Lucy drew the fur pelerine more closely about her throat.

Lord Colchester, duty done, turned and made a dignified scuttle for cover, closely pursued by a group of local worthies. Lucy was reminded that the day's trials weren't by any means over yet. She said dismally, 'I can't imagine how on earth we are going to dry them all out in time for dinner!'

Vilia returned temporarily to the present. Fortunate Lucy, to have such clear-cut problems. She said, 'Not easy.'

'If only Charlotte or Harriet had been well enough to have them at Glenbraddan! But by the time we get back to Kinveil the rain will have soaked right through, and there won't be a dry stitch on anyone.'

'Except Luke.'

'That new cloak of his? Well, at least today ought to prove whether Mr Mackintosh really *has* invented something waterproof. It's a pity it weighs so much with those heavy layers of cloth and whatever-it-is bonded in between!'

'Rubber.'

'Is it?' Lucy considered her son's tall figure as he strolled easily behind the others towards the waiting carriages. 'Although I will say he carries it off well. He has quite an air these days, don't you think? Thank heavens we sent him off on the Grand Tour, for although I would say it to no one else, I *can* say to you that he was the greatest affliction to me when he was growing up. Such a relief to find that his travels have civilized him where my own efforts had no success at all.'

Vilia never ceased to be suprised by Lucy's objectivity, which somehow didn't match the sweet placidity of her temperament. But all she said was, 'He has certainly gained in assurance.'

He had waylaid her that morning on the tower stairs, pulling her into the shelter of a doorway and straight into his arms, kissing her devouringly, and pinning her body so tightly against his that, even through all the fashionable layers of skirt and petticoats, she could feel

326

him hard and avid against her. She had struggled, furiously angry, her palm itching to slap his handsome face, and when he had raised his head a little, she had said through clenched teeth, 'Let me go this instant! I am not some chambermaid to play kiss-in-the-corner with!'

He was breathing roughly, and the lids were heavy and lax over his eyes. 'I want you. God, I want you! Tonight, *please*. I must come to you tonight!'

She clutched at the first excuse she could think of. 'No. Kinveil will be full of guests. It would be madness.'

He had one hand behind her neck and, against all her resistance, forced her mouth back within reach of his. Then, his feverish lips brushing hers, back and forth, he murmured, 'What does that matter? We *are* mad, and we need each other so much.'

'No. I know it is necessary for us to talk . . .'

His head had come up at that, the eyes sultry and mocking, and anger surged in her again.

'I really mean *talk*.' She made an intense effort to control her temper and find the right words. In a voice that was caressingly reasonable, she added, 'We must try to be wise.'

It was a relief to find that she could still dominate him, as long as brute strength wasn't involved. But she knew she couldn't rely on it if she were to find herself alone with him behind locked doors. This time, however, he dropped his arms and she was able to step back, her legs weak and trembling. As she readjusted her huge, puffed velvet beret and shook out the folds of her skirt, she said with something that was almost pleading in her voice, 'I'm not a – an incognita!'

He said nothing for a moment, and she could see that he was trying to force discipline back on his body. Then he sighed, and smiled, and dropped a light, carefully nonchalant kiss on her cheek. 'No, of course not. In that bonnet you look more like a *kugelhupf* – quite delicious.'

And so the awkward encounter had passed, and despite her anger she found she didn't regret it. Since the episode on the hill, her mind had been spinning with arguments and plans and speculations, and all of them inhibited by the nagging doubt in her mind as to whether it was really love that had driven Luke, or only the kind of hunting instinct that was snuffed out in the moment of achievement. Now, at least, she knew the answer to that.

Lucy rapped on the panel, and Willie Aird's face appeared. 'Yes, mistress?'

'Turn the coach now, Aird. We must make sure of being back at Kinveil before our guests.'

'Yes, mistress.'

Lucy settled back. 'Thank heaven we don't live in the Isles. Just think of having Lord Colchester stormbound with us for days and days and days. Not,' she added without much conviction, 'that he isn't a delightful man, of course.'

Vilia smiled faintly. 'It's just that it's like having both Houses of Parliament on your hands.'

'Precisely.' Vilia was a soothing companion. She always understood how one felt. Lucy sighed regretfully. 'What a pity you have to leave so soon.'

Tomorrow. And Vilia had still no idea what she was going to do. Two nights ago, lying drowsy and fulfilled in bed, she had thought that Fate had relieved her of responsibility, and that there was nothing to do now but go on. In the chill light of day, however, the inescapable question had presented itself – go on where?

Everthing would have been so much simpler if Luke had not come to her on the hill and played havoc with her bodily peace. Then the only question to tease her would have been whether she should, and indeed whether she could contrive to, marry him for the sake of Kinveil. Love wouldn't have entered into it. And that would have been true, too, if he had been awkward or graceless. But he hadn't been. Even the memory of his mouth and hands and smoothly muscled thighs was enough to bring her own body back to dissolving awareness. Who, she wondered, had taught him such practised sensuality? Not Kirsty Macintyre or Jinty Macleod. He must have known women far more sophisticated than they; had mistresses, perhaps, in Paris, in Rome, in Venice. She wasn't jealous of them. If things had been different, she might have considered becoming one of their number, for the idea of pleasure without responsibility had a seductive charm. She had spent thirteen joyless years paying for her one transgression, but she was older and wiser now. Between herself and Luke, there would be a kind of rightness about such a relationship, for although he had become attractive and amusing and assured, it was only her body that was in love with him.

And that was what was confusing her. English gentlemen seldom married their mistresses. If she persisted with the thought of marriage, she would have to withold her body from what it so much desired until the day she became his wife. One lapse might be forgiven to a woman supposedly carried away by love, but not a second. It wasn't coyness or lack of desire, but realism, that had made her forbid him to come to her room. With bitter amusement, she remembered that soothing 'no choice but to go on'. If she left matters to take their course, there was little doubt in her mind that the course would lead inexorably to bed, but not to the altar.

Which did she really want? Which did she want to be *sure* of? A week ago she would have said, unhesitatingly, Kinveil. And that was still true. It was just that she wasn't quite sure whether she could live with herself if she deliberately manipulated Luke into marriage. If he were to ask her voluntarily, and without pressure . . . But she didn't think he would.

If Lucy hadn't been there beside her, Vilia would have wept. She had to decide. Had to make up her mind by tomorrow. Kinveil was the stake, and she wanted it unequivocally. Feverishly searching for a way to postpone the decision, to give herself more time to think, she suddenly remembered a piece of sound business wisdom Mungo had once passed on to her. 'Folk are aye girning about having no choice, when half the time they could have had a choice. Just you remember! When you have to make a decision, look well ahead. It's like chess. If one move's bound to land you in check, and there's another that leaves you with a move open – however unpromising it looks – take the second one. If it does nothing else, it'll give you time. You have to keep your options open if you're going to suceed in business.'

It had been good advice, and at the foundry she had always followed it. She supposed it was an index of her current state of mind that, only now, did it occur to her to apply it on a personal level. If she could induce Luke, by whatever means, to ask her to marry him, that would be enough for the time being. She wouldn't have to say yes, or no, straight away. And it would give her time to come to terms with her conscience.

For what remained of the journey back to Kinveil, she devoted her mind to the problem of how to handle him.

2

It was one o'clock in the morning when at last she tumbled into bed and deep into sleep, exhausted by two wakeful nights and the seemingly interminable day. The ladies had retired at eleven, leaving the men comfortably ensconced in the Long Gallery with their whisky and brandy and the evident intention of staying up for hours more, but Vilia had thought it wise to remain fully dressed for as long as there seemed any danger of Luke coming to her room. There were no locks on Kinveil doors, and never had been. So she had sat, pretending to read, until her eyes began to close of their own accord. Then she had looked at the time, and thought that he wouldn't come now.

She didn't hear his footsteps on the stairs, or the lifting of the latch. She didn't feel him turn back the coverlet with extravagant care, or loosen the ties that held her nightshift together, and open it, and smooth its satin folds aside so that she lay exposed to him, naked and silver-pale in the fitful light of the moon. She didn't sense him, flushed and elated, steadying himself against the carved bedpost while he raked her with his eyes. He ached for her, with an ache all the more consuming for the brevity of their union on the hill. A dozen times he had relived those swift, importunate moments, thinking – God! how Silvana would have laughed to see the elegant, leisured Signor Luke, with his unequalled skill at prolonging the act of love, behave like some frantic beginner, some uninstructed schoolboy. Yet there had been beauty in it, and an overmastering relief.

Relief on more counts than one. He knew, now, that Vilia must always have been chaste except during her marriage. In the six years since he had fallen in love with her, he had scourged himself with the belief that it was impossible for such a woman, so beautiful, so unprotected, to have preserved her virtue. Sick with jealousy, he had peopled her life with a legion of lovers. Yet during those fifteen climactic minutes on the hill when, from love and weakness, she had given in to his passion, not by a word or a sigh, a movement or a caress, had she shown herself aware of the arts of seduction that, if she had known other men, she must have learned. It had been strange to him to realize that, for all her worldly success, for all her undoubted maturity, she was still so innocent. Strange, and touching.

Now, after the long evening of boredom and frustration, he was very drunk indeed. And as he gazed at her, lying asleep, every last shred of caution and sobriety vanished in his desire for her. He raised a hand and began to strip his cravat away from his throat. It was night, and they were alone, and he would teach her all the exquisite enchantments of flesh on flesh. Teach her to need him as he needed her. But just in case she said no, he would have to be firm with her at first. She wasn't, he reminded himself fuzzily, an incognita. She had to be taught.

She fought him all the way while he raped her, and although none of her struggles had any effect, she didn't give up, not for a moment. She thought, afterwards, that if she had had a weapon she might well have killed him.

When it was all over, he fell asleep on top of her and it took her a long time to drag her maltreated body free, bones and sinews as unstable as quicksilver, and wrap herself in the illusory protection of a robe. But she managed it at last, and subsided into a chair, drained of everything but shame and disgust.

It was hours before he came back to awareness, his senses spinning. He wasn't even sure where he was until he saw her shadowed face in the first grey-gold gleam of the dawn light. And then he remembered what had happened. There was nothing he could say that men hadn't been saying since time began.

Slowly he pulled himself upright and sank his head in his hands. There was a small, vicious hammer beating just behind his right temple, and the lining of his mouth felt as if it had been dredged up out of a neglected laundry basket. After a while, he said thickly, 'Will you ever forgive me? No refinements. No finesse. Just simple, brutal need.'

He forced himself to look up, and saw a shiver run over the face that had been still as an icon. Then, as if the words had been forced out of her, she said, 'Like Andrew. That was what hurt. As if I were no more than a mechanical toy, without mind or feeling, something to be used.' The tears began pouring down her pale cheeks, as she went on, 'I thought, the other day on the hill, that what was between us was something different, but it isn't, is it? I'm only a vehicle for you to vent your desire on. Whatever I am, whatever I've made of my life, there's still one thing I share with the cheapest drab in Edinburgh. Love without joy, love without tenderness. Nothing but degradation and child-bearing.'

331

Tears came to his own eyes, at that, and he stumbled to his feet and went to her, where she sat. He half-expected her to recoil, but she didn't, as if her misery were too deep, so he sank on the rug before her and took her hands in his, tightly. His voice shaking, he said, 'It doesn't have to be like that. It shouldn't be like that.'

But it was as if she hadn't heard him. Turning her face away, she whispered, not to him but to herself, 'The fault is mine, all mine. What have I done?'

He knew she didn't mean it. Even through the thick, cloying fog in his head, he knew she didn't mean it. At any moment, what he thought of as her natural, womanly shame would give way to the revulsion that she must feel at the sight of him. And then would come the rejection he deserved, which he feared more than the wrath of God.

'What have I done?' she whispered again. And then, despairingly, 'What if I should have a child?'

It was an aspect of the matter that hadn't occurred to him, either tonight, or on the hill. There had been nothing in his mind but desire. What, after all, did sordid realities have to do with a grand passion such as theirs? And then the solution came to him, suddenly, blindingly. He knew he would never stop wanting her. He thought he would die if she refused to let him touch her ever again. Somehow, he had never considered marriage, even in these last days, perhaps because he had always thought of her as independent and unattainable, and feared instinctively that if he asked he would be refused. And that would be the end of everything. But now . . . The blackmail sprang readily to his tongue, as if it had been lying there waiting for its moment.

He poured some water from the carafe on the bedside table and gave it to her, although his own throat almost cried aloud for it. 'Drink it,' he said gently, 'and let me hear no more of such nonsense. What you have done – what I have done – is beyond recall. But there is an answer to it, and only one. You must marry me.'

She looked up at him, her face colourless and drawn.

'I mean it. Don't think of Andrew. Don't think of what I forced on you tonight. That wasn't love.' He took the glass from her, and knelt at her feet again to clasp her hands in his. His lips touched to the fine, transparent skin on the inside of her wrist, he murmured, 'We *do* have something different,' and then, almost pleadingly, 'It *was* beautiful the other day on the hill. It can be even more beautiful again, I promise you. Marry me, Vilia! I love you so much.' He didn't dare to raise his eyes.

The silence seemed to stretch into eternity. She gazed down at his dark head and her mind, very slowly, began to function again. It had all come about as neatly as if she had planned it, but she hadn't. Or she didn't think she had. Her distress had been agonizingly real, and there had been space for nothing else at all in her mind. Unless that second self, that other Vilia who had taken a hand in her life once before, on a day she tried never to think of in August 1822, was hovering in the air again, calculating and contriving, putting into her mouth the magical words that, this time, would achieve the one thing above all that she wanted to achieve.

'I don't know,' she said, her voice grating. 'I don't know.'

Nothing he could say or do, no argument he could advance, was sufficient to persuade her to give him an answer then, or to prolong her stay at Kinveil until she had made up her mind.

'How can I change my plans?' she said. 'What would your parents think?'

'Does it matter? Why won't you say yes? Why won't you marry me at once – now – today? This isn't England, with its banns and licences! All we need to do is clasp hands before witnesses and declare ourselves man and wife! Then I will have the right to be with you always.'

He was still, she thought, as spoilt as when he had been a child, always expecting his wishes to be paramount. 'But I don't know! I must have time to think.'

He took her in his arms and kissed her, but she didn't respond, and after a moment he let her go again. Then an idea came to him, and he exclaimed, 'I know! It's just that I can't bear to be separated from you. Why don't you,' his voice was wheedling, 'why don't you say yes – provisionally! – and then we can tell my parents, and they'll understand why I have to come to Edinburgh with you! Please! Why not, my darling, why not?'

She could think of several reasons, including three sons who were living reminders that she was eight years older than he, and the brisk efficiency that the foundry always brought out in her and that had made him so nervous during his Oxford years. Patiently reasonable, she said, 'Calm down, my dear. We mustn't rush into marriage just because of what's happened between us. I don't want you to marry me because you feel you have to! You – we – must take the most careful thought, separately and privately, without any pressure from outside or from each other. Apart, there's a chance that we may be able to consider the future rationally. Together . . .'

His hands were on her shoulders, and his lips in the hollow of her throat, and in another moment she knew they would begin to slide downwards to where the neck of her robe had slipped open. She twisted away from him, firmly but not unkindly, saying, 'Together, we're beyond reason. But marriage is so much more than the physical. At New Year I'll come back, and then we can decide.' She hoped she was doing the wise thing. She prayed that nothing would go wrong.

Neither of them knew, when she drove away just after noon, that they would not see each other again for seven long, weary months.

3

Luke's birthday was on May sixteenth, and this year was his twenty-fifth. After a wet morning, the weather was showing signs of clearing, but he still sat at his desk in the panelled, carpeted study that had once been his grandfather's. The room had changed little since Mungo's day, although Luke had bought an elegant satinwood secretaire to replace the zebra wood monstrosity the old man had been so fond of. It had been a mistake. Designed by the younger Mr Chippendale, it was full of drawers, shelves, and pigeonholes of, one might have thought, every conceivable shape and size, but none of Luke's notes, letters or diaries fitted comfortably into any of them, so that he was hemmed in by piles of papers on all sides, some of them spilling over onto the floor. Mr Chippendale had had the doubtful distinction, at one stage in his life, of being declared bankrupt. Serve him right, Luke thought.

He threw down his pen and rose to set a taper to the fire and light one of the thin brown cigarillos he had lately begun to affect. His mother would have wrinkled her nose in disgust, but his mother had been in London since December.

The last two months of 1828 had been months of family crisis. Scarcely a week after the opening of the bridge, Charlotte Randall's illness had entered a final, acute phase, and Magnus and Lucy had spent most of November at Glenbraddan, watching her die. Luke, for the first time in his life, had felt genuinely sorry for his father, who had been fond of her in his way. And then, no more than a few days after the funeral, it had been discovered that Edward and Harriet's infant son wasn't just naturally placid, as everyone had thought, but suffering from what the doctor called a palsy of the brain. No way of telling how badly, yet, he had said, but no known cure. The only thing to do was wait and see. Harriet had clung to Lucy, and Edward, prey to a hopeless misery, had turned to Magnus, as if to the father he had never really known.

Luke had made up his mind to be extra considerate to his parents when at last they escaped from Glenbraddan, their stock of family feeling exhausted. But his good intentions had suffered a nasty setback when his mother said, 'My nerves are in tatters, and I see no possibility of mending them here. We will be much better equipped to give Edward and Harriet the support they need later on, if we take the opportunity to recruit our strength properly. In London, I should think.'

'An admirable suggestion, my love,' Magnus said. 'We both need a change.'

Hopelessly trying to salvage something from the ruin of his plans, Luke said, 'Why not wait until after the New Year? What about the guests you've invited to the house party?'

Lucy shuddered. 'House party? Heaven preserve us! No, we will have to put everyone off. I know it's short notice, but they'll understand.' It was clear that she was indifferent to whether they understood or not.

Vilia couldn't, and wouldn't, come to a house where there was no hostess to receive her, and Luke couldn't take the time to travel to Edinburgh when he had been left in undisputed charge of Kinveil for the first time in his life. Or so Vilia told him. There was no urgency, it seemed, of the kind they had feared. She would come, she promised, as soon after Magnus and Lucy's return as she reasonably could. And now it was May, and Luke's parents were due back in two weeks, and he had written to Vilia, and lied to her, and told her they would be home for his birthday and that his mother looked forward to seeing Vilia almost at once.

More than anything, he wanted Vilia to himself, and if he were forced to invent some story to account for the discrepancy in dates, what did it matter? Even a night here alone with him, unchaperoned except by the servants, would be enough to bring a new pressure to bear, to replace the unfulfilled fear of pregnancy that, in his black moods, had seemed to him the only reason why she had even considered marrying him. His own desire for her never wavered, but jealousy had gripped him again the moment she was out of sight, and he couldn't tell what decision she might have reached, away from him.

By the turn of the year, he had known he would go mad if he had nothing to occupy him but thoughts of Vilia and the undemanding routine of the estate in winter. So he had set himself to a task long postponed. He could still remember the day when his grandfather had first suggested it. 'Suggested'? Ordered, more like. The old man had summoned him to his study on his sixteenth birthday and said, 'I've a wee business proposition to discuss with you.' Rising, he'd gone to the side table and returned with two tumblers of bitters, the drink made from whisky, camomile flowers, Seville orange peel, and juniper berries that every Highland gentleman took as a stomachic before breakfast and at comforting intervals throughout the rest of the day until bedtime. 'But first things first. Luke Telfer, on your sixteenth birthday I wish you good health and happiness. *Slàinte mhor!*'

'*Slàinte!*' the boy had responded, downing a man-sized gulp. He already knew that it packed a punch, but had thought it politic to say, 'Whoof!' in a startled tone. Then he had crimsoned under the old man's cynical eye. His grandfather had an unpleasant knack of seeing straight through people. Also, he had been in a belligerent mood that day, and before he knew where he was Luke had found himself landed with the task of writing the family history.

It was the most extraordinary idea he'd ever heard, and he'd gaped at his grandfather vacantly, muttering, 'But I don't even know anything about *you*, far less your father and your grandfather!' And Mungo had said, exasperated, 'I'll tell you what you need to know about the past, but the important thing's the future. When I said family history, maybe I should have said family chronicle. I want you to keep a diary. You can pass the job on to someone else when it gets too much for you. The job and . . .' he had added cunningly, 'the annual income from a wee trust I'm going to set up to go with it.'

That had put a different complexion on the affair. Luke knew his grandfather well enough to know that the income wouldn't be miserly. No more relying on the allowance from his father; no more being called on – when his father remembered – to account for how he'd spent it. Weakly, he had said, 'Oh!'

Then he had a vision of himself marching bang up to his Aunt Charlotte, and saying, 'Tell me, aunt. Why did Uncle Perry leave you and run away to America?' He closed his eyes for a moment and then said, 'But no one will tell me anything, will they, if they realize I'm writing it all down?'

Mungo had won in the end, of course. Comfortably, he'd said, 'Och, well, they'll be protected. They won't be expecting a laddie like you to write down anything beyond the commonplace, for a start, and when you hand over the job of chronicler to someone else, you'll send everything you've written to my lawyers in Edinburgh, and they'll keep it locked away for fifty years before they hand it over to whoever's keeping the record in the 1870s, or 80s, or 90s, or whenever it is. By then, most of the folk you've written about will either be snibbed in a mortsafe or past the stage of caring.'

Luke still had no idea why his grandfather had been so set on the idea of the family chronicle, but he had given up wondering. For almost eight years now he had been collecting notes, and they were beginning to get out of hand. Faced with long weeks of boredom and loneliness, he had decided at last to do something about them.

It had been strangely soothing, sorting them, and reading them, and remembering and collating them into some kind of coherent narrative. So many things he had forgotten. So many things that began to appear in a new perspective. Had Cameron of Kinveil had any choice at all, but to sell to Mungo? Had his own parents stayed in London for so long because of his mother's health – or because they didn't really like Kinveil very much? Had his Aunt Charlotte been entirely to blame in her dealings with Perry Randall? Luke had almost forgotten that evening at the Northern Meeting ball, when Vilia had mischievously set out to teach Charlotte a lesson, and bewitched Perry into aiding and abetting her. Was Edward quite at fault in turning Glenbraddan over to sheep, when the only alternative was insolvency?

Luke had spent the afternoon and evening of the day before his birthday re-reading what he had written, and recognized for the first time how reticent he had been about his own affairs and Vilia's, especially after 1822, the year he had fallen in love with her. He had recorded nothing but the barest facts. It bothered him, even while, deep in the recesses of his mind, he knew that he had feared to expose himself – and her – to the clinical appraisal of some unknown descendant half a century on.

He had spent a wakeful night, fretting at the problem, until he had realized that the 'unknown descendant' might, just might, be a son or grandson of his marriage to Vilia. It put a different complexion on the affair. Suddenly, he wanted this stranger of the future to know something about the love that had given him life.

He sat for a long time with the fresh sheets of paper laid out before him, the inkstand and the sandcaster newly plenished. His thoughts, he believed, were in order, but there remained the problem of words. How to describe her?

According to one of the seventeenth-century poets Henry Phillpotts had forced him to read, 'Beauty and beauteous words should go together.' As Mungo would have said, 'Aye, well . . .'

Was there a beauteous word in the language that hadn't been worked to death?

Graceful, yes. Elegant, yes. Lovely, certainly. But so much more. If he were to convey the reality of her, he would have to do better than that.

Pursuing words, he found himself pursuing truth, wondering why he should be so obsessed by her – he, Luke Telfer, with his sense of property and his passion for sole ownership? When he knew that she belonged only to herself, and to Kinveil. Perhaps that was why he was jealous, because he wanted all of her, not only her body and some small, uncommitted corner of her spirit.

After a time, it became too much for him, and he abandoned the search for Herbert's 'beauteous words' and wrote, 'She will be here three days from now, and I hope and believe she will agree to marry me, although I am not without fear. Sometimes I think she loves me too little and knows me too well.' And even that wouldn't do. Frowning, he struck out the last sentence. It wasn't something to be put in words, not even to himself.

Strange to think that you, whoever you are, reading this more than half a century on, may be our son or grandson. Stranger still to think that, in the next few sentences, or paragraphs, or pages, you will find laid out before you the pattern of a life that Vilia and I have yet to live. If only I knew what kind of pattern it would be . . .

Christ! He would have himself in tears, next. He threw down the pen. This was no time to reawaken all the doubts and fears he thought he'd conquered in these last months. Three more days and he would know. Three days and he could bear to confront the future again – or not, as the case might be. He wouldn't think about that. Perhaps it would help if he tried to live the next three days hour by hour.

The sun had come out. What he needed was a hard, tiring gallop, and then perhaps he would sleep tonight.

4

There was no real reason why Perry Randall should have dismounted and scrambled down to the water's edge to gaze out over Loch an Vele, his eyes, screwed up against the westering sun, falling into the creases that had become habitual after long years of scanning the Missouri river or the mountains of Colorado, searching for grizzlies above Yellowstone, or Arapaho in the Great Plains. That period in his life was ended now, but still, instinctively, he stopped when a new vista opened before him. Stopped, and surveyed it with care.

The water was flat calm, the mountains swooping down into it and levelling out again, blue-tinted and softened and two-dimensional, aquatint replicas of themselves. New green merged with the russet of the hilltops and turned them purple-bronze above the intricate girdle of beeches, leafless still, but glowing richly mahogany in the sun, and glittering when the rain lingered on them. Round the shores were great banks of gorse, sharp and sulphurously yellow, and the ditches were spangled with primroses and dog-violets. There had been a dwelling once near where Perry stood, and the stones of it loitered still among a riot of daffodils and lilacs, watched over by an ancient crab apple, knotted and gnarled, its branches curved by the westerlies so that they looked like a woman's windblown skirts. Another week or two, and summer would be here.

It was beautiful, but Perry found little pleasure in it. It was fourteen years since he had seen it last, and he had thought at first that the circumstances of his life here had been responsible for tarnishing the whole austere and magnificent panorama in his eyes. Impossible, he had reflected, to feel nostalgia for the scene of one's own defeat. But he wasn't defeated now, and the Highlands still failed to move him.

Perhaps the landscape and the people were too old, too set in their ways. A thousand years ago, there must have been challenge here, but the landscape had won and the people had resigned themselves to living under its rule. He remembered the emigrants who had sailed with him for the New World, shivering in the discovery that their comforting, age-old fatalism was not going to be proof against the biting wind of independence. There was nothing in the world more frightening, if one stopped to think, than to have to stand on one's own feet and make one's own decisions. No conventions, no ground rules, no reassuring pattern to conform to. No one to blame but oneself. But equally, there was nothing in the world more satisfying than to succeed. Perry recognized that, in the New World, he had found his place. Despite its rough self-seeking, its lack of grace, its desperate search for identity, it was the world for him. From out of the past, a light, silvery voice said, 'You should have been an adventurer, a corsair, a Crusader.' She had been right in a way that neither of them could have envisaged.

Benjamin Briggs, standing patiently by the roadside minding the horses, saw his master's lips tighten and wondered, for the dozenth time, what was afoot. They had been two months in England while Mr Randall went about his business, aristocratic and charming when the circumstances required it, brisk and sometimes abrasive when they didn't. He didn't suffer fools gladly. Played his cards close to his chest, too. The first Briggs had known about this jaunt to what he regarded as a thoroughly God-forgotten corner of the world had been the day before they set out. No hint of precisely where they were going, or why. Since they had crossed the Border, they'd stayed in one filthy hostelry after another, with nothing to eat, day after day, but oatmeal and potatoes, sour cheese and rancid butter. Mr R. said they'd improved a lot in the last few years, but Briggs had been reminded, with loathing, of his time as a powder boy on the *Shannon*; salt beef, beans, and hardtack, and think yourself lucky. He couldn't understand why a gentleman like Mr R. didn't have rich friends to stay with, and when they'd come to the big house at Glenbraddan yesterday he'd heaved a sigh of relief. But Mr R. had stayed well out of sight and sent Briggs to inquire whether the Misses Randall were at home. *The Misses Randall?* Briggs, dumbfounded, had been as disappointed as his master to learn that the family had left for Edinburgh last week. Mr Blair was expected home in a day or two, but the young ladies anticipated remaining in Edinburgh with Mistress Blair. On instructions, Briggs had then asked whether the butler knew if Mr and Mrs Telfer were in residence at Kinveil. Forbiddingly, the butler had replied that he could not take it upon himself to say. Scaly old twiddlepoop! Briggs had thought.

The landlord at the inn by the Bridge of Braddan had been more forthcoming. Mr and Mrs Telfer, like most of the Highland gentry, had migrated south for the winter and weren't back yet. What Briggs couldn't understand was why Mr R. should be trailing along these extra, interminable miles, if there was going to be nobody at home when they got there. He wasn't the type to waste time on sentimental journeys.

Briggs looked round as a horse cantered along the road towards them, a nice-looking bay filly with a personable young fellow in his twenties astride. The gentleman nodded to Briggs, and then turned to glance at the man on the shore. The glance developed into a stare, and then into stupefied recognition. With a twitch on the reins, the newcomer took his horse slipping and sliding down on to the beach, and Briggs heard him exclaim, 'Uncle Perry? *Can* it be?'

There was a resigned, ironic smile on Mr R.'s long, firm lips. After a moment, he said, 'Luke, I take it? I don't think I'd have known you.'

They rode back together to Kinveil, two tall, limber, well-set-up figures. Briggs, looking for some family resemblance, couldn't find it, although they were alike enough on a superficial level. It seemed to Briggs, who admired his master more than anyone else on earth, that Mr Luke was no more than a callow youth beside him, easy and handsome enough, but with not a spark of his uncle's astringent vitality. A soft billet all his life, no doubt. He didn't look as if he knew what the world was about; needed a few lines of experience etched on that high-nosed, slightly sulky face of his.

Words and phrases drifted back to Briggs as they rode, sentences filleted by the clatter of hooves, or topped and tailed by a turn of the speaker's head.

'. . . dealing in guns . . . some parts they still make better in Birmingham . . . Black Ball line, twenty-three days New York to Liverpool . . . steam? across the Atlantic?' And a laugh from Mr R. 'That'll be a few years yet, I guess.'

And the young fellow. '. . . London to Leith quite often . . . parents thought me very odd . . .'

'. . . away from home?'

'Yes . . . quite on my own . . . months and months.'

And then they reached Kinveil and Briggs discovered it was a ruddy castle. The real thing. He gulped, took a firm grip on his P's and Q's, and wondered whether he'd be expected to tug his forelock. Damned if he would; he was an American now.

Later in the evening, Luke took Perry into his sanctum for brandy and a long, private gossip. Remembrance hit Perry like a blow. 'Your grandfather's study?' he said. He could still see Mungo sitting there behind the old zebra wood table, small, tough, shrewd, and unbelievably kind. A pity the old man hadn't lived to know that America had been the making, not the breaking of Perry Randall, that spineless young good-for-nothing of times past. Shame washed over him, always, when he allowed himself to think of the damage his irresponsibility had done to everyone who knew him.

'Yes.' Luke gestured towards the Chippendale secretaire. 'And one of the things he left behind – which is why my desk's so untidy – was a kind of *idée fixe* about keeping a family chronicle. I've been working on it all winter. You know he died a few years ago, of course.'

Perry's eyebrows rose. 'My dear Luke! That "of course" shows how innocent you are about communications between here and the States. There's no "of course" about it, I can assure you. I had assumed he must have died by now, but I didn't *know* until fairly recently.'

Without thinking, Luke said, 'Who told you? You mean you've seen my parents?'

'I doubt whether your father would tell me so much as the time of day, if we should have the misfortune to meet. No. It seemed to me that it might cause distress if I wrote to your grandfather here, and the letter were opened by someone else. So I addressed myself to his lawyers in Edinburgh and they told me what had happened.' He stopped, his eyes fixed on the golden contents of the glass revolving between his long fingers, and after a pause went on. 'They also told me a few weeks ago that my wife had died. They had some difficulty in reaching me, because I was travelling. It must have been bitter for Charlotte to think that all she possessed was still, in spite of everything, mine under the law. Fortunately, it wasn't much. I'm arranging for it to be put in trust for the girls.'

'Have you seen them?'

Perry shook his head. 'They're in Edinburgh, I understand.'

'Yes, I'd forgotten. Edward's taken Harriet and the baby – Harriet's his wife – to see the doctors. The baby has something wrong with its brain.'

'I'm sorry to hear that.' He was. Poor Edward, even as a boy nothing had ever gone really right for him, and it didn't sound as if things had changed.

'The girls have gone to keep Harriet company.'

Casually, as if it were a matter of little interest, Perry asked, 'What are they like?'

What were they like? Luke had never thought very much about it, and there didn't seem anything clever to say. 'Grace is sixteen, now. Quite tall and pretty in a quiet way. Brown hair. Serious-minded. More like Aunt Charlotte than you. She has rather a – a managing disposition.'

Perry laughed. '*Very* like Charlotte.'

'Not as bad as that,' his nephew replied tactlessly. 'I can't see her ever frightening the life out of anyone, the way Aunt Charlotte used to do to me.' He didn't add that she was more likely to bore one to death. If he were to be honest, he suspected that Grace was developing a *tendre* for him, although perhaps she had fallen into the habit of riding over to consult him about all her problems and difficulties because she and Edward didn't get on. She had a lot of problems and difficulties.

'And – er – Shona?'

The child born to an embittered mother after her brief, very brief, reconciliation with her second husband, the Honourable Peregrine Francis Egerton Randall. Luke still felt his chronicle was rather sketchy about that whole episode, and wondered whether it gave him sufficient justification to ask his Uncle Perry straight out. But, looking at him, he decided perhaps not.

Perry Randall, now, was not the kind of man one put impertinent questions to. The last time Luke had heard of him, he had been a travelling salesman, a 'drummer', and Luke's adolescent imagination had struggled to superimpose that seedy image on the elegant, amiable young Corinthian he remembered. It hadn't been easy, and it seemed he could have saved himself the trouble. There was nothing at all seedy about him now, and Luke wasn't sure about the amiability, either. But the elegance was very much in evidence. Perry's riding coat and breeches had been made by a tailor whose name Luke would have liked to know, and the black, frocked coat he had changed into, thigh-length and tight-waisted over narrow black trousers and a grey-damasked waistcoat, suited his lean, athletic figure to perfection. His jaw above the snowy ruffle was hard, and the creases that had always bracketed his mouth were deeply etched. Not a trace of grey marred the admirably cut black hair, but there were two short vertical lines between his brows. He reeked of authority temporarily under leash.

Luke rose and went to refill their glasses. 'Shona? The sweetest child you could imagine. A little like Aunt Charlotte to look at, but shy as a fawn.' He didn't mention that everyone ignored the poor child, except Vilia. 'She's still – unformed is the word, I suppose. Dreamy. Too sensitive for her own good, perhaps.'

'Are they happy with Edward and Harriet?'

'Oh, tol-lol. Well enough, I suppose. They miss Georgiana. You won't know that she was married last year. French fellow, very dashing. In fact, Georgy was talking about you, wishing you'd been there to lend a bit of style to the wedding.'

Perry threw back his head and laughed, almost in the old way, and Luke found himself joining in with a spontaneity that, in his growing up, he had come near to losing.

'How delightful,' Perry remarked sardonically, 'to know that at least one member of the family thinks of me with approval!' But there was no expression at all in his voice when he added, 'What do my own daughters think of me?'

'I've no real idea. Grace is a little wistful, perhaps.'

Perry rose and went to the window. It was almost ten o'clock but still daylight. One forgot how northern these latitudes were. Luke's answer was much what he had expected. Charlotte, he knew, would have been bound to discourage the girls from thinking about him, as if he had died; she could scarcely pretend he had never existed. Perry wondered whether it freed him from responsibility. Paternal feeling, common humanity, legal obligation, all told him that, now their mother was dead, he should take them to America to live with him, and relieve Edward of the burden. He wanted to, or he supposed he did. But could he really transplant two daughters he didn't know, and who didn't know him, to the big handsome empty house in Boston where he had begun to roost occasionally, when he wasn't in New York, or Philadelphia, or New Orleans? If they had been a little older, he thought, it would have been possible. But not now, not when he didn't have a wife to care for them. And if he *had* the wife he wanted, he would want to have her to himself, quite alone, for a long, long time.

Charlotte's death had freed him at last, and his own success in the last few years had given him back his pride. He had gone to Glenbraddan hoping to see his daughters, but had ridden on to Kinveil for one purpose only, and one that touched him far more nearly. He hadn't expected to see Luke, hadn't even thought about him. He had meant to drop in, casually, on Ewen Campbell, to discover what he knew about Vilia Cameron's present situation. If anyone knew, he had thought, Ewen would. He had persuaded himself that it was logical, sensible, wise, to take time to spy out the land, but the truth was that he was deliberately postponing the moment he desired and feared – the moment when, for a second time, he would throw his fate in the balance with Vilia.

It had been a long silence. 'Would you – er – like me to sound them out?' Luke ventured.

His uncle turned, and Luke, seeing the blankness in his eyes, put it down to the darkness of indoors compared with out. Rising, he lit a taper from the fire and began setting it to the candles. He had an Argand lamp, but although it was useful enough for work its glare always seemed to him harsh and unfriendly.

'That would be a kindness,' Perry said after a moment. 'Now! We seem to have talked only about me. Tell me about yourself and Kinveil. Have you taken up sheep-farming, like Edward? I saw the Cheviots on his hills.'

'Edward's sheep?' Luke gave a mock despairing groan. 'The way he's handled them is enough to turn anyone grey. It was awkward enough when he moved the first tenants off their land to make way for the damned animals, even though he did *try* to do it decently. This last few

345

months, though, he's been so sunk in misery over the tragedy with the baby that he doesn't have a thought for anyone else. He's all set to clear out some more of the clachans, and making no attempt to soften the blow. The people at Grianan have refused to accept the writs, and things could turn nasty. If they decide to make a stand on eviction day, Edward will have to use force.'

'*Have* to?' Perry surveyed him thoughtfully. 'That sounds almost as if you approve.'

'Not approve, precisely. I'm not, as it happens, a great believer in the Clearances, but I don't think there's any doubt that the future does lie with sheep. And it is, after all, a landlord's prerogative to do as he chooses with his land. No gentleman can afford to have his tenants setting up in opposition to him.'

'That doesn't sound like the Luke I used to know. However, I suppose most people's views about property change as they move from the ranks of the have-nots to the haves. No! Let it go, Luke!' He raised one long-fingered, capable hand. 'We're not likely to agree on that topic, I can see. Tell me how you've been occupying your time since you went up to Oxford. In 1822, wasn't it? I remember you were just going up when I was over here last.'

'When you were . . .' Luke's hackles had risen, as they always did, at the hint of criticism, and his voice was sharper than was courteous. 'I thought this was your first visit home since you left in 1815!'

Perry, now gracefully at ease in one of the leather chairs by the fire, didn't allow his puzzlement to show. He could understand that Vilia mightn't have mentioned his second visit to Marchfield House, but why the devil should she and Lucy Telfer have kept quiet about the first? Mungo had known he was in the country, after all. But if Luke didn't know, Magnus probably didn't either. There was something odd, here, but Perry didn't want to land Luke's mama – nice woman – in the chowder. He said non-committally, 'I was over for a short time, just, and happened to be in Edinburgh during the royal visit.'

Luke was not to be put off. 'Why didn't anyone tell me? You met someone – you must have done. Who did you meet? I should have liked to see you, and grandfather would have been delighted to have your news, even if only at second hand.'

With an internal sigh, Perry recognized that in a moment Luke's mystification would turn to suspicion. Protecting the inexplicable

Lucy, he smiled and said, 'You forget I have never been very popular with your family. But I wonder how everyone was faring, and paid a call on Mrs Lauriston as the likeliest fount of information.' Wryly, he added, 'She was even able to tell me I had a daughter of whose existence I knew nothing.'

'Shona?' Luke was temporarily diverted. 'You mean you didn't know anything about her? Jesus! Surely my aunt could have found some way of letting you know!'

'Perhaps, if she'd wanted to. Perhaps not.'

His hand on the decanter and his back turned, Luke said casually, 'I thought you and Mrs Lauriston were scarcely acquainted?'

But Perry's instinct for danger had become highly developed during his years of exile, and he sensed at once that there was something badly wrong. He didn't have an inkling of what it might be, but didn't dare hesitate. 'Very little.' Then, conscious that it hadn't been enough, despite the dismissive tone in which it had been uttered, he added, 'We met once or twice in London, by chance, when I was there in '15.'

'Oh, yes. Gold Cup day at Ascot, if I remember.'

'I believe it was, and there was another occasion. I don't quite recall. Anyway, she was able to tell me how things were at Glenbraddan and Kinveil.' His voice changed. 'So! Did you find Oxford suited you? And did you have your Grand Tour afterwards? That was something I missed. No Grand Tours for the sons of the idle gentry when the Napoleonic Wars were on.'

Luke was reminded of his grandfather. Perhaps this was one of the talents one learned in commerce – to dictate conversations as one dictated one's business affairs. How to leave one's unfortunate *vis-à-vis* with no possible way of pursuing a subject without downright rudeness. Left stranded on the shoals of his Grand Tour, Luke gave Perry the edited version that nowadays tripped almost automatically from his tongue. A little bawdier than usual, perhaps, for this was Perry Randall and Luke still felt the old compulsion to try and impress him. He managed, he thought, to be fluent and entertaining in spite of everything. In spite of the light, crisp voice echoing in his ears. 'I met him only twice, you know, the second time for no more than a few minutes at Ascot . . . I was told he went to America. Did you ever hear what became of him?'

'. . . so I came back for Georgiana's wedding last year. And then there was the opening of the new bridge over the Braddan – you crossed it on your way here. Did you know it was built with materials from Mrs Lauriston's foundry? She was here for the opening.'

Then, moved by he didn't know what – fear, suspicion, pride, self-defence – he went on, 'Indeed, Uncle Perry, although no one else knows it yet, perhaps you will wish me happy? Mrs Lauriston and I are to be married.' He watched his uncle with a fearful intensity, searching for the faintest sign that would tell him what he wanted to know. What he *didn't* want to know. The room seemed to have become intolerably hot, and the candles hurt his eyes.

'Are you?' Not a muscle of the handsome, authoritative face showed anything more than a mild surprise. 'My congratulations, Luke. A remarkably beautiful and talented woman.' His eyes dropped, and he flicked the ash from one of Luke's cigarillos into the fire. 'When is the happy day?'

'We haven't settled it yet. She will be here next week, and we expect to be married soon after.'

Next week. And it was Friday now.

Perry said, 'You'll live here at Kinveil, I suppose.' The question was superfluous.

'Oh, yes. We're both very fond of the place.'

As clearly as if she had told him, Perry knew that there could be no other reason for Vilia to marry the boy. 'She and your mother are still sufficiently good friends?' he asked drily.

It took Luke a moment to absorb that. 'Yes, of course,' he said.

'And what about the foundry?' Impossible to imagine Vilia, with her incisive mind, her habit of command, tied to someone so much younger than she in every way. If it had only been a matter of age, but it wasn't.

'I don't know yet. We haven't really discussed it. We'll probably put a manager in. It's of no great importance.'

How little you know! Perry thought grimly. If Vilia had to give up her private empire and devote her energies to Kinveil, the fur would soon start flying. She was far too vital to dwindle into placid domesticity. His ironic smile was quite genuine when he said, 'What about the two boys? Do either of them look likely to take over some day?' He raised his eyebrows at Luke's expression. The boy seemed to be taken aback, as if the question was a difficult one.

Luke floundered. Two boys? Was it possible Perry didn't know about Drew? Odd that Vilia hadn't mentioned him when she was talking about Shona, because the two were very much of an age. He said, 'Three boys. The youngest was born a few months after Andrew Lauriston died. Didn't you know?'

Perry said, 'How – how distressing for her.' It had been a struggle for him to gather enough breath even for those few words. *A few months. How many constituted 'a few'?* How could he ask? 'I'm surprised,' he remarked, 'that the shock of her husband's death wasn't enough to bring on a miscarriage.'

Luke's knowledge of feminine biology was sketchy, but nothing would have induced him to admit it. 'Indeed, yes,' he replied. 'It might well have done. As it was, I believe she had a very difficult time right up until the child was born. My grandfather brought her here afterwards to recover, and she was here for the last of the winter and the whole of spring.'

Perry had been away too long. He had forgotten that spring here didn't begin until the middle of May, and that it was rare indeed for the season to be as advanced as it was today. So the child must have been born in January or February, and couldn't be his. There was a lead weight somewhere in his chest as he thought of what Vilia must have suffered, carrying Andrew's child under such circumstances, although it would have been worse for her, he supposed, if the child *had* been his. He remembered her saying, at Marchfield House, that she had been unwell in the latter part of 1815, and wondered why she hadn't told him the reason. Had she thought it might appear to him as some kind of betrayal; that it would give him pain to know that she had been carrying Andrew's child, when it should have been his? Foolish Vilia, when the child must have been conceived before either of them had even admitted to being in love. But she had been right, of course. It was a long time since he had felt such heartache.

As if he had been thinking about Mungo, he said, 'He was a good man. Are you acquainted with the boys? It must have been difficult for Mrs Lauriston, bringing them up with no father.' *What was he to do? What the hell was he to do?* Back in the disastrous present, his mind twisting and turning like some animal in a trap, he wondered savagely what in God's name Vilia was thinking of. She must be mad. Did she need Kinveil so much? Two hours had been enough to tell him that

Luke was the same self-centred, spoilt, touchy brat he'd always been, despite his carefully cultivated urbanity. Vilia must know it. She wasn't a fool. *What the hell was he to do?*

'I haven't seen much of them lately, but they're shaping up well.'

'If they've inherited their mother's love for Kinveil, I imagine you'll see a good deal more of them in the future.'

It was a point that hadn't occurred to Luke. 'Oh, no. Theo's far too keen on the foundry, and the others follow his lead. Anyway, I certainly wouldn't encourage them in any ambition to become country gentlemen. They're Lauristons, after all, not Telfers.'

Perry studied him meditatively. The Lauriston boys' ancestors, through Vilia, had ruled over Kinveil for almost five hundred years, and it was less than thirty years since the Telfers had come to it. Yet already Luke thought his blood finer than theirs. Perry shrugged, and murmured a meaningless, 'Indeed.' He wondered whether Kinveil, now, was really all that mattered to Vilia. He could understand how tempting it must be for her, the prospect of having it back in her own hands. But she must see – surely she must see! – that love of place was barren when compared with human love such as the love they had had for each other, the love that on his side had grown deeper and stronger through their long separation. He could convince her, he believed, for he had developed a new depth and strength in these last seven years.

But before he could convince her and divert her from her chosen path, he had to see her. He had always known this meeting was not going to be easy. He had written to her more than once – short, unsentimental letters that, by their very existence, were a statement of commitment. He had hoped that the act of receiving them would mean as much to her as the act of sending them did to him. They hadn't been love letters, because love set down on the page by anyone but a poet always sounded, to Perry, cheap and immature. So he had confined himself to beginning, 'Vilia, my dearest', and ending briefly, 'Yours, Perry'. Not until these last weeks had it occurred to him that Vilia might not have understood. He had received no replies to guide him, although either letters or replies could easily have gone astray. Perhaps he had been wrong. Perhaps without the reassurance of words, however commonplace, she thought that the love of which he had failed to convince her seven years ago had proved in the end to be as insubstantial as she had claimed. This time, he thought again, he would convince her, because there was nothing in the world that would stop him. But he had to see her before her feet were irrevocably set on the path she seemed to have chosen. *Next week, Luke had said, and it was Friday now.*

He stretched himself lazily, and stifled a non-existent yawn. 'Perhaps, in time to come, Lauriston's will be able to supply me with materials for my guns. Until now, I've been content to act as agent for a number of American gunsmiths, but my next step will be to set up a manufactory of my own.' It seemed a sufficiently neutral note on which to end a conversation that was now beyond him. 'In the meantime, Luke, I think I must retire. It's been a long day, and I have to leave at dawn tomorrow. The exigencies of business, I fear. I have appointments to keep, and I have stayed away too long. I'll send Briggs down to warn them at the stables.'

They left at first light and reached Marchfield late on the evening of the Monday after the kind of journey Briggs prayed he would never have to live through again. They had scanned every carriage on the road, inquired at every inn, descended at every isolated dwelling along the way, and in between Mr R. had kept up a killing pace, regardless of whether their hired mounts were ambling old nags or half-wild youngsters scarcely broken to bridle. By the time they arrived at Marchfield, Briggs wasn't even capable of dismounting, and it was Mr R. himself, dust thick on his clothes and sketching in, like chalk on grey paper, the creases that bracketed his long mouth, who ran up the steps and set the knocker resounding through the quiet air.

And despite everything he had missed her. Despite the meticulous checking at every point on the route to make sure she wasn't there, resting for an hour, and that she hadn't been there. Despite the waits at ferries, and the mad, scrambling gallops between, and the shouldering through crowds that had clogged their way in towns and villages, his eyes raking the streets and wynds for any sight of her. He hadn't thought of her taking the canal route, which hadn't even been open when he was in Scotland last.

Mistress Lauriston had left on Friday, the butler said, and would be almost at Kinveil by now. It wass a great pity, indeed it wass, that the chentleman had not sent ahead to tell Mistress Lauriston that he wass coming.

Chapter Four

1

She descended, smiling, from the carriage Luke had sent to meet her at Fort Augustus, and Luke strolled out to welcome her with a cigarillo between his fingers and a casual, proprietary gleam in his sleepy brown eyes. 'My dear,' he said languidly, dropping a kiss on her forehead. 'How delightful to see you.'

She thought at first that he might be putting on a performance for his parents' benefit, and glanced round, but they were nowhere in sight. Indoors, perhaps. Turning, she said, 'Wait, Sorley, and I'm sure Mr Luke will send someone to help you with the traps.' It was unusual for there to be so few underlings about, for Magnus liked it to be obvious how well served he was.

'Aye, mistress.' Sorley's eyes were on Luke, waiting for a greeting, but Luke ignored him. Instead, he took Vilia's arm and turned to cross the causeway. 'A pleasant journey?'

'Blowy. Especially on the sea crossing from Greenock. But oh, such delight to feel the air fresh and clean again after the foundry!' She glanced out over the water, strands of long, silken hair teased out from under the close-fitting scarlet hat. 'Spring is early this year, isn't it? What joy to be back. Tell me, how many lambs? And have the fish been running well? And does your mother feel better for her stay in London? Such a dreadful time as they must have had at Glenbraddan!'

'Tea first,' he said.

She went to her room and freshened herself, and allowed her maid, rigid perfectionist that she was, to brush out her hair and pin it up again in the heavy, classical coil that was never either in fashion or out of it. With her hair, as with her gowns, Vilia made her own rules. She was wearing today a simple, slender travelling dress of blue-grey-green kerseymere that made no concessions to the vast uncomfortable skirts of 1829, which she donned only on social occasions and only under protest. It had long, graceful oversleeves that could be detached when the dress was worn under a pelisse. She put them on now, and went down and through the courtyard and then up to the Long Gallery.

Luke was waiting. 'A dream,' he said smoothly when he saw her. 'Straight out of some mediaeval book of hours. A lady of courtly love.'

Disregarding the drawl, she went to him and, putting her hands on his arms, raised her face to be kissed. 'My dear, I am back.' There was a hint of a question in her voice.

'Ye-e-es.' Once more, lightly, he dropped his lips to her forehead.

She could feel him shaking a little and said, puzzled, 'You don't seem precisely overjoyed to see me?' He seemed to have put on height since the autumn, and weight, too. She touched a finger to the incipient pouch of flesh at the corner of his mouth and whispered, 'Kiss me properly.'

He raised a quizzical eyebrow. 'We mustn't shock Betty Fraser. Let us possess our souls in patience, or at least until she has brought the tea-tray in.'

She knew by now that something had gone awry, and very recently; it was only a few days since she had received the last of the many letters he had written her during the months of separation, letters burdened with endearments, promises, yearning, letters that had helped her persuade herself that all would be for the best, so that she had come trailing clouds of compliance and good intentions. What could have gone wrong? Nothing very important, presumably; perhaps it was just that his vanity had become inflated by the knowledge that he had won and that she would marry him after all. Irritation stirring in her, she said, 'By all means,' and turning, sat down and settled her skirt and sleeves with care so that they fell in becoming folds from the chair to the floor.

Betty came in, bobbing and smiling, and they drank their tea and made polite conversation until Vilia asked again, 'And your mother, is she well? Did I arrive before I was expected, that she isn't here?'

Luke stared into his cup for a moment, and then replaced it on the table. His tongue flickered out to moisten his upper lip, and then he said, 'My parents are still in London, I imagine. I don't expect them here for another ten days.' He met her eyes challengingly.

'What do you mean? How long have you known this?'

'For some time.'

'Why didn't you stop me?' she asked sharply. 'How *dared* you bring me here under such circumstances!' She paused, thinking it through. 'Were you so unsure of me that you felt it necessary to compromise me? Is that what it is?'

'Compromise you?' he repeated. 'My dear Vilia, is that possible?'

It was such an extraordinary thing to say that, for a moment, the sense didn't penetrate. 'What are you talking about?' Her voice, suddenly, was uncertain.

He crossed to her and, taking her hands, pulled her to her feet and then, slowly and provocatively, into his arms. She lay there, and allowed him to kiss her, and knew, as one compelling hand slid down her back pressing her body hard against his, that some things hadn't changed. But all her instincts warned her to take care, and she didn't respond even to his lips.

After a moment, he raised his head and murmured, 'Don't be stubborn, my dear. Kiss me!'

But before he could silence her again, she turned her head away and said, 'What did you mean?'

He took a step backwards, then, and holding her hands wide in his, looked her up and down almost impersonally, as if he were assessing the points of a mare he was thinking of buying. 'How old are you, Vilia? Thirty-three, thirty-four? And fourteen years widowed. Chaste for so long? Uncompromised? You, with your beauty, and your body, and your independence?'

She didn't believe she had heard him aright. And then he added, 'Was that why you wouldn't let me come to Edinburgh? Your last taste of freedom before you submitted to the restraints of matrimony again?'

And then she thought – jealousy. The instinctive, irrational jealousy that had afflicted him as a child, and that she had thought he must have grown out of. It wasn't a very attractive characteristic, but she couldn't think that there would be much scope for it once they were married. Certainly she couldn't allow it to wreck her plans, overturn the decision she had reached after seven months of heart-searching.

She breathed incredulously, 'You're jealous? Oh no, I promise you there's no one to be jealous of. I swear to you that no man has touched me since my husband died. No man but you.' And except for a kiss, it was true. Under God, it was true. There were tears in her eyes as she returned his gaze.

'That's very good,' he said approvingly. 'You couldn't manage a sob or two as well?'

With all the strength in her, she struck him across his insolent face.

Shocked out of his sick defiance, he knew he had overdone it. He didn't really believe anything he had said or implied. It was just that, ever since his uncle had left, he had been torturing himself. Perry and Vilia. It was so obvious, so right, once one thought about it. He wouldn't have thought about it if he hadn't had the past fresh in his mind from the family chronicle, and if his uncle hadn't let something slip.

But there was one thing that nullified it all. Vilia's inexperience. Her body had been so innocent when he had made love to her on the hill; however she might deceive him, however she might twist him, intellectually, round her finger, there were some things it was impossible to simulate, and innocence was one of them. Luke could still remember honey-sweet, virginal Antoinette, in Lyon, who had fooled him not for a moment. There were touches, caresses, that a woman accustomed to men resorted to almost without realizing. From what Vilia had said that last night in October about Andrew Lauriston *using* her, Luke knew he could have taught her none of them. But if Luke's charming, handsome, devil-may-care Uncle Perry had ever taken her to bed, Vilia must have learned everything there was to know; or more, much more, than she did.

In the end, Luke had succeeded in convincing himself that, if Vilia and Perry had ever been in love, there had been nothing physical in it. But he was still sure there had been *some*thing between them, even if they had been strong enough to deny the flesh. In a way, that had made it worse for him.

One palm to his flaming cheek, he looked at her doubtfully, and it was as if she could read his feelings. The rage in her eyes faded, and she looked at him in a sad, understanding way. Vilia Cameron, the passion of his life, who loved him too little and knew him too well.

She sighed. 'Don't torture yourself so. Won't you believe me? I've spent all these months in Edinburgh, longing to be here with you. If you must be jealous, be jealous of James Moultrie and Wally Richards. Be jealous of the foundry. But of nothing and no one else.'

She could still, as she had always done, make him feel childish and uncertain. Was that why his conquest had been so sweet? He knew that, if it hadn't been for Perry Randall's visit, underlining possibilities that he had half seen and wholly ignored in the family chronicle, he would never really have doubted her, but recognized the jealousy that plagued him for what it was, a weakness that he had learned to identify but would never learn to control.

There were wheels on the gravel and he seized on the diversion. 'A carriage? Who can *that* be?' He went to one of the windows overlooking the causeway, and after a moment Vilia joined him.

It was her own carriage, from Edinburgh. Graham the footman, laughter on his face, was letting down the steps to allow three blonde-haired boys to tumble out, one after the other. Theo first, and then Gideon, and then Drew. She could see that they were bubbling over with high spirits and mischief, and knew instantly that there was nothing wrong; the foundry hadn't burned down, or the house. They had simply taken the law into their own hands, objecting to being left behind, and had no doubt raced the carriage all the way here to arrive almost as soon as she did, and surprise her. A game. A delightful game. Theo, she suspected, had been at the root of it; Theo, who never did anything for frivolous reasons, but always had his eye on the main chance. What main chance, she wondered, did he have his eye on this time? Silly Theo. He wasn't anywhere near to being as clever as he thought he was. He couldn't know about his mother and Luke Telfer.

She hadn't brought the boys, although they had been disappointed and more than a little vocal about it, because she didn't want to remind Luke that she had three adolescent sons. He had never shown any concern about the difference in age between himself and Vilia, but that didn't mean he wasn't conscious of it. Irritating Theo.

Fair, slim, tall for his age, Theo looked up and saw them at the window and smiled and waved. Gideon, too. And then Drew, thirteen years old and vivid as the sun striking on glass. He said something to his brothers, and they all laughed and looked up again, and then Drew scampered blithely across the causeway, followed more sedately by the other two, and disappeared from view. To be clutched, Vilia reflected ruefully, to the collective bosom of Jessie Graham and Betty Fraser and every other female in the castle.

'Oh, dear!' she said, in an undervoice. 'What impossible children they are! What *shall* I do with them?'

She turned away, mentally framing an apology for their lawless behaviour.

And then, from behind her, a voice she scarcely recognized breathed, 'You bitch!' She spun round. 'You whore! How dare you bring your brats to this house? No wonder you've kept them away from us! How long did you think it would be before one of us here recognized Perry Randall's bastard?'

The blood fled from her face, leaving it stark and white as a cerecloth, with all the fine, beautifully wrought bones stripped bare and the slanted brows flying over eyes that were garish as emeralds. After an eternity, she said, 'What do you mean?'

If, seeing Drew so soon after Perry, any doubts had remained to him, her face would have dispelled them. In the anguished days since Perry had left, he had worked out all the possibilities, although in his mind's eye he couldn't see any resemblance between the nine-year-old Drew he remembered and the powerful man Perry had become. But seeing the boy in the flesh again, and knowing that it *could* be, he knew without any possibility of doubt that it *was*.

'You know what I mean. Perry Randall was here a few days ago. I know what happened between you. How could I not?'

She had no more colour left to lose. 'Here? *Here?*'

He came towards her, stalking her, and she backed away. 'Here?' she said again, her voice rising.

'Why not? Should he have rushed to Edinburgh, to you? Don't be so vain, my pretty bitch! Do you think he cares any more? There are whores by the thousand in America. Why should he want you?'

One hand settled round her throat, soft and suffocating, and the other pulled her to him in a travesty of an embrace. 'You've been too clever, my dear. I've had time to think since Perry left, and I know why you wanted to marry me. Oh, yes, *wanted* to marry me. "What if I should have a child?"' he mimicked viciously. 'It's Kinveil you want, not me. You've never wanted anything else. Do you remember that very first day at St James's Square, when you screamed at me, "Kinveil is *mine!*" And then you began to work very hard indeed at bewitching the old man. And then you took Perry away from Charlotte, in case they should have a son who might be in line to inherit the place. Edward was no problem; you knew my grandfather would never leave Kinveil to him. But a son of Charlotte and Perry . . . That was another matter and you settled it very neatly. Don't think I don't give you credit for being clever, my dear. Had you thought even then that some day you might marry *me*?' He laughed unpleasantly. 'It must have been a very nasty shock for you when you heard that Charlotte was in the

357

family way again. But it turned out to be Shona. No wonder you were so kind to her last year. You could afford to be!'

Choking, she said, 'You're wrong. Quite wrong.'

In one appalling surge, all Luke's maturity had fallen away, all the amused, airy veneer he had built up so carefully that even he believed in it. Now he was down to the shell, to the real Luke who cared nothing about others except as they affected himself. Who wouldn't be crossed. Whose only interests were his own. Vilia, deep in shock, realized that he hadn't changed at all. She hadn't taken the trouble to study him deeply enough. She *wanted* him to have changed into the urbane adult he had appeared to be, because it was convenient for her to have him so. It had allowed her to justify herself – to herself.

'You're wrong,' she gasped again. 'Wrong about everything. I can't tell you how wrong you are!'

'I hope you won't try, my dear. It would be such a waste of energy.' Malevolently, his hand caressed her throat. 'You've lied to me, to all of us, ever since we knew you. You don't know how to be truthful, even in bed.' And that rankled more than anything. If she had managed to deceive even him, she must be clever and calculating beyond redemption. 'It seems a pity. I've always found the really mature harlot so rewarding. But perhaps, now that the truth is out, you'll be prepared to demonstrate some of your more esoteric talents.'

His hands pressing ruthlessly on her shoulders, he began to force her down to her knees. 'Come along now, my dear. I am in need.' He thrust his hips towards her. 'Some of your whore's tricks. A little mouth music, perhaps?'

She didn't understand the words, but she understood everything else, and somehow, in a wild flurry of movement when he wasn't expecting it, she tore herself away from him, out from under the bruising hands. She had thrown him off balance, so that despite her hampering skirts she succeeded in reaching the fireplace where the ancient swords and daggers hung on display. When she turned, there was a short, bright dirk in her hand.

For a heavy-breathing moment, neither of them moved or spoke. Then Luke lunged forward, and she responded, and when he jerked back again with a cry there was blood welling from a deep, ragged slash across the back of his wrist. He clasped his other hand round it, his eyes wide and his mouth open with shock, and the blood began to seep

358

through his fingers and trickle sluggishly back down the injured wrist to turn the white shirt-cuff scarlet.

Still holding the dirk levelled against him, she said through clenched teeth, 'Don't come near me, you *animal*! If I have lied to you, it was on one matter only, and not for my own sake but to save others from the consequences of my foolishness.'

It was clear, then, that he wasn't going to make any other move. He was a child again, terrified of being hurt. She straightened up a little, and the fury began to fade slowly from her eyes. After a long silence, when they did no more than stare at each other, their expressions unchanging, she spoke, a dozen generations of arrogant forbears ranked invisibly behind her. 'Your behaviour has been unforgivable. You haven't grown up yet, and I doubt if you ever will. Your mind, it seems, is as coarse and corrupt as your tongue. But I will make allowances for you, that you were not prepared to make for me. I know you have always been jealous and possessive, and it seems that you have allowed your imagination to become overheated. Your parents have been very good to me, and I should dislike hurting them, so I will mention this episode to no one. But don't dare – ever – to lay hands on me again.'

He scarcely felt the pain of his wrist yet, but he was almost crying with rage and frustration. His face crumpled, his voice trembling, he said, 'Don't flatter yourself that I want to. And don't condescend to me. Do you think I care whether you mention this "episode", as you call it? Because *I* will mention it, by God I will! As soon as my parents return, I'll tell them everything about you. And once I've done that, my pure, unsullied, uncompromised little trollop, you'll never be allowed to cross the threshold of Kinveil again!'

It seemed as good an exit line as his tongue was ever likely to encompass, and, turning, his eyes half-blind with self-indulgent tears, he made his way towards the door. He didn't even see Sorley McClure just outside it until he cannoned into him.

'Sorry, sir,' the fellow said, holding something out in his hand. 'Here iss a note chust come for you from Glenbraddan. Robert Fraser wass busy, so I said I would bring it up to you.'

Wordlessly, Luke accepted it and went on his way. It seemed a long time before he reached his room, at last, and was able to let the storm engulf him.

2

In spite of everything, the rules of hospitality prevailed. Bathed, changed, and unobtrusively bandaged, Luke went down to dinner at the appointed hour, presenting an appearance of calm normality except for faintly swollen eyelids and a heart that was cold and numb. Vilia was equally calm in a ruffled, high-necked gown that hid the marks on her throat and shoulders.

Only Gideon, his eye caught by the flickering reflections from his mother's wineglass, saw that her hands were shaking. He glanced at Theo, but Theo was too busy showing off to have a thought for anyone else. Gideon groaned inside and wondered what he was up to.

The three boys' escapade had been Drew's idea. None of them had been near Kinveil since they were small, and Drew was quite incensed that Mama hadn't offered to bring them. He wanted to see the place again, now that he was old enough to appreciate it; an unrelieved diet of the *Waverley* novels had done wonders for his romantic streak, and he knew that Kinveil was straight out of the Middle Ages. 'Why *shouldn't* we go, and give them all a surprise? We could race Mama by road. Why not? It would be an adventure!' He was the most disgustingly persuasive child, and couldn't believe that anyone would ever be annoyed with him. Although Theo could have squashed the idea flat, he hadn't; he hadn't even ticked Gideon off for letting Drew talk him into playing truant from Perth Academy.

Gideon had the feeling that what Theo was up to, was trying to find out what Mama was up to. And whatever *that* was seemed to have turned her into a bundle of nerves. Wondering whether it could be anything to do with Luke Telfer, Gideon decided not. Luke was just as much of a stuffed shirt as when they had last seen him at Marchfield, four years ago. Although it was Gideon's pride to be vastly tolerant, he had never cared much for Luke, and couldn't understand why Theo had such a weakness for him.

'This new hot blast process,' Theo said, pushing away the remains of his salmon and leaning back in his chair, one negligent hand in his trousers pocket and the other twirling the stem of his glass.

Oh no! Gideon moaned to himself. Not the foundry. Not again! Not now. Theo and Drew were foundry-mad, but Gideon hated the place.

'You've no idea how fascinating it is, Vilia dear!'

Vilia could never decide whether to be amused or exasperated by her eldest son's Olympian certainty that he knew more about most things than she did. 'Oh?' she said. If she gave him his head, it would at least relieve her of the need to make conversation.

'It's not just that it produces three times as much iron for the same amount of fuel, but you can use raw coal instead of coke. And fewer furnaces produce the same volume of iron. Now, those facts alone would recommend it to us. But if we look even further ahead than that, we find that the result would be to give us a great deal of spare space. So many things we could use it for. More castings, for example, and perhaps finer ones. We must think about it very seriously.'

'Yes,' Vilia said flatly. She couldn't, after all, let him go on. It was too impolite to Luke, whatever she thought of him. 'Neilson patented it only last year, and the Clyde Ironworks are turning over to it now. We'll wait and see how the system works in practice, and then discuss it again.'

Gideon giggled to himself. There was no one like Mama for putting Theo in his place.

Luke, patently bored, roused himself to ask, 'Still want to be the greatest poet and ironmaster the world has ever seen?'

Theo gave him his faun-like smile. 'Of course. Though I haven't much time for the poetry side of it these days.'

'I'm going to be just as good,' intervened Drew belligerently. 'I'm going to . . .'

'That will do,' Vilia said. 'Gideon, I'm sure Luke has had enough of the foundry. Have you nothing to contribute to the conversation?'

'Yes, Vilia. I'm sorry.' He turned politely to their host. 'You know, it's funny being at Kinveil for the first time since we were small. The castle's really very interesting, and it's quite different seeing it from just hearing about it. Sorley showed us round part of it while you and Vilia were talking before dinner. I hope you don't mind,' he added anxiously.

Drew sat up in his chair. 'I liked the listening tube best – that Laird's Lug thing – but Sorley wouldn't let me put my ear to it. He said it was rude to eavesdrop, but you wouldn't have minded, Luke, would you? Just for a minute, I mean, so that we could hear what it sounded like.' Luke simply stared at him, and Drew sighed. 'Anyway, when I argued he got quite cross and sent us all downstairs. Just so's he could have a quick listen himself, I bet!'

Gideon said, 'Drew, behave yourself!' and added apologetically to Luke, 'Perhaps we can satisfy his curiosity tomorrow, if it's not inconvenient. But I was thinking, I'm sure what's happening in the glens must be every bit as exciting as all our new industrial advances?'

'Yes.' There was no humour in Luke's smile. 'In fact, I hear there may be some very real excitement tomorrow. My cousin Edward is just back from Edinburgh, with his sister Grace, and she writes to tell me that he's evicting some of his tenants tomorrow to make way for sheep.'

'Oh, no,' Vilia exclaimed. 'Not more!'

Luke shrugged. 'He needs the space. Grace is afraid that, this time, there may be trouble. She wants me to ride over, though what she thinks I can do to prevent it I can't imagine.'

'But you'll go?'

'I suppose so.'

Drew sat up in his chair again. 'May we come, too? Oh, please may we come? It would be so interesting.'

Vilia said, 'My dear, we mustn't impose on Luke's hospitality. This is only a flying visit. We have to leave again for Marchfield, first thing in the morning.'

There was a howl of protest from the boys, even Theo. 'Oh, Vilia! No!' Drew's treble piped above the rest. 'You can't make us go. It's not *fair*!'

In a tone that none of them had ever heard before, Vilia said, 'You will do as you're told.'

The three of them stared at her, Drew looking as hurt as if she had said something quite brutal. Gideon thought how funny it was that Drew, even at thirteen, still behaved so childishly when Vilia was present, as if he were asking her to pick him up and cuddle him. Gideon and Theo had always had a very civilized relationship with their mother, who had never talked down to them, or snapped at them, or been anything but pleasantly reasonable. Certainly, Gideon couldn't remember her ever telling them – as he knew many of his friends' mothers did – that they must do as she said simply because she said so. Admittedly, he couldn't remember her ever petting or hugging them, either, but he and Theo hadn't minded. It had always suited

362

them to be treated less as children than as under-sized adults. But it was different with Drew, who badly needed to feel important. It made him very demanding. Vilia didn't like it, and Gideon had wondered more than once when Drew would begin to realize that, the more he asked, the less he was given. Vilia was determined that he must learn to stand on his own feet, and he didn't want to in the least. He was like the last of the fledglings, who wasn't going to leave the nest without a good hearty push.

His lips quivering, Drew said, 'But . . .'

And then Luke intervened. 'Unnecessary, Vilia.'

Her eyes flew to his face and then dropped again, hidden by the veiling lashes. For hours her mind had been fluttering aimlessly, looking for an escape, but now it began to work again. To leave Kinveil the very day after she had arrived could only advertise the fact that something was seriously wrong, and at least the boys' presence lent her visit an element of respectability. To leave at once, she knew, would be to leave forever. If she stayed on, it might – just – be possible to salvage something.

Luke said, 'We can talk again when I get back from Glenbraddan. And the boys may accompany me, of course, if they want to. You can send Sorley to keep an eye on them.'

He came to her room that night, in spite of everything, but she had found a length of wire in the orraman's shed and wound it round the latch. He knocked softly, and his voice, grating, said again and again, 'Let me come in. I beg of you, let me come in.' But she lay in silence, watching the faint vibrations of the latch, and neither moved nor answered. And after a while he went away.

3

Luke wondered why Sorley, riding a little ahead with Drew, had reined in so sharply when he reached the bend overlooking Grianan. He could hear Drew asking excitedly, 'What did you say, Sorley? You said something in Gaelic. You swore, you know you did! What did you say?' But Sorley, the freckles livid against his suddenly white face, was paying no attention.

Then Luke saw why. The sunny, peaceful little amphitheatre in the hills, with its dozen houses, its grazing cows, its carefully tended lazy-beds, its sparkling river, was peaceful no more. Luke's first impression was of frantic, scurrying movement, and shouting, and screaming, and greasy billowing smoke, of a scene now brightly lit, then blacked out, then lit again as the clouds raced small and dark and tempestuous across the sun. It took several moments before his eyes and ears were able to sort out what was happening, even though his mind grasped it at once. This was trouble – real trouble – and it looked as if Edward had brought it on himself.

Weeks ago, the Glenbraddan factor had delivered writs of removal to all the tenants of the little township of Grianan, folk whose parents and grandparents, and, probably, great-grandparents had lived here for a hundred years or more, sharing the evil-smelling comforts of their homes with a cow, some hens, and their pampered 'little old sheep', and supporting themselves by unambitious, careful husbandry. And now the world had caught up with them. In correct and ludicrously inappropriate legal language, the writs had told them they were under obligation 'to flit and remove themselves, Bairns, family, servants, subtenants, Cottars and dependants, Cattle, Goods, and gear, and to leave their tenancies void, redd, and patent, that the Pursuer, Mr Edward Blair of the property of Glenbraddan in the county of Inverness-shire, or others in his name, may then enter thereto and peaceably possess, occupy and enjoy the same in time coming.' All to be accomplished by the Quarter Day next occurring, the fifteenth day of May in this year of our Lord 1829.

But Edward had been in Edinburgh on the due date, and the tenants hadn't flitted and no one had made them. Luke reflected that the poor souls had probably persuaded themselves that Edward had thought better of it and would let them stay. They must have had a rude awakening this morning when they heard the tramp of his cohorts on the gravelled road that skirted the valley on its way to the coast. Luke could see several of Glenbraddan's toughest estate workers in the crowd, and there were others who could only be sheriff-officers and constables, brought along by Edward to enforce the writs. The law was undoubtedly on his side.

A hammer to crack a nut, Luke would have said if he'd been asked. Upwards of twenty-five hard-faced, strong-armed men to evict a handful of ill-nourished peasants and demolish a few hovels. If Edward hadn't wanted to be sure the people left, he wouldn't even have needed to demolish the hovels, because his precious Cheviots could have grazed over their roofs without so much as noticing they'd strayed from the surrounding heath. It was difficult enough for the human eye to pick the houses out from the landscape, consisting as they did mainly of heather-thatched roofs that sloped up from low boulder walls to meet the hill against which they nestled. Luke had never been inside one, but he had been told they were warm and dark and womb-like, cushioned against the rain by their thick stone foundations and the layers of turf that underlay the thatch; quiet even in the howling gales that ripped through the glens, because the wind never caught them flat on, but swept up and over, following the scarcely interrupted line of the slope in which they were embedded.

And now two of the houses were sluggishly on fire, and Luke could see that he would have been wrong and that twenty-five hard-faced, strong-armed men might not be too many to evict a handful of peasants. For there was far more than a handful, and although they were mostly women and children they were wild with fury, as bellicose and as dangerous as the fishwives who had marched on Versailles at the start of the French revolution.

Even as Luke watched, the Glenbraddan employees began to beat a craven retreat to where Edward sat in his gig on the far side of the valley, while a portly gentleman whom Luke didn't know scrambled hastily up the hillside towards where the Kinveil party had halted. Two sheriff-officers and a dozen men guarded his rear against the shrieking horde of women and children with their sticks and hoes and bannock spades and peat irons. Luke didn't blame the man for bolting. He'd have done the same. There weren't more than seventy or eighty on the rampage altogether, but they couldn't have been more frightening if there had been a thousand.

Half-way up the slope there was an outcrop of rock, rather like a pulpit, and the portly gentleman paused in his ignominious flight and began searching distractedly in his pockets.

Drew was pulling at Sorley's sleeve. 'Who's that, Sorley? Who's that man? What's he doing, Sorley?'

The man had found what he was looking for and, turning, faced the mob from his rocky eminence and began to read aloud. At first, Luke

365

couldn't hear above the combined hubbub of people and dogs and cows and 'little old sheep', but the people fell silent as they realized what was going on.

'. . . Sovereign Lord the King chargeth and commandeth all persons being assembled immediately to disperse themselves, and peaceably to depart . . .'

'It iss the Sheriff-Substitute,' Sorley said. 'He iss reading the Riot Act.'

'. . . upon the pains contained in the Act made in the first year of King George the First for preventing tumults and riotous assemblies . . .'

'What's it *mean*, Sorley?'

'It means that when he hass finished reading, if the people iss not going away within the hour, the law says he can use as much force as he thinks fit, in order to make them. And if anyone iss unlucky enough to be killed in the process, that iss chust too bad.'

'. . . God save the King!' The Sheriff-Substitute folded up his paper again and restored it to his pocket.

Luke said, 'Don't be a fool, Sorley. You know he won't use more force than he has to,' and Theo – at his most irritatingly superior – added coolly, 'In any case, his men seem to have no firearms. They can't do much damage with those sticks of theirs.'

Sorley didn't answer.

Luke wasn't sure what he should do. He ought to go and join Edward, either to give him moral support or apply moral pressure, he didn't know which. But to join Edward meant riding along that very exposed stretch of road with the forces of law and order on one side and the 'riotous assembly' on the other. He didn't fancy it at all, even though the stones had stopped flying for the moment and the women seemed to be busy arguing among themselves. Certainly, he couldn't take the boys with him. If anything happened to them, Vilia would never forgive him.

He gulped, and wondered how he was ever going to make his peace with her after yesterday, for at some stage during the watches of the night, the worst night he had ever spent, he had discovered that he wanted to, more than anything else on earth. His jealousy and hatred smothered by an almost death-like exhaustion, he had lain on his bed, still fully dressed, his bandaged wrist throbbing fitfully, and had faced up to the situation. And there had crept into his dulled heart a glimmer of understanding, a recognition that everything that had happened might have stemmed from no more than a single half-hour when Vilia and Perry Randall had given in to the demands of the flesh, as Vilia and he himself had done last autumn on the hill. His mind had shied away from that, because it made it all too real, too much to bear. But at some time during the hours of darkness, he had begun to grow up at last.

Drew had hopped down from his pony. 'But they're not a – a tumult and a what's-it's-name! They're just poor women who don't want to be put out of their homes. Can't we do something? Can't we tell the Sheriff-Substitute to go away? It's so silly waving a big stick at them – you can't expect them to like it!' He turned to Luke. 'And really, Luke. I do think your cousin Edward ought to be nicer to them! After all, they're *our* people.'

No one but Sorley knew why Luke was staring at the boy. The sentiments were Vilia's, but the straight eyes and long, curling mouth were unequivocally Perry Randall's.

Sorley reached out and pulled the boy towards him. 'Peace, laddie,' he said. *'Na abair do shàr-fhacal gus an oidhche roimh d'bhàs.* And before you ask, that means "save your fine words until the night before you die".'

Drew wriggled free. 'Yes, but can't we *do* something!'

He looked as if he were about to take off down the hill, and Luke stretched out a long arm and caught him. 'Stay where you are, my boy. This isn't your fight.' He looked up and caught Sorley's eye. Through his teeth, he added, 'And don't criticize *me*, Sorley McClure. It's not my fight, either.'

But somehow his mind had been made up for him. There seemed to be a temporary truce below. 'Stay here with the boys, Sorley. I'm going to ride over there and have a word with my cousin.'

'Oh, *good!*' Drew said, and Gideon thought wryly that the brat was so used to getting his own way – largely because it never occurred to him that he might not – that he probably thought Luke was going to tell Edward Blair to tell the Sheriff-Substitute to go away.

It was too much for Luke, his emotions in turmoil and his immediate desire to be anywhere other than here. 'Hold your tongue!' he snapped. 'You know nothing about anything. My cousin is perfectly entitled to do as he pleases where his people are concerned. *His*, not ours. And most certainly not yours!'

As he rode off down the hill, only one of the four pairs of eyes that followed him wasn't frowning. Theo's superior smile didn't even falter.

They watched him all the way along the road, passing between the two camps as if he were some innocent wayfarer going about his lawful business. And then he reached Edward's gig and leaned down to have a word with him, and they could see Edward shaking his head vigorously, and then looking up to where they sat, and then giving a grimace. After a few moments Edward waved one man over – 'the grieve', Sorley murmured – and then a big, sturdy fellow who looked as if he might be a shepherd, and another with the heavily-muscled arms of a forester. More time passed, and then the grieve turned his pony and took it, sure-footed, across the slope to where the Sheriff-Substitute was still sitting among the rocks, his men warily at attention around him. They spoke, and the Sheriff-Substitute pulled his watch out of his pocket and looked at it, and then called his officers to him.

Sorley hissed, '*Ceusda-chrann ort!*' It was so obviously a malediction that none of the boys even troubled to ask what it meant. For the constables were lining up now, ash sticks in their hands, and the Glenbraddan men next to them.

Gideon said suddenly, 'Why are they all women, except for those three or four old men?'

'The men iss always up in the hills at this time of year. They probably put off going until after Quarter Day. The grazing in the valley iss very thin by the time spring comes, and the beasts haff a habit of wandering off to forage for themselves. It iss not worth bringing them back until about now, and they take a bit of finding. And some of the men iss probably gone to the shore with the ponies to collect seaweed. They will be away for days, because it iss slow work, and the ponies iss not able to move fast with a great weight of wet dulse and carrageen. They use it to fertilize the potatoes in the lazybeds.'

'There aren't very many houses for all those people,' Drew said disapprovingly. 'There must be forty women at least, and almost as many children.'

Sorley wasn't really attending. 'Three or four women to a house iss not many in this part of the world, Drew. And it is in the nature of things for women to haff children.'

The floor of the little valley wasn't wide, and the line of men with their batons and staves stretched right across it. The Sheriff-Substitute raised his hand and cried, 'Clear the way!'

Clear the way to the houses that were to be demolished, the scanty belongings that were to be burned. Trample down the lazybeds. Drive the 'little old sheep' off their pastures. Send the hens squawking into the hills to become the prey of eagle and buzzard, fox and wildcat. Beat back the harridans who had shamed the majesty of the law with their bannock spades and peat irons. Skelp the living daylights out of the children who had dared to throw stones at their betters. Clear the way.

They did. They swept without mercy from road and river right up to the walls of the houses, hitting out at anyone and everyone in their path. The women, their violence dissipated by the hour of inaction, wavered and broke. One or two ran for the false shelter of their homes, others made straight for the hillsides. It was the older ones, most of their lives behind them, who rallied briefly against the baton charge before they, too, ran – grey hair flying, screaming mouths open, some with blood pouring from head injuries, some with arms or legs half paralysed – up the slopes and out of range of the panting, swearing constables with their sticks and the grieve's lads with their horsewhips. The children, wiry and half naked, fled with them, picking up missiles as they ran, and turning to hurl them at their pursuers as accurately as if they had been bringing down a hare or a rabbit for the pot.

In less than half an hour it was over. Once or twice Sorley murmured, '*Chan eil teud am chlàrsaich. Chan eil teud am chlàrsaich,*' and Theo said, with a boredom that convinced nobody, 'Really, Sorley! You *are* having an attack of the Gaelic today. To save Drew the trouble, what are you saying?'

The thin face didn't change. 'There iss no string to my harp. There iss nothing I can do.'

'We could go down and help!' Drew exclaimed, predictably. But no one was listening.

Suddenly aware of a movement on the road behind, Gideon turned to see two small, poorly clad children, tearful and forlorn. The little girl was about five, he thought, and the boy no more than three. Staring at Gideon, saucer-eyed, the girl began in a tiny, strangled voice to tell him something, but he had no idea what it was. He heard a word that might have been *mathair*, and a phrase that began *bha an t-acras* before it was swallowed up in a sniffle of misery. 'Sorley!' he said.

They were hungry and they wanted their Mam, and they couldn't find her. They had been sent off that morning to gather nettles for her dyeing and had come back to find their world in chaos. With infinite patience, Sorley succeeded in extracting a rough description of their Mam. Long black hair. And she was bigger than Mhairi though not as big as Una. She had a red plaid and a bonny silver brooch to fasten it. They couldn't see her among the women scattered on the hill, but that didn't mean much. In the end, Sorley had no choice. 'I will take them to find her,' he said. 'Theo, you are in charge. Stay here.' His tall thin figure, with the little boy perched on his shoulder and the girl by the hand, was soon lost to sight among the descending folds of bracken and heather.

The law had done what it was here to do by clearing the way, so that Edward's employees could go about the business of repossessing the land, but it was still the sheriff-officer's duty to give the final admonition. Even from where they sat, the boys could hear his stentorian voice as he looked inside each house, roared, 'Are you prepared to leave as the writ of removal requires' and then waved the burning party forward. There were women inside two of the houses. 'An hour to get all your goods out!' the sheriff-officer bellowed, and passed on to the next.

Bedding, bed frames, spinning wheels, coggs, churns, benches, tables, clothing, cauldrons and griddles swiftly began to pile up outside the doors of the unoccupied houses, thrown out by the grieve's lads with a kind of malicious vigour. The shepherds, meanwhile, were piling dry faggots against the walls, while the foresters clambered on the roofs and began to slash through the thatch and set crowbars and axes to the turfs and timber beneath. They offered an easy target to the children, making wild sallies down the hill with their stones and rocks. Two or three of them had slings. A triumphant chorus of yells ripped through the air when one of the foresters, hit above the ear by a well-placed shot, keeled over slowly and toppled the few feet to the ground.

It made no difference, of course. A few blows with the pickaxe were enough to loosen the walls, and the roofs were easy to burn. It had been a fine, warm, blowy spring, and the sun and the wind together had dried out the thatch and turf and timber so that they took readily to the flame. Thick, slow, and oily, the smoke began to roll up into the May sky. Gables collapsed, lethargically as in a dream; powdery turrets of soil and dust appeared; hesitant flames licked and curled and, sensing their power, grew and spread.

The women on the hill, sullen and scattered, sat and watched, prevented by the ring of constables from approaching any closer. But there was a low, continuous growl coming from them, and the children had fallen silent.

Suddenly, Gideon became aware that Drew had disappeared. 'Where's the brat?' he exclaimed, and Theo, furiously, replied, 'Would you care to wager that he's gone to offer the ladies the use of his pocket handkerchief?'

Gideon took one direction and Theo the other. It was just as Gideon was picking his way carefully along the foot of the hill, between the women and the constables, that the growling stopped. He turned to see why.

The burning party had reached the occupied houses now. There was a sturdy old biddy pushing her oatmeal kist out through the door of one, shrieking at the sheriff-officer with such venom that he backed away and turned to the hovel next door, where a young mother who was little more than a girl, her baby balanced on one arm, was dragging a knotted blanket full of her worldly goods to a place of safety. 'Come along, now!' he bellowed. 'We haff not got all day!' She said something to him, pleadingly, and he answered with a shake of the head. It was clear that she was asking for more time and he was refusing. Even while they talked, the foresters had climbed on the roof and begun hacking and gouging, throwing down the turf and attacking the rafters. With a cry, the girl turned and ran back inside.

But the men didn't pause in their work of demolition.

The growl started again and swelled into a roar of spine-chilling fury, and before Gideon knew what was happening he found himself caught up in a mad rush that swept the constables aside like so much chaff and thundered on almost to the walls of the houses, before it was halted by a living barrier, many-limbed as an Indian god. It was the grieve's lads on their ponies, ponies that reared and plunged and whinnied, terrified by the smoke in their dilated nostrils and the shrieks and yells, and the heat from the burning shambles behind them. Their hooves lashed out wildly, and the riders' whips rose and fell, and the women tried to pull them from their saddles, and then the constables attacked from the rear, truncheons flailing, boots kicking out at unprotected shins and grinding viciously on unshod feet and the hands of those who had fallen. The air was alive with noise, and a fierce, bitter rage.

Gideon, ducking, weaving, parrying the limbs and weapons that threatened on all sides, grimly went on searching for Drew, sure that he would be in the thick of it. An elbow drove into his diaphragm, winding him, as its owner drew back her hand to hammer at one of the foresters. Soon afterwards, he tripped headlong into a mêlée of arms and legs, where three or four infants had pinned one of the shepherds to the ground and were thumping every accessible inch of him. Still engaged in disentangling himself, Gideon looked up to see a face looming over him and a hand with an iron-shod stick in it. But the blow didn't fall, and in a moment of clarity Gideon recognized that his gentlemanly clothes had saved him; clouting the rich was no way for a grieve's lad to win advancement. His devout thankfulness tinged with a shamed anger, he struggled on, making now for the edge of the battlefield where he might be able to see more clearly. He had collected a painful number of blows, including one on the point of his shoulder that had paralysed his arm and brought tears to his eyes, before he emerged into the relatively clear space before the old biddy's house and found himself face to face with a constable whose crazed eyes told him that, this time, his clothes wouldn't save him. For a breath-stopping moment they stared at each other. Gideon, weaponless, knew that his hour had come. And then, flying out through the door of the hovel, came an enormous china object that hit the constable a tremendous blow on the side of the head and knocked him flat. Gideon, his mouth open, stared down at the unconscious figure, and at the shards of flower-painted chamber-pot surrounding him, and began to laugh a little hysterically.

Where, in God's name, was Drew? Where were Sorley and Theo? Where was Luke? As he was scanning the disreputable mob of combatants, swaying, wrestling, tussling, he heard a crash from behind. The foresters had jumped down from the roof of the young woman's house, their work half finished, when the assault began, but there was a soaring cloud of dust rising from it that probably meant the half-severed rooftree had collapsed of its own weight. While Gideon was still frantically wondering whether the girl had had the sense to get out in time, she emerged through the empty door frame, staggering, filthy, the baby still in her arms and one hand to a dazed forehead.

She was moaning something in Gaelic, but everyone who might have understood was too busy to hear. As Gideon started forward, she saw the incomprehension in his face, and stumbled towards him crying, 'My children! My bairns! The roof hass fallen on them. Help me, please help me!' Knowing that one of his arms was useless and fearing that his strength would be inadequate, he half turned to see if there was anyone who could supply some extra muscle power, but she mistook his response. Shrieking, 'Then hold my baby that I may haff two hands free!' she thrust it into his arms and turned back to the house.

And then Luke appeared. He had stayed out of it all like a rational, sensible man. There was nothing he could usefully do. He had no right to help those who were being evicted, and he couldn't quite bring himself to help those who were doing the evicting. So he had remained with Edward, standing by the gig on a slight rise, watching the progress of the battle. He had seen the girl who had been the cause of all the trouble go back into her cottage, and the men still working on the roof, and the first of the timbers falling. Then, later, his eye had caught the movement as the roof began to shift. The girl must have come out again without him seeing. Surely she must. Surely . . . He could still remember, years ago, when he had told Vilia about Wattie Gillespie being hanged, and she had lashed out at him with her tongue. 'You didn't care enough. If you had cared, you could have stopped it.'

He had left Edward at a run, sprinting round the outside of the mob, warding off a few half-hearted blows, his eyes fixed on the shifting roof. It caved in while he was still fifty yards away.

Now, he pushed the girl brusquely aside and said to Gideon, 'Stay where you are. I'll deal with this.'

It was strange inside, with some of the roof still hanging drunkenly in place while the main part, the whole of one end, was open to the sky. Before him was a nightmare jumble of heather and divots and thin timbers and ruined furniture, capped by the rooftree which had slipped down so that it was balanced like a giant seesaw weighted at one end. The floor was surprisingly empty under the raised end, where, from the looks and the smell of it, the livestock were usually penned. Thank

God the rooftree hadn't fallen quite straight. His wrist protesting painfully, he was able to pull on the high end, and swivel it until the balance shifted and he could wedge it in the angle of the wall. He hoped it would hold; he didn't need a clout from a baulk of timber to add to his troubles.

He stood for a moment, his eyes searching the debris, and a scatter of stones flew past his head. The battle had spread, and was raging on the slope above the cottage as well as in front. Apprehensively, Luke glanced up, half expecting the belligerents to slide straight off the hill and into the cottage beside him. It wasn't impossible. If only there were less noise, so that he could hear any sound the children might be making. Systematically, he began moving aside the turfs and thatch that seemed to be smothering everything beneath. The girl was standing behind him moaning, 'My bairns! My bairns!' and it was beginning to get on his nerves. 'How many?' he asked a trifle breathlessly.

'There iss two. The three-year-old and the wee one who came the Ne'erday before last. They wass in the corner by the box bed. Chust over there!' She went back to moaning again.

Suddenly, Luke was conscious of a shout from above. It was Sorley, maddeningly taking part in the scrimmage instead of looking after Vilia's boys. There was the wildest kind of fist fight going on, but even while Sorley had one arm raised to land what was shaping up to be the most almighty punch, with the other he was pointing to a spot in the rubble by the end wall. He was right.

Sourly, Luke glanced up again at his now preoccupied form and muttered, 'Thanks!'

There were two small figures, covered with dust and quite unconscious, almost hidden in the wreckage of the box bed. It was easy enough to free them, and Luke thought they weren't hurt but had probably passed out with fright. Picking up the younger one first, he pushed it unceremoniously into its mother's arms and propelled her out of the cottage before he turned to the other. The child stirred as Luke cleared the debris away, and then opened its eyes and, immediately afterwards, its mouth. It looked as if it were winding up for an earsplitting howl. Hoping to divert it, Luke stood the infant up firmly just inside the door, brushed it down somewhat cursorily, and sent it out to its mother on its own unsteady legs. And then he stood for a moment, aware of relief and a sneaking pleasure at the thought that, this time, he *had* cared enough – and that Vilia would hear about it, not from him, of course, but from Sorley and the boys.

Gideon, waiting patiently outside with an armful of damp and odoriferous baby, had spotted Theo by now, over on the left and trying to haul one of the grieve's lads from his horse, an expression of feverish and quite un-Theo-like enjoyment on his face. And Drew. With a groan, Gideon saw that Theo had been right, though it wasn't a pocket handkerchief he was offering one of the ladies, but a supporting arm. Courteously, chivalrously, he was assisting the Dame of the Chamber Pot over the assorted junk scattered on the ground before her hovel. Disbelievingly, Gideon watched him shoulder his way past a brawny female locked in mortal combat with one of the foresters, and heard him say in his high, clear voice, 'Excuse me! Let us pass, if you please! Excuse me!'

The smile still on his lips, Gideon turned back to the house and saw that Luke had paused for a moment in the doorway, watching the toddler stagger into its mother's arms. Then, quite suddenly and for no apparent reason, he dropped as if he had been poleaxed.

After a moment, Gideon went over to the young woman and politely restored the baby to her. She smiled without seeing him. Then, stepping carefully and rather slowly, he made his way to the doorway and knelt beside Luke.

It seemed a long time before he became aware of a shadow looming over him, and glanced up. It was Sorley, with Theo and Drew behind him.

'What iss it?' Sorley's expression was tense, and somehow vibrant. 'What iss wrong?'

Gideon swallowed. 'It's Luke,' he said in a voice that wasn't his own. 'I think he's dead.'

4

It was Sorley who broke the news to Vilia, because Theo had decided that he and Gideon must stay at Grianan and say what had to be said, and do what had to be done, before Luke's body could be brought home to Kinveil. It was fortunate, in a way, that the Sheriff-Substitute and his officers were there, although if they hadn't been, Luke would probably still have been alive. But with the law on the spot, it seemed likely that the inquiry into the accident would be completed with dispatch. One of the sheriff-officers thought he had seen the rooftree lurch suddenly free, to catch Mr Telfer at the base of the skull; the suggestion was that it hadn't been wedged very firmly, and the vibration caused by the fight on the slope above had been enough to dislodge it and set it swinging on its axis. Something had shifted it; of that there was no doubt.

Sorley had wanted to stay, but Theo, his face shocked but his assurance unimpaired, had pointed out that someone must go back to warn them at Kinveil, and that it would be extremely improper for Luke's guests simply to take themselves off as if nothing had happened. 'But take the brat with you,' Theo had added. So Sorley and Drew, unnaturally silent, had ridden back together.

After the first, disbelieving exclamation, Vilia sat silent and stunned, quite unable to identify her feelings, knowing only that when, after a while, all the decent, correct reactions began to float into the blankness of her mind, none of them was real. It was like writing a letter of condolence to herself on the death of someone who had been neither friend, nor in the true sense lover, but just a human being to whom she had been tied by childhood acquaintance, occasional liking, and a complexity of needs. In time, when her head released the message to her heart, she would mourn the human being and remember, with a trace of sadness, something of what had been between them. But it was the hurt to Magnus and Lucy she thought of when the first moments of shock wore off, and then, foolishly, of the hurt to Mungo, whose grandson Luke had been.

The tears glimmered in her eyes at that, and then she realized that she must have been staring through Sorley for several minutes. He was watching her with a curious expectancy on his face, and she thought suddenly – I suppose he knows about Luke and me; something, anyway. He knows me so well. So well. I suppose he knows about yesterday, too. Does he know that none of us might ever have seen Kinveil again, after yesterday?

The sword of Damocles over their heads, but the thread hadn't broken, and today the sword had been taken away. Though not as if it had never been. She hadn't wished, even for a moment, that anything like today's accident would happen, but she would never be wholly free from guilt at the relief it had brought her.

She said, 'It's all right, Sorley. I'm not going to embarrass you with tears. Were the boys upset? Perhaps you would send Drew up to me now? I am sure he is dying to tell me all about it.'

She smiled a little, ruefully, and Sorley gave a small, satisfied nod of his head, and went.

Part Four   *1829–1838*

Chapter One

1

'And Gideon must come, too,' Vilia said. But her son's attention was wandering, as it so often did during these planning conferences at the foundry. Exhaustedly, she said, 'Gideon, will you please pay attention!'

He raised his eyes and said, 'I'm sorry.' He meant it, for he knew that she was anxious to get the meeting over and done with, and for once he knew why. Though he was fond of his mother, Gideon had never shared Theo's curiosity about her, his fascination with everything she did or said, his passion for analysing her. When he was quite small, he had decided he would never understand her, so he hadn't really tried. It had been easier to take her on her own terms; cool and friendly most of the time, occasionally high-handed, sometimes – though not very often in these last few years – marvellously good fun. But this morning something had happened to make him think, and he had been brooding about it ever since.

It had been no more than a minor domestic tragedy – scarcely even that, since they had expected it for some time. A cat's nine lives didn't usually add up to much in terms of years, and the Duchess had been over eighteen, only a few weeks younger than Gideon himself. She had been showing her age for months, and then, yesterday, she had begun to die before their eyes. She hadn't been ill or sick, but compulsively restless, moving from point to point of her daily round not once, but again and again. After a time, her muscles had stopped obeying her, so that her legs failed her after a few steps and she collapsed, and then staggered to her feet for another few steps and another collapse. It had been heartbreaking to watch, but there was nothing they could do, although as the hours passed the interval between helpless collapse and obstinate rising had become longer and longer. Vilia, her eyes tormented, had sent the boys to bed soon after midnight. Theo, rational and adult, had said, 'You should go to bed, too. Domesticated or not, cats are wild animals. Leave her in peace, to die alone as animals do.' And Vilia had looked at him and replied, 'Perhaps. I don't know. But she has had no existence apart from us for all the years of her life. If I can't convey *some* sense of comfort to her now, then nothing in this whole dreadful world has any meaning.'

Gideon hadn't slept much, and had gone down to the drawing-room soon after five. The Duchess had been stretched out, small, black and lifeless, on the fireside stool where she always slept, and Vilia had been curled up on the floor nearby, arms and head buried on the seat of a chair, her hair a loose, dishevelled screen around her. She was weeping harshly, and when Gideon took her by the shoulders to raise her, he knew at once that she had been weeping for a long time.

A few controlled, sentimental tears he could have understood. But this . . . It was so unlike her.

Casting back, he couldn't remember her ever letting her emotions show. Theo said she had been very withdrawn for months after old Mungo Telfer died, but Gideon hadn't noticed. And after Luke's death four years ago, she had been strained and monosyllabic, but no more, not even during the trying days of Magnus and Lucy's return and the subsequent inquiry, when everyone had been intent on blaming everyone else but the final verdict had been that the rooftree had slipped. The court had offered its commiseration to the victim's parents, so tragically deprived of the sole prop of their declining years, which hadn't gone down very well with Magnus. He was, after all, only forty-five. There had been an odd little episode afterwards, when Vilia and the boys had returned to Marchfield House. For several days she had been unnaturally calm and supercilious. Gideon had thought she was merely relapsing into her foundry personality, but Theo was convinced that something had happened while they had been away. Angus McKirdy, the butler, had presented her with a long list of problems that had cropped up, notes that had arrived, persons who had called, and Theo had gone around for days speculating on which of McKirdy's messages had been responsible for her odd mood.

And then, last year, Lucy Telfer had died and Vilia had been more upset than her sons had ever seen her. Yet still she hadn't wept. Perhaps she hadn't had time. Cholera had reached London in February and Edinburgh a few weeks later. People had died by scores and then by hundreds as, whimsically, the plague ravaged one whole side of a street and passed the other by. The dead-carts had gone from door to door, and a sickly smell of chlorine hung in the air, and the authorities laid down overdue regulations about dunghills and cesspools. With pink, well-scrubbed Wally Richards to help her, Vilia had imposed a stringent regime of hygiene at the foundry, but even so there were men who went home from work at night and were never seen again. And then the news had come that Lucy Telfer had died of it in London. Lucy Telfer, who had borne up under her son's death far better than Magnus had done; Lucy Telfer, who had been the closest thing to a mother or sister that Vilia had ever had. Gideon had liked her, too, for she had been possessed of the same kind of gentle detachment that he was trying to cultivate for himself. Vilia had been almost less upset by Lucy's dying than by the manner of it, less hurt by her own sense of loss than by the thought of the misery something like cholera must have caused to the dainty, fastidious Lucy. At least it had been mercifully brief; only three days.

Death, Gideon supposed, must have become a familiar presence to Vilia. Her father, Theo Cameron; then her husband, the father of her sons; then grandfather Lauriston; then Mungo Telfer, whom she had been so close to; and Luke, whom she had known since childhood; and Lucy. And all the other people Gideon had only heard of – childhood mentors at Kinveil, like Meg Macleod, her nurse; and Ewen Campbell's father, Archie; and old Robbie Fraser the gardener. Yet it had been the death of a small, elderly black cat that had reduced Vilia to an extremity of misery that Gideon couldn't even have imagined. It was a mystery that had preoccupied him for most of the day.

He said again, 'I'm sorry. I *was* listening, although I may not have looked it. I know I'll never learn anything about the administration of the foundry unless I follow you around everywhere, so, obviously, I must come to London with you. How long will we be away?'

Vilia shrugged. 'It's July now. If we go next month, we should be finished by the end of November. I have a great many people to see, and so has Theo. If he is to be our railways expert, he must first find out all he needs to know, and then let everyone see that he knows it. We have to know which companies are going to be granted authority to acquire land. We have to know which are likely to be best funded, because with such a speculative enterprise it could be ruinous to become involved with someone under-capitalized. The dangers may not be very great at the moment, but when the real boom comes in about ten years from now there are bound to be any number of fly-by-nights.'

'Ten years?' Theo exclaimed. 'Less than that, surely. Why, I would expect us to be selling as much as seven or eight per cent of our total pig production to the railways in not more than three years!'

'Very possibly. But in ten years it could be nearer twenty per cent.'

Drew, who had been unusually silent, said, 'Theo's supposed to be the foundry wizard. I don't see why he wants to trample all over my territory. If I'm going to be responsible for selling, I ought to be the one who talks to all these people.'

Gideon had seen it coming, but Vilia hadn't. Drew had a knack of disconcerting her. He was seventeen now, just finishing university and due, at the end of the year, to join what would then be Lauriston Brothers as the partner responsible for selling the firm's products. He was admirably cut out to be a salesman — charming, gregarious, single-minded. But, in a subtle family, he remained a stranger to subtlety. He liked things to be simple and clear-cut, and one result was that he often came out with remarks that, to the others, sounded nothing short of idiotic. Theo and Gideon had grown used to it, but Vilia always looked at him as if she were having to make some difficult mental adjustment — as if, somehow, Drew had no right to be such a muttonhead. This was a case in point. It was obvious to everyone except Drew that, where a new, specialized, and potentially very important market was concerned, it made sense for the manufacturing specialist to be the one who had direct contact with the customers. There were going to be a great many technical problems to be ironed out, and Theo would be able to iron them out much more swiftly and effectively than Drew.

For a moment, no one said anything. Theo saw no need to defend himself, and Vilia looked as if the last straw had just been added to her burdens. Gideon said soothingly, 'Look, Drew. You should be grateful to have one time-consuming task taken off your hands. Once we start expanding our cast-iron exports to Europe, you'll have your hands full enough, and if we go into the American market as well. . .'

With a visible effort, Vilia interrupted. 'Thank you, Gideon. Drew, you don't know about the American project yet, but earlier this year Congress passed something called the Compromise Act, which allows for import tariffs to be progressively reduced over the next ten years. I hope that you or Gideon can make a visit to America next year or the year after, to find out whether it will be feasible for us to compete there.'

Gideon's heart soared. It was the first he had heard of *that* idea, and he was struck by a blinding revelation. For as long as he could remember, it had always been assumed that Theo would take over sole responsibility for the works when James Moultrie retired, as he would do soon, and that Gideon would take over from Vilia some of the administration, which had become increasingly complex as the foundry had expanded. But privately Gideon had reached the conclusion that the world of industry, however well it suited the rest of the family, was not for him. He hadn't said anything about it, because no very appealing alternative had suggested itself to him. And now, suddenly, he realized that what he really wanted to do was travel, and see new lands and new people. Hot on the heels of this discovery came another. Perhaps, afterwards, he could write about it all. His imagination flying free and disoriented, like a bird released from a darkened cage, he cleared his throat and tried to look as if he were indifferent.

'Hum,' Drew said, his handsome lips pursed. 'Why me *or* Gideon? I should have thought . . .'

Vilia couldn't face any more. There had been a lump in her throat all day. Every sentence had required a new, separate exercise of will, and every sensible, business-like word had had to be forced out past the tears that lay ready in ambush. She said, 'It won't be a selling trip, just an investigatory one. Anyway, there is time enough to decide who should go. For the moment, unless any of you has anything particular he wants to raise, I would suggest we regard this meeting as at an end.'

Firmly and deliberately, she began to gather together the papers on the desk before her. It was a much finer desk, now, than it had been in those early days seventeen years ago, and her office was no longer in a loft but in a separate block, simple and elegant, that had been put up two years ago, in 1831, when there had been unexpectedly good profits from trade with the Netherlands, and the newly installed hot blast process had begun to release furnace space for other purposes. There were quite a number of buildings now that hadn't been there in Duncan Lauriston's day – offices for the clerks, housing for the foremen, a shed for the fire engine, warehouses, moulding sheds, an engine shop and a pattern shop, a new watch house, and a brewhouse to make decent ale for the furnace men instead of the vile stuff they had always swilled in the past. Vilia had done a great deal in her years here, but at the moment she felt no pride at all. Nothing mattered to her today. There was no space in her heart or mind for anything but misery, for mourning over that small, unimportant death.

The little black cat, like Sorley, had so often comforted her simply by being there. Between them, they had offered her an unquestioning, uncomplicated, inarticulate solace that had been her only refuge since Mungo died. She knew it was weak-minded of her to care, but she did, passionately.

She looked up to find that Drew was still lingering, although the other two had gone. He said, 'I thought that, while you three are in London, I might have a holiday. It'll be the last for a while. You don't mind, do you?'

'Of course not. Where will you go?'

'Kinveil, I thought.' His eyes were bright and challenging.

'But it's all closed up. Magnus hasn't been near the place since Luke died.'

'I know, but I'm sure Ewen Campbell would have me. All I want to do is have some sport, and perhaps do some walking or hill scrambling. The place appeals to me so much, but I feel I hardly know it. You can't object, I imagine.'

She could, but not in terms that could be put into words. Her dulled mind told her that no one would see in him what she saw of Perry Randall. It was very little; no more than something about the set of the eyes and the shape of the mouth. It had been the purest mischance that Luke had seen the resemblance, and he had seen it only because he had seen Perry himself a few days earlier. Perry, she knew, had gone straight from Kinveil to Marchfield, but he had refused to leave a message and she had been glad. If she hadn't interrogated McKirdy carefully, she would never have discovered the identity of the urgent, dusty gentleman who had called. She had wondered, drearily, what had happened to the love he had declared when she last saw him; clearly, it hadn't survived. One or two brief, uncommitted letters in the years after 1822, and then nothing until he went to Kinveil and betrayed to Luke what had happened between them during those magical days in London in 1815. She would never forgive him for that. God knew what havoc it would have wrought if Luke hadn't died when he did.

She supposed that, as long as Drew didn't go to Glenbraddan – where, just possibly, Edward or some of the older servants might have better memories than she credited them with – it couldn't do any harm. 'Very well,' she said with a sigh. 'But you would be advised to give Glenbraddan a wide berth. Charlotte Randall had a silly prejudice against me, and her son has inherited it. Also, I think he half blames us for Luke's death; if it hadn't been for Gideon, he believes Luke wouldn't have intervened.'

'I wouldn't dream of going to Glenbraddan! The whole episode was entirely Blair's fault, and I don't think I could be civil to him.'

Still vaguely uneasy, but too tired to pursue it, she said merely, 'Are you sure you want to go to the Highlands? My dear, you'll be bored to tears in a week. You know what an urban mortal you are at heart.'

He wouldn't admit it, still ruffled from having been made to feel the unconsidered junior partner in the business. 'I've never had the chance to find out! Besides, I've always had a splendid time when I've stayed with the Mattiesons on the Borders!'

'That's a civilized country house. A farm cottage isn't quite the same.'

Stubbornly, he said, 'I'll find out, won't I?'

2

It was three weeks before Drew admitted to himself that his mother had been right. He was bored. The salmon season was almost over and it was too early for stalking on these hills. Ewen wasn't going to have time to teach him until late September, anyway. There were game birds enough – grouse and ptarmigan and blackcock – and pests that needed shooting, fine, fat brown hares round the crofts, and hoodie crows, and fork-tailed kites. But Drew had no gun of his own, and the one Ewen lent him was a brute, an antiquated flintlock that didn't spark until what felt like half an hour after one pulled the trigger, and then let out a blinding flash and a cloud of smoke that rivalled the total output of Auld Reekie's chimneys. And by that time, as he pointed out to Ewen, the birds he'd been aiming at were well on their way to the next glen.

Truthfully, he didn't care much for the farm, either, although it was substantial enough in a small way. Once the initial interest had worn off, he began to feel suffocated. Ewen and his wife were both in their forties, but they were still producing sturdy young regularly every couple of years, and the baby had remarkable lungs for its age. Drew wasn't used to communal living, to tripping over a graduated scale of children wherever he turned, to moving at a crouch in case he blundered into the ceiling-hung baskets and creels and nets and smoked herring and lengths of coiled rope, or barked his shins against coggs and churns and meal kists and spinning wheels. He found the fare rather plain, cooked in the big covered pot that always rested on the hearth, or the iron griddle – one of Lauriston's, a gift from Vilia – that hung over it on an intricate pot chain. There wasn't much to read, either. Stewart of Garth's *Sketches of the Character, Manners, and Present State of the Highlanders of Scotland*, eleven years out of date, a few volumes of sermons, and a well-thumbed Bible. Drew was aware that he should be grateful for not having to share his bedchamber, but he felt uncomfortable that this privacy had only been contrived by moving four of the children in with their parents. Indeed, if it weren't that Vilia had told him so, he'd have gone back to Marchfield at the beginning of September.

Ewen, who was finding the lad something of a trial, would have been relieved. But Drew was, after all, Mistress Vilia's boy and very like her except for something about the eyes that Ewen couldn't quite place. In the middle of the month, pleased to have something to offer by way of a change, he said, 'Why do you not come with me to the tryst? There iss plenty to see, if you haff neffer been to one. Though you will maybe haff been to Falkirk?'

'No! It's so near us that we're more inclined to stay away. Swearing impartially at cattle and sheep and drovers when they hold up the carriage!'

'Aye, they would. Well, you know they are haffing trysts on Skye every year, and that the drovers come from the south to buy, and then drive the beasts back to Falkirk or Crieff? It iss taking them about six weeks and by the time the beasts get there they are worn to a bone. Well, a year or two back some of us here wass thinking it would be a good idea to start a new market inland. We catch the drovers before they effer get to Skye, do you see, and it suits them fine, because they haff not so far to travel, either coming or going.'

Drew laughed. 'I don't imagine you're very popular with the people on Skye, if you're stealing their business!'

'No, indeed. They would massacre us like a shot, if they had the chance,' Ewen agreed philosophically. 'But why not come with me? It will be a new experience for you.'

It was. Drew had never seen such an assortment of people – breeders, farmers, drovers, cottars, factors, shopkeepers, shepherds, crofters, ghillies, lairds, lawyers, children of all shapes and sizes, and an astonishing number of women. The road was lined with temporary blanket shelters – cookshops whose owners reeked as powerfully of broth and mutton as the drovers did of dogs and sheep. Everyone and everything was damp, for it had been a wet night and Aonach was a bare and barren place. Most of the folk, it seemed, had either slept on the heather or sat up all night drinking and gossiping, and they were indescribably dirty and untidy. The cattle and sheep, which covered a vast area of ground, stood quietly and gazed around them, while the drovers, blowsy and unshaven, leaned on their sticks and stared at the beasts as if, with poor stock like this, it was the breeders who ought to be paying to have them taken away.

For a while, Drew wandered around eavesdropping on the bargaining.

'Ah'll guv ye three pun',' a thick, low-country voice would say, 'and no' anither bawbee.' Then the accents of someone local. 'No, neffer! Three pounds fifteen I must haff. What iss the use of you higgling? I know you are for the cows as well as the stots, so you must not be wasting my time this way.' And the first man again, in scandalized tones. 'Three pun' fifteen? Och, awa' wi' ye, man! Ah canny gie ye that kin' o' siller. Guidsakes, huv ye nae notion whit prices is like in the south the noo? Jist tak' whit Ah'm offering, and settle it yince and for a'.'

After a while, the smells of wet wool and steaming people became oppressive, and Drew drifted up the hillside to where Mistress Ewen was unpacking bannocks and cold venison while her husband, a respected fellow in these parts, conducted lordly negotiations with a succession of disreputable purchasers. By mid-afternoon, a great many stoups of whisky bitters had disappeared, and a great many bargains had been struck, but Ewen remained as courteous and unflustered and, it appeared, as sober as when he had risen from his bed this morning.

It was about five o'clock when a shy female voice said from behind, 'Hello, Mr Campbell. How are you? I wonder if you've seen my brother anywhere? I can't find him, and I expect we ought to be going home soon.'

She was the most sweetly pretty girl Drew had ever seen, with brown hair, soft brown eyes, and a flawless summer-warmed skin. There was no mistaking that she was of gentle birth, although she was dressed with propriety rather than elegance, her long curls emerging from a bonnet uncompromisingly tied under her chin and framed by a brim so modest that it could hardly even have been said to be out of fashion, far less in. Studiously, she ignored Drew, but she was blushing.

Ewen said, 'Good day to you, miss. No, I haff not seen him aal day. Not at aal.'

Her rounded chin quivered. Really, Drew thought, Ewen wasn't being very helpful. He said, 'You shouldn't be wandering un-chaperoned in a place like this! Perhaps I may be permitted to offer you my protection while we search for your brother, Miss . . .' The word hung on the air, but Ewen ignored it. Then the girl said, in her gentle voice, 'Miss Randall.'

What luck! Drew thought. What incredible, wonderful luck! 'Then we are already acquainted! You must be – surely you must be Shona? I'm Drew Lauriston. Our families know each other, and we met in Edinburgh when we were children. During the royal visit, do you remember?'

When she had seen him standing on the hillside beside Mr Campbell, she had thought him the embodiment of all her dreams – tall and slender and handsome, his bronze-gold hair sweeping back from a high forehead, his mouth smiling, and such a vivid light in his eyes. And now it seemed they were acquainted. And he was offering to escort her round this horrid hillside until she found Edward again. The son of Mrs Lauriston, who had been so kind to her.

The glow suddenly died from her eyes as she remembered Edward and Harriet's views on Mrs Lauriston and her sons. Distractedly, she murmured, 'Oh, yes. I remember you. Of course. But no, I couldn't permit . . . Such a trouble . . . I will find him . . .'

But, masterful as the young knight errant she thought him, he tucked her hand into the crook of his arm. 'We are such old friends there can be no objection. It won't be a trouble. Not at all. It will be a very real pleasure.'

His lips pursed gloomily, Ewen watched them go. Edward Blair wasn't going to like it.

It took them a while to find Edward, though it would have been quicker if they had been looking. But they had the reminiscences of almost a dozen years to draw on, and the words tumbled out, eager and breathless, as if neither of them had ever had anyone to talk to before. In no time at all, and quite unwittingly, Shona's artless revelations had led Drew to pity her deeply. He wasn't without imagination, and her life at Glenbraddan sounded to him like little short of persecution. Even if Edward and the unknown Harriet had been normal, cheerful people it would have been drab enough, but their naturally dismal temperaments seemed to have been exacerbated by the trials that beset them on every side – trials not only like the eviction episode, but one mentally retarded son, and three miscarriages before the safe arrival of a baby daughter, Isabella.

'Harriet is very devout,' Shona said in her sweet, uncritical way, and Drew had an instant vision of good works and black bombazine. 'She's had so much to vex her, and only me to lean on – apart from Edward, of course. If only Grace were still here!'

Grace, it seemed, had bitterly offended her brother by blaming him for Luke's death and had been briskly despatched to Paris to annoy Georgiana instead. 'Oh, do tell your mama that Georgy and Emile have two children now – Gabrielle is four, and little Guy is one! I'm sure she will be interested. And she'll remember meeting a young man called Peter Barber at Georgy's wedding. Well, Grace and he met again in Paris, and they're married now, and have a baby daughter, Petronella. They seem very happy. Mr Barber is a very worthy young man.'

Drew shuddered slightly. Earnest Grace and worthy Mr Barber; they sounded well suited. Gazing down at Shona with a compassionate light in his eyes that set her blushing all over again, he said, 'You must be so lonely without anyone young to bear you company!'

She hadn't thought of it that way before. 'Oh, I had my governess until I came out of the schoolroom, and I paint. Watercolours of birds, mostly. And I persuade all the old people to talk to me about the traditions of the glen. And I read a great deal, and I help Harriet with the housekeeping. I'm very busy, really, especially now that I have to keep the family chronicle.'

'The what?'

She dimpled up at him. 'It was grandfather Telfer's idea. Luke used to do it, and when he died Uncle Magnus said he was too much occupied and it was up to Edward. But Edward has no literary inclination, and no time, so he thought it would give me an interest. I'm not very good at it, but grandfather Telfer set up a trust and I have the income from that – for doing it, you understand? So I don't object! Although I do feel a fraud, because there's so little to write.'

'Oh, but it must be interesting to go back and read what Luke had to say about things that happened when you were too young to remember? What fun!' The idea appealed to him.

'No, because all that has been sent to the lawyers in Edinburgh. No one's allowed to see it for fifty years!'

'Really? What a peculiar thing! Do you suppose . . .'

There was a figure blocking their path.

Exasperated over having to search for his sister, Edward was in no mood to handle the situation with the somewhat stilted civility he might otherwise have brought to it. 'Who's this?' he rapped out before either of them could speak, and then recognized Drew. 'Young Lauriston?' His round, heavy-lidded eyes were hostile. Drew knew that he was only just thirty, but he looked like a sour old dominie.

Formally, Drew said, 'Mr Blair, sir! Good afternoon to you. I was bringing Miss Randall to your carriage. Perhaps you will allow me to call on you one day soon? I am staying near by.'

'Are you, indeed! Unfortunately, I fear that Mrs Blair is indisposed. We do not expect to be receiving visitors for quite some time. Come along, Shona. Good day to you, Lauriston.'

There was distress in her eyes as, timidly, she said good-bye and thank you. Drew's face was set as he stood and watched the carriage out of sight.

3

Several weeks later, Vilia returned to the hired house in Clarges Street, Mayfair, to find Gideon in sole occupation of the drawing-room, his nose buried in *The Times*. 'Oh, dear,' she said wearily, stripping off her gloves and sinking gratefully into a vast, padded chair. 'Such a tiresome day. I'm cold and wet, and I want my tea. Of all months in the year, I believe November is the most disagreeable.'

Gideon said, 'Shall I ring?' wondering vaguely why the day should have been so tiresome. There had been no business appointments that he knew of.

'No need. I told Frederick as I came in.'

He watched her rise again and go to the mirror to take off her grey squirrel bonnet and smooth her hair, then jumped to his feet to relieve her of the fur-lined mantle. Her hands were ice-cold, and he exclaimed, 'Where have you been? You're frozen!'

She flexed the long, slim fingers. 'It's not the weather. Nerves, that's all. I've been to call on Magnus Telfer.'

'I thought he was in Brighton.'

'He came back a week or two ago.' She sat down abruptly. 'Oh, Gideon, he looks so thin and ill, even after all these months. When Luke died, I always thought he was suffering more from losing his son-and-heir – you know what I mean? – than Luke himself. But Lucy's death has hit him very hard. He has lost all that fair-of-flesh look, and his hair is streaked with grey, and he's dreadfully apathetic. He's still wearing coats that do no more than hang on him, because he says he can't summon up the interest to see his tailor. And he was so touchingly pleased to see me, so grateful to me for coming. Magnus – *grateful*! We spent most of the afternoon talking about Lucy. "She understood me so well," he kept saying. "She knew how to make me comfortable, knew just what I liked." So you can guess why my nerves are a little frayed.'

'Yes, indeed. Very trying.'

There was a silence. Then, twisting the amethyst seal on her finger,

391

Vilia said, 'It wasn't only that. I have a confession to make. I tried to buy Kinveil from him, and he refused.'

'You *what?*'

'Why shouldn't I?' she said defensively. 'Don't look at me like that, Gideon! I wasn't proposing to use the foundry's money!'

'That's unjust. I didn't think you were.'

'I suppose not. It's what Theo would have thought, though. *Where* is that tea?' She rose and gave the bell a violent tug just as the door opened to admit a flustered maid and apologetic footman. Even after three months they hadn't learned to conform to the standards Vilia required of her servants.

When they had gone, she sat stirring her tea thoughtfully. 'Magnus hasn't been near Kinveil since Luke died and it occurred to me that he might be persuaded to part with it. I was afraid he might already be considering doing so. I've spent a good deal of time going into my finances with old Mr Pilcher, and we came to the conclusion I could raise £60,000, not more. Which is the precise sum Mungo Telfer paid my father for it.'

'But . . .'

'As you say. *But* Highland estate prices have soared since then, although less extravagantly than one might have thought. Magnus could probably sell for about £100,000. However, since he doesn't really need the money, I thought I would ask, hoping – quite unashamedly – that for sentimental reasons he might agree. But his gratitude doesn't extend as far as that. His father loved Kinveil, and he believes Luke did, too, which gave him the excuse to talk a good deal of nonsense about "sacred trusts" and the like. He spoke of going back some day when he felt strong enough to face it. I'm not sure how the sum of £130,000 crept into the conversation, but it did. So I withdrew as gracefully as I could. If it's of any interest to you, however, he hopes the Lauristons will regard Kinveil as if it were their own. If I wish the castle opened up to receive us, I have only to say so.'

'Christ! Does he mean it?'

'At the moment, yes.' Her lips smiling, she surveyed her son. 'You don't really care, Gideon, do you? Theo has a feeling for the place, and so has Drew. But not you.'

'No,' he admitted. 'It's beautiful, but it's not my kind of beauty. The climate, the people, the whole atmosphere of it' – he hesitated, wondering how far he dared to go – 'everything depresses me, some-how. It smells too strongly of fatalism and finality.'

Unexpectedly, she quoted poetry at him. 'Have you ever read Shelley's *Lines written among the Euganean Hills*? Somewhere near the beginning, he says – let me get it right – yes . . .

> . . . like that sleep
> When the dreamer seems to be
> Weltering through eternity;
> And the dim low line before
> Of a dark and distant shore
> Still recedes, as ever still
> Longing with divided will,
> But no power to seek or shun,
> He is ever drifted on
> O'er the unreposing wave
> To the haven of the grave.

That's what you feel about it, isn't it? That atmosphere. That's why you reject it – and why I'm drawn to it. I suppose that, in a way, Kinveil is *my* "dark and distant shore".' She smiled faintly. 'My haven and my grave, too, perhaps. But certainly always just a little beyond my reach.'

For a moment, the light, musical voice diverted him from the words, as did the realization that this was the first time she had ever voluntarily opened any part of her mind to him. Then he exclaimed, 'My God! How morbid of you! I hope you won't make a habit of seeing Magnus if he has this effect on you.' It wasn't, perhaps, the most sensitive or sympathetic thing to say, but he wasn't equipped to follow the revelation through, or not without thinking about it first.

'Poor Gideon,' she said, her voice brittle. 'Go back to your *Times*, my dear. Is that the afternoon mail I see over there? All for me?'

'Two for Theo, but he's out.'

It was several minutes before he became aware that the quality of the silence had changed, and looked up from his newspaper. His mother was sitting as still and stiff as a lay figure, with an open letter in her hand. Her face was mask-like. Even as he looked, she put a trembling hand to her forehead and murmured, 'Oh, God! Oh, no!' and fell back in her chair in a dead faint.

He couldn't rouse her at first. He had no idea what to do, but tugged on the bell and knelt there, chafing her hands uselessly and saying,

'Vilia! Mama! Wake up!' until the door opened and the footman appeared. 'Get the housekeeper!' he said, with vague thoughts of burnt feathers and sal volatile. They laid her on a sofa with her feet above her head, and if Gideon hadn't been so worried he would have laughed at the housekeeper's concern over the danger of her mistress's skirt slipping and showing her ankles.

She came to, after a while, and pulled herself dizzily up to a sitting position. When she took the cup of tea one of the maids was holding out to her, the cup rattled in its saucer like harness jingling. 'Thank you,' she murmured. 'I've never fainted before. I . . .' There was panic in her eyes, and Gideon turned to the servants and dismissed them.

Wordlessly, she gave him back the cup of lukewarm tea, and when he said, 'Shall I order fresh?' shook her head.

'What is it? What's the matter?'

She gestured towards the letter, still lying on the floor, and then covered her face with her hands, her head moving from side to side as if she were denying something quite unthinkable.

Gideon picked it up. It was from Edward Blair at Glenbraddan. 'Madam – I have to inform you, in case you are not already apprised of the fact, that your son, Mr Andrew Lauriston, has seen fit to abduct my unfortunate sister, Miss Shona Randall.' Jesus! Gideon thought, darting a swift glance at his mother. It couldn't be true.

Although I forbade them to meet, your son chose to ignore all the rules of gentlemanly conduct. For the last two months, it seems, he has been persuading her into clandestine meetings, with results, no doubt, that must be considered inevitable when a gently bred and innocent girl falls into the hands of a youth whose morals are such as no decent man could contemplate without loathing. Yesterday, during my absence on business in Elgin, they ran away together. It seems, from the note my unfortunate sister was so obliging as to leave behind, that she believes he intends to marry her. For her sake I hope this is so. But I wish to make it clear to your son, through you, madam, that under no circumstances will I permit either of them to cross the threshold of Glenbraddan again. I have too much respect for my wife and daughter to permit them to be contaminated by contact with two people who have shown themselves so wanton, so shameless, so contemptuous of all the tenets of Christian morality, and who have forfeited all right to be received in decent society. Yours &c – Edward Blair.

After the first shock, Gideon's only feeling was exasperation. He didn't for a moment believe Drew had seduced the girl, but he had obviously fallen head over heels in love, and been carried away by that extremely trying romanticism of his. It was very bad, of course. Gentlemen weren't supposed to elope with innocent girls. But if Drew had become convinced that she was unhappy at Glenbraddan, and if it was Scotland where one came of age at sixteen and could be married by simple declaration . . . Young Lochinvar, Gideon reflected gloomily. What a pest of a boy he was!

He went over and knelt beside his mother, recognizing that it would be a mistake to try and make light of it. Looking up at her, he said firmly, 'It's not so dreadful, truly it isn't! Don't distress yourself so. I know it's not the way one would have wished Drew to go about things, but you mustn't be too shocked at him. He's fallen in love, that's all, and persuaded the girl it would be romantic to elope. I remember you telling me once what a sweet, biddable child she was, and Drew can be abominably convincing when he chooses. You know that as well as I do!'

But she was still sitting, shaking her head, silver rivulets running down her cheeks. 'It's impossible,' she murmured, her voice breaking.

What was impossible? 'If you mean he wouldn't seduce her, of course he wouldn't! No, Mama. Truly, it could have been worse. We can hush it all up. You'll see – they'll be safely married by now!'

Her face dissolving, she cried, 'No! No, no, no! Gideon, you must stop them! You must stop them somehow! Take the night Mail north and find them. You must find them and stop them before they do anything irrevocable. You *must*!'

All he had done was make things worse, and he couldn't understand why. If the situation had been put before him, merely as a subject for speculation, he would have said that Vilia's response would have been simple, straightforward annoyance at Drew's idiocy. It really wasn't as disastrous as she was making it appear. He would *never* understand her.

Gideon stared at her blankly. 'But this letter must have taken a week to get here. If they were going to do anything irrevocable, they'll have done it by now.'

'They might not. Gideon, they might not! I've just thought – Drew may have taken her to Marchfield just to get her away from Edward. She was probably very unhappy. Really, Gideon, *really* he'll have

395

taken her there. You know he'll want to do everything in proper style. He'll have taken her there! Perhaps he's written to me already, so that we can go home for the wedding. That would be like him, wouldn't it, Gideon?'

She was almost frantic, gripping his arm with a strength he wouldn't have believed she possessed. He said gently, 'Oh, Mama! You don't know Drew at all, do you! He's a dashing hero, a knight in silver armour throwing the blushing maiden up into the saddle before him and riding off with her into the setting sun. He's more likely to have married her with only a hill shepherd and his blasted dog for witnesses!'

'No, that's not true. *You must go!*'

'Vilia, if I thought there were any purpose in it, I'd go tonight, but there's no purpose *at all!*' He tried to be reasonable. 'You must reconcile yourself. It's not a bad match, you know, and I won't go on such a wild goose chase, not even for you. God knows where they may be; certainly not at Marchfield. That would be far too mundane for the beginning of a lifetime idyll!'

But she was determined, single-minded. 'Gideon, do as I tell you! You must go. You must stop them.'

'But why? I don't understand why.'

'You don't have to understand. Just do what I say!'

'No, Vilia. I'm sorry, but I'm eighteen now, and I don't have to do something that seems to me foolish beyond permission.' He was shaking a little himself, now. He'd never stood up to his mother before; had never needed to.

She dropped her hand from his arm, and sat up straight and rigid. 'Then find Theo,' she said sharply. 'He must go.'

It made a change, and Gideon thought that by the time he had found Theo she might, perhaps, have cooled down a little.

4

At first he couldn't discover where Theo had gone. The butler had no idea. All he could say was that Mr Lauriston had driven off in a hackney. Theo's valet had no idea, either, but he was so wooden about it that Gideon became suspicious and went off in search of Sorley.

'Don't pretend you don't know, Sorley. You know everything that goes on in this household. I assume he's found some little ladybird – why be so secretive about it? I must find him, and soon. It's important.'

Sorley, who had just come in, said with a faintly satirical look in his eye, 'I would not go chasing after him if I wass you, Gideon. He will not like it at aal.'

'I don't care whether he likes it or not! Mother wants him in a hurry.' But Sorley just smiled. 'Look!' Gideon exclaimed irritably. 'You're bound to find out sooner or later. Drew's eloped with the youngest Glenbraddan girl – Shona Randall, you know? – and mother's in a dreadful state. God knows why, but she wants Theo to rush off on the Mail and try and prevent them from getting married.' And that, he noted with a certain satisfaction, had wiped the smile off Sorley's face. 'In my own opinion, it's too late already, but perhaps Theo will see things differently. So where is he, Sorley?'

'He hass gone to Theresa Berkley's – Mistress Berkley's. It iss at 28 Charlotte Street.'

The address didn't mean anything to Gideon, although when he found a hackney its jarvey cast him an unpleasantly knowing look.

The moment he crossed the threshold, Gideon recognized why. There could be no doubt what Mrs Berkley's profession was. His stomach turning slightly at the blast of warm and perfumed air that met him, Gideon addressed himself to the porter, an ex-bruiser if ever he'd seen one. And not so ex, either. He'd be the bully-back as well, as happy to throw some of Madame's customers out as to welcome others in.

Gideon knew enough not to say he'd come looking for his brother. Instead doing his best to look like an embarrassed greenhorn – which he wasn't, quite – he murmured tentatively, 'I wonder if I might see Mistress Berkley? Just to discuss what – er – services she can offer. If you know what I mean?'

The porter knew precisely what the young gentleman meant; better, as Gideon later discovered, than he did himself. 'Busy right now,' he said, shaking his head. 'Mebbe one of the other young ladies could help you?'

Gideon swallowed his relief. 'I'd – er – prefer Mistress Berkley herself, I think. I've been told that she's very – um – very understanding.'

The porter didn't say anything, but just stared at him thoughtfully.

Gideon would have preferred to wait in the hall and catch Theo on the way out, but Theo had left a message that he wouldn't be in to dinner and Gideon couldn't risk having to stay here for hours. There had to be a waiting room of some kind, from which he might be able to make a foray into the more secluded part of the establishment. 'Perhaps I might wait until she's free? Somewhere not quite as – er – public as here?'

'Why not make an appointment and come back later?' But the young gentleman didn't seem to favour the idea much, and there was plenty of time before the evening rush. Pursing his lips and remembering the old bitch's fondness for blond boys – she was playing games with one of them right now – the porter relented. 'Orright,' he said. 'Not know about the services? Mebbe you'd like to watch. She don't usually mind with pleasant young gents like you.'

Speechless, Gideon stared at the man. *Watch?* If he said no, the fellow would probably turn surly. And it was probably the quickest way to find Theo. But Christ! he thought. He'll kill me! His voice creaked a little as he said, 'That would – er – be very – er – instructive.'

The porter rang a bell and summoned a younger edition of himself. 'Sam'll look after you. Number seven, Sam.'

Gideon had just enough presence of mind to toss the porter a sovereign before he was led through a heavy wooden door with an eye-level grille in it. The staircase beyond had wide, shallow, thickly carpeted treads, and the walls were invisible behind draped red plush, innumerable candelabra, and more mirrors than Gideon had ever seen in his life. The silence was total. Half-way up, they came to a door set among the drapes and only then did Gideon realize that they had probably passed other doors on the way. Sam, ushering him through, paused for a moment to loosen a couple of ties, and the plush fell with a soft swish to obscure the door from outside. It was, Gideon supposed, as good a way as any of indicating that the room was occupied. He stood in suffocating pitch darkness for a moment, and then there was a whisper of sound as Sam drew back some curtains to allow a glimmer of light into the room.

Nervously, Gideon looked round, but there was nothing here except a sturdy chair drawn up to the right-hand wall. The light appeared to be coming from some kind of picture next to it, a big, amateurish thing consisting of flat areas of paint and very little detail. He looked at Sam and opened his mouth, but Sam wagged a finger at him and waved him to the chair. Obediently, Gideon sat. It wasn't quiet any more, but he couldn't identify the sounds.

And then he discovered that the picture wasn't quite what it seemed. It wasn't the source of the light, but a transmitter. He was on the wrong side of a glass painting, set directly into the wall, and the light was coming from the room next door. He'd heard about things like this; erotic paintings executed on the underside of a sheet of glass, so that from one side they appeared perfectly ordinary, while from the other – the back – it was possible to look right through, in the places where the paint had been thinly applied. The Chinese were said to be experts in what was undoubtedly this rather specialized field; it was as much as they could do, apparently, to keep up with the orders that flooded in from the bawdy-houses of Europe. Feeling more than a little uneasy, Gideon forced himself to look through what appeared to be a wide and placid river – there were ducks on it, and a water-lily or two – knowing that, although he could see them, the people on the other side couldn't see him at all. Even if they had been looking.

But they were much too busy. Gideon, his mind reeling, discovered that Mrs Berkley's was not an ordinary brothel.

He knew, of course, that there were men with unorthodox sexual needs, men who had to be whipped, beaten, flogged, before they could find release. He had known, too, that there were women who specialized in meeting such needs. But he had never dreamed that Theo . . .

He couldn't, at first, make sense of what was going on, and closed his eyes. Then he opened them again and looked more carefully. It was hideous, horrifying, disgusting, obscene. It was also very funny in a macabre kind of way. The room was heavily draped in black plush, with swags of it over the curtained windows and on the walls, and coy garlands of scarlet, presumably artificial, roses. Gilt-framed mirrors, interspersed with some fairly explicit pictures, covered most of the free space, and there were great gilt candelabra held aloft in the hands of four marble statues of naked females.

One of the candelabra shook slightly, and the statue's free hand came up to rub the place where some hot wax had dripped. Gideon gave a choke of laughter, and Sam murmured, 'Quiet, sir, if you please.'

Here and there, scattered about the room on small, ornate Louis

Quinze tables, were Chinese porcelain vases filled not with flowers but with canes, switches, branches of holly, and stiff, nail-studded leather straps.

Reluctantly, Gideon dragged his eyes back to the centre of the room. There was a contraption not unlike a stepladder stretched at an angle between floor and ceiling, its length parallel to the wall behind which Gideon sat so that he had an admirable view of it, above and below. His stomach griping, he stared at the three people engaged on activities he could never have imagined. There was a temporary lull, but even through the glass he could feel the scene vibrating with anticipation, while one of the women carefully selected something from a Chinese porcelain vase. When she turned, she had in her hand a gold-handled, many-lashed whip. She was a big woman, and powerful, with coarse dark red hair pinned up under a hunting beaver, and large feet encased in spurred riding boots. The other woman was much younger, with long black hair tumbling down her back and a nosegay of holly pinned to her bosom. She was seated on a polished leather saddle below and in front of the stepladder.

And on the ladder was the naked body of a man, spreadeagled face down on its black velvet rungs, wrists and ankles manacled to the uprights, and his waist confined by a thin, studded horse harness.

Theo.

There could be no doubt about it. There was a scarlet, eye-slitted hangman's hood drawn over his head, but Gideon could never have mistaken the lithe, finely muscled body of his brother. It was sheened now with perspiration, golden where the candlelight caught it and shimmered on the stretched, quivering muscles of shoulders and hips, and over the rib cage, whose movement betrayed the quickened breath with which he waited for what was to come.

The big woman stood for a moment, thoughtfully drawing the whip through her fingers, and then, catching the girl's eye, nodded and stepped back a pace.

Theo screamed. God, but he screamed! Gideon, his hand tight over his mouth, sat and shuddered in the echo of it, and then, his stomach still in his throat, heard Theo – incredibly – begin to laugh. There was a wild, ecstatic, triumphant note in it, and the girl grinned, and the big woman nodded in satisfaction, and raised her powerful arm and brought down the whip.

400

It went on and on forever, although sometimes there were a few moments when the women allowed Theo to rest. Cool, smiling, superior Theo. Gideon tried to drag his eyes away but couldn't, until the black-haired girl, with no weapons but lessoned hands and lascivious mouth, began to take over the major role from the red-haired harridan. And then Gideon's own loins stirred violently, and he threw himself away from the glass and closed his eyes and clapped his hands over his ears, and waited, breath suspended, until some seventh sense told him everything was over.

Shaking, nauseated, his pose of amused detachment in rags and tatters about him, he said to Sam, 'Perhaps it would be best if I returned to wait in the front hall. I don't imagine the gentleman would care to know that I had been watching.'

The man ran his tongue over his lips. 'That's the reason for the mask, your honour. Most gentlemen don't care much whether they're being watched while they're on Madame's horse, but it might make for awkwardness if they were to be recognized outside. Very nice class of customer we have, sir, which means that sometimes they're acquainted.'

'Quite,' Gideon said, and gave the fellow a sovereign. He looked as if he enjoyed his work.

It was almost half an hour before Theo appeared, a little flushed. Once or twice before, Gideon had seen him with that cat-at-the-cream look and had wondered what it meant. Never again.

There was a cold, unfriendly glitter in Theo's eyes. 'Why, Gideon, dear boy, what a delightful surprise! Were you looking for me?' Taking his brother hard by the arm, he tossed a coin to the surprised porter. 'Thank you, Hocking. I'll see you again. Now then, Gideon . . .'

5

All the way back to Clarges Street they talked about Drew; never a mention of Mrs Berkley. Gideon knew there never would be.

Sorley waylaid them the moment they got in. '*Dia*, but you took your time! For the love of God, go in to her. She will not take anything to eat or drink. She will not lie down or even sit down. She iss chust walking the floor, and there iss nothing I can say or do. Go in, and do whateffer she wants you to, if you love her at aal.'

All their lives they had regarded Sorley as if he were almost a member of the family. He had guided them, and bullied them, and conspired with them, and even spoilt them a little. But they knew his dedication to Vilia was absolute and unquestioning, and that if it came to a choice no one else in the world really mattered to him. He worshipped her. They didn't know how they knew it, because it didn't show, but it was as much a fact of their lives as the existence of the foundry. None of them had ever thought of Sorley as a servant. But now, Theo snapped, 'You're forgetting your place, Sorley!' and turned his back on him and stalked away. Gideon, catching the spark in Sorley's eye, raised his brows in a half-embarrassed, half-derisive way, and followed his brother into the drawing-room.

Vilia was in an even worse state than when he had left her. Some of the pins that held her hair in place had come loose, and a long, silver-gilt coil lay on her shoulder, the fine-stranded threads of it drifting and shimmering in the breeze stirred up by her compulsive pacing back and forth, back and forth. There were tears soaked into her cheeks, and her lips were scarlet where she had bitten them.

She whirled round as they came in. 'Has Gideon told you?' Her voice was rough with anguish. 'You must go, Theo. *You must go* and put a stop to it!'

Gideon could see that his brother had thought he was exaggerating, but not now. Theo's face changed, and the tight expression disappeared to be replaced with one of the most intense interest. Walking over to Vilia, he took her by the arms and forced her into a chair. 'She needs a stiff whisky, Gideon,' he said. 'And so do I, for that matter. Pour them. Now, mother dear, why such extravagance?'

She took a deep breath and made an obvious effort to speak calmly. 'Drew is only seventeen, the girl even younger. It is folly for them to marry. If Gideon is right and Drew's principles wouldn't allow him to seduce her, then it isn't too late. *Pray God* it isn't too late!' Gideon put a glass in her hand. Her voice ragged, she went on, 'We can sort everything out somehow, as long as we can stop them. I'm convinced they must be at Marchfield.'

Theo said, 'They'll be married by now, you know, otherwise why run away at all? If they'd wanted us at the ceremony, they could have postponed their romantic flight for a few weeks. It's not as if Edward's been holding the girl in durance vile. Or has he?'

'Don't be frivolous. Drew might have thought we would be opposed to it, unless he presented us with a *fait accompli*.'

'You can hardly call running away from one drearily respectable house to another drearily respectable house – sorry, Mama – much of a *fait accompli*. Anyway, have you ever known Drew do other than thrive on opposition? They're married by now. They must be.'

Almost beseechingly, Vilia said, 'However remote the chance that they're not, we must make the effort. Theo, you can go tonight. You can still catch the Mail and be in Edinburgh in forty-eight hours.'

'Thank you, Mama,' Theo replied and then, after a moment's artificial hesitation, added, 'But I don't think I will.'

'*Yes*, Theo. Yes, yes, yes – you will!'

He shook his head. 'No. I'm tired, and I don't fancy the journey. If I didn't get there in time, there wouldn't be any point in it, and if I did – if I did . . .'

Gideon watched his brother with a kind of horrified fascination.

'. . . perhaps you'll tell me *how* I could persuade my incorrigible young brother to abandon a course of action that may, I grant you, be ill advised, but is hardly the grand tragedy you seem bent on making of it?'

There was a speculative glint in his eyes, and Gideon knew what he was up to. Drew and Shona's immaturity wasn't, by any stretch, enough to account for Vilia's extreme reaction, and Theo was desperate to know what was.

Vilia also knew what he was up to, but she still went on fighting the inevitable. The unthinkable truth, the impossible revelation of it. 'You have no need to "persuade" him. You will tell him that he *mustn't* do it.'

Theo's slanting brows, so like hers, rose delicately. 'But he's of age in legal terms, my dear. He can do as he wishes.' And then, with exaggerated enlightenment, 'Oh-h-h-h! Are you thinking of filial duty and family feeling? But I remember you once describing those as – what was it? – the triumph of hope over experience. Have you come to believe in them after all?'

'Don't be impertinent.' She stared into her glass for a moment, and then said flatly, 'Then I'll take the travelling carriage and go myself.'

'You can't!' Gideon was shocked. 'It would be far too exhausting for you!'

'And besides,' Theo interrupted smoothly. 'Chalmers tells me he's had to call in the wheelwright. There's something wrong with the axle.'

Gideon looked at him suspiciously, but his face was unreadable.

For an eternity, Vilia went on staring into her glass, while Theo and Gideon stood and watched her.

At last she raised her head and, clearing her throat, said, 'There is one incontrovertible argument against this marriage. I had hoped you'd never have to be told.' She looked from Theo to Gideon and then dropped her eyes again and chose her words with meticulous care. 'I'm afraid that Drew and Shona are – or may be – brother and sister.'

They heard the rain begin again, pattering irresolutely against the windows and sizzling on the gas lantern outside. A carriage rattled down the street towards Piccadilly, and someone thumped impatiently on a front door nearby. A couple of pedestrians went past on unsteady feet, their voices drunkenly quarrelsome. Inside the drawing-room, the coal settled with a gritty sigh among the embers, and one of the candles guttered.

Abruptly, Theo sat down. In other circumstances, Gideon would have laughed at the spasm of pain that crossed his face.

Theo, his eyelids still fluttering with it, breathed, 'What do you mean?'

He wasn't shocked. Vilia knew, chillingly, that he was excited. She had borne him when she was just over eighteen, and had even welcomed him. He was a year older now than she had been then, but still very young despite the sophisticated facade and the competitive manner he always assumed with her. Competitive, and possessive, as if the two of them had a special, unique relationship. As indeed they had, for they knew each other better than most mothers and sons, even if in some ways they scarcely knew each other at all. Even through her horror and despair, she had recognized, the moment he walked into the room, that he was bathed in the afterglow of some cataclysmic experience. Sexual experience? She didn't know and would probably never know. To Theo, like herself, privacy mattered almost more than anything. It was just that, sometimes, she would have been easier in her mind if she had known what he was being private about.

She sighed. 'I mean precisely what I said. Shona's father, Perry Randall, may – possibly – have been Drew's father, too.' Perry Randall was only a name to them, scarcely even that. Their questions shimmered on the silent air like heat above a flame, and she had no choice but to go on. 'A few days after your father left for Brussels, I met Mr Randall. We had met casually once or twice before. He was troubled and unhappy and I, perhaps, was over-emotional at the time. I can't – I won't – excuse myself for what happened. He came to the house to see your father, but he had gone. Mr Randall was a very attractive man, and I didn't – resist him as strongly as I should.' The words were truthful enough, she thought dismally, however false the impression they conveyed. Even now, despite everything that had happened, she couldn't bear to lay the pale, wild ghost of that long-ago happiness, to exorcize it by reducing it to some crude, inadequate form of words.

Theo said, 'And Drew was born in March 1816.'

'Afterwards, Mr Randall went back to his wife, although he stayed only a few weeks and then sailed on an emigrant ship for Nova Scotia. I was told that he later went to America and became a gun salesman. More than that I don't know. Shona was born in June 1816, some months after he sailed.' What more did they need to know? What more did anyone need to know?

Gideon went over and took her hand in his, genuine sorrow and sympathy in his face. 'It must have been dreadful for you. To be seduced, and then not to know afterwards . . .'

'Couldn't you have screamed?' Theo asked softly.

'Oh, yes. I could have screamed. I could have ruined my reputation, and Mr Randall's, and Charlotte Randall's whole life. I could have screamed, but I didn't.'

'And you truly don't know whose son Drew is? I thought women were supposed to know those things.'

'You thought wrongly.' A wave of nausea gripped her. 'And the risk is too great. They must be stopped.'

'Dear me, yes,' Theo said, calmly. 'This does put a different complexion on things. You'd better ring, Gideon. We need our traps packed in a hurry.'

'You'll go?'

'We'll both go.'

It was a relief, of a sort. She said, almost inaudibly, 'Don't tell Drew unless there's no other way. He's so proud of his – his father's heroism.'

'No, Mama.' Theo's smile was ambiguous. 'You must tell us about him some time, though.'

6

Theo and Gideon reached Marchfield House after a killing forty-eight hours on the Mail and another two in a hired carriage. Theo was restless, and clearly in some discomfort all the way, and his eyes were feverish by the time they walked into the hall to be met by Drew and Shona, enchantedly happy. They had arrived earlier the same evening.

Proudly, Shona held out her hand with the wedding band on it, made from pale, pure, Scottish-mined gold, she said proudly. Gideon, embracing his new sister, exclaimed over how pretty it was, and Theo, after a moment, followed his example.

It didn't even occur to Drew to ask them why they had come home on the Mail.

Chapter Two

1

As Gideon swung his hired buggy in through a Gothic ruin of an entrance, complete with broken, ivied walls and fallen blocks of masonry, he hoped he had come to the right place. The light was failing, but to his right he could see, elegantly embowered in trees, something that looked uncommonly like a Greek temple while on the left lay the calm waters of an ornamental lake. He'd been told the house was new, so he hadn't exactly bargained for a stately home when he had accepted the unknown Tylers' invitation. He hoped to God he was properly dressed.

Jonathan Marsden, Lauristons' agent in New York – though not for much longer, if Gideon had any say in the matter – had given him an introduction to Mr Tyler in Baltimore. 'If you handle him right,' he'd said, 'he can fix for you to see over the Government Manufactory of Firearms at Harper's Ferry.' It was Gideon's opinion that, if Marsden had been worth his retainer, he'd have been able to fix it himself without bothering Mr Tyler. Even so, it had been with a thrill of anticipation that he'd set off on the complicated journey to Baltimore – steamboat to Amboy, railroad to the Delaware, and across the river to Philadelphia. Then, after a night at the American Hotel, back on the Delaware again, railroad to the Chesapeake, and finally to Baltimore on another steamboat. He wasn't convinced that his bath under the hotel pump had freed him from the rich smells of smoking and spitting, the gin sling, brandy, sweat and smuts, that had impregnated him, and his clothes, and his baggage. Steamboat cabins in the New World were frowsty places.

When his civil note to Mr Tyler had brought an invitation to the party Mr Tyler's good lady was giving for some of the young folks that night, Gideon hadn't been unduly worried. In his limited experience of America, he wasn't likely to get close enough to any lady for there to be a risk of offending her sensibilities. He knew that American hospitality was overpowering. His hand had been shaken so often that he suspected it would never be the same again, and he had been given more introductions to people from New York to New Orleans than he could conceivably have taken up in the course of a year or more. But he had found that it was the custom at most social gatherings for the men to congregate at one end of the room, smoking and drinking and talking business or politics, while the ladies gravitated towards the other, studying one another's dresses until they must have known every stitch by heart, and discussing Parson Whatsit's recent sermon on the Day of Judgement, or Doctor Whosit's wonderful new dyspepsia pills. There had even been one party when the gentlemen had sat down to supper in one room, while the ladies – immobilized by whalebone, hugely puffed sleeves, and gargantuan skirts – had taken theirs, standing, in another. Although Gideon remembered vaguely that the French had the same system, he thought it quite uncivilized. There were few occupations more pleasant than talking to a pretty girl, and American girls, from what he had been able to see, were not only pretty, but lively and extremely self-possessed.

Torn between uncertainty and hope, he scanned the carriage front of the Tyler place. If it were anything to go by, things might be different here. It was imposing, to say the least – pure Gothic revival, and spanking new despite the delicately traceried oriel windows, battlemented parapet, and slender, octagonal tower. Gideon's vulgar commercial instincts poked him in the ribs and muttered, 'Money!' and he grinned to himself. Repressing a craven desire to scuttle back to the hotel for another bath, he followed a servant through a hall magnificent with groined vaults and tessellated marble pavements, wainscotted walls, gilded cornices, and stained glass. There was a babble of talk coming from the great double doors on the left, broken suddenly, to Gideon's horrified disbelief, by the familiar, bloodcurdling wail of a piper launching into the *urlar*. His grace notes were terrible. Gideon's ears cringed.

He waited patiently beside his beaming host until it was all over, and when the last erratic warble had died, Mr Tyler shook him vigorously by the hand for a second time, exclaiming, 'Doesn't that make you feel great, Mr Lauriston? Say, it ought to make you feel at home, too! You're from Scotland, ain't you?' Gideon admitted it.

Mr Tyler was a large, jovial fellow, splendid in dark blue tailcoat, embroidered waistcoat, and an exuberantly frilled shirt in which was embedded a massive gold brooch, and he had the air of one who would be happy to talk to someone from the Old Country all night, if only he didn't have a hundred other guests to be hospitable to. It was clear he had never got over the breathless experience of a visit to Abbotsford eight years earlier, when he had been deeply honoured to meet the great man himself, Sir Walter Scott. 'The greatest moment of my life,' he said solemnly. 'An inspiration. A real inspiration, sir.' He waved a large hand at his surroundings. 'I might even say that this, my home, was in some small measure inspired by his genius. I was deeply grieved to hear of his passing on to that undiscovered country from whose bourn no traveller returns. As your great poet, William Shakespeare, has it.'

Firmly repressing the temptation to say, '*Hamlet*, Act three, Scene one', Gideon agreed that Sir Walter had been a remarkable man. 'My mother was slightly acquainted with him. They had interests in common. In fact, she was born in a mediaeval castle in the Highlands, though it is nowhere near as – er – impressive as this!' It had been the right thing to say. Mr Tyler – 'Call me Tom!' – was delighted.

It was a splendid party. Gideon had found that Americans were sensitive to English accents, as if they expected them to utter nothing but criticisms, real or implied. But, here, no one seemed to notice, and his wasn't even mentioned until half-way through the evening, when he was sitting in the extreme corner of a Gothic sofa, the rest of which was occupied by the rose-coloured skirts of a remarkably pretty girl with merry blue eyes, a profusion of dark curls, and the longest, sootiest lashes he had ever seen.

'But your accent is so quaint!' she exclaimed. 'And I just love your English manners!'

He laughed. 'Not *English* manners, please. I'm Scottish, through and through, for I don't know how many generations. As a matter of fact . . .'

He had lost her attention. There was a tall gentleman bowing over her hand, a satirical smile on his handsome face. 'Undoubtedly the belle of Baltimore, Angelina,' he was saying. 'You *have* grown up since I was here last.'

The sooty lashes fluttered provocatively at him, and his smile deepened. 'Spare me, my dear. Not even you can deflect me from my purpose. It's your companion I'm interested in right now.' He turned to a surprised Gideon and said, 'Lauriston?'

Someone from the Firearms Manufactory? Gideon bowed and said, 'Sir?'

The gentleman took him by the arm and, with a nod at the pouting Miss Angelina, drew him aside. When Gideon glanced back apologetically, he murmured, 'Don't worry, there will soon be bees enough around the honeypot.'

Then, from his slight advantage of height, his grey eyes looked quizzically into Gideon's and he said, 'Allow me to introduce myself. I'm an old acquaintance of your family and friends. My name is Randall.'

For a moment, Gideon felt as if the floor had risen up and hit him over the head. His mouth opened, and closed again, and then he stammered, 'Perry – I mean the Honourable Peregrine Randall?'

The man laughed. 'Only if you insist, and I hope you won't. I've spent the better part of twenty years trying to slough off my effete Englishness. All I admit to is Perry.'

'Yes. I mean, no! But fancy meeting you here, of all places!'

'Very appropriate, I should have thought. Brighton Pavilion crossed with Fonthill Abbey, wouldn't you say?'

Gideon didn't know whether he was being serious or not. 'I – er – hadn't realized the *Waverley* novels had made quite such an impression on this side of the Atlantic.'

'Not usually on this scale, I grant you. But the further south you go, the more widespread you'll find Scott's influence becomes. My dear boy' – his voice was unmistakably sardonic now – 'I can't tell you what pleasures await you in Dixie! Chivalry in full war paint. Jousting and tourneys, Knights of the Green Garter, Knights of the Silver Lance. Knights of the Jumping Bean, for all I know. Have some tea.'

Gideon looked at the profferred tray doubtfully, and then at the servant holding it. The spoons obviously had some significance, but he couldn't think what. Some were in the cups, some in the saucers.

'Green tea or black?' Mr Randall asked helpfully. 'Spoon in the cup means green, spoon in the saucer black. File it away in your head; it's quite a common practice.'

His smile, now, was one of uncomplicated amusement. 'And now that you've had time to recover from your surprise, perhaps you'll tell me which of the Lauriston boys you are. Tom Tyler doesn't know.'

'I'm Gideon, the middle one. But how on earth did you make the connection?'

The strong, straight eyebrows rose. 'Lauriston – Scotsman – mediaeval castle – Firearms Manufactory. It really wasn't difficult.'

Disconcerted, Gideon said, 'I suppose not, but . . .' Then he remembered. 'Dammit! I'd forgotten. You're a gun salesman.'

'Past tense. An independent manufacturer now, with a very pretty little new project up my sleeve. I visit at Harper's Ferry now and again, to see what the opposition's up to, and stay with the Tylers on my way. We're old friends. Not such a coincidence after all, you see.'

So this was Perry Randall! Gideon didn't know what he had expected. What little he knew of the man's history had suggested weakness and irresponsibility, even though he had never been able to imagine his mother being swept off her feet – unwillingly or not, and he had certain doubts about that – by anyone ordinary. He could see that Perry Randall had never been ordinary. To Gideon, the man looked positively formidable. He must be in his mid-forties by now, Gideon calculated, but he showed scarcely a sign of it. The waving black hair was touched with grey at the temples, and the creases round the eyes were pronounced, but his lean, muscular figure in its admirable tailoring was easy and athletic, his jaw hard, his mouth long and firm, and his eyes uncomfortably penetrating. He looked like someone it would be dangerous to tangle with.

Gideon, feeling rather young and immature, said breathlessly, 'This is a very real pleasure, sir.' He had already learned always to say 'sir' to Americans.

Perry Randall grinned.

Gideon said, 'I . . . My . . . Your . . . Yes, well.' Before he had sailed, Shona had taken him aside and said to him, in that sweet, innocent way of hers, 'I've never known my father, or anything about him, and I've always wanted to, so badly! Oh, Gideon, do you think – do you *think* when you're in America you might try to find out what's happened to him? I know it's a huge country, but if you're travelling around . . . And it's just possible, isn't it? I so long to know what happened to him!' Gideon, privately horrified, had said, 'Of course, Shona, I'll try. But there are God knows how many people in America. I can't promise anything.' He had felt slightly faint at the thought of the complications that would ensue if he found the man, and had hoped, very devoutly indeed, that his and Perry Randall's paths wouldn't cross.

'As it happens,' he said firmly, 'I have been commissioned to look for you.'

Perry Randall's face suddenly became very still. 'You have? By whom?'

'By my sister-in-law. Your daughter Shona.' He hesitated. 'You probably don't know, but Shona married my brother Drew – my younger brother – at the end of '33. They've a new baby now; he's called Jermyn.' The only reason for the name had been that Shona liked it. With a twist of humour, Gideon wondered how it felt for a man like this to be told he was a grandfather. It had made Gideon, at nineteen, feel old to become an uncle. Theo was fascinated by the baby, but Gideon, once he had reassured himself that it didn't have two heads or six arms, had come to the conclusion he was a jolly little fellow and given up thinking about him. Vilia couldn't bear to look at him.

After a moment, Randall said, 'Oh. They're happy?'

411

'Indecently.'

There was a dry note in the other man's voice. 'Forgive me, but your brother can't be as much as twenty yet. Is he able to keep her in the – er – in the style to which she was accustomed under her half-brother's roof?'

'My God, yes. At least we don't pinch pennies at Marchfield!' It wasn't the most tactful thing to say, but Mr Randall didn't seem to mind. 'Please don't worry about that. She really *is* happy. She has a talent for it. She's the sweetest person I've ever known, and she and Drew adore each other.' Again, he hesitated. 'I don't know very much about love, but theirs seems to me the kind that will last. She worships him, and he's dedicated to her. He's a very staunch kind of person.'

Perry Randall's expression softened. 'Thank you, Gideon. Even so, they were married very young. Didn't your mother object?'

Without a trace of hesitation this time, Gideon replied, 'Only on principle. They were young, yes. But . . .' It was now or never. 'Drew's very like our father. Once his mind is made up, nothing will stop him.'

How ironic, Perry Randall was thinking. How unbelievably ironic. Not only the alliance of the two children, but that he and Vilia should have a grandson in common, when all he had ever wanted was that they should have children in common. Not even that, for posterity didn't mean much to him. Only Vilia did. 'How is Mrs – your mother?' he asked politely. 'It's many years since I've seen her.'

And there Gideon wasn't going to be drawn. 'Very well, thank you. If you know her, you'll know she thrives on being occupied.'

'And beautiful as ever, I have no doubt.'

Gideon smiled. 'It's funny, you know. She's quite ageless. She doesn't seem to have become a year older since I was a child.'

'Enjoying life?'

'I think so.' Vilia didn't know what Shona had asked of him, and although he hadn't deliberately kept it from her, he hadn't felt any compulsion to mention it. He had no idea what his mother felt about Perry Randall now; dislike and contempt, probably, but there was no telling. At the moment, it scarcely mattered. What mattered was steering the conversation away from this extremely delicate subject. Gideon suspected that Perry Randall was much too clever for comfort. He didn't think he had given anything away, but he preferred not to run unnecessary risks.

He didn't know that Perry had noted his reserve and put it down – temporarily – to British reticence. Thinking hurriedly, he wasn't even conscious of the silence while Perry fought down his desire to ask more about Vilia.

Was she happy with Luke? Did they have children? Those were the questions that had tormented Perry for six years, questions that, now, seemed to him more bearable than the answers could possibly be. He didn't think he wanted to know.

Gideon said politely, 'Shona will be delighted to know we've met, even if it was no thanks to me. I hadn't a notion where to start looking for you.'

'I have a house in Boston, though I'm seldom there. It's big, and rather cheerless, I'm afraid. I bought it in '28 for what' – there was an almost derisive smile on his lips – 'for what seemed a good reason at the time. Nothing came of it, but I've never been able to bring myself to get rid of the place. You'd like Boston. It's very civilized. Much of the time I'm in New York, however. I've a house in La Grange Terrace, on Lafayette Place, that I bought a couple of years ago. I hope you'll visit me there. The chances are, you know, that we'd have met anyway. I travel about a good deal, to the same places you'll be visiting, since we're both interested in metals. I'm in Philadelphia regularly on business . . .'

'I can't imagine anyone going there on pleasure! Is it true what someone told me, that they put chains across the streets on Sundays, so that people can't profane the Sabbath by using their carriages?'

'It is. And on weekday evenings it's just like a graveyard, except when they're having a riot, of course, which is one of their newer and less attractive habits. Mind you, most American towns are pretty lifeless after dark. That's because we all work so hard and rise so early. You'll discover that as you learn more about us. You're here on business for the ironworks, of course?'

'Yes. Theo's the practical one of the family, and Drew's in charge of sales. He should have been the one to come, but he couldn't leave Shona and the baby. Administration's my field.' Belatedly, the sense of Perry Randall's remark about them both being interested in metals got through to him. This was the very man he needed. 'If you're in guns,' he said, 'you must know all about iron. I'm here to sound out the

413

market, and I scarcely know how to begin, the field's so vast. Would it be an imposition for me to ask your advice?'

An imposition? Perry looked at the boy – pleasant, well bred, naive. He had none of Vilia's strength; indeed, he wasn't even very like her except in his fairness and the size and beauty of his eyes, though his were nearer hazel than green. But it didn't matter. Gideon Lauriston was Vilia's son, and there was only one other person in the world Perry would rather have been with. 'I'll give you any advice I can. Why don't you come with me to Harper's Ferry tomorrow? We can talk on the way.'

'That would be splendid!' Gideon's face lit up.

'Fine. Where are you staying? I'll pick you up at seven.'

2

The road ran along the Patapsco, with thick undergrowth and tall trees framing the craggy banks. Gideon, prejudiced, thought he had seen more beautiful scenery in the Highlands, but even so he drew breath for a moment where the Potomac and the Shenandoah met and burst their way through the rocks, under a shading of steep cliffs and green-black pines. In some ways, it was like the Pass of Brander in Argyll, but the Blue Ridge Mountains and the Alleghenies lent a dimension to the scene that Brander lacked. From the heights above Harper's Ferry the view was glorious.

Gideon was so used to the smell of coal smoke and the clank of hammers that he scarcely even noticed the Firearms Manufactory below until Perry Randall, amused, pointed out to him that as a tourist he ought to be complaining about it. Gideon laughed and flopped down on the turf, beginning to feel more comfortable with the other man. 'I wish *our* foundry was in a spot like this!' Chewing a stalk of young grass, he asked, 'Is it silly? My being here, I mean. We thought the Compromise Act would open new markets, and it all looked fairly simple from the other side of the Atlantic. But I've been here only a little over three weeks and, as far as I can see, the whole of America is a market! I don't know where to start. How can I talk to potential customers when every man I meet is a potential customer?'

Perry stretched himself out and breathed contentedly, as if the open air were his natural element, but there was nothing bucolic in what he had to say. 'You're right. All America *is* your market. You're ahead of us in some ways, because Britain's very compactness helps the process and dissemination of invention. And even on the most fundamental level, America's population is too small to do all the things that need to be done. We'll catch up with you some day, but in the meantime you could sell us as many cooking cauldrons as you like to produce. Now, and for years to come.'

He paused, and then exhaled lightly. 'I remember my early days here, when people who'd never heard any accent but their own took me for a swindling Yankee pedlar. No one would even give me a hearing except in the log cabins in the backwoods, where they wanted my gossip as much as my guns. No money, of course, so I became an expert at barter. After a while, I invested in an ancient Conestoga wagon and loaded it to the gills with every kind of firearm – lock, stock and barrel – I could lay my hands on. Sky blue, the wagon was,' he said reminiscently, 'with four old nags to pull it. Took me a year before I could get them to acknowledge I even existed, far less obey me. Anyway, the log cabins were still there, and so were the backwoods, and they're still there now. They'll probably still be there fifty years on. There's a lot of continent to cover.'

Gideon was interested. He'd always thought Scotland was empty, but even three weeks had begun to open his eyes to what real emptiness was. 'It must be a very strange, lonely life. In the cabins, I mean. What's it like?'

'Well, when you come in view of one, you let out a loud, "Hello-o-o-o! The house!" and you wind your way somehow in amongst the stumps and half-burned log piles until they can see you properly. And there's a good, stout log hut, and a corn crib, and a smoke house, and half a dozen hogs snoring in the shade. And the smells run out to meet you. Woodsmoke from the fire, and the rancid fat-and-lye mixture of soap boiling, and the stink of coon or muskrat or mink skins drying, and bare-arsed infants and unwashed hound dogs. And you know "the old woman" isn't a day over thirty, though she looks fifty. And every single thing in and around the house is home made, except the gun, if there is one, and the iron cauldron. They call it a "kettle" here. It's the most valued thing they possess, and the most difficult to replace. They cook in it, and use it as a wash boiler, and reduce maple sugar in it, and scald the hogs in it at killing time, and boil soap in it. I tell you, Gideon, there'll be backwoodsmen for another half century and they'll all need kettles. Hell, I wish I could buy a million from you and give them away free to those stubborn damned fools. They're building something from nothing in a way even I never had to do.'

Gideon was silent for a moment, taken aback by the depth of feeling in this surprising man's voice. Then Perry Randall sat up and laughed. 'Philanthropy – the curse of the money-grubbing classes. Forget it! Let out a yell for Briggs, will you? He's got some food and drink in the hamper there.'

With a slice of hickory-smoked ham in one hand and a wedge of squash pie in the other, Gideon said, 'The thing that's struck me in the time I've been here is the tremendous building activity. Canals, steamboats, railroads, and houses as well, of course. I've no way of judging whether or not we're more advanced at home. Is there anything we can supply that's better than what America's producing for itself? Or is it simply a matter of quantity?'

Perry shrugged. 'Quantity's important, of course. In your small islands you don't have the sheer difficulties of scale we have here. But scale introduces other problems you mightn't expect. Your steamboat engineers know that squeezing out an extra knot an hour won't get his passengers where they're going all that much sooner. Here it's different. Fast trips mean more profit and more prestige. It's not unheard-of for riverboat engineers to tie down the safety valve if they're in a hurry, or feed the fireboxes with bacon from the cargo, or timbers from the superstructure, if the fuel's running low. And then the boiler blows up, of course or the whole damned boat goes up in flames. Invent an unblockable safety valve, or an unburstable boiler, and you'd make a fortune. The same applies to the railroads. On the new line out of Charleston, South Carolina, a year or two back, the fireman held down the safety valve just because the hissing was getting on his nerves, and there was an almighty bang as a result. But no one's about to stop using the Iron Horse when it's averaging fifteen miles an hour compared with the six we're used to. We don't have many ten-mile-an-hour highways here. The main problem on the railroads, I'm told, is how to design rails, ties and ballast that will hold the tracks parallel and level.'

'That's Theo's speciality. I'll talk to him about it!'

'We've got canal fever, too, especially since Ohio finished a couple of stretches that let you go all the way from New York to New Orleans by water. Oh, yes, Gideon my lad! You've plenty of scope. Cauldrons for the backwoodsmen, boilers for the steamboats, rails for the railroads, lock gates for the canals.' Perry turned his head. 'And most American bridges are wood-built, and they have to be roofed to protect the roadbed and piling from the weather. Iron would be an improvement. And hell, Gideon! Someone even put up a cast-iron bank front in Pottsville five years ago. Just think! Iron-fronted stores, iron-framed buildings maybe even iron-built steamships one day. That's a project they're working on already.'

Amused, he watched the boy's face as he considered the staggering possibilities. Gideon said, 'Iron ships could be bigger, couldn't they? And they'd take more and heavier cargoes. And that'd bring the cost of shipping our iron down a good deal. And . . .'

'Hold on, hold on! Don't get too far ahead of yourself. Think how much coal they'd use if they were really big. If they carried enough for an Atlantic crossing they might have no space left for cargo. Coaling stations would have to be set up at – where? – the Azores? Newfoundland? Unless someone invents a way of producing more steam from less coal.'

Gideon stared at him. 'It's fantastic, isn't it? All those opportunities. All those *incredible* opportunities!'

'You're up in the air, boy. Come on down. Your brothers will have your head on a platter if you go home with nothing but dreams and visions.'

'I know. But that's how my mind works. Theo's the practical one, I'm the imaginative one, and Drew's the hard-headed romantic!'

'That sounds contradictory.' Never before had it occurred to Perry what a joy it would be, to have a son like this.

'What? Hard-headed romanticism? Not really. Commerce being vulgar and modern, Drew treats it as such. He reserves his romance for long-established things, like love and chivalry and mouldering ruins. Quite logical, really.'

Perry grinned at him. 'One foot in the future and one in the past. The perfect man for our times.'

'Yes, well. But what do I do, Mr Randall?'

'Perry.'

'Er – thank you.' He meant it. 'If all America's in the market for iron, how do I find out who's *most* in the market for it?'

He was a nice boy, and quite shrewd, but he didn't know anything about business at all. Perry said, 'You use your eyes and your intelligence. You also head straight for your competitors, and find out what they're up to. There's no better way of learning where the most important business is coming from. Besides, *they* know more about America than you do. Pick their brains. If you're clever, they'll never even cotton on to the fact you're doing it.'

Doubtfully, Gideon said, 'It's not awfully ethical, is it?' and Perry threw back his head and laughed.

'I'll give you some introductions. There's a belt of coal and iron that appears to run from Chicago to St Louis and over into Kentucky. Chicago's only a village right now, but it won't be long before it's a city. Go and see it. Another belt runs from the Smoky City – that's Pittsburgh – all the way down to Alabama. I reckon it might be worth going to South Carolina, too. They import more than any other state in the Union, and it was their resistance to import tariffs that led to the Compromise Act you were talking about. But to start with – go west, young man!'

His mind filled with visions, Gideon couldn't concentrate on the Firearms Manufactory. Lauristons' had never made rifles or cannons, and it was clear that the Manufactory didn't need any more suppliers of raw materials. No market here, he thought, listening with only half his attention to the technicalities that ricocheted round his head. He did wonder vaguely why the name of a gentleman called Sam Colt kept cropping up, but couldn't raise any enthusiasm for a new type of revolver, just about to be patented, when the whole world was determinedly at peace and seemed likely to remain so.

All the way back to Baltimore next day they talked about where Gideon should go and whom he should see. Then, just before they reached their destination, Perry stopped the carriage so that he could show Gideon his favourite view of the town.

From the hillside, they could see not only the neat, pretty houses but the harbour and shipping beyond. 'Beautiful, isn't it?' Perry said. 'That schooner there, the long, low one – that's the *Ann McKim*, Baltimore-built three years ago. She's what we call a clipper, because of her speed. Not much space for cargo, of course.'

Gideon sighed. 'She's lovely.' With a little difficulty, he went on, 'I know I can get excited about iron, and making it, and selling it, but that's my upbringing speaking, not my instincts. What I want to do is travel. Where do ships like the *Ann McKim* go?'

'Everywhere. I don't know what the *Ann*'s run is these days, but there's a friend of mine, a captain from Salem, who knows the India and China seas as well as he knows the coast of New England. He's been to Riga, too, and Arabia Felix, and Zanzibar, and Patagonia – everywhere! – trading one kind of goods for another at every port he visits. It's a strange, rootless, exacting kind of existence, but quite enthralling. Sometimes I think it's the kind of life I should have had myself, but I didn't see the attractions until too late. My first experience of the sea – from Fort William to Nova Scotia on an emigrant ship – put me off voyaging for a long time. I guess that's why I've only been back to Europe twice since I left.'

'Twice? I didn't know you'd been back at all.'

'Why should you? You were scarcely out of short petticoats. It was back in 1822 and again in '29.'

Without thinking, Gideon said, 'Poof! I remember those two years very well. The royal visit to Edinburgh, and the year Luke Telfer died.'

The air was still, for day was giving way to evening and the sea breeze had faded and the land breeze not yet begun to blow. Gideon sat and enjoyed it, and didn't notice how long it was before Perry said, 'Luke Telfer?'

'Yes, did you know him? But you must have done, of course. He'd be your – your nephew by marriage?'

The other man drew his long, flexible fingers absently over his forehead, smoothing out the two little creases between his brows. Abruptly, he said, 'Yeah!' It was the first time Gideon had consciously noticed him sounding like an American. 'I saw him in '29 at Kinveil – not long before he died, I guess. What happened?'

'At Kinveil? I didn't know you'd been there.' It was a silly remark, Gideon thought belatedly, considering he hadn't even known that Perry Randall had been in the country.

'What happened?' the other man asked again.

'It was an accident. He was caught up in a Clearance episode. We all were, in fact. Edward Blair was evicting some tenants at Grianan, and there was a good deal of stone-throwing, and houses collapsing, and

419

that kind of thing. Luke was hit by a falling rooftree. There was the most appalling fuss about it afterwards.'

'I imagine there was. When did this happen?'

The date was engraved on Gideon's memory. 'May twenty-first.'

Perry had left Kinveil on the seventeenth and reached Marchfield late on the nineteenth. The butler had said Mrs Lauriston would be almost at Kinveil by then. Almost . . . Almost . . . And Luke had died two days later. Perry, his stomach churning inside him, could scarcely bear to go on. Was it possible – was it conceivably possible! – that the marriage hadn't taken place after all? That he had spent six barren years trying, and failing, to resign himself to something that hadn't even happened? Fighting until a few months ago when, cursing himself for a fool, he had begun to pay court to Miss Sara Fontaine, of Beacon Street, Boston. Nothing had yet been said between them, but he knew that Sara, twenty-two years old but mature for her age, self-assured, impeccably well bred, would be a willing partner in a marriage of convenience. She was plump and brown-haired, and he suspected that the blood which ran in her veins was as cool as it was blue. It would be an excellent match.

Even after twenty years, he hadn't the right to ask about Vilia, straight out. Into the silence, he said, 'Tragic for his parents.'

'Yes. Fortunately or unfortunately, they were in London at the time. It was my mother who took the brunt of it all.'

'That must have been harrowing for her.'

'Well, it was, though it could have been worse. I doubt she ever really cared for Luke very much. She'd known him a long time, of course, so it wasn't easy.'

Clearly, she hadn't married him. *She hadn't married him.* And it sounded as if her sons hadn't even known she'd been thinking of it. What game had Luke been playing with him that evening? What game had Vilia been playing? And *why?*

He almost missed what Gideon was saying. '. . . more upset when his mother died three years later. Cholera. Lucy Telfer had been a very good friend to her.'

Automatically, Perry said, 'I'm sorry about that. She was a nice woman.'

'Yes, Magnus was dreadfully cut up about it, though he's beginning to pull himself together now. Vilia says he ought to marry again, and I'm sure she's right.'

And that went altogether too far. *That's one thing you won't do, my girl! That is one thing you – will – not – do. Not while there's breath in my body.*

He rose to his feet and stood smiling down at Gideon. 'Time to be getting back,' he said.

Most of the light had gone, but Gideon could see the hard line of Perry Randall's jaw, and the flash of white teeth against the sunbronzed skin, and the glitter as his eyes caught a reflection from the lantern Briggs had just lit on the carriage. He had been kind to Gideon, and extremely tolerant of someone who must have seemed very callow to him. Gideon was grateful to him not only in a positive sense, but because he knew he wasn't equipped to deal with such a man if he had chosen to be less than cordial. Just at the moment, he looked about as domesticated as a jungle cat. Gideon scrambled to his feet with an alacrity that would have astounded his family and friends. Though perhaps not Vilia, he reflected. If even his strong-minded mama had capitulated to Perry Randall, it wasn't likely her peace-loving second son was going to do better.

3

Two days later, armed with a route plan and a walletful of letters of introduction Gideon set off on his travels. 'Happy hunting!' said Perry Randall with a grin as he saw him off at Columbia on the canal boat that was to take him to Pittsburg. 'You'll find it's like going to John o' Groats by way of Land's End, but it's as good a way as any of discovering the mad expedients we're driven to in this new land of ours!'

Nothing in Gideon's experience had prepared him for the days and weeks that followed. No one in the Lauriston family was accustomed to idleness, so it was pleasant at first to sit on deck in the sun and watch the country slide by, even if, all too soon, he became aware that it would have been quicker to walk. The nights took even more getting used to. Before he entered the long, narrow cabin with its thirty-nine other occupants, he had thought that his passage on the steamboat had broken him of being over-nice in his sensibilities. But it was an illusion. Since he was slightly built, he was allocated one of the top tier of bunks, the lower ones being reserved for gentlemen whose avoirdupois was greater. He wasn't reassured by being told that this was to minimize injury in case the supports gave way. For the first time, he learned the absolute truth of the statement that hot air rose. So did smells. From the ripe, overall blend certain high notes emerged, distinct and individual – raw whiskey, tobacco smoke, rancid frying fat, sweaty socks, mattresses matured by years of use. Then someone made the understandable mistake of opening the cabin windows, and to the cacophonous noise of the massed choirs of bullfrogs on the canal banks was added the hazard of massed regiments of mosquitoes in the cabin. Next morning, Gideon noted in his journal, 'As far as murdering sleep is concerned, Macbeth was the merest tyro compared with the fauna of these parts.' By the time the canal boat floated over the aqueduct into Pittsburgh, he felt much as the original engineers must have felt when, with relief, they contemplated the results of their labours. Perry Randall had been right about mad expedients, for after the first 172 miles, when the canal meandered along by the Susquehenna and Juniata rivers into the hills at Hollidaysburg, the boat was taken apart, hauled up over the Allegheny summit by steam winch, and then let down to be reassembled at Johnstown for the remaining 150 miles of the journey. Virtuously, Gideon had counted all 174 locks. It added up to a lot of gates. How Drew's eyes would gleam when he heard!

And so began a strange, months-long interlude in which a few days of talk and smoke and heat and noise alternated, again and again, with weeks of travelling by every means humanity had yet devised, through every kind of countryside – hills and mountains, valleys wooded and bare, rivers quiet and bustling, furiously active new towns set amid great solitudes, where the colours were gaudy and the temperatures high, and the only sign of life was the blue jay, bright and delicate as a flying flower. Gideon learned a good deal about iron, but more about travel and more still about people and the huge, wide continent of America. He even learned to be amused at himself when he caught himself doing what all Americans did, eating his breakfast on the run. No loitering or lounging, no dipping into the newspapers, no pause between mouthfuls of eggs and oysters, steak and peaches, ham and chicken, hot biscuits and corn bread and buckwheat cakes and maple syrup. He noted it down, as he noted down everything, so that after a while he had to throw out one of his coats to make space for his journals.

From Pittsburgh to Cleveland, and then to Chicago, raw and busy and bare on the prairie above Lake Michigan, its houses fresh and new in the rough landscape as if they had been tumbled out of some giant's toybox and set up where they had fallen, stranded among rank grass and tree stumps along half-built streets. Then south again to join the Wabash, and on to the Ohio river, and then the great Mississippi. He left it at Memphis to travel cross-country to Alabama and a new, more violent society where there seemed to be none but the very rich and very poor and there were two sides to every man – silky deference to the ladies and lordly inhumanity to the slaves, a soft drawl in the voice and a sharp knife in the pocket. And after Alabama, on to South Carolina and the mellow, beautiful, blue-blooded city of Charleston.

Gideon had planned to go north from there to Richmond, Virginia, to see the Tredegar Iron Works, and then on to Washington and back to New York. But in Charleston he fell in love.

4

Long before that, Perry Randall had sailed for England.

Shona was almost speechless with excitement when his letter arrived from Fortune's Tavern in Edinburgh, and the nurserymaid thought she had taken leave of her senses, walking the floor all afternoon with nine-month-old Jermyn in her arms, cuddling him and whispering to him until, with a faint, bored gurgle, he fell asleep.

Drew was almost as excited as she was when he arrived home and heard about it, and said at once, 'We must invite him to stay, of course we must!' No one could have had a more wonderful husband.

Theo remarked thoughtfully, 'Fortune's Tavern? Well, he isn't penniless, at all events.' Then, after a moment, 'And Vilia is away. How very annoying.'

'I don't see why!' Drew exclaimed, showing hackle. 'Shona is perfectly capable of entertaining a house guest, and the man *is* her father!'

'True,' Theo replied with one of his most exasperating smiles. 'True, indeed.'

Perry Randall, when he walked through the front door next day, expected Marchfield House to seem smaller than he remembered it; places from the past always did, and this was no exception. But it was pleasant, and elegant, and handsomely furnished, and had a lived-in feel that his own two houses lacked. For a moment, his eyes rested on the Cameron family portraits, and then he turned back to his daughter.

Slim, brown-haired, and shyly pretty, there was nothing in her to surprise him. She looked like Charlotte, but gentler. Smiling, he held out his arms in a way that didn't come easily to him, and hugged her. She was laughing and crying, and quite incoherent, and he looked ruefully over her shining head at the two young men standing politely just inside the door. The one with the pleased, proprietary look on his face was presumably Drew, and the other, several degrees fairer and an inch or so taller, must be Theo. It was Theo who returned his glance, and even through the confusion of his own emotions, Perry noted the particular quality of his smile and groaned to himself. He wondered whether Vilia knew.

Where was she?

Next, he had to meet his grandson, and chuck him under his sleepy chin. Thank God no one suggested he might like to hold him. Then they all went in to dinner, and it was necessary to explain about meeting Gideon, and to relate something of his own recent history, and hear about theirs. Everything was painfully stilted. Perry had almost forgotten how oppressively polite the young were here, in comparison with young Americans. Gideon had been right, he thought, about Shona and Drew. They were admirably suited. How on earth had he and Charlotte managed to produce a daughter so sweet, and loving, and uncritical? She scarcely uttered a sentence that didn't include the words, 'Drew says', and when Drew was talking it was as if he were handing down the gospels from Sinai. She wasn't very clever, and she had no sense of humour at all, but she was a darling, although the kind of darling, Perry was beginning to feel after an hour or two, who might very easily drive one to distraction. Or was there something mortally wrong with his paternal instincts?

Having met Gideon, Perry would have recognized Theo and Drew anywhere. The resemblance was strong, particularly about the eyes and in their general height and fairness. Theo looked more like his mother than the other two, and Drew least like her. There was a stubborn set to his mouth. Gideon had said he was uncomplicated, and that was probably true. Theo, on the other hand, practical man or not, looked to be a mass of complications, for the people who dealt with him, even if not within himself. Perry wasn't sure that he cared for Theo, not because of his sexual proclivities – which didn't bother him – but because there was a hint of intellectual vanity in his smooth charm. It didn't show much. To Perry, his manner was pleasantly deprecating even when the talk veered round to metals and foundry work, and Shona, with a gentle smile, left the gentlemen to their port with a request that they shouldn't linger too long. Drew hurried them through it as if their lives depended on it.

Where was Vilia?

'My plans are fluid,' Perry said, 'but I have business in London, so I will be able to call on Grace and her husband.'

'Yes,' Drew said, clearly not very enthusiastic about his sister-in-law. 'They have two children now. Grace manages them admirably. You won't be going to Glenbraddan to see your stepson, I take it?'

'No. Even before my – er – marital troubles, Edward never warmed to me; nor, if the truth be told, did I to him. My fault, perhaps.'

Theo said, 'Did you know that his sister lives in Paris now? Vilia is on a visit to her at the moment.'

Is she, by God? He smiled. 'Georgy was, I think, seven when I last saw her, an engaging little scamp. Has she calmed down with the years?'

'Goodness, no!' Shona said. 'She's *so* full of life, and she adores Paris. She has been writing to us forever to come on a visit, and at last we persuaded mama-in-law to go. She has always wanted to, and I feel quite guilty because I know she would have gone sooner if it hadn't been for me, and wanting to be sure I was settled and happy first. You can't imagine how kind she has been to me! And she has promised to bring back all the latest frills and furbelows. It's so exciting!'

Perry had no intention, this time, of rushing off and missing her on the way. Absently, he said, 'I'm sure it is. Does she make a long stay?'

'Until the end of September.'

Another seven weeks. 'Then I may have the pleasure of renewing her acquaintance. I was considering going to France on a matter of patent

425

registration, and I would of course call on Georgy if I did.' *Hell! Not the most intelligent thing to say.* He looked at his daughter, one of the vast legion, he suspected, of under-occupied young ladies who spent most of their time writing letters. 'Don't, though, warn your sister to expect me. It's possible I might be held up in London, and never get to Paris at all.'

'Oh, no! But what a delightful surprise it will be for her. She will be as confounded as I was when your letter arrived.'

It was five days before Shona could bear to let him go, by which time he knew everything he could ever have wanted to know about Marchfield, and Drew, and Glenbraddan, and the foundry, and a wide range of friends, connections, and acquaintances, including several he had never heard of, and several he remembered well. Including Magnus Telfer, who had not reopened Kinveil, but was now greatly recovered from the shock of his wife's death and living most of the time in London, a sociable and eligible widower. Although Vilia didn't go out much when she was at home, when she was in town Magnus often escorted her to parties and balls.

5

Vilia, who had little time to spare for milliners and mantua-makers, and a natural disinclination to follow any dictates but her own – even the dictates of fashion – had always pleased herself in the matter of what she wore. Not by the wildest stretch of imagination could vast bonnets, ballooning sleeves, and skirts as wide and weighty as a steeple bell have been said to suit her everyday life, jogging back and forth to the foundry, shuttling in and out of carriages, and sometimes – more often than she would have wished – in and out of warehouses, engine rooms, and furnace sheds. She had become used to slender clothes and, by the exercise of a little malicious ingenuity, had been so successful in giving them a picturesque, subtly mediaeval look, that most of her acquaintances had come to believe that she was not careless of fashion, but contemptuous of it. No one could possibly have called her a dowdy. Indeed, more than one lady of mode, burdened by a dozen yards of printed satin, by petticoats and stays and bustles and sleeve-wadding, had thought wistfully that she would have liked to follow Mrs Lauriston's lead, if only she had the courage.

But in Paris even Vilia's courage had failed her. Graciously summoned with M. and Mme Savarin to a court ball at the Tuileries, she had hesitated, and listened to Georgiana, and been lost. She didn't know enough about France to know whether particularity of dress might not be taken for *lèse-majesté*, even if the *majesté* in question was the commonplace Louis-Philippe, the Citizen King, of whom she had no opinion at all. On the whole, however, she thought as she threw a last look at herself in the glass, the result was not as dreadful as she had feared. She had said a firm no to flowered damask, and an even firmer no to maroon brocade over rose-coloured satin, and settled for blonde lace over blonde satin. The wide, low neckline displayed her shoulders to advantage, and the cross-draped bodice was flattering even if the 'Imbecile' sleeves were fuller than she would have liked. She was not altogether sure that she was going to be able to manage the ample skirt, looped up on one side to display the underdress, and fastened with a veritable chandelier of pearl and crystal drops. There were pearl and crystal earrings to match, but her throat was bare. Ruefully, she thought that she would have been bowed under the weight of it all if the boning hadn't held her in place.

She forgot her discomfort when they arrived at the Tuileries, overcome by an almost childish excitement at the sheer gorgeousness of the scene. Though the Citizen King might be every bit as dull and bourgeois as bluff old Sailor Billy across the Channel, there was nothing mean or penny-pinching here. For a nostalgic moment, she remembered the Peers's ball in Edinburgh during George IV's visit in 1822. That had been quite different, noisy and colourful and not altogether civilized, but there had been the same exhilarating feeling of being at the centre of things. She had come to France because she had an imperative need to escape for a time from a situation in which she was reminded, day after day, of all the things it was important that she should learn to forget, or at least ignore. Here, she had thought, in the decent anonymity of a country where she knew almost no one, she might be able to come to terms with it all. And now, looking round the Tuileries, for a few moments she was able to forget the foundry, and Marchfield House, and Edinburgh, where taste and culture, as in Paris, were little more than a veil drawn over the coarsest squalor. She forgot even London and its tedious respectability, and the way Magnus Telfer was coming more and more to rely on her advice and judgement.

The whole length of the palace was glittering with lights and diamonds and feathers and uniforms, all the connecting chambers thrown open to give a perspective that dazzled the eyes and the senses. The walls and ceilings had been newly gilded and painted, the servants were arrayed in magnificent liveries, and medals gleamed profusely on the chests of a good many of the male guests. Vilia knew that some who should have been there were missing; victims of the infernal machine with which an assassin had tried to kill the king a month ago. But Louis-Philippe and his queen moved freely enough among the three thousand guests, gracious and civil – too civil, perhaps – exchanging a word here with a duke or princess, there with a national guardsman or a private soldier. Democracy at work, Vilia thought, amused. The guests came from all strata of society, although every woman there seemed to be decked out with a ransom in jewellery. Could there be so many diamonds in the world? The men were easier to place. There were uniforms of course, and a few frock coats, but the majority wore formal tailcoats, cut across at the waist and fastened low to display exotic waistcoats and exquisite shirts. Vilia giggled to herself. By their nether garments shall ye judge them, she thought. Some, as if declaring that they would have no truck with royalist display, wore trousers, as they would have done to any evening event, but others were turned out in the knee breeches, silk stockings, and pumps that court etiquette preferred. How much handsomer they looked, Vilia thought, when they had the figure for it.

There was dancing in several rooms, and the most extravagant supper Vilia had ever seen set out on tables in the theatre. Every dish was a work of art as well as of culinary genius. It seemed a pity that whalebone prevented most of the ladies from savouring more than a mouthful of *homard à la crème* or *caille à la vigneronne*, but at least the sorbets were refreshing in the oppressive heat of candles, people, and one's own gripping, stifling, abominable gown, in which one couldn't even sit down with any comfort.

To escort Vilia, the Savarins had roped in the Comte de Marcabrun, a good-looking young man in his mid-twenties with a fulsome line in compliments and some pretensions to wit. He had literary ambitions, too, and during a pause in the dancing took the opportunity – which he had clearly been hoping for all evening – to regale herself and Emile with the story of his recent luncheon with the distinguished but absent-minded M. de Balzac.

'Not until I arrived did he warn me that he lunched like a monk, and there was I hungry as a wolf! Will you believe me? Three raisins and two penny rolls, and a glass of Rhine wine with which we drank a toast to "God, the foremost novelist of the world". I swear to you, on my honour!'

The orchestra struck up a waltz and Vilia, still smiling, became aware that someone was standing behind her; some gentleman, no doubt, who hoped she might honour him with this dance. She could see from Savarin's face that it was no one he knew, and turned, gracious rejection already on her lips.

She didn't feel anything at all. The music and the lights and the dancers vanished, leaving her insensate as a marble statue staring at another marble statue. After the initial shock, her eyes, disbelieving, passed a tentative message to her mind, and her mind said, it's impossible. It can't be.

It was thirteen years since she had sent him away, someone she didn't really know, with harsh lines on his face that hadn't been there before, and a tension in his manner that suggested struggle unrelieved by success. Since then, for very cogent reasons of her own, she had persuaded herself that by now he would be lined and middle-aged, his muscles slack, his hair receding, his manners coarsened by thirteen more years of effortful failure. Her mind said again that it couldn't be Perry Randall, but it was.

Impeccably groomed, faultlessly arrayed in black coat, white waistcoat, and knee breeches, he bowed and said with a trace of mockery, 'Perhaps you will give me the pleasure, Mrs Lauriston?'

She took his arm and he led her to the floor. Neither of them spoke, she because she couldn't, he because he had planned every last detail of his strategy. Their steps matched as perfectly as they had done on the only other occasion when they had ever danced together, at the Northern Meeting ball in Inverness in 1814. Twenty-one years ago. After a while, as if she had voiced her thought, he said, 'You were wearing blonde lace that evening, too, I remember.' There was no caress in the words, spoken with a faint accent she didn't recognize,

429

only a chilling matter-of-factness. She smiled as if she had forgotten. 'Was I?' And that was all.

Afterwards, he restored her to her party. Georgy was back, and knew who he was before he had the opportunity to say a word. '*Mon dieu!*' she squealed. 'My erring papa! Where in the world have you sprung from? *Ça, c'est renversant!* Emile, it's *mon beau-père*, the second husband of my mama! The one who ran away to America!' It was Georgy's habit to lard her English as liberally with French as her French with English; as good a way as any, Vilia had thought, of disguising her inadequacy in the tongue of her adopted country.

It didn't disconcert Perry Randall at all. There was laughter in his eyes as he said, 'How clever of you, my child, for I certainly would not have recognized you. If I hadn't run across young Gideon Lauriston in Maryland a few weeks ago, I wouldn't even have known you lived in Paris. I was aiming to call on you tomorrow.'

Vilia hadn't heard from Gideon since the letter from New York, saying he was going to Baltimore. Was that in Maryland?

Georgy squeaked, 'Oh, do! When did you arrive? Where are you staying? How long will you be here?'

'I arrived a couple of days ago. I'm racking up at the embassy. And I'll be around for three or four weeks. You haven't changed after all, have you! As volatile as ever, in spite of two children and – but I guess I shouldn't mention how many years of growing up!'

Georgiana blushed and giggled. 'You can't *wish* to stay at a dreary embassy. Oh, and gracious heavens – I suppose it must be the *American* embassy. Pray, do come to us instead. We have room and to spare. It would be such fun! Emile and I would be *enchantés* to have you.'

Her husband, who was looking anything but enchanted, added his voice to hers, but Perry said, 'Thank you, no. The secretary is a personal friend of mine, and it would be discourteous to spurn his hospitality. We Americans set great store by hospitality, you know!' There was a gleam in his eye as he bowed, saying, 'Tomorrow, though. Mrs Lauriston. Georgy. Your servant, sir, and yours, Savarin.' He turned away and vanished in the crowd.

After that, somehow, the ball seemed to lose its glitter. It was raining when the time came to leave, and a gusty wind had come up. The waiting carriages seemed to stretch for miles, and the palace servants, scornful of the democracy that reigned indoors, summoned them up in strictest order of precedence. M. Savarin did not stand high in the social register, and Vilia had the feeling that, if this had been a private house, the footmen would already have begun snuffing the candles by the time they got away. She also had the feeling that, regardless of rank, the tall formidable-looking gentleman from her past had probably been among the first to drive off. By the time Savarin's coach reached the Avenue Matignon, even Georgy's relentless vivacity was showing signs of wear.

Vilia didn't sleep at all that night. How *dared* he treat her so politely, so distantly, as if there had never been anything between them! He who had fathered her child; who had come to her again in 1822, wanting only her body; who had scarcely even troubled to write to her afterwards, despite all his protestations. And who, carelessly or of intent, had told Luke Telfer in 1829 things that could still have wrecked her life, and almost had. Afterwards, he had paid a single visit to Marchfield House, wanting only her body again, she supposed – but not very much, for he had not come a second time. Since then, she had taught herself to hate him. It had been the shock, the surprise, she told herself, that had caused her temporarily to forget it.

In the morning, she left the house at eleven, a good hour before he could be expected to call. When Georgy protested, she said, 'My dear, I hardly know the man, and I'm sure you would prefer to have him to yourself. I am going sightseeing. No, don't fret. I don't need any other protector than Sorley. His French may be rough and ready, but even if my own were not perfectly adequate, his smile removes obstacles in France just as effectively as it does at home.'

She knew there was no danger of Perry Randall being pressed to stay to dinner, since they were dining out, but Georgy couldn't stop talking about him. He had admired little Gabrielle and Guy, of course, and complimented Georgiana on becoming a true Parisienne, envying her accent. His own, he said, once perfectly respectable, was scarcely understood in Paris now, for he was used to talking the patois of Louisiana, where he travelled much on business. 'And he is, *évidemment*, a success, for he has a house in Boston and another in New York! I wonder why he hasn't married again?' she said thoughtfully, and Vilia felt a queer, twisting sensation in her diaphragm. 'For one must admit, *n'est-ce pas*, that he doesn't look like a man vowed to celibacy!'

Later, Vilia discovered that she need not have troubled to stay out all day. It was Perry Randall's first visit to Paris, as it was hers, and Georgy, more than a little dazzled by her stepfather's looks and style, had volunteered to act as his and Vilia's guide to the city. Vilia, about to demur, caught Emile Savarin's eye. He was not very tall, verging on rotundity, and vaguely dissipated in a lethargic way. She didn't care for him, but she could well see why he would prefer her to take part in any such expeditions. Georgy's sense of propriety was not to be relied on, even if – to do Perry Randall reluctant justice – his almost certainly was. In any case, Vilia could think of no legitimate reason for refusing.

Next day they went to the Louvre, which had been stripped in 1814 and 1815 of many of its greatest paintings. 'An outrage!' Georgiana claimed, as if they had not, in fact, merely been restored to the owners from whom Napoleon had plundered them. Many of the antiquities and the Vatican sculptures had gone, too, but their place had been taken by newly-discovered treasures from Assyria, a fine display of Classical vases and bronzes, and a growing collection of *objets d'art* from the Middle Ages. Even when Georgiana relapsed into silence, there was plenty for two intelligent adults to talk about, even two who were determined, at all costs, to avoid touching on any matter bordering on the personal.

On the second day, they all went riding in the Bois, which had the advantage of ruling out a great deal of conversation. Mr Randall, in any case, only had an hour to spare.

On the third day, they picked their way through the narrow, crooked streets to Notre Dame, and admired the great rose windows, still with their centuries-old stained glass, and the flying buttresses and sculptured portals. They listened to Georgy explain how the long, galleried row of the Kings of Judah had lost their heads – decapitated, she said, by a revolutionary mob who had thought they represented the Kings of France. Then, still smiling politely, they returned to where the carriage was waiting. Perry Randall's groom was standing beside it with Mr Randall's horse. Easily, Mr Randall mounted, and with a smile and a wave, left them.

The day after that, Vilia pleaded a headache. Next day, she feared she might be contracting a cold and would be wise to stay indoors. And on the morning that followed, she took the opportunity to say good-bye to Mr Randall. She was about to leave for the country, and would not be returning to Paris. How charming it had been, she said, to renew their acquaintance.

To drive her out of Paris had been his aim. He was pleased to have achieved it so quickly.

6

Versailles, once the home of so much grandeur, was an empty, abandoned shell, although rumour said that it was soon to be restored. But its neglected saloons and galleries, its overgrown avenues and parterres, its dry fountains, suited Vilia's mood. She sat on a grassy bank and leaned her tired head against a tree. Her maid and Sorley, a discreet distance away, were squabbling amiably over the remains of the picnic, and the postboys were fast asleep in the shade of the carriage.

The strain had been intolerable. She had nursed her resentment at first, clung to her hatred as if it were a lifeline, and had succeeded in upsetting only herself. It had been like hating a cast-iron canopy or a length of railroad track, for he had accepted her chill politeness just as he had accepted Georgiana's hard-working vivacity – as if he were impervious, as if his own manners and breeding were too much part of him to be flawed by the pettiness or immaturity of others. He had been, and had remained, an eminently civilized companion, and perfectly at ease. There hadn't even been anything ironic in his courtesy, no extra shade of meaning when the satirical gleam came to his eye and the creases round his mouth deepened at something that, in other circumstances, would have amused her, too. There had been no hint of tension in him when he spoke to her, no suggestion of a tremor in his hand when he took her elbow to guide her across the street, nothing to suggest that he remembered they had even met before. Except for that one remark about blonde lace.

It was as if there were an unspoken agreement between them to let the dead past bury its dead. Only, for her it wasn't dead. She had, indeed, sent him away thirteen years ago, telling him that she didn't believe his love was either deep or durable; but almost at once, thinking over what he had said – again and again, interminably – she had begun to wonder. And then Mungo had died, and the first sorrow

433

had been absorbed in the second, and then both had been absorbed in a third – the long banishment from Kinveil. Perhaps because that was something it had seemed possible to rectify, she had allowed it to possess her mind to the exclusion of everything else. But no sooner was she back at Kinveil than she had begun to long for Perry Randall again, and had been desperate enough to persuade herself that Luke might be his substitute. And then Perry had come back, without seeing her, and had betrayed her to Luke.

She told herself, again, that she hated him. But still, she craved an explanation of it all, even though it looked, now, as if he had accepted that ill-judged dismissal, thinking she meant it; which wasn't surprising. She had relived their last meeting in her mind so many times, and she knew how convincing she had been because of her fear of being hurt again. More, almost, than anything in the world, she wanted to know how and when his feelings for her had changed, not on any general level, but in every tiny, desolate, masochistic detail. She wanted, she supposed, to have everything out with him, to quarrel with him, to justify herself, to prove to him that he had been wrong, yet again, and had failed her, yet again. She wanted to bare her soul, and his.

And she couldn't. There was no possible way of resurrecting the past with this stranger. This strikingly handsome, authoritative, wholly self-contained stranger. Almost everything he had said had made her realize how little she knew about him now. And that was what had made everything quite intolerable in the end. For if he had *really* been a stranger, she would have been in love with him, and he with her.

So she had fled. With Georgiana she had planned an itinerary that would take her, slowly drifting, back to the coast, stopping for a day here or a week there as the fancy took her. Emile had given her introductions to friends who would be happy to welcome her, if she should prefer a civilized house to an hotel or hostelry.

She spent that night not far from Versailles, and set out next day through the valley of the Chevreuse. The sun was warm, the hills were green, and there were pleasant orchards and tree-lined glades. The fields and the farms, the thatched houses and nestling villages, were well tended, well-endowed, peaceful, so that she herself was more composed when they found an inn not far from Dampierre, an elegant jewel of a château with domed corner turrets and a moat of running water, all in a sylvan setting of woods and lakes and trees. 'The château of Dampierre,' Emile had said, 'does not resemble the château of Kinveil in the smallest particular.' With something that was almost a laugh, she recognized that he had been right. The inn was comfortable and friendly, and she told the *patron* that next day she intended to go on to Rambouillet.

Yet still, that night, she dreamed about him. Half waking, half asleep, she remembered their one brief week together, those days in 1815 when nothing had mattered in the world except him. When all her senses had been focused, like the sun through a burning glass, on what was between them. She had known, in a compartment of her mind, that he was almost distracted with worry. She had known that by every standard of morality her own behaviour was wrong. She had thought of his wife and child and stepchildren, of her own husband and her two little sons – and it had been as if they all existed on another planet. Nothing had mattered except that they should be together again, she and Perry, their bodies, like their spirits, melting together into something above and beyond themselves. The whole infinitely more beautiful than the sum of the parts. Still, sometimes, she was able to take their love out, like a jewel from a velvet pouch, and run her fingers over its smooth, perfect surfaces, and turn it to the light and admire the radiance of it and the lancing fires. She thought about it now, drowsily, and after a while ecstasy took her, and a tearing, resplendent agony.

Slowly, gaspingly, she came back to the present and threw off the feather-stuffed quilt. Gazing blindly out through the thinly curtained window at the dawn she wondered for the first time what would happen if the Perry Randall of 1815 were to reappear before her, older perhaps, but otherwise unchanged; unshadowed by all the betrayals between. Would she still want him? The charming, passionate, unreal lover she herself had created and perpetuated. She didn't know.

There was a different chaise that day, and the postboys were new; something about a forty-kilometre limit from Paris. She didn't really pay much attention, because the countryside was soothing and the picnic by the banks of a little stream delightful. Could Mrs McKirdy learn to make bread like this, she wondered, and charcuterie? But it wasn't easy to get good pork in Edinburgh. As they approached Rambouillet the sun was setting, but Vilia leaned out of the coach hoping to see the fourteenth-century tower of the château, or perhaps Marie-Antoinette's dairy. It was odd how different latitudes affected the angle of the sun. She would have thought them a little further north than they really were. Anyway, she couldn't see the château.

She knew nothing about the hotel where she intended to stay that night, except that it was supposed to be good, but she was a little surprised to find it so plain and unassuming. No blaze of lights, no glasses clinking, no sound of talk, no ostlers, and only one other coach in the grassy forecourt. But the postboys seemed to have no doubts, so, with a little grimace, Vilia trod up the broad, shallow stone steps.

There was a man in some kind of livery holding open the front door, and with a nod she passed through. Momentarily dazzled, she was aware that the hall was empty save for one man. The *patron*, no doubt.

And then her sight cleared, and she saw it was Perry Randall. There was a sardonic smile on his lips, but his eyes were unreadable.

7

He stood aside to allow her to enter one of the ground floor rooms, and she went in without speaking, since it seemed that was what he wanted. It was a welcoming room, charmingly furnished, and the curtains were drawn, the candles lit, and a fire of scented logs burned in the hearth. There was a table laid out with silver, crystal, and porcelain, and an array of covered dishes. A faint, appetizing aroma came from a chafing dish on an ornate burner. As if in a trance, she moved toward the scrolled mirror set in the overmantel and began to remove her bonnet; a few wisps of hair had come loose from her chignon and, automatically, she tucked them in again. Then the door closed, and he was behind her, taking the light, gauzy carriage shawl from her shoulders. Their eyes met in the glass, and she heard the slight catch in his breathing, but he walked over to another door and opened it for her. It was a small retiring room with a gilded dressing stand, basins and ewers, towels, mirrors, and water closet. She was grateful after the journey.

When she returned, he was pouring wine into two slim, tapering glasses. He handed one to her and then, his eyes brilliant, raised his own and said, 'To you! To us!' She gazed back at him, her own eyes green and translucent in the candlelight, and then smiled faintly and raised the glass to her lips.

She had no real desire for food, but it was excellent, and she ate some in recognition of all the trouble someone had gone to. They didn't speak except for the courtesies of the table; there seemed no need.

After a time, she thought of something, and said, 'Where are we?'

'At a house called the Chaumière de la Reine, near Montfort-l'Amaury, a few kilometres north of Rambouillet.'

'You bribed the postboys?'

'Of course.'

'How did you know?'

'Your route? From Savarin. He didn't even realize he had told me.'

When they had finished, he crossed to the bellpull and two servants came in to clear away, and then to bring a tray of decanters and set up a little folding table with a coffee pot, cups, and sweetmeats on it. Then they were alone again.

She was sitting, half reclining, on a chaise longue by the fire, her eyes fixed on the heart of the flames and a faint, almost imperceptible lift at the corners of her mouth. Perry stood, quietly watching her. He had expected resistance, anger, even a cold fury. Any of them would have been justified. Personal considerations apart, it was hardly good *ton* to abduct a beautiful woman travelling alone in a foreign country, protected only by her servants. But at least, he reflected with a gleam of self-mockery, if one had to go in for abduction it was the easiest way to do it.

He had known better than to show anything of his feelings for her in Paris, for he didn't delude himself about her probable attitude to his reappearance after all these years. It was necessary for them to be alone, not just for an hour or two and always in danger of interruption, but much longer than that. And in Paris it was impossible. There were too many difficulties, perfectly real ones involving convention, propriety, and possible scandal, and some less real but potent enough to offer refuge if she chose not to face what he wanted her to face. As she might do. She had been forced too young into maturity, burdened too early with other people's weaknesses, other people's needs, other people's demands. Her defences against the world had been thrown up too quickly, so that some were irrational and ill-considered; and because she had never been granted the leisure to take them down again and rebuild more wisely, some were too strong. From remarks Gideon and Shona had made, Perry thought that, over the years, she had come to hold herself aloof from human involvements and was not, perhaps, always as discerning as she might be in her dealings with people. He didn't know how she felt about him – it was almost the only thing he didn't know about her – but he was certain that, if he still meant anything to her, she would see him as a threat to her cherished self-reliance, just as she had done in 1822.

He was prepared to expend all the patience he possessed on breaking down her barricades. Although she could be cool, detached, sexless, as she had been in Paris, or headstrong and hurtful as when she had sent him away from Marchfield House, he knew that she had a true capacity for love. And that was something that never died, even if love itself did. That was why he was here, why they were both here. He thought she had probably stopped loving the Perry Randall of 1815. But he would make her love the Perry Randall of 1835 as deeply, or more deeply than the weak, irresponsible ghost of twenty years past.

He had had many mistresses over the years, most of them beautiful, some of them amusing, a few of them clever, but his love had been reserved only for her. However confused his mind, however difficult his life, he had never deviated. Nothing she could say or do would ever change his feeling for her, although she might drive him to anger or even despair. For he knew her through and through, far better than she knew him. He had a kind of instinct where she was concerned. Even from five thousand miles away he could tell, without conscious thought, how her mind was working. The difficulty had always been that he didn't know, until too late, about the circumstances that provoked her mind to action. It was the only thing that frightened him.

He needed to have her alone, which was why he had borrowed this isolated house from one of the officials at the embassy, and was prepared to hold her here, ruthlessly as some feudal lord, for as long as he had to. He would have been prepared, if necessary, to lock up her only protector – her footman McClure – in one of the attics. But he had a feeling it wouldn't be necessary. He had observed that lanky Highlander carefully in Paris, and suspected that the only thing he cared about in the world was that his mistress should be happy; he suspected, too, that McClure remembered that she *had* been happy during that strange, dreamlike week in June 1815.

Now looking at her, Perry could see he wasn't going to have to fight after all. No tantrums, no resistance, just a calm content as if she had come home after some long, stormy voyage. When she had fled from Paris so quickly, he had known that her defences weren't impregnable, but he hadn't dared to hope that she would destroy them of her own will.

Oh, Vilia, my very dearest. Why? Tell me why.

He moved at last and knelt beside her, taking both her hands in his own hard grip. And then, just as he was about to speak, her eyes came round to his, wide and clear, candid as a child's. For a long time, they remained there, their gazes blending in a communion far beyond words until gradually, he sensed a change in her and said, softly, 'There is a room prepared for us. Come, let me show you.'

The phrase echoed oddly in her head as he led her upstairs in the shelter of his arm. Something to do with Kinveil. Something to do with Mungo. Something to do with happiness. Across the years, her own voice came back to her. 'There's nowhere as fine as here. Come, let me show you.'

She turned and smiled up at Perry Randall as he closed the door behind them. And then he took her in his arms, where she belonged.

8

Day followed day, and night night, separately and independently beautiful, like baroque pearls strung on a threat of purest happiness.

It was as if they had dropped out of the world, out of time. Everything conspired, even the soft September weather, to foster the illusion of having been born anew into a landscape of sun and clear skies and gentle breezes, where there was no pain or heartache and never could be. They rose late, drowsy with pleasure, and broke their fast on coffee and fruit, warm rolls and fresh sweet butter, then rode through the peaceful countryside, or explored the ancient streets of Montfort, with its centuries-old church and little cemetery in an arcaded gallery. Sometimes they went no further than the gardens of the house, strolling the hours away, hand in hand along grassy paths heavy with the scent of late roses, and cool with the hiss and tinkle of fountains. And sometimes they went nowhere at all, but sat on the balustered terrace of the house, not speaking, or thinking, or even moving except when, now and again, their eyes met and locked, smiling.

Perry was forty-five and Vilia thirty-nine, but age had nothing to do with anything that concerned them. Vilia had always been Perry's grand passion, while she, who had thought him her first and only love, now knew that he had also become, by some strange alchemy, her second and last love. There was, to begin with, a kind of wonderment in the discovery that this stranger, who in Paris had set her pulses tingling with his sheer, animal magnetism, should have lips and hands so familiar, and should know so well how to rouse her with his very first touch. Caressed into delight again and again, brought with passion and tenderness to the knowledge of continuing joy, she gave herself up to him completely. Often enough before, she had lived each day as if it were the only day of her life, because she would not otherwise have had the strength to see it through to its end; because tomorrow was unthinkable, and the next day, and the day after that. But here, in the house called the Chaumière de la Reine, yesterday and today and tomorrow merged into one another, day into night into day again, a single blur of love and joy and fulfilment, without beginning and without end.

Perry, himself enchanted out of touch with past and future, saw and marvelled at the change in her. The just perceptible lines of care and sadness and self-will vanished almost overnight, to leave her smooth-skinned and ageless. Even the flawless grooming, a deliberate state-ment of her attitude to the world, was abandoned. She began to tie her hair loosely, so that fine, sunstreaked tendrils curled round her forehead and her neck. She cast aside the formal trimmings and chemisettes and neat pelerine collars of her gowns, and wore them low-necked and frivolous and summery. She looked fresh, and young, and vulnerable. With a touch of sadness, he recognized that she had been transformed, not into the girl she had been, but into the girl she might have been if the circumstances of her life had been different. Loving and giving, free, happy. Such a waste – all those years of loneliness.

Everything was perfect, too perfect, and he couldn't bring himself to talk of the things that had to be talked about. Not because they were unpleasant – far from it – but because they involved decisions, and arrangements, and all the ordinary commerce of the world that, for the moment, was too well lost. There was time enough, he thought.

They talked very little, and mostly of nothing. From fear of dimming the iridescent bubble of their joy in each other, they asked no questions except unimportant ones. She said once, 'How was Gideon? Will he be all right?' and he replied, 'Oh, yes. A nice boy, my darling. Young, but he'll grow up quickly in America. Don't worry about him.'

On another occasion, out of some fugitive train of thought, he asked about Sorley. 'Is it fair to him? To keep him slave to Vilia Cameron for all these years? Does he have no life of his own?'

She gurgled delightfully. 'I suspect he has a very active life of his own! It's funny, though. We never have anything that could be called a conversation. Sometimes I talk to him as if he were a kind of confessor, or even just part of the furniture. And all he says is, "Yes, Mistress Vilia," or "No, Mistress Vilia." But he comforts me, I suppose because I know he's entirely on my side. He has no sense at all of what's right or wrong. In fact, I think the christening fairy must have forgotten morality altogether when she was bestowing his birth-gifts on him. I'm sure he approves of *our* relationship in a way no self-respecting pillar of the kirk would do for a moment. Dear Sorley – I can't imagine life without him.'

Once, carelessly, Perry mentioned that he had been to Marchfield and seen Shona and Drew, and for a moment all the cares of the world came back. But he was quick to say, 'I can't imagine how you can bear to have them in the house. Do they dote *all* the time?' And she laughed, and the moment passed.

After the first few days of hunger for each other, intense and insatiable, they ventured into new fields of pleasure. It began when, one evening, blushing like some innocent bride, she asked shyly that she should be allowed to sleep alone. It was so unexpected that, for a moment, he didn't grasp what she was trying to say. Then he took her in his arms, his eyes dancing, and said, 'Do you want to? For five whole nights?' So he taught her what she had never known – how she could give *him* pleasure – and taught her, too, some of the games lovers played. Deliberately, he made it all light-hearted, and she responded, and they laughed a good deal. Afterwards, their relationship was the richer for it.

But the time came when he had no choice but to talk about the future. It would be the end of this idyll; he simply hoped that, understanding now how much they needed each other, she would accept that the future could be an idyll of another kind.

When she opened her eyes one morning, he was there beside her as on other mornings, his dark head propped on one fist, the single waving lock drooping as it always did. His grey eyes were smiling into hers, and the long humorous mouth was disarmingly curved. He kissed her lightly on one sleepy eyelid, and she wriggled and stretched like a kitten, and then moved her body into the curve of his and closed her eyes again.

'No,' he said, laughing. 'Pay attention. I have a business, and money, and a house in Boston and another in New York. All of them are empty and meaningless without you. And so am I. When will you marry me?'

It wasn't fair, he knew. Her mind was slow to wake in the morning, and that was why he had chosen it. He wanted an answer uncomplicated by thought, by all the obstacles he knew that, given time, she would raise.

The translucent green eyes opened again. 'Marry you?' she repeated hazily. And then, after a long moment, 'Why?' He knew, then, that she had indeed been living in a state of thought suspended, and hadn't given a moment's consideration to anything beyond the present.

He swung himself on top of her, and then, at once, inside her. His hands caressing her, his mouth hovering over hers, he whispered mockingly, 'You ask why?' It wasn't what she had meant, and he knew it wasn't, but it was one kind of answer.

A long time afterwards, while they lay, bodies still locked, in temporary peace, she opened her eyes and murmured, 'America? Couldn't we . . . Isn't it possible . . . Couldn't you come back and settle in Scotland?'

His hard jaw tightened, but there was a smile on his face as he said, 'Oh, no, my darling!' and began, tantalizingly, to move again. And even as her body responded, swift and achingly impatient as it always was, even as she opened her lips to his and sent her hands straying over the long, flexible muscles of his back, she breathed, 'Damn you, Perry Randall. Oh, damn you! Damn you!'

And that, he knew instinctively, meant *Damn you for making me love you. Damn you for making me need you just when Kinveil is almost in my grasp.*

Another man, knowing it, might have been harsh with her, but he loved her too much. Even so, there was a controlled violence in him as he took her, this time, that he had never let her sense before.

He recovered himself quickly. Why, after all, should he be hurt by a truth he had already accepted? He had learned, within limits, to laugh at himself, and knew that he had been suffering from injured vanity. Not one of the more constructive emotions. Half dreaming, he lay beside her, marshalling his forces for the next stage of the battle between himself and Kinveil.

She, diverted by this new facet of him, turned her head in the web of shining hair and said pensively, 'Isn't it strange? We know so little about each other, in spite of everything. Even the most ordinary things – like what size of gloves, and what kind of music, and birthdays . . .'

His eyes crinkled in lazy amusement. 'Eight inches, and Vivaldi, and March twenty-fifth, 1790.'

'March? Really?' She raised her head and dimpled at him, looking absurdly youthful. 'Do you believe in the stars? Why should all the men I love have been born in March?'

He raised a quizzical eyebrow. '*All* the men you love?'

'Well, there's you,' she said mischievously. 'And Theo, and Gideon, and Drew . . .'

It was as if the sun suddenly went out, and the sounds of the countryside faded and the air closed in about him, thick and suffocating.

The words defied utterance, but he spoke them at last. 'Drew? I thought he was born earlier in the year.'

She might have deceived him if she hadn't still been languid with pleasure, if she hadn't been gazing straight into his eyes, if she hadn't been so close to him that her hair was brushing his cheek and her perfume filling his nostrils. But when his meaning reached her, he saw the warmth fade from the fine-textured skin and her eyes turn blank.

She said, 'No. I had a very difficult time with him. He was late. He was overdue.' She laid her head back on the pillows, as if there was no more to be said.

A lifetime later, he raised himself and leaned over her, but she turned her face away and he had to wind his hand in the silver-gold tangle of her hair to force her to look at him. He said, 'When was he born, Vilia? Don't lie to me. I can find out easily enough.'

'The eighteenth of March. He was late. He was overdue.'

His eyes went on staring into hers, grey as ice floes, and she knew he was working through the calendar, carefully, laboriously, week by week. She could imagine how his mind must be recoiling from it, but all she saw were the hard lines of his face, the set jaw, the deeply incised brackets round his mouth, and the two short vertical creases between the dark brows. She felt sick, horribly sick, and there was a lump in her throat, obstructing her breathing.

'Two weeks, almost three weeks late if he was Andrew's,' he said at last. And then, through his teeth, 'He's *my* son, isn't he? *Isn't he, Vilia?*'

She tried unavailingly to shake her head. Tears, spilling over, ran down her temples and into her hair.

He had her by the shoulders now, his grip so powerful that it seemed thumb and fingers must meet through the soft cavity below her collarbone. '*He – is – my – son!*'

And then he flung himself away from her, and when she opened her eyes again he was standing by the window, his back to her, the long, limber body haloed in the sunlight that was streaming in as it had streamed in every morning for three uninterrupted weeks of happiness. She supposed, dully, that it was fear of this that had led her to block out the world so completely. It had been foolish, because the contrast only made it worse.

His voice when he spoke was crisp and business-like, the kind of voice she used herself at the boardroom table. 'My son. Married to *my* daughter.'

She remembered walking the floor at Clarges Street, her mind paralysed at the thought of Drew marrying his half-sister, but the horror of that seemed pale compared to the unequivocal '*my* son . . . *my* daughter.'

She could hear voices coming from the direction of the stables, and there was a jingle of harness. The clip-clip-clip of shears floated up from the gardens. The birds were singing their hearts out, and a female chaffinch landed with a faint scrabble on one of the window bars and pecked at the glass, puzzled to find a barrier in the clear air.

Inside the room, there was no sound at all. It was if they had both stopped breathing.

Into the reverberant silence, he said, 'How could you let it happen?'

If she had not been who she was, she would have gone on her knees to him and cried, 'Forgive me! I was upset at the time. I didn't think. It never occurred to me that they would meet. I had almost forgotten Shona's existence; anonymous, retiring little Shona. And when I knew, I tried desperately to stop it.' But she had never been accountable to anyone for her actions. If he had said, 'How did it happen?' it might have been different. But, too shocked to choose his words, even for her, he had said, 'How could *you let it* happen?'

She was lying where he had left her, the pillows no whiter than her face. She felt cold in every nerve and pore. If he had loved her at all, he must have known that she had done everything in her power to stop it. But he didn't know. So she was still, in spite of everything, alone, as she had been for so much of her life. No haven, after all. No haven but the grave.

'How could you let it happen?' he said again. 'Surely you could have stopped it.'

The effort of speech was almost beyond her, the voice she forced out past locked throat muscles flat and colourless. 'Drew went to Kinveil alone. I was in London. When I heard about it, it was too late.'

After a time, he turned, but his face was still invisible, lost in the silhouette of dark head and strong shoulders and smoothly-muscled thighs. Then he moved towards the bed and sat down in the chair beside it, leaning forward, with his crossed forearms resting light and relaxed on his knees. She had never seen such an expression in any man's eyes.

Patiently, he said, 'I don't understand. Ever since he was born you must have recognized the danger.'

'No.' Her voice scraped a little.

'Why not? Because you cut it out of your mind, as you cut out everything you don't want to know about?'

'That's not true.' *And if it is, why not? Why shouldn't I? How could I go on living if I couldn't stop myself from thinking?*

'Then why didn't you take steps to prevent something like this from happening?'

'How could I? *How could I?*'

'You could have told the boy when he was a child, when he would have accepted it without much thought.'

Even through the grief that was not only for herself, but for him, she gave something that was almost a laugh. 'Oh, yes! "By the way, darling, the hero of Waterloo whom you so idolize wasn't, as it happens, your father . . ." Oh, yes, I could have told him!'

'Don't be juvenile. It would have been difficult, no more.' He paused, and then resumed, 'You were afraid of losing his love and trust. I see that. But then you should have made sure the children never met.'

'I did! They saw each other only once, when they were six years old. We had nothing to do with Glenbraddan. No contact. Charlotte hated me. But how could I put a guard on them when they were growing up? I did my best. Until they disobeyed me, the year Luke died, the boys had never been to Glenbraddan, and not even, since they were babies, to Kinveil.'

'Ah, yes,' he said. 'Luke.'

His voice was still perfectly reasonable, but her head began spinning. What next? What next?

'You were prepared to marry him for the sake of Kinveil. You wanted Kinveil so badly you were prepared to run any risk for it.' With all the humour and vitality gone, and in his eyes nothing but anguish, he looked his age. 'I understand that you might feel that way. But there are some risks nothing can justify. If anything had come of that, it would have been impossible to keep the children apart.' He was frowning a little. 'You do see that, don't you? You should have considered the risks.'

For the space of a heartbeat, she remembered the long, lonely journey through the arches of the years, with no respite from her burdens, and no hope of peace except one.

And then, '*Should I?*' she flared, and springing out of bed snatched at her night-robe, voice and hands shaking uncontrollably as she struggled to fasten it. 'You don't understand anything at all. How dare you hand down judgements from on high! How dare you speak as if it were all my fault! Yes, Drew *is* your child. Why should you start caring after all these years? You loved me and left me – isn't that what they say in the ballads? You loved Charlotte and left her, too! How many other children have you begotten on wives and mistresses I know nothing of? How many other girls should I have kept Drew away from, in case they were his sisters, too? How . . .'

His hard hand on her shoulder whirled her round, and with the other he dealt her a blow on the cheek that sent her reeling into the corner between the *garderobe* and the wall.

She gasped, and after a moment began to weep, her sobs rising on a hysterical crescendo that was dreadful to listen to, her arms clasped around herself not as protection against him, but against her own heartbreak.

He wouldn't spare her. He stood scarcely a yard away, desolation in his eyes and an exhausted anger in his voice. 'You don't know what love is, do you. It's more than passion, more than the – the felicitous matching of two personalities, more even than slaving to provide for those who need and depend on you. It's being able to understand them completely, to know them through and through and *still* love them. As I do you. It's foreseeing what might hurt them, and doing everything to prevent it, even if it means sacrificing yourself in the process. It's bringing your intelligence to bear on everything that affects them. And many other things, too. You have to love, or at least feel for the human race, if your love for individuals is to be worth anything.'

She tried to protest, through her tears, but he stopped her. 'No, let me finish. Don't tell me how you've worked, how you've made a success at the foundry. I know you have, and I know how hard it must have been for you. But don't deceive yourself, Vilia. I have no doubt you think you have done it all for the boys, but you haven't. You wanted success for yourself, as much as for them. More, perhaps. And you want Kinveil entirely for yourself. I've never quite known why you have such an obsession about the place, but even if you marry Magnus tomorrow, he will never bequeath it to the boys.' He paused for a moment, and then went on heavily, 'Did you think you and he might have children? It's still possible.'

Stunned, disbelieving, cornered not only by his body but by the mind that seemed to know everything about her, she could only stare at him. After a long, long time, answering her unspoken question, he said, '*I know you.*'

Then he turned away and began to don the riding dress his

447

manservant had laid out the night before. She watched him, motionless, as he pulled on his boots and then stood up to transfer coins and notes and keys from the dressing chest to the pockets of his coat.

'You're very stupid, sometimes,' he said, as he stood before the glass fixing the pin in his cravat, the gold pin in the form of a serpent with opal eyes that she remembered Mungo had given him. 'You didn't recognize what a fool of a romantic our son was. Do you know that Gideon hates the foundry, that all he wants to do is travel and write? Do you know that Theo . . . Do you know that his sexual inclinations are – unorthodox? And very illegal. There's quite a recent Act of Parliament that says, "Every person convicted of the abominable Crime of Buggery committed either with Mankind or with any Animal, shall suffer death as a Felon". I checked it when I was in London. You don't know what buggery is, my dear, do you? It's what the Bible calls sodomy. And Theo is heading that way, even if he hasn't got there yet. If you love him, remember that.'

He came to stand before her again. 'I've told you about Theo because I love you. If you know now, it may save you a greater hurt later.'

The pain still raw in his eyes, he took her chin lightly between his fingers and raised her face so that he could kiss her. Marble lips to marble lips. 'We both need to be alone, to think. I'm going riding. Good-bye, my dear.'

When he returned many hours later, she was gone. He had expected it. Nor could he bring himself to follow her.

Chapter Three

1

Gideon ducked as a pot of butter launched itself past his head with the velocity of a cannonball, and made a snatch at a cut of corned beef that looked about to leap off the table and bolt through the door of one of the staterooms. An apple dumpling skidded along the board, dead in line for his lap. He repelled it. All he wanted was a small egg, lightly scrambled, that would sit still in front of him and allow itself to be eaten.

Abruptly, he realized that he didn't even want that, and, rising to his feet, made his apologies to the captain and took himself up on deck.

The fresh air helped, although it was still blowing a gale and the sound of timbers creaking and wind whistling through the rigging reminded him of the Norse legends Vilia had given him to read as a child, legends of the storm god Wotan, and the Wild Hunt and the Raging Host. They were all abroad this morning, running free over the wide ocean with its great, grey, foam-topped waves and mountainous billows, huge and black, bursting into spray with a roar like all the furnaces of hell rolled into one.

After a while, feeling less squeamish, he went below to the cabin where Elinor lay, her skin green-white against the damp mahogany of her hair. 'Oh, Gideon,' she moaned.'I want to die.' Her soft Charleston drawl slurred the word 'die', dragging it out until it seemed as if it would never end. As he had done every morning for the last ten storm-tossed days, he took her hand in a sustaining grip and said, 'Not much longer, my darling. We should sight Liverpool soon.' And he thought again, as he had thought every day, 'We should have waited. Madness to face the Atlantic in March. The foundry can't need me as urgently as this!'

At the beginning of February, less than a week before he and his new bride had been due to set off from Charleston on a round of honeymoon visits, a letter had arrived from Theo. It was dated December tenth.

Gideon, dear boy – We were all, of course, charmed to hear that the beautiful Miss Langley has consented to make you the happiest man in the world. Drew, while prepared to dispute the title with you, begs me to convey his felicitations, as well as a great many reflections on the joys of matrimony. I do not propose to clutter the page with them, as it should place no great strain on your imagination to work them out for yourself.

Greatly though it pains me, however, I must ask you not to prolong your lotus-eating any more than necessary. The sad truth is that we need you here. Indeed, I cannot answer for what will happen to the administration of the foundry without you. I am much too busy to concern myself with it, Drew is not equipped, and Vilia, at the moment, is more of a hindrance than a help. Impossible to credit, perhaps, but there it is! She returned from Paris at the end of September in a high state of nerves, and although she has not granted us the favour of an explanation, I have my own suspicions. I merely *mention* the fact that our American friend, visiting Marchfield in August, expressed his intention of going on to Paris and calling on his stepdaughter, Georgiana Blair.

Intrigued? And rightly so. Anyway, Vilia has scarcely smiled since her return, and jumps out of her elegant skin if anyone so much as sneezes. Mistakes at the foundry are multiplying. I cannot feel that is *good* for business to send a gross of Mr Bramah's unpickable locks – without keys, I may add – to a customer who has ordered a single furnace-bottom.

Vilia excuses herself – and at least she *does* excuse herself – by saying she has not been sleeping well. But she refuses to resort to laudanum. I thought, a week or two ago, that she was beginning to improve, but alas! it was a false dawn. I fear that her relapse may have had something to do with dear Shona's ecstatic discovery that she is increasing again, and if that is so, then we can expect no real improvement until the brat makes its entry into the world in June or July. Hence the present *cri de coeur*.

One more thing. With a sad want of foresight, and remembering your remarks about Marsden's deficiencies, Drew and I proposed to Mr Randall when he was here that he might care to represent Lauriston Brothers in America. Just possibly, he may now view the proposal with less favour. If you are sailing from New York, I do think it would be wise to see him and sort the matter out. I won't disguise the fact that I will be interested – really, *most* interested – to hear what happens. Don't, I beg of you, let the agreement fall through if you can help it!

Pray apologize to your bride for Vilia's not having written to her. So fortunate that ladies always seem to understand other ladies' indispositions!

We will see you as soon as you can contrive, won't we, dear boy? – Yours, Theo.

To Gideon – lotus-eating, as his brother had so accurately surmised – it had all brought back that incredible day at Clarges Street just over two years ago, the day he would never really forget if he lived to be a hundred. Did he want to go home to it all? he wondered, as he ran up the stairs of the house on the Battery to break it to Elinor. She had been disappointed, for, like all Southern girls, she had looked forward to showing her husband off to every last relative and connection she possessed, but she had overcome it almost at once, and smiled at him, and exclaimed, 'No, of course I don't mind, Gideon honey. We must go if your family needs you!'

Mr and Mrs James Langley, who had hoped to persuade Gideon to stay and be the son they had never had, saw them off reluctantly, and Elinor had hugged her mother and sisters convulsively, and between them they had wept enough to raise the water in the harbour by a good two inches. Fortunately, the journey north had taken her mind off it. Fortunately, too, by the time they reached New York she had ceased to laugh gaily at her husband's frequent mentions of warm gowns and furred pelisses, when all she had ever worn were muslins and taffetas and organdies. When it turned out that Perry Randall wasn't in New York but in Boston, Gideon took his wife's Mammy aside and explained to her in detail what Miz Elinor was going to need, and then, with a parting injunction to buy something warm for herself and the maids as well, removed himself from the fray. He had a momentary vision of Mammy settling in at Marchfield, and shuddered violently, thinking – not for the first time – sufficient unto the day.

It was with relief that he checked in at the Tremont House. All he had heard about it was true – the neat facade, the fine portico, the sumptuous public rooms, the chandeliers, the galleries, the piazzas. More, it had what his soul craved after all the months of overwhelming hospitality – privacy. There were single bedchambers for gentlemen who didn't wish to share, chambers with locks on the doors; and personal bars of soap, and bathrooms with running water nearby. So, although it was on the very corner of Beacon Street, he waited until next day before sending a note to Perry Randall at the house across the road.

The scrawled message that came back said, 'Welcome to Boston. I expect to be tied up for most of the day, but my wife and I would be happy to have you dine with us tonight. We'll expect you just after six. – Yours, Perry R.'

2

The house was red brick, mellow and spacious. 'Charles Bulfinch,' Perry said, greeting his guest. 'Like all the most select houses in Boston!' The name was meaningless to Gideon, and it must have shown on his face, but Perry Randall didn't pursue it. Instead, 'Come and let me make you known to Mrs Randall. Your good wishes will be in order. We are only recently married.'

The marriage had been surprise enough, but Mrs Randall was another. Gideon would have expected someone rather stylish, yet she was scarcely even pretty. She couldn't, he supposed, be more than five years older than Elinor, but whereas Elinor had no thought in her head

451

beyond enjoying life and – he hoped – being in love with him, Mrs Randall was calm, composed, and a little austere. Her hair lay in flat braids on her cheeks under a matronly lace cap, and her smoky blue velvet gown was draped with a demure lace fichu. She looked as if she had been married for years, and the only word for her manner was gracious.

But at least it provided Gideon with an opening which allowed him to break the news of his own marriage without making too much of an occasion of it. What bothered him, as course followed course in the quiet dining-room, with its eighteenth-century portraits, gleaming table, and lyre-backed chairs, was whether he was going to be given the opportunity for a serious discussion with Perry. Was Boston etiquette like European? Would she leave them to their port and madeira? He hoped so, for he was in no doubt that it would be the worst of solecisms to mention anything as vulgar as commerce at this cultivated table.

Perry was looking strained, and his smile didn't reach his eyes when he remarked, 'I've never yet seen a Southern belle without her retinue of Mammy and maids. Are you taking them all to Scotland with you?'

Gideon said, weakly, 'There doesn't seem much alternative.'

'It may not have occurred to you, Mr Lauriston,' remarked Mrs Randall in her level, slightly nasal voice, 'that you may be doing them a disservice. From what Mr Randall tells me, I cannot think that Southern negroes would thrive in Scotland, however attached they may be to their mistress. Which I have no doubt they are,' she added kindly. 'As their owner, you might find it preferable to offer them their freedom while they are still here, in the country of their birth. Their bonds will, of course, be worthless on the other side of the Atlantic.'

Despite the papers Mr Langley had given him, Gideon hadn't thought of the slaves as anything other than ordinary servants. Without realizing it, he knew that he must have blocked out the awareness of being legal owner of three other human beings. Now, he felt all kinds of a fool, and an embarrassed one. He looked at Perry, questioningly.

'It's good sense, Gideon. You will have nothing but trouble if you take them with you.' Then, spontaneously, he laughed. 'Can you imagine your wife's Mammy having it out with Mrs McKirdy? "Ah ain' gwine ter stand by an' see mah lamb 'spekted ter eat dat hawg swill yo call pawridge, sho 'nuff!" '

452

Gideon clapped his hand to his forehead. 'Gemini! I hadn't thought of Mrs McKirdy. You're right, she'd have a fit! "Mistress Lauriston! If yon woman sets foot in my kitchen one more time, I'll not answer for the consequences!" But what can I do? I shouldn't think Elinor could manage without her servants.' It didn't need Perry's quizzical eyebrow to remind him that, however much he adored his bride, marrying her hadn't been the most intelligent thing he'd ever done. In Charleston, he had contemplated her adjustment to a new life with unalloyed optimism, but it had faded with every mile of the journey north.

Mrs Randall looked at her husband. 'My dear, I wonder whether Miss Tully might answer?'

Miss Tully, it transpired, was an Englishwoman who had been abigail to several ladies of the first consequence before coming, at last, to the regretful conclusion that she was not entirely in sympathy with the New World. For some time, she had been wanting to go home, but could do so only if she found a lady willing to employ her. It was not easy for an abigail, even one as superior as Miss Tully, to save money. Mrs Randall promised that, as soon as Elinor agreed, she would arrange matters. Gideon could have embraced her. Suddenly, she looked a great deal prettier.

Even so, he was relieved when Perry rose to draw back his wife's chair and she said, smiling faintly, 'I am sure you have things to discuss. I will tell Fogarty to take the decanters to your study, my dear. You will be more comfortable there.'

'Thank you, Sara.' Gideon could see that they understood each other.

The study was comfortable, smelling of leather and books and tobacco. Gideon, a few months older now and several years wiser, wondered whether Perry's reserve was new since they had met in Baltimore, or whether he himself – so concerned with choosing his words in case he should betray the truth about Drew – had been less observant than he might have been. Then, with a mental shrug, he did as Theo had instructed and raised the matter of representation.

Perry wasn't encouraging. He was not, he said, about to back out of the arrangement they had discussed, but since his return home he had become concerned over the way things were going. Speculation was wild, and getting wilder by the hour. 'Another year and there could be an almighty crash. God knows, this country can't exist without credit, but credit's dangerous if expansion doesn't keep pace with it, and I don't see how it can. My advice to Lauristons' would be, keep your horns in for now, as I'm doing myself. If you start exporting here in the next few months, you may find you've trouble getting paid.'

'It's like that, is it?'

'And could get worse, if the banks were to close their doors – which they might. Leave it for now, Gideon. Let Marsden go on for the time being, and make it clear to him you want every cent the moment it's due. If the crash comes, it could come fast. Let things ride for a couple of years and then we can think about it again.'

Perry, studying the boy, hoped he had convinced him. The argument was valid, sure enough, but, only too aware of the fact that the arrangement had been discussed with Theo and Drew before he had gone to France, Perry's main concern was to leave Vilia a way of wriggling out of it without too much fuss. Did he want out of it himself? He didn't know any more. He had sailed home direct from France with nothing in his heart but shock, a dull despair, and an overpowering need to cut the ties that had bound him for so long. Well, they were cut now, he supposed. And yet . . . And yet . . . And yet he still wasn't free. Even the prospect of seeing Gideon today had been almost too much for him. Sara had noticed, of course; marriage of convenience or not, she had her own perceptions. He had no intention of hurting her, and in time, perhaps, he would forget. He said, 'Have you heard from home? How is everyone?'

Gideon made the lie sound as convincing as he could. 'Very well indeed, I gather. And by the way, you will soon be a grandfather again, if you don't already know. Shona is expecting another baby in June.'

There was an infinitesimal pause, while Perry lit another cigarillo. He seemed to have been smoking a great deal this evening, Gideon thought. Then he raised his eyes from the glowing tip and said, 'How delightful. I imagine she would like a girl this time?'

Gideon said, 'I imagine so.' The pause must have been coincidental, mustn't it? Perry Randall couldn't *possibly* know. Gideon put it firmly out of his mind, in case he might make the mistake of mentioning it to Theo when he got home.

3

The ship docked at last, and Gideon thought the worst was over. But it had scarcely begun.

By the time they reached Edinburgh, even Miss Tully, a tower of strength on the voyage, had abandoned her patriotic commentary on the beauties of the countryside and the thriving industry of the towns, for the landscape looked dour and grey, and the towns full not only of warehouses and factories, but of sickly, dirty, hollow-cheeked people, and gin shops, and poverty, and squalor. Edinburgh itself was half hidden in smoke and mist, the air reeking of coal, fog, and sleet, and by the time they reached Marchfield they could scarcely see it through the dirty yellow blanket that enveloped it, broken only by the incandescent glare of the lamps flanking the door.

As Gideon helped Elinor down from the carriage and led her up the front steps, slippery with damp, he was overcome by a wave of guilt at having brought this pampered child of sun and warmth and leisure to such a grey, grim land. He squeezed her elbow and murmured, 'Don't worry. They'll all adore you and you'll feel at home in no time.' But her answering smile was tremulous, and their welcome was not what he had hoped.

The fog had filtered into the hall and hung, a dulling miasma, over everything and everyone. When Vilia came forward, smiling, to kiss Elinor's cheek, her bright hair was colourless, her complexion drained, and her eyes lightless and blank over the sombre grey morning gown. She moved like an automaton, and her smile had no meaning. Gideon torn between shock at her appearance and fearfulness for his wife, threw an agonized glance at his brothers, but Theo had clearly no intention of becoming involved, and Drew was simply standing there with his company smile on his face and his arm round Shona's ample waist.

And then Shona, darling that she was, ran clumsily forward and threw her arms round Elinor, the words of welcome spilling out in an inane but comforting stream. 'We're so *happy* to have you here, but you must be chilled to the bone in this horrid weather. Do come and get warm, and then I can show you the rooms we've prepared for you. I'm sure you'll like them. Goodness, but you look so pretty and smart! You make me feel like a dowdy. Mama and I stayed in our morning gowns so that you wouldn't have to change out of your travelling dress, but . . .'

Still chattering, she led Elinor into the drawing-room, and the awkward moment had passed.

Gideon kissed his mother's raised cheek. 'How are you?'

'Very well, my dear. I hope you had a pleasant' – she frowned as if she couldn't quite remember why he had been away – 'a pleasant visit?'

He could never have mistaken it for sarcasm, and, catching Theo's eye, knew that the distress must show in his own.

In the privacy of their room that night, Gideon turned to Elinor, needing her as desperately as he thought she must need him. But she didn't. All the way from Charleston to New York they had gone laughing to bed together, however tiring the day's journey, however poor the hotel. He had been unfailingly gentle, unfailingly careful with her, and he had thought she was learning to enjoy making love. Even though the spell had been broken five days out of New York, he had told himself that it would all come right again when they were able to lie together peacefully at home, in their own bed at last. Afterwards, he realized that he had asked too much of her, too soon. She was unresponsive at first, and then pettish, and then reluctantly cooperative until the moment when, fully and urgently aroused, he was half inside her; and then with a wail of 'No!' she tore herself away from him and curled herself into a ball at the farthest side of the bed, and began to cry as if her heart would break. He cried himself, soundlessly, while he brought his body back under control. She was lost, poor lamb, a helpless stranger in an alien world. She wouldn't let him touch her for a long time, but at last she fell asleep with his arms about her.

He had no choice next morning but to leave her for the foundry, and it was to be several weeks – weeks of working seven days a week, from seven in the morning until seven or eight at night – before he was able to spare a whole day for her. He knew how unhappy she was; she who had always been the centre of attraction at home, the eldest of three pretty sisters, her days filled with visits, and parties, and flirtations. And now she had been brought to a strange house where no one had any time for her, not even her husband. Where she had only Shona for company – Shona who couldn't appear in public now that she was pregnant, couldn't ride, or drive in to Edinburgh to look at the shops and warehouses; who didn't, in fact, want to, but was happier to stay at home and play with Jermyn, or sew for the baby, or gossip. Gideon, harassed, promised that the moment it could be arranged he would take Elinor out to meet new people, perhaps even to stay with friends on the Borders.

But it was an empty promise. Mentally and physically, Gideon was soon wearier than he had ever been in his life before. It wasn't a matter simply of isolating and then correcting all the errors that had been made in the past months, but of trying to extract from Vilia what had been done that shouldn't have been done, and what hadn't been done that should. He was in and out of her office like a jack-in-the-box, and found her, time after time, sitting at her desk staring into infinity. When she spoke, it was with the slow exactitude of someone who was exceedingly drunk.

Tiredly, he said to Theo on one occasion, 'The moment I have things straight, I'm going to suggest she goes away somewhere for a change and a rest. She must know she needs it!' And Theo replied, his slanting brows raised, 'You can try. But my own view is that's she clinging to the foundry as if it were her only anchor.'

At home in the evenings, conversation was difficult. Normally, they would have talked about work most of the time. Shona was used to it by now. But for Elinor's sake they made an effort, and she, unbelievably bored, starved for companionship, responded with some of the sparkle that had made Gideon love her.

And then, about ten days after they arrived, Gideon came running down late to dinner and exclaimed, dropping a kiss on her forehead, 'That's a very fetching shawl, love! I haven't seen it before, have I?'

'I don't recall, honey. I bought it when you were in Boston.'

Gideon pulled out his chair, and prayed. He had told Theo, briefly, of his meeting with Perry Randall, and they had agreed that Vilia shouldn't know. So they had kept it from Drew and Shona, too, who would have seen no reason not to talk about it. But he hadn't been long enough married to think of warning Elinor.

His prayer went unanswered. Shona, on a faint shriek, exclaimed, 'Oh, *Gideon!* Does that mean you saw my father? Why didn't you tell me?'

He made something of a business of settling, and unfolding his napkin. 'There has been so much else to talk about, and you must admit I gave you the fullest report of my meetings with him in Baltimore. Yes, I saw him again, and yes, he was well, though I thought he looked tired. I suppose that, like me, he found himself with a lot to catch up with after being away. Drew, you can serve me some of that soup. It smells good and I'm famished.'

Before Shona could say anything more, Theo intervened suavely, 'I can't think it was very chivalrous of you to leave your bride alone in New York, Gideon. Or were the shops of Broadway tempting enough to make up for his absence?' He looked at Elinor, and smiled in the way that women always responded to.

She smiled back, the dimples in her cheeks looking like fingerprints in cream. 'They were just darling, and Gideon had said I might spoil myself, so I did – didn't I, honey? I didn't miss him one little bit. And when he came back, he'd arranged with Miz Randall for Tully to come as my maid, so it all worked out just beautifully.'

The silence was total. Gideon, grateful that the last mouthful of soup had slipped past his epiglottis just in time to prevent him from choking on it, waited fatalistically. Theo raised his brows exaggeratedly at him, as if to say he'd done his best.

Faintly, Shona repeated, 'Miz Randall?' and then, on a higher note, 'Mrs Randall? Gideon, you don't mean my father has *married* again?'

'Er – as a matter of fact – yes. Quite recently.'

'But what on earth is she *like*? Heavens, Gideon, why didn't you tell us *at once*?'

He slithered past it. 'Very pleasant, very quiet and restrained. I only met her once. I don't know what else to say about her.'

Shona, exasperated, exclaimed, 'Men! What does she *look* like?'

'Brown-haired, slightly plump, refined rather than pretty. I suppose she must be in her mid-twenties.'

'Is he *happy*?'

'Really, Shona! How should I know? They seemed . . .'

Vilia's voice broke in. 'Drew, I wish you would remove the soup plates, McKirdy seems to have disappeared and it's Sorley's evening off. Elinor will think this a very peculiar household, where we all sit round with empty plates in front of us. Gideon may carve the beef, and you, Theo, pray do something about that chicken instead of letting it sit there congealing before you. Elinor, will you have beef or chicken? Our beef is really very good here. I imagine you may not be accustomed to beef. Cattle don't thrive in a hot climate, do they? I suppose our food must seem very dull to you, but with so many people to cook for Mrs

McKirdy hasn't time for elegant sauces and all the little extras that I am sure you must be used to. Do you have potatoes in Charleston? Oh, and I have been meaning to say to you that fruit is something we rarely see here except in summer. But there is a delicious apple pie to follow. Mrs McKirdy is very good at that, isn't she, Shona? Drew, do get up and see if the horseradish sauce is over on the sideboard. We can't eat beef without that. Have you ever tasted horseradish sauce, Elinor? Isn't it there, Drew? How vexing. No, you serve the girls with vegetables, and I will go and see what has happened to it.'

Drew, dutifully spooning potatoes and carrots and cabbage greens onto a protesting Elinor's plate, grinned at her. 'I hope Gideon has told you mama isn't always like this? Don't let it bother you. He hasn't really brought you back to a madhouse!'

Ten minutes later, McKirdy appeared to say that Mistress Lauriston was rather tired tonight, and perhaps they would forgive her if she didn't rejoin them.

The worst thing about it all, Gideon slowly came to realize, was that Vilia now began to make Elinor the focus of her misery, like some Roman emperor executing the messenger who brought bad tidings. He didn't notice it at first. All he noticed was that, when one of the servants dropped a knife, or Drew gave his customary ear-splitting cough before speaking, Vilia had to hold herself tight to prevent herself from screaming. And then he saw that, with Elinor, she was holding herself in all the time. Soon, everyone became over-sensitive to Elinor's mannerisms, her indolence, her increasing petulance, and above all, her drawl. Theo said to him one day, 'Your wife is a charming girl, dear boy – don't think I don't mean it. But can't you, for God's sake, persuade her to keep quiet when Vilia's there? Dear Elinor's drawl is driving her to distraction. Indeed, if Elinor goes boring on much longer about Maa and Paa, and Gidyun-honey, and Chalst'n and wo-ohn' do this, or cain't do thaat, there's going to be an eruption. And if mama bursts out and screams at your petted little Southern belle – dammit, Gideon, don't try to deny she's spoilt! – you'll have even more trouble on your hands than you have already.'

But the trouble, when it came, took a different form. Returning home one evening in May, Gideon found his wife face down on her bed, wearing nothing but her shift and with her hair in a mad tangle over her shoulders, screaming and kicking like a frustrated two-year-old. Miss Tully, standing by the bedside, had a resigned expression on her face and a comb and hairbrush in her hands.

'What's the matter?' Gideon exclaimed, crossing the floor in two strides, and Miss Tully said with a sigh, 'Madam is a little upset, sir. Would you wish me to leave you with her? I will do her hair later.'

Gideon laid his hands on Elinor's shoulders and leaned over, burying his mouth in the nape of her neck. But all she did was screech more loudly. She was in a very juvenile tantrum, and it wasn't easy to take her seriously. He waited, but it showed no sign of diminishing, so he said eventually, 'Hush! You'll make yourself ill. What's the matter? Tell me.'

The face that turned towards his was scarlet with fury, and there was something very like hysteria in her voice. 'It's all your fault! I hate you! I hate you! I want to die! I'm going to have a baby. It's all your fault!'

The first thought that sprang irrepressibly to his mind was, 'Well, there's something in that, as the actress said to the bishop!' And then he was ashamed and delighted, both at the same time. Pulling her upright, he cradled her against his shoulder, brushing the red-brown hair gently back from her damp forehead. 'It's the most wonderful news I've ever heard. Why so upset, my darling? I'm so happy I can't believe it!'

'Well, I'm not,' she wailed. 'I don't want it. I'm frightened. I don't want to have a baby in this horrid house where no one likes me! *I can't bear it.* I want to go home. I want my Ma. *Oh, I'm so miserable!*'

Gideon's amusement vanished, and he felt only compassion for her. She was so young and helpless – like a bright, tropical flower, he thought, wilting at the first cool kiss of a northern breeze. All the conventional words of comfort sprang to his lips, about how wrong she was, and how much everyone loved her under their reserved British exteriors, and how kind Vilia would be as soon as she knew about the baby, almost like Elinor's own mother.

None of it was true. Gideon knew that even if Vilia had been her normal self she wouldn't have warmed to Elinor; neither would Theo or Drew. With hurtful clarity, he recognized what an intruder she must seem to them – spoilt, demanding, immature, sparkling at them over the dinner table every evening when they were all too tired even to be entertained. But she needed an audience so badly, and Gideon, however loving, wasn't enough.

460

He wondered suddenly how it had happened that, for all of them, Marchfield had stopped being a home and become an extension of the foundry. It hadn't been like that once. He could remember when none of them had been expected to turn up for dinner unless they wanted to. Neither Vilia nor Mrs McKirdy, God bless her, had complained if one of the boys chose to make do with just a sandwich and a glass of wine in the library. The turning point, he supposed, had been when Shona had come, and he and Theo had felt it was only proper to present themselves dutifully at table. Afterwards, the custom established, it wasn't easy to break, and after the first few awkwardly courteous weeks when they had struggled to talk of anything and everything, the conversation had gravitated inevitably towards the foundry. Shona didn't seem to mind, and it was better than sitting silent or forcing their minds into the small talk that didn't come easily to their tongues. The result was that, now, none of them could forget the foundry until they were shut away in the privacy of their own rooms. It couldn't possibly be good for them.

He said as much to Shona next day, and she, sounding less like Drew's mouthpiece than usual, replied, 'You're right. We do live too much in one another's pockets, but Vilia was such a tower of strength to me at first that I wouldn't have known what to do without her. I think that, after the baby comes, Drew and I might find a little house of our own. But don't take Elinor away now, Gideon. However unhappy she may think herself, she needs us, and she isn't very well equipped to manage for herself. In a year or two things will be different.' Reflectively, she added, 'I think it might be good for Vilia, too, to call her house her own again. But in the meantime, I am *sure* Vilia will become accustomed to Elinor, and then everything will be all right!'

Gideon gave her a hug. 'How do you stay so sane in this ridiculous place?'

There was a shy little twinkle in her eyes. 'Because I love you all so dearly, that's how!'

Vilia didn't become accustomed to Elinor. Night after night she sat, hands clasped together, bone white on bone, until no matter how hard they tried to ignore it everyone knew she couldn't stand it for much longer. Then she would rise and excuse herself, and no one would see her again until next morning when, with lagging steps, she would go out to the carriage that took her to the foundry.

With anyone else, the tension would have snapped and there would have been a majestic row, which would have done everyone a great deal of good, Gideon thought. But for as long as her sons could remember, Vilia had held the most inflexible views on courtesy and self-control. It had seemed to them, sometimes, as if good manners were the be-all and end-all of existence. Drew had complained once, when he was about five, 'I don't see why I should be polite to everybody when I don't *feel* polite!' and Vilia had told him, 'Apart from anything else, my dear, courtesy greases the wheels of social intercourse; self-control helps to preserve your self-respect.' It had all been rather beyond Drew at the time, but Gideon, growing up, had found it persuasive. Now, however, her nerves strained to the uttermost, Vilia was unable to see that her own hard-held control was more painful to all of them than the wildest kind of screaming match would have been.

Gideon worried about her a good deal, but there seemed nothing anyone could do. Talking to her was useless. Her only response was to smile absently and say, 'Yes, my dear, I am sure you're right.' Drew, typically, left his worrying to Shona, and all Theo would say was, 'Leave her alone, Gideon. All the tragedies of her life have caught up with her at once – and there have probably been far more tragedies than we know of. But she's strong, deep down, and she'll realize in time that she can't go throwing fits every time Drew and Shona have another child. Let's hope this one's all right, too. Leave her to herself, and she'll pull out of it.'

For once, Theo was wrong. Even after Lavinia was born, a lovely baby, Vilia didn't pull out of it. Instead, three weeks later, she suddenly became worse. Her last reserves of energy deserted her, and she was no longer able even to drag herself to the foundry. She spent more and more of each day in her bedchamber, and after a while gave up joining the others for dinner. It was as if facing the world was more, now, than she could manage.

Gideon and Theo couldn't understand it at all.

4

Magnus Telfer was extremely embarrassed to receive Vilia's letter and wondered if there were any possible way of leaving it to Henry

Phillpotts to answer. That was what secretaries were for, dammit.

Magnus couldn't imagine Vilia tired and unwell, far less admitting to it. He had always found her vitality, her cleverness, her strength of will, rather overpowering. While freely conceding that she was a brave little woman, he liked females to be gentler and more submissive. He sighed sentimentally. Lucy had been such a perfect wife to him, except in one way, and he had never had any difficulty in satisfying his physical needs elsewhere. He'd thought, sometimes, what an admirable arrangement it was, giving him the benefit of variety and relieving him completely of the bedchamber disputes that, according to all his friends, were the bane of married life. He and Lucy had never quarrelled in all the twenty-nine years they had been together. The only thing he had ever regretted was that they hadn't had more children, and even that hadn't troubled him until Luke died. It wasn't that he specially wanted children; he didn't. He had no idea how to deal with them when they were young, and when they grew older they made demands. But as things stood the Telfer money and estates would go to Edward Blair, and Magnus didn't like Edward much. He had been feeling lonely, too, these last years. Although there was a rather dashing high-flyer who was pleased to see him once every week or two, that kind of thing did nothing to dispel the emptiness at St James's Square, or at the neat little house he had bought on the sea front at Brighton.

It was Vilia who had set him thinking, at the beginning of last year. He had escorted her to a party and made some genial remark about what a pleasure it was to have a pretty woman on his arm again. And she had laughed up at him – she really was a very pretty woman! – and said, 'You should marry again, Magnus. You know how well it suits you to be looked after, and Lucy always said you made an admirable husband.'

'Did she?' He had been a little touched.

Considering it afterwards, it had struck him that Vilia herself would do very well in the role of second Mrs Telfer. They had known each other for years, and he thought he ought to marry someone decently mature. He couldn't face breaking in some blushing debutante who had no idea how to run one household, far less three and would probably wear him out by being coy in the bedroom. Especially as there had been one or two occasions lately when he'd needed a bit of help;

regrettable, but only to be expected when one reached the age of fifty-two. No, he didn't want a debutante. There was the point, too, that Vilia had been very close to Lucy and knew exactly what Lucy had done to make him comfortable. By and large, he thought she would do him credit as a wife. Her fair fragility set off his own stalwart looks rather well. They would make a distinguished pair, and she was sufficiently young-looking not to make him look elderly – always a problem, he'd noticed, when a wife aged more quickly than her husband. He couldn't stand seeing well set up fellows of his own age dancing attendance on stout, grey-haired matrons. And Vilia had three sons, so she must know what that side of life was about. It had occurred to him, too, that she might take some of his business problems off his shoulders; he couldn't leave everything to Henry Phillpotts. It would do him a world of good to be relieved of worry, and she would probably enjoy managing things, especially Kinveil, which was always a headache. Yes, he had thought, it was a real possibility. But he wasn't going to rush things. He'd sound her out next time she was in London.

He had understood he would see her on her way back from Paris last September, but she had gone straight home to Marchfield – something to do with urgent business at the foundry that only she was equipped to deal with. He had no doubt she would deal with it very effectively. The nagging little voice in his head grew louder. As a wife, might she not be too efficient for comfort? Magnus couldn't stand people being brisk with him. And perhaps she wouldn't let him have his own way as readily as Lucy had done. Lucy had known that, because of the very fact of his being a man, his judgement must necessarily be superior to hers, but Vilia might not see things in quite the same way. But he still went on feeling that she would be the best wife for him until it occurred to him to work out what age she was. When she had come to live at St James's Square in November 1811, she had been not quite sixteen, which meant that on the ninth of December last she must have been – good God! – forty. Not too old to produce a son and heir, but too dashed near it!

Then, by the greatest good fortune, Magnus had met Julia Osmond, who was twenty-seven and rather like Lucy, not in appearance but in temperament. She couldn't hold a candle to Vilia for looks, but she was calm and placid and had been running her father's house for some years now. Magnus decided she would know just how to make him comfortable, and had wasted very little time in asking her to do so. They were to be married in September.

He looked at Vilia's letter again. '. . . tired and unwell . . . would benefit greatly from spending a few weeks at Kinveil. You said once that you would open it up for me whenever I wished . . . have always felt it too much to ask of you . . . but now my need is great . . .'

He couldn't leave it to Henry Phillpotts, he supposed. And he had to break the news to her some time, so it might as well be now.

'July the third 1836,' he wrote. 'My dear Vilia – I am greatly distressed to hear of your indisposition. It appears to me that you have asked too much of yourself for too many years. The female constitution was not, after all, designed for the rigours that a man may face without flinching. However, I am sure that a period of rest and repose will suffice to restore you.' That part was easy enough, but several rewritings were entailed before he was satisfied with what came next. The final, fair copy that Vilia received three weeks after Drew and Shona's second child was born, went on,

Unfortunately, having already decided to open up Kinveil again, I have thrown in an army of workmen to make good the ravages of the last few years. In consequence, it is not fit to receive you. The workmen will not be finished until September, a date I have set for a purpose – a happy one for me. Remembering your advice that I should marry again, I know you will rejoice with me that Miss Julia Osmond, of Crawley Hall in Wiltshire, has consented to be my wife. Since Miss Osmond is very attached to the country, I anticipate that we will spend the better part of each year at Kinveil.

I hope you may find yourself sufficiently recovered by September to be present at the ceremony in Wiltshire. If not, we will be delighted to welcome you at Kinveil when we are settled in, possibly in the summer of next year. I am sure you will become as attached to Miss Osmond as you were to my dear, lamented Lucy, God rest her soul.

Please accept my sincere wishes for your early recovery, and convey also my regards to my niece Shona and her husband. Yours &c – Magnus Telfer.

5

It was almost six months before Vilia's recovery began.

One day in January 1837 when, sunk in the apathy that had possessed her for she didn't know how long, she was lying listlessly in bed, she heard a howl from Elinor's four-week-old Lizzie and an instant, echoing screech from six-month-old Lavinia. The sounds came from just outside her door, and she knew that the babies' nannies, shushing vigorously, were taking them out for the afternoon walk that all nannies insisted on, torrent, gale, blizzard notwithstanding. This afternoon there was a combination of all three. Vilia couldn't even be grateful that she herself was lying on a warm, soft bed, with candles to repel the gloom, and a pile of new novels beside her that she couldn't summon the interest to open. All she cared about was being left alone in her cocoon, dead to feeling.

Even so, she was hazily pleased that Lavinia was such a healthy child, and quite unflawed. Funny, gurgling, and far more positive than her brother Jermyn. More like Drew than Shona, she thought. And more like the man who had fathered both of them. Even that didn't mean much any more, so that she was able to think about it – just. She couldn't think about *him*, yet, and when she tried to, her mind always slid away on to some other track, or no track at all.

Shona had told her that there was soon going to be a baby in the house on Beacon Street in Boston, and Vilia had managed to say how exciting it would be for Shona to have a new half-brother or sister. She had been distantly proud of herself, as if she had achieved something rather splendid, even if her mind had recoiled from defining what the something splendid was. The news hadn't been unexpected, of course. Considered coolly, it had been as inevitable as the news Grace had just passed on from London, that the new Mrs Magnus Telfer was also in the family way. 'Already!' Grace had exclaimed with uncharacteristic malice.

The world, suddenly, seemed full of babies, and all of them – with the sole exception of little Lizzie – associated in Vilia's mind with her own pain. With the blasphemous alliance between Drew and Shona. With *his* second – third – desertion, worse almost than the first. With her own final severing from Kinveil. Vilia had no doubt that Julia Telfer's child would be a boy; a boy to inherit.

And yet . . . And yet . . .

She turned on her side, her eyes blind to the pretty room with its washed greens and silvers, its graceful furniture, its flowered hangings. She hoped those silly women would have enough sense to bring the girls back in again. And yet . . . All of it, she supposed, meant that there was nothing more the world could do to hurt her; no longer any blow left for Fate to deal.

Laboriously, she considered it. She considered it all afternoon, and again in the evening, after the boys had paid their duty visit before going down to dinner. The past, with its agonies, was past. There was nothing the future could possibly do to her.

She slept that night for four whole hours without waking.

It was a week, still, before she was strong enough to rise from her bed, and almost two months before she ventured downstairs for dinner. She wanted to be sure that she didn't quiver like a frightened mare when Shòna fussed over her, or Elinor mentioned Charleston, or Theo put Drew in his place with some clever, cutting remark.

By April, she was strong enough to write to Magnus and say that she would so much like to make the acquaintance of his dearest Julia, and hoped it would be convenient if she came on a visit at the end of May. Theo insisted on escorting her, although she told him Sorley could look after her perfectly well.

6

Dearest Julia died early in the morning after they arrived, giving birth to a seven-month child. There had been no warning, and the midwife wasn't due for a month or the fashionable London doctor for six weeks. Even the man from Fort Augustus couldn't be found in time.

Magnus hurried across the causeway to greet them in the soft, moist air of early evening. Foliage and grass were tropically lush, and the range of greens almost oppressive. There was no wind, and the rain had lifted a little so that all the insect life of the countryside had emerged from hiding. The midges were swarming – vicious, hungry little bloodsuckers, the plague of overcast days and still water, landing and biting before one even knew they were there. Magnus, sweating with fear, wore them like a nimbus round his head.

'Can you do something?' he gasped. 'Can you do something for her?

She's dying I know she is, and there's no one to help but the servants! You've had three children, you must know what to do. Help her, Vilia. Help her!'

There was nothing she *could* do. The girl who lay on the bed, uselessly swathed in towels and napkins and wadded sheets, her fair hair still braided but her cheeks waxen and her eyes ringed with purple, had been too frightened and too ignorant to let the village women do what might have saved her. 'It wass the wrong way round, Mistress Vilia,' Morag Bain murmured to her. 'And she would not be letting uss turn it because the pain wass too great. She wass screaming and fighting, she wass, aal the time. It iss a miracle the baby iss aal right, but there iss no way that we can stop the bleeding. Poor soul. Poor soul.'

When, at last, Julia Telfer lay straight, still and lifeless under a fresh white sheet, and the child Juliana had been lulled to sleep at Morag Bain's breast, Vilia went out to stand on the sea wall. After a while, Theo, who had been filling Magnus up with whisky, came silently to join her. It should have been dawn, but the sky had turned black as pitch and so lowering that it seemed near enough to touch. Minute by minute, the world closed in around the two quiet figures on the parapet until they could see nothing beyond a dozen yards. And then the rain came, sudden and violent as if it had been emptied out of some cosmic bucket, pouring down the castle walls in great, thick, moiré ripples, like molten lead, until the courtyard was awash and Vilia and Theo as drenched as two corpses from the deep. The lightning followed, wild, brilliant, ragged flashes of it, ripping the sky to north, and west, and then to south, illuminating the five great peaks at the end of the loch with an unearthly glare, flickering so that it seemed almost as if the mountains themselves had begun to move. The thunder rolled and reverberated unceasingly, echoing over water and hills like the ultimate meeting of the upper and the nether millstones.

When it began to die away at last, with Kinveil, miraculously, still standing solid and four-square as it had stood for more than five long centuries, Theo, far from sober, murmured, 'Cheap symbolism, Vilia dear! Come indoors and dry yourself. Remember you have been ill.'

7

A year almost to the day after Julia died, Magnus Telfer came to Vilia and asked her to marry him.

He had recovered well from his third loss in eight years, although there was more grey in his hair, and the well-furnished face was marked with lines that had not been there before. She was a little surprised at the simplicity, and the honesty, of his declaration.

'I have never been a passionate or demonstrative man,' he said, 'and I cannot change now. What I feel for you is warmth, and fondness, and the greatest admiration. Gratitude, too, for the way you tried to help Julia last year. Perhaps you may think that none of this is enough. But there is Kinveil as well, and I know what it means to you. If you consented to marry me, you would have to give up the foundry, but the boys must be able to manage that by now. Will you take me, and my little Juliana, and Kinveil, instead?'

Although in most ways she was well again, there remained a numbness of heart and feeling that she thought, now, might never leave her. She didn't want them to, because they gave her the kind of armour she had been trying to create for herself ever since Mungo died. She had even lost interest in the foundry, which demanded too much of her. Besides, it was right that the boys should be left to fight their own battles without her interference.

Looking at Magnus, with the unfamiliarly open, almost anxious smile round his eyes, she realized that, although two or three years ago she had schemed to bring a marriage with him about, it would have stood, then, only a moderate chance of success. Alive and alert, she would have been bound to try to do things, and probably to manage him as well, and they would have ended by irritating each other beyond bearing. But now, when he knew he needed her, and when she had no more tears to shed, she thought they might do better. Indeed, she thought they might do quite well.

The wedding took place at Kinveil in July, and there was a special gaiety about it, spilling over from the coronation, a fortnight earlier, of the new young queen, Victoria, with all its promise of a brighter future and glittering new horizons.

It was a calm, beautiful day, and Loch an Vele was alive with boats, small and large, some of them sparkling with brass and fresh paintwork, others still slippery with fish scales, but all of them bravely flying flags and bunting. There was scarcely a Highland landowner who hadn't turned up with his family and retainers, and guests had come from as far afield as Edinburgh and London. Georgy and Emile had even made the trip from Paris, bringing little Gabrielle and Guy for a first sight of their mother's native heath. And from all over Kinveil and Glenbraddan the tenants and crofters had come, spruce and clean in their best clothes, travelling in carts or gigs, on foot or on Highland ponies.

After the ceremony in the courtyard of the castle, the invited guests sat down to a magnificent banquet in the Great Hall while the tenants and crofters picnicked on the mainland, and then, at eight, the two parties came together in Kinveil's big stone barn for the traditional *ceilidh*. It was another Mackinnon now – old Dougal's son – who strode up and down outside the barn, but the sound of the pipes, handsomely played, was multiplied and mellowed as of old by the echoes, as the sun went down, burnished gold against an aquamarine sky. The water was like softly creased satin.

Neither Gideon nor Theo nor Drew had ever seen their mother look so beautiful except, perhaps, on that long-ago evening of the royal ball in Edinburgh. And perhaps, Drew said, childhood innocence had invested her that evening with a special splendour. They had never seen her dressed up before, and never so happy. Gideon caught Theo's eye and knew that he, too, was thinking they had never seen her so happy again. But that was not something to remember on this carefree day. Even Elinor, who had achieved a kind of truce with her mother-in-law, had to exclaim over how lovely she looked in the low-necked pelisse robe of palest water-green muslin, with its tiny flower print, and the belt of fresh rosebuds round her waist. There was a nonsensical green ruffled hat on her head, with a single rose under the brim.

Vilia, smiling on her new husband and her family and guests, found her eyes coming to rest most often on the people of Kinveil, all the dear, familiar faces from long ago, many of them old and wrinkled now, and others whom she had known only as children. *Her* people now in reality, as they had always been in her heart. Was she imagining it, or did they all seem especially happy today – because a Cameron had come home again to Kinveil? She caught Sorley's glance. He was forty now, as lanky and freckled as ever, as unobtrusive, as unswervingly devoted as he had always been. She smiled at him, and he smiled back, the blinding, beautiful smile that was associated in her mind with days when she herself had been happy. As if he smiled *for* her, more than at her.

When there was no light outdoors but the afterglow, she slipped out of the barn and across the causeway to the castle. There, alone on the sea wall, she sipped from the glass she had brought with her, and then took a rosebud from her belt. Slowly, carefully, she poured what remained in the glass in a fine, thin stream into the sea, and then dropped the rosebud after it. A sentimental offering to the memory of Mungo Telfer. And to Kinveil.

She stayed only for a moment, and then turned away back to the *ceilidh*. She didn't know whether Mungo would have been disappointed in her, or happy for her. She didn't know, herself, whether she was happy. But at least she was content.

Part Five   *1838–1864*

Chapter One

1

As the fishing smack nosed its way in to the shore, water creaming softly under its bows, Gideon grinned to himself. Ahead lay a wide, magnificent, mile-long stretch of beach, virgin and empty as on the fourth day of Creation – except for one intrusive element.

'Robinson Crusoe, doing things in style,' he murmured.

Vilia laughed. 'You can't think Magnus would forego his comforts merely because of a family picnic?'

She waved, and the figure on the beach raised a stately hand in response. Gideon was irresistibly reminded of some solitary explorer upholding civilization in the heart of the desert, for Magnus was seated on a large, comfortable chair behind a linen-draped table laid out with crystal and crockery; he had a glass in one hand and some kind of *bonne bouche* in the other, and there was a liveried footman standing at attention behind him. Otherwise, there wasn't a soul in sight.

'Not Robinson Crusoe,' Gideon said with a chuckle. 'Ozymandias, king of kings. "Round the decay of that colossal wreck, boundless and bare, the lone and level sands stretch far away."'

'Yes, well,' his mother replied prosaically. 'Don't let Magnus hear you. He may be approaching the colossal, but not even three years of marriage to me have made a wreck of him. Yet.'

Gideon didn't pursue it. From a distance, when one couldn't see his unhealthy colour or the pouches under his eyes, the old boy made an impressive figure. The white shirt, black cravat, and nankeen frock coat lent him a faintly rakish air, and the tall, wide-brimmed straw hat

473

revealed a profusion of grizzled curls over his ears while concealing the fact that, on top, his hair had retreated almost to vanishing point. Defiantly, he had also begun cultivating a moustache which sat on his upper lip like an extra pair of eyebrows. Facial hair was coming 'in', and Magnus prided himself on keeping abreast of fashion. But he was undoubtedly getting fat.

Responding to the small hand that tugged at his, Gideon looked down into the big blue eyes of Magnus's four-year-old daughter. She had been clinging to him ever since they left Kinveil, prey to the unreasoning alarm that the unfamiliar always seemed to rouse in her. There, she was like her father – *very* like her father, Vilia said – although what demoralized Juliana were sights and sounds rather than new ideas or unexpected suggestions. Magnus's automatic rejection of what he wasn't prepared for was becoming a family joke, but luckily Juliana was easier to deal with. Reassurance, for her, consisted quite simply of a strong male hand to cling to. Gideon smiled at her. The waif-like prettiness and big blue eyes, their colour midway between sapphire and cornflower, were irresistible. She was going to be a real honeypot when she grew up.

She said pleadingly, 'Are we nearly there, Gideon? Is that papa on the beach?'

'Yes. Very soon now. Look, he's saying something to Macdonald.'

They watched the footman turn away towards the rocky outcrop at the northern end of the sands, and Gideon added to his mama, 'The question is, has he gone to make sure that the wine is decently cooled, or merely to tell the others we've arrived?' It was a baking hot June day, and he knew what his own priorities would have been.

'Undoubtedly the wine,' Vilia said. 'No one could possibly have failed to hear us coming. Even if they have Grace holding forth on the subject of parliamentary reform, they could scarcely remain deaf to the approach of a seaborne monkey-house!'

It wasn't a bad description. In addition to the crew, the *Maggie May* was carrying six adults – Peter Barber, Theo, Drew, and Sorley McClure, as well as Vilia and Gideon – and six children ranging in age from eight to four. The voyage had been longer than expected since the breeze had suddenly dropped, and the children were on the verge of becoming fractious. Even so, the sail up the coast had been enjoyable, and Gideon was glad he hadn't accepted Magnus's invitation to join the party travelling by road. Magnus was not happy on boats and neither was anyone who was so ill-advised as to sail with him: the thought of Magnus at sea with half a dozen children was very unnerving indeed. Vilia, arranging the expedition, had handled him beautifully, and Elinor and Grace Barber had accompanied him willingly enough, Elinor because her first and only Atlantic crossing had given her a distaste for the sea, and Grace because she considered fishing smacks insanitary. Shona, who would have preferred to be with Drew, had gone with them only for the sake of little Peregrine James, who was too young at the tender age of one to be committed to the mighty deep. The sixth member of the carriage party, Grace's daughter Petronella, had tagged along – as far as Gideon could discover – only because it seemed to emphasize her ten-year-old superiority over 'the little ones'. Yes, Gideon thought again, he was glad he hadn't gone by road. Absently, he wondered if Grace had talked *all* the way.

As the children were being decanted from the rowing boat on to the sand, the girls emerged from the shelter of the rocks; even on such a day as this they had been too concerned with their complexions to yield to the lure of the sun. Elinor was looking exceedingly pretty, her husband thought, in a blue tarlatan gown with flower-sprigged stripes, her mahogany ringlets bunched at the sides under the deep poke of her bonnet. The brim was lined with pale blue, and when she bent to kiss little Lizzie, running across the beach towards her, her skin seemed white as milk. They were much alike in looks and, to some extent, in temperament, for Lizzie, child of northern climes, had acquired some of her mother's Southern languor. It worried Gideon. Languor had a purpose in hot climates, but on this side of the Atlantic it too easily deteriorated into lethargy. Lizzie was timid, too; her father didn't know whether it was because Elinor always complained that her head ached when children were exuberant, or because Lizzie was dominated by Cousin Lavinia, six months older, and a bright, lively, forward little madam. Lavinia was more like Drew than Shona, and more like Vilia than either of them, and Lizzie trailed around in her wake like the rowing boat in the wake of the *Maggie May*.

The picnic was excellent. Afterwards, replete, Theo, Gideon and Drew lay back on the sand, coats and cravats off, near where Magnus sat somnolent in his chair, half in sun and half in shade. The girls had retreated again to the shelter of the rocks, but Vilia, accustomed to being outdoors, was propped against an outcrop, her eyes closed, her softly tanned face turned towards the warmth, and her uncovered hair bleached every shade from cream through topaz to citrine. She looked marvellously exotic, Gideon thought. The children had been dispatched to play among the rock pools in Peter Barber's charge. There had been a faint echo of dissidence at first, when Lavinia, who didn't like being ordered about, had objected to Petronella's telling her to move over so that *everyone* could see the crabs in the pool, but even that had moderated to no more than an occasional sleepy murmur.

Not a cloud marred the sky, and the sea stretched glittering to the far horizon, bounded by a low line of mist that might have been a mirage but was, in fact, the island of Harris, forty miles away. It was the kind of day, Gideon thought, that belonged to childhood – bright, innocent, flawless. Something to treasure secretly in one's heart as an amulet against all that was petty and hurtful in the everyday world. In the eight years since that unforgettable day in Clarges Street, Gideon had begun to understand a little of what Vilia felt about the Highlands, her need for, her sense of one-ness with, the empty places. There had been times when he too, stranger to tragedy though he was, had been aware of strung nerves crying out for refuge. But he didn't think he could ever renounce the rough vitality of ordinary life for the kind of peace Kinveil had to offer, the emotional peace that sprang from rejecting all challenge. Not permanently, anyway – even if, on a temporary basis, Kinveil was unbeatable as a place to restore and refresh the spirit. Idly, Gideon wondered how his mother felt about it now, after three years. Before that, she hadn't spent more than eight consecutive weeks here since she was a child.

A bee droned past, and Gideon opened his eyes, squinting against the brilliance of sun, sea and sand, to follow its progress in search of the tufted heads of sea pinks, rising from their neat green cushions on the rocks. Young Jermyn further down the beach with Sorley keeping a lazy eye on him, didn't even raise his head from the sandcastle he was building. Gideon knew that, although he wasn't yet seven and still wearing a childish smock over his pantaloons, his castle would be neat, intricate, and constructed with an instinctive knowledge of strains and stresses. Was it because Perry Randall's blood ran in both Drew and Shona that they had produced a son who looked set to become a technical prodigy? It wasn't a thought he was inclined to pursue on such a day. As he laid his head down again, Gideon heard Peter Barber's soft voice say to eight-year-old Ian, 'Tell me, Ian, in Greek if you please, what Hesiod had to say about bee-keeping.' The boy's Greek was very good; his father had begun teaching it to him at the age of three. Gideon smiled and drifted off to sleep.

He returned to the present to hear Theo's voice, sun-filled and drowsy, saying, 'Gideon should do it, don't you think?'

Gideon sat up and stretched. 'I disagree. Gideon should not do it. Gideon has enough to do already.' He yawned. 'Anyway – do what?'

'Take over the Telfer chronicle, dear boy. After all, we Lauristons are now part of the family, so it would be legitimate. And who better qualified than you to bring literary distinction to it? Shona herself says that, in twelve years, she hasn't recorded very much, and is perfectly ready to admit that her style lacks that certain something. One *would* like the Telfers to have a chronicler worthy of them.'

Magnus grunted. 'That's true. I can't think Shona's done more than write down a lot of women's gossip.'

Gideon stared at his brother. Show Theo a hornets' nest and he could always be relied on to stir it up, wearing an air of the most perfect innocence the while. Gideon had taken some care to avoid finding out whether Theo still patronized brothels like Mrs Berkley's, but it was clear he hadn't lost his taste for excitement.

Drew looked as if he were about to have an apoplexy, and Gideon intervened hastily. 'Nonsense, Theo. I'm sure Shona is making an admirable job of it.'

But Drew wasn't to be diverted. 'By God, but you've a sly tongue, haven't you, Theo!' he exclaimed, his handsome face scarlet. 'What has literary style to do with it? Shona's spent a lot of time on the chronicle all these years. She's forever writing letters, and filing them, and making notes and God knows what else. She's worked *damned* hard at it and been *damned* conscientious – and look what she gets in the way of thanks!' He glared at Magnus.

Magnus wasn't accustomed to being snapped at. In his world, he was the one who did the snapping. His eyes glazed for a moment, and his chin dropped. Then, looking very much like an offended fish, he replied, 'Don't take that tone with me, young man!'

'I'll take whatever tone I choose, when you're unpleasant about my wife. Your own niece, too. It really won't do, Magnus!'

'Niece? Humph! She's more her father's daughter than she is my sister's.'

'And what do you mean by that?' Drew inquired bodingly.

'I mean her father was a damned irresponsible ne'er-do-well, that's what I mean. And your wife's inherited it.' When Magnus was angry, he cared for no one's feelings but his own. It was one of his least likeable characteristics. 'Never been any doubt in my mind about that,' he went on, clinching his point, 'since she agreed to elope with you. Disgraceful!' As if to signify that the subject was now closed, he leaned his head back and snapped his eyes and lips firmly shut.

Drew, on his feet, breathed in heavily. 'And that goes too far! I am going to fetch my wife, Magnus, *and you will apologize to her!*' He stalked off.

Magnus's nostrils flared, but his eyes remained stubbornly closed.

'Dear me. How very fortunate that duelling has gone out of fashion,' said Theo, his voice at its blandest, adding, in response to an exasperated glance from Gideon, 'Only trying to help, dear boy. Think how useful the income would be to you.'

Gideon had forgotten the income from Mungo Telfer's trust. Useful, indeed. For years now, he had racked his brains to think of some way of achieving financial independence, but because of Elinor and Lizzie had seen no way of cutting loose from the foundry, which paid him a salary and a share of the profits. They couldn't live on the profit-share alone. Even so, Gideon had nourished his hopes by making every preparation he could think of. He had taken on and trained a high-level deputy, Felix von Sandemann, who had been sent over from his family's ironworks in Bohemia to study British methods and was showing a disposition to stay. He was an arrogant bastard, but very efficient. At the same time, Gideon had begun to teach himself shorthand and had written some speculative articles about industrial prospects in America. Two of them had been published. But he couldn't give up the foundry and move to London on the strength of two newspaper articles. More than once, Elinor had suggested that they could live on her dowry until his writing began to pay, but Gideon wouldn't hear of it. The money was hers, he had said, and should be kept for a rainy day. 'Rainy day?' Elinor had wailed. 'Gideon honey, I don't recall a day since I came here that *hasn't* been rainy!' She still hadn't settled to life in Scotland, and Gideon was beginning to think she never would. April was the worst month. He always knew, when he found her gazing out at the grey landscape, shivering in the biting east winds of spring, that she was homesick for warm breezes and the heavy scent of flowers and the plaintive cry of the mocking birds. This April, he had sensed that she was very near to packing her bags and going home to Charleston, and had been dismayed to realize that, if it hadn't been for the fear of losing Lizzie, he wouldn't have minded very much. Although they hadn't yet fallen quite out of love, most of the time they bored each other.

The income from the trust might make all the difference. Gideon didn't know how much it was, but he supposed that Theo did. How badly did Drew and Shona need it? Not too badly, Gideon suspected, for Drew had his sales commission as well as his salary and share of the profits. Even so . . . Gideon decided to remain silent on the matter, or as silent as he was allowed to. He glanced at Vilia and caught her faint, amused smile as she watched Drew returning with a worried Shona in tow. A little distance behind – far enough behind to be tactful, but not so far as to miss anything that might be said – followed Grace and Elinor, their faces expressive of polite concern rather than the very human curiosity that Gideon knew must be consuming them. He held out a hand to his wife, and she sank gracefully down on the sand beside him.

Drew came to a stiff-necked halt before the seemingly oblivious form of his stepfather. 'You were going to apologize, Magnus.'

Magnus drew a long-suffering breath. 'Oh, no, I wasn't! And don't loom over me like that. You're blocking the sun.'

'You were going to thank Shona for keeping the family chronicle, and tell her you didn't mean what you said about her father.'

Magnus opened his eyes. 'In-cred-ible!' he exclaimed on an explosive huff. It was one of his favourite words. 'Anyway, Shona wouldn't *know* what I said about her father if you hadn't told her. It's all of a piece. No sense. Not that I've ever concealed what I think about that fellow Randall. A wastrel. Ruined my sister's life. Bad blood. No sense of responsibility, and Shona takes after him or she wouldn't have agreed to run away with you. Blood will tell, and maybe she can't help it – but what does that have to do with anything? All I say is, you're well suited, the pair of you.'

'You've never liked me, have you, Magnus?'

If there was one thing Magnus loathed more than being contradicted or criticized, it was having a straight question put to him – an odd quirk, Gideon had often thought, because he wasn't usually backward about stating his opinions, whether he knew anything about the subject under discussion or not. Left to himself, he would have been perfectly capable of volunteering the information that no, he did *not* like Drew. But, under pressure, what he did was roll his eyes heaven-ward and say again, 'In-cred-ible!'

Vilia's quiet voice broke in. All she said was, 'Drew!' but there was no mistaking her meaning.

Drew grimaced. 'Oh, very well, mama. Perhaps I shouldn't have said that, but I don't see why Magnus should keep harping on irresponsi-bility. I sincerely hope he's not daring to criticize *my* father, too!'

Studiously, Gideon avoided catching Theo's eye.

Ignoring the latter part of Drew's speech, Magnus said with heavy sarcasm, 'Indeed! You think eloping with an innocent girl is *respon-sible*, do you?'

'Thanks to Edward, yes. We had no alternative.'

They glowered at each other.

Shona, her eyes enormous in the sweet, anxious face, threw herself into the breach. 'You're not being fair, Uncle Magnus. But we don't mind. At least, not very much,' she amended conscientiously. '*We know* we weren't wrong or irresponsible. But I think it's very unkind of you to blame my father for what we did. After all, Grace is his daughter, too, and she has never done anything that even the severest critic could complain of.'

Anyone other than Magnus would have conceded the point, but that would have been as good as admitting that he was wrong. 'Maybe,' he grunted. 'But she's had Peter Barber to guide her, and I expect he's the one to thank for it. *He* doesn't go round flying up in the boughs and contradicting people all the time. He's a good influence, you can see it in the children.'

Grace's face was a study. Gideon, glancing towards her husband to discover whether he had overheard this encomium, was met with a small, controlled smile. It was true that Barber didn't, in fact, make a practice of contradicting Magnus but that was because he was an economical soul who didn't like waste, even waste of breath. Gideon grinned at him.

Drew, just about to take offence at the suggestion that he himself was an unsatisfactory father, closed his mouth resentfully as Vilia forestalled him. 'I think,' she remarked placidly, 'that we have rather lost sight of the point at issue. Shona, my dear, would you be distressed at giving up the family chronicle?'

'No, truly! If Gideon would do it, I should be delighted. He would be so much better at it, too.' She smiled at him. She really was a darling.

Miraculously, Drew held his tongue, and Vilia said, 'If you were to sit down, Drew, we should all feel more comfortable. Thank you. Now, Gideon, what do you think about it?'

'Well, I . . . Yes, I'd be happy and' – he glanced at Magnus – 'and honoured. And if I were to give up my work at the foundry, as I've been intending, I would have sufficient time to devote to it.'

This edited version of his plans had the happy effect of taking Magnus's mind off Drew's delinquencies. 'Give up the foundry?' he echoed, thunderstruck. 'To do what? You'll have to do *something*.'

Gideon wasn't misled into thinking that Magnus regarded him as one of Nature's activists. Biting back a slightly tart rejoinder in which his stepfather's idleness, inherited capital, and income from rents would all have figured, he said merely, 'I hope to write.'

'Good God!' Magnus looked as if he didn't fancy having a writing johnny in the family. 'Can you make a living at it?'

'I hope so.'

'What'll you write? Stories? Not long-winded things like that new fellow – what's his name? Dickens? – keeps turning out. How do people think that kind of thing up? I don't understand it.'

'No, I want to try my hand at reporting, writing about politics, religion, the people of other countries. That's more my line.'

'Well, I hope you know what you're doing.' Clearly, he doubted it.

'So do I.'

'Will you really be able to make a living at it?'

'With application, and perhaps a little luck.'

'You mean fellows like Dickens make a living out of it?'

'Yes.'

'Incredible. A decent living?'

'I imagine so.'

Silence. Then, 'How *do* they think that kind of thing up? Stories, I mean. I don't understand where they get it all from.'

Gideon, only too aware that the inquisition could go on for ever, flicked a glance at his mother, and she came amusedly to his rescue. 'One thing occurs to me about the chronicle, Magnus, if I may just interrupt for a moment? Since Edward still refuses to allow Drew or Shona to set foot in Glenbraddan, it's been difficult for Shona to write as much as she should have done about the Blair side of the family. But Gideon, at least, is on reasonable terms with Edward, so things would be easier for him. And Mungo *did* mean the chronicle to take in Charlotte's descendants as well as yours. What do you think?'

Magnus hesitated only for a moment. Truth to tell, he hadn't until today given so much as a thought to the family chronicle since he had shuffled it off on to Edward, and subsequently Shona, after Luke had died a dozen years before. What did he think about it? He didn't know, and didn't care very much. Restored to humour by the ill-founded belief that he had put young Drew firmly in his place, he said benignly enough, 'There's something in that, certainly.'

As the salmon said when it swallowed the fly! Gideon thought. It looked as if Magnus might be hooked. *Please, Magnus!*

After a century or two, Magnus said again, 'Yes, there's something in that. If the thing is to be done at all, it ought to be done properly.' He looked round to be sure that everyone was properly appreciative of this highly original thought. Only Drew seemed less than impressed, and it was enough to make Magnus's mind up. He said, 'Remind me when we get home, Vilia, and I'll arrange to have everything legally transferred to Gideon.'

'Yes, my dear. Of course,' she replied with a smile.

2

Vilia, at some cost to herself, had become very good at managing Magnus. She had known, before they were married, that she would have to make concessions, and not just the ordinary concessions necessary between two reasonable people who had chosen to live together. They were by no means twin souls, and 'reasonable' wasn't the first adjective that sprang to mind where Magnus was concerned. She had been acquainted with him for long enough to know that he needed specially delicate handling, but she remembered Lucy's technique with him and foresaw no real problems. Admittedly, he was self-centred. Admittedly, he had delusions of infallibility. Admittedly, his temper was uncertain and sudden. But if Lucy Clive had been able to keep him in a reasonably equable frame of mind, then surely she, Vilia Cameron, should be able to do as well. It seemed a small price to pay for the gift of Kinveil.

That had been before she began to live with him twenty-four hours a day, seven days a week, fifty-two weeks a year.

The early days of their marriage had been marked by an almost excessive goodwill on the part of both of them. Right from the start, Magnus had handed over to her most of the responsibility for running Kinveil, remarking sentimentally, 'You, after all, are far better equipped than I am.' That, Vilia had thought drily, was one way of putting it. The truth was that Magnus had a rooted dislike for responsibility of any kind, and was not only prepared but eager to shuffle it off.

Not that she could complain at having her dearest wish granted so readily. In the first few weeks, it had been all she wanted of delight just to be at Kinveil again, to lay her forehead against one of the turret windows and look out over the loch and the village and the mountains, to run her fingers over the smooth-rough walls, to slip out when the dew was still on the heather and walk over the hills for an hour before returning to the castle to oversee the dusting, polishing and repairing that were needed to restore it to what it ought to be. It was a long time before she recognized that, in her walks, she consistently avoided the little hollow in the hillside where Luke Telfer had found her on that autumn day in 1828.

Then she had set about rectifying, with a vigour to which in recent years she had been a stranger, all that had gone wrong on the estate during a decade of carelessness and neglect. Within two or three seasons, she had effected a transformation. The tenants' and crofters' houses no longer leaked. The arable land was properly seeded and weeded. The cattle were fatter and gave more milk. The trees grew more sturdily once the undergrowth had been cleared away. More lobsters were caught, more salmon smoked, more venison sent to the markets of Glasgow and Edinburgh. She had closed down the little alkali factory Bannister had built on the coast in an attempt to exploit the kelp that no one wanted nowadays; far more productive to use the seaweed as fertilizer. Giving in to economic realities, she had even imported a small flock of Cheviots, sending them over to Aberdeenshire to be wintered, so that they didn't ruin the grazing for everyone else. With the wool, she planned to bring cash spinning and weaving to Kinveil, for she was convinced that naturally dyed yarns and handwoven cloth could still compete with the manufactory product.

It was just when everything was going beautifully on the estate that things had begun to go wrong with Magnus. First he had taken to complaining, in a kind of paternally reproving tone, about the money she was spending. She had said, 'But, my dear, once the estate is thriving, it will return the outlay tenfold – a hundredfold!' He didn't understand, or he didn't want to, and for a while she was puzzled by her own inability to convey to him the truth of what seemed to her a perfectly obvious business proposition. Intrigued, despite herself, she had begun to study him more minutely than she had ever studied anyone before.

Until then, she had been too preoccupied with the estate to pay much attention to him. She had made sure that he was comfortable, that nothing occurred to ruffle him, and that she herself was never less than charming and sympathetic in his company. That had been difficult sometimes, because he had an obsessive need to talk and a habit of repeating what he said, not once but several times, as if repetition gave weight to even the most commonplace remark. Since he didn't even have Henry Phillpotts to talk to now – Henry having resigned precipitately as soon as he discovered who the third Mrs Telfer was to be – Vilia was his only audience, and the steady trickle of platitude soon began to affect her like some Chinese water torture. She had managed, however, to smile and appear to be listening, just as she had managed to show wifely concern whenever he found something to complain of, which was often. But since she had always known that he derived a positive pleasure from complaining, she had paid no real attention at first.

When, at last, she did begin to pay attention, she quickly discovered that he was suffering from resentment, strongly tinged with envy. She had been too efficient, and it hadn't occurred to her to hide it – which had been a mistake, for Magnus, it seemed, felt that her talents had the effect of diminishing his. It mattered deeply to him that he should feel superior, and she was making it difficult for him. So, true to her promises – to herself, and to the shade of Mungo Telfer – she had set about becoming the kind of wife Magnus wanted. A little queasily, she had resorted to barefaced flattery when he was pleased with himself about something; she had become deprecating about her own achievements, and as unobtrusive as she knew how in everything to do with the estate. She had even begun asking his opinion about it – and *that* had qualified as self-sacrifice carried to its extreme limit. Magnus, who had never before troubled to ask what she was doing on the estate, now never stopped asking, so that she had to expend a great deal of time and energy and subtlety on manoeuvring him into believing that all her ideas had, in fact, originated with him.

It had been worth it, she supposed, for Magnus's temper, once he felt he was being deferred to, improved considerably.

Except in bed. Vilia hadn't expected to enjoy that, but neither had she expected that Magnus's initial, prideful virility would so soon degenerate into impotence. Even at the beginning, she had found him uncongenial; not gross, but flabby, and heavy, and toilsome. She had tried not to let her feelings show, but within weeks it had all become rather embarrassing. Time after time, when he had worked his way conscientiously through the preliminaries that had the effect, not of arousing her but of boring her into the most complete apathy, he had finished by rolling away with a dissatisfied grunt and a petulant plea of 'tiredness, or something'. She had made all the appropriately soothing remarks about it not being of any consequence, and that these things happened, but it was clear that he wasn't used to them happening so often. She knew that he blamed her, and perhaps he was right. She would have liked to know how he performed with the girl who had succeeded Jinty in the village, but she couldn't very well ask. It was a relief when he stopped coming to her bed. But it was also a kind of death.

It was strange, she sometimes thought, how living with Magnus had proved to be such a natural sequel to the years before their marriage, dulling emotions that had already lost their edge, sealing the last chinks in her armour against the world. For ever? She didn't know. But there were no more agonies now, no more tears, no feelings stronger than acute irritation. She didn't care about anything very deeply, except that she was back at Kinveil, and that Kinveil and its people were thriving. She still wished that it could belong genuinely, and legally, and for all time to come, to herself, not Magnus. Vain wish! But at least she herself was thriving, too; she couldn't remember having felt so unequivocally healthy since she was a child. She didn't feel forty-five, and still found it a little ridiculous that she was four times a grandmother.

Her glance veiled, she looked at Drew, silhouetted against the sea, with the sun rimming his head and bringing out bright highlights in the hair that had become so much darker than his brothers'. She couldn't explain her uneasy sense of *déjà vu*. It wasn't as if Drew was particularly like – him – except in build, and perhaps in something about the mouth and eyes. But she wished he would learn calm and tact. It couldn't be good for him to lose his temper so readily. If he were as choleric as this at twenty-five, he'd be dead before he was fifty. Not like Theo, inhumanly even-tempered, the son who had always been closest to her, and probably knew more about her than she did about him. Though that was partly by her own choice, for she didn't want to know the details of his life. She had enough problems. It was time he was married, she thought. That, surely, should solve everything.

And Gideon? Her over-civilized changeling, who had achieved at twenty-six a quite impressive detachment. She had once heard it said of someone that he would bleed for a nation, but wouldn't pour a pot of tea over you if you were in flames at his feet. That was Gideon. A born spectator.

She smiled quizzically at him as the monkey-house re-embarked. 'Satisfied?'

He smiled back. 'My God, yes. I can't believe it. It's incredible!'

Vilia shuddered theatrically.

3

By the end of the year, Gideon, Elinor and Lizzie were installed in a charming little house in London, and by the end of the following year Gideon had begun to forget that he had ever been anything but a journalist.

He had been lucky. Armed with a folder of beautifully polished specimens of his prose, he had set out in search of commissions, expecting it to be a long haul. But the very first editor he approached had almost fallen on his neck. The *Times-Graphic* was a new weekly, liberally embellished with woodcuts and quite unblushingly modelled on the scarcely less new, but conspicuously successful, *Illustrated London News*. Fanshawe, the editor, had set the whole thing up rather quickly, and the first two issues had brought an exceedingly surly postbag, full of complaints about inaccurate reporting – especially on the industrial front – and slovenly English. So when Gideon walked in – a man who knew all about iron, and railroads, and the structure of industry; who wanted to be a reporter; and who was not only university-educated but literate, by God! – Fanshawe welcomed him with tears in his eyes.

It was a varied life, and Gideon loved it. Fast bowling versus slow at Lord's. The Britannic Universal Alphabet for the Blind. The Thames tunnel from Rotherhithe to Wapping. Her Majesty's first railway journey, with Mr Isambard Kingdom Brunel driving – *very* carefully. Recent railway disasters, which wasn't such fun; Gideon hoped that Theo hadn't taken out a subscription to the *Times-Graphic*. And Mr William Henson's design for a steam-propelled 'aerial carriage' that would take people to China or India in no more than a day or two. Gideon wasn't sure the idea was quite as exquisitely funny as everybody else seemed to think.

Then, in the spring of 1843, Fanshawe sent him up to Edinburgh, where the General Assembly of the Church of Scotland was due to meet. Fanshawe didn't know much about the Church of Scotland, except that it was a good deal more strait-laced than its English counterpart. But his large, red-veined nose was sensitive to more than the fumes of stale beer, and he had heard there were going to be ructions. What he wanted to know was – *interesting* ructions?

Gideon thought for a moment. 'Yes, very possibly. The right to choose a minister for the parish has always belonged to the lairds and landowners, and there are a good many ministers of the kirk who hold their appointments because they're distant cousins of the laird's bailiff, or hard-up youngest sons of some cousin or other. That means they're often English or Lowlanders.'

Fanshawe peered at Gideon over his spectacles. 'So? Does it matter?'

'It matters all right. From a Highlander's point of view, it's little short of blasphemy.'

'What'll happen, then?'

'I think things have reached the stage where half the ministers at the Assembly will walk out. They'll simply secede from the established church – and perhaps form a new one.' He grinned. 'It's an old Scottish custom.'

'Using what for money?'

'That's the question. The lairds will forbid them to use existing church buildings, and they'll certainly be paid no stipend. They'll probably have to preach in the open, and live on voluntary contributions from their congregations.'

'Will they *have* congregations?'

'Oh, yes. The people will follow them.'

Fanshawe's nose twitched, and he emitted the long, squeaky, triple sniff that meant he had reached a decision. 'Fine,' he said. 'The Assembly meets on the eighteenth of May. After that, you can go on a tour of the parishes. What we need is some good, meaty stuff. Plenty of drama. Preachers in their wayside pulpits, Bible-reading in the rain, some of those lugubrious psalms of theirs floating up to heaven on the pure Highland air. It *is* pure, I suppose? Good. Let's have the tears pouring down our readers' cheeks over the sacrifices people will make to have the right to worship their God in any way they choose.' He clapped his hands, making a crack like a pistol shot, and then rubbed them together, palm to palm, with the enthusiasm of a glutton sitting down to a banquet. 'Just the thing, my boy! Just what the paper needs. We've been neglecting the Almighty of late!'

4

John Gunn, minister of the parishes of Kinveil and Glenbraddan, was one of the 451 clergymen who walked out of the established Church of Scotland to form the Free Presbyterian Church on the eighteenth of May, 1843.

Magnus was furious.

Gideon hadn't been near Kinveil for two years, but it had struck him as a good idea to base his final article about the Disruption on its effects in the Highland parish he knew best. He arrived late one evening in October. It had been wet earlier, but now a three-quarters moon was riding high in a clear patch of sky, gleaming on the fallen leaves so that the ground looked like a rippling extension of the loch. Gusty winds shook and rustled the branches of the wild cherry trees and sent grey, fleecy, silver-edged clouds scudding across the sky. The castle might have seemed no more than a black and silver rock in the black and silver landscape if it had not been for the golden pinpricks of candle-light coming from the Long Gallery and the tower.

He found his mother almost at screaming point. 'I don't know whether to be glad or sorry to see you,' she exclaimed, hugging him shakily. 'You're bound to set Magnus off again, and I don't think I can bear it! He was just beginning to run out of steam. He only mentioned the Disruption five times yesterday, and Mr Gunn's ingratitude four. It's been quite awful!'

She was looking tired, and even in the flattering candlelight he could see the lines of strain about her mouth and the heaviness in her eyes. 'As bad as that?'

She led him over to the fire and said, 'Sit down and thaw. Betty will bring a tray up for you directly. Magnus has gone to bed – always the perfect host!' She sighed. '"As bad as that?" Worse, far worse. He hasn't stopped since May, and you know how he goes on!'

Gideon smiled. 'He doesn't like to let a subject drop, certainly. But that's Magnus, isn't it?' For better or worse. Most people had irritating habits of one kind or another, and Magnus's seemed to Gideon to be moderately harmless. He wouldn't have chosen to live with his stepfather, of course, but Vilia must have known what she was letting herself in for. Gideon hoped the pair of them weren't at war, because he had no intention of getting involved. 'I take it he doesn't approve of the Disruption?'

His mother looked at him. 'Gideon, dear, are you perfectly well? You don't have a fever, or anything? *What* a silly question! Of course he doesn't approve of the Disruption. It might, though I doubt it, have been different if our own minister had stayed with the established kirk. Magnus is always prepared to be tolerant towards troublemakers who make *other* people's lives difficult, and it would have given him a good deal of satisfaction for our neighbours to be in a pickle, and us not.'

'That's not a very kind thing to say.'

'Kind!' Vilia almost shrieked. 'It's all very well for you. You can afford to be indulgent and superior when you live six hundred miles away. But you'll see! And don't think you aren't going to hear about it, too, at the greatest possible length. Especially since Magnus thinks it's all my fault. It was *I* who persuaded him to give the appointment to Mr

Gunn. He was far and away the best man – stern and saintly, you know the type. Just the kind of minister to appeal to our people. But *of course* he seceded and *of course* Magnus says that if he'd followed his own inclination and appointed young Ellbert – the dreariest man! – *he* wouldn't have had the gumption to join the Free Kirk and *we* wouldn't have a crisis on our hands.'

Gideon laughed, and his mother said, '*It isn't funny!* Especially as all our tenants and crofters are unequivocally on Gunn's side. And so am I. But I haven't argued with Magnus – *not once!* And I haven't lost my temper. I have been sweet reasonableness incarnate, and it has been a very great strain.'

'Has it had any effect?'

'None.' She shrugged fatalistically. 'Oh, well. You don't want to hear about my woes after your wearying day. Tell me, how are Elinor and Lizzie? You've left them at Marchfield?'

'Yes. Too tiring for them to be dragged around the country with me. I'm going back next week, and then I've promised to take Elinor down to Tim Lawrie's for a few days' hunting before we set off home again.'

When Gideon went downstairs next morning, he found Magnus alone, staring despisingly at his breakfast eggs. Without looking up he muttered, 'Kickshaws! What I want is some rare beef and a mug of ale to wash it down. But your mother says I'm putting on weight, and it isn't good for me. *I* don't think I'm fat. Just a little bit of a paunch, and I'm tall enough to carry it, don't you think? She's just trying to worry me – as if I hadn't enough to worry me already with all this fuss about the kirk.'

'Good morning, Magnus.' Gideon helped himself to some kidneys and bacon from the covered dishes on the sideboard, and sat down. 'May I trouble you for the mustard?'

'Mmmm? Oh. Morning. Sorry I'd gone to bed last night by the time you arrived. I get very tired these days. I don't sleep well.'

'Oh, dear.'

'Your mother says it's because I don't get enough exercise. But where am I supposed to find the energy for exercise when I'm so tired all the time? I ask you!'

'A vicious circle.'

'Eh? Yes, I suppose so. It's worry that keeps me awake. If it's not one thing it's another. Pass me over the bannocks and marmalade, will you? Oh, and the butter, too. Betty Munro never sets this table properly, and your mother's too busy encouraging the tenants to bite the hand that feeds them to have time to tell her.'

Gideon, never at his best at breakfast, sighed to himself. 'Oh, dear,' he said again non-committally.

'You wouldn't believe the ingratitude I've had to put up with! When I think how much hard-earned money I've put into the estate . . . You wouldn't suppose it was asking too much to be allowed to appoint the minister, now would you? That's all I ask. Not their life's blood. I suppose I must be one of the most considerate, easygoing landlords in the whole of the Highlands!' Magnus looked as if he were about to cry. 'But it won't do for them, oh no. It's incredible, quite incredible. And that fellow Gunn. *I* appointed him. *I* gave him a piece of land for his cow and his hens. Dammit, I even invited him to dinner. And what thanks do I get? He walks out, without so much as a by-your-leave. Just like that. The ingratitude of the fellow. It's beyond belief.'

Gideon mumbled sympathetically, through a mouthful of bacon.

'Anyway, he can't complain if I put my foot down, now can he?'

'I shouldn't think so.' Gideon hesitated for a moment, but although he had a pretty shrewd idea of what the answer would be, he knew that Magnus expected him to ask the question. 'What are you going to do?' he said. Ten to one Magnus was going to do what the Duke of Sutherland had done.

He was. 'Well, the fellow can't go on living at the manse, and he can't preach in any of the existing kirks. So when he had the incredible audacity to come to me and demand – yes, *demand* – a piece of land to build a new manse and a Free kirk, I told him, politely but firmly, mind you, that he could take his demands elsewhere. "And don't bother to take them to Glenbraddan," I said, "because Mr Blair is entirely in agreement with me! There's far too much free-thinking around these days. That's what's the trouble with this country! Dangerous, seditious nonsense, that's what it is. Nothing but harm can come of it. Look what happened in France in '89," I said.'

Gideon choked over his coffee. 'I hope Mr Gunn isn't a second Robespierre. I shouldn't like to think of you in a tumbril!'

Magnus snorted. If Vilia's boys weren't being damned impertinent, like Drew, they were being frivolous like this one. Theo was the only one with a decent respect for his elders. 'You never know where this kind of thing can lead,' he said repressively. 'Anyway, Edward and I have settled that we shan't let Gunn have an inch of land either on Kinveil or Glenbraddan. Unless he's prepared to hold those dour, depressing services of his on the roadside or the beach, he'll have to leave the district. And then the people won't have any choice but to go back to the proper church again.'

'Have you found an orthodox minister to replace him?'

'Edward has. He arrived last week. Officious fellow called Abernethy. Not that I'm interested. I've washed my hands of the whole business.'

But he hadn't, really, as Gideon soon found out. When Sunday came, Magnus announced that the entire household, servants and all, would turn out to give Abernethy moral support on the occasion of his first service. It was as well they did, because the new minister would otherwise have been preaching to a completely empty kirk. Afterwards, however, he made the tactical error of reproaching Magnus for his failure to persuade, blackmail, browbeat, or otherwise encourage his tenants and crofters to attend, thus reducing Magnus to a state bordering on apoplexy. 'Fine thanks for turning up to support the fellow!' that gentleman spluttered. 'Especially when I'm an Episcopalian, not even a Presbyterian at all!'

Tactfully, Gideon waited until after lunch, when Magnus went to lie down and recover from his exertions, before saying to Vilia, 'Well, that was instructive in a negative kind of way! If I stay over until next Sunday, can I go to a Free Church service? What arrangements does Mr Gunn make?'

Vilia hesitated. 'Complicated ones. Strictly speaking, he's legally within his rights only if he preaches on the beach or the public roads, but that would be quite impracticable. So he's been holding his services in the hills, sometimes on Edward's land and sometimes on ours. He changes the site every week, but there's always a danger. You remember how stupidly obstinate Edward was about the Clearances, and what the result was? Well, he feels just as strongly about this, and the law of trespass would apply if he chose to take repressive measures. So you mustn't, on any account, breathe a word. Next week is especially important because it's communion, and I should think every tenant and crofter for miles around will be there. I'll come with you –

Sorley will know where it's being held – but I repeat, you must promise not to let Magnus or Edward find out!'

Gideon promised, and on the following Sunday they set out with only Sorley in attendance. By the greatest good fortune, it was a beautiful day, bright and crisp, with a clear blue sky and the hills aflame with autumn colour. Just the kind of day when they might really have been setting out for the hill walk that was their avowed purpose. Magnus, who hadn't been up a hill for years, saw them off with a confident flow of unreliable advice about where to leave the pony cart, and which was the shortest and least exhausting way to the finest viewpoint.

Gideon's mouth opened in astonishment when they arrived at the natural amphitheatre Mr Gunn had found for his service. It was oval in shape, set high above the glen, and bare except for a scattering of firs and a throng of people whose number Gideon estimated at almost three thousand. 'Where have they all come from?' he gasped. 'This must be the entire population for forty miles around!'

Vilia nodded her fair head, with its plain, unobtrusive woollen tam. 'Very nearly. That's Archie Mackay from Fort Augustus over there, isn't it, Sorley? And Donnie Mor and his family from Strome. And . . . Gracious me, everyone's here, and they've all come on their own feet so they must have set out last night.'

In a real church, the communion tables would have been laid out in front of the pulpit and fenced off from the congregation, but today what lay in front of the preaching-box – which reminded Gideon irresistibly of a Punch-and-Judy stand – was an array of plaids spread on the ground. Lacking a fence, Mr Gunn made do with stern exhortations. 'None but they who cleave tae the paths of virtue shall be permitted to approach the Lord's Table. Let me no' see fornicators or whores, or sabbath-breakers, or adulterers, or frequenters of concert halls or dancing assemblies, or other such seminaries of lasciviousness and debauchery. Beware the wrath of the Lord!'

Mischievously, Vilia whispered to her son, 'That means no communion for you, my boy!'

In the last few weeks, Gideon had listened to more kirk services than he had heard in the whole of his life before, and more than he proposed ever to listen to again. He had no religious bent, and was never comfortable in the presence of the devout, largely because although he

493

prided himself on knowing how people's minds worked he had come to the conclusion that they didn't work at all where religion was concerned. He couldn't understand how, in this new, scientific age of the nineteenth century, people could still abandon themselves to blind, unreasoning faith. Especially people who, twenty or thirty years before, had been anything but zealous.

He had asked Vilia about it, knowing her own attitude to be ambivalent, but she had said frankly, 'I don't know. When I was small, everyone's attitude to the kirk was perfunctory, but now . . . Something to do with the spread of learning, perhaps. Well over half the new schools in the Highlands and Islands owe their existence to the Society for the Propagation of Christian Knowledge, or to the Gaelic Societies, which are no less evangelical. No reading, writing or arithmetic, without an equivalent amount of Bible study. But I suspect it's more than that. In the last hundred years the clan system has begun to lose its identity and its purpose. And with the estates changing hands the people can't rely on the lairds the way they used to. The Clearances haven't helped, either. The laird and the clan used to act as a kind of feather-bed for the people, so that there was always someone to turn to. But now there's no one, except God.'

Gideon, from his position on the extreme fringe of the crowd, allowed his eyes to wander over the congregation. People of all shapes and sizes and ages, proclaiming their differences even in the backs of their heads, which was all he could see of most of them. Under the toories and tams and old-fashioned blue bonnets, the men's hair showed grey, black, red, or fair, and the set of their shoulders beneath the coarse dark blue or brown homespun proclaimed six of the seven ages of man; the seventh, the infants, lay mewling and puking in their mothers' arms in the best Shakespearian tradition. Unmarried girls were easy to distinguish since they went bare-headed, their hair neatly braided and bound with a snood of coloured woollen thread, whereas matrons all wore the curtch, a large triangle of white linen tied under the chin. A few of the girls wore garish dresses and amber beads, but most were in sober, home-dyed linsey-wolsey.

'*What* was that?' Gideon suddenly asked his mother. His Gaelic was perfectly up to the demands of everyday conversation, but Mr Gunn's magniloquence went rather beyond the limits of his vocabulary. 'What's he talking about?'

494

'Original sin.' Her face was suspiciously lacking in expression.

'Translate, please?'

'. . . as full of sin as a toad is of poison . . . our hearts are foul sinks of atheism . . . sodomy, blasphemy, murder . . . whoredom, adultery, witchcraft, buggery . . . if we have any good thing in us, it is but as a . . . drop of rosewater in a bucket of filth.'

'Yes,' Gideon said. 'Thank you very much. I wonder why he left out cannibalism?'

There were prayers, then psalms with the congregation following the precentor line by line, then more prayers, more psalms, more exhortations. After two-and-a-half hours Mr Gunn gave himself and the congregation a breather preparatory to starting all over again in English.

Gideon, casting a hungry eye over the picnic Sorley was unpacking, noted that it wasn't up to Kinveil's usual standard. Oatcakes, cheese, and two flasks of straw-coloured liquid.

'No cooking on the Sabbath,' Vilia said. 'No gluttony or other excess, and no fetching water from the well. I forgot to remind you not to wash or shave this morning, either.'

Contemplating the flasks, Gideon said, 'But drinking is all right?'

She looked at him with exaggerated surprise. 'Of course! Everyone knows that yesterday's water is flat and unhealthy, so that one must put plenty of whisky in it to render it wholesome. You and Sorley can share that flask between you. The paler one is mine. White wine.'

Gideon hadn't much cared for Mr Gunn in the Gaelic, and in English he was even less attractive. Gaelic was a guttural, muscular kind of language, but although the native Gaelic-speaker, by some strange alchemy, developed a soft and rather pleasant lilt in English, Mr Gunn wasn't a native Gaelic-speaker. In both tongues his voice was harsh, and now that Gideon was able to understand him better, he discovered that his mind was made to match. Of the many secessionist ministers Gideon had listened to, this thickset, florid man, with a mouth like a rat trap and a head of hair as creamy white and tightly curled as a cauliflower, was easily the most frightening. It was bigotry such as his that had sent men to be broken on the wheel and stoked the fires of the Inquisition, Gideon reflected, casting a sideways glance at Vilia and wondering how she could give her support to such a man. But she had said he was the kind of minister the people trusted, and that was what mattered.

And there the people still sat, all three thousand of them, listening to Mr Gunn's tirades in a sober, concentrated silence broken only by an occasional wail from a baby or snarl from the dogs.

Then, all of a sudden, things began to look up. 'The unrighteous shall perish,' thundered Mr Gunn, 'and the fires of Hell shall be fanned for adulterers and fornicators.' His arm shot out, pointing. 'For folk like *you*, Angus Macdonell!'

Every eye swivelled in the direction of his finger.

'Aye, you, Angus Macdonell! For the Lord's gaze is upon you. *He* saw you sneaking into yon house on Mearns Street when ye went up tae Inverness last week – yon house where lewd women are permitted to dwell, to the everlasting shame of the provost and corporation!'

There was no mistaking the unfortunate Angus, sitting about half-way back and slightly to the side of the congregation. The nape of his neck was scarlet, and the woman beside him was looking at him with an expression that suggested he wasn't going to have to wait long to meet his doom. No longer than it took her to get him home.

The minister's arm changed direction. 'And you, Maggie Tosh, with your bairn in your arms and you wed not three months past! Woe unto you, you lightsome woman! The Lord's eye is upon you, too, and dinna you forget it!'

Mr Gunn's own eye roved for a moment, and then – while the congregation began to look exceedingly shifty – pounced. This time it was Archie Macpherson, guilty of playing golf on the Sabbath; and then Mary Maginty of the whoreson smile; and Ellie Meikle, who practised abominations with eggshells and mutton bones. 'Beware the wrath of the Lord!'

Gideon, quite unable to imagine what kind of abomination anyone could possibly practise with an eggshell, turned to Vilia for enlightenment. 'Fortune-telling,' she murmured.

It was at that point that Mr Gunn turned his attention to absent friends – in the persons of Magnus Telfer and Edward Blair. He had a fine talent for invective when his heart was really in it, and no nonsense about turning the other cheek when someone offended him. Magnus had offended him considerably. 'He will not, devil's spawn that he is, consent to see the light, but clings like a barnacle to yon rotting hulk that calls itself the Established Kirk, yon midden, yon rubbish dump of the carnal-minded and the dead of soul, yon apology for a kirk, wallowing like a sow in the mire of Erastian heresy.'

Gideon, sorely tried, succeeded in keeping a straight face, though he didn't dare glance at Vilia to see how she was taking it.

'Idle, impious and parsimonious . . . cock on a dunghill . . . offspring of Belial . . . pride and self-glory that will turn into a reproach and a hissing . . . Vengeance is mine, saith the Lord; I will repay!'

With horrified delight, Gideon waited to hear what Mr Gunn was going to say about Edward, but, in the event, it wasn't funny at all. 'Five bairns has his wife failed to carry to their full term, and the boy that lived, lived but for ten years in a state of idiocy. There is none to follow Edward Blair but a wee lassie. You would think, would ye not, that the warnings of the Lord had been clear enough? But Edward Blair hasna heeded them . . .'

Gideon had just turned to Vilia to comment, with distaste, on Mr Gunn's total disregard for human decency, when he saw her mouth open in blankest astonishment. Then the minister's voice roared, 'And that a woman from this impious family should defile the kirk by being here today is a blasphemy against the Lord's name!'

He was pointing fully at Vilia. Her mouth closed again with a snap, and the hot colour flooded to her cheeks only to drain away as swiftly as it had come.

'A woman contaminated by contact with sinners like these – aye! But a sinner in her own right, too!'

Vilia's face was unreadable, but Gideon knew that her mind must be racing, as his was. What the hell did Gunn know? He was hideously well informed. And whatever he knew, nothing was going to stop him telling three thousand people about it. Gideon listened as if all five of his senses were merged into his hearing alone.

The minister started off innocuously enough. 'It is the duty of a wife to persuade her man against unrighteousness, to lead him into the paths of sanctity. Only that way can she atone for the sins of Eve, yon first accursed woman who led Adam astray, and all men after him. But does Mistress Cameron do any such thing? No! Born herself a child of these parts, bound by her paternity, and by tradition, and by the Lord's command to cherish her people as if they were the bairns of her own body, yet has she failed them! Failed to persuade her man to see the light. Failed to make him forsake the trimmers, the time-servers, and follow the Free Kirk of the Lord.'

Very gently, Gideon began to let out his breath.

'Failed to bring him round to the knowledge that the onus lies on him to give to me, the Lord's anointed, and to you, with whom his bounden duty lies, even a few paltry yards of the Eternal Father's soil for the building of a kirk for His worship and a manse for His minister!'

Mr Gunn had an axe to grind, and the sound of it was sweet to Gideon's ears. As long as he was more interested in squeezing a few acres out of Magnus than he was in Magnus's wife's personal imperfections . . .

'You would think, would you not, that sins like these would be enough for any woman? But are they? No, I tell you, they are not.'

Gideon closed his eyes. He could feel Vilia, beside him, taut as a bowstring.

'You would think, would you not, that it was enough to fail to lead folks into the paths of righteousness? But this woman, like her sister Eve, beckons them into the paths of evil. There can be – *there can be, I say!* – no more flagrant proof of defection from the way of the Lord, no more sinful opening of the floodgates of licence, no fouler blot on the pure faith of the Gospels than what this woman has seen fit to lend her name to!'

Vilia's gasp was scarcely audible. It sounded to Gideon, for a disbelieving moment, as if she had choked back a laugh.

She had. For the next word that the minister bellowed was, 'Dancing!' Gideon blinked.

'Promiscuous dancing! This woman, no more than three weeks since, flaunted her name at the head o' a piece of paper wanting folks to buy tickets for *a ball* in Inverness! Patroness, she called herself! Patroness of an assembly for that profane and dissolute pastime practised by the Israelites during their base and brutal worship of the Golden Calf at Bethel! Practised by that unhappy lass who danced the head off John the Baptist! Practised by yon perverts of Sodom and Gomorrah before the Lord in his wisdom rained down fire and brimstone upon them as they jigged away to their fiddlers' tunes! Did the fiddle strings themselves not vanish in flame, and did all those unnatural sinners for a distance of thirty miles around not pay for their iniquities? For the Lord made them fry in their skins! But this woman – aye, you, Mistress Cameron! – this woman lent her name to these selfsame intemperate, lewd and lascivious practices. Take heed, woman! Take heed, for the Lord's eye is upon you!'

Without moving her lips, Vilia murmured in a tone of hurt remonstrance, 'But it was a *charity* ball, Mr Gunn, dear.'

And at last the minister's tone changed, and it seemed he was coming to an end.

His voice flat, and the words contemptuously spaced, he said, 'There may be some among you who say that, in the past, this woman has done you a kindness. But *I* say to you that whatever shows like goodness in her or hers, it is nae mair nor the light that shines from a creeping insect on the braeside at night. Bright in the dark, aye! But when the morn comes and the sun rises, you see that it is but a crawling kail-worm after all. Be not deceived by the Philistines and the Pharisees, but see their kindness for what it is – a hypocritical mask on the sour and raddled face of anti-Christ. We will now say the Lord's Prayer. Our father, which art in heaven . . .'

Offensive and vulgar! Coming from Mr Gunn, what else? But not damaging. Gideon, feeling as if his nerves had been scrubbed, wrung out, and hung to dry in an equinoctial gale, took a deep breath and, turning to his mother, said calmly, 'Can we go now?'

5

It was an index, Gideon realized later, of the tension Vilia had been under for the last few months that her amusement over Mr Gunn's denunciations didn't sound convincing. Although her mouth smiled and her brows lifted in mock affliction as she recalled special gems from the minister's invective, her eyes were dark and opaque. Her son thought drily that, deep down, she was as resentful over the minister's ingratitude to her – who was on his side – as Magnus had been with less justification.

Gideon's own mind was churning as he tried to sort out his impressions of the service and the congregation, and his head felt full of words, not only the preacher's but the ones he himself was going to use in his article for the *Times-Graphic*. He knew instinctively that it would be the best thing he had ever written. The moment they got back to Kinveil, he would have to start getting it all down on paper. And then he remembered, irritably, that Magnus would be suspicious if he sat down to scribble busily after what had supposedly been an innocuous day's fresh air and exercise in the hills.

It was almost dark when they reached Kinveil, and Magnus took it as a personal affront that they had been out for so long. 'Never been able to understand what's so wonderful about struggling up a hill just to look at a view. I ask you, Gideon, do *you* understand these fellows who go in for climbing mountains just because they're there? Silliest thing *I* ever heard. Your mother says it's the challenge, and the mental and – what was it, Vilia?'

'Mental and bodily discipline.'

'Oh, yes. That's right. Mental and bodily discipline. But I don't see it myself. Fancy putting yourself to all that discomfort when there's no useful purpose in it. It's incredible. Beyond belief.'

'Every man to his taste, my dear,' Vilia murmured. 'You'll forgive me if I go and change.'

Gideon sensed impending trouble all the way through dinner, though Magnus was as impervious as always, prosing on about nothing in particular with the relentless fluency of one who knew that his every word was worth more than rubies. His pauses were traps even for the wary. His voice was inclined to drop at the end of a sentence, making it sound – especially to two people who weren't listening to him – as if he had finished what he was saying. Sometimes he waited long enough for Vilia or Gideon to open their mouths before cutting them off in mid-breath by resuming his monologue. Sometimes he even went so far as to allow them a sentence or two, before taking advantage of the first opening to go on, reprovingly, 'So what could I say to the fellow after that, except . . .'

For the first time, his own equanimity frayed by tiredness and strain, Gideon had a glimpse of what Vilia must have been through in the last five years. Until this evening, he had suffered Magnus with a kind of amused resignation, taking wagers with himself as to what Magnus's opinion would be on any given subject and, when that palled – as it soon did, for he was tiresomely predictable – experimenting to see if there were any way of diverting him from his chosen subject, short of getting up and walking out of the room. There wasn't. Magnus would have made an excellent politician, for he had the born politician's gift for moving sideways from any question he was asked, in such a way as to enable him to answer the question he would have *preferred* to be asked. With a mental shrug, Gideon had accepted the inevitable and learned how to listen to Magnus while devoting his mind to other matters.

But tonight Magnus was remarkably difficult to shrug off. Although Gideon had noticed, often enough, that he tended to become less blandly assured and more dogmatic as the wine level in the decanter sank, he hadn't previously sensed the note of petty viciousness. Was the old boy more alive to other people's moods than one gave him credit for? Yet although Vilia's nerves were undoubtedly overstrung, she was behaving impeccably. When Magnus declared, idiotically, that these new adhesive postage stamps were damned unhygienic and probably responsible for half the disease in the country, what with people licking them, and so on, she merely said, 'But only one person licks them, my dear.' Though her tone was perfectly – indeed, commendably – polite, Magnus snapped back at her as if she had offered him a deliberate insult.

Later, in the Long Gallery, she went to a cupboard for the chess set, and Magnus, perfectly aware of her intention, stayed where he was, blocking her way. With a smile, she said, 'Excuse me, my dear. I'd like to get into that cupboard.' He jerked away. 'Well, *I* don't know what you're doing, do I? You might have been going to fetch my newspapers for me. But you wouldn't think of that, would you? Oh, no!'

Wordlessly, she handed him the topmost of the pile of newspapers that always arrived on Saturdays. It was the wrong one, of course. 'I've read that one. You just don't think, do you? It's Wednesday's I want.'

'Is it? I'm sorry.'

For a few beautiful moments there was silence, broken only by the almost inaudible sound of Vilia setting up the chessboard and the rather more audible crack of Magnus shaking out the pages of his newspaper.

Gideon studied the board, looking forward to an hour of peaceful concentration.

'Well, *that*'s something to be grateful for!' Magnus exclaimed.

Automatically, Vilia responded as he expected of her. 'What is?'

'That agitator fellow, O'Connell. The Irishman. You probably don't know, since you never read the papers . . .' Vilia's lips tightened.

'. . . but he cancelled a mass meeting in favour of Repeal of the Union with Ireland at Clontarf last month. It says here they've arrested him. Conspiracy and sedition. Splendid! I hope they hang him.'

Gideon, catching his mother's eye, swallowed his startled objection and turned his attention back to the board again.

Magnus flapped over another page, and Vilia made her opening move. Gideon, recognizing the gambit, grinned at her as he reached for his pawn.

'Incredible!' said Magnus. 'Gideon, you know that fellow Mathews, that priest who was preaching temperance all over London last month? It says here that he gulled half a million people into signing the pledge. It's outrageous. Shouldn't be allowed. Fellows like that should be stopped. The government should do something about it.'

'Yes,' Gideon said peaceably.

'Damned dangerous nonsense, this teetotalism. You never know what things like that can lead to.'

'No,' Gideon agreed.

'It's all these dissenters and nonconformists, you know! A deliberate attack on the whole fabric of the country, trying to undermine the established institutions.'

'Yes.'

Magnus sniffed, and relapsed into silence again.

After a while, Gideon became aware that his stepfather had trans-ferred his attention from his newspaper to the chess game, possibly – Gideon thought uncharitably – because the chessmen provided a larger and clearer focus for his slightly inebriated gaze.

'There you are!' he exclaimed suddenly. 'If you hadn't moved your knight, Vilia, Gideon wouldn't have moved his.'

The truth of what he said was incontrovertible. Vilia smiled.

Then, 'It's a dull game, chess,' Magnus announced, not troubling to smother a yawn. 'I've never seen any point in it. Do you really enjoy it, Gideon?'

'Yes.'

'I can't imagine why. Never understand what people find in games like that.' There was a gurgling sound as more brandy disappeared down his throat. 'Play cards much?'

'Sometimes.' Gideon, trying hard to concentrate, moved a pawn.

'Funny how people can get obsessed with card games. I've seen fellows sit playing whist for hours at a stretch. You'd have thought their lives depended on it. I don't understand it. I've never found cards very interesting.'

Vilia's hand, hovering over her bishop, had begun to tremble slightly.

Gideon knew how she felt. Moving his queen, he said, 'Check.'

'Beating her, are you?' Magnus asked with satisfaction. 'Good for you. Won't do her any harm. She always wins when she plays with me. I'm not interested in chess, you see, so I never really work at it. It would be different if I did, of course.'

Vilia's concentration on the board was almost tangible.

'Look at her! Poring over it like that. And it's only a game. That's one of the reasons I don't care for it much. People take it so seriously. You can't even make a casual remark without getting your nose bitten off. Very boring, I think.'

Picking up his knight, Gideon found that his own hand was shaking, and was aware of a powerful desire to pick up the board and clout Magnus with it.

Magnus remarked, 'It's supposed to be good mental exercise, don't they say?' There was no mistaking the scorn in his tone, even through the slight thickening of alcohol. 'Did they teach it to you at school, Gideon?'

Gideon took a firm grip on himself. 'They didn't have to. Vilia taught us all when we were quite small. In any case, it would have come a pretty poor second to natural science and geometry and logic and navigation, and all the other subjects they were concerned to din into us at the Academy.'

But Magnus wasn't listening, although he did have the courtesy to wait until Gideon had finished before he said, 'Talking of school, there's something I forgot to tell you, Vilia. You know our parish schoolmaster joined those pigheaded Free Churchmen? More fool he. Well, I hear he's been dismissed for it. That'll teach the fellow!'

There was a small, sharp clunk as Vilia, white-knuckled, slammed her king down on the board. Her voice tight, she said, 'And what happens about the children's education?' The atmosphere, suddenly, wasn't just irritable.

Magnus looked at her glassily. 'How should I know? They'll send someone else, I suppose.'

'And do you think Free Church parents are going to send their children to an Established Church schoolmaster?'

'How should I know?' Magnus said again. 'Anyway, that's their problem, isn't it?' He rose to refill his glass.

Vilia watched him, her green eyes ice-cold in a face suddenly turned white. Gideon could feel her struggling to control herself.

Magnus had difficulty lining his glass up with the neck of the decanter, and some of the brandy spilled on to the tray.

Of all his stepfather's more trying characteristics, Gideon had always found least supportable his habit of reacting to pettifogging irritations as if they were mortal insults. A teaspoon slipping out of his grasp was enough to rouse him to fury, as if the whole world, animate and inanimate, had entered into some kind of conspiracy against him. He would turn scarlet, and his face and voice would begin to shake, and he would blurt out a string of extraordinarily silly complaints. The teaspoon was badly designed, or slippery with grease, or not properly dried, or too well polished. His spurts of rage were quickly over, but they induced in Gideon, brought up to regard self-control and courtesy as the first of the ten commandments, an almost physical revulsion.

Now, watching the spilled brandy drip from the base of his glass, Magnus ran true to form. With more energy than he ever displayed in any useful cause, he pulled a handkerchief from his pocket and began to mop furiously at the tray, exclaiming, 'Why are there never any cloths when they're needed! This stupid decanter never pours properly. The lip's badly designed, and you can never get a decent grip on the neck. How's anyone supposed to pour from it, I ask you! I've been telling you to throw it out for years, but you never pay any attention, do you? Oh, no! It's got the Cameron crest on it, so that means it has to be perfect, no matter what *I* say!' He threw the sodden handkerchief down on the tray, and raised the glass to his lips.

Finally and irrevocably, Vilia's temper snapped.

There was release from five years' self-discipline in the violence with which she jumped up from her chair. It toppled over with a crash, and Magnus turned, the automatic grievance springing to his lips and the high, swift colour returning to cheeks from which it had just begun to fade. But she didn't, for once, allow him to have his say. Instead, her voice rose high-pitched and bitterly angry over his.

'You don't care, do you! It doesn't matter to you if the children grow up illiterate because of some idiotic quarrel between fanatics who don't even know what true Christianity is about. All they're concerned with is proving *they* are right. All *you're* concerned with is that your side should win. Because that will allow you to feel superior, won't it, Magnus? *What have you ever done, to be superior?* What do you ever do but wallow in your own self-esteem? What do you know about ordinary people's struggle for existence? What do you know about anything other than your own comfort? *Nothing, nothing, nothing!*' Her voice searing, she went on, 'Oh, yes! You're a big man, Magnus. You're rich and handsome and distinguished-looking. You're good at impressing people who don't know you. But inside, you're still only four years old, a spoilt little boy who thinks the world has been made for his convenience. You've never grown up, and you never will. Because you don't want to. I thank God – *how* I thank God! that your father isn't alive today to know what a hollow man you have become.' Her voice was breaking, and she was quivering from head to foot.

Gideon, almost as stupefied as Magnus, stared at her. Never in his life had he seen her in a rage, and he didn't like it. Yet even while he sympathized – within limits – he wasn't going to be involved in what promised to be a very nasty quarrel. Hoping he would be allowed to get away with it, he rose to his feet and made for the door. He was almost there when his mother's voice rapped, 'Gideon! Where are you going?'

'I – er . . .'

'Stay!'

Magnus, looking very much like an outraged cod, suddenly found his voice. 'So that's what you think, is it? My, but you *have* changed your tune. I wonder what happened to all that sweetness and charm you had when you were so anxious to marry me? You don't need it, now you've got what you wanted. I know you think I'm stupid, but I've always known it was Kinveil you wanted, not me. Don't interrupt!' He stopped for a moment. 'Perhaps you're right, though, in a way. Perhaps I *am* stupid. I was always surprised you'd stayed a widow for so long. It didn't dawn on me that other men had too much sense to ask you to marry them. They must have seen what I didn't – how self-centred and arrogant and *cold* you are under all those fine looks!' It was obvious that he thought he had scored with the word 'cold'. His tone was hectoring as he went on. 'But just take care what you say to me! Don't dare criticize, and don't ever raise your voice to me again. Just remember whose house this is, because if you don't, by God I'll make you sorry for it!'

Vilia laughed. It wasn't a pleasant sound. 'You'll make me sorry for it? *How*, you stupid man? There hasn't been an hour in these five years when I haven't been sorry I married you. If you tried from now until Doomsday, you couldn't think of any way to make me sorrier than I already am!'

'Oh, couldn't I?' His mouth was viciously tight. 'Just remember that I hold the purse strings, madam! You live here because I permit it. I pay for every stitch on your back and every mouthful you eat. I can throw you out of this house any time I want. What would you do then, eh? Go back to your wonderful sons at Marchfield? I wonder how pleased *they*'d be to see you back after five years of having things their own way? Oh, no. Make no mistake about it. You need *me*. But I don't need you!'

Be careful! Gideon willed his mother not to give Magnus the answer that must have sprung to her mind, as it had done to his. For before she had married Magnus she had made arrangements to safeguard her independence. Gideon wasn't supposed to know about them, but Theo had told him. 'Our mama is not a fool, dear boy. Anything but. She doesn't trust Magnus, and who can blame her? So she has set up an arrangement to cover almost three-quarters of her capital – in my favour, though not outright. Can it be', he had wondered mournfully, 'that she doesn't trust me either? Ah, well. It's all exceedingly complicated and terribly, terribly legal. Ingenious, too. The income comes to me for seven years – nominally, of course. I imagine she'd have a fit if I were to spend it. And at the end of seven years, she can review or revoke it. A very pretty notion, and it means that she will be able to stalk out of Magnus's life whenever she feels inclined. Always remembering that she would have to stalk out of Kinveil, too, about which she might be more hesitant.' Gideon had been not only amused but admiring. It had always seemed inhuman to him that a married woman's property should belong, in the eyes of the law, absolutely to her husband.

To let Magnus find out would be disastrous. As long as he didn't know, there remained some possibility of patching up the quarrel, and Gideon knew that, for the sake of Kinveil, Vilia *would* patch it up when she recovered her equanimity, no matter what it cost her in strain and nervous tension and secret grief. Kinveil. Her dark and distant shore, her haven and her grave. Remembering the words, Gideon felt a shiver run through him. But, strangely, they reassured him, too. This outburst was too uncharacteristic, too unrelated to the things that really mattered, to have any lasting effect – even if it would take some time to smooth Magnus down again. Magnus, Gideon supposed, must never have seen Vilia in a rage before.

He, himself, couldn't even remember seeing her helplessly upset except on two occasions on the night when the Duchess was dying, and again, a few months later, on that harrowing day in Clarges Street. Even in his most private thoughts, he never defined The Day more clearly than that. A funny thing, emotion. With the vast majority of people, Gideon believed, emotion dominated the mind. In the case of the minority – among which he included himself – it was the mind that was in control. Now, for the first time, he wondered whether he was inclined to over-simplify. Was there another group of people for whom mind and emotion existed in a state of balance? He knew that Vilia's feeling for Kinveil was emotional, but he suspected that her mind was capable of assessing the fact; that she knew, coolly and rationally, how obsessed she was. He *thought* that she had learned to accept it. But had she, perhaps, begun to make concessions to her emotions in the interests of peace of mind? To feed them deliberately, as one might lay out rabbits to divert the golden eagle from the new-born lamb, or tie out a goat to divert the man-eating tiger?

He blinked. Perhaps, he thought, himself a little light-headed after too much fresh air and too much tension, Magnus wasn't the only one who'd had more than enough to drink. Certainly, Vilia wasn't going to tip rat poison into Magnus's brandy! Although, if the old fool tripped on the stairs, Gideon had the feeling she wouldn't precisely rush to save him.

Showing scarcely a sign of her forty-eight years except for the tiny lines, shallow but incised now for life, round the eyes and at the corners of her mouth, Vilia stood there and confronted her husband. Her eyes, as luminous and green as they had ever been, glittered inimically in the candlelight. 'So you think you don't need me, Magnus? You don't even need me to run the castle, and manage the servants, and deal with the estate, and pamper you, and give in to your whims, and listen to your endless monologues? Well, we'll see. I'll give you the opportunity to find out. Gideon is returning to Marchfield tomorrow, and I will go with him. I'll take Juliana with me.' Surprisingly, Magnus made no protest. 'I don't know how long we'll be away. Certainly for a few weeks, possibly for some months.'

'Good!' Magnus responded with an exaggerated sneer. 'I won't sit up for you. G' night, Gideon.' Turning, he made his slightly unsteady way towards the door.

He almost collided with Sorley, who was just outside.

Sorley looked after him, his face expressionless.

'Damn you, Sorley!' Gideon exclaimed, venting some of his nervous unease. 'Have you been listening at the Laird's Lug?'

'Would I do that, Gideon?'

'Like a shot!'

There was a scarcely perceptible crinkle of amusement about Sorley's narrow hazel eyes as he turned to Vilia. 'I came to ask if you wanted anything before I smoored over the fires for the night?'

'Yes,' Vilia said. 'I want my maid and Juliana's nurse here, right now. And pack your own traps. We're leaving for Marchfield in the morning, and we'll be away until New Year at least.'

'Yes, mistress.'

Chapter Two

1

As she picked her way through the iron jungle of the engineering shop, Vilia had to fight hard to still the fluttering in her diaphragm and the scurrying chaos in her head. The place was full of unfamiliar hazards, of massive chains, hooked and lethal, hanging from the roof; giant cogwheels, relentless as the mills of God, revolving within inches of her skirts; great pistons thudding with the undeviating violence of anvil hammers in some steam-powered hell. There were machines crammed into every available foot of floor space, and a great many men she had never seen before, who glanced at her curiously before they turned back to the job in hand. The smell was suffocating, a compound of hot metal and axle grease and dust and unwashed humanity, and the noise and vibration shook the earth, the air and the walls, making

Vilia feel as if her very bones were rattling in their sockets and her brains ricocheting around in her skull.

The engineering shop was Theo's pride and joy, and all the machinery in it was new. The strangeness, here, didn't surprise her. But elsewhere she had been taken aback to discover that she had forgotten the unforgettable. The sheer, naked savagery of the foundry, the heat, the glare, the stench and the din, had hit her with an impact as brutal as on that day in 1814 when her father-in-law, Duncan Lauriston, had introduced her to it for the first time. Later, during the twenty years when this had been her world, she had learned the trick of subordinating the whole to the parts, disciplining herself into a kind of selective awareness so that, in the end, she had been amused by the undisguised horror which was most visitors' reaction to it, and their greater horror at the thought of a delicately bred woman being exposed to it day after day, week after week. But she had been away from it all, in the flesh, for five years now, and in the spirit for three years before that, and she had lost her immunity. Even so, she wouldn't have thought it possible for her to feel like this – stunned, panicky, irrelevant – in a place that had once been so much her own.

It wasn't only the foundry that was doing it. The man who walked beside her was partly to blame, for although in looks, style and background Felix von Sandemann bore not the slightest resemblance to Duncan Lauriston, his manner recalled the old man unequivocally to her mind. Her initial encounter with Gideon's successor had taken place, accidentally, just inside the main gate, and had been stiff and exceedingly stilted. Even while she scrupulously made allowances for his English, she had been annoyed over having to introduce herself to an employee in her own foundry. She had, perhaps, been a little abrupt with him. But gradually it had begun to dawn on her that the trouble lay not with her, nor indeed with his grasp of the language, but with his attitude towards her. Under the automatic courtesy was something that might have been impatience or irritation but, she realized with sudden, speechless fury, was more like contempt. Did he – *dared* he? – consider her as no more than a nuisance of a woman, the interfering mother of the men who employed him?

The effect was curiously demoralizing. Vilia was long past the age of being upset by other people's antipathy; making enemies was a normal business risk, and only the incompetent could be assured of universal liking. But the people who had hated V. Lauriston, ironmaster, had also respected her – and Felix von Sandemann didn't. She wished very much she had told Theo she was coming today; she hadn't, only because she had hoped to get the feel of the place again on her own, and wanted no ironically solicitous guide at her elbow. She couldn't have foreseen that von Sandemann would wish himself on her instead.

He said something that she didn't catch. 'I beg your pardon?' But she seemed to have lost the ability to pitch her voice on the level that, effortlessly, cut through the clamour, and had to repeat herself on something very near a shriek. *'I beg your pardon?'*

'We have in the forge from tilt hammers to the new steam hammers to change begun. Steam has more power, and more control offers. We may now beams and plates larger make.'

Even his cavalier way with verbs didn't obscure the fact that he was talking to her as if she were a complete ignoramus. Her lips snapped together. Although it was difficult to be curt at the pitch of one's voice, she didn't grudge the effort. 'Mr von Sandemann,' she exclaimed, 'I am really very well acquainted with the principles and advantages of steam power. I should perhaps point out . . .'

Infuriatingly, he wasn't attending, but had turned away to consult with a sturdy, grime-smeared workman about some problem to do with temperatures. It was like that all the way round the foundry, every time she tried to respond to his grossly over-simplified explanations of metal planing machines and punching machines, copying lathes and screw-cutting lathes, water-cooled coils for the tuyers, cast-iron bottom plates and rounded hearths, and the Württemberg system of using waste gases to preheat the blast – something Mungo Telfer had put into her own mind as far back as 1816, but that she had never quite managed to translate into practical terms. There had been an astonishing number of technical advances in these last few years, she reflected, and Theo and Drew had taken advantage of them all.

Perhaps her frustration over being continually talked down to had something to do with the weakness that assailed her when they were outside Number Three furnace shed. Either that, or one of the unaccountable leaps in body temperature that struck her sometimes without warning. A symptom of her age, she had been told. She felt the perspiration start from every pore, and her head began to swim, and it was as if all her limbs had turned to jelly. Her only desire was to strip off her bonnet and veil, her heavy pardessus and the gown and chemise beneath, and stand naked in a cool breeze until she became herself again. Weakly, she leaned against the wall of the furnace shed, seething with the knowledge that von Sandemann had probably been expecting her, all afternoon, to succumb to an attack of the vapours. That, after all, was what most females would have done. She inserted a hand between her throat and the high, constricting collar of her pardessus, and wondered how to say, without admitting defeat, that she would prefer not to go into the furnace shed.

As she straightened up, beginning to recover, he turned away as if to lead her towards the warehouses. He was not motivated by consideration, she was sure. And he certainly *ought* to take her into Number Three shed, where the new wet-puddling process had been introduced. With creditable decisiveness, she said, 'I should like to see the new wet-puddling process, please.'

'It differs not from the dry.'

She raised her eyebrows. 'Surely! I understood it was no longer necessary to use men for stirring the metal in the furnace. I should like to see.'

He sighed extravagantly. 'The furnace floor is with pieces of cooled slag coated. With the molten metal this combines a boiling effect to give. That is all.'

The funny thing was that his accent was almost flawless. She repeated, 'I wish to see it.'

The hard brown eyes, with their yellow lights, looked down at her athwart a nose that was thin-boned and sharply hooked. He was an angular man in his late thirties, not much above the average height, with thick jet-black hair and tight, clean-shaven cheeks shadowed with blue-black near the jaw. There was a harsh distinction about his looks that might well be ruined, she reflected astringently, by anything as human as a smile.

'If you insist,' he said.

The air inside was pullulating with heat, but there was a group of men gathered close round one of the furnaces, their backs to the newcomers. Their sweating skins gleamed red-gold with the reflection from the fires. Overcoming her recoil at the searing temperature, and taking a moment to adjust to the contrast between the overall darkness and the pools of flame in the open furnace doors, Vilia recognized Theo in the centre of the group. His bright hair was stranded with damp, and he was clad in nothing but a pair of filthy under-breeches. It looked as if he were explaining something, for the men nodded, and one of them asked a question. Theo, replying, raised one arm and laid it round the shoulders of a brawny fellow beside him, the muscles of his back rippling smoothly under the marked skin. The fellow turned his head a little, and grinned as Theo's hand tightened on his shoulder.

There was something disturbingly private and intimate about the scene that shattered as von Sandemann, with Vilia at his heels, approached the group. The quality of Theo's smile, taut and vivid, changed, although she couldn't read his eyes behind the darkened goggles.

'Felix, dear boy,' he drawled, 'you should have warned me. I don't believe my mother has seen me stripped since I was in the nursery.'

Was there a discordant note under the lightly sardonic words? Vilia couldn't tell. Her mind was preoccupied with the threadlike tracery of scars she had seen on his back, most of them white and healed, but a few still angrily red. She could scarcely ask about them in front of the men, without sounding nauseatingly maternal.

Theo, tipping up his goggles, extended a hand sideways and snapped his fingers. One of the men picked up a shirt from a bench and handed it to him.

Shrugging himself into it, Theo smiled again more naturally and asked, 'Has Felix explained wet puddling to you?'

She replied, acidly polite. 'No. I believe Mr von Sandemann considers it beyond my poor female comprehension.'

Her son threw back his head and laughed. 'For shame, Felix! My mother is not just a female, you know, however decorative. She probably knows more about iron than you do. I hope – I truly hope – that you have not damned yourself irrevocably by being condescending to her?'

Von Sandemann, Vilia was pleased to see, was wearing the faintest trace of a frown.

'Vilia, my dear,' Theo went on. 'Come and look. It's a very neat way of using chemical reactions to save puddlers like Jock and Willie here a good deal of heavy labour. They remember Joseph Hall in their prayers every night, don't you, dear boys? We line the furnace floor with roasted slag – "bulldog", you remember – and when we put the pig iron in, the oxide in the slag combines with the carbon in the pig to produce carbon monoxide under the surface of the metal. It comes to a kind of independent boil, and of course the pig decarbonizes at the same time. Fast, and far less wasteful than with human puddlers, even when I do it myself.'

The men didn't seem to mind. They even nodded in agreement, and one of them said, 'Aye, there's nae doubt you're the best, Mr Theo.'

She looked at them with a touch of puzzlement and Theo, as so often, read her mind. 'It doesn't cut human labour out altogether,' he said. 'Far from it. The metal still has to be worked up until it's malleable, but the boiling makes that a less heavy task.'

'I see. Well, I'm relieved that Jock – was it? – and Willie and the others haven't been put out of a job by the new process.' She smiled at them, and they bobbed their heads, embarrassed. She had the feeling she recognized one or two of them from the old days, although she had made it a rule to stay out of the furnace sheds – for the men's sake, not her own. Smiling at them again, more directly, she turned back to Theo. 'Is it economical?'

'In some ways, though it uses more fuel.'

'That's minor enough.' She stopped herself with a sigh. 'My goodness, I remember when we had to coke all our coal, and fuel was almost like gold dust. Changed days!'

Taking her by the elbow, he began to lead her towards the door. 'I worked it out recently,' he remarked. 'What the hot blast process has done for us since we installed it, and the saving from raw coal. Do you realize that since 1828 we've cut the cost of pig by almost two thirds? We're producing today at £1.15s a ton, while in the south they haven't got below £3 yet. They're being very slow to change to the hot blast. It's a pity we haven't been able to make similar savings on the refining and finishing sides.'

'I shouldn't let it worry you,' she said thoughtfully. 'There's always going to be a demand for pig iron, whereas I have the feeling that someone – quite soon perhaps – may well find the answer to cheap steel production. And that could make a nasty dent in the wrought-iron market.'

'Thank you!' her son said with a grimace. 'Don't let the puddlers hear you say that, please!'

'It's beautiful stuff, steel. I've always been interested in it. I believe you would be well advised to consider the possibilities.' Do you remember when you were a child, and I had some steel experiments done here? I couldn't afford to go into it, far too expensive, but I had some very handsome jewellery made. I have it still.'

'You wore it to the Peers' ball in '22, when George IV was here. I remember it very well.' He looked at her consideringly. 'Do I detect a note of revived interest in the foundry? I thought Kinveil had replaced it in your affections. You haven't even wanted to hear about it for the last five years, and now . . .'

'And now I do!' Her smile was vivid, lighting up the dull November afternoon. The furnace flames, darting upwards to lick at the clouds, were reflected back to give a glow of colour to her face. 'I want to talk shop! I've been turning into a vegetable, Theo, and it's time I began thinking again. My mind needs exercise. You must tell me all about what's going on!'

There was amused resignation on her son's face. Felix von Sandemann, she noted with satisfaction, was looking distinctly sour.

2

She was tired of being tactful. They were back in Theo's office, drinking a civilized glass of wine and nibbling shortbread, crisp and not too sweet. Theo was his usual elegantly groomed self again, clean and fully dressed. He had always kept spare shirts and neck-cloths at the foundry, but Vilia wondered whether he was still wearing the filthy pantaloons under his fashionable checked trousers. Perhaps not. He had looked very much at home in the furnace shed. Although he had always said he would never ask the men to do what he wouldn't or couldn't do himself, she hadn't realized he took the principle to quite such lengths: she had always assumed, without really thinking about it, that he didn't do more than make a few token motions with the stirring-bar. And yet – 'There's nae doubt you're the best, Mr Theo'! In some ways, different ways, all her sons were a mystery to her.

Theo's office, which had once been hers, had changed very little although it now had a satiny gleam that suggested he used it seldom, and mainly for entertaining customers. She had been startled to see two portraits on the wall that she had consigned, long ago, to the darkest corner of the cellars at Marchfield House. Duncan Lauriston and his wife, painted by some journeyman artist whose inspiration hadn't extended to mastery of facial expression. With all trace of personality bleached out of his features, Duncan Lauriston had been quite a good-looking man. Shuddering, Vilia had averted her eyes, only to meet those of Felix von Sandemann. She shuddered again.

What would his office be like? Stern, efficient, austere, or ponderously ornate? He had been talking at length about 'modern taste' but she couldn't tell whether such taste was his. She was much concerned lest he should impose it on Lauriston Brothers', ruining the reputation for craftsmanly simplicity that she had been at such pains to build up. Drew, it seemed, was enthusiastically on von Sandemann's side. He would be.

'I think you are being extremely short-sighted,' she said, abandoning her pretence of detachment. 'Yes, Theo, I know the future lies with the railroads, but is there really going to be such a construction mania as you expect? And if there is, will it last? There is, after all, a limit to the number of lines that can be profitable, and if too many contractors are chasing too few concessions, nothing but trouble can result. Something of the sort happened in the Highlands when I was no more than a child. The Parliamentary Roads commissioners were inundated with applicants for the road contracts, and granted some of them to builders who weren't equipped for the work, although they had sounded very good. Half a dozen of them, at least, either went bankrupt or else had to abandon the work before it was complete. You must be sure to deal only with the most reputable companies, and don't, please, set your hopes too high! You seem to me to be over-committed. Once the railroads are built that will surely be an end to it – unless, of course, the quality of rail you are supplying is so poor that there will be a constant demand for replacement sections!'

'Cold feet, mama? And yet I remember you forecasting, almost ten years ago, that twenty per cent of our total pig-iron production would go in railway orders. You were right, and more right than you could have foreseen now that we've cut the wastage in refining to a third of what it was. We're at twenty per cent now, and nowhere near the height of the boom yet.'

'Yes, my dear!' Her voice was exasperated. 'But I'll forecast again, if you like. Booms are usually followed by slumps, and in another ten years you may well find yourself back where you were in 1833, with only six or seven per cent taken up. And what do you do then with your excess capacity, if you have been over committed?'

'Felix will tell you.'

She had been incensed to discover that von Sandemann's verbs slid neatly into their proper place when Theo was present. When the man had left them for a few moments to sign some urgent correspondence, she had remarked to Theo that she hoped the clerk was sufficiently literate to polish up his superior's syntax – 'because, *really*, Theo, it makes me cold all over to think of Lauristons' being faulted on English grammar!'

'Tiresome, isn't it?' he replied with malicious sympathy. 'I had to take him very severely to task when he first came. The men were becoming quite exhausted chasing his verbs around. We have very little trouble now, except when he isn't paying attention.'

'And what am I to deduce from that?'

Theo had smiled his slanting smile. 'That since you were merely a woman, he felt no need to pay attention.'

'Does he not like women?'

'Oh, don't mistake me! In some ways he likes them very well. But not for their minds. Not in the way I do.'

She couldn't read the curve of his lips or the expression in his eyes. Worse, he clearly knew that she couldn't. A deliberately forgotten voice whispered in her head, 'Do you know that his sexual inclinations are unorthodox?'

Impatiently, she said, 'Don't be foolish. It's high time you were married.'

'Is it? I don't agree, even if early marriage does seem to run in the family. After all, I'm not yet thirty and I have no great desire to settle down into domestic bliss.'

She looked at von Sandemann and waited. Despite what had been said, she suspected that he still underrated her. It would be almost like old times having to prove herself to the superior male. As she had learned to do a quarter of a century ago, she pushed her chin up a little and her shoulders down, clasped her hands loosely on the desk before her, and looked coolly into the dark brown, golden-flecked eyes.

He said, 'When the British market for railway lines weakens, there will of course be other markets in France and the Zollverein – the

Prussian Customs Union, you understand? – and America, where our associate, Mr Randall, tells us that interest again quickens after the depression. But all that is the – what is the expression? – the province of Theo. Drew and I are agreed that we should expand our fine art castings in line with modern taste.'

Vilia's heart sank.

'Lauriston Brothers have a reputation for architectural ironmongery of the old-fashioned kind . . .'

A faint chuckle came from Theo, but Vilia had no trouble preserving her gravity. 'Yes?' she said encouragingly.

'. . . by which I mean,' von Sandemann went on with surprising smoothness, 'the traditional kind. Producing admirable examples in cast iron of products that have a history of having been made in wrought iron or bronze – but always in metal. But it now is possible to copy, even to improve, objects that have formerly been made of wood, perhaps, or pottery.'

'Such as?'

'Such as gates, and garden ornaments, weather vanes, ornamental fountains, garden vases, jardinières, chairs, tables, mirror frames, hat stands, chimney-pieces, statuettes. There are many ideas that we have yet to study.'

Chairs, statues, mirror frames? 'I cannot believe,' Vilia said flatly, 'that you will find many customers. A funereal border to one's mirror scarcely flatters the complexion, and a vast black expanse round the hearth – no, really, it would be too oppressive.'

It was a mistake to be dogmatic. Von Sandemann smiled coldly. 'Oppressive? Once, perhaps. But modern taste favours ornamentation, and Gothic and rococo give lightness and – *Lebhaftigkeit* – yes, liveliness to such things. And it is necessary no longer that they should be black. Three years since, the company of Elkington, Mason in Birmingham developed a process that makes it possible to lay a deposit of gilt or bronze over the iron. You see? Golden gates, and bronze statuettes at a small fraction of what they would otherwise cost. We cannot fail to find customers, and Drew believes there will be many.'

Theo, with his usual almost uncanny accuracy, diagnosed his mother's frown. 'The Germans have been ahead of us in the art of design, and in metalworking skills, for some years now. You need have no fears about quality, with Felix in charge.'

517

With the frankness that could, she knew, be disarming, she said, 'Personal prejudice on my part! I am not in sympathy with what Mr von Sandemann calls "modern taste", and I am sure he knows more about it than I do. But taste aside, think of the number of moulds for all these things! So much investment, so much space needed, for such frivolous things, things that people don't need! Don't think I have anything against luxuries, but they are very dangerous to base a business on – the first items to suffer when times are hard. And fashion in luxuries is so fluid. I'm sorry, but I don't care for the idea at all.'

She met her son's eyes squarely, and after a moment he remarked, 'We're a family business. What would you suggest?'

It didn't occur to her that he was being generous. He could have said, 'I, on the other hand, do care for the idea. And the foundry isn't yours any more.' She said unhesitatingly, 'Structural work. The usual railings, gates, balconies, of course, and staircases and gas lamps. Bridges, as always. But especially the skeletons for shop fronts and other kinds of building. There's bound to be a tremendous demand when people realize the advantages over traditional methods of construction. Just consider! The population of England and Wales has almost doubled in the last fifty years, and in Scotland far more than doubled. And unless marriage and children go out of fashion, it *must* go on. There simply has to be an urgent, and increasing demand for houses, and shops, and manufactories, and business premises. The potential markets are at least as great as with railroads, and certainly far greater than with art castings!'

Reflectively, Theo said, 'How delightful to hear you sounding like your old self again. Yes, I take your point. Standardized units and interchangeable parts. The Americans are doing quite a lot along those lines, I'm told, though mainly with guns, clocks, and pumps. No reason why it shouldn't work on a much larger scale. Vilia, dear, you are a constant refreshment. I didn't realize how much I had missed you.' Blandly, he turned to von Sandemann. 'No criticism of you, Felix, dear boy. Of course.'

Von Sandemann's face was like a thundercloud. 'Will you then support for my ideas withdraw?'

'Verbs, dear boy. Verbs.' Vilia could almost have sympathized with the man. Theo had a genius for being offensive. 'Withdraw my support?' he went on. 'I really don't know. Probably not, but I think we might reduce our commitment. We must talk about it when Drew gets back from London.'

There was a knock on the door, and Theo's clerk entered with a note in his hand. Theo glanced at it, and raised his brows. 'From Gideon, and addressed to me urgently. By messenger, too.' Opening it, he scanned the message rapidly, and then went back to the beginning again. 'Dear me,' he said at last. 'How very distressing. It seems that Elinor has broken her neck.'

3

Dully, Gideon wondered whether funerals had been invented for the purpose of keeping the bereaved occupied until the first edge of grief had been blunted, for no sooner had Elinor been carried back from the hunting field to the Lawries' calm and gracious house than he was faced with the question of where she was to be buried. The decision was his alone. Momentarily, he grieved for her parents and sisters in Charleston, who would know nothing until it was over, and long over.

In the end, it seemed best to him that she should be buried here among the quiet rolling hills where Scotland merged almost insensibly into England – the Scotland she had married into and hated, and the England where, briefly happier, she had still been a stranger. At this moment, his sense of loss was largely overshadowed by feelings of guilt and self-reproach for having torn her, ridiculously immature, from the warm, loving, cushioned world she knew and brought her to a land and life that were its diametric and Calvinistic opposite. With his help and understanding she might, in time, have grown into it, but he had expected too much of her, and his love had degenerated into an automatic affection overlaid with resentment at her dependence on him. He wondered, with a flash of insight, how much his own upbringing had to do with this failure of his. His mother's love for himself, and Theo, and Drew, had waxed and waned, he thought, according to how successful they were in standing on their own feet. Drew had always been the emotionally dependent one, and there had been times when Vilia had seemed to withdraw her love altogether, as if in that way she could force him into maturity. Looking back, Gideon could see that Drew's headlong marriage to Shona had been an inevitable result; he had simply transferred his emotional dependence from mother to wife. Even now, despite his air of assurance, his looks, his charm, without Shona he was lost. And perhaps he had the best of it.

A cold thing, independence, however much one treasured it – and Gideon treasured it most of the time. But now, standing under the pale, washed-out blue of the Border sky, with the Cheviots to south and east flattening into the featureless grey silhouette that meant snow to come, he found it wanting.

He wished he had been able to respond with more than a mechanical smile last night when, gazing out of their bedroom window at the moon sailing free and clear silvering the fallen leaves in the orchard, Elinor had exclaimed, 'Frost, Gideon honey! The going should be just perfect tomorrow!' But he took no pleasure in riding to hounds, even though, after eight years of marriage, he had learned to welcome anything that smoothed out the petulant creases from around his wife's mouth.

He wished he had stayed by her side, too, at the meet, but his own mount, a herring-gutted piebald, hadn't been in the same class as Elinor's mare, which took off like a train in the wake of the Huntsman when the hounds caught the scent. Gideon, a long way behind, had been relieved to see that the mare knew how to jump, and enjoyed it, and had turned his attention back to his own animal, which showed no disposition to lark over fences but made a pusillanimous bee-line for any gap that could be shouldered through or scrambled over. He didn't even see the mare, when she came to an inoffensive-looking brook, dig her heels in abruptly, pecking as she slithered to a halt. Elinor had been told that the animal hated water, but must have forgotten, expecting her to go flying over as she had flown over the fences. Instead, it was Elinor who had gone flying over the mare's head, straight into the rock-strewn bed of the inoffensive-looking brook. By the time Gideon reached her, someone had lifted her on to the bank, where she lay soaked and broken, like some chestnut-haired Desdemona dripping fallen leaves and hairpins. Her hat still bobbed upside-down in the stream, trapped in an eddy of the current. He had bent down and salvaged it, laying it beside her on the makeshift stretcher. She had never taken a step outdoors without something to protect her complexion.

He had failed her, always; marrying her before he recognized that it was part of his nature to keep his distance from the human race. He wouldn't make that mistake again.

He supposed that Vilia and Theo would come to the funeral, and wondered distantly whether they would be embarrassed by his knowing that they had never taken to Elinor. Probably not. Shona, for whom it was inconceivable not to love anyone close to her, would be upset; it was as well that she and Drew couldn't arrive from London in time to be present. What emotional and organizational complications there would be in another few years, when the railway made it possible to travel from London to Scotland in a day. There would be no more legitimate excuses for not being where one didn't want to be, or for not inviting someone to an occasion one didn't want them to attend.

Christ! Gideon thought. What if Vilia brings the child?

But Vilia, unsentimental though she was about children and despite her feeling that seven-year-old Lizzie's spine badly needed stiffening, was not heartless.

'I left her with Lavinia and Juliana, my dear,' she said, kissing her son's lean cheek and taking his chilled hand in hers. 'Why are you standing out here in the cold?'

'Escaping from sympathy, I would imagine,' Theo remarked. He didn't grip Gideon's shoulders sustainingly, as another man might have done, but went on, 'And suffering from remorse? Don't, dear boy. You can't guard people from their destiny, not even your wife. Or yourself.' He smiled slightly. 'Anyway, here we are – for what it's worth. I'll deal with anything you feel is beyond you.'

He was damnably perceptive, and his cool realism oddly comforting. Gideon had never tried to analyse what he felt about Theo. Though there was only a year between them in age, it had always seemed as if there were a century in terms of experience. Theo had been adult by the time he was five.

Three days later, with relief, they said good-bye to the Lawries' kind, uneasy house, Tim still deeply chagrined – despite all Gideon could say – that a horse from his stables should have been responsible for Elinor's death. It had been as much as Gideon could do to persuade him not to have the mare shot.

There had been little opportunity for the three Lauristons to find any peace or quiet, and for the first twenty miles they scarcely spoke. Only when the landscape began to change and they could see ahead the

Forth and Clyde valley, did Gideon brace himself to confront what must happen next. He didn't think Lizzie would respond other than quietly to the news that her mother was not coming back; he had been troubled to see how much happier she was with Lavinia and, after a few days, Juliana, at Marchfield House than she had ever been at home in London. But after that, what?

Vilia said suddenly, 'You mustn't take Lizzie back with you to an empty house in London. She would be acutely unhappy.'

'Your father took *you*.'

'Yes. And although you think I was born strong, I can assure you I wasn't. I was miserable, but I survived – perhaps because what I missed was a place, and I knew that it wouldn't change, or not in essence, while I was away. Lizzie is different. She seems to have no sense of place at all, only of people. It matters deeply to her who she is with. Take her away, especially from Lavinia, and leave her to some governess for a few years, and you will be performing an act of something very near cruelty.'

'She would have *me*.' He was aware of the defensive note in his voice.

'Oh, Gideon! Don't be foolish. Above all, don't be commonplace! That might be all very well if you led the kind of regular life that suits a child, and if you were soon going to settle down again into cosy domesticity. Are you?'

'No.' The answer came out more uncompromisingly than he had intended.

'You love your daughter but don't, please, try to persuade us that you would consider abandoning, or even adjusting, your career for her.'

He dropped his eyes and plucked at a thread adhering to the knee of his trousers. 'No,' he said again, after a moment. 'Do you have an answer to the problem?'

'Ideally, she should stay at Marchfield. Shona would have no objection. She would love the child just as she loves her own. She has a natural turn for motherhood.'

It was, of course, the sensible solution, but Theo intervened drily, 'If it were only Shona!'

Vilia stared at him. 'And what do you mean by that?'

'Just that Drew has a say in the matter, too, and he has never forgiven Gideon for stealing the family chronicle. Or, to put it vulgarly, the income that goes with it. Very reprehensible, no doubt, but there it is.'

'He can't possibly need the money?'

'No. But I can envisage his thought processes, can't you? The family chronicle money was, morally, Shona's. With it, she would have been perfectly at liberty to bring up as many motherless children as she liked. But where *his* income is concerned, he cannot feel justified in depriving his own family – etcetera, etcetera.'

Gideon exclaimed, 'That's easily settled! I wouldn't dream of asking them to take care of Lizzie without contributing to her keep.'

Theo's particular smile gave his face wings. The slanting brows, so like Vilia's; the curly, upcurving nostrils; and the way his lips lifted at the corners. 'But Drew could never bring himself to take money *from his brother* for looking after a poor, orphaned little niece!'

There was a nonplussed silence.

Vilia said, 'You're being ridiculous, Theo. I never heard such nonsense!'

'But you don't know Drew very well, do you?' It was said gently, but his mother's face stiffened. He went on, 'That, I assure you, is how he will think. Not being very subtle, he might even put some of it into words. Checkmate?'

Gideon said, 'It *is* ridiculous, you know!'

'When has that ever bothered our brother? We didn't call him "the brat" for nothing when he was young.'

4

It was just as Theo had said, although Drew – conventional Drew – took the greatest care not to mention anything as crude as money. A gentleman didn't, even within the family circle. Gideon found it hard enough even to catch his brother in an unoccupied moment, for when he wasn't arguing out the merits of fine art versus functional castings, he was furiously trying to catch up on a backlog of work. What he did constantly – and, to Gideon's extreme irritation, with every evidence of sincerity – was sympathize.

Vilia and Theo were no help. They didn't even try to make the right kind of conversational opening when Drew was trapped at the dinner table. Vilia, in fact, had fallen into the oddest mood after a few days back at Marchfield. Her puzzled second son could only define it as jaunty, and he felt let down by it. Illogically, he knew. Why, after all, should Vilia weep for Elinor when she had never liked her?

As it happened, although Vilia had always thought her late daughter-in-law shallow, vain, and unsuitable, Elinor had been driven completely out of her mind by an incident that had satisfied her vanity as much as it had offended her sense of fitness.

Soon after Drew's return, she had been passing von Sandemann's office at the foundry, and moved partly by curiosity and partly by an honest desire to find out what he meant by 'good taste' in castings, she had knocked and gone in. He had been sitting behind his desk – a perfectly ordinary desk – and his expression when he rose to greet her had been what she thought of as his Number One expression. Number Two – and he only had two – differed simply by being a few degrees sourer.

'Have you drawings for some of your projected designs?' she began, and then stopped. The next words were wrenched out of her. 'What an *extraordinary* . . . Good heavens! Is that a chair?'

Since he had been sitting on it, the question was rhetorical. He said, 'What you might call a piece of experiment.'

'Experimental piece,' she corrected him automatically. 'It can't be comfortable, surely? And it most certainly isn't beautiful! I thought German design was supposed to be advanced.'

The chair looked as if someone had knocked together a few offcuts from the workshop floor – flat bits of metal, sections of gas tubing, and a thick slab of wood for the seat. It was the ugliest thing she had ever seen.

There was an edge of something that was almost amusement in von Sandemann's voice. 'Oh, it is,' he said. 'But this chair was designed by an Englishman. You don't like it? But you can scarcely complain that it is ornate.'

She felt her face tighten in annoyance.

'Perhaps you prefer that?' He pointed.

'That' was equally odd, in a different way. It was as if someone had taken a piece of rope and allowed it to fall into graceful loops, and then fossilized it. She said, 'I . . . What is it?'

'Bentwood. Wood that has been boiled and moulded. It was made by

524

a family friend of ours called Michael Thonet. He has been commissioned to furnish the Liechtenstein palace. Interesting, is it not?'

'I suppose so.'

'You don't see, do you?'

'See what?'

'The shape! This chair I am sitting in is ugly, but strong. That one has a kind of beauty, but it is weak. Yet it is a shape we could *make* strong, in cast iron.'

She hesitated. It was like nothing she had ever seen before, like something that had grown rather than been made. Frowning, she tried to visualize it in iron, and shook her head. Whether black, gilded, or bronzed, it would look heavy. Painted white, perhaps? But no one would ever buy white furniture; there wasn't a house in the country it would fit into.

'No,' she said, her chin up. 'You and I, Mr von Sandemann, may see a certain elegance about it, but this foundry can't afford to make things to be sold only in tens or hundreds. I am afraid you will have to do better than that before you have any support from me.'

She turned away. There was a real, if reprehensible, pleasure in laying down the law, secure in an authority that needed to make no concessions to others. For five years of marriage she had guarded her words every day, muted her opinions, expressed her feelings as circuitously and softly as if she were dealing with a rattlesnake. But not here, not at the foundry. And especially not now, when Theo had suggested she might like to become involved in the management again.

Two heavy hands grasped her by the arms and whirled her round. 'You arrogant – you arrogant . . .' Von Sandemann bit off some word that, from his expression, would have been unforgivable. 'Will you *never* admit you might be wrong? While you have been hidden in your Highland castle the world has changed, but you see it not. You come back here acting as if you never away have been. *Ja!* I know that it was you who built this foundry and ruled it like some petty tyrant! I honour you for it. You are a formidable woman. But it gives you not the right to say, here and now, I will have this, or I will have that!'

She had never felt such emanations of violence since that day in 1814 when she had faced up to Duncan Lauriston in the workshop; it had been almost a week before the bruises faded from her shoulders.

Mesmerized, she stared up into Felix von Sandemann's eyes, all of her concentrated in her mind, estimating, assessing, and in a suspended way, waiting. She didn't even know that her own eyes were wide and water-green and empty, her face soft and smooth, and its muscles as relaxed as in sleep or death.

Sharply, he drew in his breath and then, without warning, his grip changed and his mouth came down hard on hers. There was nothing lover-like in the kiss, only a need to impose himself on her, in this way if he could contrive it in no other. But even while she fought, outraged, her body played her false, and a betraying quiver sprang up somewhere in the small of her back and ran, like molten fire, down into her loins. She struggled even harder, then, but his iron grip only tightened and he dragged her crudely against him, locking her arms to her body with one of his, and dropping the other hand to the base of her spine. And that was too much! Her anger won, and with a violent effort she managed to free one arm and tried to push him away. She didn't succeed, but she forced him to shift his grip, and that momentary relaxation was all she needed. Raising her right foot as high as she could, she stamped it down on his with all her strength. By good fortune, her foot was at an angle, and the heel of her shoe ground cripplingly into the base of his toes.

He froze for a moment, and then growled somewhere deep in his throat. Suddenly she was frightened. But as the paralysis travelled up his leg and began to cramp his calf muscles, he released her, his hands splaying out, his shoulders a little bent, and his mouth so tightly shut that his lips were invisible. She backed away, watching him, and after a while he let out his breath again and said, '*Danke Schön*. Thank you. Thank you very much.'

She could feel the coil of her hair slipping – silver-blonde again as it had been in her youth, instead of the warmer gold of the years between – and she reached up to adjust the pins, her heart pounding in her breast and her arms trembling. For a traitorous moment, she wished she hadn't stopped him so soon. Why had she, when her body cried out with starvation? For convention's sake, or because this wasn't the man? She had tried to forget what it was to be hungry, tried to convince herself that that side of life was over for her. But whatever von Sandemann's motives had been, they had included a strong element of the physical. She lowered her eyes, in case the smile deep inside her showed through. After the atrophied years with Magnus, who had made her feel plain and middle-aged, it was like being born again. The life essence began to flow back into her.

She had to say something, and the circumstances seemed to require that it be something repressive. 'Do the ladies of your country not object, Mr von Sandemann, to being treated as if they are no more than objects to satisfy men's baser needs? Why should you think physical strength is a proof of mental superiority? In this country, Mr von Sandemann, it is the custom for gentlemen to show respect to ladies. Since you are a stranger here, I propose to overlook this episode, but you will oblige me by remembering that I am not accustomed to being treated so, and that I will not tolerate it!' And that, she thought, a bubble of laughter welling up inside her, was probably one of the silliest speeches she had ever made. She wanted respect for her mind, certainly, but why was it so impossible to admit that she wanted other things, too? Was she alone in that? Was there something peculiar about her? If only it were possible to talk to someone about it, but it wasn't, and she didn't know the answer. Once, in a very roundabout way, she had tried to find out whether Shona enjoyed the pleasures of the bed, but Shona had turned scarlet even when Vilia asked whether the mattress was comfortable, making Vilia feel that there was something very indelicate about pursuing the subject. She brushed aside the thought that there was one person in the world – one man – who might have told her, if ever she had thought to ask. But the question hadn't mattered, then.

Von Sandemann didn't look in the least crestfallen. He was wearing his Number Two expression. Patronizingly, she said, 'In the matter of the foundry, I see no reason why our differences of opinion should be so intense. You must have had differences with my sons before now. Did those make you so angry?'

His nostrils flared and then he replied, after a moment's hesitation, 'You are correct. They did not.' He drew himself up, and clicked his heels together.

It was quite impossible for her not to giggle at the spasm of pain that crossed his face. With a faint gasp, she said. 'I believe a cold compress is the sovereign remedy for bruises.' Then she turned and fled.

If the circumstances had been different – and the man. Perhaps, or perhaps not. All she knew was that she felt revivified. In two weeks she would be forty-eight years old, though she knew she didn't look it. Now, she didn't feel it, either. When she had married Magnus, so that Kinveil had been restored to her, she had gained something beyond price and at the same time lost the one thing that had kept her going through so much of her life, her sense of purpose. She hadn't noticed the loss at first; she had been too busy setting the estate to rights. And then everything had deteriorated until it seemed that her only ambition was to keep Magnus pampered and peaceful. None of it had diminished her feeling for Kinveil, but her sense of looking forward, of having a positive objective in life, had been doused like some useless candle. It was as if all Fate held in store for her was to spend the next twenty or thirty years, as she had seen other people do, waiting resignedly for death.

Effervescently, she thought that Fate was due for a surprise.

No one, perhaps, but Meg, the nurse of her childhood, would have recognized the mood that took her in its grip. The boys, certainly, had never seen their mother when she was looking for mischief.

One evening at dinner, she said bracingly, 'Now, this problem over what is to be done about Lizzie!'

Gideon looked up warily. 'It seems to me that I have no choice but to take her back to London with me.'

Drew laid down his fork and looked at Shona who, in turn, glanced at McKirdy, who was in his sixties now but whose eyes were as blue and his smile as open as they had ever been. Obedient to her signal, he nodded to one of the footmen to remove the plates, and himself made ready to bring one of his wife's magnificent puddings to table.

Vilia ignored the byplay. 'On the contrary,' she said, 'I will take the child back to Kinveil with *me*.'

Drew said, 'Pudding, Vilia?'

'What is it? Mrs McKirdy's apple crumble? Yes, please.'

Gideon's relief was fleeting. 'But what about Magnus?'

His mother said, her eyes wide and disingenuous, 'What *about* Magnus?'

'Won't he mind?'

She smiled limpidly at her apple crumble, and raised her spoon. 'Why should he, my dear?'

Gideon could think of any number of reasons. After a moment's reflection, he himself was not too sure of the scheme, and voiced his own doubts. 'He's hardly a man to want children round his feet. His own daughter is one thing, but Lizzie as well . . .'

'Pooh!' she said.

'What Gideon is trying tactfully to say, Vilia,' Theo intervened, 'is that it is scarcely a house for children. With respect, a little – er – middle-aged.'

Gideon was annoyed. It was precisely what he had meant, but there was no need for Theo to be so elephantine about it.

'Pooh!' Vilia said again through a mouthful of pudding.

It troubled Gideon that she didn't say she would like to have Lizzie with her, or even more to the point, that the child would be company for Juliana. Hesitantly, he said, 'She and Juliana are much of an age. Would Magnus really not object?'

'Why should he?' she repeated.

Gideon caught Theo's eye and could see that the same thought was in his mind. Two birds with one stone. Help Gideon out of a fix, and annoy Magnus at the same time. Surely not? He didn't want Lizzie caught in that kind of cross-fire.

Theo, having rejected the pudding, was peeling a pear. He had long, capable fingers, perfectly controlled. His eyes on his task, he said softly, 'Don't I remember some complaint that, even as it was, you didn't devote sufficient time to Juliana?'

She chuckled. 'That was part of his campaign to stop me from being quite so busy about the estate. He found my energy exhausting.'

Drew spoke for the first time. 'Embarrassing, too, I should hope. His idleness is beyond anything.' Shona murmured something inaudible, and he said, 'No, my dear. I am sure your uncle has many virtues, but responsibility is not one of them. Goodness knows where the estate would be without Vilia.'

'*Goodness* knows?' Vilia repeated, amused. 'My dear, the whole world knows. Between ourselves I have made no secret of the – difficult – aspects of my husband's personality, although I wouldn't, of course, talk about it to anyone else. But I have not been able to prevent it from becoming common knowledge that he neither wants, nor is competent, to manage Kinveil. I only wish he would give me a rather freer hand with it. He has a regrettably public habit of countermanding my orders.'

Theo paddled his fingers in the bowl of scented water before him, and began to dry them on a napkin. 'He can't last forever,' he said with rare candour.

'Fine consolation!' Gideon found her amusement vaguely shocking.

'Has he reached any conclusions?'

'Conclusions? Magnus?' Her brows rose over satirical eyes. 'It's one of his favourite topics of conversation, and if he were to make up his mind the whole game would be spoiled.' She glanced quizzically at Gideon. 'We're talking about Magnus's Will, in case you hadn't guessed. He's almost sixty and knows he *ought* to have made up his mind about it; on the other hand, he likes to think there is plenty of time. So he changes it regularly, once a month.'

Gideon said, 'There can't be many permutations. Surely everything must go to you and Juliana?'

She laughed. ' "Aye, well," as Mungo Telfer used to say. You might think so, but you're leaving Magnus's views on women out of account. Especially managing ones, of whom he considers me a prime example. He's terrified of encouraging the same tendency in Juliana. It would be different if she were married. A husband and a son or two would solve all his problems, but that happy day isn't likely to come for a while yet. After all, she's only six. He can't decide what provisions to make in the meantime – who's to be responsible for running Kinveil, I mean.'

'You, of course,' Drew exclaimed.

'Of course,' she agreed dulcetly. 'But Magnus feels it ought to be a man.'

'Edward Blair?'

'He's one possibility. There's Peter Barber, too. And in another few years there will be young Ian, and of course Guy Savarin. He must be twelve or thirteen by now. And you know, Drew, you ought to be a possibility yourself, if you hadn't such a talent for offending Magnus. You're just as much married to one of his nieces as Peter Barber is!'

Drew grinned. 'I can just see me trying to manage Kinveil! No, thank you, I have enough troubles already, and I really wouldn't be suitable.'

'You could hardly be less suitable than Peter Barber. It turns my hair grey to think of a philosopher trying to manage thirty thousand acres of Highland Hills. Now, if only Theo would marry some nice girl and settle down . . .'

530

With his blandest smile, Theo said, 'I thought Magnus wanted to keep everything in the Telfer family.'

'Well, he does, but you seem to have the knack of handling him. He might be persuaded, you know.'

'And then you could continue to run the place as if nothing had changed?'

'My dear Theo! *Would* I?'

'Yes.'

She laughed. 'Well, I should certainly have something to say if you tried to interfere. What's the point of having sons if they don't do what mother tells them?' The signs of strain that Gideon had noticed at Kinveil had vanished in the last few weeks under the stimulus of the foundry and the relief of separation from Magnus, and he thought that she looked more like Theo's sister than his mother.

Theo smiled again, unreadably.

'It would fairly upset Magnus's apple cart if anything happened to Juliana,' Drew remarked, shocking his tender-hearted wife.

'Drew! What a dreadful thing to say!'

He was unrepentant. 'Well, it would, wouldn't it?'

Vilia said, 'Don't worry, Shona. She's a disgustingly healthy child. In fact, Gideon, to return to the subject, I think – if you insist on being sombre and serious about it – that she might be good for Lizzie. Being younger, she won't dominate the child as Lavinia does, but she's a bright little thing on her home ground and might be able to put more of a sparkle into her.'

Gideon didn't enjoy having it pointed out that his daughter, of whom he was genuinely fond, was such a timid mouse. 'I suppose so. You'll have to break Juliana of that habit of shying away from anything unfamiliar, though, or she'll have a hard time growing up.'

Vilia stared at him. 'Is that a criticism?'

He sighed, ashamed of himself for trying to hit back. 'No. Merely a comment. I suppose she'll be all right as long as she has someone to cling to.' Casting one more look at Drew and Shona, he sighed again and said, 'Well, if you feel able to contend with Lizzie as well as Juliana, all I can say is, thank you. I'm grateful. I don't know what I'd have done otherwise.'

Vilia rose, smoothing down the smoky green wool of her skirt. She smiled in the business-like way so long familiar to all of them. 'Let's try it for a few months and see how she settles down, shall we? She will have a week or two to become used to the idea. I think, despite everything, we ought to be back at Kinveil by Christmas, otherwise Magnus will be angry enough to pull up the drawbridge. And that would be bad tactics on my part, when I want him not only to accept an extra child about the place, but to accustom himself to the idea of my being back on the board of the foundry again. Dear me, poor Magnus!'

5

Magnus, who had a very selective memory, welcomed Vilia back not with relief or forgiveness, but with a large tolerance that was almost as informative. He clearly found it more comfortable not to remember what they had said at parting, and had also missed someone to talk at. Vilia was a little – a very little – touched when he accepted Lizzie with no more than a pessimistic mutter, and decided to save the foundry until later.

She watched Lizzie carefully for the first few weeks, but she was an opaque child compared with Juliana, and Vilia couldn't tell whether she was settling down contentedly or not. She knew the nursery routine would be different from what Lizzie was used to, for at Kinveil, as in most Highland houses, there were no concessions to luxury, and in winter it was often necessary to break the ice on the washstand ewer for one's morning sponge-down. At least, Vilia though bracingly, it might wake the child up a bit. She had the most maddening ability to dawdle around looking languid, and was very slow to learn. Vilia herself taught the children French and arithmetic, while their governess, a kindly, cheerful, but limited young woman whose name was Emily Harper, instructed them in singing and geography, sketching and stitchery, and set them to learn reams of the sickliest poetry by heart. Lizzie had an aptitude with pencil and paintbrush, but no other talent that Vilia could discern. It was fortunate that she was going to be such a beauty some day.

The winter was a tiring one. It seemed as if the wind never dropped, whistling round Kinveil day after day, night after night, battering against the walls, finding its way through every invisible crack, howling in the chimneys. Sometimes it was laden with rain, sometimes with snow, but more usually with a bitter, soaking sleet. Even Vilia, hardened to it, found it required an increasing effort of will to venture outdoors for the early afternoon walk that was part of her unvarying routine. Juliana complained, but Lizzie didn't.

Vilia's own frame of mind was oddly suspenseful, as if she were waiting for something to happen, she didn't know what. She had half expected a few weeks' exposure to Magnus to drain her of the vitality her encounter with Felix von Sandemann had given back to her, but it didn't. All that happened was that the desire to *do* something, deprived of outlet, went on simmering inside her.

In March, the weather suddenly improved. Juliana very nearly danced with glee, for March was the time for 'the floating', an event at which she had been present last year for the first time, and couldn't wait to see again.

'Extraordinary the things that catch a child's fancy!' her father grumbled, and privately Vilia agreed with him, although she knew she might have felt differently if it had been a feature of her own childhood. But Kinveil, unlike Glenbraddan, had never been timber country.

Edward Blair, however, had begun to fell more trees, and more systematically, than ever before, anxious to clear extra land for sheep. The days of casual forestry and lonely little sawmills had gone. Now the trees were felled in autumn, and the foresters spent the winter lopping the branches and stripping the bark. When the spring thaws came, the logs were sent tumbling down the mountain streams to the Braddan, there to be gathered on the banks for the great floating, when merchants from the eastern side of the country sent their own men to help dispatch the piled logs towards the loch and the big sawmills that would convert them into planks at a speed undreamed of by the foresters of the glen.

When the spring floods came, and the salmon were running, that was the time for the floating. The sluices were opened and the river roared into a torrent that tossed the logs towards their destination as if they were so many stalks of grass.

'It's so exciting, Lizzie!' Juliana assured her cousin importantly. Since it was demonstrably silly to think of Juliana as Lizzie's step-aunt, 'cousin' had been agreed on as a compromise. 'I'll explain it all to you when we get there. You can't understand without seeing it, you know.'

'Stop showing off, Juliana!' Vilia told her, suppressing her amusement. Lizzie was fated to go through life with people telling her, 'you won't understand unless . . .'

Next day, Juliana bustled around greeting the floaters as familiarly as some old lady who had known them all since the cradle, and the men grinned and ducked their heads appreciatively, thinking it was wonderful what a year could do for a little girl. Very shy and retiring she'd been, last year, as if she were frightened of them. But now that Juliana no longer felt herself among strangers, her wide blue eyes smiled at them and her fair curls tossed merrily under the scarf that held her bonnet in place. Only when she encountered a few men who were new this year did her brightness falter.

Officiously, she introduced Lizzie to the log rollers, whose task it was to lever the tree trunks into the river; then to the pole men, who manoeuvred the logs into the middle of the current, pushing waist deep into the icy water to deal with jams and obstructions; and then to the clippers, the youngest and most active of all, who raced along the river bank with their long hooked rods, ready to pounce on any log that deviated from the main stream or seemed about to obstruct the ones that followed it. Sometimes the clippers hopped athletically on to the fast-moving, slippery logs themselves, keeping their balance as if by magic.

On a bright, crisp blue day by a picturesque river, with the sound of shouts and laughter and Gaelic oaths and the roar of the water, it was marvellously exhilarating.

And then it all went hideously wrong. Juliana, with a shriek of 'I can do it, too! Watch me, Lizzie!' skipped from the bank on to the nearest log, and then to the next, and then the next. She found herself on a trunk that had grown smooth and straight, without any excrescences to weight it in the water. Smooth, even, resistless, it turned again and again as the current took it, so that she had to dance to stay upright. After the first, startled moment she caught the trick of it, and giggled pleasedly at the horrified faces on the bank.

Standing beside Vilia, eleven-year-old Isa Blair shrieked, 'Oh! Oh! The pool and then the spout! Do something, Aunt Vilia! You must do something!'

Vilia was frozen, her mind estimating, calculating. Not very far away was the calm pool from which the only exit was the deep, roaring waterfall known as the spout, through which the logs shot one by one into the loch below. As the river opened into the pool there was a wild mêlée, the logs erupting from the river into the wider water, crashing and whirling. And then the spout sucked them one by one, willy-nilly, into the rocky conduit. If she ever reached there, the child would be broken. Even in the pool, the slack before the cataract, she couldn't help but slip and fall, to be crushed among the chaos of jostling trunks.

Harriet Blair was on her knees, praying, while Edward stood uselessly muttering, 'My God! My God!' It was a blessing Magnus had decided not to come.

Isa Blair was still shrieking. 'Be quiet, you stupid child!' Vilia said, and when Isa paid no attention turned and, with unthinking force, struck her across the face. The shrieks stopped, shocked, and Vilia, scarcely aware of what she had done, turned back to look at Juliana. The child was frightened now, and fear was robbing her of her precarious stability. One of the clippers had jumped on to a log and was trying to reach her, but the current was running faster and more erratically, and although he stretched out his arms Juliana was too young and too distracted to risk a lunge that would carry her into the arms of someone she didn't know. Didn't know, and therefore didn't trust. Vilia began to run, breathing fast, cursing the luck that had put one of the new men nearest to the child.

Was Juliana closer to this bank or the other one? Looking across, Vilia saw Sorley prepare to try and reach her, but knew that he wouldn't manage it. He knew it, too, for he backed away again and resumed his scrambling run along the rough bank, keeping pace with the child. Vilia did the same, sobbing with rage at the skirts that hampered her, tangling in her legs, threatening to trip her up every time she stumbled over a rock. One of the clippers beside her exclaimed, 'Och, the poor wee bairn!' and made a leap, but the log whirled as his hasty feet landed on it and he slipped into the water, the violent splash of his falling setting up eddies that diverted the nearest logs from their path and rattled Juliana's, so that it rolled again and side-swiped another, and drew from her a hysterical yelp of terror.

Still, miraculously, she succeeded in keeping her feet. But the pool wasn't far now. Regardless of rocks and lichen and slimy mud, Vilia succeeded in tearing her boots off and, as she ran, began kilting up her skirts, tucking the hem into her belt and giving thanks that she had never succumbed to the fashion for a dozen petticoats.

Somehow, she gained a little on the child, just enough to allow her to take care as she stepped on to the first log. Even with one of the clippers running level, holding his pole out to give her something to grip while she found her balance, it was terrifying, as if the whole world were revolving under her feet. She gasped, and clung to the clip pole. Her soaking feet were bleeding from the rocks, and as she looked down she could see little tendrils of blood coming from them, to be snatched away into the whirling water like smoke in a gale. Then, conquering her shaking limbs, she released the pole and turned towards the middle of the stream.

Raising her voice above the shouts of the men and the roaring of the water, she cried, 'Don't be afraid, Juliana. I am here, and so is Sorley. Everything will be all right if you do as I say.' Unless, she thought grimly, I slip at the vital moment and we both go down.

Her heart and her stomach seemed to have changed places, but gradually she worked her way towards the child. Sorley was matching her own progress from the opposite direction. How much further to the pool, dear God? Juliana, her feet still slipping and slithering desperately on the rolling log, was turning her head back and forth, from Vilia to Sorley. Don't! Vilia thought. Don't move like that or you might lose your footing. Don't do anything at all!

And then she was almost within reach. But, upright, Vilia couldn't stretch out or the child would be bound to lean towards her, and then they would both go under. Desperately, Vilia glanced back towards the bank. The man who had supported her with his pole pushed it out towards her again. There was something attached to the tip. She could just reach. A belt? Two belts knotted together? What were they for? The man pointed urgently towards her feet. After a moment of utter blankness, she realized that if she could strap her log to the next one, it would stabilize them both and make a kind of raft. Somehow she kept her balance; somehow she succeeded in looping the belts round the two logs; somehow she retreated to the first log again and pulled the makeshift rope tight. Would it work? She was soaked to the skin and her hands felt crushed and raw, but the belts held. And then she was able to slip down into a crouch and hold her hands out to Juliana.

536

Sorley, on the child's other side, sat astride his single tree trunk. He, too, was holding out his hands.

But neither of them was quite close enough.

For an appalling moment, they both rested there, arms outstretched and Juliana turned first to one and then the other. But she couldn't reach. Inches that might as well have been miles.

Vilia readjusted her balance and stretched again, and so did Sorley. But the fingers that would have given the child enough reassurance to take the one, crucial step, still didn't make contact.

Knowing that her arms were extended to their very maximum, Vilia looked at Juliana's crumpled, tearful face, and was conscious that her own face must betray her, for Juliana let out a wail of pure terror. There was something impossibly wrong! Vilia *could* reach the child. She knew, if only she tried. But she *was* trying – wasn't she? Momentarily paralysed, she let her eyes slip past Juliana to Sorley. He was watching her, not the child. *Watching her as if he were waiting to see whether she wanted him to make the effort or not!* His gaze said, I will do what you will do.

With an inarticulate moan, she forced her frozen muscles to life again and reached out, and this time touched the child and grasped her fingers. At the same moment Sorley reached her, too, and steadied her from behind. After that it was only a matter of coaxing and balancing the frightened little girl, with Sorley gliding nimbly from log to log behind them, and three of the clippers coming out from the bank to help. The pool was only yards away.

'Dia!' one of the men exclaimed when they reached the bank safely at last. 'There wass a moment when we wass thinking you wass not going to reach her. When your muscles iss chilled they do not stretch so far. Och, but, Mistress Cameron, you wass a real heroine there. Chust so, you wass!'

She had only fainted once in her life before, and on that occasion, too, she had been trying to escape. Sorley carried her to the coach, and then Juliana, wrapped in a plaid. Then he shooed a wide-eyed Lizzie in beside them.

Harriet Blair, alternately giving thanks to God and criticizing Juliana's lack of discipline, gave them the cold comfort of Glenbraddan for the night. They had been invited to stay there, anyway, so Vilia was able to make light of the whole thing when they reached home the next day. Juliana, a disgustingly healthy child, didn't even catch the chill she deserved.

Chapter Three

1

'What, *more* children?' Magnus exclaimed, making it sound as if Kinveil were bursting at the seams with them. 'No, really, Vilia! It won't do. I won't have it.'

His face had the taut, scarlet look she knew so well, as if the flesh had been inflated under the skin.

He would give in ultimately. He always did, because she took care never to suggest anything unreasonable, and to allow him several days without badgering to follow the arguments through in his mind and reach the conclusion that it had all been his own idea in the first place. But it was tiresome, especially when her own thought processes were swift and efficient, and sometimes she found it difficult not to snap.

'But the epidemic is becoming serious, you know!' She didn't specify which epidemic. The mere mention of the word cholera was enough to plunge Magnus into an orgy of self-pity, although it was sixteen years since Lucy had died. Vilia didn't resent it, but there was a limit to how long one could go on making soothing noises about something that had happened so long ago. 'Harriet tells me Grace and Peter Barber are sending Petronella and Ian up to Glenbraddan, which must mean they're worried. And it takes a good deal to worry the Barbers.'

'Yes, well,' he mumbled. 'I suppose that's true. They don't fly up in the boughs for nothing.'

Vilia, who found the Barbers' ostentatious calm somewhat oppressive, accepted this gratefully. 'Everyone says that, bad as it is in England, it's worse in Scotland. I think it perfectly natural that Drew and Shona should be anxious to send the children away.'

'I don't see why. Marchfield's a clean enough place; no bad smells that I can remember. It's breathing an atmosphere full of – what d'ye call it? – "pestilential miasmas" that spreads the disease. That's what those doctor johnnies say, at any rate.'

538

'Yes, I know. But Jermyn is at university in Edinburgh, and Lavinia and Peregrine James at school there, and you know the Old Town smells like a pigsty. There were forty cases last week and thirty of them fatal.'

'Why don't they go back to Marchfield, then?'

Shona's letter had said, 'I would simply bring them back here until the epidemic wears itself out. But you know how strong-minded they all are! The boys, especially Jermyn, will not be persuaded that a mere outbreak of cholera should be allowed to divert them from their studies, and Lavinia, of course, feels bound to agree with them. At least if they were at Kinveil there would be no fear of them taking a quick trip into town to see their friends, or collect a few books, or listen to some lecture that it would be a pity to miss!'

There was no denying that they were a headstrong trio, but Vilia felt it would be a mistake to mention the fact to Magnus, who hadn't seen them for seven years. She said, 'It might not do. There's a new theory that the – er – epidemic may be caused not by the presence of pestilential miasma, but by the absence of ozone. If that's true, the children would be much better off here.'

Magnus glowered at her. 'Ozone? We've certainly got plenty of *that*! But I don't like it. I don't want them here.'

'What a pity.' It was said resignedly. 'Juliana is so anxious for them to come. She and Lizzie have so little youthful companionship.' And that, she thought, was the point at which to let the matter drop for the time being. Juliana was twelve now, and Jermyn fifteen, and it seemed to Vilia desirable that they should get to know each other better. If they were to make a match of it . . . It would give her almost inconceivable satisfaction to know that Kinveil would go, in the end, to a child who had Cameron blood in his veins, as if it were a kind of vindication of all the miseries and misdeeds that had resulted from her own early banishment from Kinveil. Though Magnus wouldn't approve; not because he disliked Jermyn – indeed, he was scarcely even aware of him – but because he was Drew's son and Vilia's grandson.

For more than two years after Vilia's return to Kinveil at the end of 1843, she and Magnus had rubbed along quite well. He had reconciled himself to Lizzie's arrival, smiling on the child when something happened to draw his attention to her, and ignoring her for the rest of the time. He had even reconciled himself to Vilia's involvement in the foundry; indeed, she thought that once his initial disapproval had faded he rather welcomed it. It gave them a rest from each other and there were always two or three weeks of something very near benevolence when she returned from her periodic visits south. She, too, was always in a good humour when she returned. Kinveil didn't bore her – never that! – but it was invigorating to exercise her mind in another field.

Then, in 1846, she and Magnus had clashed irrevocably. It was worse than their disagreement over the Disruption of the kirk, because this time it was a matter of life and death. The potato blight that had destroyed the previous summer's crop in Belgium, Denmark, Sweden and Canada, as well as in Ireland, had passed Scotland by, but everyone knew that this year it would strike. The portents, whether real or mystical, lent themselves to only one interpretation. And more than two-thirds of the people of the Highlands lived almost exclusively on potatoes for nine months in the year.

'Well, they'll simply have to live on something else, won't they!' Magnus had exclaimed peevishly. 'Can't be good for them eating the same thing all the time!'

Even coming from Magnus, this statement had a blinding irrelevance that momentarily deprived Vilia of speech. She said, 'But they grow the potatoes themselves. They would have to pay for any alternatives.'

'Well? It's not unheard-of to have to open one's purse to buy food, is it?'

She took a deep breath. 'But there is nothing *in* their purses.'

'Rubbish!' he replied. 'I daresay nine out of ten of them have a sock full of money hidden away under the bed.'

'Very clever of them, considering they live mainly by barter! Where would they get it, do you suppose?'

'How should *I* know! Really, Vilia, it's no concern of yours. They have to learn to sort out their own problems. Besides, it'll probably turn out to be a storm in a teapot. It seems the farmers have started opening up the storage pits and there's nothing wrong with the potatoes in them at all, so even if the new crop fails there will still be the old one to fall back on.'

But then the pits were opened at Lochcarron, and then in Ross and Sutherland and the Isles, and the potatoes in them had rotted. It was the same at Kinveil. Vilia racked her brains trying to discover some way of helping, but there was nothing she could do. Magnus had flatly forbidden her to lay out any money, and he meant it. She did, however, write to Theo and tell him to buy seed potatoes and send them to Kinveil. He was to use her private funds, although she would imply to Magnus that a collection had been made at the foundry and that the men had been generous. At least it would give the people of the estate something to plant, something to give them hope.

In July, even after weeks of drought, followed by unnatural storms and floods, the potato fields looked rich and green.

Magnus said, 'There you are! I told you it was a fuss about nothing.'

Then, in August, drifting invisibly in with the rain and mist, the blight arrived. The plants drooped, their leaves turning black and slimy. When a spade was dug in, the potatoes it turned up were grey and oozing and smelt of decay. The transformation took place in the space of no more than two days. From survival to starvation in forty-eight hours. Within weeks, the whole potato crop of the High-lands had failed.

As winter began to set in, with cruel winds and snow and black ice, the authorities at last began to act – 'if,' as Vilia said bitterly, 'running around squawking like decapitated hens can be called acting'. What it all added up to was recommendations and road-mending. The starving were to buy oatmeal, peas and beans and cabbages, with the money they earned from working on specially devised road schemes. No one knew where the oatmeal, the peas, beans and cabbages, were to come from, and there were too few roads to mend for the number of people who needed to work on them.

But miraculously, some of the great Highland proprietors put their hands into their own pockets and Magnus felt he owed it to his position to follow their example. 'Not charity, mind you!' he warned Vilia. 'I don't believe in it. But there's no denying it would be useful to have some kind of road over the Black Mount to the Summer Loch. You can get the people working on that, if you like.'

'Thank you,' Vilia replied tightly.

Already, she had set Shona the task of raising public donations in Edinburgh, and Shona had cooperated with all her gentle heart. Grace, in London, was preoccupied with a charity gala designed to benefit the people of Glenbraddan – although Vilia suspected that by the time the gala took place it would all be too late – but Gideon, with the money raised by Shona, was able to buy barleymeal at a competitive price and send it north. 'Blackmail, pure and simple,' he wrote to his mother. 'I tell the merchants I am considering an article for the *Times-Graphic* on the subject of excessive profits in the food retailing trade, and the price comes down with a bump!'

Even so, there was crisis after crisis. It was madness to try and build a road over the mountains in the depths of winter, but Magnus wouldn't hear of paying the men unless some work was done; it was twenty years since he had been up in the hills and he had forgotten what they were like. Sometimes, the food dispatched by Gideon couldn't get through because the roads were blocked. And when Destitution Boards were set up in Edinburgh and Glasgow to collect and administer funds from public appeals, Shona found more difficulty in raising money; the Boards themselves were incompetent and wasteful.

Every day during that long, dreadful winter, the penniless and the starving drifted over the causeway to Kinveil in search of aid. All over the countryside people had left their homes looking for somewhere more kindly – whole families, fathers, mothers with children in their arms and others, bare of head and foot, at their skirts, sleeping where they could, begging a few salt herring or a bowl of thin broth where such was to be had. To the east and in the Lowlands, there were riots, but the people who wandered the Highlands showed a fatalism that broke Vilia's heart.

Harriet Blair, of all people, proved to be a tower of strength. Vilia almost forgave her for her black bombazine and the sermons she served with the soup, because she never turned away the unfortunates whom Vilia sent on to Glenbraddan from Kinveil. Even Edward showed a flicker or two of humanity, if only because whatever Harriet did must be right.

It put them firmly back in Magnus's black books. After the first few weeks of basking in the euphoria of good works, he began to relapse into a more normal frame of mind. Vilia was tiring herself out, he said, and uselessly. It was foolish to think she could save the world single-handed. Besides, she was neglecting her domestic duties. His study hadn't been cleaned for days; what were the maids doing with their time? Juliana hadn't had a French lesson since last October. He was tired of nothing but salmon and mutton every night; it was time she started giving some attention to the menu again. It was time she sent someone out stalking; he fancied some venison for a change. Had she noticed that the share market was unstable? Were rail shares going to collapse? What did Theo say about it? Should he sell the script Theo had talked him into buying? He couldn't afford to lose money, not when Vilia was spending it like water.

It went on and on, and in the end — one day when for some impenetrable reason he had walked into the castle kitchen and found Juliana and Lizzie timidly serving mutton broth to some thin, filthy, and probably disease-ridden children, the explosion came. What he and Vilia said to each other was, in effect, no more than what had been said over the Disruption, but underneath it was a far deeper bitterness. This time, Vilia could neither forgive nor forget his selfishness. And this time, because she refused utterly to obey him, he did not forget, either.

It had all happened more than two years ago now, two years during which they had lived in a state of armed truce, in a state of coexistence that was sometimes amicable enough but always and unfailingly distant. They heard each other, but didn't listen, and neither of them cared at all.

2

Jermyn, Lavinia, and Peregrine James Lauriston arrived at Kinveil in November 1848, and not even Magnus was able to fault them at first. They had the most beautiful manners. Even Jermyn, who would have been too clever for Magnus's comfort, was quick to recognize that intelligent conversation was not what was required and lapsed almost at once into a dreamy, absent politeness that gave his step-grandfather a very good opinion of him. Lavinia, too, found favour. She was a bright, pert child who was not in the least afraid of him, and he was disarmed. Indeed, as Juliana remarked crossly to Lizzie, he laughed at conduct in Lavinia that he would not have tolerated in them! Only about Peregrine James did he have reservations, detecting in him too much of his father — not in looks, but in that celestial belief in himself that had always been a source of acute irritation in Drew. 'What's he got to be so pleased with himself about?' Magnus muttered to Vilia, who – herself far from doting where her youngest grandchild was concerned – replied, 'He *is* only eight years old, and boys are often difficult at that age.' Magnus harrumphed, and said he hoped he would improve soon, or he would wear out his welcome.

Christmas came and went, and New Year, and spring, marked by great floods that brought widespread damage, wrecking bridges and causing the Caledonian Canal to burst its banks. Summer arrived and the children were still at Kinveil, for the cholera epidemic was still increasing. By August more than a thousand people were dying every week in London alone.

Kinveil had settled down to a peaceful routine. Lavinia shared her schooling with Juliana and Lizzie, while Jermyn alternated between setting Peregrine James exercises that his brother complained were far beyond him and flying for refuge to the temporary laboratory that Vilia had allowed him to set up in the disused topmost room of the Kitchen Block. No one was quite sure what he did there, and since the day when he had tried to explain to Vilia about patent electric light, and long-distance explosions, and electric guns – about which he seemed alarmingly well informed – she thought, on the whole, it was safer not to ask. All she insisted on was that he spend some time outdoors every day. Three more ponies had to be acquired and stabled with Juliana's and Lizzie's pair, who were known as Honey and Oatcake because, as Juliana said, they went so well together.

In September, Theo arrived on a visit. 'How gratifying,' he remarked, as he surveyed all the faces assembled to welcome him. 'If I were not naturally modest, I should be persuaded you were all delighted to see me.'

He exaggerated very little. Only Lizzie, a stranger to any sensation as positive as delight, and Lavinia, whose self-assurance was not proof against the satire in her uncle's smile, greeted him with reserve.

Vilia had never seen him looking tired before, but his body seemed to have lost some of its resilience, and there was strain behind the suavity of his expression. The last three or four years, of course, would have been enough to exhaust Vulcan himself. The railway mania of 1845 had meant urgent pressure at the foundry, and the 'battle of the gauges' that followed had added its own problems. It made little difference to Lauristons' whether the Great Western's seven-foot gauge was generally adopted, or whether the royal commission settled for four feet eight inches as most other railways preferred, but there had been a flood of orders for extra rails from companies struck by the idea of trying a mixed gauge, with a third rail between the other two. Next had come the financial crisis of 1847, when the bottom dropped out of the railway market and shares became unsaleable. That was when Vilia had annoyed Theo quite deeply by finding herself unable to resist saying, 'I told you so'. But although banks all across the country had been forced to stop payment, Lauristons' was stable enough to ride the storm. Prudently, Theo had turned his attention to diversification. And still the crises had continued. One of them had been utterly unforeseen. In 1848, when it seemed as if all the continent of Europe was going up in flames, Her Majesty's foreign secretary had been sufficiently perturbed to pass an Act for the deportation of 'aliens of disreputable character, whose presence and conduct may be deemed dangerous to the peace and social order of these realms.' And that had been the end of Felix von Sandemann, who was neither disreputable nor dangerous, but had succeeded in making personal enemies of one or two people who had done their best to make him appear so. That, anyway, was what Theo said, and Vilia – despite her private amusement – was bound to admit that he was hardly the kind of man to consort with revolutionaries.

However, Theo said, it looked as if things were beginning to calm down, if only for the moment. 'What I have to do now is think and plan. Because on Perry Randall's advice we are about to enter the American market at last.'

'Indeed? It's a long time since I have heard news of – Mr Randall. He and his family are well?'

'I believe so.'

'I don't recall,' she said airily. 'How many of a family do they have now?'

'Three. The two boys, Francis and Benson, and a girl, Reine. Odd name, isn't it?'

He couldn't know. He *couldn't* know of those weeks in France at the house called La Chaumière de la Reine – 'the queen's cottage'. She said, 'Yes, it is. But tell me, what are your plans for America?' She was a little out of touch.

'You know about the Gold Rush in California? Hundreds – thousands – of people looking for gold, and no roof over their heads in

545

the meantime? Well, we have just shipped prefabricated, self-build houses to them in corrugated iron, each with three rooms and a store. We produced them in a matter of weeks; it was easy enough once the idea presented itself. And I expect they will sell very well.'

'Ingenious!'

'Yes. I can say so because it was the Moulding Shop foreman's idea, not mine. He has a cousin among the gold-seekers. And the next step – although I scarcely dare mention railways to you nowadays! – is precisely that. Or should I say "those"? Last November, the Galena and Chicago Union Railroad shipped its first carload of grain into the city. Perry believes that the Great Plains will soon be opened up, producing all the meat and corn the Eastern states will ever need, and that the railroad will make it possible.'

'But if the – what was it? – Galena and Chicago company already exists, is it not too late?'

'Well,' Theo replied consideringly, 'when I tell you that the first famous carload was transported over a whole ten miles of track . . .'

She laughed. 'I see! And the Great Plains stretch for hundreds, I assume?'

He was opening his mouth to reply when there was a sudden roar, as if thunder had rolled within feet of their heads. The very walls seemed to shake, and the window was obscured for a moment by an avalanche of dust and what sounded like tiny pebbles or hailstones.

'My God!' Vilia exclaimed, her hand at her throat. *'Jermyn!'*

3

Juliana, listening with deceptive interest to Jermyn's explanation of the manufacture and uses of nitro-glycerine, wondered fretfully what Lavinia and Lizzie were doing. Had they gone along the beach towards the village? Lavinia had been saying for days that she must collect some more shells for the shell picture she was doing. It was going to be quite pretty. Juliana would have liked to help. She wished her stepmother didn't insist on her spending so much time with Jermyn when she would rather have been with the girls. It had been all very well when the Lauristons first arrived, but now, after almost a year, the reasons didn't seem convincing any more.

Vilia had said, 'You are their hostess, remember, because this is your home. You are of an age now when you must begin to learn what responsibility means.'

Jermyn said, 'Pay attention, Juliana, for goodness' sake. I'm not explaining all this to you just for fun, you know!'

'Well, *I* don't want to know how to make nitro-whatever-it-is! Why should I?'

'Girls! Always asking what things have to do with *them*! Can't you be interested in knowledge for its own sake?'

'No.'

'Well, you should be. Pay attention. What you do is mix concentrated nitric and sulphuric acid, like this . . .'

Juliana sighed. Vilia had said, 'It would be considerate to allow Lizzie to have Lavinia all to herself, just for a while. You know how close they used to be, and how distressed Lizzie was to be separated from her. I know you have done a great deal to make Lizzie happy here. In fact, I am very pleased with you.' Juliana had stared, and then turned pink. Commendation from her stepmother was something quite out of the common run. Not that Vilia was ever unkind, but she was inclined to be cool and sometimes impatient when Juliana employed the helpless feminine tricks that pleased her papa so much. 'However, you mustn't be too obvious about it. Lavinia would feel very unwelcome if you left her alone with Lizzie for no good reason. I suggest what you do is look after Jermyn. Peregrine James is really too young to be a companion to him. And then everyone will be happy.' Except Peregrine James, Juliana had thought – but that was before she had met him. The youngest of the Lauristons was eminently capable of filling in his time without assistance from anyone. He was the most astonishingly self-contained and self-assured child.

'*Juliana!*'

'Yes, Jermyn.'

She didn't understand him at all. His head was stuffed full of facts and figures and equations and what he called 'formulae'. She wasn't quite sure what formulae were except that they included a great many strings of forgettable letters and numbers of which the only one that stuck in her mind was H_2O for water. Why couldn't he just say 'water' and be done with it? He was preoccupied with chemistry at the moment, but thought he would soon move over to mechanical engineering. She didn't know what that was, either, but he said he thought it would suit his cast of mind better. She was, however, perfectly able to recognize that he found the task of trying to explain things to her exceedingly wearisome and only did it out of courtesy, and because, too, the very act of explaining seemed to force him into asking questions of himself. More than once, he had stopped himself in the middle of a sentence to say thoughtfully, 'Now, that's a possibility, isn't it!' And because she had learned when she was quite small to open her eyes wide and look admiring whenever any grown-up male seemed to think he had done something clever, she had said, 'Is it? How exciting!' But from that point of view Jermyn wasn't very satisfactory. She was used to a responsive smile, and a reassuring hug or pat on the shoulder, whereas all Jermyn did was look at her as if she wasn't there.

Now he said, 'Are you watching? Once it's properly cooled, I'll treat purified glycerine with it, and we'll finish up with a heavy, oily-looking liquid.' He began to lay out a variety of old saucepans and jars, and what looked like a porridge spurtle. 'I have to stir it,' he said, 'and it's very important to do it slowly and gently, otherwise it might blow up. I don't suppose you know that stirring things is sometimes enough to generate its own heat?'

'*Blow up?*' she almost shrieked.

'Oh, don't worry, and stop capering around. It doesn't like sudden vibrations, either.'

She had withdrawn a hurried few steps, but stopped dead. In a breathy little voice, she exclaimed, 'You must be mad! Why are you playing about with it if it's likely to blow up?'

Calmly measuring something from a thick glass flask, he replied, 'Because it's meant to, stupid. That's what nitro-glycerine is. An Italian chemist called Sobrero discovered it two or three years ago. People have been looking for something to improve on gunpowder for ages and ages, and the most promising alternatives seem to be either this or gun cotton. But when Schönbei – that's the man who discovered gun cotton – tried to make it commercially the year before last, he managed to blow up the whole works. It must have been quite a bang, because there were twenty-four people killed.' He looked at Juliana, white as a sheet, and added kindly, 'That was gun cotton – nitro-cellulose. Nitro-glycerine's different, and it's perfectly safe as long as you know what you're doing.'

'But why do you want to do it *at all*?'

'I should have thought it was obvious. With Lauristons' so deeply involved in railway construction, it would be extremely advantageous to us if we could supply blasting explosive to prepare the tracks as well as the lines to lay on them! Now, be quiet for a moment, will you?'

She gulped, and watched as he carefully began stirring his mixture with the spurtle. At last, he said, 'I'll let it rest for a few moments now.'

'But – but what are you going to do with it when you've finished making it?'

'I'm going to take it up into the hills and see if I can blow up some rocks.' He grinned suddenly. 'Quite a long way into the hills! Grand-mother would have a fit if she thought I was doing damage to her precious Kinveil, even if I'm only shifting a boulder or two. Don't you dare tell her!'

Like all the Lauristons, he was a good-looking boy. Until now, Juliana had thought how attractive he was when he smiled; he had a kind of gentleness, even when he was being impatient with her, and she had felt comfortable with him. But not now. It was the horridly matter-of-fact way he talked about what he was doing, as if blowing up rocks – and people – was a perfectly commonplace affair. She would have felt far less frightened, and appreciably safer, if he had been breathless and keyed-up and wary. She stared at him saucer-eyed.

'Just one more time,' he said thoughtfully, 'and then I think we can leave it for a while.' Gently, he stirred, and gently laid aside the spurtle. Then he turned and saw Juliana's expression. 'Poor Juley!' he exclaimed with a chuckle. 'You look frightened to death. Come along, then, and let's forget about it. I could do with a cup of tea, couldn't you? Do you think we might persuade them to make us some in the kitchen?'

He was very disarming, and she was so relieved she could have hugged him. As they emerged, hand in hand, from the laboratory, the fresh air coming up the staircase made her realize what nasty smells she had been breathing for the last hour. 'Pooh!' she said with a giggle. 'We don't want those disgusting smells spreading all over the place.'

And slammed the door.

Jermyn's mouth was just opening when the bang came. It was the most terrifying experience of Juliana's life, even counting that day when she had almost been drowned at the floating. It was the suddenness of it, and the loudness, and the way the floor shook, and plaster started raining down. It was the way the door she had just slammed groaned and creaked and then, slowly as in a nightmare, toppled out towards her and then jammed with a horrifying crash in the angle of the staircase. It was the nauseating, suffocating fumes that came with it. It was Jermyn pushing her and pulling her, his hands like steel claws on her arms, hurrying her downstairs and ignoring her screams and wails as she tripped and almost fell to her knees, and dragging her ruthlessly upright again. When they reached the courtyard, he released her abruptly, and with a crisp instruction to fetch Theo, vanished back into the doorway through which they had come. A greasy black cloud rolled sluggishly out of the gap.

But Juliana simply stood, weeping hysterically, far beyond common sense, as the courtyard filled with startled people. It was Theo she ran to and clung to, sobbing incoherently, and he had to take a moment to comfort her before he could make any sense of what she was saying through her hiccoughing gasps. Then, his fair brows lifting in a face profoundly unimpressed, he thrust the child into Vilia's arms and himself plunged into the smoke. Sorley disappeared in his wake, and then three of the house servants. The others, on Vilia's instructions, stayed where they were. 'If help is needed,' she said, 'we will know soon enough.'

Magnus appeared just when Theo and the others had emerged again, coughing, spluttering and filthy. 'Item,' Theo was saying, 'one hole in roof. Item, large crack in wall. Item, one splintered floor. Item, one coat of filthy grease over everything. Item, one tanning of Master Jermyn Lauriston's hide. And by God, Jermyn, if you were a couple of years younger, I'd mean that literally! What were you playing at?'

Ghostly white under the dirt, Jermyn said, 'It was an accident. Nobody's fault.'

From the doorway of the Day Block, Magnus squawked, 'Accident? Am I to understand you have blown the roof off Kinveil and you call it an accident?' He was wearing a rather splendid embroidered dressing-gown, and his eyes were blurred, as if he had been woken violently from his afternoon nap.

Almost without thinking, Vilia began to soothe him, leading him back to his room with assurances that the damage was only superficial and best left to Theo to deal with. But when he showed a disposition to lay down the law, she handed him briskly over to his valet and returned to the fray.

It was three hours before a semblance of calm returned to Kinveil, and Vilia and Theo could retreat to chairs set up on the sea wall, where they would have ample warning of interruption, and lie back soaking in the evening peace. Theo had the decanter within easy reach, and Vilia, breaking her usual custom, held a glass containing not white wine but a stiff, neat, pale whisky. Gratefully, she murmured, 'What a relief! Thank heaven Lavinia and Lizzie were out of the way at the time. Two more neurotic children would have been quite beyond bearing.' Jermyn, extremely crestfallen, had been banished to his room with Peregrine James who had, at one point, been so supercilious as almost to earn himself a box on the ear from his exasperated grandmother. A returned Lavinia and Lizzie, after hovering inquisitively and getting under everyone's feet, had been similarly dispatched, this time to the schoolroom. Magnus had retired to his bed to recover from the shock, and Juliana, her tears dried at last, had been tucked up with a cup of hot milk laced with honey. Sorley, with assistance, was clearing up the mess.

'Oh, dear!' Vilia sighed. 'Other catastrophes apart, I suppose this afternoon's episode has put an end to any hope of Juliana and Jermyn developing an attachment for each other. With Juliana shaking at the very sight of Jermyn, and Jermyn nobly taking the blame for something that was very clearly her fault – though I can't think how! – it looks as if my plans have been as mortally injured as the roof. My poor castle. My *poor* castle!'

Lazily, Theo said, 'Modern times, my dear. Once it was enemy slingshot, then Redcoat guns, now nitro-glycerine. Only another episode in history, another of Kinveil's honourable scars. Does it really upset you so much?'

'Yes, it does. Every stone in the place means something to me. I remember the corner I used to run to, when I was unhappy as a child. I remember which part of which wall I used to lean against, to pull off my boots before I went indoors. I remember which step I always rested on to get my breath back, when I was climbing to the top of the tower. I remember Jessie Graham sending me up to that very room Jermyn's just blown the roof off, to see whether the salt-smuggler was on his way up from Inverbeg. I remember the torrent that used to come in through

551

that same roof when the snow melted. And I remember who had it mended. Mungo Telfer.' There wasn't any humour in her laugh. 'Sentiment, I suppose. Oh, well. So much for Juliana marrying into the Lauriston family! It was as much as I could do to prevent Magnus from sending Jermyn packing, here and now. I don't think I've ever seen him so angry. Do you think Peregrine James would do instead?' She sighed. 'I can't see it, I must admit.'

Theo smiled. 'No. On the other hand, my own hardened bachelor heart was touched when Juliana ran to me today. Perhaps I might marry her myself in a few years.'

After a long moment, Vilia withdrew her eyes from his face and gazed out towards Skye, an indigo silhouette against the pale green evening heavens. There was a sliver of new moon beginning to show. What age was he? Thirty-five? And Juliana a dainty, immature twelve, straight and undeveloped as a boy. But in another five or six years the chasm would be much narrower. It wouldn't be a man and a child any longer, but two adults. There was nothing at all unusual in a girl marrying someone much older, and it was true that Juliana was very ready to turn to Theo for coaxing and reassurance. The idea hadn't occurred to Vilia before, but it would be a perfect – a splendid solution to all her designs. *Such* a splendid solution. She said without inflexion, 'Do you mean that?'

'You tell me often enough that it's time I was married. And if I must, then why not Juliana? You wouldn't have any objection, would you? And we're not blood relations, so the church could have none. Magnus could be persuaded, I imagine. All we have to do is convince Juliana herself. Perhaps you could handle that aspect of the matter?'

He was still smiling. Her eyes blind and her mind whirling, she smiled back at him. To persuade the child to see Theo as her surest – her only – refuge. To discourage her from running to anyone else. Magnus's approval was important. If it were possible to set him at odds with everyone who presented a challenge to Theo – not only as husband but as trustee – it might all work out.

'Perhaps I could,' she said.

Chapter Four

1

As the royal carriages drew up at the main entrance to the Crystal Palace at noon on the first of May 1851, the sky cleared and the sun came out in full force, setting the raindrops sparkling on almost three hundred thousand panes of glass so that, against all the odds, the place really did look as if it had been made from crystal. Gideon, sliding unobtrusively indoors through one of the less distinguished entrances, grinned to himself. It appealed to him that the world's first great international exhibition of industry should be housed in a building that had been designed by a former gardener – on the model of the Duke of Devonshire's lily house, no less – and nicknamed 'crystal palace' by some humorist on *Punch*. He wondered if Her Majesty had been amused. Probably not.

The battery across the Serpentine fired a salute, and there was a flourish of trumpets at the north end of the transept. In dutiful response, twenty-five thousand voices hit the cathedral-like vaulting in one vast, reverberating cheer. Gideon flinched and glanced up as the sound bounced back from the hundred-foot ridge and volleyed from one end to the other of the long glass nave. He was certainly going to be the *Times-Graphic*'s man-on-the-spot if the roof fell in. But it didn't, although the decorative palms and flowers and the great elms swayed and shuddered, and Gideon had the impression that one or two of the rather dubious statues lining the transept had shifted slightly on their plinths.

The interior gates stood open waiting for the royal party to pass through, gates intricately cast in iron coated with bronze, marvels of floriation and curlicue, of finials and crowns and stags' heads, one of the principal exhibits from the Darby foundry at Coalbrookdale. Gideon wondered what Theo thought of them. Stretching to his fullest height, he looked around hoping, though not very seriously, to catch sight of someone he knew. Theo, Drew, and probably Jermyn would be stationed as near as possible to the Lauriston exhibition stands – four in all; one each in the machinery, civil engineering, hardware, and metalwork sections – but Vilia ought to be here somewhere with Magnus and the two girls, and Shona with Lavinia and Peregrine

James. Vilia had intended to find a vantage point as near the dais as possible.

The Barbers had said they were coming, too, with their house guests, young Isa Blair from Glenbraddan, and the Savarins, who had come over from Paris for the occasion. Grace, uncharacteristically harassed when Gideon had last seen her, had remarked that she couldn't imagine *why* they were coming, since she had seldom known anyone less interested in industry than Emile. But nineteen-year-old Guy, it seemed, was passionately concerned about 'modern design', which no doubt explained it. His mama regarded it as *très important* to encourage artistic tendencies in one's *enfants*. Gideon hadn't met the Savarins since Vilia's wedding, but he remembered Georgy very well – a most improbable sister for someone like Edward Blair.

Scanning the crowd, his eyes were suddenly arrested by a glimpse of someone on the other side of the aisle, a grey-haired man with a boy of about fourteen by his side. Gideon didn't believe his eyes at first. It couldn't be! There was a surge of people behind the retaining ropes and the face disappeared. But surely it *had* been Perry Randall! Gideon hadn't seen him for fifteen years, but he couldn't be mistaken. Had anyone known he was coming? Theo hadn't said anything about it. Pleasure warred in Gideon's breast with something that, after a moment, he identified as apprehension. This was going to cause a flutter in the Telfer dovecote.

His mind reeling, Gideon turned to watch the entry of the royal party. The Prince Consort came first for once, a step ahead of his queen. He seemed to be leading her, with justifiable pride, into the exhibition he had done so much to promote. Gideon wasn't a royalist, but he found it rather touching. Little Princess Vicky, in white satin and lace, was clinging to her father's left hand, while the ten-year-old Prince of Wales, self-consciously attired in full Highland dress – kilt, sporran, brightly-paned hose, feathered bonnet and all – grimly clasped his mother's right. Victoria herself was a vision in pink and silver and what looked like every diamond in the royal treasury. Well, *almost* every diamond; the recently acquired Koh-i-noor was on display here at the exhibition, in a sturdy metal cage with a crown on top.

From their place on the other side of the aisle, strategically positioned between the Coalbrookdale gates and the ceremonial dais with its great canopy, Perry Randall and his son Francis watched the plump and rather coarse-skinned young woman make her way along the corridor of heralds and Beefeaters, past groups of Exhibition Commissioners and officials and officers of the Household troops in their garish uniforms – all of them clashing nastily with her own pink and silver – while, Perry reflected, she hadn't even been born when he had left her realm for the New World. It reminded him of something he preferred not to think of, that he was more than sixty years old now. The last few weeks had tired him a little, but not much. Anyway, they would have been enough to tire a man half his age.

As the organs, backed by two hundred instruments and a well-schooled choir of six hundred voices, did their best with the National Anthem, Perry wondered for the dozenth time in the last hour how the men were getting on with unpacking his exhibits. All those damned Colt revolvers to be separately mounted on a twelve-foot targe, in the pattern traditionally used in the Highlands for displaying swords and dirks! Perry had thought it would be a compliment Her Balmoral-mad Majesty might appreciate, but he wished now the idea had never occurred to him. Just one revolver out of line and the effect would be ruined. He should have been at the stand, supervising, but he couldn't deprive his son of this opportunity to see royalty in full plumage. Yet last-minute rush or not, he was still ahead of most of his compatriots. America had made an almighty fuss about having enough space for its displays, and then had done little to justify it. Making a brisk sortie to the American court just before noon, Perry had been dismayed to see no more than a haphazard scattering of rocking-chairs, blocks of copper, barrels of flour, and very little else. He hoped to God someone was going to do something before America became a laughing stock. Even though the queen's programme for today didn't include a visit of inspection to the foreign wing of the exhibition, there ought to have been more signs of hustle than there were.

When the music had droned to its conclusion, the Prince Consort, in his thick accent, began reading out The Report, which told his wife what she presumably already knew – that there were fourteen thousand exhibitors, half of them British; that forty foreign countries were participating; that there were ten miles of frontage for the display of exhibits; and that the exhibition was divided into general classes consisting of raw materials, machinery, manufactures, and sculpture and fine arts. The crowd cheered and clapped. The queen raised her voice in a brief reply that might well have been briefer, the sum and substance of it being, 'How splendid!' and the crowd cheered and clapped again. The Archbishop of Canterbury offered up a prayer that could also, with benefit, have been briefer. Then, when organs and choir had disposed of the Hallelujah Chorus, the grand procession began. Up to the far end of the nave and down again, with a military band adding its mite to the general rumpus. How many ladies, Perry wondered, were going to have to resort to laudanum when they reached home? Even Her Majesty's head must be splitting by now.

And then it was over. Lord Breadalbane, at the pitch of his lungs, announced, 'Her Majesty commands me to declare this exhibition open', and there was another flourish of trumpets to see the royal party off the premises.

'Father,' said a voice at Perry's side, 'I don't know whether you would wish to be informed, but there is a gentleman over there who appears anxious to attract your attention. At least,' he added worriedly, 'I *think* it is you.' Francis was a source of recurring joy and wonder to his father. Slender, quiet, and amazingly courteous, he could have been reared nowhere but on Beacon Hill, Boston. Perry, who had left his upbringing to Sara, had no idea how it was possible for a fourteen-year-old to be so open-hearted, naive, and utterly charming. With a smile, he followed Francis's glance, expecting to see some harassed official wondering how much longer Mr Randall expected to need the dozen or so labourers and porters he had been allotted. But instead he saw Gideon Lauriston, waving cheerfully, his face fifteen years leaner, fifteen years more observant than when they had last met, but still unmistakably Gideon. Still unmistakably Vilia Cameron's son.

Perry had known they were bound to meet, although his arrangements had been made at such speed that he hadn't taken time to tell anyone that he was coming. He waved back, his eyes – beyond control – travelling past Gideon to the people around him. But there was no other face that he knew. What would she look like after all these years? How would she have changed? That fine complexion must be lined now, and at fifty-five her hair would be nearer white than blonde; he hoped it hadn't turned that yellow-white pepper colour. Would she be thin, now, instead of slim? But such questions didn't matter, or not very much. What mattered was how she felt about him. On that last day at the Chaumière de la Reine, he had wounded her deeply, and, made thoughtless by shock and bitterness, had criticized her without guarding his tongue. The wounds she might forgive, but the criticism never. By now her hatred might have faded, for she was too intelligent to cherish such a wasteful emotion, but what would be there instead? He hoped not nothingness, which would be too hard to bear.

One thing he had come to accept as a fact of life. Although he loved his children very deeply and had both respect and affection for his wife, he was still in thrall to Vilia. Consumingly, he wanted to see her again, to see if by some miracle there were still laughter and sparkle in her eyes. Desperately, he didn't want to see her again, because she would destroy the calm he had built up with such pains. He felt as he had felt when he went to Kinveil in '29, postponing the day of reckoning, except that this time there was no ounce of hope to weigh in the scales. He wished he had stayed at home in Boston, but business had almost forced him to come, and Francis's eagerness had been the ultimate, irresistible factor. At some time in these next weeks, he was going to see her. And she was going to be cool and distant with him. And he, for the sake of his pride, and his children, and his marriage, was going to be distant, too. He had no idea what he would do if, against all the odds, he saw that particular light in her eye.

'It's Gideon Lauriston,' he said to Francis. 'The renegade from the foundry. Hang on to my coat and we'll try and fight our way through. You'll like him.'

Gideon's smile was a little guarded now, but still delightful, and Perry clapped him on the shoulder and said, 'How goes it? This is my son Francis.'

He didn't disguise his pride in the boy, and Gideon, for the second time that morning, felt oddly touched. Perry had put on a few pounds in weight, and his hair was iron grey, but it only gave him added distinction. The deep-cut marks of satire round his mouth had softened, and the controlled tension seemed to have gone altogether, as if he no longer needed it. Gideon had always thought of him as a springing tiger. Now he was more like an elder statesman, despite his still admirable figure and equally admirable dark frock coat and plaid trousers. His eyes danced, and his mouth was as decisive as of old, but his air was that of a man who, secure in his own achievement, had learned to look on the world with an encompassing tolerance.

Gideon said, 'I'm fine, and you two look like walking advertisements for the American way of life! Are you exhibiting? Why didn't you let us know you were coming? Have you a few minutes to spare? Everybody's here – but God knows where! Let's try and find them.'

In the end, they found only Theo and Drew, who were precisely where Gideon had expected them to be. Gideon was torn between relief and exasperation at having caught not so much as a glimpse of the Kinveil party.

That, although he didn't know it, was because one member of the Kinveil party had caught a glimpse of them first. She had turned so pale that Shona, seeing it, had exclaimed, 'Are you all right, Vilia? It's the heat and the noise!' and with the gentle efficiency that had come to her with maturity had swiftly marshalled adults and children out of the Crystal Palace and into the waiting carriages, and told the coachman to drive home.

2

Gideon's jaw dropped. 'A family dinner party?' he echoed. 'Shona, are you mad? Magnus at the same table as Perry Randall! And you know he doesn't have any opinion of Savarin – or Drew or Jermyn, come to that.'

'I don't care,' she said, surprisingly. The eyes in her round, pretty face were as innocent as they had ever been, but she was stubborn now in defence of what she cared about and there was the merest trace of the kind of moral rectitude that had always been one of her sister's most irritating characteristics. 'It seems to me perfectly ridiculous that Uncle Magnus should keep up a silly, purposeless feud that began before I was even born, for the antagonism is all on his side, you know! My father is quite impartial about it.'

'Then why bother?'

'Because it makes everyone else uncomfortable. Grace and I can't even mention father's name in Uncle Magnus's hearing without being treated to one of his tirades, and besides, it gives the children a very odd idea of their grandfather. I can't explain to them why Uncle Magnus dislikes him so. His behaviour to my mother was really not very gentlemanly, after all. But it was all so long ago, and apart from that his conduct has been quite irreproachable.'

Gideon stared at her for a moment. Was women's intuition no more than a myth, or was it just that Shona was constitutionally incapable of seeing beyond Drew? Their devotion to each other never ceased to astonish him; it made him feel a little queasy. After a moment, he said hopefully, 'Perhaps Magnus won't come.'

She sat up sharply, her soft brown ringlets tossing above the blue foulard gown with its modish waistcoat bodice. 'Really, Gideon! I thought you at least would be on my side.'

'Isn't Drew?'

'He says I must do as I wish. He's been too rushed to discuss it with me. And all Theo will do is smile in that maddening way of his. But Grace agrees that it is a very good idea.'

'And Vilia?'

Her self-confidence faltered. 'I'm not sure. She says she thinks it is very strong-minded of me, which isn't precisely encouraging. But I still think I should make the effort, and next Thursday seems to be the only possible day. Georgy and Emile are going back to Paris on Saturday, and my father and Francis sail on the Monday after. I think we *should* have the Savarins at the party, don't you? Uncle Magnus hasn't even met Gabrielle and Guy yet, and after Edward, Guy would be his heir if anything happened to Juliana.'

Gideon grinned. 'You think they might divert Uncle Magnus from your father?'

'Nothing of the sort.' Her soft eyes gleamed. 'Although I feel quite giddy when I try to work out a seating plan for the table.'

'I'm not surprised! Are you having the children as well?'

'Oh, yes, all except Peregrine James. He's really too young and it would make the numbers uneven. But I think it would be nice to invite Francis, and of course if he comes all the rest must, too. Twenty-one altogether. Surprising, isn't it? I've never added them up before.'

'You'll forgive me for saying that most people wouldn't think of twenty-one as an *even* number?'

She giggled. 'I know. The thing is that even without Peregrine James I need an extra lady. That was what I wanted to talk to you about.'

'Oh, yes?' He surveyed her warily.

'I can't think of *anyone* except Mrs Armstrong – you know, Peter

559

Barber's widowed cousin who lives with them? And while she is a very good sort of person, she is not at all sociable.'

'Fine!' he said promptly. 'You can seat her beside Magnus. They should get on very well.'

'So I wondered . . . Isn't there someone *you* would like me to invite?'

'Someone?'

'Well, some – some lady of your acquaintance. Someone who wouldn't consider it – er – odd to be invited to a Lauriston family party.'

So she *could* see beyond Drew sometimes! Gideon had thought that no one knew anything about Miss Selina Parker. The hair rising slightly on the back of his neck, he tried to imagine Selina let loose at Shona's party. Selina was vivid, intelligent, and opinionated – with some justification, for she had been one of the first salaried female employees on a national newspaper and considered it the worst of misfortune that she had narrowly missed beating Eliza Linton into becoming *the* first. It was a subject of which, regrettably, she never tired. But, apart from that, she was excellent company and one of those rare women who, while having no wish to be married, saw no reason to deprive herself of the pleasures of that state; she and Gideon had a very satisfactory arrangement. It was one thing to have an emancipated mistress, however, and quite another to introduce her into the bosom of one's family. The morality of it didn't worry Gideon unduly. It was just that Selina saw no need to gloss over their relationship, and while that was all very well in the circles in which they were accustomed to move, it would not be very kindly received by certain of Shona's guests. Magnus, for example. It would be little short of cruelty to the old boy to expect him to swallow Selina as well as Perry Randall.

'No,' he said firmly.

'Are you sure?'

'*Quite* sure!'

'Oh. Well, I suppose it will have to be Mrs Armstrong, then. I hope she has no other engagement. You wouldn't think it possible that next Thursday is the first evening for six whole weeks when everyone admits to being free!'

Gideon thought the 'admits to' was only a turn of speech. Shona had no reason to suspect that her most important guest had simply run out of excuses, even if, for the first week, these had been perfectly valid. Perry, he knew, had been fully occupied in setting his exhibit to rights under the pressure of constant interruption from a stream of visitors. But after that there had been an easier spell until the twenty-sixth of May, when the Monday-to-Thursday admission fee had been reduced to a shilling and more crowds had flowed in at a rate of over fifty thousand a day. Even Theo and Drew had returned to the hired house in Audley Street limp and exhausted, although Theo's machinery attracted only a small number of well-informed visitors, and Drew's hardware a large number of husbands and wives who were fortunately more interested in looking than in asking questions. But there didn't seem to be a man in London, Perry said, who wasn't curious to know precisely how the Colt revolver worked. 'Mind you,' he had added with a laugh, 'I shouldn't complain. Sam Colt's having a much harder time than I am. He's displaying a hundred *different* designs, which makes for a lot more questions and a deal more time spent answering. I guess I have the best of it.'

Even the less hectic days had still been long and tiring, and the evenings had been committed to a string of receptions, official, semi-official, and unofficial. But it was as if everyone had been playing an unadmitted game of hide and seek. Perry had attended the assembly given by the association of exhibitors, but Vilia, invited in her capacity as a director of Lauristons', hadn't been able to persuade Magnus to accompany her and had tactfully not gone alone. Theo and Drew had appeared at the Austrian ambassador's party, but Perry hadn't. Vilia had declared herself too tired to go to the French soirée. Perry had been there. When Vilia was at the machinery manufacturers' ball, Perry was drinking tea with the Barbers. And so it had gone on ever since the beginning of May. It couldn't be deliberate, but could it really be all coincidence? For no specific reason, Gideon found himself thinking of Sorley, and of Perry Randall's housekeeper, plump, fortyish, and not unprepossessing, who had been hired with the house in Manchester Square. Sorley, even at fifty-something, still had a way with women. A spy in the camp?

On the following Thursday, at Shona's earnest request, Gideon presented himself at Audley Street half an hour before the appointed time. 'Just think if Drew and Theo should be kept late at the exhibition!' she had said. 'I don't believe I could face it on my own.'

Despite the prospect ahead, he was in the best of humours, having that very afternoon signed a contract to write a book about America. Not the vulgar, incomprehensible America described in the many works that, over the last twenty years, had induced nothing but fascinated horror in the British reading public, but a serious, constructive, and above all friendly assessment of the exciting present and expanding future of a great subcontinent. It gave him immense satisfaction to think that, now, he would be able to put some of his literary predecessors in their place – including that fellow Dickens, whose *American Notes*, besides being exceedingly dull, displayed a misunderstanding of country and people that, in Gideon's view, was little short of scandalous.

Shona and the children were already in the drawing-room when Gideon entered, Lavinia saying with a fifteen-year-old sigh, 'Mama, you are beginning to twitter! Pray don't. It is, after all, only a family party, and I have no doubt that Papa will be here almost at once to give you his support.'

'Oh, I do hope so. Gideon, how providential that you should have arrived early!'

'You asked me to.'

'Did I? Heavens, how clever of me! Lavinia, dearest, do just run down to the housekeeper and make sure everything is all right in the kitchen.'

'*Again?*'

'It's so difficult to know what one should serve at a family party,' Shona complained distractedly when her daughter had gone. 'If one provides an interesting menu – well, Grace is bound to accuse me of extravagance! And Uncle Magnus doesn't like kickshaws. But if one doesn't, Georgy is sure to start talking about French chefs and that certain *je ne sais quoi* that enables them to elevate even the most trivial dishes into something *extraordinaire*.' It wasn't a bad imitation. 'But at least' – and she tweaked a ringlet into place before the mirror – 'she will have less excuse here than at the Barbers'. I can't imagine why the food at philosophers' tables should always be so plain and wholesome. Was there something in Socrates about it? Heavens, here they are!' Smoothing down the bodice of her gown and fluffing out its rose-figured skirts, she turned towards the door and waited, rigid as a prisoner in the dock.

It was the Barbers, with the unwanted Mrs Armstrong in their train. Grace was clad in a practical, mud-coloured satin that didn't tone very well with her 'archaeological' scarab necklace, while Mrs Armstrong, a woman in her mid-thirties, was so unobtrusive that she was almost invisible. Petronella, however, made up for them both, though it had clearly been in the teeth of parental opposition. Scarcely had the preliminary greetings been exchanged than she said in ringing tones, 'I appeal to you, Gideon! Tell mama that the world is changing and that females have as much right as gentlemen to dress as they choose. She considers this gown quite fast, merely because it is colourful.' It was. 'But I may tell you that, if it hadn't been that I have no wish to shock Uncle Magnus, I would have chosen to wear trousers. Have you heard of Mrs Bloomer? I understand some of her disciples are coming here later in the year to spread her gospel. And high time, too. A good dose of Bloomerism is just what British womanhood needs!'

Mercifully, they were spared a discussion of Bloomerism by the arrival of the Savarins and Isa Blair. Grace had said that, though one scarcely noticed dear Isa, the Savarins made the house feel exceedingly full. Gideon could see what she meant. And then his eyes skidded past the overdressed Georgy to the two young people behind, and he whistled under his breath. Gabrielle and Guy. How in the world had the Savarins managed to produce this pair? They were very much alike, tall and willowy, with hair like thick amber silk, glowing dark eyes, and beautiful mouths. Too beautiful in the boy's case, although the years would probably harden it. Gideon studied him with closer attention than he might have done, because he knew Theo was interested in him – not, Gideon had been relieved to discover, because of his looks, but because of his relationship to Magnus.

'Ignoring the distaff side of the family,' Theo had said, 'and disregarding Edward Blair – which one would be only too delighted to do – Guy is the eldest of Magnus's blood relatives, and consequently in direct line to inherit Kinveil if anything should happen to Juliana. One cannot, therefore, help being interested.'

'Can't one?'

'No, dear boy,' Theo had replied with a trace of asperity. 'You may not care what happens to Kinveil, but Vilia does, and so do I. Guy is

563

the first in line, followed by Ian Barber, and then by our very own nephews Jermyn and Peregrine James. Just think if the place were to go to Jermyn! Vilia becomes perfectly beatific at the thought of it reverting to a descendant of the Camerons.'

'Does she, indeed? Well, it seems to me a great waste of energy. Juliana's a healthy enough child and, besides, she's a sweet little thing. I sincerely hope nothing *does* happen to her.'

'So do we all, dear boy. So do we all. But even so, I look forward to seeing how Magnus reacts to Guy. If he dislikes him as much as he dislikes Jermyn – or more – then we should only be left with Ian. And, you know, Guy starts with the appalling disadvantage of being French, and compounds it by being artistic with a capital A. You'll see what I mean when you meet him. He would be quite intolerable if it weren't for the fact that he really means it. But Magnus won't care for him. What a pity the Barber boy is so unequivocally worthy!'

'Come on, Theo! He's a perfectly reasonable youngster, and a damned sight more reliable than most. He'll probably grow out of his stuffiness.'

'Playing devil's advocate?' There had been a malicious twist to Theo's smile, but he had dropped the subject.

Looking at Guy now, Gideon saw what Theo had meant. The boy was obviously shaping up to be a full-blown romantic of the kind that Magnus, who prided himself on being a man of plain common sense, couldn't abide. He probably remembered Guy as he had been at the wedding in 1838, an obstreperous infant with a very inadequate command of English. Gabrielle, two or three years his senior, hadn't looked much more promising. But now . . . Gideon whistled to himself again and, despite Selina's teaching, caught himself wondering why she wasn't married. Mlle Gaby didn't look like a girl wedded to independence – or to lifelong chastity. He caught her thoughtful gaze, and gave her his best bow and most charming smile. He wondered who was going to have the tantalizing experience of sitting next to her at dinner.

Drew came running downstairs just then, full of apologies. He was always under pressure, always in a rush. Gideon knew that Theo had arrived home at the same time and thought, with amusement, that he was going to have difficulty in reconciling his usual pose of leisureliness with his undoubted desire to be present at Magnus's first encounter with Perry. And Perry's with Vilia. Neither Gideon nor Theo had ever seen Perry and Vilia together. Indeed, as far as they knew, the two hadn't met since their portentous encounter in 1815. As far as they *knew*.

Lavinia, returning from yet another embassy to the kitchen, cocked an ear and murmured, 'A carriage. I think it must be grandfather's. It doesn't have the *weighty* sound of Uncle Magnus's!' Gideon grinned. He liked Lavinia.

With impeccable timing, Theo, who didn't like Lavinia, reached the upstairs hall just as the Randalls did. 'What a pleasure!' Gideon heard him say. 'We can have a civilized conversation for once, instead of all these disconnected expressions of goodwill we seem to have been tossing each other in passing over the last few weeks. And Francis, too. How splendid.'

Perry, neatly cornered, winked at Gideon, who had himself been transfixed by Peter Barber. The seconds ticked by, and the minutes, and then the drawing-room clock chimed the quarter – *Home, ho-ome!* – and then the half – *Home, ho-ome! sweet, sweet home!* – and then the three-quarters – *Home, ho-ome! sweet, sweet home! There's no-oh place like ho-ome*, – and Gideon gritted his teeth and hoped something would happen to prevent him having to listen to the whole damned verse. The rest of the company, scattered around the narrow, double drawing-room, was showing an increasing tendency to fidget, and Shona clearly wasn't hearing a word Mrs Armstrong was saying to her. Dusk was falling, and a servant came in to light the gas wall lamps, extravagant creations of plated bronze supported on voluptuous brackets adorned with winged tritons. Gideon didn't care for them at all, but they and the opulently carved furniture and richly patterned walls were the main reasons why Shona had hired the house. 'Drew thinks it *so* important that we should have somewhere up-to-date, because he will be entertaining any number of prospective customers, you know.' Gideon's own small house just north of Hyde Park was still lacking, like most others in London, the convenience of gas, but at least when you sat down the chairs didn't threaten to impale you on an antler, or throttle you with some creeper from an ebonized jungle vine.

And then, at last, the Kinveil party arrived.

Theo was just saying to Perry, 'I hope you lunched late today?' when there was a bustle on the stairs. Perry, replying, 'I didn't have time to lunch at all', turned towards the door, and waited, as everyone else was doing.

Magnus was standing there, his attention still focused on the hall. He was obviously saying something snappish, leaning on a stick and, with his right hand, making beckoning, hurrying gestures. It came as a shock to Perry to see that he was an old man, although there couldn't be more than half a dozen years between them. Not that Magnus, even in his twenties, had ever been young.

Two subdued-looking girls of about the same age as Francis scuttled – there was no other word for it – into the room, and after a somewhat distrait embrace from Shona, the taller, auburn-haired one made straight for Gideon. That was presumably Lizzie; Perry remembered Gideon, a lifetime ago, rhapsodizing about his new bride's autumn-leaf hair. Which meant that the other one, making for Theo and himself, had to be Magnus's daughter Juliana. Smilingly, Perry acknowledged her curtsey, and then turned back to the door, aware that he had been holding his breath and that Theo Lauriston's damnably interested eyes were still on him. Very gently, he exhaled. Why the devil hadn't Vilia forced her son into matrimony with some girl or other? Or hadn't she understood what he told her that last morning in France? But at least, Perry reflected, it was preferable for Theo to be interested in him rather than Francis.

Then Magnus, sighing heavily, ushered his wife through the door. Unbelievably, she was as slim, fair, and erect as ever. Her hair was paler, perhaps, but not blanched, and there was a heaviness about her eyes and a sharpness about the corners of her mouth that probably meant crow's feet and creases. Perry's vision nowadays wasn't what it had been, and he couldn't tell from this distance. She was smiling, and her eyes, still green, had a disquieting glitter in the harsh gaslight. Her gown was the colour of lichen, its bodice silky and close-fitting, and its wide, though not extravagant skirts made of layer upon layer of some diaphanous fabric, fluid as a waterfall. There were emeralds at her ears and wrists.

Her smile would have chilled a glacier as it swept the room, settling on no one, and then she said in the light, silvery voice that hadn't changed at all, 'Shona, my dear. I am so sorry, but we were delayed by a small domestic crisis. Please forgive us.'

Juliana, stationed between Theo and Perry, murmured, 'Papa said he wasn't coming, and Vilia said yes he was, and Papa said no he wasn't. "Domestic crisis" makes it sound like something wrong with the plumbing.'

Shona exclaimed, 'It's quite all right! I ordered dinner for much later than usual, on the principle that someone or other was bound to be held up.'

'*Dear* Shona!' said Theo in an under-voice, watching her coax Magnus to a chair. 'Always so considerate of other people's feelings. How can one possibly cavil at being left to die of slow starvation in such a good cause?'

Magnus was overweight and almost bald, though the white side-burns curled luxuriantly down by his ears and half-way along his jaw. There were heavy pouches at the corners of his mouth and thick folds of skin under his eyes. And having, it seemed, been forced to come, he didn't propose to put himself out any further. Sardonically, Perry watched him, secure in his role as head of the family, sit enthroned and wait for everyone to pay their respects. Everyone did. Perry noted that, while he seemed to approve of the Barbers, he deplored the Savarins, root and – after a momentary stare – branch. Young Guy, unmistakably artistic and too good-looking by half, did not improve matters by paying his uncle a good many Frenchified compliments, and although it was, perhaps, his faulty English that caused him to describe the castle as 'primitive', Magnus didn't like it at all. There was a strangled chuckle from Theo, back at Perry's side, and a murmur of, 'Well done! Keep it up, dear boy.'

Magnus was just asking Isa Blair, a colourless girl, whether she had remembered to write home to her mama to say how much she was enjoying London, when Perry became aware that Drew was bringing Vilia over to meet him. It was extraordinary, but Drew didn't seem to know that they were acquainted.

Vilia's expression had the kind of courteous impersonality it might have had if she had been listening to someone explain a new, but rather commonplace, piece of machinery to her. Her lips were very slightly upcurved into something that was nowhere near a smile, and her eyes looked without seeing. She said, 'Yes, my dear. Mr Randall and I met once or twice a very long time ago, and again briefly in Paris in the '30s. How delightful to see you again, Mr Randall. I understand you have quite settled in America now? I hear about your business interests from my sons occasionally, and of course Shona and Grace await your letters with the most anxious interest. And this must be – Francis, is it? How do you do?'

Overdoing it, my dearest love! Remember, Theo is listening, and he is cleverer – much, much cleverer – than our son.

Their son – his and hers – was standing with a complacent smile on his face, as if presiding over a meeting between two valued associates. In his mid-thirties now, he was showing his years more than either Theo or Gideon. Handsome still, he nevertheless had an air of strain, and his mouth looked as if it smiled only for customers – though perhaps sometimes, and more genuinely, for Shona. Perry hoped so. Drew was a stranger to him, and could never, even under quite different circumstances, have been anything else. Fathers and sons were not always compatible.

Francis bowed beautifully, and then Perry said, contriving to sound as distant as she, 'Indeed, Mrs Telfer, it is a pleasure to see you, too. I need not ask if you are well. You look to be in high force.'

Still, the arbitrary green gaze did not focus on him, even while she acknowledged the compliment. 'Thank you. I wish we could have longer to talk, but I must ask you to excuse me. I am most anxious to have a little time with Georgiana before she returns to Paris. We see her very seldom.'

And that was that.

The end. Finis. He knew she would say nothing more to him at all, unless she was forced into a formal 'please' or 'thank you'. She could scarcely have told him more clearly that they were now worlds apart, that there was no future for them at all, even if they had been free. And Perry, in any case, did not expect to be free in what remained of his life. He believed – and indeed, in ordinary human decency, hoped – that Sara would outlive him, for she was more than twenty years younger. Which made it quite irrelevant that Vilia was a dozen years younger than Magnus.

Theo's voice, verging on the unctuous, interrupted his useless train of thought. 'Ageless, isn't she?'

After a moment, Perry said, 'A remarkable woman.' He wished, deeply, that he could take his leave now, this moment.

He couldn't, of course. He was left wondering what happened next. What happened next was – nothing at all. Unnaturally sensitive to every vibration, Perry was aware that very few of the company, except perhaps Gideon and young Jermyn – whose involvement with science seemed to be matched only by his lack of involvement with people – could be described as wholly at ease. But no one made a scene, no one fainted or had hysterics, no one walked out. The ingredients of drama might be there, but the evening turned, almost at once, into a slightly sour *comédie humaine*.

Just as Shona was leading Perry over, at last, for the confrontation with Magnus that in prospect had woken her, shaking with nerves, at three o'clock every morning for a week, dinner was announced. She wavered, and murmured distractedly, and half turned, looking to Drew for support. Magnus, in the meantime – rummaging around for his stick, glaring at his wife's oblivious back, and struggling to rise – accepted the arm Perry offered without even noticing whose it was. When he did, he muttered, 'Oh, it's you. How d'ye do?' and then turned to his niece and demanded, 'Who am I taking in to dinner? You, I suppose?' Her face the most comical mixture of bewilderment and relief, she stammered, 'Yes, Uncle Magnus. If you please, Uncle Magnus,' and, taking his arm, swivelled him round in the direction of the door and the stairs down to the dining-room.

Perry found himself, at dinner, seated on his daughter's left with the negative Mrs Armstrong on his other side, and Magnus opposite. There were eight people separating him from Vilia at the other end of the table. He was grateful that Shona favoured the newly fashionable *service à la russe*, which left everything to the servants, so that there were no distracting voices breaking in on one's thoughts with, 'A slice from that duck before you, Randall, if you please,' or 'I believe Miss This-or-That might be tempted by the salmi of hare, Mr Randall, if you would be so very obliging as to serve some to her!' It was possible just to sit and observe, contributing occasionally to the small talk, and showing no sign of the assessments one was making, or the thoughts that were milling around in one's head.

His absorption didn't prevent him from keeping an eye on Francis, who was having a hard time, poor kid. Jermyn, leaning across his sister Lavinia, was interrogating him about the heating effect of firing several shots in succession through a single gun barrel. 'It must cause expansion, surely, and that could lead to a burst, couldn't it?'

Francis, who hadn't been in the Randall workshop more than half a dozen times in his life, didn't have the remotest idea, but to disappoint Jermyn would have run counter to all his ideas of politeness. 'I am not entirely sure,' he said, 'but I guess it has something to do with the speed of firing.'

'I know *that!*' Jermyn was impatient. 'I thought you might have made systematic tests. It seems to me one could develop a tremendously useful military weapon by adapting the revolver principle to something the size of a rifle, but it wouldn't be worth while unless it could fire at least a hundred balls in quick succession. And a longer barrel would be likely to generate more heat than a short one in such circumstances, don't you think?'

'Well, I guess . . .' Francis began, doing his valiant best, and was saved by Lavinia, who chose to put her foot down.

'Do stop talking across me!' she exclaimed to her brother. 'It's not at all polite, and besides, who cares about your boring old guns!' She giggled. 'You can see that Uncle Francis doesn't!'

Francis turned scarlet, though it wasn't clear whether this was because of the 'uncle' or Lavinia's uncomfortable bluntness.

Jermyn said, 'I suppose he is. How funny! He must be almost *every*body's uncle!'

The boy wasn't very far wrong, Perry thought. Stepbrother to Grace and Shona, Francis was step-uncle to Petronella and Ian Barber, as well as to all three Lauriston children. And what? – step-step-uncle? – to Isa Blair and the two young Savarins? Perry himself felt like everybody's grandfather.

'He's not *my* uncle!' Juliana exclaimed, fair curls bobbing and the big, sapphire eyes sparkling. Her early nervousness of Francis seemed to have evaporated. 'In fact, I'm probably his aunt!'

'Don't be silly, you can't be. You're only a kind of cousin, if that.'

'I don't see why! If Francis's father used to be *my* father's brother-in-law, then . . .'

'That will do, Juliana!' Vilia's voice, floating down the table, was sharper than the circumstances warranted, but just then there came a fortunate distraction in the shape of a burst of laughter from further up. Perry, reluctantly amused, caught Grace's outraged eye. Laughing aloud was *very* ill-bred. The culprit, surprisingly, was Gideon, who looked as if he were in his element, sandwiched between Perry's dashing granddaughter Petronella and the seductive Gabrielle. Not even the most charitable onlooker could have denied that the girls were flirting outrageously – or that Gideon was encouraging them. Two pretty, competitive kitties who didn't like each other above half. Mlle Gaby was also fluttering her eyelashes at Theo, seated opposite her between Juliana and a silent Lizzie, and Theo – clever bastard – was responding very convincingly indeed.

After a time, inescapably, the conversation came round to the Exhibition, about which Gideon was blithely irreverent, and Theo, who had been honoured by a visit from Her Majesty, scarcely less so.

'I don't believe she understood more than a quarter of what I so carefully explained to her,' he drawled, 'though I had a thirst like a Border reiver by the time I was done.'

Magnus broke his silence at last. 'Lollipops!' he muttered, sinking a spoon in the maraschino soufflé.

There was a moment's nonplussed silence, and then Ian Barber asked politely, 'Don't you care for lollipops, sir?'

Perry had often noticed that clever boys lacked ordinary common sense, but even for one who had mastered Greek and Latin by the time he was five, it was a surpassingly silly question.

'Should he?' Theo asked slyly.

'Well, I think he might, you know. They're very refreshing.'

'I believe your uncle is of the opinion that the Exhibition restaurants should sell something better than lollipops and cold coffee.'

'The coffee isn't *meant* to be cold, Uncle Magnus, and I am sure if you asked for tea, they would provide it.'

His teeth clenched, Magnus said, 'When your Aunt Vilia and your cousins have dragged me all round the world from China to Peru, and from Land's End to John o' Groats, what I want is a large glass of whisky bitters. I would even make do with ale, at a pinch. Lollipops or cold coffee, indeed!'

'Oh, I see! But you can't deny that if the restaurants sold alcohol, a great many men might become a trifle – er – bosky, and that could do nothing but ruin the pleasure of all the *respectable* visitors. Perhaps you have not tried the ices? They are very thirst-quenching, you know.'

Theo opened his mouth again and Perry hoped that he was going to take pity on Magnus, who looked as if he were about to have an apoplexy. But instead of changing the subject, he said, 'Does one take it that you have reservations about alcohol, Ian?' Perry frowned. It sounded like deliberate provocation.

'Well, yes, I do. I believe it to be responsible for a great deal of expenditure by people who can't afford it, and productive of much domestic discord. And there can be no doubt that it is exceedingly bad for the constitution.'

'Stuff!' exclaimed Magnus. 'Have you been listening to those teetotallers? Queer in their attics, every last one of them.'

Isa Blair's prim voice emerged from lips no less prim, but she was pink with annoyance. 'My *mama* subscribes to the National Temperance Society.'

'Hah!' Magnus erupted, but before he could annihilate the girl, Peter Barber interrupted. 'Come now, Uncle Magnus,' he said in his usual measured tones. 'You should not allow yourself to be blinded by your own lifetime's preferences, you know. There is much to be said in favour of temperance, and more in favour of total abstinence. I should not be displeased if Ian chose to ally himself with either branch of the movement.'

'Oh, wouldn't you? Well, I tell you here and now that I would! And don't be so damned magisterial, either!' His approval of the Barbers seemed to be suffering a reverse.

None of Peter Barber's face muscles actually moved – not the eyes, nor the somewhat bony nose, nor the lips half hidden between moustache and goatee beard – and yet somehow his brow deepened, as if his already receding hair had moved back an inch. Everyone except Magnus could see that the philosopher was ruffled.

Tartly, Grace raised her voice. 'I am surprised Uncle Magnus hasn't discovered Mr Soyer's Gastronomic Symposium. I believe it has something called an American bar that serves a number of stimulating beverages with names like sherry cobbler and mint julep and brandy smash!'

'Just so, miss!' her uncle snapped, the sarcasm passing right over his head. 'Why should I have to trail all the way across to Gore House to be offered foreign rubbish like that, eh?'

Shona, not before time, rose and gathered the ladies together with her eyes, and then Drew, to Magnus's disgust and Perry's relief, allowed the port to circulate only twice before saying, 'Shall we join the ladies?'

Perry estimated that in another fifteen minutes or so he and Francis could decently take their leave. They were going out of town in the morning, and had to be up early. As an excuse, it had the merit of being true.

In the drawing-room, as they entered, Juliana was saying, 'How I should love to go to India. Vilia could scarcely tear me away from the Indian exhibits. Wasn't that howdah unbelievably gorgeous? And the other trappings on the elephant, so rich and majestic!'

Gideon, a trifle above par, chuckled and said, 'You know where the elephant came from, of course?'

'No.'

'The museum at Saffron Walden, in Essex. The committee had a terrible time finding one the right size and shape.'

There was a general laugh, but Juliana said stoutly, 'I don't care! It must have come from India once. I should love to see real live elephants, with their trunks waving, and rajas riding on them.'

'Wearing all their jewels, of course!' It was Lavinia, caustic little monkey.

Gabrielle came to the rescue, showing a considerateness Perry wouldn't have expected of her. 'Do you want to go to India, Juliana? *Vraiment?*' Her accent was charming. 'I think it is most brave of you. I read somewhere that one calls it the graveyard of the British because so many die there, and quite young, also.'

'Rubbish!' said Magnus. The French had always had their eye on the East Indies, and Britain had sent them about their business. 'Stuff and nonsense! No more dangerous there than it is anywhere else.'

Lizzie, who hadn't spoken a word all evening, suddenly said in a soft, expressionless voice, 'The mediaeval court was pretty, too.' A strangely passive child, Perry thought, with promise of great beauty in her small, regular features, stately neck, and mass of copper hair. An empty vessel to be filled, a silent instrument to be played upon? It depended on whether the passivity covered a natural reserve – or a nothingness. It was hard to tell. No one, not even her father, had paid any attention to her for hours.

But now, Guy Savarin gave vent to an unexpected and penetratingly Gallic 'Ah!' and bent on her the look of one who had found his soulmate.

'Don't do that!' said Magnus testily. 'Can't stand fellows who go

573

ooh-ing and aah-ing all over the place, frightening people out of their skins!'

Guy ignored him. 'You found the mediaeval court a revelation, also?' It wasn't quite what Lizzie had said, but a glow came to her eyes and she gave an infinitesimal nod. He made an expansive gesture, leaving his hands extended, rather like Atlas waiting to catch the world when it was tossed to him. 'Such perception! Such feeling for beauty! You have a soul, Lizzie!'

Lizzie, overcome, began to blush, and Vilia, sharing a peculiarly hideous tête-à-tête double chair with Mrs Armstrong, remarked prosaically, 'We all have souls, Guy. Why should admiration of Mr Pugin's Gothic fantasies be proof of it?' And *that* was deliberate provocation, too, Perry thought. Poor Magnus.

It was all the encouragement Guy needed. The words came tumbling over one another, and even if sometimes his listeners had to be nippy with their French, there was no mistaking what he was trying to say. Design was, *évidemment*, a matter for the artist, who was not a menial or a drudge, but something between craftsman and priest, with beauty and truth as his gospel. Design such as this was to be seen nowhere in all the Great Exhibition except in the mediaeval court. Everything else, every other thing *sans exception*, was coarse, vulgar, barbaric, because it was made by machine and designed – *mon Dieu!* – by menials and drudges working with sham materials and sham techniques. Carpets in imitation of the Persian, machine-woven by men who had never studied a leaf or a tree, skins of precious metal plated on to common iron by machine-minders who derived no more satisfaction from working with gold than they would have done with brass . . .

There was a great deal along these lines, and at last it became too much for Drew. 'Now, see here, Guy!' he objected, his colour high. 'There's nothing wrong with what the machines produce. Dammit, very few people can afford real Persian carpets or real gold plate. Why shouldn't they have something incomparably cheaper and almost as good? It's all very well for you artistic johnnies to claim that things were better in the fourteenth century, but a fine pickle we'd all be in if we were still stuck there!'

Guy, drawing a graceful hand over his flowing amber mane, said, 'But you do not understand. The machine will be the downfall of true

574

aesthetics – do you have that word in English? All this elaboration comes from ignorance and insincerity. What the machine produces is incongruous, whereas the artist finds inspiration in natural truths – in mountains and lakes and flowers – and in the beauty of the work his hands have wrought.'

Magnus's mouth was slightly open, but Vilia didn't make the slightest effort to change the subject. It was clear to Perry now that she was encouraging the boy to display the whole range of his ill-digested views on art and taste, and give voluble tongue to that rather tired philosophy of art for art's sake that was bound to offend anyone who prided himself on being a plain, down-to-earth sort of fellow. Like Magnus. What was she up to? Wilfully upsetting the old boy, to pay him out for being so recalcitrant about coming this evening? She was certainly succeeding. Magnus was getting angrier and angrier.

Perry watched her from his seat across the room. The disquieting glitter that had been in her eyes when the evening began was long gone. She was perfectly cool now, and still perfectly groomed although the evening was uncomfortably stuffy. Her colouring, after the richer middle years, had returned to the almost ethereal pallor that had marked it in her youth. Perry's vision suddenly blurred, and he saw her as if she were a drawing of the girl he had first fallen in love with, a delicate sketch, defined and yet faintly blurred, in chalk and pencil on softly tinted paper. A foolish conceit. There had been such warmth, such a capacity for love in her then. Had it gone – all of it?

The crisp voice said, 'But to come back to Mr Pugin, Guy. I think even he has not hit the true Gothic note. Indeed, if you wish to become a real artist, I believe you must come and spend some weeks at Kinveil to study the mediaeval at first hand.'

It verged on the brutal. Magnus almost choked. And then Theo, who had shown every sign of enjoying Guy's torrential eloquence, contributed his mite. 'What an admirable suggestion,' he drawled. 'And not only the mediaeval, but a positive cornucopia of – er – natural truths, I think you called them. Mountains and clouds and things.'

Perry found that, little though he cared for Magnus, he couldn't go on watching him rise to every fly that Vilia and Theo chose to cast. Whatever they were up to, Perry didn't want to know.

Abruptly, he stood up. 'Come, Francis. I hope you will all forgive us,

575

but we have to leave for Brighton very early in the morning. Shona, my dear, thank you for a delightful evening.' His glance travelled, smiling, round the room. 'We sail on Monday and I guess we won't see most of you again. So we will say not only good night, but good-bye.'

Good-bye, Vilia. My heart's love.

And then, as three times before, he walked away from her.

3

The party broke up soon afterwards. The younger ones all seemed to have enjoyed it inordinately, and even Lizzie scarcely stopped talking all the way home. She and Juliana considered cousin Guy the most romantic young man they had ever met.

Every part of Vilia's body ached, with the dragging ache of muscles harshly stressed after long disuse. It required every shred of will-power she possessed to prevent the nervous shudders that racked her from becoming noticeable.

So many years of trying to convince herself that everything was over, and yet knowing within herself that it wasn't. Or not for her. But tonight had shown her that, for him, it was. She had expected it, of course, and behaved distantly to him, and yet all the time she had been waiting – and waiting – for some sign, some spark of contact. There had been none. All he had done was look at her as if he were summing her up, and not greatly liking what he saw. So he had gone, and it was over. Over. This time the blade was finally withdrawn from her heart, and the torture at an end. Let the numbing scar tissue form soon, she prayed. Let me accept the knowledge, and learn to live with it. *Never again, never again.* The refrain from her childhood came back to her.

She was sick, relentlessly and repeatedly sick, all night.

When the girls came to see how she was in the morning, she said it was nothing. Just that the mackerel patties had disagreed with her.

Chapter Five

1

Gideon couldn't remember ever feeling so cold, not even at Kinveil. It was as much exhaustion, he knew, as the Crimean wind soughing through the holes in his tent, and the mud seeping up through the floorboards, and the fact that he had had nothing to eat since a hasty breakfast twenty hours ago. He didn't want anything now, which was as well. No fires were to be lit, by order, in case the Russians mounted another attack. He thought of the poor devils of soldiers who had lived through today's battle at Balaclava on dry biscuit and a single ration tot of rum, and were living through tonight on nothing at all.

He had finished his report now, and didn't need a clear head any longer, yet it was with distaste that he poured out half a tumbler of brandy and tossed it back. He hoped it would warm him, but knew, too, that it would deepen the depression this hideous day had bred in him.

From the heights above Balaclava, side by side with Billy Russell of *The Times* he had watched with horror as a few hundred Hussars, Dragoons and Lancers had trotted under parade-ground discipline straight into the heart of the Russian army; 673 men armed with lances and swords against fifty-eight heavy field guns, four thousand cavalry, and nineteen battalions of infantry. By some miracle, almost two hundred had returned alive. The onlookers on the heights, tears pouring down their cheeks, had watched them staggering, limping, crawling back, a few dragging their bleeding horses with them. From the moment when the trumpet had sounded the advance until the last survivor reeled in, it had taken only twenty minutes. Someone had told Gideon that one of the French generals, watching, had commented, '*C'est magnifique, mais ce n'est pas la guerre.*' But wasn't it? What was war, if not wanton, senseless destruction?

Until the charge of the Light Brigade, the battle had seemed quite unreal. The mists of dawn had dissolved to give a bright blue morning, clear and sharp, so that the valley had seemed like a toy landscape peopled by toy soldiers. From where Gideon had stood, a couple of dozen yards from Lord Raglan and his staff, the plain had looked as flat as a board, although in fact there were hillocks and ridges blocking the sight and impeding the hearing of the men on the ground. The watchers on the hill could see, dreamlike, thousands of drab-coated Russian cavalry advance in a great oblivious block to within a few hundred yards of where half their number of British cavalry stood, no less oblivious, clad in brilliant uniforms and heavy bearskins and glinting helmets. The air had been unnaturally still, so that there had drifted up quite clearly the champing of bits and the clink of sabres and, after a while, Sir Colin Campbell's rich Glasgow accents rebuking the thin red line of his Highlanders when they seemed disposed to charge a body of horsemen that outnumbered them four to one. The thin red line stood fast, and the Russians withdrew, and the road to Balaclava was saved. Everyone on the hill had cheered except Gideon, too busy swallowing his pride in the Highlanders and his furious anger at the politicians who valued their lives so cheaply.

But then the Russians had begun to move the guns from a redoubt they had captured from Britain's Turkish allies. Once, it had been a cardinal rule of war that the enemy should never be allowed to take the standard; today, every army felt the same about its guns. So Raglan had sent an order down to the plain instructing the cavalry to make sure of the guns, and there had been a mistake, and the cavalry commander, who couldn't see the redoubt, had understood that it was the *Russian* guns that were meant. And so the Light Brigade had ridden to its destruction. And it had no longer been a toy landscape peopled by toy soldiers.

Afterwards, Lord Cardigan, who had taken part in the charge, had ridden back with a few superficial wounds to his yacht in Balaclava harbour, partaken of dinner and a bottle of champagne and gone to bed. His superior officer and brother-in-law, Lord Lucan, had had a flaming row with the commander-in-chief, and then retired to brood in his tent. In the meantime, the dead and wounded were carried back from the silent valley under a flag of truce, while the farriers roamed the field and dispatched the survivors of the five hundred horses that had fallen in the charge. Gideon didn't think he would ever forget the flat, melancholy, repetitive crack of their pistols.

It had been a good shooting season at Kinveil, too.

Desperate to sleep, but knowing that he wouldn't, Gideon looked for the letters he had received from home that morning and only glanced at. It was a long time since he had received news from home. He had been with the allied armies for months now, first at Gallipoli, and then at Varna, and for the last six weeks in the Crimea. But the army authorities abominated newspaper correspondents – largely because of Billy Russell's searing reports in *The Times* – and treated them with rather less consideration than they afforded the TGs, the 'Travelling Gentlemen' or tourists who turned up in a thin but inquisitive stream, hoping to fit a battle in between the Parthenon and Schönbrunn. It was a continuing headache trying to get one's stories out, and incoming mail had to take its chances. The only advantage was that Billy couldn't be pestered by Delane, nor Gideon by Fanshawe. Editors had to take it or leave it.

His fingers clumsy with cold, he drew the lamp towards him and trimmed its wick, and then turned it down a fraction. Already, it was difficult to find oil for it. He turned up the collar of his greatcoat and began to draw on his thick woollen gloves, but stripped them off again when he found they were still damp with caked mud. Then, shoulders hunched and hands sunk in his pockets, he gave his attention to the letter from Vilia.

Fifty brace of partridge to date, and two hundred of grouse, as well as a few Black Game and ptarmigan. And already we have a larderful of venison. A good shooting season, in fact, although some of our guests go stalking with a paintbrush rather than a rifle. Their style, however, is not that of Mr Landseer. Dear me, no, although I would be at a loss to tell you why. I fancy it may be because people actually pay *money* to buy his paintings, which means he cannot be a true artist.

How clever of you to guess that I am talking of Guy Savarin and his friends! We have always had rather small parties for the shooting, but I decided that this year something must be done. Even on the Black Sea you must be aware that your daughter and Juliana will be making their come-out in the spring, so that it now becomes urgent for them to learn how to be at ease with strangers. Sometimes I despair! While I have succeeded in teaching Lizzie how to appear remote and mysterious, instead of stupidly shy – my dear, how *did* you and Elinor contrive to produce such a retiring child? – I am still quite defeated by Juliana, who is thrown into the most complete state of nerves by people she doesn't know. It seemed to me that Guy, who has been in London for some months now – an ardent disciple of Rossetti and Holman Hunt and their 'brotherhood' – might be the answer. He is, after all, family, and the girls met him once three years ago, if you remember.

Gideon remembered very well. That gruesome family party during the Exhibition when Vilia and Theo had been doing their best, with considerable success, to give Magnus a dislike of his potential heir, and Gideon himself had been too merry to do anything about it. Not that he'd have done much sober, either. He had always made it a principle not to interfere in what didn't concern him. He frowned tiredly, wondering what Vilia's real reason for inviting Guy to Kinveil had been.

It has not, alas, proved to be one of my happier inspirations. Magnus likes Guy no more than he did before, and certainly his somewhat fulsome attention to the girls might be described as ill-judged. However, I hope they are learning something from the experience.

Your brother, I may add, has done nothing to assist harmony in the home! Guy brought with him two friends, one who claims to be an artist and the other an art critic. When Lavinia arrived – she was in London for her first Season this year – it transpired that she was not only acquainted with the critic but madly in love with him. Unfortunately, Theo has struck up a close friendship with the young man, and they have become practically inseparable, which annoys Lavinia intensely. Theo, when I remonstrate with him, does no more than smile in that maddening way of his and say that Lavinia must learn that the world has not been created for her sole convenience. Heigh ho!

I need hardly say that we follow your reports in the *Times Graphic* with the closest attention. Your Mr Fanshawe always displays them very prominently, which must afford you the greatest satisfaction. Write to us when you can, my dear. Magnus sends you his regards.

Gideon had learned a good deal about the world since that day in Mrs Berkley's brothel so long ago, but Theo had guarded his privacy well, and, watching him when there were pretty women around, Gideon had persuaded himself that even if he continued to crave excitement, Theo's tastes were still what society called 'normal'. But tonight, depressed to his boots, he was incapable of turning a blind eye. Deep down, he had known for years. He only prayed that Theo, whose vanity should have been enough to save him from really serious involvement, hadn't succumbed at last. So stupid, so dangerous. So unlike Theo to be careless. Damn him, he was forty years old and ought to know better. For the first time, Gideon wondered how much Vilia knew, but it took only a moment's reflection to convince him that, however puzzled she might be by Theo's continuing bachelorhood, she couldn't have any idea of the truth. There was a universal male conspiracy to protect well-bred women from that kind of knowledge, and although Theo was closer to Vilia than anyone, Gideon didn't think that even he would break the great unwritten law. Especially when to do so would be to reveal that he had needs, which in Theo's book would be tantamount to admitting weakness. His attitude even to Gideon had been subtly different ever since the day of Mrs Berkley's brothel; and that same day had seen a change in his relationship with Sorley. It was clear that he had hated Sorley knowing what he was up to, though he showed it only occasionally in references to 'old family retainers; such a tiresome breed!'

Gideon sighed and turned to the other letters, one from Theo himself and one from Juliana. He didn't know whether he wanted to read Theo's. On the other hand, at least it was legible, which was more than could be said for Juliana's dramatic scrawl.

In fact, Theo's was no more than a note, enclosing a string of questions Jermyn wanted answered. There was no shadow of doubt that Jermyn was a born engineer, with a swift and penetrating vision and a mind as precise as one of Joseph Whitworth's machine tools, and he was still devouringly interested in guns. Gideon was in the enviable position of being able to watch artillery in action, Jermyn said, and would oblige his nephew very much by taking particular note of how different guns functioned under the conditions for which they were intended. 'The heat of battle must undoubtedly produce effects that are not apparent to Ordnance Factory test ranges. It is also my impression that the army is seriously hampered by the smallness of its field guns. I imagine that if an eighteen-pounder – what we now regard essentially as a siege gun – could be designed on more manoeuvrable lines, it would be of inestimable benefit on the field of battle. I do hope you can investigate these matters for me. Mama sends you her love, as do Father and Peregrine James, who has now quite made up his mind to a career in the law. Father is exceedingly disappointed that he is not coming in to the foundry, but you know what an obstinate little devil he is!'

Impossible, after the day just gone, to think of field guns purely as pieces of engineering. Gideon stared sightlessly at Jermyn's letter for a long time before he laid it aside. All Theo's covering note had said was, 'Jermyn asks me to forward this to you. Kinveil is looking particularly handsome this autumn – as is our respected mama – and the guest list is a cut above the usual. Quite entertaining, on the whole. Take care of yourself, dear boy.'

Juliana's letter was worse almost than Jermyn's. Gideon was very fond of her, for she was a taking little thing, and he couldn't imagine any red-blooded male capable of withstanding her pretty face and confiding ways. But she was such a child still, despite her seventeen years, her letters so girlishly irrelevant to everything outside her own experience. Half-way through reading he stopped and pulled on an extra pair of socks and found some dry gloves, and then, pouring himself some more brandy and hanging the lamp from a hook in the tent pole above his bed, lay down and forced himself to finish it.

Dearest Gideon – Vilia says she is too busy to write to you at any length, and that Lizzie would be bound to leave a great many things out, so I have been given the task of sending you all the gossip.

It must be dreadful in the Crimea! I read your article about the battle of the Alma and really felt quite sick. What a pity Jermyn can't be with you. I am sure he would be in his element with great big guns booming all over the place! Are you *really* keeping up the family chronicle even there? Vilia says you are, but I should think it must be awfully difficult.

Nothing terribly important has happened, as a matter of fact. You know that Ian Barber married Isa Blair last year, and that her father didn't approve at first because they were cousins. And Vilia said, nonsense, they were only step-cousins and no two young people could be better suited. Lizzie and I had great difficulty in smothering our giggles, because we knew what Vilia meant by *that*. But fortunately Edward thought she was paying them a compliment, so all was well. Anyway, they had a baby a few months ago, a daughter called – guess what! – Harriet, who is known as Etta to distinguish her from her grandmother.

Gaby Savarin was also married recently. Vilia was quite taken aback to discover that she knew the young man, and that he wasn't young at all. Her eyes went that funny absent way they do sometimes, and then she said, 'Marcabrun? Gracious, I met him in Paris in the '30s, and it *must* be the same man. What age is Gaby – twenty-four, twenty-five? Then he's a good twenty years older than she is. However, it sometimes works very well for a girl to marry a man considerably her senior.' Theo was there, and he said, 'If that is to my address, Vilia dear, I should forget it. My interest is not what it was.' She looked awfully angry, but you know Theo. He just smiled. I have no idea what he meant, but perhaps you do.

Gideon didn't, as it happened. He could only assume that Vilia thought she had found some suitable wife for Theo, and that he was resisting. Because of the art critic? He flicked his eyes down the page, full of conscientious detail about the estate, and Glenbraddan, and Petronella Barber's visit to America to study the woman suffrage movement that had grown out of the meeting at Seneca Falls. Peter Barber, it seemed, was suffering from some illness and bearing it – as Juliana remarked unfeelingly – with the stoicism to be expected of a philosopher. Ian was girding his loins preparatory to embarking on a political campaign of the greatest social consequence; Juliana had to confess, regretfully, that she wasn't quite sure what it was.

At last she had arrived at the Kinveil guest list. Even through his depression, Gideon was grateful not to be there. Such a collection of drearily respectable people, all distinguished in one way or another, and scarcely one of them under fifty. He was distantly acquainted with most of them. The art critic's name, it appeared, was Dominic Harvey.

Lavinia had a very successful Season, but disappointed all the older members of the family by refusing several very flattering offers because she has given her heart to Mr Harvey. Lavinia says he will become very famous and distinguished some day. It is just that, now, he is forced to make his own way and cannot contemplate making an offer for her because he is quite unable to keep her in the style to which she is accustomed. She says she will wait for him – forever, if need be. I think it is truly romantic. If only I were sure that Mr Harvey is quite as much in love with her as she is with him! He does seem to neglect her, rather, and is forever out on the hill with Theo, who likes him very much. Indeed, he says he is surprised to find Lavinia has such good taste. Only funning, you understand! But Lavinia is upset, and it *is* trying, because it makes the numbers uneven. As well as Mr Harvey, you see, Guy brought up a very nice man called John Gaunt, one of these modern artists whose work does not immediately strike one as very *good*, but I'm sure it is really. He's very big and comforting, and I'm not at all nervous of him any more. The thing is that Guy and Mr Harvey and Mr Gaunt *should* act as escorts to Lavinia, Lizzie and me, but of course with Mr Harvey always disappearing with Theo, we are left with one gentleman short.

Strictly between ourselves, I think that Vilia's plans have gone awry. I am almost sure that she hoped Guy and I would become attached, which would have been very convenient in some ways. It would have saved me from facing the Season without having a single gentleman I know to turn to – an ordeal I positively *dread*. But it is *your daughter* who has captured Guy's heart. I think perhaps I should tell you that he has captured hers, too. You don't mind, do you? He is excessively handsome, you know, and so clever that Lizzie and I are perfectly in awe of him. He is trying to elevate our minds and souls so that we will understand true art, which I think shows great sensibility in him. Ian Barber says he has a sense of social purpose, which gives me a better opinion of Ian than I ever remember, considering he has no patience at all with artists. *Neither does Papa!* Indeed, I think if Guy and I had fallen in love, the family shotgun would have been unearthed from the closet and Guy dispatched back to London at the greatest possible speed! But in Lizzie's case he doesn't feel compelled to interfere, thank goodness. I'm just worried that Vilia might. Because Lizzie is really smitten! Anyway, I think she will probably write to you quite soon and tell you all about it. Much love from us both, dearest Gideon.

It was too much for Gideon's exhausted mind to take in. What on earth could Vilia be up to where Guy was concerned? There seemed no sense in it. Poor Lizzie. Gideon hoped she wasn't too much in love with Guy, or she would be made very unhappy. It would be a quite unsuitable match. Guy, not too plump in the pocket, and with his head somewhere in the clouds, could never care for timid, gentle, not very clever Lizzie in the way she needed to be cared for.

The lamp was beginning to smoke, and the flame was edged with black. Gideon turned it out and lay back, still shivering, on his bed. Vilia would put a stop to it, he knew.

After a long time he drifted off into a troubled sleep, and dreams in which Balaclava and Kinveil were inextricably mingled, and it was Vilia who touched the match to the Russian guns, after Theo had pushed home the ramrod. Lizzie was wearing a scarlet crossbelt, and there were tears in her eyes.

2

Vilia was waiting, not patiently, when Sorley brought Lizzie and Guy – the first quaking and the second defiant – back from the hill in the light of a full, frosty moon. They had been out alone, unchaperoned, for eight hours. And with unbelievable stupidity they had missed dinner, so that their absence had caused remark.

Magnanimously, Guy was prepared to apologize. They had perhaps been thoughtless and had undoubtedly misjudged the time, but they had already been on their way back when Sorley found them. 'There was a stag, you understand, outlined against the sky, and it was necessary that I should commit every detail to paper before my memory lost the *ambiance*. And then I prevailed on Miss Lizzie to take me to a corrie – I have that right? – where there was likely to be a stag with his hinds, and on our way we saw a most magnificent beast rising from a – a peat wallow. Quite superb! And then at the corrie *such* a scene, *such* an experience! Imagine to yourself two great stags locked in battle! The agility, the plunging and the circling, the . . .'

'Quite!' Vilia interrupted. 'I do not require a description of something I have seen often enough for myself. What I require is an explanation of why you and Lizzie were on the hill at all. I am aware that in *artistic* circles' – there was a wealth of contempt in her tone – 'it may be perfectly acceptable for a young couple to elude friends and chaperons and spend a whole day together, but you must know that more conventional persons are inclined to put an extremely undesirable interpretation on such an escapade.'

'*That* for conventional persons!' Guy exclaimed, snapping his fingers in a very adolescent fashion. 'How is it possible for spirit to talk to spirit, and soul to soul, in the presence of your "friends and chaperons"?'

He really was the most impossible young man. 'Spare me these theatricals!' Vilia snapped. 'What I am concerned with is my granddaughter's wellbeing!'

'Ahhhhh! You suspect impropriety? Then you will permit me to say that I had not expected a reaction so *bourgeoise* from you, madame!'

Before Lizzie's terrified eyes, her grandmother turned white with anger, but Guy went on, oblivious. 'I must tell you that I worship the ground on which Miss Lizzie walks. So pure, so trusting! It is inconceivable that I should so much as touch the hem of her gown. You insult me by suggesting that I could ever harm her!'

'All very fine, Guy.' Vilia's voice had dropped several tones, and flattened, as it always did when she was at the end of her patience. Then her arbitrary gaze swivelled towards Lizzie. 'The fault, however, is not entirely yours. Perhaps Lizzie will be so good as to explain to me why, despite everything she has ever been taught, she was so vulgarly ill bred as to agree to this expedition?'

Lizzie could still remember, as a child, how distraught she had been when her mother was angry with her papa. It hadn't happened very often, but it had petrified her. Once, in a rare moment of communication, she had said as much to him, but he had belittled her fears and told her that mama's tantrums didn't mean anything except that, perhaps, and just for a little, she wasn't her usual happy self. Lizzie hadn't been reassured. Always, and unfailingly, angry voices reduced her to a jelly.

If that had been all, it would have been enough. In the years of her growing up, few adults had ever spoken to her angrily, and they had always been disarmed by her patent misery. But she had discovered there was another kind of anger, that wasn't loud but quiet and cold, and she had no idea what to do about it other than fall back on silence. It didn't help much. Grandmother Vilia had never been unkind to her, but she was brisk and sometimes imperious, and Lizzie knew only too well that her own mute refusal to fight irritated her grandmother very much. Lizzie was terrified of her.

'Answer me, please, Lizzie!'

Even the room they were in, Vilia's private drawing-room, was always enough to throw Lizzie into a state of nerves. It was so cool, so stylish, so impeccably tidy, so unpropitious to clutter, whether of possessions or emotions. Vilia stood with her back to the window, and the moonlight reflecting off the water lit her hair with frosted silver and blanched the lines of her neck and cheek. Her mouth was set uncompromisingly, and her eyes were dark and unreadable.

'I am waiting, Lizzie.'

Lizzie's breath caught raggedly in her throat, but all she could do was stammer; she knew that never in her life before had she done anything so dreadful.

Vilia stared at her, as much depressed as angry. Lizzie was one of Nature's victims, whose passivity would never bring her anything but hurt. Vilia had tried to rouse her, to armour her against the brutal realities of life, but she had recognized long ago that it was useless. If there was anything to be done for Lizzie, she was the wrong person to do it. She suspected that the only treatment Lizzie would respond to would be a slow, gentle, infinitely careful drawing out. She didn't even know whether there *was* anything to draw out, but thought probably not. And she herself hadn't the patience for it, or the self-denying heart. Only a cleverer Shona – or a less self-centred Lucy Telfer – could have done it. What strange quirk of heredity, she wondered, for the hundredth time, had produced a child like Lizzie? There was nothing of Gideon in her at all, except perhaps his detachment carried to impossible extremes. And Elinor, who had been neither clever nor astute, had at least had a kind of vivacity.

Gideon had married Elinor for her pretty face and taking ways, and had salved his conscience when she died by convincing himself, not that he had erred in his judgement of her, but that marriage was a state that wasn't for him. He was certainly being slow to embark on it again. Shona had told her two or three years ago, with extreme confidentiality, that there *was* a lady, handsome and terribly intellectual, a newspaper writer. But nothing seemed to have come of it in the end. Vilia's eyes on her granddaughter didn't flicker. Lizzie was one of her failures, and she wasn't used to failing. There were times when the girl exasperated her almost beyond endurance.

'*Lizzie!*'

And then Guy began to bluster. 'Madame, you must not speak to Miss Lizzie so! It is not right that you should persecute one so young, so sensitive. Indeed, I will not permit it!'

The lids heavy over her eyes, she turned her head unhurriedly towards him. '*You* will not permit it? My dear Guy, you have nothing whatever to say in the matter. Lizzie is not your concern.'

'*Mon dieu*, but she is! Madame, I must tell you that I worship and adore her!'

Heaven preserve her from callow youth! Vilia thought. He knew nothing – *nothing*. 'Do you, indeed? I am sorry for it, because there can be no question of your suit being acceptable. Your Uncle Magnus is exceedingly angry over today's escapade, and has asked me to tell you that you are no longer welcome at Kinveil. Since your instant departure might give rise to precisely the kind of talk we wish to avoid, you may remain for another three days. No more than that. And during that time you will make no attempt to see Lizzie alone. Perhaps it would be as well if your friends left at the same time. That is all.' She could hear herself, as if from another planet. If there had been someone to cut *her* ruthlessly off from Perry Randall, before their love took hold, how different her life would have been. A few months' tears, perhaps, in place of forty years' tragedy. Oh, Lizzie! Stupid little Lizzie. Do as I say.

And then Lizzie found her voice at last. 'No. No, it isn't all! You can't send him away. I love him. I'll *die* if you separate me from him!'

'Don't be foolish.'

The child was clinging to Guy's arm as if she had no other support in the world. 'That's what you always say! "Don't be foolish, Lizzie!" You think I'm stupid and weak, and that I don't have any feelings. Well, I do. I have feelings just like anyone else. But you've always hated me . . .' Vilia opened her mouth. 'Yes, you have. You've always thought me contemptible. I know I'm not clever, like everyone else in the family, but Guy doesn't mind. He cares for me, because I'm *me*. I love him and I won't be parted from him. I won't!'

Her auburn hair was tumbled after the day on the hill, and her skin flushed, but there was no expression at all on her lovely, immobile face.

Vilia stared at her, confounded. Never in the whole of her life had Lizzie answered her back. And *what* a time to start, when sober discussion might just have won concessions that defiance never would.

Guy, his face radiant, clasped his free hand over Lizzie's, and gazed worshipfully into her eyes.

Two shallow children infatuated by the trappings of romance, he by her beauty and vulnerability, she by his poetical good looks and articulate self-esteem. The worst kind of match possible. Vilia said, 'Please refrain from edifying me with such sentiments, Lizzie. They do you no credit. However, if you are sincere, I imagine that your Uncle Magnus might be prepared to reconsider the situation in two or three years, assuming that in the meantime Guy has made some progress with his career, and that you both feel as you do now.'

Lizzie exclaimed, 'But it has nothing to do with Uncle Magnus! It is my father who is my guardian. I will write to him – *he* will support me!'

'Do you think so? I am afraid, Lizzie, that even if your father did not have more important things on his mind at this moment, you would find his opinion in the most complete agreement with mine. You are too young to know your own mind yet, and Guy is not in a position to support a wife. I have no knowledge of what expectations he may have from his father, but I can assure you that he will certainly have none from Uncle Magnus unless he behaves in future with considerably more sense of responsibility and decorum than he has done in the past. No, don't interrupt me! I wish to hear no more about it. Guy, you will go and join the company in the Long Gallery for what remains of the evening. Lizzie will go to her room. *That is all.*'

When they had gone, Vilia sank into a chair and rested her forehead for a moment on forefinger and thumb. She was tired, and there was a steady throb in her head that made it difficult to concentrate, more difficult still to exert tact or understanding in a situation that filled her with a weary indifference. She knew she had mishandled it, but she scarcely cared. If today had done nothing else, at least it had confirmed Magnus's rooted dislike for a young man to whom he might otherwise some day – just might – have bequeathed Kinveil.

3

'Well, it's perfectly simple!' Lavinia exclaimed to the distraught young lovers. 'You must do what my parents did. Run away! It's quite legal in Scotland, you know. You can be married without any difficulty at all.'

Juliana gazed at her in awe. 'Did your parents run away? I didn't know that.'

'Goodness, yes. I suppose Vilia must have been annoyed at the time, but it soon wore off. My mama says she couldn't have been kinder to her, once the deed was done.'

'Run away?' Lizzie's small voice was completely devoid of expression. 'Oh, I couldn't.'

But Guy, to whom the Middle Ages and tales of Gothic romance and courtly love meant more than the present ever could, grasped her limp hands and exclaimed, '*Pourquoi pas?* Why not, *ma mie?* Why not, *ma petite fleur?* Was I not born to be the knight who plucks the one perfect bloom in the garden of love?'

Juliana's mouth was very slightly open, and Lavinia said, in a kindly aside, 'The *Roman de la Rose*, you remember?'

Juliana didn't. 'Oh,' she said.

'I couldn't,' Lizzie repeated. 'It's wrong, I know it's wrong.'

'Don't be silly,' Lavinia said. 'In the law of Scotland, you don't have to be married in church, and you don't need your parents' consent if you're over sixteen. Even if you just live together, that's known as "marriage by habit and repute". Then there's marriage by declaration *de praesenti*; before witnesses, in other words.' She ticked it off on her fingers. 'And marriage by promise *subsequenti copula*. That means – oh, well, perhaps it doesn't matter. Anyway, I don't think it's relevant. But you see, whatever happens, you'll be legally married, so it *must* be all right.'

Three pairs of eyes were on her. 'How do you know all that?' Juliana asked.

'Oh, pooh!' said Lavinia airily. 'Everyone knows it. Besides, I asked Peregrine James.'

'Why?'

Lavinia cast her a repressive look. 'Because I was interested.'

Juliana remembered that Lavinia had designs on Mr Harvey. Rounding her mouth into a silent 'Oh!' she reflected that Lavinia was really the most determined girl.

Lizzie said doubtfully, 'But I would like to be married in church.'

Guy clasped her to his bosom. 'You will, *ma mie*! You will.'

'That's all very well,' Lavinia objected. 'But it isn't quite as simple as that. I wouldn't *dream* of encouraging you to run away together unless you were to be married at once, and you can't arrange *that* in a church!' Her thin, vivid face was unnaturally virtuous.

'Then we will be married before witnesses first, and later we will be married properly in church! Say you will, *chérie*! Say you will!'

Lizzie's face had cleared a little. 'Would that be all right?'

He misunderstood her hesitation, and indeed, she would have been puzzled to put it into words, for she scarcely understood it herself. He exclaimed, 'Is it that you think we will not be truly wed until our union will have been blessed by God? Then I swear to you that, like the troubadours of old, I will lay not so much as a finger on my Lady until that time!' He carried her hand to his lips.

'You had better start practising now,' Lavinia recommended briskly, 'because I hear somebody coming.'

Fortunately, the newcomer proved to be Mr John Gaunt, who settled himself comfortably in a chair, stretched his legs out before him, plunged his hands in his trousers pockets and, when all was revealed to him, considered it a splendid lark. 'By God, yes!' he exploded. 'Bring Miss Lizzie to London right away, old fellow, though I warn you that you'll probably find yourself cut out in no time at all. Not an artist in the whole metropolis who won't want her for a model.' He corrected himself. 'Not one of the *new* school artists, that's to say.'

Guy was quick to show hackle, especially when he saw his beloved's faint and perfectly beautiful blush, but Gaunt interrupted him. 'Don't want to spoil sport, old fellow, but isn't there a little matter of religion? I thought all you French stuck to the Romish faith.'

There was silence. Then Juliana said, 'Guy *can't* be a Catholic. I know your parents were married in the kirk at Glenbraddan, Guy, because I remember Papa telling me that Luke – my dead half-brother, you know? – was a groomsman.'

Guy said carelessly, 'Yes, but they were married again in Paris, according to Catholic rites. I believe that *Maman* chose not to reveal to her brother Edward that she had been accepted into the faith.'

Lavinia's eyebrows were in her hair. 'Good heavens! Don't tell me *Aunt Georgy* goes to Mass and confession and all that? I don't believe it!'

'*Oh, Guy!*' Lizzie's voice quavered. 'Will I have to become a Catholic? I don't think I could.'

'But it is so beautiful! You will find it warms your spirit as this cold Scottish kirk could never do. Beauty, and light, and colour. You will be instructed in the faith, and learn to love it as I do, and then we will be married.' What, he implied, could be simpler?

Lavinia, watching the pair of them, knew exactly how her grandmother would have felt if she had been present, which thank heavens she wasn't. For that silly young man to have ignored the whole question of religion, when he must have known . . . And for Lizzie to sit there looking as if she would be consigned to eternal hellfire if she never again sat on a hard, freezing cold bench, and listened to an endless sermon, and raised her voice in a melancholy, metrical psalm. What an exasperating girl she was!

'Don't be silly, Lizzie,' she said bracingly. 'It's the same God, after all, and the choice is between doing as Guy says – or never seeing him again!' She sounded *just* like Vilia.

Lizzie's soulful eyes filled with tears. 'I'm not silly, even if grandmother says I am. She only says it because she doesn't love me the least little bit. Sometimes when she looks at me, in that way she does, I think she hates me.'

'Of course she doesn't!' Juliana intervened. 'What an idiotic thing to say!'

Lizzie's voice rose. 'You see! You're doing it, too!' She burst into hysterical tears. 'Take me away, Guy. Please take me away! I'll join your church, I'll do anything you like, but I don't want to live without you!'

Taking a deep breath, Juliana said, 'I have a confession to make. When I wrote to your papa, I told him you and Guy were in love. I thought it might prepare the ground for you. I hope you don't mind.'

Lizzie raised her face from Guy's magnificently damasked bosom; there was a dark patch where her tears had soaked into the silvery cloth. 'Oh, Juliana! But grandmother says that he will feel just as she does about it. Oh, what if he is already on his way home to stop us!'

'I shouldn't think he will be,' Juliana said after a moment. 'He can't just rush off and leave his work, and he must be awfully busy with all those battles.' Her brow lightened. 'And you know, I do think that if he was seriously against it, he would have written back right away. So perhaps he doesn't mind.'

Lavinia said judiciously, 'Of course we don't know how long it takes letters to arrive there. When did you write?'

'A month ago.'

'Oh, well, that should be enough.' But she could see that Lizzie wasn't convinced. It didn't really matter. If they were going to run away, the sooner they did it the better. Lavinia had her own reasons for wishing to see Guy and his friends off the premises. She was most anxious to separate Mr Harvey from dear Uncle Theo.

She said, 'Now, you must make plans. It seems to me that Guy and Mr Gaunt and Mr Harvey should leave the day after tomorrow, as Uncle Magnus wishes, and stop at Inverbeg or somewhere. Then Lizzie and Juliana and I can set out for a ride, and join you there.'

Juliana said in a small voice, 'But when just the two of us come back, everyone will know what's happened. And we'll be blamed.'

Lavinia hadn't thought of that, but she said, 'Don't think up difficulties! We can work all that out later. And it will be perfectly unexceptionable. Mr Gaunt and Mr Harvey will be able to chaperon Guy and Lizzie for as long as necessary.'

It was by no means the end of the discussion, although Lavinia said very little from then on. Only when everything had been settled did she remark thoughtfully, 'You know, I believe it would be unwise to let Mr Harvey know what we have planned. You can explain it all to him after you've left Kinveil.' Everyone saw the force of this, except Lizzie.

Impatiently, Lavinia said, 'Well, you don't want him telling Uncle Theo, do you! And it might be as well to take care that Sorley doesn't find out, either.'

'Oh, no!' Lizzie gasped. 'He'd be sure to tell grandmother.'

'Well, he might not,' said Lavinia fairly. 'He doesn't tell tales. But from something dear Uncle Theo said once – I can't remember what it was – I have the impression that Sorley is more than capable of putting a stop to things on his own account, especially if they're things he knows grandmother wouldn't like. And it's *much* better to be safe than sorry.'

4

The *Times-Graphic* had sent an illustrator out to join Gideon, although Gideon had warned them that the man would probably have to beg a ride over almost four hundred miles of the Black Sea to Constantinople in order to send his drawings off with any certainty of their arriving. And then one day at the beginning of November a message came up from the harbour at Balaclava; a man called Fred Tyler had just disembarked and was waiting for instructions. Gideon went down as soon as he could. There was only one man there who could possibly be Tyler, slung around with satchels and surrounded by baggage that included a number of large, flat packages. He went over to him.

'Jesus bloody Christ!' the man said, his eyes fixed on the water. 'Is it all like this?'

Dimly visible under the surface were piles of arms and legs that had been amputated after the battle, the uniform sleeves and trousers still on them. There was a half-clad, headless corpse fouling the cable of the ship that had just docked. And every few minutes the bright green scum that coated the water was broken as a dead body, bloated and grotesque, was drifted upwards by some malevolent current, only to sink again or float sluggishly away. The air reeked of decay and cholera and sulphuretted hydrogen.

'More or less,' Gideon said. 'And one doesn't get used to it. I take it you're the illustrator. Why not start with this?'

'Jesus!' the man said again. '*Should* I?'

The very next day had come the battle of Inkerman, fierce and bloody beyond imagining. At one stage less than five thousand British and French troops were engaged against seventeen thousand Russians. But the allied forces won, and spent the next three days burying not only their own but four thousand Russian dead, Prince Mentschikoff having pointed out from the comfort of besieged Sebastopol that it was customary, as he understood it, for such work to be done by those left in possession of the battlefield. The whole countryside seemed to be covered with wounded, lying day and night on the wet ground, starving and screaming in agony and dying. The British hauled them up on to mules lent by the French, and took them to the hospital enclosures. If they didn't die on the way, they usually died under the surgeon's knife.

The healthy were in no better case. Icy winds now blew on the troops besieging Sebastopol, and there was no fuel. Every bush, every twig was consumed, not for warmth but to cook the dried peas and salt meat that was the men's only food apart from ship's biscuit. There was no tea, even, only green coffee beans that they had to roast and grind themselves, if they could. Without the two daily glasses of rum, life would have been insupportable. It seemed, at least, that things could only get better.

But then the hurricane struck. Tents were torn up and whirled off, never to be seen again. Stones flew through the air, ripping and smashing and tearing anything or anyone in their path. Heavy wagons were thrown down and swept along the ground, dragging the oxen with them as if they were kittens. Hospital marquees collapsed on the sick and dying. There was scarcely a ship in Balaclava harbour that didn't go down, and among them the supply fleet that had just arrived. Everything the army had been waiting for – hundreds of tons of gunpowder, millions of cartridges, forty thousand desperately needed greatcoats, thousands of pairs of boots for men whose footwear was already paper thin, and stores whose value was to be reckoned in terms of lives, not money.

In the weeks that followed there was hail and rain and snow, and more rain, and sleet, and more rain. Transport animals died or became too weak to work; the men's rations were curtailed; the camps outside Sebastopol were vast sheets of mud, and the trenches knee deep in it. There were few tents now, few men who were not reduced to rags, none who could remember what it was to be warm and dry and well fed. Night after night, the men died at their posts from cold and exhaustion. Those who didn't began to suffer from typhus, respiratory diseases, dysentery, frostbite, boils and ulcers, and there wasn't a man in the army who didn't have diarrhoea.

By the end of the month, Gideon had discovered that Fred Tyler was not only an extremely good artist, but a kindly, reliable fellow who could be left to watch events at Sebastopol while Gideon himself did what he had been trying to do for some time, and paid a visit to the base hospital at Scutari. It meant at least two weeks away, and two crossings of the Black Sea in vile weather, but he needed to confirm the reports he had heard. A lady called Miss Nightingale had arrived three weeks earlier with a party of forty women nurses. The army authorities didn't seem to want her much, and the doctors certainly didn't, but the men, it seemed, were already counting her among the angels. Gideon, sick and shivering, thought Scutari couldn't be worse than here.

He struggled down to Balaclava to find the town in chaos. Ships would arrive without notice, and no one knew what was in them. Sometimes they were sent all the way back to Constantinople, only to be turned round and sent back again. No one knew how many ships there were, or where they could refuel. The sick and wounded were being crammed into ordinary transports dignified by the name of 'hospital ship'; Gideon heard of one that, fitted out to receive 250 men, set sail with nearer fifteen hundred, men with amputations, men with cholera, packed close together, so that when the ship rolled, they rolled on top of one another. He sailed on one that wasn't quite as bad as that, but nearly.

Gideon had thought that, by now, he was physically inured to any sight, that it was only his mind that recoiled. But Scutari was indescribable. The wards were packed, and all the corridors were lined with men lying on the unwashed, rotting floors, crawling with vermin. There were no pillows and no blankets. The men propped their heads on their boots, and wrapped themselves in their own filthy greatcoats, stiff with blood and mud and excrement. The doctors were working for twenty-four hours at a stretch, but there were still men who had lain ten days in the hospital before a doctor reached them. More than a thousand of the patients were suffering from acute diarrhoea but in the whole hospital there were only twenty chamber-pots with, in each ward, a huge wooden tub, usually but not always emptied once a day. The smell was worse even than the smell outside Sebastopol, where it was compounded of gunsmoke and urine and the putrefying corpses of animals and men, sweet and cloying and unmistakable.

Within hours, Gideon had forgotten why he was supposed to be there. He had a saucepan thrust into his hands and was told brusquely to go down to the pier and dispense its contents to the wounded in a newly arrived transport. Afterwards, he was sent to the corridors with his note pads to take down messages from the dying; within minutes his papers were crawling with lice. Next day he found himself assisting at an amputation, supporting the shoulders of a man whose leg was being removed; the operating table was only three feet long. He hadn't slept in the interim, and he didn't know when he was going to.

He stayed at Scutari for two weeks instead of the two days he had intended, for more and more sick were arriving every day, hundreds of them, and he didn't know how to leave when he was able to do something, however little. He knew, now, that Miss Nightingale *was* an angel, but an angel of steel. He could think of only two women who could have done what she was doing – Vilia, and Selina. Or perhaps not even them, for Vilia was too fastidious, and Selina too self-centred.

Fred Tyler welcomed him back to Sebastopol in December without remarking on his haggard face, over-lean body, or obvious exhaustion. All he said was, 'I hope you brought some supplies with you from Constantinople, like champagne and caviar? What – only brandy and tinned ham? They'll do. There are some letters here for you; I'd have sent them on if I'd known you were going to be away for so long.'

Underslept, seasick, and racked by bowel pains, Gideon wrapped himself in one of the blankets he had brought and lay down on the second of the camp beds Fred had managed to buy from an Albanian merchant who had set up shop in Balaclava. There were letters from Fanshawe, and one from his publisher, and another from a different publisher inquiring whether he was likely to put his Crimean reports together to make a book. Billy Russell had sent him a copy of *The Examiner*, drawing his attention to a poem by Alfred Tennyson.

'Half a league, half a league, Half a league onward . . . "Forward, the Light Brigade, Charge for the guns!" he said . . . Theirs not to reason why, Theirs but to do and die . . .' Gideon would have been sick if there had been anything left in his stomach. He had held one of the Light Brigade down while the doctor had taken his arm off, but the man had died two days later. He remembered picking a handful of maggots from the bandage round another man's chest; the dressing hadn't been changed for three weeks because there weren't enough bandages.

He, Gideon Lauriston, who had always tried to remain detached, uncommitted, could be so no more. The sights he had seen and the problem of writing about them obsessed his mind now to the exclusion of all else. It was with scarcely more than lukewarm interest that he turned to the two family letters awaiting him. There was one from Theo and one from Lizzie. Theo's was dated first so he opened it first.

Vilia should be writing this letter, but she is, I suspect, too embarrassed. Gideon, dear boy, I much regret to tell you that Lizzie has run off with Guy Savarin. This may not come as a complete surprise to you, since Juliana tells me she wrote to you that they were attracted, and elopement, it seems, runs in the family. I will not weary you with all the details. Suffice it to say that they went, and that Vilia then instructed me to go after them and put a stop to it. I, as you may imagine, said, 'What, again?' which was not at all well received. In the end, I pursued them to London, and had no difficulty in finding them, since Guy had taken Lizzie to his apartment at Blackfriars, a romantic place overhanging the river and smelling of it quite strongly.

Unfortunately, it appears that they are not married. Guy turns out to be a Catholic and declares that a civil ceremony has no meaning, and Lizzie – *such* an impressionable girl – has agreed that, since they propose to live in perfect chastity until she is received into the church of Rome – when they will be married 'properly' – the formalities of a civil ceremony are superfluous. They appear to be sincere.

I see no way by which Lizzie can be saved from Guy, except possibly by an appeal from you – mine had *no* effect! – or by due process of law, which would still require your presence. In Scots law, there would be nothing at all one could do about it, since they would be regarded as legally married 'according to custom', or whatever the phrase is. But English law may be different; Lizzie is not of age by English standards, and most certainly not married. Unfortunately, even Peregrine James doesn't appear to know whether Scots or English law would apply. In any case, neither Vilia nor I has any legal jurisdiction over the child. So you must decide.

We are all genuinely sorry about this. Vilia considers she should have foreseen it, and Magnus, as you may imagine, is being quite intolerable about the bad blood that causes Lauristons to elope left, right and centre. As if the bad blood in the Randalls wasn't enough! How one wishes that Edward Blair would do something wildly improper, and take the Telfer strain down a peg or two.

Anyway, let me know, dear boy, if there is anything I can do, although I can't think what it might be. Try not to get in the way of any of those nasty, noisy guns.

It was another world, Gideon thought, a world filled with characters as cut off from him as if he were seeing them through glass or reading about them in the pages of some penny novelette. He recognized that his daughter had done something extremely foolish, and that she hadn't done it without being pushed – by someone, or some circumstance. She was such a biddable girl. If someone had been there to say, 'Don't!' when Guy said, 'Do!' she would still be safely at Kinveil. He hoped no one had been unkind to her. But Guy had probably filled her head with rosy visions, painted a glowing picture of the life they would have together in some neo-mediaeval paradise. Just the thing that would appeal to Lizzie. He remembered vaguely that Guy had been besotted by the Middle Ages; so had Drew once, but at least he knew how to keep his misguided ideas of chivalry separate from the demands of modern life, and Gideon wasn't sure that young Guy did. He sighed, and opened the letter from his daughter.

Poor little Lizzie. She had tried to give herself confidence by searching for a suitable model in *The Lady's Indispensible Letter Writer*, and had found some genteel paper – horribly gilt-edged and deckled – with a matching envelope. She had sealed it with lilac wax. Even her handwriting, for the first few lines, was all that a lady's should be.

Dearest papa – May I commence by inquiring after your health? I hope the weather is more clement with you than it is here in London. The purpose of this letter is to inform you that I am shortly to be married to M. Guillaume Savarin, a connection of Uncle Magnus Telfer's, who had the pleasure of making your acquaintance at the time of the Great Exhibition in 1851. I hope you will be pleased.

But here the reference model had begun to let her down.

For reasons which it would impose on your patience for me to relate, I have come to London somewhat in advance of the wedding, which I hope will take place quite soon. M. Savarin has been so kind as to offer me his hospitality in the meantime.

And then, as if she had realized that there was no possibility of wrapping it all up in clean linen, the timid, worried girl began to show through.

I do assure you, dearest Papa, that there is nothing whatever improper in this situation. M. Savarin is the most perfect gentleman. It is just that Uncle Theo has been here, and I think he wants to separate us, and I could not *bear* that. He said he would write to you about it, and if he does, please *please* don't pay any attention to any horrid things he says about Guy or the way we ran away together which we had to otherwise grandmother would have parted us and I would have *died* because she was already cross with us and Uncle Magnus said he wouldn't have Guy in the house any longer and he was to go away. So you see we *had* to leave and we didn't even say good-bye which was very ill-bred of us.

Gideon sank his head into his hands. Poor child, poor child. The appalling thing was that all he could feel about it was a mild, rueful resignation. Strange how war put the triumphs and tragedies of ordinary life into a different perspective. The suffering, degradation and death he had observed on such a massive scale for so many weeks now reduced his daughter's troubles to no more than a problem of etiquette. She would have to learn to face the world as others did, and grow up on her own; though if Guy truly loved her, and Gideon hoped he did, she would not be wholly on her own.

There was nothing Gideon could do; nothing, perhaps, he would do even if he could. Tomorrow, he would write her a note of reassurance and give it to someone who was going down to Balaclava and could send it off. He fell asleep with a bleak half-smile on the lips that were hidden, these days, under four months' growth of beard.

5

Vilia, with some idea of keeping an eye on Lizzie, went to London early in January, taking Juliana with her. Juliana was to make her come-out in a few weeks, and Vilia told Magnus there was a great deal of shopping to be done first. It was a relief even for Juliana, dutifully and unthinkingly fond of her father, to get away from him, for he showed no sign of easing up on his complaints about Guy, Lizzie, and Lizzie's grandmother. In response, Lizzie's grandmother had been becoming progressively sharper-tongued, and although Magnus bore the brunt of it, Juliana had not escaped. Vilia had been swift to recognize that a large part of the blame for Lizzie's flight could be laid at the door of the other two girls, and Juliana and Lavinia had emerged, shaking, from an interview that Juliana still preferred not to remember. Lavinia had been able to stalk off back to Marchfield, but for Juliana there had been no escape. She was beginning to wonder if Vilia would ever forgive her, and wasn't sure that she cared. Vilia had never been the kind of stepmother one ran to for warmth and comfort and perfumed embraces, but until about three years ago she had been briskly understanding and sympathetic. And then, suddenly, after the Great Exhibition, she had just stopped being interested, as if she didn't like anyone any more. Juliana wondered wistfully, sometimes, what her own mother had been like. In her portrait she looked soft, and pretty, and – cosy.

They did some shopping, mostly in Regent Street, thick with carriages and horsemen, and debutantes with their mothers, sisters and aunts, especially in the late afternoon, when the whole world seemed to congregate in Swan and Edgar's silk shop, or Allison's, where the latest fashions and materials were to be had. London seemed to Juliana to be terrifyingly busy.

As soon as they had settled into the Brook Street house they had taken, Vilia summoned Jermyn from the War Office, where he was involved in a series of complex discussions about military equipment. With his usual, faintly absent-minded air, he set off as instructed for Guy Savarin's apartments at Blackfriars and returned, equally absent-mindedly, to report that Lizzie had announced that nothing in the world would persuade her to see her grandmother, who would only bully her. 'Overwrought,' Jermyn remarked laconically, 'and I don't wonder. That Savarin fellow seems to live with his head in the clouds, and poor Lizzie doesn't have the wits to realize that there's nothing up there. In the clouds, I mean. He's kind enough to her, but she feels horribly inferior, poor girl. Anyway, she says she'll see Juliana. Do you want me to take you, Juley? I can't spare any more time now, but we'll go this evening.'

It was dark and eerily quiet by the river, and the gas lamp outside the house was reflected in the oily surface of the Thames, not once, but again and again and again. Outlined against the faint luminescence of the sky Juliana could see St Paul's and, where the buildings were lower and more squalid, the rigging and masts of tall ships; the silence was full of stealthy murmurings which, at last, she identified as the river gurgling and sucking round the wharves, and barges moving gently on the current or snubbing the rotting wood of the wharf piles. There was a sickly mist over all, evidence of the sewers that poured into the water, day and night, the refuse of one of the greatest cities in the world. 'It can't be healthy,' she whispered to Jermyn. She had no reason on earth to be whispering, but once the carriage had drawn to a halt, there was no single sound that did not reek of darkness and secrecy.

'It is the most delightful room for a party,' Lizzie said in her small voice when she had greeted them and taken Juliana's cloak. No servants, Juliana noted in disbelief. 'There are windows on all sides, you see, and there is a balcony over the water where Guy sits and paints when he is here. The weather has not been very clement, of course, but we have had one or two beautiful days. When the wind is fresh and the sun is shining, it is very exciting and beautiful. And there is so much activity on the river.'

'Hmmm,' Jermyn said. 'And when the fog comes down, the mud-banks are bare and putrid, and the air must be thick with cholera and typhoid. It's not right for you, Lizzie, you know, especially when you're used to a place like Kinveil. I'd get Guy to find somewhere else, if I were you.'

Her eyes dilated. 'Oh, but Guy loves it!'

'No doubt. This one of his paintings? Dante and Beatrice, I take it, in a Tuscan landscape? Well, he doesn't need the Thames for that, does he? Were you the model?'

'Yes.'

'Mmm. He's certainly caught that blank look of yours. To the life.'

'Jermyn!' Juliana exclaimed. '*Will* you go and wait in the coach while Lizzie and I talk. How can you expect Lizzie to feel comfortable when you are criticizing all the time.'

'I'm not criticizing.' It was said without heat. 'All right, I'll go. Guy's out, is he, Lizzie?'

'He's gone to dine with Mr Swinburne.'

'Oh. Well, call when you want me, Juley.'

It took a long, long time to break down Lizzie's brittle little barricades. She talked as if Juliana were some new acquaintance to whom it was necessary to say all the hostessly things, offer all the correct refreshments, make all the polite responses. It was as if her physical beauty were all that existed. Beyond that, there seemed to be nothing there at all. And yet they had grown up together, lived together for twenty-four hours a day for more than ten years of their lives.

In the end, Juliana exclaimed, 'For heaven's sake, Lizzie! This is me – *me, me!* Are you all right? Truly, that's all I want to know!'

She was wearing some strange drapery that had nothing to do with fashion, and the beautiful copper hair, no longer disciplined into modish waves and knots, flowed smoothly and silkily over her sloping shoulders. The column of her neck was like cream. She sat, upright and motionless, hands gracefully clasped in her lap, in a massively built, straight-backed chair that looked as if it would take four strong men to move it. 'I am very well, thank you,' she replied with no perceptible change of tone or expression.

Juliana, petite, fair and fashionable, hopped briskly to her feet and marched over, then, taking Lizzie by the shoulders, shook her vigorously. '*Lizzie!* You aren't here at all, are you! Come back this minute and talk to me as if you were a human being instead of an automaton!'

Lizzie's wide eyes, so much darker than Juliana's, blinked and then settled on the other girl with something akin to alarm. 'I *am* perfectly well,' she said in the small, bell-like voice that somehow didn't match her looks. A statue, Juliana had always felt, should never speak at all, or should have a voice that was cool, low and musical.

'Well, you look positively mournful to me! Don't tell me there isn't something wrong.'

'It's only – well, I don't understand things.'

Juliana sighed. 'You've never been awfully quick, you know! What kind of things?'

'We can't be married until I have been received into the church, and I can't be received until the priest thinks I'm fit. And I won't be fit until I understand all the things he explains to me – and I *can't!*' It was a wail.

'Surely you can pretend to?'

'Oh, no. That wouldn't be right.'

'Have you told him you don't understand?'

'Oh, no.'

'Well, why not try? He might be able to explain everything differently, so that you could.'

Doubtfully, Lizzie said, 'Do you think so? The dreadful thing is that I don't understand Guy either, most of the time.' She rose and drifted over to a settle with painted cupboards over it, occupying one of the bewildering number of nooks and alcoves in the walls. Opening one of the cupboards, she brought out a box of sweetmeats, but when she turned her eyes were full of tears.

'About art, you mean?'

'And its – its verity, and purpose and significance. I can draw, Juliana, you know I can, but I don't seem able to put my *soul* into it. At least, Guy says I don't, and I'm sure he's right, because I don't understand *how* one puts one's soul into it. If only I weren't so stupid!'

'You aren't stupid,' Juliana replied automatically. 'Besides, none of it matters if Guy loves you.'

'But what if he stopped loving me?'

'My dear Lizzie, if you always look as beautiful as you do now, it's highly unlikely. I shouldn't think there's a man on earth who wouldn't fall head over heels in love with you if you so much as smiled. Though I do think,' she added judiciously, 'that it would be better if you could make your smile a little less wan and sorrowing.' She looked like some early Christian martyr.

'But that's what Guy and all his friends admire so much. They all want to paint me because I look so remote and unattainable. It's very tiring sitting for them, you know. Guy says I personify the abstraction of Love, rather than the reality of the beloved. I don't know what that means.'

Neither did Juliana, but she didn't like the sound of it at all. 'Stuff!' she exclaimed. 'Spiritual passion is all very well, but it seems to me that the sooner you settle things with the priest the better. You'll feel so much more comfortable when you are married.' Not being wholly ignorant, she went on a little hesitantly, 'I'm sure it must be very hard for Guy living with you like a monk. Perhaps he talks about – what was it? – abstractions of Love to take his mind off – er – other things.'

'That's what *terrifies* me!' Lizzie whispered tragically. She was leaning on the back of the monumental chair, her white hands gripping its Gothic peak. 'If anything should happen – you know? – without us being married, it would be the most dreadful thing. I could never hold up my head again. I would kill myself.'

'I can't see why,' Juliana said prosaically. 'No one would know, would they? And if they did, they could hardly blame *you*!'

Even Lizzie was capable of spotting the flaws in that ill-considered

603

speech. 'Couldn't they? Everyone would say I had brought it on myself. *No one* would truly feel for me. And, oh, Juliana, I wrote to Papa to tell him what has happened, and he hasn't answered! Do you think he has washed his hands of me too? I'm so frightened! *Everyone* has deserted me, and I can't bear it alone!'

'*Don't be silly!*'

She could have bitten her tongue out. Two great tears welled up in Lizzie's eyes and began to roll down her cheeks, impairing her beauty not at all. Tragically, she moaned, 'Guy has begun to say that, too!'

An exasperated Juliana didn't altogether blame him. 'Well, if you will go on about how inadequate you are, when you're not inadequate at all, it's not to be wondered at. For heaven's sake, Lizzie, pull yourself together. I'll come and see you again as often as you like, and you'll feel much more cheerful for being able to talk to someone. It seems to me that you have worked yourself up into a terrible state! If Guy is out a lot in the evenings – which, I must say, seems to me *most* thoughtless of him – you are obviously left too much alone, and you have never been used to that. You have allowed your fears to get the better of you. Shall I come again one evening next week?'

Sadly, this bracing little homily had no effect at all. Juliana didn't realize how like Vilia she had sounded. Dealing with Lizzie, it was hard not to.

Lizzie's heavy-lidded eyes became vacant, and her voice, when she spoke, was apathetic. 'Yes. No. I don't know. You see, when Guy is at home he likes to work at his easel, and I don't think he should be interrupted. He is a very great artist, you know. But I don't always know when he is going to be out. Mr Ruskin has arranged for him to teach at the new Working Men's College, you see. It's very exciting. Guy says that Christian Socialism is humanity's one great hope for the future. He goes there quite often in the evenings, sometimes even when he has no classes to take.'

Juliana, drawing on her gloves, said with a trace of asperity, 'You mean it would be more convenient if I only come when I am invited? Very well, Lizzie. But I warn you, if you don't invite me, I shall come anyway. I don't think it's good for you being on your own.'

Lizzie didn't invite her, and Juliana heard nothing for several weeks. More than once, knowing her cousin's lethargy too well, she hesitated about descending on her, but then did nothing. Already, she was caught up in the round of parties and receptions, luncheons and suppers, that preceded the real start of the Season, and Vilia insisted that she must attend them so that she could extend her acquaintance. Then she would not be quite among strangers later on. To Juliana it made little difference; it was just as much of a trial making new acquaintances in a private house as it would have been at a grand ball.

At last, in the middle of March, she received a note from Lizzie. But she told no one about it, because by the time it arrived, Lizzie was dead.

6

The news reached Gideon less than two weeks after he himself had turned the corner between life and death.

Late in January, when there were eleven thousand men besieging Sebastopol, and twelve thousand lying in hospital at Scutari, sick with acute scurvy as well as all the other diseases that ravaged the army, Gideon had decided he must visit the hospital again. It had a morbid fascination for him. For more than a month he had scarcely thought of anything but the extraordinary gentleness of the men who lay so patiently in their loathsome surroundings, suffering horribly, screaming sometimes, and yet never allowing a single coarse word to pass their lips in case it might distress the gentlewomen who nursed them; the ill, the dying, the nurses, all rising with heartbreaking dignity above conditions that no human being could be expected to endure. And they were all being betrayed, time and time again, and in everything, by the stupidity, the incompetence, the indifference of politicians, administrators, and petty officials. Gideon knew that in December twenty thousand pounds of lime juice, the surest specific against scurvy, had arrived at Balaclava but that none of it had been issued, because army orders made no provision for its inclusion in the ration. In January, a shipload of cabbages had been thrown into the harbour because it was not consigned to any particular department. And huge quantities of warm clothing and preserved foods had been sent out from England only to disappear in the bottomless pit of the Turkish Customs House. Fretting, miserable, feeling himself useless at Sebastopol where nothing was happening to justify the presence of a newspaperman,

Gideon was drawn as if by a magnet to Scutari where he might, perhaps, be able to help just a little.

The wards were cleaner now, the lavatories unstopped, and the food almost eatable, even if men with scurvy were unable to masticate it. Miss Nightingale had worked wonders. But outside there was a sea of decaying filth, so that the very walls of the hospital were soaked in it, and every breath of air blew gases from the choked, overloaded sewers back through the privies and into the wards and corridors. One of the nurses told Gideon that patients in the beds nearest the privies never survived.

An epidemic of what some of the nurses called Asiatic cholera and others 'famine fever' had broken out earlier in the month, and four surgeons and three nurses had already died of it. At any other period of his life Gideon would have walked sensibly away from a place of danger where he had no need to be. But now, obsessed, he stayed.

He stayed, fetching and carrying, taking down messages from men who were sick, in agony, almost too weak to talk. He stayed as the death toll steadily mounted, and the Turks tipped the bodies into large shallow pits because the British couldn't muster a fatigue party of men strong enough to dig. He stayed, and helped, and at the end of February himself went down with cholera.

Just before that, he had received a letter from Lizzie, a sad and at the same time hysterical letter reproaching him for having deserted her. He had written to her from Sebastopol, but it seemed she had not received his note; the messenger with whom he had sent it to Balaclava must have been killed on the way.

Poor Lizzie. This was a cry from the heart. 'I am so alone; I have no one to turn to if I do not have you.'

He had known already that he had caught something in the hospital, so he had scrubbed his hands with extreme care before he sat down to reply, and touched nothing but pen and paper while he wrote. But he could still smell the sickness around him, feel it as tangibly as if it had soaked into his shirt, as if it were tangled in the hairs on his forearms, as if it lay like a sheen of perspiration over all his skin.

Somehow he had finished the letter, somehow explained to her the situation he was in, somehow collected together as many short, reassuring words as he could think of. And then, reporting to the medical staff as a patient, he had begged one of the nurses to see his letter dispatched, explaining a little of it to her before he was gripped by the first brutal, cramping pains. He had watched men beyond counting die of cholera. He knew it was uncomfortable at first, but no more; like a touch of dysentery. Then, within hours, it became the 'bloody flux' that had devastated armies in the past, ravaged cities, killed more people in famine zones than famine itself. After that, the cramps really took hold, and the sick man wasted away before one's eyes, his face shrinking, eyes receding, nose losing all its flesh until it became pointed and pinched and skeletal. His skin became wrinkled and dead, so that even a finger's pressure remained like a potter's thumbprint in clay. The stomach cramps had spread throughout his body by now, reaching the throat so that breathing was constricted and to swallow impossible; it was then that panic began to show in a man's eyes.

Most of the men at Scutari had gone quickly on from there, because they were undernourished and exhausted even before the disease struck. The fortunate ones – those who had been born in slums, starved in youth, harshly tested in maturity – went in less than two days sometimes, from start to finish. The well-fed took longer. Gideon knew what lay ahead of him.

But, somehow, he survived, although it was three long weeks before he was capable even of standing on his feet again.

When the letter from Vilia arrived, he was sitting at the little deal table in Miss Nightingale's storeroom making fair copies of correspondence for her. She was inundated with paperwork, for she had no one to act as her secretary. She nursed, and she managed the wards, and the supplies; she dealt with an endless stream of questions and demands from anyone who had anything to do with the hospital – nurses, merchants, doctors, chaplains, the captains of the sick transports. And she wrote home for the men, with their dying messages; for the nurses, to their children; occasionally to her own family; and almost daily there was a stream of official letters, and reports, and requisitions. The light in her room was never put out. Her stamina was perhaps the most remarkable thing about her. For a little time at least, Gideon hoped he might take some of the burden from her shoulders.

Vilia's letter was brief.

It seems that Lizzie had been suffering from neuralgia, and the pain, as well as a natural unease of mind, were making it difficult for her to sleep. Guy went out at about nine o'clock to the Working Men's College, where he teaches in the evening, and when he returned some time after eleven she was unconscious. An empty phial of laudanum was on the table beside her bed. She died a few hours later. It seems possible that she took a normal dose of the drug and fell asleep and then, waking again soon after, dazed and confused, took more without realizing quite how much it was. I believe this to be probable as well as possible, for even when she was in full possession of her faculties poor Lizzie was too often inclined not to concentrate on what she was doing. Guy is distraught with grief and remorse, and blames himself entirely.

I need hardly say how deeply distressed we all are over this tragedy. I don't know what you will wish to do – whether you will come home, or whether it would be better for you not to – but Theo has arranged for Lizzie to be taken back to Marchfield and buried in the little cemetery of the village kirk. We hope that is what you would have wished. All my love and sympathy, my dear. What else is there that I can say?

7

Gideon did go home when he was fit to travel, although there seemed little purpose in it. He had failed Lizzie just as he had failed Elinor, and couldn't judge how that weighed in the balance against the hundreds, thousands of lives he had been trying to save by staying in the Crimea and observing, and exposing, and writing the articles for the *Times-Graphic* that had helped to force the newly elected government at home to send out a Sanitary Commission to investigate the state of the military hospitals. It was a question to which there wasn't any answer, but he thought it was a question he would never be able to forget.

By the time he arrived in London, gaunt as a scarecrow and scarcely recognizable there was no longer any sign that a crisis had been reached between Vilia and Juliana.

Juliana, blaming herself for not having given Lizzie support when she needed it, had turned on Vilia and laid it all at her door.

'My dear Juliana,' Vilia had said with exactitude. 'An accidental overdose of laudanum is something for which no one can be blamed except poor Lizzie.'

'Poor Lizzie! *Poor Lizzie*! If you hadn't patronized her with your "poor Lizzie" all these years, she'd still be alive now! You made her feel silly, and stupid, and unloved. She would never have run away with Guy if she had thought there was any other choice. You never gave her any softness or comfort, and she needed them so badly. She was like me, in a way; she needed someone to hold on to. The kind of help Lavinia and I could give her was no use, because she knew we were as young and ineffectual as she was.'

'Juliana, *really*!' Vilia interrupted, her voice taut. 'Lizzie was a sweet but stupid girl, who died by an unfortunate accident. I am aware that you must be upset – *as I am* – but I would be obliged if you would control your tongue. I thought, at least, that I had managed to instil some idea of self-discipline into you in these last seventeen years!'

'Oh, yes!' Juliana exclaimed hysterically. '*Oh, yes*! You've been very firm with me. You were so firm with Lizzie, too, that she came to think you hated her. If it hadn't been for that . . . But she thought she would be happy with Guy, happy for the first time in her life. And then you said no! You didn't show her even the tiniest hint of sympathy when she fell in love, though it was the most wonderful and the most – the most *difficult* thing that had ever happened to her. I don't understand you. I don't understand you at all! I don't think you know what love *is*!'

When Juliana at last rushed from the room, leaving her stepmother in a state of ice-cold fury, she had said more than she would ever have dreamed herself capable of saying. There was only one thing she had held back.

The note Lizzie had written her on the day before she died had been scrawled, and blotted with tears, but its message had been unmistakable. Life, in the end, had become too much for her.

I don't understand anything any more, and I feel as if my head is going to burst, and even Guy thinks I am stupid. I know it will be like this for as long as I live, and I can't bear it. I feel so alone, so *alone*. There is only one thing I can do, isn't there, Juley? I know you meant well when you came to see me, but it isn't enough. There is only one thing I can do, and even if I *am* stupid, I am still capable of *that*. Please tell my papa I am sorry. If only he had been here. I'm sorry! I'm sorry! Good-bye, dear Juley.

Juliana had told no one about the note, because she thought only Gideon had the right to know that his daughter hadn't died by accident; only he who could decide what, if anything, to do about it. But when she saw him, she found that showing him the note was quite beyond her power. He had suffered enough. And besides, she couldn't see what good it would do.

Chapter Six

1

A year after Lizzie's death, Dr Richard Henry Curtis of the Bengal Medical Service approached Magnus with some trepidation and asked for his daughter's hand in marriage. Juliana had warned him that her father would say no, because he always said no on principle.

But his prospective father-in-law's glassy stare discomposed Richard more than a little. Not being able to read Magnus's mind, he couldn't tell that the old man was suffering from an attack of *déjà vu*, remembering St James's Square forty years ago and another army fellow asking permission to take another young woman off his hands. Vilia Cameron. By God, he wished someone would come and ask him again now!

He exhaled gustily through his lips. 'No, no. Couldn't consider it,' he said. 'What, take my little girl away from the only home she's ever known to a nasty, dangerous country on the other side of the world? The graveyard of the British, they call it! No. Definitely no.'

'But I *am* a doctor, Mr Telfer, and I've had five years in India already. So I know what I'm talking about. She'll be perfectly safe with me, I assure you.'

Magnus ignored him. 'Anyway, strange people and places have always frightened her. Nervous little thing, you know. In fact, I don't know what's got into her. D'you tell me she *wants* to marry you? Why should she? Why should she want to go gallivanting off to goodness knows where with you?'

Richard gulped. 'Well, sir, we are very much attached to each other, and she says that, if she has me, she will be perfectly comfortable even in a strange land.'

'Humph!'

No more than Richard was Magnus aware of his daughter's increasingly desperate need to get away from Kinveil, and as far away as humanly possible. The first few months after Lizzie died had been predictably awful. Juliana's Season had had to be abandoned, which she didn't regret, and Gideon had returned with herself and Vilia and, for a brief space, Theo, to the Highlands. Theo had been particularly kind and sympathetic to her, but he hadn't been able to stay long and hadn't been back since, because railway speculation was running riot in America and Lauriston Brothers' was very much under pressure. Vilia had been very curt with him for some reason. Gideon hadn't stayed as long as he might, either. The peace and inactivity of Kinveil seemed to fret him rather than soothe him. It was as if he had locked Lizzie's death up inside himself, for he spoke of nothing but the war in the Crimea and of no one but Miss Nightingale. When a news item appeared in *The Times* saying that she was dangerously ill, he had announced at last, 'I must go back.'

'Because of Miss Nightingale?' Vilia's eyebrows had gone up. 'But why? There is certainly nothing whatever that you can do.'

'No. I just know that I have to go. Anyway, Fanshawe has been very forbearing, and little though one might think it, here, the world beyond Kinveil continues to turn.'

Juliana had known she would miss Lizzie, but she hadn't known how much. Nor had she realized how inevitably she would be thrown into her stepmother's company. And that was worse than anything, because Vilia, deeply and it seemed irrevocably angered by Juliana's outburst after Lizzie's death, treated her now with a distant, elaborate politeness that was more hurtful than Juliana would have believed possible. She felt completely isolated, and only now began to understand fully what Lizzie had meant when she had talked of being alone.

She didn't know how to escape. And then Jermyn, blandly ignoring Magnus's dislike of him, had come up on a visit, bringing with him a young man, home on leave from India, whom he had met through some old university friends. Richard Curtis was almost twenty-nine, but he had pleasant good looks and a charming, boyish enthusiasm that had the almost instantaneous effect of lifting the clouds. Never in her life had Juliana felt at ease with anyone so quickly. She liked him very much and thought she might come to love him. And she had always wanted to visit India, ever since the Great Exhibition.

So, when Dr Curtis, captivated by her piquant little face and obvious pleasure in his company, had gone down romantically on one knee and begged her to be his wife, she had said yes. If Papa would permit it.

In the end, it was Vilia who persuaded Papa to agree by being dubious, and hesitant, and voicing a great many arguments for Magnus to shoot down. Juliana, expecting Vilia to be on her side – not because she had any sympathy for young lovers, but because Juliana assumed she would be as glad to see her go as she herself would be to leave – had gone to Vilia first. Her response had been tolerant. 'It's serious, is it? But an army doctor? With no money and no prospects, unless he has ambitions to become Surgeon-General, or whatever it is?'

Juliana, nettled, exclaimed, 'If he marries me, we will have Kinveil!'

There was quite a long silence, then Vilia said, 'That's true.'

Juliana didn't like her tone. 'We might not, of course, if we were forced to run away together, in the old family tradition. But I don't think even that would cause Papa to cut me off. Do you?'

'Probably not. In any case, I think a complete change of scene would do you good, and India has the merit of being exotic.' Her lips curled satirically. 'And think of all those Cashmir shawls I couldn't drag you away from at the Great Exhibition! But I don't imagine India is all shawls and rajas. I hope you will remember your upbringing. The poor need your respect and consideration far more than the rich. Don't forget it.'

Richard, who had joined them, exclaimed, 'Forgive me, Mrs Telfer – er – Cameron but there will be no question of Juliana having any contact with the natives, except for the princes and officials, of course. The bazaars are never free from epidemics of one kind or another, and the British don't have the inbred resistance to them that the natives do.'

'Afraid of a few germs, Richard? And you a doctor!' Vilia said mockingly. 'How fortunate that Juliana has always been so healthy. I don't remember her ever catching anything, even a cold.'

Richard looked as if he were about to embark on a lecture, so Juliana said hurriedly, 'Oh, well! Since we will have at least twenty servants – because Richard says they are very firm about not encroaching on one another's duties – I expect I will learn quite as much as I want to about the lower classes without going near the bazaars!'

It hadn't been the happiest choice of phrase, she recognized, seeing Vilia's frown. Her father was always talking about 'the lower classes', and it never failed to irritate Vilia, who didn't believe in 'classes'.

The wedding took place in May at Kinveil, though Edinburgh would have been more convenient. But Magnus was over seventy and found travelling too much for him, so Juliana had to begin organizing her trousseau without recourse to shops or warehouses. Shona and Lavinia sent materials up by the bale for all the things Juliana had been told she would need. She hadn't believed the first list she was sent by a lady who had resided in India for fifteen years, but others confirmed it – and there were a great many others. Indeed, it seemed as if half the gentlewomen in the Highlands were, or had been, married to husbands who had seen service in the East India Company.

'Two dozen cotton chemises, six flannel vests, six lightweight petticoats, and ten flannel ones!' she exclaimed to Vilia.

'And Mrs Lyon says that two of the flannel ones must be red,' Vilia replied drily. 'Jenny Meneriskay can make them for you.'

'Four crinoline petticoats, four pairs of corsets with washable covers, two dozen pairs of cotton drawers, three dozen pairs of gloves. And three dozen pairs of stockings with double-woven heels, because Indian dust is as bad as sandpaper, and no lacy-patterned ones because they give the mosquitoes an opening.'

'Well, we know all about *that*, don't we! It sounds as if mosquitoes belong to the same persuasion as midges. What else?'

Juliana looked at the list doubtfully. 'Soap, knives and forks, Eno's fruit salts, lace for antimacassars, a piano. A *piano*?'

'How fortunate that you're not musical!' Vilia said cordially. 'You can cross that off.'

Juliana sighed. 'And gowns, hats, boots, shoes, not to mention furniture for the cabin on the ship, if we don't want to spend sixteen weeks sleeping on the floor. How will I ever be ready in time!'

But at least it took her mind off the wedding itself, and what came after. Juliana was sufficiently a child of the countryside to understand Vilia's somewhat cryptic references to the Kinveil bull and his harem, and to believe that a young wife's marital duties might not be pleasurable at first. But it was all right after all. Richard was wonderfully gentle with her, and almost as nervous as she. Perhaps he ought to explain to her what was going to happen, he said. Being a doctor made it *quite* all right for him to talk about it. Did she think that would be a good idea? He looked pink, and harassed, and just a little pompous, so that Juliana couldn't help but giggle. And then he laughed, too, and after the first few nights, once she was used to it, she began quite to enjoy it.

By the time they embarked on the *Southampton* at the end of July, she was already wondering whether she might be carrying a child. It was a natural sequel to marriage, but hard to believe that it could be happening to her, Juliana Curtis, who had very little experience of life and none at all of babies. She wished now that her father, as much to annoy Vilia as anything else, hadn't flatly forbidden her ever to set foot in any of the houses on Kinveil, which always seemed to be full of babies. 'You never know what you might catch.' Thank goodness she had Richard, who was a doctor and would look after her.

She turned to Gideon, who had come to see them off. The war in the Crimea over, he was home again, thinner and more serious, with a good many silver hairs scattered among the fair, and sidewhiskers that were almost white against his weathered skin. But his smile was still full of charm.

He said, 'I've brought you a small parting gift.'

She had to open it there and then. It was a beautiful diary, a big, fat one bound in sapphire-blue leather, with her new name in gold on the cover. 'Gideon!' she gasped.

'You have to fill it, remember. And with the kind of things you won't be ashamed for other people to read. Think of your duty to the family chronicle. I depend on you!'

'Heavens! I haven't kept a diary since I was twelve, and that most certainly wasn't fit for other people to read. Full of adolescent yearnings and deep thoughts.' She laughed, remembering. She had been frantically in love with the gamekeeper's son at the time. 'I'll do my best, and Richard will help me. Good-bye, Gideon dear. You will write to me, won't you?'

'I already have the timetable for the overland mail.' He patted his pocket. 'And I'll expect you to answer, dear Mrs Curtis.' She blushed enchantingly, and looked at her husband. Gideon hoped to God she was going to be all right. She was so young still, and so very vulnerable.

2

Even Gideon, more aware than most of what was going on in the world, could never have foreseen that, on the first anniversary of her wedding, Juliana would be sweltering in a bungalow in northern India, terrified for her life and the life of the seven-week-old baby who lay, gurgling peaceably, in his cot beside her. She jumped like a cat at every sound, silencing her own sobbing breath while her ears strained for the approach of danger.

The mail went next day, and she knew she must write, because it might be the last opportunity for a long time. She had already, with much difficulty, finished a serious but carefully unalarming letter to her father and Vilia, and it had nearly drained her of the little courage she had left. At least she could be more honest with Gideon, who would understand.

May 29, 1857. My dear Gideon – I seldom put off writing until so late, but the last two weeks have been quite dreadful. You probably know by now that the native soldiers, the sepoys, who make up such a large part of the British army here in India, mutinied at Meerut on the 10th, and massacred their white officers before setting off for Delhi to do the same thing there. They seem to have run mad, for they have murdered women and helpless babies as well, people who have never done them any harm. During these last days, we have had reports of sepoys on other stations rising in support of their comrades. You may know more at home than we do here, in our lonely outpost, where every tiny fact arrives embedded in a whole snowball of rumour.

She stopped, forcing back the tears. Snowball! Such a word to choose! May here was the hottest month of the year, although in April she couldn't have believed it possible for the heat to get worse. Her hands were sticky with perspiration and coated with grit from the dust storm that had just passed, the searing wind of it finding its way through every crack. The only way to stay sane in the hot weather, she had been told, was to lie on a sofa and not move at all. But she couldn't do that. There wasn't time. Dashing the back of her hand across her forehead, and running a parched tongue over her lips, she began to write again.

We hope that our own regiment will stand firm, but who can tell? We are only a dozen Europeans in this great sea of dark and threatening faces – seven officers, Richard and myself and baby Luke, and Mrs Clark (the wife of one of the officers) and her baby. None of us, I suspect, is able to think properly, although we all try to hide it.

If only I were stronger! But the birth of my darling boy, and the dreadful heat and the insects and all the things that are so horrible and strange about India have combined to leave me fit for nothing, except to weep miserably to myself when Richard is not here to see. Oh, Gideon! I do try to be brave, but I am such a dreadful coward inside! Richard is out now, helping to fortify one of the

615

bungalows. It has to be done secretly, in case it goads the sepoys into the mutiny we still pray may not happen. And what use will it be, I wonder, against hundreds of bloodthirsty sepoys with flint and tinder. They burned the houses down at Meerut, with people inside.

It must be done, I suppose, but left alone here with the servants I become convinced that they are all in league with the mutineers. Our dhobi (washerman) has a cousin at Meerut, and the grass-cutter's brother was employed in the Native Lines there.

Richard says that if only General Anson would make some move, even the three thousand white troops at Peshawar could make mincemeat of any number of sepoys, but in the meantime we scarcely dare close our eyes at night. I keep a sword under my pillow, and Richard has his pistols ready loaded, prepared to start up at the slightest sound. He has promised that, if things come to the worst, he will put an end to baby and me with his own hands. How unreal it all sounds, doesn't it? Like one of those trashy tales in *Reynolds' Miscellany*. But it is true.

Again, she stopped. But the creaking noises were only the sound of the house settling again after the dust storm.

Such a world. Such a world. Richard has become so dear to me that I can almost contemplate dying *with* him, but not being separated from him. He is so anxious to send me to what he calls the "safety" of Lucknow, which at least has the merit of being defensible, but I *will not go* unless the baby's life depends on it. Richard and the baby *are* my life, and I pray I will never be faced with having to make such a terrible choice.

Once or twice over these last days, I have wondered how Vilia would act in my situation, for she is the strongest person I know. But all it does is sink me deeper into despair, because I know she would do *something* – even if it were only to line the sepoys up and give them a good talking to. The trouble is that I am not like Vilia, but just very ordinary, and very weak, and so frightened that I can't even think. God preserve us all, through whatever may come. Oh, Gideon! How can such awful things happen? I must stop now. All my affection – Juliana.

And even there, she had succeeded in sounding braver than she felt. She laid her pen down and wept.

Ten days later, a message came from Sikrora, sixteen miles away, to say that there was an officer there, with an armed guard and transport elephants, to escort the women and children of the district to Lucknow. They must leave at once. Richard rushed Juliana round the house, one arm on her elbow, saying 'What will you need?' and picking up and discarding all sorts of useless things until she stopped him at last, gasping, 'But you're coming, too?'

Then he gave up the pretence, and put his hands on her shoulders and said, the boyish smile still breaking through all the new-cut lines of exhaustion and worry, 'Poor kitten! Lucknow is for refugees, and fighting men to protect them. I'm not a fighting man, and I'd only be a useless extra mouth. I have to stay and help the people who will be trying to bring back order and sanity. No! Don't argue, because I won't listen. Don't be frightened, my darling. It won't be long.'

3

Lucknow, July 1. My pretty diary, where are you now? With all those pages I filled so dutifully after we sailed from England. Still in my writing desk, or in ashes? Oh, Richard, if only I could know what has happened to you, where you are! Do *you* know that, here in Lucknow, we are besieged after a terrible battle yesterday? There are wounded men all over the place, and their screams as the surgeons do their work are the most horrifying things I have ever heard. I tried to go with some of the other ladies to give them comfort, but I fainted the moment I set foot in the hospital. So I was sent back here, because the doctors said they didn't need swooning ladies under their feet, to add to all their other troubles. I am so *ashamed!*

The mutineers are all round us now, and their guns are firing, and when they score a hit, the walls begin to fall down – first a bang, and then a grinding noise, and then a kind of soft crash and a hissing. I can hardly write because my hand is shaking so, even in this windowless, underground room, where the baby and I are safe – at least from the guns. But the noise and the heat . . .

When I recovered consciousness I hugged the baby so convulsively, and cried over him so much, that I have made him cry too. So I thought that if I began a new diary, it might concentrate my mind. *There is nothing else I can think of to do.*

We have been in Lucknow for more than two weeks now. It is unbelievably hot, and the place swarms with flies and mosquitoes and other insects that I can't – and don't want to – identify. 'The place' is an old native house with three onion domes on top, called the Begum Kothi. I am told it was formerly the residence of one of the King of Oudh's wives. I suppose it must have been luxurious once, but now it is empty of everything except people. Our first night here we slept fifteen in one room, and all in the centre, because someone had contrived to have a punkah – a big fan – fitted, and we were all gasping for a breath of air, no matter how hot and dusty and evil-smelling.

Lucknow itself is beautiful. As we approached it that first day, weary and overwrought as we were, we couldn't help but stop to admire it. There were no mutineers in sight, then, and it was a perfect vision of palaces, minarets, domes and spires of azure and gold glittering in the sun, long arcaded buildings, terraced roofs, all rising out of a wide, calm landscape that is the colour of champagne, though when the rains come it will all turn green again. It looks rich, magnificent, enormous.

Since this morning, most of the city is occupied by the mutineers, mad with delight over their victory yesterday. There are said to be ten thousand of them. We British are confined in what is called the Residency area, a group of about twenty buildings inside a kind of enclosure (I have had no real opportunity, or inclination, to count) ranging from a sheep pen to a church. It used to be the headquarters of the East India Company's representative in the state of Oudh. After yesterday's battle there remain only about 1,600 men to defend us, and they include 700 so-called 'loyal' sepoys. No one knows whether they will continue to remain loyal when they are asked to shoot at their fellow-sepoys outside the walls. There are about 500 women and children here, most of them refugees from the outlying military stations, and goodness knows how many servants and coolies. I don't know whether to envy their masters and mistresses, or to fear for us all, with so many Indians inside our defences. Mrs Clark and I have no one, having rushed off from home so quickly.

Oh, Richard, my darling! You were wrong when you said we would find everything we needed here, and shouldn't burden ourselves. The fugitives are very ill supplied. I hadn't even a change of clothes for the baby, poor mite, until Mrs Captain Germon sent me some linen, as well as some china, of which we had none, and a table. Her husband has been stationed in Lucknow for some months, so she was able to bring a good many comforts into the Residency with her. How funny it

618

is to refer to someone as Mrs *Captain* Germon! There is Mrs *Colonel* Inglis, too, and Mrs *Colonel* Case – although since yesterday, poor soul, she has been Mrs *The-late-colonel* Case. India is so conscious of rank and precedence! It is necessary for ignorant provincials like us to know precisely where everyone stands in the hierarchy. As far as I can discover, Mrs *Doctor* Curtis stands nowhere.

The first days here were awful. Everyone was too taken up with their own troubles and anxieties to care for anyone else's, myself included. Separated from Richard, not knowing what had become of him, without servants for the first time in my life, quite ignorant of how to care for my baby, and thrown all alone among strangers – I veered from moment to moment between numbness and hysteria. We have settled into some kind of routine now; ten women and their children in one room.

What am I saying? Nine women since two days ago. It was Mrs Hale, whom I scarcely knew. She became ill quite suddenly, and was dead within hours, despite what the doctors could do. It was cholera. She lost consciousness just before the end, and her brow was damp, as if there were dew on it. Mr Harris, one of the chaplains, came and read some of the Visitation Service, and we stood and watched her pass quietly away. I have never seen anyone dead before.

There are other sicknesses in the Begum Kothi, too. Baby and I have been suffering from prickly heat, and my poor pet is miserably unhappy, but someone in one of the other rooms has smallpox, and there are two or three cases of dysentery. Until the chaos after the battle yesterday, none of us had seen anyone but doctors and chaplains for days. Sir Henry Lawrence was determined that the infections should not spread, so we were all left here in a kind of lazzaretto, to live if we could, or die if we must.

Oh, Richard, Richard! I could have faced death with you in the open, but I cannot, I *cannot* face it here without you, in an underground room where the heat is suffocating, and everyone fevered in body and mind, and the little ones beginning to sicken. We can't even tell what the food is when it is placed on the table, because it is no more than a black and crawling mass of flies. I found a rat in my bedding last night. Everyone told me things would be better when the rains broke, but it poured on Saturday night, and everything now is far, far worse. The floor of our room is sodden and green, and the walls steam, and my skin is as soft and clammy and wrinkled as if it had been soaked in water. Every movement is an indescribable effort, and our regiments of crawling things have become armies. The cockroaches are disgusting. Mrs Clark is due to be confined with her second child some time this month. Poor soul, poor soul!

Every day since our arrival there has been alarming news of some kind. All the little babies at Sitapur were cruelly bayoneted by the sepoys, and their bodies tossed in a heap like so much refuse. There was a massacre at Sultanpore, too, and we have heard the most frightening reports from Cawnpore, where General Wheeler had only two hundred men to defend four hundred women and children. They are said to have surrendered, and all been massacred.

We have been told not to go outdoors because of the shot and shell flying about so the days are little different from the nights, which are so hot and wearisome that we have to sit up in turns to fan the children, so that they can have some rest. My heart aches for them. Even my own plump baby is growing thin and fractious before my eyes with this unnatural life. Today we are being served out rations – flour for chapatis, rice, dried peas, salt, and meat weighed with the bone still in, which I think isn't fair, because it means that some people will have far more eatable meat than others.

July 2   There was the most terrible explosion in the middle of the night that made us all think our last hour had come, because it sounded as if the sepoys had blown up our defences and forced their way in. We all sprang from our beds, and when we lit a candle the whole room was so thick with dust we could scarcely see one another. The bricks and mortar had fallen from the ceiling and the children were screaming with terror. But it turned out that some of our soldiers had been cut off from the Residency in an old fort near-by, and had been ordered to blow it up and make a bolt for safety under cover of the noise. It all went off very well, from their point of view. It's just that I'm surprised half the garrison didn't die of shock.

We have no way of cooking, and the native servants who have agreed to cook our rations for us say everything must be put in together, because there are so few pots. They have only one, of untinned copper, and the horrible stew that emerged from it today was perfectly green. It *cannot* be good for us, eating verdigris, and the children, who have

620

little appetite because of the heat, wouldn't touch it at all. I am so afraid for Luke, because although I try to feed him, I have not enough milk after all the stresses and strains of the last weeks. Dear God, surely someone must come to our rescue soon!

July 4   Sir Henry Lawrence, the good, kind man who has been in charge here, died this morning from a wound he received two days ago. It is said that even he will have no privacy in the grave, but will be sewn up, like everyone else, in his own bedding, and consigned to the pit dug every night for those who have died in the day. So *many* are dying every day – men, and sometimes women, killed or injured in the dreadful bombardment that seems as if it will never stop. The mutineers are using the guns they captured from us at Chinhut a few days ago.

July 12   I have not felt able to write for some days. On the 8th I was standing in the doorway of our room, with the baby in my arms, hoping for a breath of air. There was a little girl playing in the courtyard of the building, and even as I watched, something flew through the air and . . .

I can't write it. I can't think about it. There was a funny noise, and then a spray of red all round her, and I fainted dead away. Thank God I had tied little Luke to my waist to relieve me of some of his weight, or I would have dropped him. I have only now recovered enough strength to do more than sit and hold him to me, and try not to think. I don't know whose daughter the little girl was.

Mr Ommanney, of the Civil Service, died the other day, and Mr Polehampton, one of the chaplains, was wounded, but not seriously. He was actually in the hospital when it happened. Fifteen or twenty people die every day, and have to be buried after dark. One of the ladies in our room is ill today. It is said to be smallpox. How I tremble for my poor baby. We are so confined, and there is no fresh air. The mosquitoes are fearful. Perhaps Mrs Thomas doesn't have smallpox. We are all suffering from boils now; it might be that.

July 16   Mrs Thomas died this morning. It was smallpox, but no one else has caught it yet.

July 20   Mr Polehampton, after recovering from his wound, has died of cholera. His widow is coming to occupy the room next to ours; may God comfort her. Mrs Clark gave birth to a daughter this morning. I don't believe either of them will live. Her mind is wandering, and I sit beside her and hold her hand, but I can't make out what she is saying.

July 30   Mrs Clark died this evening, poor thing, scarcely older than I am, and such a gentle person. Her infant daughter seems unlikely to survive.

August 3   It has happened, as I knew it must. Last night, Dr Wells told me that my baby was dying. He has cholera, and he is so small. Mrs Polehampton came to help me nurse him. We gave him the strongest remedies the doctor said could be given to one so young. I have been kneeling at his bedside all night, and today I believe – God, I pray! – that he is better. But he is so weak from the cholera and the remedies that I don't dare hope.

August 8   The baby is a little better, but I have been ill myself. Mrs Clark's orphaned daughter died yesterday, and we have just put Mrs Kendall's sweet little girl in an ammunition box that someone found for a coffin. The enemy have been firing all night lately, hoping to reduce the garrison by exhaustion since they have not yet succeeded by other means. They found the range of the Begum Kothi one night last week and several shells exploded in the upper part of the building. I believe someone was killed. It was the night we thought Luke was dying of cholera.

It can't go on like this. Everyone is ill some way or other. My fingers are covered with boils, and Dr Darby has lanced some of them. He says I mustn't use my hands, but I have to. Feeble though I am, I am the strongest of the ladies still left in this room, and there is so much to do, especially now that we have no one to cook for us. I can't keep everyone and everything clean on my own, but I try. It is so important for things to be clean when there is disease about. I remember Gideon telling me how insistent Miss Nightingale was about that at Scutari. The trouble is that my hands are so painful, and it makes everything so slow and clumsy. It takes hours to get the lice out of the baby's hair, and I try to do Mrs Kendall's, too. Although she is almost prostrate, she does mine in return, but not very well because nervous exhaustion has taken all the strength from her. It is the flies that are the worst; Lucknow is famous for them. When I open my mouth to swallow my boiled-lentil soup, the flies swarm into it instead. And then they fall in the plate and float about, and I can't face trying to eat any more of it.

I feel so sorry for Dr Darby. His wife was at Cawnpore, and we have heard that although most of the hundreds of unfortunates there were massacred, a few escaped. He doesn't know whether she is alive or dead; almost worse, if she is dead it was not peacefully, or quickly. The tales we hear are horrible beyond belief. Poor Dr Darby. Poor me. Richard, my dearest, if only I knew whether *you* were alive or dead. If only I knew anything at all!

Nothing has been heard of anyone coming to our aid here.

August 19   One of the officers who escorted us here from Sikrora has shot himself.

August 20   Baby is still so weak and poorly. I have no milk now, and am feeding him mostly on arrowroot that Dr Darby brings me, and a little goat's milk that Mrs Martin gives me every day. It is as precious as gold. It is very difficult to cook now because of building a fire. The wood is so wet that it won't burn. A soldier brought me some that was dry, but I have only a dinner knife to chop it with, so it is very difficult. Our rations are to be reduced, which means, I suppose, that there is no likelihood of the garrison being relieved yet. All our problems were near to being solved two days ago, when the enemy blew a great breach in the defences, but nothing came of it.

September 18   I have written nothing these last weeks. My hands have been too bad, and there seems little purpose in repeating a catalogue of miseries and worries and disappointments. All that happens is that the people in the Residency become steadily fewer. The Rev. Mr Harris now not only reads the burial service at nights in the cemetery, but has to dig the graves himself.

There is a partial eclipse of the sun today, from which the natives foretell famine. If we were still capable of laughing, we would. We are all so accustomed to being hungry that words like famine have no meaning at all. The bombardment goes on, and on, and every so often there is an assault in which the enemy are repulsed and a few more of the garrison die. The soldiers are beyond admiration. They loot when they can, and steal when they have the opportunity, and get drunk when by some miracle liquor comes in their way. They are walking skeletons, clad in rags or in other soldiers' cast-offs that they have bought on credit at the auction of some corpse's effects. They bid astonishing sums, because everyone is agreed that the accounting date shall be when their next pay is disbursed, and none of them expects to live to see it. And yet somehow they fight on, with a kind of dogged madness that nothing can overcome. I believe the plan is to blow up the entrenchments, with all of us inside, rather than give up. I was thinking, just the other day, how utterly insane such an idea would have seemed to me a year ago. And yet now it sounds perfectly reasonable.

There is no news at all from the outside world, or none that filters through to Mrs Kendall and myself in our underground cell. Perhaps Colonel Inglis knows something. Perhaps *Mrs* Colonel Inglis knows something.

Fortunate Mrs Colonel Inglis!

September 23   There is a rumour that the relieving force is on its way at last. Do I believe it? I don't know. I prefer to doubt it, because the disappointment will not be so great.

Oh, God! *Can* it be true?

Later   It *is* true. We can hear the guns. Dr Darby says they are no more than three miles away. General Havelock and Sir James Outram are in command. Is Richard with them? *Is Richard with them?*

September 24   No sleep last night. My poor, weak little baby lies there and stares at me, his eyes enormous with wonderment at something he has never seen before – his mama not only smiling, but laughing with excitement. The guns seem further away this morning, but it may just be a trick of sound. The important thing is that we are not forgotten, not deserted. That has been harder to bear than almost anything. Oh, Richard! Can it be that after all these weary months we will soon be together again? You *must* be with General Havelock, mustn't you?

September 25   A bad night, with the enemy attacking us violently several times, as if in a last effort to break into the Residency before General Havelock arrives. But this morning there is no doubt that the General has already reached the outskirts of the city.

I know it was silly and vain of me, but I spent most of yesterday trying to make myself pretty again for Richard. I rubbed and rubbed at my second gown – poor Mrs Clark's – but it is so difficult to get it clean without soap or even *dhal*, and plain water has no effect on the grease marks or the insects, bred, born, reared and fattened as they are on monsoon rains and human perspiration. So I put a few grains from our tiny salt ration on every one I could see. Mrs Kendall says salt only kills greenfly, not lice or fleas. But whether because of the salt or my vigorous rubbing, most of them seem to have gone. If only there were some way of ironing things! But baby and I are clean, at least, if somewhat creased. My hair is so lank, and my face so hollow; my hands so swollen and scarred; and all of me covered with bruises. Dr Darby says that, like everyone else, I am suffering from scurvy because of the lack of fresh vegetables, which is why even the slightest bump produces a bruise. But Richard won't mind – will you, my dearest? When we are restored to each other, I will be myself in no time at all, you'll see!

We have all been most sternly instructed to stay under cover until the relief force is actually within the gates. But it is so hard to be patient now, after all we have been through! Eighty-seven days since the siege began.

Later   There is so much shouting going on! I think I hear someone beginning to cheer. I must go out. I *must* go out!

4

September 25. Eight o'clock   It is so strange to see how immaculate our saviours are, the generals in their shooting coats and solar topees, and all the soldiers in their beautiful uniforms, only a little dusty. They look so stout and healthy, throwing their arms round our own poor fellows, who appear like the worst kind of bandit by comparison. The pipers of the 78th Highlanders – first in, *of course!* – were playing, which nearly made an end of me. I could see nothing for the tears in my eyes and streaming down my cheeks. Everyone was shaking hands with everyone else, and the rough-bearded soldiers holding the babies up in the air, and crying and laughing and thanking God they had arrived in time to save them from the fate that had overtaken the poor little mites at Cawnpore.

I am trying to write this very slowly and legibly to calm myself down. For I must be patient just a little longer before I can be reunited with Richard. The very first officer I asked told me he shared a makeshift tent with Richard just last night, so I know now that he *is* with the force. But I have been walking up and down by the Baillie Guard gate for almost three hours and he has not come in. Someone told me at last that 'young Curtis' is with the rearguard, and will probably pass the night at the old palace, the Moti Mahal, before breaking through the mutineers still in the city during the course of tomorrow. So I must be patient. I must be patient. And I think I can be, now I know he is so near. But my heart is so full I don't expect to sleep.

Such a noise, still. I can hear the Highlanders dancing a reel, and a good deal of singing and laughing. My dear, *dear* Highlanders. I promise I will never say a word against the bagpipes again! There, another splash of tears on my beautiful calligraphy! I must try to stop crying or my face will be all swollen in the morning. I never knew what happiness was, until now.

September 26   I'm not *really* worried. I have been waiting all day, but Richard has not come yet. I thought it best to sit by the door, because he is sure to ask directions as soon as he comes in and I must be here. It is surer than for me to wander around with baby in the hope of seeing him arrive. Mr Freeling promised me this morning that Richard would certainly be here today; he said they had been together for a good part of the march, and that Richard was in the wildest spirits yesterday at the prospect of seeing his wife and child again. So it is very disappointing that he has not come yet. But *no more than* disappointing.

September 27   It is noon, and he has not come yet. I am afraid. Dear God, I am so afraid.

It was the last entry Juliana made in her diary. In the afternoon, Dr Darby came to see her, his face drawn. She knew already that the relief force had brought with it bitter news for some of the garrison. Dr

Darby's wife had given birth to their baby during the siege at Cawnpore, with no other shelter than one of the guns in the entrenchment. Afterwards, she and the child had died in the massacre, cut to pieces by the butchers from the bazaar and tossed down into a well in the grounds, already crammed with women and children, dead or dying.

Dr Darby said nothing of it, and neither did Juliana. All she said was, 'It's so strange that my husband has not come in yet.'

He found he hadn't the strength to tell her, pretty, helpless child that she was. What was she doing in this heathen land? What were any of them doing in this heathen land! 'It is strange,' he said. 'Will you forgive me if I leave you? I must go and see to my patients.'

She knew, then.

The baby was asleep on the bed, thin and pale, but she didn't wake him. Kneeling beside him, she buried her face in her poor, scarred hands and, this time, couldn't weep. Because she had been expecting it for hours, there was no blessed numbness to take the edge off her agony. If she could have died then, she would. But grief didn't kill, or not quickly, and the refrain that had haunted her all these months, that had kept her on her feet despite everything, ran through her head still – 'Who will look after the baby?' Now, for a moment, she remembered Lizzie and envied her.

Mrs Polehampton came in to her after a while and sat with her, saying little.

Once, Juliana gasped, 'Poor baby. All these weeks when he has been sick, I have said to him, "When Papa comes, baby will get well again."'

And later, 'I can't endure it.'

And, hours afterwards, 'You are so serene, but your husband was a chaplain. Does that help? Is that what gives you strength? I don't have that kind of faith.'

Mrs Polehampton had her own wisdom. 'Strength comes from whatever matters most to you.'

Juliana raised her head, and it was as if her eyes, ringed with great purple shadows, were all that existed in the white, piquant little face. 'Luke?' Then, after a long, long pause, 'Yes.'

The following day, two of Richard's native servants appeared with their master's handsome black horse, the horse Juliana herself had ridden during her first few weeks in India. They brought a few of his personal possessions, too – his watch and his fob; his purse; and his wedding band. Still, the tears didn't come.

They didn't come the day after, when Dr Darby brought a newcomer to see her, another doctor who had been with Richard when he was killed.

There had been a fearsome attack on the rearguard, for all the mutineers – thousands of them – had turned on it in frustrated fury. Richard had gone to the other surgeon to ask for his help with some wounded, and as they had made their way towards the litters, the surgeon had flinched at the shots whistling all round and exclaimed, 'I hope we may get out of this!'

Richard, laughing, had replied, 'What! With my wife and child only a mile away? Nothing can touch us!' And then had come the shot that killed him. It was immediate – or so the surgeon said – and he hadn't suffered.

No one knew what had happened to his body. The fighting had been too severe.

5

The days passed, and it soon became clear that the relieving force had brought not relief, but more trouble. Strong enough to break into the Residency, it wasn't strong enough to break out again. In their haste to relieve Lucknow, Havelock and Outram had even left their stores behind at the Alambagh, four miles away, and with sepoys thicker than cockroaches on the ground between, there was no possibility of getting them in to where they were so desperately needed. Rations were cut again; six ounces of meat, half of it bone, three-quarters of a pound of unground wheat; one and a half ounces of rice; half an ounce of salt.

Juliana found that she wasn't hungry, anyway, though she drank a great deal of toast water, the liquid in which scorched chapatis, made from the wheat ration, had been soaked to provide a kind of substitute for tea. She passed the six dreary weeks following the so-called 'relief' in a kind of trance, doing everything she had done before without even being aware of it. Sometimes she would stop and wonder whether she had, in fact, washed baby Luke that morning, because she had no recollection of it at all. Sometimes she would frown for a long time over the strange noises she could hear upstairs in the Begum Kothi, until she remembered that it was a hospital annexe now. And, conscientiously, she still stayed indoors even though Havelock and Outram, in a few wild sorties, had flung the mutineers back from the walls of the Residency and extended the perimeter.

She was in the world but not of it. There was nothing to look forward to but difficulties she couldn't even contemplate. If the city were to be properly relieved, her rough cocoon would be stripped from her and she would be all alone except for the baby. Where would she go? Where else was there but Kinveil? But she would have to find her way to Calcutta, and she didn't know how. And have to arrange a sailing; how did one do that? She had very little money left, and had no idea whether there were still banks in existence. Everything was beyond her.

On November sixteenth there was intensive fighting outside, and on the seventeenth Mrs Polehampton and Mrs Kendall gently but relentlessly forced her to go outdoors with them to watch the arrival of the second relief force. Sir Colin Campbell was in command.

'The soldiers are coming in now,' Mrs Polehampton said. 'Come. These terrible months will soon be over.'

The soldiers this time were as clean and sturdy as the now thin, dirty and tattered men of the first relief had been. Incongruously, six hundred miles from the sea, there were straw-hatted sailors with them. Juliana spoke politely to one or two of them, and smiled, and shook hands, and allowed them to tickle baby Luke under the chin. Then she went back indoors again.

After a while, vaguely aware that there was someone standing in the doorway, she looked up from where she had been sitting emptily beside the bed. It was a tall man in civilian clothes, and he was watching her gravely.

At last she whispered, 'Gideon?'

6

Gideon had been on his way to China for the *Times-Graphic*. He had become very restless after a few months at home, and the Chinese at Canton had taken a high-handed line with what they claimed was a pirate ship that happened to be flying the British flag. All the Western powers had been looking for a chance to get a foot in China's door, and this one was too good to miss. So Lord Elgin had been briskly dispatched with a few gunboats, and Gideon had succeeded in negotiating a passage with him. News of the Mutiny in India had come while they were at sea, and Elgin decided to leave the war steamers *Shannon* and *Pearl* at Calcutta for use against the mutineers. Gideon had stayed with them. There was no conflict that he could see between his duty to his paper and his personal anxiety for Juliana and young Curtis. The tragedy in India was far more important than a petty war of imperialism in China.

With the Naval Brigade from the *Shannon* and the *Pearl*, Gideon had travelled with agonizing slowness from Calcutta to Allahabad, and then, after a rousing battle at Kujwa, on to Cawnpore to join up with the commander-in-chief's forces there. Sir Colin Campbell, his lips pursed, had said, 'Aye, I remember you from the Crimea, Mr Lauriston. You and Mr Russell of *The Times*. You hadn't many good words to say about the army then; some of the officers were wondering just whose side you were on. I trust that this time you don't have any doubt about where your sympathies lie?'

For three months, Gideon had heard nothing but tales of the atrocities committed by the mutineers, and neither had anybody else. He knew that the Highlanders now were in the habit of shooting or bayoneting any wounded 'Jack Pandy' left on the field of battle – 'to put them out o' their misery. They're just animals, you see' – and though he didn't like it, he could sympathize. If Juliana had been one of the victims of the Cawnpore massacre . . . Until he reached Cawnpore on November first, he hadn't known for sure, although he had been repeating to himself over and over for three months that she was more likely to be in Lucknow, which was nearer where Richard had been stationed. If she had succeeded in getting a letter out, Gideon hadn't received it before he sailed from England.

With a sigh, he replied, 'No, Sir Colin. No doubts this time. And I was never on anyone's side but the men's. It was the high command I criticized.'

'Aye, well,' Campbell had said with a snort of laughter. 'Oblige me by remembering that *I'm* the high command now! And you can tell Mr Russell, too, when he gets here, as I've no doubt he will.'

In the two weeks since then, Gideon had discovered what a good officer Campbell was. Even if he moved so slowly that he was called 'Sir Crawling Camel' by his impatient men, it was better than moving too fast, as Havelock and Outram had done. When Sir Colin relieved Lucknow, it would be the genuine article.

And now they were here. Gideon had stayed with the Naval Brigade, a rollicking lot who viewed army discipline with jovial contempt. Their talent for survival was a source of wonder to Gideon, for they liked nothing more than a good bout of hand-to-hand fighting, and their captain encouraged them by behaving in the field very much as if he were laying the *Shannon* alongside an enemy frigate. Gideon had been surprised to arrive intact.

It hadn't been difficult to find Juliana. The third scarecrow he had asked had directed him to the Begum Kothi, and a lady who had been standing hesitantly outside the door – Mrs Polehampton, she said – had told him what had happened, as soon as she knew who he was.

'Mrs Curtis needs to weep. Help her if you can,' she had concluded, and then, sizing him up with exhausted eyes, added, 'I have been trying to nerve myself to tell her that Dr Darby, who has been very good to her, has been wounded and is not expected to live.'

'Leave that to me. I'll choose my moment.'

She had nodded. 'I will see that no one comes in to interrupt you for a while.'

Juliana whispered again, 'Gideon?'

She looked as if she would fall apart if he touched her. Her bones were thin as a sparrow's, her eyes huge and sunken, and her lips had no more colour than her cheeks. She was wearing a limp black gown two or three sizes too large.

He moved forward, his heart breaking for her. It cost him a good deal to say, half derisively, 'My poor pet. What have they been doing to you?'

Familiar, reassuring Gideon, who had only that moment discovered how much she meant to him.

And then she was in his arms – his kindly, reliable arms – clinging to his coat lapels with astonishing strength, quite unable to speak but breathing in harsh, jerky little gasps. He thought that, left to herself, she would never let go, so after a time he dropped a kiss on her forehead and, unclasping her fingers, persuaded her to sit down again.

'A large handkerchief, or a large whisky?' he asked provocatively.

And that was all it took. Half laughing, she wailed, 'Oh, Gideon!' and then the dam broke and her tears flowed as if they would never stop.

He cradled her while she wept, deep, racking, rending tears, his fingers smoothing the elflocks back from her brow, and loosening the mass of hair that clung to the nape of her neck. Lice, of course, poor lamb, he thought unromantically, and glanced round the dismal cell where she had lived for five months without comfort or privacy. The stone walls were pitted with holes where the mortar had crumbled and been shaken loose by the gunfire and explosions outside, and the plaster hung from the ceiling in thick, ragged flakes, like discarded pieces of jigsaw puzzle. Perched on one of them, staring down at him, was a scorpion. The beaten earth floor was powdered with dust and mortar fragments, and there were cockroaches on the piles of rubble someone had swept into the corners. A tide mark ran round the walls, a foot or so up from the floor, faintly green where fungus had grown during the rains. The only furniture consisted of a scarred table, a few boxes, a large covered object in one corner, presumably the privy, and half a dozen hammock-like beds, two of them neatly made but the others rumpled and slept in. An emaciated child of six or seven months lay on the neat bed by which Juliana had been sitting his eyes – blue and dark-ringed like his mother's – gazing towards her, wide open and empty. The room was dim, sour-smelling and oppressively close, for the only light and ventilation came from the doorway, which itself was half underground. The flies, fat and loathsome, were everywhere. Gideon's mind fled for a moment to Kinveil, cool, fresh, and orderly, and his arms tightened round the girl convulsively. Poor, helpless, unprepared Juliana. He found himself cursing the ghost of the young man she had married. Surely he must have seen trouble coming? Surely he could have got her away to safety before it happened!

Finally, he said, 'That's my last clean handkerchief, I warn you. Come along, my pet. Blow your nose and sit up like a good girl. I have something for you.' He rummaged in the bag still slung over his shoulder. 'Not silks or jewels or looted treasure, although God knows there's enough of that about. But . . .' One by one he dumped a number of small packages on the table, itemizing them as he went. 'Tea, real bread, fresh butter, milk, sugar, and oranges for the baby.

Now, for heaven's sake, don't start crying again! Where can I boil up some water for the tea? Have you anything to use as a teapot?'

The bracing treatment helped, as he had hoped it would. After months steamy with emotion, he thought there was probably nothing she needed more than a sense of normal, commonplace reality.

The effect of being transported from the depths of despair to, not the seventh, but at least the second or third heaven, was to produce a slightly delirious euphoria. Extravagantly, she began to pour out to him the tale of everything that had happened inside the Residency during the siege, in a breathless, uncoordinated stream, exclaiming, every dozen words or so, 'Oh, Gideon!' as if his name were a kind of talisman. He had no idea how long this state would last; a few days at least, he hoped, because what still lay ahead was going to test everyone's nerve and stamina to the uttermost, and he didn't want Juliana suffering from the nervous collapse that was bound to come. She still hadn't mentioned Richard at all, and he thought perhaps she wouldn't until Lucknow was far behind them.

It occurred to her, at last, that she hadn't asked what he was doing here, but he said, 'Never mind that. Are you going to be able to pack fairly quickly?'

'Pack? Why?'

Could she possibly be imagining that Campbell had dispersed the mutineers, so that everyone could drift off, at will, after a round of social good-byes? In fact, the commander-in-chief's only course of action was to evacuate the place, postponing the final confrontation with the mutineers until he was fully reinforced. And the evacuation was not going to be funny, because Campbell had to hold together a body of men strong enough to do battle, if necessary, with thousands of mutineers, while detailing a massive escort for the column of sick and wounded, women and children, from the Residency, a column that couldn't, Gideon estimated, be less than a mile long, probably much more. There were few pack animals, few litters or bearers, and even fewer carriages, and no one knew whether the hundreds of people who had survived the siege would be strong enough to walk the first five, and most hazardous, miles.

'Campbell wants to move everybody out, either tonight or tomorrow night, while the enemy is still disorganized and not expecting anything.'

Juliana, with a forlorn attempt at brightness, said, 'Oh, I have nothing to pack. We can go this moment, if you like! I had only the gown I stood up in at first, and then that fell to pieces. So I wore Mrs Clark's. She died, you know. And then, when . . . And then a few weeks ago Mrs Polehampton gave me this one. It doesn't fit very well. Baby has two little dresses and a shawl. So, you see . . .'

'Dammit!' Gideon exclaimed. 'I knew there was something else.' And burrowing again in his satchel he produced a Cashmir shawl of exquisite beauty and workmanship. He had looted it because, if he didn't, someone else would, and he had thought Juliana would like it.

He said, 'I've never forgotten the look in your eyes at that dreadful family dinner party – during the Great Exhibition, do you remember? – when you had just seen your first Cashmir shawl, and were quite besotted with the idea of India, and elephants, and rajas wearing all their jewels. There you are. Something extra to pack!'

She fingered the shawl, her eyes filling with tears again. 'I haven't seen a raja all my time in India, and I don't suppose I shall, now. Gideon, you are so good to me. It's beautiful, far too beautiful. I look such a wreck.'

Leaning over, he smoothed out the lines on her brow with a tender forefinger. He didn't say, 'You're being silly.' He didn't say, 'You will never be less than beautiful to me.' He said, 'Well, do something about it, my pet.'

She had combed her hair, and rinsed the tears off her cheeks, and was smoothing her eyebrows into shape with a dampened finger when she said, 'I must send a message to Dr Darby, to tell him you're here and I am all right now. He had promised to take care of me on the way to Calcutta.'

It was now or never. 'I understand he's not – not feeling very fit. He's been wounded.'

Her finger froze for a moment, and then she said, carefully smoothing the other brow, 'He'll die, I expect. He wants to, after what happened to his wife and baby at Cawnpore. He has no one to live for.'

Gideon's eyes turned towards the baby, peacefully asleep after his orange juice and then back to Juliana. He felt a surge of fear for her.

He slept fitfully on the ground outside the Begum Kothi that night, because Juliana couldn't bear for him to go beyond call, and neither could he, and they spent most of next day talking, and drinking gallons of tea, and tidying the room. Gideon, who didn't like tea very much, was feeling slightly awash, and wryly amused over the care Juliana was taking to leave everything neat and clean for the mutineers who would soon be moving in, though she didn't seem to realize it.

There was a difficult moment when Juliana was packing her few possessions. Suddenly, staring at some stained and blotted pages of closely written paper, she exclaimed, 'Oh, Gideon! Your beautiful diary – the one you gave me at Gravesend! I – I don't know what's happened to it. I wrote it all up very carefully, but it's probably been destroyed by now. Your – your beautiful diary!'

Of all the ludicrous things to weep over! Summoning up his best imitation of Magnus, Gideon said grumpily, 'Well, you'll oblige me by taking more care of the shawl!' It was touch and go for a moment, and then her tears changed into a watery giggle.

She put the papers in his hand. 'I haven't written anything since . . . I haven't written . . . Anyway, you might as well have the notes I kept for the first few weeks. They're rather dirty, but I don't suppose it's of any consequence.'

7

They reached Calcutta ten weeks later, after a journey that would live in Gideon's memory for ever. The first ten days were a nightmare of heat and dust and enemy harassment, from which he was quite unable to shield Juliana, and after that they were beset by a constant succession of lesser alarms.

She couldn't make the adjustment to being back in the world again. Gideon, watching her, knew there was nothing he could do except be there, tortured by the knowledge that she was discovering, at last, that having a strong male hand to cling to wasn't always enough to set everything automatically to rights. Superficially, she was calm enough, submitting docilely to whatever arrangements he chose to make, but he could see that she was fighting her own personal battle, inside herself, and that because of the child, wasting away before their eyes, she wasn't winning.

Without making an issue of it, he arranged for the baby to be seen by a succession of doctors, but they all shook their heads privately to him afterwards, and murmured something about the effects of long privation on the system of such a very young child. Blindly, Juliana insisted that he was improving a little – 'for although he is weak, he is quite quiet, you know, and not in any kind of pain'. And Gideon, helplessly, tried to think of yet another way of phrasing the only possible answer, which was concerned with the beneficial properties of sea air.

On February tenth, he saw her on board the ship with the baby and the boxes of medicines and comforts and new clothes he had insisted on buying for her at the Auckland Hotel where, blessedly, there was a whole shopping mall complete with dressmaker, haberdasher, and provision dealer. Otherwise, she would have sailed with enough supplies for a whole army of children, and nothing for herself but the old black gown she stood up in.

The ship was to sail on the evening tide on the eleventh, but when Gideon, who was staying at the Bengal Club, went on board that morning, he heard that it had been postponed for twenty-four hours. He went down to Juliana's cabin.

Mrs Polehampton, who was travelling home with her, was there when he entered. She was sitting with Juliana's hand in hers – and she was saying, softly, 'My dear, you must prepare yourself. The doctor says the baby is very ill.'

She meant well, no doubt, but when she looked up and caught Gideon's eye, he knew that his own face, like Juliana's, must be a stiff mask of rejection. She rose to her feet then, and said quietly, 'Will you forgive me for a little time? I have something to attend to. I will be within call.'

Throughout that long, dreadful day, Gideon remained with Juliana in almost complete silence, interrupted only when Mrs Polehampton came in with tea or bouillon.

The little cabin was cut off, as if by some fathomless abyss, from the noise and bustle and brightness of the world outside. The sun was shining, and the temperature was like that of a fine summer day in England. A forest of masts lay in the river below the great pile of Fort William – lean, well-trimmed American vessels; Chinese ships, with an eye painted on either side of the bows, so that they could see their way; clumsy country boats laden with produce; the green, goose-shaped budgerows used for river travel; and thousands of small boats dashing in and out among them all, back and forth to a landing stage crowded with people of all shapes, sizes, colours, and occupations. The wind was blowing from the sea, so that not even the smell of the city's open drains spoiled the attractions of the scene.

Inside the cabin, Juliana sat by the bed, her hand limp in Gideon's and her face like a sleepwalker's, watching the baby. He lay, perfectly quiet, in a kind of daze, his eyes opening occasionally and then falling closed again as if the effort were too great.

Once, Juliana said in a flat, expressionless voice, 'I *cannot* spare him.' And again, when Mrs Polehampton had been in, 'If God is merciful, I don't see how He *can* take him away when I have nothing else left.' And, when evening was falling, 'It's my fault. All my fault.'

Gideon turned her gently towards him. 'No. Nothing of what has happened in this last terrible year has been your fault. You mustn't think like that.'

But her eyes were empty. 'It is my fault. When he was born, I knew his *ayah* would care for him, so I didn't learn how to care for him myself. And then there was no *ayah*, and I had to. It is my own ignorance that has brought him to this.'

'My dear, there are other far more experienced mothers whose experience hasn't saved their children.'

But all she would do was shake her head stubbornly. 'No. My fault, my fault.'

Night came, and he couldn't leave her. Mrs Polehampton seemed to be forever in and out, and it was a while before Gideon realized that she thought she was protecting Juliana. 'Propriety!' he thought savagely. 'At a time like this!' But she was right, he knew. Although the baby was dying, the other passengers would remember all through the long voyage that lay ahead that young Mrs Curtis had been alone with a man, all night, in her cabin.

The crisis came, as crises so often did, in the bleakest watches of the night. The child, without warning, became restless, and Juliana picked him up and walked the cabin with him, murmuring to him, kissing him, rocking him, her face stark. This time, it was Gideon who went to Mrs Polehampton. 'There *must* be something we can do.'

She went back to the cabin with him, treading softly, to find the baby struggling weakly in his mother's arms.

'Sit down, my dear, and take him in your lap.'

Gideon stood, his back against the door, and watched.

After what seemed a very long time, Juliana turned her gaze away from the baby gasping helplessly in her lap, her eyes wide blue pools of agony in her blanched face. She said something then, but her voice was so choked that the sense didn't reach Gideon at first.

'I *cannot* see my child die.'

Mrs Polehampton murmured, soft but clear, 'Look, my dear, how bright his eyes are growing. Too bright for ours to look on.'

But Juliana couldn't turn her head. And still, she couldn't turn it when the child's limbs became suddenly, weakly, convulsed and then quite still. It was Mrs Polehampton who stretched out her hand and closed the staring eyes. 'So He giveth His beloved sleep,' she said quietly, and lifted the thin, inanimate little body and soothed down the lacy white cotton robe, and laid him on the bed.

Juliana sat with Gideon's arms around her for all that remained of the night, and only when dawn came did she turn her eyes towards the bed. With a gasp, she said. 'So peaceful. Your papa will look after you now, my darling.' She stopped, but after a moment went on, 'I only had you for ten months. Only ten months.'

In the late afternoon, Dr Fayrer, who had been in Lucknow, too, came to fasten down the lid of the little coffin, and he and Gideon carried it, light as it was, to the grave in Park Street cemetery. Somehow, the news had reached almost all the Lucknow refugees, and it was that that almost broke Juliana. So many who had suffered what she had suffered, even if she had scarcely even seen them in all the long months; their presence was a mute recognition of what they had shared.

When Gideon took Juliana back to the ship an hour before it sailed, Mrs Polehampton had tidied away every reminder of the tragedy. Everything but a bright, woolly ball on a cotton cord, that lay almost hidden behind the clothes chest.

Gideon, for an hour or two, had been tempted to abandon all he should be doing in India to sail home with her. But the ship was full, and besides, it would be better for her to go alone, to come to terms with things in her own way. He didn't want to over-protect her, to smother her. And he knew now that he loved her too much to do otherwise.

Some time, perhaps, things would come right for them. It didn't matter – did it? – that he was twice her age.

But he knew that it did.

He said, 'One of the family will meet you when you land, my dear. And during the time between, try to find strength.' He kissed her then, fleetingly, on the cheek, and turned away.

As he reached the door, she said her only good-bye. 'Thank you, Gideon. If it weren't for you, I don't think . . .' And then, with seeming irrelevance, 'I don't want their sympathy, you know.'

He nodded and went, leaving her seated, a frail little figure, alone beside the bed.

8

Gideon was still in India, more than eight months later, when Theo's letter arrived.

Gideon, dear boy, where the devil are you? I am addressing this care of Sir Hugh Rose's headquarters, as my study of the newspapers suggests that the pair of you – with assistance, no doubt – are probably chasing Tantia Topi around Central India. What a pity the Rani of Jhansi came to such an untimely end; there is something so appealing about a pretty woman leading her troops into battle, don't you think? Wouldn't Vilia have revelled in it, given the chance!

Thank you for your letters about Juliana. What a difficult time the poor child has had. We all – Magnus excepted – took due note of your instructions and refrained from weeping all over her when she arrived, although I doubt whether she would have noticed if we had. I think she may have developed some kind of protective shell on the voyage home, for she is politely distant to us all; not melancholic, thank God, but bright and faintly brittle.

I met her myself when the ship docked, and not without inconvenience, I may tell you. Last year's financial panic in the States, and here, was too closely tied to railway speculation not to cause us a good deal of trouble, and Drew, Jermyn and I have been engaged on an intensive salvage operation. Vilia has been very tiresome. If only she would say, 'I told you so' straight out, instead of holding her tongue so ostentatiously! However, we are now agreed that the time has come to bow gracefully out of railways and into armaments. Jermyn, clever boy, has designed a very interesting rifled field gun. It means we will have to go into steel, but I don't object. Our main competition is going to come from

Krupps, although I suspect Armstrong, who is irritatingly well in with the War Office, may also give us trouble. We might find ourselves competing with Randalls', too; we had to cut our connection with them last year to save our own elegant hides, because every British company with American associations found itself not only suspect, but positively hunted! When I tell you that over £32 million in American debt was held by British investors, you will understand why. Did you know that Perry has retired now? His younger son, Benson, who is about eighteen and has the same inborn technical wizardry as Jermyn, is running things – under supervision, of course. Francis, whom we met in '51, appears to have no ambitions in that direction, *his* only wish being to study human nature. So delightful for him to be the idle – and idolized – son of a rich father.

Gideon smiled to himself. It was refreshing to hear from Theo. Vilia wrote occasionally, but her letters in the years since Lizzie died – and before, now he thought about it – had been rather impersonal, while Shona's were a conscientious chronicle of small beer.

There had been two or three notes from Juliana, written on the voyage, but nothing since. Two or three? Two, to be exact. The first one had come at the beginning of May, just before the battle of Bareilly, and had expressed her dutiful thanks for all he had done for her. Her guard had slipped only once, when she wrote, 'I wish that everyone on the ship was less well informed about my misfortunes, and less oppressively kind to me.' On the second occasion, Gideon had been prostrate with sunstroke in one of Rose's field hospitals; despite the gruelling June heat, the British had just captured the fortress of Gwalior. She had written, 'I have learned now to defend myself against the sympathy I don't deserve. Looking back, I know that Richard's and little Luke's deaths must both be laid at my door. Richard died coming to save *me*, and the baby died because I didn't know how to save *him*. The burden of that knowledge is enough; what sympathy does is heap more guilt upon me. The ship docks tomorrow, and the most important episode in my life is over. And my life itself, in the only way that matters. I don't care very much about anything, any more. Thank you again, Gideon dear. And don't worry about me.'

Gideon, with a headache of staggering proportions, had wept for her. When he recovered, he had written begging her not to think in such terms, and had wondered at intervals during the months since then whether there was any significance in the fact that she didn't reply.

It was November now, and he was at Allahabad, where the governor-general had just read out, to a predominantly British audience, a long and faintly illiterate royal proclamation. India had been fought over, and won, and ruled for a hundred years by a company of merchants, the Honourable East India Company. But now no more. The British Crown, carefully refraining from any suggestion that the Company had made a hash of things, was taking over.

The proclamation was couched in antique language that probably dated back five hundred years. Gideon shook his head; one wouldn't have thought this was the second half of the nineteenth century. He must remember to quote some of the better bits when he wrote back to Theo.

The smile was still on his face when he began reading again.

Yes, dear boy, I *am* about to get to the point. A few weeks ago, I found myself trapped over the brandy decanter by Magnus, who has tried everyone's patience to the uttermost on the subject of Juliana's misfortunes, though I don't believe he has the remotest idea of what the poor girl has been through. He is, as usual, irksomely repetitive, alternating between distraction over the loss of his grandson, and criticism of Vilia who, he claims, wilfully encouraged Juliana to leave for the graveyard of the British (how *weary* I am of that phrase!) in the face of all his own cogently stated objections. One would think, to hear him, that Juley herself hadn't had a word to say in the matter. Anyway, after he had moaned for an hour in the most maudlin way imaginable about who was going to look after his little girl when he has gone – as, with his customary pessimism, he expects to do any day now – I felt the least I could do was volunteer.

When Gideon's mind began to function again, his heart was beating like a trip hammer and his hands were shaking. With difficulty he focused his eyes.

She has, you know, always been inclined to run to me when in trouble, and as Vilia says with monotonous frequency – she seems to have picked up the habit of repetition from the old man! – it *is* time I was married.

'A few weeks ago,' the letter said, and it had taken another two months from the date of writing for it to reach Allahabad.

Also, it seems to me that Juliana ought to be removed from Kinveil. I hadn't realized that, during the year before her ill-judged marriage, she and Vilia hadn't been on the most amicable terms. Vilia herself agrees that, deeply though she feels for the child, it would be unthinkable for them both to live permanently at Kinveil. 'One should never go back,' she said to me the other day. 'It is always a mistake to go back, to situations, or places, or – or people.' I *wonder* what she meant by that?

My suggestion cheered the old man up a good deal. I am, after all, very nearly the only one of his connections of whom he unequivocally approves; he has even been gracious enough, on occasion, to commend my wisdom in staying single. You, I may say, are not at all in his good books, despite your services to Juley. All this gadding about, when you should be settled down here at home like a sober, God-fearing citizen!

Need I say that the question of who should inherit Kinveil, after the unfortunate demise of Luke the Second, exercises what he calls his mind very seriously. He is most anxious for a replacement as soon as possible; several, for preference.

Gideon had never known whether Theo was as heartless as his conversation and letters often made him sound. It wasn't lack of sensitivity; he was far too perceptive for that to be the explanation. And it was more than just his particular brand of cleverness.

So there it is. My affianced bride is not – alas for my vanity! – delirious with joy over our approaching nuptials, but neither am I. On the other hand, neither of us has anyone else in mind, and she seems content enough. So we will do our best to provide Magnus with what he so badly wants. Vilia, too. For Kinveil's heir to have Cameron blood in his veins, dear boy! All her ambitions will be realized! As far as I am concerned, marriage will be a new experience, and, as you know, I always find new experiences so stimulating.

It had all been settled, then. Gideon felt sick to his heart. He remembered how relieved he had been to see Theo flirting with Gaby Savarin at that damned dinner party of Shona's, because, at the time, he had seemed dangerously friendly with the muscular, monosyllabic young man who did the smithing at Kinveil. Still searching for the stimulus of brutality, Gideon had wondered, or something more? But Gaby hadn't meant anything, and in the autumn of '54 there had been the awkward business with – what was his name? Dominic Harvey? –

the art critic with whom Lavinia had been smitten. Gideon had drawn the inevitable conclusion. But surely even Theo, with his Olympian self-interest, wouldn't embark on marriage – and marriage with *Juliana* – unless he were capable? And prepared. Was it possible that his relationships with the blacksmith and Harvey had really been no more than what people nowadays had begun to call 'passionate friendships'?

It would take six weeks at least to get a message home by the overland route saying, 'Stop!' If only, *if only* there were something like the new Atlantic Telegraph to connect London with Calcutta as quickly as with New York!

And then he read on and discovered that it was already too late.

We have set October eighteenth as the date. Juliana has no recollection of the weeks between the first and second reliefs of Lucknow, so there is no danger of precipitating an emotional crisis over the anniversary. Incidentally, I have had to be exceedingly careful to prevent her from seeing any of the appalling epics that have been pouring from the pens of our poets about the Mutiny in general and Lucknow in particular. Have you seen Mr Tennyson's latest? It scans with difficulty and rhymes only – presumably! – if one has that gentleman's rather thick Lincolnshire accent. He claims that they kept the flag flying all through the siege? Did they, do you know? Juliana doesn't.

Yes, I *am* straying from the point. Put it down to the natural diffidence of a forty-four-year-old bachelor about to embark on matrimony with a chit of twenty-one. And don't look like that, dear boy! We all have our sensitive spots. I imagine the great day will have passed by the time this reaches you, and will therefore take your fraternal good wishes for granted.

Now, what else has been happening that I ought to cram into my remaining space?

Gideon found he couldn't read any more for a time. Blankly, he sat and gazed from the window at a scene little changed since Juliana and he had frittered away the weeks, almost a year before, waiting for the steamer to take them down to Calcutta. Desolate still, with the great castle of Akbar brooding over the burnt-out ruins that the Mutiny had left, although they had already been softened a little by the sun, and the scavengers, and the monsoon rains.

He knew, even while he denied Juliana the same bitter comfort, what it meant to feel one had failed the people one loved. He had failed Elinor because he had seen no need to gallop hell-for-leather by her

643

side, and remind her that her mare wouldn't jump water. He had failed Lizzie, and she had died from a drug she mightn't have needed to take if he had not been too preoccupied with other people to give her the support she needed. And he had failed Juliana herself, because he had chosen not to sail home with her, where he might have protected her from a marriage that could only be disastrous. Suddenly, he remembered Vilia saying to him just after Elinor died, 'You love your daughter, but don't try to persuade us that you would consider abandoning, or even adjusting, your career for her.' The same hadn't been true – *surely* it hadn't been true – in the case of Juliana, despite the little voice in his head that, telling him she would be better on her own, had also told him that he must remember his duty to the *Times-Graphic*, especially now that his friend and arch-rival, Billy Russell of *The Times*, had just landed in India. Surely he hadn't been as selfish as that? Not this time. Not with Juliana.

Eventually, he dropped his eyes to Theo's concluding paragraphs. Guy Savarin had become a chloral addict, 'which should put a period to his existence before very long; he still tries to paint, but the virtue has gone out of him.' Ian Barber and his wife now had three children, all models of what children should be except that they were all girls; 'so frustrating for them. Vilia made the tactical error of remarking in Magnus's presence that Ian is becoming intolerably sanctimonious; it has shown rather strongly of late in his views on our entry into the armaments business. But Magnus, devoted to Britain's imperial adventures and thus, one might expect, to any weapon that can enforce them, promptly forgot everything in his desire to put Vilia in her place. Ian, he said, was a thoroughly responsible young fellow. Such a pity Magnus doesn't know the meaning of consistency. He never learns anything, and never forgets anything.'

Peregrine James, it seemed, was developing the most astonishing resemblance to Perry Randall, 'for which excellent reason, Magnus can't stand him. Vilia can't, either, but I won't expand on that. Personally, I can't imagine Perry ever looking down his pompous young nose at people in the way P.J. does.'

And, finally, Lavinia. Gideon frowned. 'She is soon to marry a very good friend of mine, Dominic Harvey, who was also a friend of Guy's in their salad days. An intriguing match, which I pride myself on having helped to bring about. With Dominic a true aesthete and Lavinia such a dashing and down-to-earth girl, I can hardly wait to see what they produce in the way of little Harveys. If any.'

That was all, and it was enough. Oh, Juliana. Juliana!

Chapter Seven

1

'Juley, you aren't paying attention!'

'Yes, I am.'

'No. There's all the difference in the world between hearing what I am saying and *listening* to what I am saying! Do wake up, for goodness' sake.'

Lavinia hadn't changed at all in more than three years of marriage to her art critic, although her face, always a little too sharp for prettiness, had become even thinner and her manner more decided. 'I have something very particular to say to you. Is Theo out? Because I warn you, if he comes strolling in and tries to condescend to me in that way he has, I shall probably do him an injury.'

'He's out. I shouldn't think he will be back till late. He seldom is.'

With a sound that came perilously near a snort, Lavinia removed her hat and placed it with care on a side table, where it sat like a black velvet flowerpot full of exotic pink blooms. 'It's a pet of a hat, isn't it?' she said pleasedly. 'I do like these new little ones, so much more flattering than the boring great bonnets we used to wear. And look, Juley! Have you noticed my new crinoline? It's quite the latest, and this slightly flattened front does wonders for one's waistline. See? You really must get one. You're much too tiny ever to look your best in what we've been wearing these last few years.'

What Lavinia lacked in beauty, she made up in style, and her taste was excellent. Her new crinoline supported a charming white gown bordered with a Greek key design in black velvet, its skirt looped up to reveal a pleated petticoat in a soft cerise colour. Juliana's interest in clothes was tepid, although Theo had twice taken her to Paris to buy from M. Worth, the new French royal dressmaker. She said dutifully,

645

'Yes, Lavvy. I like that swept-back effect, but, you know, M. Worth's skirts are wider than ever this spring.'

'Pooh! What does that matter? We've copied the French quite long enough, even if M. Worth is English!' She giggled. 'And if he is responsible for that gown you're wearing, he should be ashamed of himself. I grant you that the ribbon interlacing is becoming, but the colour!'

'It matches my eyes!'

'That's what I'm complaining about. So commonplace. And why do you have that horrid piece of lace on your head? It makes you look quite frumpish.'

Juliana sighed. 'Oh, Lavinia! You know perfectly well that most respectable married ladies wear caps, and unlike you I don't want to be different.'

'Pooh!' Lavinia said again. 'How spiritless! Who cares about "most" married ladies? Vilia has never worn one, and it hasn't stopped her from reaching the impeccably respectable heights of great-grandmother-hood.' She stopped. It was a ticklish point. One never quite knew how Juley was going to react to even the most incidental references to motherhood. Not that she ever went off into a fit of tears, but she sometimes became even more self-contained than usual – which, in her cousin's view, was a remarkable, and quite undesirable, achieve-ment. Lavinia, in fact, was very worried about her, and wasn't looking forward at all to what she had come to say. She wished she could have talked to someone else first, but couldn't think of anyone. Her mother was too innocent, her father would have been outraged, Jermyn was four hundred miles away at the foundry, and Peregrine James was far too wrapped up in himself. To write to Vilia would have been to invite an extremely arbitrary reply, and there were excellent reasons why she couldn't discuss things with either her husband or Uncle Theo. It was a very great pity that Gideon was still in China. Such a busy place, what with Arrow wars, and Opium wars, and coups d'état, and now the Taiping rebellion.

Airily, she said, 'Jermyn never takes time to write to me, but I had a letter from Bella the other day. She says the baby is very well, and very forward for her age. She has just had her first tooth, and Bella is as gratified as if she had written her first symphony. I can't imagine why Jermyn ever married that girl!'

'She's perfectly pleasant.'

'Exactly! She doesn't have as much personality as one could put in a thimble. My own opinion is that Jermyn became so tired of Vilia telling him it was time he was married that he asked the only girl he knew who wouldn't make any demands on him, not even conversational ones. Do you remember her mother at that party of ours during the Great Exhibition, sitting sandwiched between Grandfather Randall and Ian Barber, and not uttering even a murmur the whole evening?'

'Yes, but Bella isn't quite as tongue-tied as Mrs Armstrong! Would you like some tea?'

'No, because then the servants would be in and out all the time, and I want to talk to you very privately.' She fixed her bright hazel eyes on Juliana, and said, 'I've never asked you before, but how do you like being married to Theo?'

Juliana's own eyes widened a little. She had agreed to marry Theo because her father and Vilia had both seemed anxious that she should, and she hadn't cared enough not to. She still had no particular feelings about him, except an occasional puzzlement, just as she had no feelings about marriage. It was a convenient enough state for her, and it meant she didn't have to live at Kinveil, or even in Edinburgh. Theo had celebrated their engagement by deciding that Lauristons' needed him more in London than at the foundry, and had bought a handsome house in Belgrave Square that Juliana thought too large for them. But her father had said it was a good thing to have spacious nursery floors, and Theo had smiled, and Juliana had never again referred to the size of the house. Only once had she even mounted the last flights of stairs to the empty, echoing top floors, and had suggested to Theo afterwards that the servants might be moved into one of them, instead of lying in cramped conditions in the attics. But Theo had replied, 'My dear child, think of all the trouble we would have persuading them back up to the attics again when we need the space! No, leave things as they are.' That had been almost four years ago, and the nursery floors were still unoccupied.

How did she like being married to Theo? 'Well enough,' she said. 'What a funny question.'

Lavinia shifted slightly on her sofa and then, bending, proceeded to free the buckle of her smart cerise shoe from between the two lowest hoops of her crinoline cage. Her face was conveniently hidden when she went on, 'I asked because – well, you've been married before, and I wondered whether you had noticed anything – anything different this time?' She sat up again, her cheeks scarlet.

'Different? Well, of course.' Juliana's eyes, momentarily unseeing, slipped past her cousin to the tall windows overlooking the square, but she didn't, as Lavinia had half feared, relapse into a reverie. Instead, she said calmly, 'Richard was young, and full of spirits, and he adored me. As I did him. Theo is not young, and he is reserved by nature, and although I think he is fond of me, he has other interests. There isn't really any basis for comparison.'

Although Lavinia was a modern young woman, she found it even more difficult than she had expected to go on from there. 'I wasn't talking about that kind of thing. I meant, aren't things different in – in . . . What I am trying to say is . . . Oh, Juley, for heaven's sake! Can't you see I'm trying to ask you about your more – your more *intimate* moments?'

Juliana gave a little gasp of laughter. 'Does he hold my hand when we're alone together, do you mean?'

'Damnation!' Lavinia exclaimed violently, and with extreme impropriety. 'That is *not* what I mean. Must you be so obtuse? I mean in bed!' She flounced to her feet and staggered, as her shoe buckle caught again. 'Oh, *perdition!*'

Lips slightly apart, Juliana stared at her, scarcely even noticing that one of the occasional tables had gone flying under the impact of the swinging hoops.

Lavinia's voice, still uneven, floated back from where she stood looking out of the window. 'What I want to know is, do you even *have* intimate moments?'

'Yes, of course.' Not very often, for which she was grateful, but Theo was forty-eight now, after all. And she couldn't complain that he was lethargic when he came to her. Rather the opposite, for although in the early days of their marriage things had been strained and unhappy, he had learned not to try so hard, and now came to her only when he was in a particular mood, already half aroused and sometimes almost febrile in his eagerness. It was one of the most surprising things about cool, amused, supercilious Theo, but Juliana had accepted it as she now accepted whatever life inflicted on her, without comment, or complaint, or any real interest. At least it meant that everything was over quickly.

Lavinia had come back to stand facing her. 'And do you enjoy them?'

Juliana couldn't imagine why she wanted to know, but there seemed no reason to lie about it. 'Not particularly,' she said.

And then Lavinia – pert, modern, self-assured Lavinia – let out a childish wail of misery and sank abruptly to the floor in a billow of skirts, her face sunk in her hands. 'Even *that* would be something!' she sobbed. 'I've never had the chance to find out!'

It seemed the most extraordinary thing to say. Dominic Harvey was a handsome, charming man, if somewhat opinionated, and he and Lavinia had always seemed perfectly contented. Mystified, and a little touched by Lavinia's distress, Juliana leaned forward and, taking her cousin by the wrists, pulled her hands away from her face. A small, uninvolved voice in her head remarked that crinolines might have been invented to stop people from doing such things; it was almost impossible to approach anyone closer than a yard. 'What on earth are you talking about?'

'Oh, Juley, I'm so unhappy! Dominic can't – can't – *do* anything. And he doesn't want to, either. I don't know what a proper marriage is!'

'Heavens!' Juliana sat back and surveyed her in astonishment. 'You mean you were really trying to ask me whether it was enjoyable? Well, it can be. Richard, dear Richard, made it a joy for me.'

Lavinia's strangled voice asked, 'And Theo doesn't?'

'No. But our whole relationship is quite different.' She wouldn't allow the ordinary, vulgarly inquisitive part of her mind to follow Lavinia's revelation through.

And then Lavinia raised a streaming face. 'That's because he's like Dominic. Didn't you know? Theo just doesn't *like* women. That's why I was asking, to find out whether we were both in the same rotten, miserable boat.' She had brought her sobs a little under control, and sniffed drearily as she began to fumble for a handkerchief.

After a stunned moment, Juliana said, 'For goodness' sake, get up. I don't care whether you want it or not, but I am going to ring for tea. You can stand over at the window when the servants come in. You look a mess, and your gown will be ruined if you sit on it like that any longer.'

When the servants had gone, she held out a plate. 'Have a pastry.'

'I couldn't! It would choke me!'

'Don't put on airs, Lavvy. Besides, they're from Gunter's.'

'Oh.' She took one.

Juliana said at last, 'I assume you know what you're talking about. Perhaps you could start at the beginning.'

With frequent relapses when her words were reduced almost to incomprehensibility, Lavinia stumbled through the whole pitiable tale, and before long Juliana began to feel quite sorry for her. For someone like Lavinia to keep such unhappiness bottled up inside her for three years must have been an appalling strain, and went far to explain why she was so distracted and unlike herself now. Juliana felt like a priest in the confessional. Sympathetic, but in a detached and lack-lustre way neither very surprised nor very involved.

'It was all my fault,' Lavinia declared tragically. 'I was so anxious to marry him. I never dreamed that he agreed only because marriage is a kind of protection for people like him. Everyone thinks that if a man is married he *must* be all right. But he wasn't in love with me. He was in love with Theo.'

Juliana said, 'Go on.'

'It's so dangerous for men to be like that. They can be sent to prison for life if anyone finds out! So he and Theo decided to take out – to take out insurance! That's what they called it.' Her voice dissolved into a wail again.

Very slowly, Juliana was remembering what it felt like to be angry. She didn't really care that Theo wasn't like other men. She did care that he had coldly made use of her. If he had told her, she would still have married him. She didn't want him in her bed; she didn't want children; she didn't care whether she inherited Kinveil or not. But her father cared, and because of that, and from the mental and physical apathy that possessed her, she had done what everyone wanted her to do. If it meant that her father would die happy, it made no difference at all to her. But it seemed that Theo, smiling, reassuring Theo, had been dishonest with her from the first. One thing she had learned in Lucknow, where everyone had been stripped down to their essential selves, was to value honesty at its real worth. Afterwards, coming home, she had been repelled by the hypocrisy of civilized society. She hadn't known what hypocrisy there was in her own house.

'I don't understand,' she said. 'You say that Dominic can't – can't *do* anything? But Theo can.'

'Dominic says that Theo's past isn't as *refined* as his. He says if Theo is roused by – by someone else, he can manage, even with a woman.'

'By someone else?'

'Or something else.'

'What on earth do you mean?'

'Dominic says perhaps Theo asks you to beat him.'

'To *beat* him?' Juliana was floundering now. 'What . . . ?'

Even in her distress, Lavinia was surprised. 'Don't you know that some men need pain to excite them?'

She shook her head.

'Oh, yes! There are some women who do it professionally. Did you really not know that?'

She shook her head again.

'Well, I can tell you that Theo likes it! That, or men, or . . .' Lavinia's voice dropped a little. 'Or boys.'

'*Boys?*'

'Oh, not children! But someone between about twelve and sixteen. The ancient Greeks were like that, too, you know. Dominic says it was an attitude of mind that was responsible for all the creativity of Classical Greek art and sculpture.'

'Indeed?' Juliana's voice was unwontedly caustic. 'And that, I suppose, makes it all right for a modern art critic?'

Lavinia pouted. 'Of course it doesn't. I'm only telling you what Dominic says.'

Roused by someone, or something, else. And then Theo could manage, *even with a woman*. Was that why he was always so urgent when he came to her room? Brought already by someone or something else to a state where he could 'manage'? Juliana, queasily, thought of the sturdy, rosy-cheeked, fifteen-year-old boy Theo employed as a messenger. He was in and out of the house at all hours. Juliana tried to avoid him because he was so impertinent to her.

'Is Dominic still in love with Theo?'

'I don't know and I don't care. Because I've decided I can't stand it any more. I really came to tell you that I'm going to seek an annulment of my marriage. I can do it, on grounds of non-consummation.'

'But Lavinia, the scandal!'

'I don't care. I *won't* spend the rest of my life like this, covering up for someone who doesn't want me. And what does the scandal matter? *I'm* the one who has suffered.'

'You know people don't look at it like that. Their sympathy's always with the man.'

'I don't care,' Lavinia repeated stubbornly. 'The family will probably cut me off, but I don't care about that, either. It's *my* life, and it's time I began to live it.'

'Papa will have a fit!'

'He's your papa, not mine.' Lavinia's face changed. 'As for my papa – you know, Juley, I don't believe he will live much longer. He looks so ill since that trouble he had with his heart. His eyes are all pouched, and he – I don't know how to put it – he has none of his old energy. He sags when he walks. Mama is in a dreadful state, because you know how close they have always been.'

'Nonsense, Lavvy. He's younger than Theo! You're making mountains out of molehills. He uses up too much energy, that's all. He needs a holiday.'

'No. It's gone far beyond that. So bright and beautiful he used to be, do you remember? Oh, well . . . What are you going to do about Theo? I don't know whether I've done right or wrong in telling you. I half thought you knew.'

'I didn't, although I understand some things better now. Do? Nothing, I suppose. His hypocrisy sickens me, but it hardly seems worth making a fuss about. I really don't care, you know. And my father is almost eighty now, and I should be sorry to ruin his hopes, even though I know what they're worth. Perhaps, when he goes, I may think again.'

2

A few nights later, Theo came to her room and she found that it was not going to be as easy as she thought. All very well to face her new knowledge impersonally, and decide it didn't matter very much. The reality was different.

Juliana was in bed reading when he tapped on the door and walked in without waiting for an answer, then turned the key in the lock. Her eyes took in the beautifully damasked scarlet dressing-gown, floor length, that he wore only when he was wearing nothing else, and the feverish glitter in his eyes that meant he was in a hurry. 'Good evening, my dear wife,' he said, as he always did on such occasions, his voice soft and reverberant like a satisfied cat's.

Wretchedly, knowing that it did matter after all, she drew the coverlet higher about her shoulders, and said, 'Not tonight, Theo, please. I would much rather not, if you don't mind.'

His expression didn't change. 'But I do mind, my dear. Very much. You must not neglect your – what do they call it? – wifely duty.' He smiled, as if the phrase amused him.

'Please, Theo. I would rather not.'

The muscles of his jaw tightened a little, but the glitter in his eyes didn't fade. Instead, it became more pronounced. 'Why not?'

She blurted out the only commonplace excuse she could think of. 'It's the wrong time of the month.'

At that, his slanting brows rose and his smile deepened. 'Really? How very odd. My memory for *that* is usually infallible.' He stood for the briefest of moments surveying her, his lower lip delicately gripped between his teeth, and then, before she realized what he was about, took three swift steps across to the bed, tore the coverlet from her fingers, grasped the neck of her night-robe in two iron hands and ripped it, in a single movement, from throat to hem.

Even as she cried out in protest and shock, he threw the gown open and scanned the length of her body.

After a moment he murmured reproachfully, 'Really, my pet. You should have pleaded a headache, and then I might have believed you and gone away.'

'Theo, no! Please don't. I don't want . . .'

But already he was stripping off the magnificent robe, and she closed her eyes against the still elegant figure, pale-skinned and smoothly muscled, and frighteningly aroused. 'No!' she gasped. '*Please*, no.'

Poised by the side of the bed, he said pleasantly, 'Yes, I had the feeling you knew. Lavinia, I presume? *Dear* Lavinia. But never mind. You understand now why . . .' He ran his hands lasciviously, not over her body but his own. 'You understand now why we mustn't waste it, must we?'

Always before, he had taken the trouble to be careful with her, but

653

tonight she could sense the fury in him. No one, in all her life, had treated her roughly, not even in small things. Even in Lucknow, there had been a kind of impartiality in the way the Fates had scattered misery and suffering on everyone. But this violent, burning invasion of her flesh was hers alone, and that made it worse. She would have doubled up, writhing, under the hard, deliberate torment of it, if all his weight had not been upon her. She cried out on a high, gasping note, and he grinned down at her, as if hurting her gave him pleasure. Through the haze in her mind, she realized that it probably did, and that if only she could stay limp and silent she would deprive him of it, and then perhaps it would be over sooner. But the driving agony was too much for her and she screamed out again and again, 'Stop! Oh, stop! You're hurting me! *Stop!*'

'Oh, no – my – pet!' He spoke through his teeth, biting the words off to the cruel relentless rhythm that was tearing her apart. 'You – know – how – much – Magnus – wants – another – heir.' Then he laughed, deep in his throat. 'Luke the Third.'

The sheer brutality of it, she realized long afterwards, achieved precisely what he wanted to achieve. A wild rage surged through her and she began to fight him, tooth and claw, throwing her slight body from side to side, tearing her head away from his, jerking her legs and knees viciously between the iron thighs that knelt astride her, ripping with sharp, manicured nails at his back and chest and the face that, laughing triumphantly, he succeeded in always twisting beyond her reach.

And all the time until, exhausted and heartbroken, she could fight no more, she could hear his excited voice gasping, 'Excellent! Splendid! Keep it up, my dear! Superb!' The more she fought, the more he laughed, and the more powerful and pitiless his assault became. In the end, when her head fell back on the pillow and all her rage was drained from her, she looked up into the face angled above hers and found that it was wearing the most beautiful smile she had ever seen on it.

Breathing hard, ecstatically, he whispered, 'Don't stop! Persevere! Persevere my pet. Please try! Go on. For *me!*'

It was her turn to laugh then, and she did so, weakly and hysterically, her body jerking convulsively as he forced himself through the last urgent strokes until his body arched, and became rigid, and he gave a single, strident groan – and then they were free of each other.

When he spoke, a few moments later, his voice was his own again, cool and ironic. 'An improvement, without doubt. Ordinarily, my pet, you are a little docile for me, but that was a definite improvement. Almost thou persuadeth me!' He rose, and belting the magnificent dressing-gown about him, went on solicitously, 'You must get some rest now. I'm sure you are tired.'

He spoke only once more before he left, turning to look back from the door at where she lay, just as he had left her, in the wreck of the pretty bed. Softly, smilingly, he said, 'It was really quite exhilarating. We must do it more often.'

She lay for a long time before she was able to drag herself up and make her painful, stumbling way towards the door, to turn the key in the lock. She didn't know whether she would ever have the courage to unlock it again.

3

Magnus was ready to die, and claimed in weak and querulous tones that he wanted to die, but to part with anything that belonged to him – even, or especially, his life – was to violate the principles that had guided him for almost eighty years. He had taken to his bed, for no good reason but with an air of finality, at the end of 1861. The only difference being bedridden had made to his way of life was that it saved him the trouble of getting dressed every day.

Twice in the two years since then, he had summoned the family to his death-bed, but on the first occasion Juliana had been suffering from a bout of the fever that had attacked her at intervals ever since her return from India, and had been unable to travel. And the second time, six months ago, Shona had been prostrate after losing Drew. He had gone home from the foundry one evening, tired and tense as always, and had fallen asleep in his chair. He hadn't woken again. For him an easy way to go, but for Shona a shock that had almost killed her, too.

Vilia herself had been more upset than she would have expected. Drew had always been the most irritating of her sons, and as soon as falling in love with Shona had given him someone else to centre his emotions on, he had grown right away from her. For more than half his life, it had hurt Vilia terribly to look at Drew and be reminded of the joy and pain that had given him birth. But now the dead past had buried its dead. All else that remained to her of that past had been extinguished on a June night in 1851 when, racked by nervous nausea after Shona's dinner party, she had brought herself to recognize that the distant, courteous man Perry Randall had become regarded her with as little interest as she had pretended to regard him. She had been almost sick before the evening began, with her long-suppressed need for him, and then they had met as if they were the merest acquaintances. And if the spark no longer lived in him, her pride forbade that it should survive in her. She hadn't known how much warmth that tiny, lingering spark had generated in her heart, until at last she had snuffed it out. She had heard from Shona the other day that Perry's wife was ill, and not expected to live, but it woke no interest in her. She was far more interested in what kind of profits young Benson Randall was making out of the Civil War.

She would be sixty-eight next month, but her mind was as sharp as ever, even if her body was less reliable than it had been. Her hair was pure white now, which she didn't mind, but her once flawless skin was marked with innumerable tiny lines, which she minded very much. Even so, the only thing that made her feel her age was the funerals of so many people who were younger than she was. There had been Drew, of course; and Peter Barber, who had died at fifty-three; and Edward Blair's saintly wife Harriet, just a few weeks after Drew. She had been fifty-seven. Vilia supposed that Sara Randall couldn't be much more than fifty.

It seemed unjust that Magnus, who had never done a hand's turn in his life, should be allowed to potter on until he was almost eighty. Fat, over-fed, over-lubricated, bone idle, he should have succumbed to his weaknesses years ago. But, Vilia thought sardonically, this time he might really go, when he had the audience he craved; most of the family was due to arrive in the next few days. Trust Magnus to be as stubborn and crotchety about dying as he had been about living. Well, he kept saying, as he had been saying off and on for five years now, they would all find out soon enough what he had ultimately decided to do about Kinveil.

It was his secret, to be clasped to his bosom with childish glee, but Vilia had a shrewd idea of the dispositions. In fact, if Ian and Isa

Barber, after five girls in a row, hadn't at last succeeded in producing a son a few months ago, she would have been moderately satisfied. As far as she could tell, Magnus had, typically, wriggled out of making a final decision by leaving Kinveil to Vilia herself for her lifetime, though probably with a whole law book of provisos. When she died – which she didn't intend to do for another thirty years at least – he wanted it to go to a son of Juliana and Theo, or, failing such, to Ian Barber or his male heirs. If by any chance Vilia outlived them, Jermyn's male heirs were next in line; not Jermyn himself, whom Magnus had never forgiven for blowing the roof off the Kitchen Block all those years ago. Jermyn had only one child so far, a daughter Drusilla, but there was another on the way. If the worst came to the worst, the only other possible legatee now that Guy Savarin was dead was young Peregrine James, that infuriating young man who, despite his strong physical resemblance to Perry Randall, seemed to Vilia to be more of a Cameron than any of them.

Voicing her thoughts to Sorley, striding along behind her by the side of the loch, she said, 'Who does Peregrine James remind you of?'

He took a moment to answer, because he didn't think she meant the formidable gentleman who had wafted in and out of her life like some fallen angel, giving her love for an hour and pain for an aeon. 'Och, he reminds me of Himself, for sure. He iss chust like the old laird, chust like your father.'

'He is, isn't he?' Just like the cool, self-centred, cosmopolitan gentleman who, by selling Kinveil, had shaped the whole pattern of his daughter's life. It was more than fifty years since he had died, but Vilia still had not forgiven him.

'If only it weren't for the Barbers,' she murmured. Ian himself, and the baby John Stuart, christened after John Stuart Mill, the philosopher. Such commonplace names. Vilia had already decided that she, at least, would call the child Jay. If it weren't for the Barbers, there would be Cameron blood in the veins of all the potential heirs to Kinveil. It was a thought that, increasingly, had come to obsess her.

There should have been no doubt. What, she wondered, had gone wrong between Theo and Juliana, that five years of marriage hadn't even produced the beginning of a pregnancy? Theo was in excellent physical condition, and Vilia had warned him to make sure that Juliana wasn't taking precautions; one never could tell, and she had been tiresomely introverted since her return from India. Sometimes Vilia wished that Gideon had been sensible enough to escort the girl home instead of vanishing back into the Indian heartland and, afterwards, to China. He might have made a better husband for her. No one had ever expressed any doubts about *his* virility, and he had already fathered one child. As always when she thought of Lizzie, Vilia's mind sheered off again.

It was too late now, in any case, though why Gideon should have chosen to marry another American, Vilia failed to understand. Miss Amy Stevenson wasn't a day under thirty, and to judge from the inscrutable Chinese portrait Gideon had sent home, no beauty, either. She was the daughter of a Boston family that had been in the China trade for many years, first at Canton and then at Shanghai, and although Gideon had been typically uncommunicative, it seemed he had been instrumental in saving her from some dreadful fate or other when the Taiping rebels had menaced the outskirts of Shanghai early last year. It hardly seemed a good enough reason for marrying her, but Vilia supposed it could have been worse; she could have been, not a merchant's daughter, but a missionary's. And there were quite enough sanctimonious people in the family already.

4

Kinveil was still full of family six weeks later, for Magnus, even yet, was taking an unconscionable time a-dying.

Glancing round the dinner table, Theo inquired suavely, 'Is it possible that anyone has any real idea *why* we are all here, like a gathering of vultures? I can't recall, offhand, any other instance of the prey insisting on the presence of the scavengers.'

It was hardly in the best of taste, but only Shona and Jermyn's wife, Bella, showed any inclination to cavil. Even the saintly Ian's patience was wearing thin. 'While I would not resort quite to such terms, I confess to thinking that it was somewhat ill-judged of Great-uncle Magnus to invite us, especially in words which no person of reasonable sensitivity could decently refuse.'

'Quite!' responded Theo fulsomely, earning a reproving glance from his mother. 'I do so agree. I found that part about wishing to see me once more before he dies excessively touching. Who would have thought that Magnus, of all people, would be anxious to have all his family around him in his final hours! Well, *almost* all.' He turned towards Gaby Savarin, amber-haired, liquid-eyed, and in maturity even more seductive than she had been at twenty-two. 'We have all had too much delicacy to ask, Gaby dear. Your respected parents? And your even more respected husband?'

She smiled limpidly at him. '*Ma mère* enjoys indifferent health, and it is *necessaire* that my father remains with her. My husband, M. le comte, was desolated to have engagements that it was not possible for him to break.'

'Alas! But so vairy interrr-resting that Magnus invited them!'

Gaby said nothing, although her gaze on him was heavy as sour cream. It dawned on Juliana for the first time that Gaby, indolent though she was, disliked Theo very much.

His decadent hazel eyes turned towards Vilia. 'Should I ask? Dear Mama, tell us. Was Lavinia invited?'

Vilia said, 'No. And I think that will do, Theo.'

Lavinia had gone home to her parents, and instituted proceedings for the annulment of her marriage to Dominic Harvey, who had behaved remarkably well, considering that his impotence was declared in open court. Very soon afterwards, Lavinia had remarried, but not soon enough. Little Andrew de Rokeby had been born just a few weeks too early for even the most charitable to be left in doubt about the date of his conception. Lavinia seemed very happy with her new husband, an artist of irreproachable Royal Academy orthodoxy, but Magnus had been so offended by the attendant publicity that he had sworn never to have anything to do with Lavinia again. He had even announced that he was going to put it in his Will, in black and white, that under no circumstances should any descendant of hers ever be considered a potential heir to Kinveil. For several months he had gone on arguing with himself, interminably, about whether it was Lavinia's heritage from Vilia through Drew, or from Perry Randall through Shona, that had been responsible for her doing what she had done.

Another absentee from the scavengers' feast was Peregrine James. He had – to everyone's surprise – condescended to turn up, but after two weeks had told his grandmother that, since he had a great many things to attend to, he would take his leave. 'If it upsets the old man,

I'm sorry,' he said, making no attempt to sound convincing. 'But in my own opinion, he's good for another month yet, and I can't spare the time.'

Juliana couldn't understand why Jermyn hadn't gone, too. Bella was abominably pregnant and forever complaining of being cold and uncomfortable. Even Juliana, accustomed to the spartan conditions of Kinveil, was finding this winter something of an ordeal; nor could she forget that her own mother and Vilia's – the last two women to be brought to bed here – had both died in childbirth. But she couldn't say it outright, and Bella told her Jermyn was working on a technical problem to do with his repeating fieldgun, and quite immune to anything else. With a shrug, Juliana turned back to her own affairs.

On a day in early January, one of the most beautiful days she ever remembered, she decided at last that she must have it out with Theo. Keeping up appearances, they had set out after lunch for a walk through the brilliant, snow-shrouded landscape. The low sun, shining from a cloudless, pale blue sky, struck ice sparks from the drifts that lay like whorled cream against the dykes, but the wind that had shaped the drifts had also swept the road almost clear. One had to walk with care, for there had been a heavy frost the night before, but at least it *was* possible to walk.

The scenery was breathtaking. The sun, skimming the mountain tops, turned the slope above Kinveil into a fall of creased silver satin and touched its wind-cleared outcrops into great nuggets of rough gold. Across the loch, the woods that began at the shore and climbed steeply to the tree line lay like a delicate and complex study in *grisaille* – majestic pines, their heads of molten ebony arched with white; spruces with snow lying along every branch and twig, so that they looked from a distance like finger-combed ermine; and the birches a fine, attenuated tracery in white and darkest mahogany. The sky was too mild to lend even a tint to the loch itself, which stretched smooth and shining, grey and insubstantial as polished smoke, to the shores of Skye. Today the Cuillins – sometimes indigo, sometimes red, more often black and menacing – lay white and pure and rounded, caressed by some invisible hand into kindly, rolling hills.

Juliana had never seen the snow lie right down to the water's edge, and only once did she remember the mountain torrents frozen in mid-cataract. Tumbling down in spate from the high tops, leaping and bounding over hidden rocks, they had been stopped dead in their busy progress, transformed in a second of time into marble sculptures, thick and opaque. Here and there, the illusory warmth of the sun had begun to thaw the icicles that festooned the banks, tipping them with clear glass that, in another hour, would turn back to marble again.

It was crisp and marvellously invigorating, and it gave Juliana the stimulus she needed. Tucking her thickly gloved hands deeper into the pockets of her sealskin mantlet, she said, 'Theo. You know that our marriage is not what it should be. I don't believe it will improve, although I've said nothing until now because of my father. But he will be gone soon, and then I would like . . . I would like a divorce. I can't see that you should have any objection.'

He said nothing for a while, continuing to walk, and when she stole a glance at his face she couldn't read anything in it. Then he said agreeably, 'If you insist on locking your door against me, my dear, it is scarcely surprising that our marriage isn't "what it should be". I believe a child would persuade you to look at the matter in an entirely different light.'

'No.' It came out more sharply than she had intended. There had been no physical contact between them since that night two years ago, but Theo had never spoken of it before. She had lain tensely for weeks, waiting for a tap on the door and a rattling of the handle, but it had never come. Eventually, she had realized that he must have found out from one of the servants, and wouldn't subject his pride to such an insult. 'No,' she said again, and had to curb her tongue to stop herself from adding, 'I want no child of yours.' She couldn't afford to offend him any more than was absolutely necessary, because without his assent there could be no divorce. She had asked Peregrine James about that.

Theo said, absently slashing at some birch seedlings with his cane, so that they burst into a shower of snow-blossoms, 'Can it be that you are not happy with me? Why, I wonder? I am pleasant to you, and accommodating; I make no demands. I place no limit on your pin money. We have a handsome house. There are even a few people who consider themselves our friends. And you cannot be suggesting, can you . . .' His eyes met hers, pensively. 'You cannot be suggesting that I am ever unfaithful to you?'

And that was the kind of remark that would have been too much even for the apathetic Juliana who had come home from Lucknow. It still took the most extreme provocation to stir her to emotion, but she had developed a fastidious contempt for her husband's vanity and the bland hypocrisy that marked all his dealings with the world.

She said, 'Please, Theo. It is simply that, for whatever reason, I find I can no longer live with you. Set me free.'

'To do what?'

'I don't know.' The trees were full of small birds, chaffinches and yellow-hammers, blue tits and great tits, elegant little dunnocks, and a fat, fluffed-out robin redbreast. They were shifting and fidgetting at the human intrusion into their landscape, and their movement was enough to send a shower of frost crystals loose to drift on the sun-bright air like a powdering of diamonds. 'I thought I might go away for a while. Stay with Gaby, perhaps . . .'

'My dear! One thing you will not do is take up residence in that household!'

'Why not?'

'I have only met Marcabrun once, but from what Gaby has let drop it is clear to me that they are no more than vulgar appendages of the demi-monde, a couple who live on their wits on the fringes of the imperial court. It is certainly not a world to which I could permit any wife, or ex-wife, of mine to belong. Really, my dear! What would people think if it became known that you preferred that kind of society to mine!'

'Oh, Theo!' she exclaimed in exasperation. 'As if you cared for such gossip! What possible difference can it make to you?'

He gave a dry little chuckle. 'You think my reputation doesn't matter to me? But it does. It's all very fine for artistic gentlemen like my friend Dominic to make themselves the centre of cheap tattle-mongering, but in the nasty, cut-throat world of commerce only respectability will do. Lauristons' would lose customers like water down a drain if my character were put in question.'

'Why should it be? I am asking you to divorce me!'

'Well, naturally.' The patronizing eyes stared at her. 'Short of following Lavinia's regrettable example – and you can hardly claim that I am impotent! – you have very little choice. Indeed, I could commit adultery thrice nightly, and no court in the land would consider it adequate grounds for divorce unless I beat you thrice nightly as well, or deserted you.'

She had been completely frank with Peregrine James, her spirit cringing at it. But P.J. had merely sighed and said what a pity it was that a man as intelligent as Theo should indulge in such adolescent pastimes. 'Adolescent?' she had asked, and he had explained that it was a stage most boys went through, and most boys grew out of. For a dark moment, she had thought of baby Luke as he might have been at fourteen; a younger, thinner edition of Richard. Then she had said, 'What can I do?' Not very much, P.J. had told her. Without Theo's cooperation she would have to have iron-clad grounds. 'The pederastic element would probably do it, but it would be an unsavoury case. And win or lose, you would be laying Theo and his friends open to imprisonment for anything from ten years to life. The law is harsh, but it *is* the law. Would you be prepared to go as far as that?' There had been no need for her even to think about her answer. There were some prices that were too high to pay.

The sun was going now, flushing the hilltops and sky with the faintest apricot, except towards the Cuillins, where the light was a pure lemon colour.

'Shall we turn?' Theo suggested. 'We appear to have a sufficiency of problems without adding frostbite to them.'

She waited, but he didn't go on and resentment stirred in her. 'That is all you have to say, is it? Then I will simply leave you.'

He laughed. 'I could win a court order that would bring you back before you'd gone a dozen miles! Especially if I could show that you were likely to fall into bad company, such as the Marcabruns'. Erring wives have very little latitude in the eyes of the law, you know.' His footsteps crunching softly, he went on, 'And to introduce sordid realism into this conversation, what would you live on?'

She said nothing, because there was nothing to say. When she married him, all she possessed had become his by law, as anything her father chose to leave her would become his. Peregrine James had said, 'The 1857 Marriage and Divorce Act allows you to resume possession of your own property if you are divorced, but not otherwise. If you simply leave Theo, you leave him in possession of all your worldly goods. And don't look so scandalized, Juley. Before 1857 things were a good deal worse.'

'No, my dear,' Theo continued. 'I see no reason why I should forego the very useful dowry your father gave you, or whatever he leaves you in this much-heralded Will of his. And you know, for me, being married is the best possible insurance, all things considered.'

That, Juliana remembered, was what Dominic Harvey had said to Lavinia. 'Is there nothing that will make you change your mind?'

'Nothing at all.'

They were at the landward end of the causeway, where the rowan tree stood guard, tall and shapely, its trunk furred with ice needles, and its branches like fine white lace. All colour had gone from the landscape now. Even the sky was white, and a ghostly mist hovered over the loch. The thin film of ice, close in to the shore, tinkled faintly in the cooling air, and the castle loomed black and golden-windowed against the grey-white dusk.

Theo put his hand on Juliana's arm and drew her into the shelter of the rowan, where they could not be seen from the castle. 'But I will make one concession. Magnus wants Kinveil to go to our son. If you care to look ⌐ quite privately, you know! – for another man to father him, I won't object.' His tone changed and the smile came back. 'But do, my dear, find someone tall and fair, I beg of you! A family resemblance is so desirable. It would be such a waste to go to all that trouble, only to have someone question the result.'

She tore her arm free from him then, and backed away, revulsion and something very like hatred in her heart.

When the dim, spinning world came into focus again, she found she was clinging to the trunk of the rowan, the magic tree that protected those it guarded – unless they were cursed on it. Grasping it with all her strength, she said, her voice breaking, 'Damn you, Theo Lauriston! Damn you! *Damn you for ever!*'

Theo threw back his head and laughed. It was the most spontaneous and carefree sound she had ever heard him utter.

5

A few days later, Vilia sent for Juliana to tell her that her father was asking for her. 'The end has come, the doctor says. We don't believe he will survive the night. I need hardly advise you not to upset him. He will die happier if he believes you are happy.'

Juliana looked at her curiously. 'Do you care if he dies happy or unhappy?'

The domineering green eyes didn't flicker. 'A foolish question, Juliana, and an impertinent one. Your father and I have often disagreed, and I would be the last to deny that ours has scarcely been an ideal marriage. But whether death is an end or a beginning, whether it is the last mystery or no mystery at all, I happen to believe that every human being has the right to face it with a mind at peace.'

'You mean that personal considerations don't enter into it?'

'I mean nothing of the sort. I have lived with your father for twenty-five years, and that creates a bond, however the bond may chafe. I am sad that he is going, but sad for it in a great many ways that you will never understand.' Her voice softened a little. 'Don't let us pursue it, my dear. Believe what you want to believe about me, but go in now and set your father's worries at rest.'

He was lying very still in the bedchamber that had once been his own father's, the warmest and most comfortable in the castle. Somehow, he had caught a cold and it had flown straight to his lungs, and fighting it had taken all the strength that remained to him. His face on the pillow was sunken, and he hadn't been shaved for several days, so that the handsome sidewhiskers of which he had been so proud looked as if they had begun to melt and spread over his cheeks and chin. Juliana had never known her father in his prime, greying and distinguished, when he had been tall, and not too fat, and still had all his hair. He had never been anything but an old man to her, willing to pet her when she ran to him, and making a great issue of his fondness for her. But none of it had ever seemed very real, and it was only now, when it was much too late, that she realized she scarcely knew him. Until the death of Lizzie, she had always been closer to Vilia than Magnus, and had picked up Vilia's habit of treating him with a respect that was quite hollow at the core. Now, she regretted it. She had never tried to penetrate the facade of quirks and grumbles and complaints to find out what lay beneath. Perhaps Vilia was right; perhaps nothing did. But she should have tried.

The candles were shaded, and there was a local woman sitting quietly in the corner, knitting. When Juliana smiled at her, she rose and left them alone.

Magnus's eyes were closed and his breathing was erratic. There was a faint, medicinal smell in the room, half drowned by the tang of wood smoke, but not quite masking the smell of old age. After a moment, Juliana leaned over and took her father's hand. It was cold, and automatically she began chafing it. 'Father!' she said in a low voice.

He opened his eyes as if it required a great effort. There was an unseeing look about them. 'Juley?'

'Yes, Father.'

'Are you all right?' His voice was faint and jerky.

'What a question! That's what I'm supposed to ask *you*!' But he had never responded to the light touch, and she quickly retrieved her error. 'Yes, Papa. I'm all right, I assure you.'

'That fever . . .'

'It comes and goes. I must learn to live with it. It's called malaria.'

'That terrible place. Should never have gone. All your stepmother's fault.'

A choking cough shook him, and she said, 'You mustn't talk.' But even on his death-bed Magnus wouldn't have any truck with all that forgiving and forgetting nonsense. '*She* encouraged you. Quite incredible. Always knew it was wrong. Graveyard of the British . . .'

'Yes, Papa. But it's all over now, and you mustn't worry.'

He had closed his eyes, but now they opened again as if the lids were on springs. '*Mustn't worry?*' he echoed strongly. 'How can I help but worry. If I only knew you were properly settled!'

She wondered if his memory was failing. 'I *am* settled, remember? Theo and I have a beautiful house, and we are very comfortable, and do very well.'

'Not enough. Children. Son to inherit Kinveil.' Suddenly, he was a picture of decrepitude. 'Should have started a family as soon as you were married. I don't hold with this putting off. How's a fellow expected to die in peace if his own daughter won't do as she ought. It worries me, you know.' He looked as if all the world was conspiring against him.

She began chafing his hand again, gazing back into the eyes that were now an indeterminate buff colour under the pale lids. Such a comfortable death-bed. A warm, handsome room, soft pillows, a doctor, nurse, wife and daughter all dedicated solely to him, and any number of others waiting in the wings to provide whatever he needed or required. She remembered the cramped little cabin on the *Himalaya* at Calcutta, and the other death-beds in the filthy, vermin-ridden, evil-smelling underground room in the Begum Kothi. And one other, on the hard ground.

She had been useless then. But perhaps she could do something now, when all it needed was a few words, a few lies. 'It's a secret still,' she said, making a great show of whispering. 'I was saving it until you were better. But if you are truly anxious . . . Well, you needn't be. There is going to be a child, and I am sure it must be a son.'

Slowly, his eyes filled with tears, and he sniffed gustily as they rolled down his cheeks.

She said, 'But don't you dare tell anyone! Promise?'

'Don't want them all fussing?'

'That's right. Not for a while yet, anyway.'

'Very wise. Can't stand people fussing, myself, and they *will* do it. Incredible!' He blinked, and gave another painful, tight little cough. 'Um – er – will you call him – er – Luke?'

She swallowed. 'Luke Magnus, I thought. Every boy needs two Christian names.'

Another pair of fat, comfortable tears rolled down his cheeks.

'Well, anyway,' she said. 'I've set your mind at rest, haven't I? No need to worry any more.'

'No need to worry,' he repeated, his breath rasping. 'That's a good girl.'

He said nothing more after that, but it seemed as if his muscles had eased, and his breathing became quieter. He was very white, and his hand was very cold.

She sat there for an hour or more. She could see he was still breathing, and he gripped her hand with surprising power as if he were afraid she would go away, but she knew that soon the faint sound from his lips and the almost invisible movement of his chest would stop.

She knew that she couldn't bear to stay for it.

He mumbled as she freed her hand from his and quietly rose and went to the door. Vilia and the woman from the village were just outside, and Juliana said, 'I think you should go in.'

For most of the night, she sat staring into the fire. She had lied to help him, but by leaving she had failed him. He had wanted her to stay with him, she knew. And now there was yet another failure to add to the tally of her dead.

Part Six   1864–1895

Chapter One

1

'What could be more discouraging?' Gideon asked, surveying the luncheon table with disfavour. 'Here am I, back on English soil for the first time in eight years, and is the family drawn up in serried ranks, panting to clasp me to its collective bosom? Is it, I ask you? No. In fact, everyone seems to have done a disappearing trick. Afraid, no doubt,' he went on dispassionately, helping himself to a large slice of game pie, 'of being blinded by the light of my countenance, or suffocated by Eastern wisdom and patchouli.'

Amy Lauriston chuckled, and her husband grinned at her. 'It's perfectly true,' he said. 'They've all vanished, every last one of them.' He didn't mind for himself, but he thought that for Amy's sake someone might have had the decency to stay and utter a word of welcome.

She said, 'They can't have. Pass your plate and I'll give you some of this salad. Now be serious, and tell me. Are all the houses closed up?'

'Yes. Vilia's at Kinveil, which is only to be expected at this time of year. But the house in Belgrave Square – that's Theo and Juliana's – looks as if it's been closed up for weeks, and as far as I can see the Barbers' place is as empty as if they've moved out altogether. I thought young Peregrine James would be able to tell me what was going on. But no. The man who owns the house where he has his apartment said he understood Mr Lauriston was in Scotland for some weeks, and I almost had to tear the address out of him by force. Marchfield, of course, but I can't imagine why he was so reluctant to tell me. I don't look like a debt collector, do I?'

'Ummm,' she said consideringly. 'I have no notion of what English debt collectors look like, of course, but I shouldn't think so. But he might have thought you were a foreigner, and that would be even worse!' Gideon's silky beard and thickly waving white hair made an exotic contrast with his tanned skin and still youthful face, and indeed, on that dreadful evening outside Shanghai when he had rescued her from the Taiping vedettes, she herself had taken him for French. His looks aside, she had never come across a Britisher who had gone to the trouble of learning to speak Mandarin, far less its Nankingese version. She admired and loved her husband very deeply in her own quiet way.

His lean face creased with amusement. 'Take care what you say, my girl! It's not for a New Englander to criticize John Bull's prejudices. Anyway, at least Lavinia is still in town. She was out when I called, but I've left a message.'

'How very daring of you! I thought her name had been obliterated from the family tree?'

'Only the *Telfer* family tree!'

Lavinia swept into their hotel suite in thin, vivid, stylish person, not two hours later, and hugged Gideon with the greatest vigour. 'How good it is to see you again! Yes, I know you said you would call this evening, but we are going out and, anyway, I couldn't wait. Oh, I'm so sorry. You must be Amy. Please forgive me for not seeing you at first, but having Gideon back is like having sanity restored to a mad world.'

Sinking into a chair, and chattering briskly to Gideon about her own affairs as the easiest way of covering the first awkward moments, she covertly surveyed Amy, half a dozen years older than herself, and, she supposed, about fifteen years younger than Gideon. The difference wasn't particularly marked, because Gideon's white hair was completely belied by his eyes, a little tired but still full of youthful charm. Lavinia had always considered it grossly unfair for a man to have such eyes, *and* such eyelashes. Amy was a surprise – not at all dashing, as one would have expected of a young woman who had lived in China, and been captured by rebels, and goodness knew what else. She was quite tall, and the high-necked, fitted bodice of her glacé tartan gown – dark blue and white, with a fine scarlet line through it – hinted at an elegantly curved figure. But although she had a mass of glossy hair wound into a long, oval chignon that stretched from the top of her

670

head to the nape of her neck, it was an unremarkable dark mouse colour. Her nose was unfashionably hooked, and her brows straight and heavy. On the other hand, there were dimples at the corners of her mouth, and her blue-grey eyes looked kind and understanding. They were also perceptive, and Lavinia made a mental note not to underestimate Aunt Amy. 'Must I call you aunt?' she exclaimed. 'It seems so silly, when we're almost of an age – and I've never called Gideon uncle!'

'I should hope not,' Gideon said, outraged. 'What's more, that brat of yours would be calling me "Great-uncle" in no time at all, and I won't have it! I'm sure Amy feels the same.'

The dimples at the corners of Amy's mouth deepened. 'And that, you see, disposes of any opinions *I* might have on the subject! The master has spoken. Amy it shall be.'

'Good heavens, Gideon! That sounds as if Amy has a mind of her own!'

He grinned. Stretching luxuriously, he sank his hands into the pockets of his trousers and said, 'God, it's good to be home. And now, young woman, perhaps you'll tell me what's happened to the rest of the family? Why this unanimous flight from the metropolis?'

'Unanimous? You don't mean to tell me Peregrine James has gone, too? Well, really! It gets more like musical chairs every day. You know everyone's moving house, of course, and . . .'

'I don't know any such thing. I'm at least six months out of date. We haven't heard anything since Shanghai, and even *that* news had taken a couple of months to reach us. We've been on the high seas for the last one hundred and seven days.'

'How very precise of you! Did you count?'

'Didn't have to,' Gideon replied laconically. 'Everyone else did it for us. We came back on one of the tea clippers from Foochow, racing another one all the way. We won. Of course.'

There was a tap on the door, and Amy said melodiously, 'Ah, the tea!'

Her husband sat up. 'No, really, Amy!' and then, surveying the trays, sank back with a sigh of relief. 'You're a wicked woman. I thought you meant it.'

Amy giggled. 'Tea for you, Lavinia, but neither of us ever wants to see the stuff again. Coffee or chocolate, Gideon?'

Lavinia decided she liked Amy. 'You mustn't allow Vilia to intimidate you,' she said suddenly.

Gideon gave a choke of laughter. 'She's not easy to intimidate!'

Amy was a splendid woman, and not a day passed without him thanking God he had met her. The pain of losing Juliana had faded by then into a dull, empty ache, but even though he had scorned himself for making a grand tragedy out of it, he had been convinced that he would never be freed from the depression that dogged him. And yet somehow Amy had managed it, without even knowing its cause. Except when she landed herself in idiotic scrapes by behaving as if the world were a rational place, when it wasn't – which was what had happened in the Taiping episode – she was extremely intelligent and had a quiet mischief that had attracted him almost against his will. He knew that she had emerged from school in Boston a perfect specimen of New England womanhood, annihilatingly correct, exquisitely polished, completely purified of any taint of unconventionality; an impeccable wife for even the most discriminating gentleman. But since Europe in 1848 was no place for a young lady to round off her education, she had been sent to her aunt and uncle in China, instead, and had liked it so much that she had stayed. In no time at all, she had stopped being a perfect specimen of New England womanhood and become a real and positive person, with views of her own and no hesitation about expressing them. She had been a sore trial to her aunt and uncle, who had been embarrassingly ready to relinquish her to the foreign correspondent of the *Times-Graphic*. Amy, perfectly aware of it, had chuckled about it for weeks. She had a delightful chuckle. Gideon wasn't in love with her, for his heart would always be Juliana's, but his affection for her went very deep, and their relationship had an uncomplicated warmth and harmony that was quite new in his experience.

He said, 'Anyway, she's been warned, not only about Vilia but everyone else! So come on, girl, let me have all the news!'

There was a good deal of it. The Barbers were going to live at Glenbraddan, to keep Edward company – Grace, Isa, five little girls, one infant philosopher, and Ian, although Ian was involved in the campaign for the Second Reform Bill and proposed keeping a base in London. Jermyn's wife Bella had died giving birth to a second daughter early the previous year. Gideon knew that, but he didn't know that

Jermyn had married again. 'Well, you know what he's like,' Lavinia said. 'Vilia was pestering him to marry again, and he'll do anything to be left in peace with his boring old guns. So he promptly married Madge. *Not* a doormat like Bella – far from it! The most enterprising girl. She was an actress on tour in Edinburgh with her own company, and the peculiar thing is that I think she and Jermyn are really in love!'

'Well, it does happen,' Gideon said. 'Can she act?'

'I don't know, but Mr Dickens gave her a very good notice.'

'Oh, dear!' he said with a sepulchral groan. 'And?'

Lavinia glared at him. 'And she is – she is in an interesting condition.'

'When?'

'October. Won't it be marvellous if it's a boy? Vilia will be so pleased. Oh, and after mother's seen Madge through the next few months, she's going to leave Marchfield to Jermyn and her, and go to live with Vilia at Kinveil. Yes, truly! It was mother's idea, but Vilia doesn't seem to mind.'

'What an eventful life everyone leads!'

There were changes at the foundry, too, it seemed. After Drew's death, Theo had overridden Peregrine James's objection to being involved in something as vulgar as business, and it had been agreed that P.J. would take over the London end where, as Lavinia said, it didn't much matter if he didn't know a tuyer from a trip hammer. His legal mind would be very handy when it came to contracts and things. Theo was going back to the foundry.

'And what does Juliana feel about a move back to Edinburgh?' He saw at once that there was something wrong, and very wrong.

After a moment, Lavinia said, 'Juliana? Well . . .' And then, in a rush, 'Well, it was all very unfortunate. A few weeks ago, she left Theo. For good.'

'Left Theo?' My *poor darling, my poor love!* 'Where has she gone? Kinveil?'

'That's the trouble. We don't know.'

'You – don't – know? What do you mean?'

'Theo wouldn't agree to a divorce, and she ran away, and no one knows where.'

It was difficult to say, but he managed. 'Was there some other man?'

'No, I'm sure not. Theo thought she might have gone to Paris, to

Gaby, so he went there, but Gaby said no. Then he thought of Petronella Barber. She's just back from America, and quite insufferable about women's right to do what they choose. But she hadn't seen Juley either. Much too busy supporting Mr John Stuart Mill's election campaign, now that he's come out in favour of women's suffrage, and . . .'

'Oh, to hell with that!' Gideon was on his feet, towering over his niece. 'It's Juliana I'm concerned about. Is that all Theo's done?' She nodded. 'Did Juley take anything with her? Clothes? Money? Jewels?'

'Don't bully me, Gideon! It's not *my* fault, it's your horrid brother's, and I don't blame Juley one little bit! She didn't walk into the river, if that's what you're worried about. She took three trunks of clothes, and every jewel she possessed, and as much cash as she could raise. Quite a few hundred pounds. Really, she won't starve.'

'What do you mean, it's Theo's fault?'

They had both forgotten Amy was there. She, acutely sensitive in everything that concerned her husband, had always known that there was someone else in his life who was, or had been, very important to him. Now she knew who it was.

Lavinia exclaimed, 'For heaven's sake, you know as well as I do! I'm not acquainted with the polite word, if there is one. He's a she-shirt, a pooff, a nancy, and you can hardly expect any self-respecting wife to live with *that*!'

He stared at her for a long moment. 'Sodomite is the word you want. Lavinia, did you go through the same thing with Dominic? Was that the reason for the annulment?'

'More or less.' Her colour high, she went on. 'Dominic was impotent with – with women, which made the annulment possible. It wasn't necessary to give the reason why, in court. But I gather it's different with Theo.'

'I see.' *I see what I sent her home from India to face alone. God forgive me.* 'Has everything possible been done to find her? Do you think Theo has seriously tried?'

'He seems to have. I can't tell, for he and I have never been on the best of terms. But, Gideon, if he finds her, the law will force her to go back to him! There was a case when the court ruled that a husband was within his rights in *kidnapping* his runaway wife and keeping her under

674

lock and key to protect her from the wicked world. And she was a very respectable lady!'

'Nonsense.'

'It's true! Peregrine James told me. It happened about twenty years ago now, but he says precedents can be very dangerous things.'

Gideon was silent, and Lavinia went on after a moment. 'You can't do anything, Gideon. All that would happen would be that Juliana would be forced to come back to live with Theo again. She'd be worse off than before.'

'Yes,' he said. 'I suppose you're right. It's just that she's so very much alone, and it makes me think of Lizzie. And even Lizzie had young Savarin, and me, however little use we were to her. Juliana has no one, and she has been so lost, all her life, when she has had no one to lean on.'

Amy intervened gently. 'Lizzie was scarcely more than a child, my dear. Juliana is a woman.'

'Is she? I don't see it as a sign of maturity to run away.'

'Perhaps not. But she may have run *to* something, as well as away. I could understand that. How can one turn one's back on a hateful past, except by starting life again, somewhere else?'

2

During the course of the next four weeks, Gideon and Amy found themselves a house in London, and Gideon went to Paris to see Gaby Savarin.

Amy expressed a desire for 'quite a small house, with a garden. A garden all round. Why does everyone live in terraced houses with only a pocket handkerchief at the back?'

'Because until fifty years ago, it was a matter of cramming maximum people into minimum space, and unless you were a Duke, you lived in a terraced house and liked it. Unless, of course, you were prepared to be shabby-genteel and live out in a village like Kensington or Islington.'

'Let's be shabby-genteel!'

'No need. Most of the outer villages are inner suburbs now! I favour St John's Wood.' He offered her his arm. 'Shall we go, madam?'

They found an enchanting villa, faintly Gothic without, simple and pleasantly proportioned within, and Amy said, 'Perfect! Quite perfect!'

And then Gideon said, 'Will you forgive me if I leave you to see to the furnishings while I make a foray across the Channel to see the Marcabruns? I feel responsible for Juliana. Can you understand?'

She understood better than he knew. 'Of course,' she said. It would be time enough to fight if things ever came out into the open. A little to her own surprise, she found herself thinking, 'Poor Juliana! Poor Gideon!'

He did find out something. Juliana had foreseen that Theo would look for her with Gaby, and had not gone there until she thought it was safe. 'But I have to tell you,' Gaby added, 'that I would have protected her from him, even had she been here. I do not care for your brother, *mon cher.*' And then Juliana had gone again, and Gaby had no idea where. 'She would not tell me, so that I have no need to lie.'

'No hint?' Gaby shook her head.

Worried stiff, Gideon found it difficult to settle in the new house, with its highly unconventional mixture of Queen Anne and Mr William Morris. He didn't know how Amy had dared, but, fortunately, he wasn't a purist and he liked it. It was just that there was something that had to be got over before either of them could face the very private problems of adjusting themselves to married life in their own home.

In the middle of October, therefore, they set out for Scotland, to stay at Marchfield for a few weeks and possibly go on to Kinveil.

If any ghosts from thirty years ago hovered over the threshold of Marchfield House as Gideon entered it with his second American bride, only the stones were aware of it. It was a bright afternoon, and the hall was warm and welcoming, and there was a smile on every face. Instead of a distraught Vilia and a pregnant Shona, there were Shona as sweet and serene, despite her mourning, as if she knew Drew were still there beside her, and Madge, two weeks past the birth of her son, Neil, and standing with an expression of friendly interest on her pretty, heart-shaped face that instantly endeared her to Gideon. He had been afraid that she might resent yielding the limelight, however temporarily, to Amy. And instead of Theo and Drew, there were Theo, Jermyn and Peregrine James. Theo's smile was bland and satirical, as it always was and always had been, but it altered almost imperceptibly as he noted the coolness in Gideon's eyes. Jermyn hadn't changed much, but Peregrine James, who had been seventeen when Gideon last saw him, was very different. Very like Perry Randall, as Theo had written, but without Perry's aura of leashed power. P.J. had his own power, but it was of the sleek and faintly inhuman kind.

And then, in the background, Gideon saw another familiar figure, who had changed distressingly in the last eight years. 'Sorley!' he exclaimed with genuine pleasure. 'What are you doing here? How splendid!' But he had become an old man, his shoulders bent a little under the smoke-coloured velvet tunic with its old-fashioned white neck-cloth, and his hair untrimmed and bone white. He looked as if he hadn't shaved for a day or two, and the pouches under his eyes were portmanteau-sized, but his smile still had the same awesome beauty.

'Och, Gideon, it iss good to see you, and your lady, too.' He bowed to Amy with charming politeness. 'Mistress Vilia went back a few days since, but she wass wanting me to take home some of Mistress Shona's things, so I am still here.'

Shona said, 'Admit, it, Sorley! It isn't that at all. You want to hear Ian Barber speaking at the National Reform League meeting in Edinburgh tomorrow night, don't you!'

'Och, well. I will not be wanting to miss that. It iss chust that I will like to know if there iss any chance of me getting the vote before I die.'

'Oh, God!' Gideon exclaimed. 'Electoral reform? I suppose we all have to turn up, do we?'

He cornered Theo the next afternoon and had it out with him, or tried to.

Theo wasn't cooperative. 'My dear wife,' he said coolly, 'was upset to discover the catholicity of my tastes. It was Lavinia, of course, who let the cat out of the bag. Before that, we had been managing perfectly well.'

Gideon repeated astringently, 'The catholicity of your tastes?' but his brother didn't respond. 'Did Juliana leave as soon as she found out?'

'No.' Theo leaned back and surveyed the tips of his well-kept toes.

'Why not?'

'Magnus, of course. She didn't want to depress dear papa, who cherished hopes of an heir to Kinveil.' He sighed extravagantly.

'But she stayed on after that. She stayed on for more than a year after

677

he died. Why?' He was trying to make it sound as if he were no more than mildly curious.

'If I had been in my dear wife's confidence, I might be able to answer that. But I was not. I knew nothing until I came home one evening to discover she had gone. I imagine she may have been trying to gather some ready money together.'

With hard-held calm, Gideon said, 'Have you really found no trace at all? A girl like Juliana can't simply vanish, just like that. She must have made some arrangements in advance.'

'No doubt. What would you have had me do? Call in the Peelers to look for her?'

'Of course not.'

'Precisely. I have done everything possible, short of that.'

Gideon felt his temper rising. 'But now you've washed your hands of it, have you? That's the end, and you don't intend to go to any more trouble. Don't you care that she may be in difficulties? She's always been so damnably helpless!' He didn't know why he was stirring everything up. Lavinia was right. Juliana shouldn't be forced to live with Theo again. But Gideon was frightened of her being on her own, and thought, in a muddled way, that now he was home again he might be able to put pressure on Theo to give her the divorce she wanted. If only they knew where she was!

Theo steepled his fingers before his lips, and studied Gideon. His eyes weren't bland any more, but ice cold. 'Be careful, dear boy. I want my wife back, and I want her in an amenable state of mind. I know what I'm doing. We could still produce a son and, as I told her, a child would almost certainly persuade her to see our marriage in a different light. Don't, by the way, think I can't perform, dear boy. I can, when I must. Yes, Juliana is ignorant of the world. After a few months, or even a year or two, of fighting it all on her own, she'll come back to me of her own accord.'

Gideon sprang to his feet. 'Are you telling me you *want* her to be hurt? Because you think that will bring her to heel? God damn you, Theo. I always thought you had a normal, human heart under that supercilious exterior of yours, but you haven't, have you! Well, I tell you – if Juliana should ever come to me for help or advice, I'll do my utmost to see that, under no circumstances, does she ever return to you. What she needs is warmth and loving, and what you have given her is . . .' His disgust was so great that it robbed him of speech. Abruptly he sat down again and buried his face in his hands.

After a very long time, Theo said, 'Gideon, dear boy!' It was like acid dripping, and Gideon looked up. 'I would prefer – I really *would* prefer you to keep your prying journalistic nose out of my affairs. My wife is *not your concern.*'

Gideon met his gaze squarely. He had never quarrelled with Theo before, seldom even criticized him. They had scarcely seen each other since Gideon went to the Crimea, where he had lost the vast self-satisfied tolerance that had always characterized his dealings with Theo, as with others. He knew now that tolerance was a fine thing in its place, but that there were some places where it didn't belong.

He said, 'Your wife may not be my concern, but Juliana is. Have you no pity at all for her? Already, she has suffered more than most people do in a !ifetime.'

He might have saved his breath. Theo had said all he intended to say. Smiling, he rose to his feet. 'You sound quite like a Biblical tract, dear boy! Now, shall we set out for this tedious Reform meeting? Jermyn and the others have gone ahead.'

3

As soon as they walked into the hall, they could see there was going to be trouble. The place was packed, every seat taken, and more than a hundred people standing at the back and spilling down the passages at the sides. Most of the early arrivals had the look of honest craftsmen and small tradesmen, although there was a sprinkling of the middle and upper classes, but the men at the back were of a different order. Even from the door, which was in the middle of one of the long sides of the hall, Gideon caught the mixed blast of axle grease and linseed oil. 'The Amalgamated Society of Engineers I would guess,' Theo murmured. 'Ah, there's Jermyn! Such a dear boy, but surely he might have found seats nearer the door?'

As they fought their way round the back of the hall, a new scent was added to the melange. Whisky. There was a good deal of jostling going on, and plenty of raucous laughter. Gideon caught the tail end of one or two jokes that were very coarse indeed, and only just saved himself from tripping over the outstretched legs of a cadaverous fellow who had settled down, oblivious of the crush, with his back against the wall and a bottle in his hand. He was waving it tipsily in time to the song he was warbling to himself, a version of 'Barbara Allan' that wasn't usually to be found in the song books. Gideon grinned at him and struggled on after Theo, whose appearance was productive of a hearty cheer from some of the men on the outskirts of the scrum, and some vigorous clapping on the back. Affecting to recoil, Theo murmured, 'Good God! If this is democracy at work, I shall be compelled to vote against it!' A roar of delighted laughter greeted this sally, and he remarked to Gideon as they reached their seats, 'Some of the lads from the foundry. Jermyn, dear boy, why is the ancient retainer all by himself back there, instead of sitting with us?' He was an observant bastard. Gideon hadn't noticed Sorley.

'What? Oh, not fitting for him to sit with the gentry, or something. You know what antiquated notions he has.'

Theo sighed. 'Chust so.'

Almost at once, the platform party made its appearance, led by the chairman, a local worthy commonly known as Honest John – largely because his surname happened to be Cockshut. As a rule, his equals mispronounced it into unintelligibility, and his inferiors called him 'sir'. But not tonight. With one accord, those at the back of the hall launched into a song known to initiates as 'Frisky Johnny'. Clearly, it wasn't spontaneous, but it *was* funny, especially as the platform party took it at first for a simple rendering of 'Bonnie Laddie', the tune to which it was sung, and beamed appreciatively all through the first verse.

> 'Tell me what is that I spy,
> Frisky Johnny, randy Johnny . . .'

Thanks to the vocalists' somewhat glottal enunciation, realization didn't fully dawn until the third verse, by which time the man next to Gideon was convulsed with mirth and even Peregrine James was grinning like a normal human idiot.

> 'It's round and long, with moss 'tis spread,
> Honest Johnny, frisky Johnny,

And just like coral is its head,
    Honest Johnny, randy Johnny,
To press it, many a lass hath griev'd,
    Honest Johnny, cocky Johnny . . .'

The chairman thumped sternly with his gavel, and the song wandered to its death amid a storm of hushing from the front rows.

Jermyn, his eyes fixed thoughtfully on Ian Barber, said, 'You know, I don't believe Ian understood that.' Theo gave a splutter of laughter, and Gideon, glancing up at the platform, saw that Jermyn was right. The boyish face in the frame of untidy brown hair and reddish whiskers wore the expression that had always meant Ian wasn't sure about something.

Gideon looked forward with mild interest to how the young man was going to acquit himself on the platform. With an audience like this, he thought pessimistically, not well.

The chairman, intent on putting a damper on the proceedings, began the meeting with a long-winded summary of the aims and objects of the National Reform League. It was thirty-three years, he droned, since the 1832 Reform Act that had given the vote to the middle classes – 'the weel-aff ones, at ony rate.' Every effort since then to extend the franchise to the workers had failed to find the necessary support in parliament.

'Aw, poaliticians!' came in a stentorian bellow from the back. 'We a' know whit they're worth. Bloody revolution, that's whit we want!'

'Now, now, my man!' said the chairman, peering over his spectacles. 'That's no' whit we want at all. The greatest stumbling block to progress was aye Lord Palmerston, but he's gone now . . .' Cheers and stamping from the back. '. . . and we just have tae persevere. Whit we want is for every honest working man to have the right to vote . . .'

'*Honest?*' roared a dismayed voice. 'Och, that lets me an' Wullie oot, dinnit?' Sounds of a scuffle suggested that Wullie was taking exception to this, and the chairman rapped furiously with his gavel. 'I canny have it, you know! I'll have tae pit ye oot if ye go on like this!'

'Awa'! You and who else? Jist you come doon here an' Ah'll melt you!'

But a chorus of be-quiets from the better regulated classes was enough to silence the hecklers, for the time being, and the chairman said, 'Aye, that's better.'

The first speaker, one Sebastian Donkin, didn't have much trouble with the hecklers, boring them so much that they lapsed into a coma, but he was followed by an experienced rabble-rouser, who had them awake again in no time. And then it was Ian's turn.

Disastrously, the chairman announced that Mr Barber had come all the way from London for this meeting, and what emerged from the immediate chorus of boos and hisses and catcalls was the general impression that the wee blankety-blank Sassenach should go blankety-blank back to where he blankety-blank came from. But the hullabaloo died down at last in response to cries from the front of 'Order', 'Fair play', and 'Let the wee fellow speak his piece, can ye not!'

There was an uneasy silence during the first part of Ian's speech, and then after about ten minutes a huge and uninhibited yawn from the side. A little later, a kindly voice from the rear said, 'Aw, hey! Mr Chairman, sir, your honour. Gie him a dunt and wake him up, heh?'

Somehow Ian struggled on in his own pedantic way. Gideon could only assume that no one was actually listening, because what he was saying was 'more haste, less speed', which was the precise opposite of what most of the audience wanted to hear. His thesis, as far as Gideon could discover, was that to ask too much in the way of reform would result in being given nothing, whereas to ask only a little, and then a little more, and a little more again, would bring far greater rewards in the end. Gideon had his doubts. But, for a while, Ian's style of oratory was enough to confuse even that part of the audience that had cheered the mention of 'bloody revolution'.

It was too good to last. 'The honour and glory of the ordinary man,' Ian said, 'is that he can respond internally to wise and noble things, and involves himself in no sophistical confusions in his response to them. However, I propose to ask myself a question . . .'

'God!' remarked a long-suffering voice. 'Ye'll get a bloody boring answer, too!'

What Ian had proposed to ask himself was lost in the ensuing grumble of restlessness. Gideon heard someone behind say, 'Och, this wusny worth comin' for. Ah've had enough. Ah'm gaun hame, are ye comin', Erchie?' He didn't catch Erchie's reply, but no one made a move.

On the platform, draped with a bright yellow banner that clashed nastily with the toast-and-marmalade hues of walls and ceiling, Ian raised his voice in vain against the growing volume of sound. He would have been wiser to give up, for by the purest bad luck a silence fell just as he reached his peroration, which concerned what would happen on the glorious day when working men received the franchise. 'Then,' Ian declaimed, 'they will bring morality into public life . . .'

There was a howl. 'Who will? Jock and Wullie? Ye huv tae be joking!'

'. . . and cast their vote decisively against all whose vested interests are responsible for the great evils that beset us today . . .'

'That's mair like it! That's the wee boy!'

'. . . against bribery and intimidation . . .'

'Aw, hear, hear!'

'. . . the imposition of British rule on alien peoples . . .'

'Whit was that?'

'. . . against the manufacture of armaments . . .'

There was a low growl, and Theo murmured, 'Oh, *dear*! My lads don't like that!'

'. . . against drunkenness . . .'

And that did it. There was a concerted roar of '*What?*' and pandemonium broke out. There was a surge of movement, as if the whole hall was shifting, and Gideon turned to discover that at least half a dozen fist fights had already broken out, presumably between the rowdies and some of the sturdier Blue Ribbon supporters in the back stalls. It was disturbing to see that several fists had broken bottles in them, and there was some very hearty pushing and shoving going on, as some of the hooligans tried to force their way forward, impeded by a general movement of the cannier members of the audience, who were intent on making a rapid exit through the door.

Gideon grasped Theo's arm. 'Where the hell's Sorley? Can you see him? I hope to God he isn't caught up in that mob!'

Theo said, 'Dear me, I'd forgotten about the ancient retainer. Vilia would never forgive us if anything happened to him. Jermyn! P.J.! Can you see the old fellow anywhere? No, don't stand up, Jermyn, unless you want to invite trouble!'

The roughs had begun throwing things, now. Gideon could see that one man had a peashooter, and two or three others were fitting missiles

– coins, and bottle tops, he supposed – into the kind of pocket sling Sorley had taught him to use as a boy. He'd never quite matched Sorley's ability to bring down a hoodie crow on the wing. Then a whisky bottle went hurtling past his ear and he dived for the floor. 'Memories of the Crimea, dear boy?' Theo laughed, joining him a moment later. 'What was yours? A bottle? How commonplace. I, on the other hand, have just come near to being decapitated by a cabbage, though why the devil anyone should be carrying a cabbage at a political meeting I can't imagine!'

Gideon said grimly, 'They came prepared, that's clear enough, and a well-aimed cabbage could do plenty of damage. I hope to God the platform party knows how to duck. Move over, you're blocking my line of vision. What's happening?'

Theo raised his head and lowered it again hurriedly. 'They're hastening slowly – in the interests of their dignity, no doubt.'

Jermyn's voice suddenly drifted along to them. He was sitting cross-legged on the floor, protected by the benches. 'It's not uninteresting, you know. The bottle tops seem to be travelling faster than the coins. A combination of velocity, and spin, and wind resistance, I suppose.'

Peregrine James inquired politely, 'So? If one has to be hit by one of them, which would you recommend?'

The volley of missiles began to slacken after a while, and the shouting became more ragged, as if the militant element was losing its enthusiasm. Gideon could hear separate voices from behind. 'Come on, Jock! Come *on*! Let's get oot o' here.' And another one – 'Jamie! Och, Jamie! Gie's a hand. My legs is a' dwaibly!' And a third. 'Ah tellt ye! Did Ah no' tell ye? There's gonny be hell tae pay. Ah'm off. Ah'm no' waiting!'

Gideon and the others rose tentatively to their feet to see that most of what remained of the audience was massed round the door, each man's eyes studiously on the back of the man before him. But there were a few people clustered round the platform where the chairman, white as a sheet and looking as if he were about to be sick, had subsided into his chair again. Sebastian Donkin was kneeling on the floor beside Ian Barber, who lay spreadeagled and very still among the debris, his face a mask of blood.

4

From where Vilia sat on a rock on the hill, with Sorley perched quietly on another a few feet away, she could see no more than fifteen or twenty yards into the mist that surrounded them. There was a sharp drop in front, an almost vertical slope faced with boulders and scree, leggy heathers and yellowing bracken that tumbled straight down to the floor of the glen. She knew it was there, but she couldn't see it, because the glen itself was full of thin, teased-out masses of dirty white vapour. The wet wind tore at the shawl she had tied round her head, and tugged at the thick, enveloping coat, snatching the collar up to plaster it against her face. She was soaked through, and there was a relentless trickle of water running down her spine, and it felt as if there was at least a gallon of it in each of her boots. But she didn't mind, although she could no longer afford to ignore it.

She glanced over at Sorley, swathed in an enormous plaid, his wild white mane emerging from under a dejected-looking woollen toorie. Always thin, he had become as attenuated as a thread in this last year or so, and never seemed free of the congestion in his lungs. Nothing she could say would persuade him to stay indoors and cosset himself. He shouldn't have come up on the hill with her today, but she might as well have saved her breath, for all he had done was smile and follow her just the same. She must see that he had a hot toddy as soon as they got back, and tell Jenny in the kitchen to bully him into giving her every last stitch of his clothes for drying. Vilia smiled to herself, conscious of mothering Sorley more than she had ever mothered her sons. But she couldn't afford to lose him, the first friend she had ever had, and still, as he always had been, a part of her life.

Suddenly the wind dropped, as it so often did at this time of year, and it was possible to make oneself heard again.

'Did they find out what it was that hit him?'

'Och, no. It could haff been anything, they said. Something small, though. An inch further over, and it would maybe haff killed him. But except for losing his eye, he iss aal right. He wass lucky.'

'He was certainly lucky that Jermyn was there.' With the extreme efficiency that seldom, if ever, showed in his manner, Jermyn had made swift arrangements for Ian Barber to have the best medical attention, and hadn't hesitated to drag three of his acquaintances at the Edinburgh School of Medicine out of their beds in the middle of the night when it seemed that things weren't going too well. Theo had remarked, in the note Sorley had brought her, 'Such a strange thing, human nature. Only Ian Barber and young Jay standing between Jermyn's infant son and possession of Kinveil, and yet there was papa working harder than any of us to maintain the status quo!'

She shivered a little. It was the damp air. It would be the supreme irony if she were to catch pneumonia and find herself following Magnus so quickly to the grave, like some Indian widow committing suttee. And another kind of irony, since Perry Randall was due to arrive tomorrow.

If she could have stopped him from coming, she would. But it seemed he had landed at Liverpool just over a week before, and his letter had reached her only this morning. Kinveil wasn't the kind of place from which one could decamp at the drop of a hat, nor was it the kind of place where one told one's butler to say that madam was not at home.

She wondered what he was like now, at seventy-five. Such an attractive young man he had been all those years ago. In spite of everything, she still remembered her sense of dazzlement during that week in London in 1815, and the feeling that she lived and breathed only when he was with her. So exciting, so exhilarating, that innocent certainty that love was a kind of magic that would make everything right.

He hadn't said in his letter why he was coming. If he had been going to Glenbraddan, she might have understood it, although it was hard to believe that he should want to pay a last visit to the scenes of his youth. But old men sometimes had strange fancies, and . . .

She sniffed, brought back to the present by the realization that for some minutes the wind had been carrying to where she sat, motionless and shapeless like a rock atop another rock, a heavy, rank, familiar odour, sour and yet cloying – the smell of a stag in rut. Turning her head infinitely slowly, she peered into the shifting veils of mist to her right, but could see nothing other than mist-shapes, shadows and darkenings that might or might not have substance.

Sorley's whisper was so low that it scarcely disturbed the air. 'Nearer the cliff, mistress. He iss ferry close.'

And then, quite without warning and hugely magnified by echoes from cloud and mountain, there broke out the first low, grumbling roar of the stag calling. After a moment, it tightened and began to rise, higher and higher, wild and elemental, with challenge in it, and anguish, and a primeval desolation. Vilia sat transfixed, all her senses concentrated on the mad, deafening music, the anarchic call of the wild. At last, slowly, it began to die, burdened by echoes and re-echoes and the answers of other stags on the mountainside across the invisible glen.

'There!' Sorley breathed, just as she herself saw the familiar red deer antlers, huge and branched, and then the stag himself, the faint grey puff of breath from his last explosive grunt still hanging on the air before him, his head high, and the wide scarf of thick long hair round his neck clinging in lank elf locks. It was the end of October, and the weeks of feverish activity had taken their toll, so that he was in poor condition, but nothing could altogether diminish a stag's splendour. He was staring straight at them, but they didn't move a muscle and they were upwind of him, so that he hadn't caught their scent. Vilia could see, now, the twitching ears of a hind standing a little back from him, and, she thought, another beyond.

The wind gusted, and the mist enveloping their cloud room swirled and reformed, and the scudding clouds above raced faster.

And out of them, with shocking unexpectedness and silent at first as the mist itself, coasted a golden eagle riding on the wind. It was so large that it had to be a female, and she came in, not too low, over the stag's left shoulder. For a dreamlike moment it seemed as if she would glide on, on her great seven-foot wing span, past the misshapen rocks that were Vilia and Sorley, and disappear again into the mist.

But just as she reached it, the whole illusion was violently shattered. With a harsh, rasping shriek of air through the great pinion feathers of her wings, she soared into a powerful, banking turn and, side-slipping to lose height, swept back at terrifying speed straight towards the deer.

Fear of eagles bred into them from birth, the two hinds were already in panic-stricken flight before she made her turn, but they had impeded the stag and he was trapped between them and the precipice. As the eagle rushed upon him, her head with its dark predatory beak drawn back and the vicious yellow-framed talons extended on muscular, feathered legs, he tried to defend himself, backing a step and stamping, dropping the great spread of his antlers against the attack. The bird, frustrated, swept up and over him, high towards the roof of their eerie cavern in the clouds where, magnificent and menacing, she hung for the space of no more than a moment and then, half folding her tremendous wings, dropped like a stone in a dive of astonishing, perfectly controlled power, straight back for the stag, still blindly butting the air where she had been only seconds before.

'The neck!' Sorley breathed. 'She iss going for the neck!'

The stag recognized it, too, for he threw up his head almost at the last moment, and reared, his hooves striking out wildly at the mist, and the eagle, once more frustrated, pulled out of its stoop with a murderous screech of air and turned into another climb. Three times she tried it, and three times the stag drove her off, and then she changed her tactics. Vilia and Sorley, frozen on their rocks, had heard of eagles driving a deer over a precipice to its death, but had never seen it happen. The great bird used her wings now, not her talons, and the stag, at each ferocious swoop, recoiled a little further, and a little further, blind and crazed with terror. It seemed as if he were no longer aware of the cruel beak, the piercing talons, the bright, malevolent eyes, but only of the vast wings that rent the air fearsomely before him as the eagle plunged, and plunged, and plunged again.

Afterwards, Vilia realized that the whole drama had taken less than five minutes. They didn't see the end, which had never been in doubt, only the stag retreating back into the mist – staggering and unstable on its hind legs – and the eagle's wings closing for another stoop, and fanning out with a thunderous crack as, yet again, she pulled clear. But they heard it. Heard the scrabbling hooves on the loose scree, and the sound that was half squeal and half bark, and the rattling thud of a two-hundred-pound body hitting the cliff face once, twice, and then no more. The eagle, they knew, would be diving smoothly down beside her prey, half-folded wings held in close to her body so that she took the shape of a trident reversed.

Vilia let out her breath, slowly, at last, and after a while Sorley sighed, and murmured, 'Aye, well.'

She had no idea how long they had been sitting there, but she felt chilled and exhausted. Rising, she said, 'Yes. It will be dark soon.'

They scarcely spoke as they made their careful way downhill by the same route as they had come, choosing their footholds knowledgeably, stepping from heather tuft to heather tuft through the treacherous stretches of bog, following the swollen streams and skirting the great boulders, slippery with moss and lichen, that marked their path as surely as any signpost.

They were almost home when Vilia voiced the question that had been exercising her mind. 'That first attack. Eagles don't usually attack adult deer directly. Do you think she expected it to work?'

'*Dia!* Who knows? There wass an opportunity and she took it, wise bird. With the stupid beast roaring like that, she knew chust where he wass, and thought he would haff no time to run.'

'And when it didn't work, she wouldn't be put off.'

Wheezing a little, Sorley said, '*Ged bheirear tràigh dhiom, cha toirear timcheall.*' Though I cannot go by the shore, I can go the long way round.

Vilia stared at him. 'Or to put it another way,' she said, 'if at first you don't succeed . . .'

'Chust so. Chust so.'

5

Perry Randall sat back in his carriage, trying to find a position out of the draught. Although it was almost November, the cutting wind sweeping down Loch an Vele reminded him of nothing so much as the wind of the Hudson in March, but there the resemblance ended. The barren, compact grandeur of this land of his early manhood had nothing in common with the undulating plains of Westchester, open, and quiet, and affluent. It was thirty-six years since he had last travelled this road, and another fourteen before that, and his view of it had changed, as it had changed before. In '29 he had thanked God that this wasn't his country any more, but now he was a little less sure. The American Civil War, six months over, had distorted all the things he loved most about his adopted land. The rough idealism had turned sour and self-seeking; the wide open spaces were closing in and would soon crush the Indians who belonged there; and the wide open American heart was closing, too. All unavoidable developments, he supposed, but as the real pioneering days had gone, so had gone the eager spirit. America, now was not so very different from Europe; it was only its problems that differed.

He sighed, and shrugged to himself. It made no odds now. What remained of his life would be lived out between Boston and New York. His choice had been made too long ago.

The carriage rounded the last bend and Kinveil came into view. It didn't welcome him. It never had. It was too stiff-necked and arrogant, there on its rock; too alone and self-contained. Only when the sun shone, and white clouds scudded across a blue sky, and there was colour in the landscape, had he ever responded to it; only when the wind was the kind that stirred the blood instead of chilling it. Strange that for fifty years he should have been obsessed by the woman who was so much a part of it. Stranger still that he had never quite drawn the parallel until now. Which mood? Which mood, now that she was no longer young, or middle-aged, but old? He had no idea. Too much had happened in these absent years for him to read her mind as once he had thought he could. Drawing the furred collar of his coat more closely about him, he leaned forward to tell the coachman to stop under the rowan tree.

Vilia stood at the window of the Long Gallery and watched him descend from the britzscha, wondering whether his choice of carriage meant that he now found it necessary to lie down on long journeys. He was almost six years older than she was, and his physical condition must have deteriorated since she had last seen him, fourteen years ago at Shona's famous dinner party. She hoped that he wasn't really *old*, because that would offend her in a foolish kind of way. And yet better, perhaps, that he was.

She saw him speak to the stable boy who had come running, another sprig of the tribe of Frasers who had served Kinveil for as long as she could remember. The boy grinned and bobbed his head, and then Perry, with a word to his coachman and another to his valet, turned and set his foot on the causeway. He was wearing a broad-brimmed, low-crowned wideawake hat, and the new style of caped travelling coat known as an Inverness. Was that coincidence, or was there a trace of his old habit of irony about it? The soft brown tweed of the cape was lined with fur, and he turned the fur collar up against the damp wind that was whipping in from the west. Vilia couldn't tell whether he had put on weight, or whether it was age that had taken the spring from his step. At least he wasn't leaning on a cane.

He glanced up, as if he knew she must be there, and raised his hat an inch or two and smiled. It was a shock to see his face so heavily lined, and the brows that had always been straight and dark now white as salt. The neatly trimmed sidewhiskers curved down to stop at either side of his chin, but he was otherwise clean shaven. Even from this distance, she could see that the old, familiar sparkle was still in his eyes, although Shona had told her that his sight was failing. So instead of merely smiling in return, she raised her hand in acknowledgement.

Perry had known there wouldn't be a servant in the place he had ever met before, but the butler admitted to being a Fraser and Perry was able to say, 'Robert's son?'

'Indeed, yess, Mr Randall, sir. And if I may make so bold, there iss many a time he hass been speaking to me of you.'

'Kindly, I hope?'

'Gootness, gracious, yess, sir! Now, will you be wishing to freshen after your chourney, before I take you to Mistress Cameron?'

Cameron? That old Highland habit of women keeping their maiden names. He smiled a little. 'Yes. Thank you, Fraser.'

He had been given a room at the foot of the tower. Did she think he was too old to climb a few stairs? He washed, shivering a little, and changed into the fresh shirt his valet laid out for him, then shivered again as Fraser led him across the courtyard, through the Great Hall, and up to the Gallery. Thank God there was a fire.

She rose to welcome him. 'It has been a long time. You look cold. Come and warm yourself, and tea will be here directly.' He was a marvellously handsome man still, despite the lines, and hadn't shrunk with age, as so many people did. Except for a slight stoop about the shoulders, he held himself erect, and although his figure had thickened he was tall enough to stand it. His coat fitted him to perfection, and she was glad to see he hadn't succumbed to the four-in-hand necktie, but still wore something like the cravat of his youth. And still with the opal-eyed serpent pin in it that Mungo had given him. She faltered for a moment, at that.

She had given some thought as to how she should treat him. Not as the merest acquaintance. There was, after all, no one else to see. As someone she had known well, long ago, and had lost touch with? Better. And it had the merit of being true.

She walked over to him and took his hand to lead him to the fire. His fingers were cold as ice, and she exclaimed, 'Goodness! You're frozen. Do come and warm yourself.'

But he was in some kind of dream, staring at her as if there were something he didn't understand. She thought that perhaps he didn't see her very well, and that would be a pity, for she had taken the greatest trouble to look her best. She had touched her cheeks and lips with rouge, and chosen her most flattering gown. Only since her hair had turned white had she begun wearing the soft rose colours she had shunned in the past; fair-haired women in pink had always been ten a penny. But she'd had to give up wearing green now, because it made her eyes look hard as chips of emerald against the pallor of skin and hair.

He shook himself free of his daze, and the glinting smile came back. 'Do you realize that I have never seen you at Kinveil before? Here, in your natural habitat? This is the first time we have ever been perched on this benighted rock together.'

She laughed a little tightly. 'Was that why you were staring at me so strangely?'

His smile broadened. He looked very like himself. 'Strangely? Anything but that. I was merely stunned by the combined impact of recollection and your indestructible beauty.'

'Thank you.' Her tone was noticeably dry.

He knew better than to pursue it. 'I can still see Mungo Telfer standing where you are now, wearing that kindly but suspicious expression that always came over his face when I put in an appearance. I was a sad trial to him, I fear.'

'Not altogether.' She bent to stir the logs. 'He spoke of you when he was dying, you know. Your failings didn't escape him, but he was fond of you. Dear Mungo. The kindest man I have ever known.'

'Yes.' He was silent for a moment. 'It's difficult to realize that this is only my second visit to Kinveil since he died. The first time in '29, when there was no one here but Luke.'

He was fishing, but he didn't catch anything except a bitten-off 'Yes'.

She was reminded, just the same, of Luke's vicious denunciation of her, in this very room, three or four days after Perry had been here and talked too much, either of intent, or by mistake. Luke had called her a whore, and treated her like one. He had died next day. She had always wondered what Perry had said, and why. Should she ask him, now that it didn't matter any more? Or let the question lie – for that same reason.

A maid came in with the tea. Another Fraser, Perry wondered? She had the look of it. He said, 'Is Sorley still with you? How is he?'

'Oh, well enough. Milk? Lemon? These macaroons are very good. His chest is troubling him. I can't persuade him to take things easier, and settle down peaceably in his new cottage, and indeed I don't think I could bear it if he did. He has always been so much part of my life. So he goes on living here, as always, and makes an occasional trip to inspect his cottage as if it were the show piece in some exhibition of domestic design. Quite funny, really, but a little sad.' She cleared her throat. 'You know, of course, that a number of your old acquaintances have died in these last few years. Including Drew. Shona must have written to you.'

'Yes. I was sad to hear it.' The child of joy, whose birth had brought nothing but pain and tragedy. The irresponsibly begotten son of two unhappy people who had fallen too much in love; the son Perry had known only as a stranger.

He went on, 'I understand that Shona intends coming to live with you here.' His mind reeled at the thought. It was thirty years since that incestuous marriage, but time had changed nothing. With Vilia and Shona alone in each other's company all the year round, it would be so easy for Vilia to make a slip. And if Shona were to discover the truth, Perry thought the knowledge might kill her. It would, certainly, destroy her serenity for ever.

'Yes. Marchfield is too full of memories for her, and she thinks that Jermyn and Madge and the children – you won't know yet that they have a new son? – should have the house to themselves. We will be company for each other, and might even rub along quite well.'

'Is it wise?'

She had never tolerated criticism. Coldly, she said, 'Wise?'

He shrugged, and didn't pursue that, either. Foolishly, he had forgotten how many topics had always been barred to the two of them. Everything he thought of seemed to lead back, somehow, to things that couldn't be spoken of. Their relationship had been so episodic, and each episode had brought its own repercussions. The fateful evening at the Northern Meeting ball, that had brought the rift between himself and Charlotte into the open. That single week in 1815 when they had been wholly in love, and Drew had been conceived. Then the meeting at Marchfield seven years later; he had gone away from that filled with a driving need for success; she had almost married Luke Telfer. There had been thirteen years between the meeting at Marchfield and the idyll at the Chaumière de la Reine, and this time he had left with another need – to cut her out of his heart, and the knowledge of Drew and Shona out of his consciousness. So he had married Sara, who had given him three other children; and Vilia had come home to Scotland and married Magnus, who had given her Kinveil. Since then, there had been only the dinner party in 1851, and Perry didn't know what repercussions there had been from that, if any. He only knew that, since then, he had never quite stopped worrying about the change in her. He had never seen her like that before, implacably cold and brittle; hell-bent on some purpose he hadn't been able to identify.

There wasn't a name he could mention, a subject he could broach, without reminding them both of the troubles they had shared. And yet not shared. That was the real difficulty, that they had been forced to bear what should have been joint burdens, not together, but alone. Only by talking could they drain away the poisons of the past, and yet talk of any real significance was impossible while they remained on such circumspect terms. Later, perhaps, he told himself, when they had spoken of what he had come to speak about – even though, from the moment he had set foot in the Long Gallery, he had become increasingly afraid that she had strayed too far from him. As if it were yesterday, he remembered that same feeling, that same sense of doom, when he had gone to her on a Monday evening at Marchfield in 1822.

Somehow, they carried on a desultory conversation until it was time to change for dinner, and at table they found safe topics in steel, and armaments, and what would happen in world markets now that the Civil War was over. Afterwards, he said, 'An admirable dinner, Vilia. Thank you. I had forgotten the excellence of the hill mutton here-abouts. May I bring my brandy to the drawing-room?'

'Of course. You may have whisky, if you'd rather. I'm sure Sorley wouldn't object to your sampling his own private product. It's very pale, and quite distinctive.'

'Bought up the exciseman, has he?'

The drawing-room, nowadays, was in what had once been Mungo's study, and subsequently Luke's. Perhaps Magnus's, too; Perry didn't know. But he could still hear the breathless, waiting note in Luke's voice when he had said, 'Wish me happy, Uncle Perry. Vilia and I are to be married.'

For Kinveil, it was an indulgent, civilized room, with carpets and pine panelling instead of slate floors and rough walls, and there were curtains to shut out the bleak night. The chairs and sofas belonged to no particular period and were notable only for being comfortable. There wasn't even a family portrait on the walls. Perry took out his spectacles to study a pair of watercolour landscapes. 'I like these. They have a look of Turner about them, but they're not, are they?'

'A young man called MacTaggart.'

He raised his hand to remove his spectacles again.

'Don't take them off on my account.'

It was so unmistakably malicious that it broke the spell that had been binding him. He laughed aloud. 'Yes,' he said. 'And don't try to tell me you haven't been stifling an "ouch" every time you've had to bend down. A touch of rheumatism, my dear?' With his glasses on, he could see that she had been adding colour to her face, and not very competently, either.

'Certainly not. It's merely that I slipped on the hill the other day, and pulled a muscle.'

'I see. And you're using the only comfortable room in the castle because it has sentimental memories of Mungo, no doubt?'

'As a matter of fact, yes,' she said, and added rashly, 'Why else?'

'I can think of several reasons. I recall Mungo saying that, much though he loved Kinveil, his ageing bones didn't.'

'That was Mungo. He wasn't used to stone walls.'

'Oh, Vilia! Vilia! Admit it! In another few weeks you will be seventy years old. There's nothing illegal in a little self-indulgence.' He sat down opposite her, and leaned forward, his forearms resting on his thighs and his hands clasped, in a way she well remembered. 'Do you know why I have come here?'

'No.'

'Sara is dead, rest her soul, and so is Magnus. You and I haven't very much time left. For fifty years our lives have been entangled, and the

695

way has never been clear for us. Now it is, and, God help me, I still love you. I came to ask whether, late though it is, we mightn't perhaps spend our last years together.'

Her eyes snapped open, exaggeratedly. 'Are you asking me to marry you?'

'Yes, my dear. Is that so hard to believe?'

She was looking at him as if he were some laboratory specimen under the microscope. 'Yes, it is.'

'Why?'

'Why?' she repeated. 'Do you not remember that night at Shona's? You treated me as if you scarcely knew me, as if all contact between us was dead. I was ill with nerves, and you scarcely gave me a look or a word. It seemed almost as if you were summing me up, and not liking what you saw. For fifteen – sixteen? – years I had *tried* to convince myself that everything was over, but I didn't want it to be. And then you told me as clearly as if you had said it in words that I was no longer of any interest to you at all.'

He could remember the tension in her, and how he had put it down to Magnus's recalcitrance because he had been so sure that their last parting had alienated her from him, and that the tension couldn't be on his account. And yet that wasn't quite true. While he had hoped that everything wasn't over between them, even more, he had feared that it wasn't – because that would be an end of his precarious peace of mind. On that evening in 1851, he had almost wanted to assume that she no longer cared about him, but the assumption hadn't stood the test of time, and in the years since then he had perversely chosen to treat the memory of that evening as if it hadn't happened, or hadn't mattered; had chosen to pretend to himself that the only barrier between them was the barrier that had been set up on their last morning in France. A barrier that – surely – must have begun to crumble by now. If he hadn't brought himself to believe that, he would not have been here at Kinveil today.

He said, 'Were we both acting, then? I was trying to protect you, you know. Everyone in that room thought we were only the barest acquaintances, but I had the feeling that Theo was watching us all the time. Perhaps I was over careful.'

'As far as Theo was concerned, certainly you were. He knows all about us.' She said it quite casually.

'*Theo* knows? *All* about us?' He took a deep breath. 'And who else, may I ask?'

'There's no need to look so thunderous! I didn't mean "all". I meant only about our – our involvement in 1815.' He was staring at her and, astoundingly, she giggled. 'He thinks you more or less raped me, by the way.'

'Thank you very much! *Who else knows?*'

'No one but Gideon.' Suddenly, her eyes were hostile. 'You are wondering why I should have told them? Very well. I told them when Drew ran away with Shona. You accused me once of "letting that happen". You seemed to think I had made no attempt to stop it, and that hurt me so much that I wasn't prepared to enlighten you. Well, I will tell you now. I was driven to such desperation when I couldn't persuade Theo or Gideon to go after them, and stop them, that I had no choice but to explain why it was necessary. It convinced them, but they arrived too late.' She paused for a moment, and then went on with a shrug, 'Theo is inquisitive. It's possible he may have guessed that we met again in France.'

So she had tried, after all. He had never, deep in his heart, thought otherwise. 'Should I apologize?'

She shrugged again, dismissively. 'It's of no importance now.'

'Isn't it?' It had always been a weakness that she couldn't look into other people's hearts, except perhaps Mungo's, and, for a little time – when she was young and loving – his own. He said, 'I don't think you understand, even yet, how I feel about you. There have been occasions when I haven't relished what you have said or done. I still believe you should have insured against Shona and Drew ever meeting in the first place. I still find it totally impossible to understand why you didn't tell me about Drew when he was still a child, and I came to you at Marchfield. And at Shona's dinner party I found that, quite simply, I couldn't watch you goading Magnus in the way you did, a man whose mind was no match for yours. But all those things are quite irrelevant. However much I may disapprove, they make no difference at all to the fact that I love you.'

'Don't they? Perhaps you should have told me that before. I saw you watching me when I was "goading" Magnus, as you put it, and your distaste could scarcely have been more evident. And because I thought *you* didn't care, I went on, just to prove that I didn't care. What a chapter of misunderstandings our life has been.' She sat, turning the Kinveil ring on her finger, as he had so often seen her do in the past when she was thinking something over, trying to decide what to say next. After a while, she looked up. 'I *don't* care now, Perry. I learned my lesson that night, and I don't think you can complain if I learned it too well. That was the end, for me. There is nothing left at all now, and hasn't been for years.'

'Not even a lingering warmth?'

There was death in his eyes if she had looked, or if, looking, she had perceived it. But, her gaze on the ring again, she said, 'Not even that. What would be the purpose?'

'Must there always be a purpose?'

Her surprise was real. 'Of course! It's purpose, surely, that keeps one alive. How else can one survive hardship, and misery, and tragedy?'

'Yes, but . . .' Suddenly, a great weariness overcame him, and he felt the familiar tightening in his chest and the fluttering sensation that warned him he must be calm. There was a flaw in her argument, he knew, but it didn't seem worth making an issue of it. He smiled crookedly, and said, 'And what happens when the purpose fails?'

'I don't know.'

Neither did he – but he would find out, now that his was gone. The end. The bitter end. The end of an old song that had first been sung fifty years ago, when for the space of one brief week they had been wholly themselves, without artifice, in each other's company.

There were tears in his throat, but his voice sounded normal enough when he said, 'You don't know? But returning to Kinveil was always your purpose, and you have achieved that. Is there some other purpose now?'

She was grateful for an opportunity to change the subject, because although she had no feeling for Perry Randall now, and doubted his for her, she had always disliked resurrecting the past. It was always a mistake to go back, to a door that had been closed, or a coffin screwed down.

'Yes, in a way,' she said, pursing her lips, and then unpursing them, because she knew it emphasized the lines. 'I only have Kinveil for my lifetime – and, of course, only if I don't remarry.'

She smiled charmingly, as if she knew he would understand that this hadn't been a factor in her refusal of him, but only a minor element in a different equation.

If he hadn't felt so tired, he could almost have laughed at her sublime faith in her ability to mislead him. 'Indeed?' he said. 'What an inconsiderate provision.'

She gazed thoughtfully into the fire. 'Magnus never succeeded in getting the better of me in life, but thought that death gave him the opportunity he had been looking for. The marriage provision doesn't worry me greatly, as it happens.'

'No.'

She looked at him sharply, but he went on, 'You can't have expected him to leave the place to you outright. What about his daughter – Juliana, isn't it?' Distantly, he remembered a pretty child with enormous blue eyes. There had been some kind of tragedy a few years ago, he couldn't remember what. So much easier nowadays to remember the happenings of fifty years ago than of five.

'He had a prejudice against managing women, I can't think why.' There was a gleam of wicked humour in her eyes, and he responded to it. 'He was afraid Juley might turn into one, so he bequeathed Kinveil to her eldest son.'

'Does she have one?'

'No. She did – Shona *must* have told you! – but he died in India.'

'I can't imagine what Magnus was thinking of, allowing his daughter to go out there. Couldn't you have stopped it?'

Vilia shrugged. 'She thought she was in love. And really, it's silly to talk of the place as if it's a death-trap for Europeans. Clearly, it can't be, otherwise there wouldn't be an Indian empire, because all the empire-builders would have been killed off.'

'So you made no attempt to stop her?'

'Why should I?'

He was remembering now. The girl's husband and child had died in India, but she had survived. And come back to marry Theo. He said, without expression, 'So she's married to Theo now, is she?'

'Well, she was, but she's left him. I've no idea why, but she's simply disappeared into thin air.'

She didn't seem troubled, which struck Perry as extremely odd. He remembered thinking he could detect her fine Italian hand in that piece of matchmaking, and had assumed she was hoping the pair of them would have children. 'You've no idea why?' he repeated drily.

She tossed her head. 'Oh, *that*? That was all nonsense, despite what you said. He has been a perfectly good husband to her.'

'Did he tell you so?'

'Of course not. It's scarcely the kind of thing a son discusses with his mother. Anyway, Ian Barber is the heir, and a fine mess he will make of it, especially if he tries to run Glenbraddan and Kinveil in harness.'

'Will he?'

'I imagine so. Edward Blair is at his last gasp, and Glenbraddan will go to Isa, which means Ian. Did you know he had an accident a week ago, speaking at one of those rowdy Reform meetings? There was a riot, and he was hit on the temple. He lost the sight of his right eye, but he could very easily have been killed.'

Perry remembered the clever-stupid seventeen-year-old at Shona's party. Ian was his grandson, but he always found it hard to think of him as such. It would hurt Vilia to think Kinveil was going to Ian. 'He and Isa have a son now, haven't they, after a string of daughters?'

'Yes, and *so* annoying of them! Otherwise, if I had outlived Ian, which I fully intend to do – for I have made up my mind to go on to a hundred, and Ian has always struck me as one of those men who worries himself into an early grave – it would have gone to Jermyn's new son, Neil. Or to Peregrine James's son, when he deigns to marry. He is *sure* to have sons, dozens of them! He's that kind of young man!'

Perry couldn't help but laugh. That was the real Vilia speaking, the Vilia he loved, and he knew just what she meant even though he'd never set eyes on Peregrine James. Another of his grandsons! A rush of longing came over him, and he said, 'Vilia, my dearest dear. Won't you think again? Even if we only had a few good years together, wouldn't it be worth something? What do a pile of rocks and a few acres mean, that you should be so concerned about their destiny? Does it really matter whether the Barber child rules over them, or someone of Cameron blood? You can't measure happiness or fulfilment in those terms!'

Her eyes turned to him, the water-nymph's eyes that had drained his soul away fifty years ago. 'Can't I? Oh, *can't* I? Kinveil has mattered to me too much, for too long. All the awfulness, all the misery, all the betrayals. My father took Kinveil from me when I was seven years old. I've always wanted it back, and I *will* have it back, wholly and completely.'

Which mood? he had wondered. Which mood, now that she was no longer young, or middle-aged, but old. He had his answer, and he could feel the chill settling in his bones.

He rose to his feet, as he had done once before in this room, with Luke Telfer, when to continue the conversation had been beyond him. He said, as he had said then, 'Forgive me, but I have had a tiring day, and I must make an early start in the morning.'

She was taken aback but not distressed. 'So soon? I had expected you to stay longer.'

He swallowed with some difficulty, trying to prevent the exhaustion and defeat from showing in his face, and said, 'Stay? No, I think not. You have given me my answer. Good-bye, Vilia. For the last time. Good-bye, my very dearest.'

Then he took her hand, and kissed it, and went. It was as much as he could do to reach his room before the tears blinded him.

6

All Paris was at Longchamp on June sixth, 1867, to see the grand review of the French army. Some people said there were to be sixty thousand soldiers assembled, but others, watching the furious last-minute brushing and polishing going on before the arrival of the sovereigns, put the number at only half that. It didn't matter. There were a lot. And they looked magnificent – grenadiers in their tall bearskin shakos; riflemen in yellow-striped tunics; green-plumed chasseurs; turbaned, baggy-trousered zouaves in red and blue, with *vivandières* skipping pertly along beside them with brandy kegs slung from their shoulders.

The ceremonial cannon thundered out from high above the racecourse, and then the Emperor Napoleon III rode into sight, mounted on a magnificent black charger and surrounded by Spahis. On his right was the Czar of Russia and on his left King Wilhelm of Prussia. They had come to Paris not to see the army showing off, but to visit the Exposition Universelle; however, *noblesse* obliged, and if Louis-Napoleon wanted them to admire his troops, they were prepared to do the decent thing. Bismarck, in the King of Prussia's train, was genuinely interested.

Led by Marshal Canrobert, hero of Africa and the Crimea, foot-soldiers and cavalry and artillery marched past the imperial stand, spotless, impeccably polished, and splendidly dashing, and the climax was a tremendous charge of ten thousand cavalry – lancers, hussars, cuirassiers, and Chasseurs d'Afrique – who swept across the field at full gallop to pull up, all standing, no more than fifteen feet away from the royal party. Saluting with drawn sabres, they cried out 'Vive l'Empereur!' and their homage was echoed in a great roar from every corner of the field.

'Poof! It's warm,' Juliana said when it was all over. 'Arsène, I must go back now. Do you intend to stay?'

The tall young man with the flowing brown hair turned to look down at her, his eyes glowing. 'Is it not magnificent? This is France – the France of Malakoff, and Magenta, and Solferino, the greatest military power in Europe!'

'Yes, Arsène. But I must go.'

He grasped her hand. 'Why must you? It is such a beautiful day. Why don't we go down to one of those little inns by the river, and have a glass of wine, and sit there and rest our souls?'

'It sounds delightful, but I can't. Monsieur would murder me.'

'Why? Surely he can spare you to me for a little?'

She smiled. 'Tonight, of all nights? It would be as much as my life is worth. It was only as a very special concession that I was given leave to come at all, and I shall have to stay late to make up for it.'

'You would, anyway,' he said gloomily. 'You always do on such occasions.'

She smiled. 'You make it sound as if it was by choice! But I can see you have no intention of accompanying me, so I shall go alone.' She stood on tiptoe to kiss his cheek, and then turned and began to struggle away through the throng.

In the fiacre, she suddenly felt weary. The baby was due in less than two months, but Madame, who had worked through her own pregnancies, had been very understanding about it. Not for the first time, Juliana began trying to calculate whether her small savings, added to what remained of the money she had brought with her to France, would be enough. Arsène earned almost nothing from his writing although he was convinced he would, one day, and she couldn't go to Gaby, who had made it very clear that the Marcabruns lived at a level of debt that Juliana could scarcely envisage. But she thought she would be able to manage – just. Theo had been right about one thing; she did want a child. But she also wanted a worthwhile relationship with its father. She had hoped to find it with Arsène, the charming Bohemian student whose dedication to literature was tempered by the crude honesty of the *demi-monde*. Juliana, recognizing the vulgarity of that world, found it indescribably refreshing after the hypocrisy and self-delusion that had contaminated the whole of her six-year marriage to Theo. But she knew now that the life she shared with Arsène wouldn't last, although she could not tell whether that was because of some weakness in him, or the emotional numbness that still possessed her, making it hard to give and almost impossible to receive.

They reached the rue de la Paix at last, and she descended before No. 7, the tall, iron-balconied building that housed the Maison Worth et Bobergh, to be greeted by Monsieur Carlsson, *premier commis*, with the information that Miss Mary and Miss Esther had been screaming for her this thirty minutes past. Juliana didn't like Isidor Carlsson, or any of the other young men whose province was the selling of fabrics. With their curled hair, pearl tie-pins, turquoise rings, and tight-fitting coats, they all seemed to be trying to pretend they were diplomatic *attachés*. She said 'Thank you', and began, heavily, to climb the stairs. She couldn't understand why Miss Mary and Miss Esther, *premières vendeuses*, should want her. Juliana's province was the records department. Worth and Bobergh had customers throughout the civilized world, some of whom rarely visited Paris, and it was Juliana's responsibility to keep an up-to-date record of every lady's size, height, colouring, peculiarities, and tastes. It was of paramount importance to be sure that two Russian duchesses, ordering by letter, didn't find themselves wearing the same gown at the same soirée in far-off St Petersburg.

Juliana's path rarely crossed that of Monsieur Worth and his lady assistants. Racking her brain, she could think of no crisis that might have occurred in her domain during her few hours' absence, and indeed none had. The crisis that had arisen was of the kind that involved the entire house.

As the Czar had been driving back with the emperor from Long-champ, someone – a Polish patriot, it was believed, but what did *that* matter? said Miss Esther, who knew her priorities – had leaped out of the crowd and fired a pistol at him. No, no, said Miss Esther, no one had been hurt, but just think of the problems of protocol! Should tonight's great ball at the Tuileries be cancelled? And what of the dinner at the Russian embassy preceding it? In the end, it had been decided that everything should go ahead as planned, but the Empress Eugénie felt that the sumptuous gown Worth had made for the occasion was no longer appropriate. Something quieter, something tactfully sympathetic, would be more suitable, and Worth and Bobergh had just three-and-a-half hours in which to produce it. The empress never appeared in the same gown twice.

'Monsieur is already at the palace,' Miss Esther said. 'But I can spare none of the *vendeuses* to assist him. We have all the other ladies to prepare for as well.' Worth insisted that, on the evening of any great occasion, his customers all came to the rue de la Paix so that he or one of his senior assistants might take a last look and see that everything was as it should be. Sometimes he might make a minor adjustment, sometimes alter the accessories; what he produced was not a gown but a whole toilette. As a result, at ten o'clock on the evening of a fashionable ball, there was a whole queue of princesses, duchesses, and countesses in his salons, consuming Madeira and *pâté de foie gras* while they waited to pass his inspection.

'*You* must go, therefore,' Miss Esther said. 'I have made a selection of fabrics for you to take, and you will also take four of the seamstresses, not the machine girls, but those who are nimble with their fingers. One of the salesmen will accompany you, in case Monsieur wishes to send back for anything.'

The empress's chamberlains had been warned, and Miss Juliana and her girls were tossed like hot chestnuts from one blue-and-silver-cuffed hand to another, along the endless corridors of the Tuileries and up to the wardrobe room, housed immediately above the imperial dressing-room. Monsieur Worth, who had not wasted time changing into court dress, was reclining dreamily on a chaise longue, neat and spruce in his velvet-collared black coat, floppy tie, and gold-buttoned shirt, his drooping moustaches twitching a little, and his high brow furrowed in meditation as he contemplated the plain white gown already draped over a crinoline cage on one of the four lay figures, made to Her Imperial Majesty's precise measurements, that permanently inhabited the wardrobe. Worth's hallmark was perfection of cut and fit and finish, and there was no question of producing an entirely new gown in such a short time; alteration was necessary. But since Worth was Worth, that meant transformation.

For the next two hours, the wardrobe was a scene of furious activity, no less urgent for the deferential silence that ruled. Off with the existing trimmings, said Monsieur in his Fenland French, and on with – no, not that. That, perhaps? No. This, possibly? Umm, no. What about this? Just possible; drape it more to the left, Miss Juliana. No; try the right. No. That white tulle, the one with the silver stitches. One layer over the skirt. Two layers. Three layers. From time to time, a lady-in-waiting's voice would come up through the speaking tube from the dressing-room below. How was Monsieur Worth progressing? Monsieur waved to Miss Juliana to deal with it.

But at last it was done, and there was a new white-and-silver gown ready for the empress to wear, luxuriously quiet and unimpeachably tactful. Gloves, fan and shoes were entrusted to a lady-in-waiting, and the lay figure itself was set in an elevator that descended through the floor directly into the dressing-room below. Monsieur made his way downstairs by the more orthodox route to ensure that Her Imperial Majesty was correctly jewelled for the toilette.

Juliana and the seamstresses, on the way out, passed the covered courtyard where supper was to be served that night. It looked very inviting with its floor crowded with tables, trailing greenery round the Corinthian marble columns, the swagged frieze gleaming gold, the chandeliers glittering, and flowers massed in the great blue vases with their imperial 'N'. There were garlands of little electric lights in the gardens, and Strauss himself was to conduct the orchestra. Juliana almost wished she had been invited.

Wishing for the moon! She shrugged, and hurried the girls back to the rue de la Paix. There was so much still to do, and scarcely time to swallow a mouthful of *pâté* and a glass of Madeira purloined from the salon before the great ladies began to arrive. Miss Mary and Miss Esther didn't need Juliana's files for the Princess von Metternich, scarlet-lipped, large-nosed, and looking, as she herself said, like a rather chic monkey; or the mischievous Comtesse de Pourtalès; or the impossible Princess Rimsky-Korsakov. But there were others, not dozens but scores, who were not quite such *habituées*, and about whom memories had to be refreshed. It was well into the small hours by the time Juliana was free to go home.

She thought at first that the pains were only colic, but then, exhausted and frightened, realized that they weren't. She wasn't ready, and nothing had been arranged. Loosening her vice-like grip on Arsène's arm, she gasped, 'Go for Madame Louis, *please*! She will know what to do. She has had . . .' The pain tore through her, but after a few moments, she was able to go on. 'She has had five children. Go, *please*.'

Frantically, she tried to remember what had happened before, and everything Richard had said before little Luke was born. There was something . . .

When the concierge arrived, Juliana stammered, 'There was something a Hungarian doctor discovered, something to do with . . . What was it? *What was it?*'

'*Ce qu'il y a de certain, c'est qu'il n'y a pas de quoi fouetter un chat!* What should a Hungarian doctor know, *enfin*? Calm yourself, madame!'

'No, it was important. Something to do with the after-birth fever that women die from. What was it? *What was it?*'

She remembered, just before all power to think deserted her. 'Chlorine water!' she moaned. 'Please, Madame Louis. Please wash your hands in chlorine water!' And then it all began.

She had no idea how long it was before she became conscious of the sound of a small, reedy wail. Somewhere in the suffocatingly warm world outside her body, she could hear Madame Louis grumbling away to herself, in the way concierges always did, and then the words took shape.

'My fourth came early, monsieur, you know. Keep him cosy, they told me, and I did, and look what a fine, strapping lad he's turned out to be! You couldn't wish for a finer, now could you, Monsieur Victor? But I am a better shape for children than madame, *bien entendu*, so it's all for the best. And you'll like having a little girl, won't you, monsieur?'

Juliana smiled, and then sighed, and drifted off into an empty, aching sleep.

7

Vilia was not altogether surprised when she heard in the summer of 1867 that Perry Randall was dead. Although she had thought him physically well-looking, she had noticed that by the end of the evening he had seemed unnaturally tired and drawn. What a very short marriage theirs would have been, she reflected with a faint smile, if by some aberration she had said yes.

The news didn't even send her back to the past, remembering. She had been through all that, so often, in the five or six years after 1851, when she had never been quite herself. Now, all she did was shake her head as if it had been someone else who had been involved, someone else who had been blinded by his charm all those years ago and had remained, inexplicably, under his spell until at last, slowly and with great labour, she had freed herself from it. Now, all she felt was a faint, lingering scorn for that long-ago weakness. If he had been stronger, how different her life would have been. What a wasteful thing human love was! So much passion, so much anguish, and all to no purpose. Better, infinitely better, to lavish one's ardour on earth and stone, lasting, predictable – responsive, even, in a comforting, unemotional way. Kinveil would still be here when she was dust.

She thought of all the others who were already dust, and for a moment had the curious sensation of having mislaid the greater part of her life. So many of the people who had touched it were gone. Andrew, and dear Mungo, and Luke. Drew, Magnus, and now Perry. And Charlotte Blair, and Harriet; and Edward, on a dark, sleeting day in February. Of all her contemporaries, there was no one left but Sorley, the first of them all. It was as if the two of them, now, had been transported back into childhood, when Kinveil was their world and belonged only to them. Was that, she wondered, why she had begun to see things again with the uncluttered vision of her early years, when problems were clearly defined and their solutions self-evident, and all that was needed to settle them was a little application? Or was it just a sign of age? She didn't think so, because the oddest thing about growing old, she had found, was that she felt just the same inside as she had always done. It was as if, running through her veins and nerves, there was some kind of basic, unchanging essence of Vilia.

She laughed, mocking herself, and turned her face towards the sea.

Chapter Two

1

When, in November 1867, Vilia yielded to Shona's pleading and summoned the family to Kinveil for Christmas and the New Year, no one but Amy was pleased.

'What?' Lavinia exclaimed to Gideon. 'Spend weeks on end in that freezing barracks of a place – because, take my word for it, the roads will be impassable by New Year and we'll never get away again! No, thank you. *What* a pity I have so many commitments in London! Besides, William and Vilia don't get on. She thinks he's stuffy.'

Peregrine James didn't even bother to manufacture an excuse, but his letter of regret was a model of its kind.

Otherwise, Gideon was interested to note, everyone had turned up, including the Barbers from Glenbraddan – Grace, Ian, Isa, the five girls, and four-year-old Jay, as well as Petronella, now in her mid-thirties, still a suffragist, and proving it by still being single. Theo had come up from Marchfield with Jermyn and Madge and the children, little Drusilla, Sophie, and two-year-old Neil. Jermyn said he and Madge both had work to do – he on his repeating field gun, and she on a play script – and they had thought they might as well work at Kinveil as anywhere else, while Theo announced plaintively that he needed a rest after steering Lauristons' through yet another period of financial crisis and bank collapses. 'Peregrine James says, and I agree with him, that the time has come to turn Lauristons' into a limited liability company. Capital of about £155,000 in £100 shares, dear boy, and we haven't settled the family holding yet. Problems, problems! I can't imagine how I keep so calm.'

There was another guest, who was a surprise. Francis Randall. His father, it seemed, had left a few personal bequests. 'Private mementoes,' Francis said, 'that he wished me to deliver in person. It is a very real pleasure for me to do so.' He was thirty years old now, but he still had the same slightly deprecating charm that Gideon remembered in him as a boy, and the same dark good looks that were Perry's, and yet not Perry's. 'I would like to say that I am honoured to have been invited here to spend this festive season with you. New Year is not generally celebrated in my country, and I look forward to it with the most intense interest.'

Vilia wasn't used to the American style of conversation, and found his formality a trifle oppressive. 'Quite so,' she said. 'Although I cannot see that being honoured enters into it. You are, after all, brother to Grace and Shona, and uncle to several of the children.'

'*Pure* Beacon Hill!' Amy murmured irrepressibly to her husband. 'I could recognize the breed blindfold at a hundred paces.' Aloud, she said, 'Mr Randall, I believe our families must be acquainted.'

They were, but Vilia put an imperious stop to what showed signs of developing into an enjoyable gossip, by remarking, 'I am sure that Grace and Shona are most anxious to have the mementoes of their father, Francis!'

Francis flushed slightly. His father, wilfully allowing life to slip from his grasp, had told him something of his own and Vilia Cameron's history. 'You are interested in people,' he had said, 'but I wonder if you'll ever know how predictable and yet unpredictable they can be. Or how they can be shaped by circumstance, and accident, and other, perfectly ordinary people, so that . . .' He hadn't gone on. All he had said was, 'I want you to meet her, and I want you to give her something from me. You can make that your excuse.' Francis now found that it was going to take a real feat of imagination before he could see, in this intimidating dowager, what his father had seen in the girl of fifty years before.

There was a pretty Paul Revere rose bowl for Grace, and a sweetmeat basket for Shona; for Petronella, a miniature bust of Susan B. Anthony, and for Ian a copy of Tom Paine; for Jermyn, a perfect scale model of a fifteenth-century cannon. Francis said, 'My father also wished me to give mementoes to you, Mistress Cameron, and to Theo and Gideon, for although there is no blood relationship, he remembers – remembered – your business association with the greatest kindness.'

Gideon wondered if perhaps there had been a trace of malice in Theo's packet of shares in a Mid-West railroad company; certainly, there was a deliberate aptness where his own gift, a first edition of Ogilby's *America*, was concerned, but he thought only a friendly irony had been intended. He had sent Perry a copy of the first edition of Lauriston's *America*, years ago, and Perry had approved.

They had to ask – or, at least, Theo did – before they discovered what was in Vilia's package, which she had been staring at for quite a long time, without speaking. 'A pin. A scarf pin,' she replied without any particular expression, and held it out for them to see. It wasn't valuable, but it had great charm and the workmanship was fine. The head was made in the form of a small, coiled snake, handsomely wrought in gold, with fire opals for eyes. 'How lovely!' Amy exclaimed, and after a moment, Vilia said, 'Yes. Most considerate of your father, Francis, but there was no need for him to remember me.' Gideon could see that Theo had recognized the pin, as he did, but no one else showed anything but polite appreciation. Or – was there a trace of puzzlement in Shona's eyes? It was an extremely *personal* gift, when one remembered Perry's fondness for it.

Amy, conscious of undercurrents, was intrigued. She knew very little about Perry Randall; clearly, it behoved her to know more, though not right now, when she had quite enough to interest her. It was the first time she had been to Kinveil, and the first time she had met Vilia. The proposed visit at the end of '65 had had to be cancelled, because Fanshawe – scantier of hair and more purple of nose, but otherwise unchanged – had summoned Gideon hastily back from Marchfield; ratification of the slavery amendment to the U.S. constitution was almost complete and Fanshawe wanted an authoritative article, complete with interviews. Then, in the summer of '66, Amy had become pregnant, and the doctors had said that a first child at the age of thirty-five was not what they would have recommended. She was to indulge in no exertion at all, and certainly no long and difficult journeys. For the first two or three months, Steven had been a delicate baby, but had subsequently begun to develop at the most amazing rate, as if, Gideon remarked, having elected to remain in the world, he were determined to make the most of it.

Vilia, unlike most grandmothers, didn't seem to be much enamoured of babies. 'They're so unrewarding,' she said. 'Especially when you consider how much effort you put into them. They have no rational conversation at all and, what's worse, you know they *won't* have any for twenty years at least!'

Amy laughed, bouncing the child on her lap. 'Ah, but it's worth waiting for, isn't it? To have tall, handsome, clever sons?'

'Is it? I suppose so, though I have always thought the popular attachment to the idea of close-knit families a little sickly. Gideon and

Theo and I are on excellent terms, but when they aren't here I don't miss them in the least, and I'm very sure they don't miss me.'

'You shouldn't have brought them up to be so independent.'

Her mother-in-law sighed austerely. 'My dear Amy, I had very little choice. The foundry was more important. It was a choice between working to feed them – and neglecting them a little – or pampering them and starving.' She studied the suitably crushed Amy for a moment, and then went on, 'You should have an occupation. You're intelligent enough, it seems, and I don't believe in women frittering away their lives in domesticity.'

'What would you suggest?'

'How should I know? Not, I beg of you, temperance, or soup kitchens for the poor, or Bibles for the heathen. That kind of thing doesn't need brains, only goodwill. You must have learned something in China, surely? About trade, or painting, or Ming vases, or opium.'

Amy chuckled. 'I can't imagine any kind of respectable occupation where a knowledge of opium would come in useful – if I had any! Except medicine, I suppose. But I do know quite a lot about Chinese art.' She said it thoughtfully, because it *was* an idea.

'There you are, then. Antiques.' It was said as if all that was needed was a little application.

Vilia fascinated Amy, who loved beautiful things. She could see that her mama-in-law must have been exquisite when young. She still was – thin, delicately made, brittle. Not unlike a piece of fine porcelain without the translucence. Definitely without the translucence. Amy had no idea what she was thinking behind that crisp manner, sometimes charming, occasionally domineering, always enigmatic. She knew that she herself had been summed up, but had no notion of whether she had been found wanting. Gideon didn't know either.

'My dear, I gave up trying to analyse Vilia when I was five. Take her as you find her. At least she doesn't patronize you – or Madge, for that matter – as she does poor Isa. She's always been impatient with what she calls "wilting lilies". I've sometimes thought she was the worst possible person to bring up my unfortunate little Lizzie. Juliana, too, for that matter.'

Amy had become very good at putting two and two together, and thought she now had a picture of what had happened with Gideon and Juliana. He, who had always tried to detach himself from human involvement, had found himself pitchforked, at a moment of complex inner turmoil, into a situation that would have touched a harder heart than his. Amy didn't think that any normal man, finding Juliana alone and desolate in Lucknow, could have failed to become involved, especially – she reflected with a pang – as it seemed that Juliana was small and pretty, and had very taking ways. Amy had always regretted her own height, and air of competence, and undistinguished looks. In recent months, however, she had stopped being quite so afraid of Juliana, because her marriage to Gideon had developed a feeling of solid stability. It still lacked the passion that, wistfully, she would have hoped for, but they were true kindred spirits, and knew it. The baby had helped, too.

Before they came, Gideon, who had paid three hurried visits north since their return from China, had warned Amy to control her tongue on the subject of Kinveil, for where that was concerned Vilia had no sense of humour at all.

'And where other things are concerned?'

He had wrinkled his brows a little and said, 'I don't know, any more. I suppose humour doesn't die, but hers has been rather in abeyance for a long time now. She hasn't had an easy time; never in all her life, when one thinks about it. It doesn't show in obvious ways, but I can tell you that nowadays she's a damned autocratic old lady!'

The autocratic old lady, presiding over the Christmas festivities, showed a distinct tendency to patronize Ian Barber as well as his wife; their astonishingly dull daughters, the eldest of whom was now fourteen, she simply ignored. Ian had recovered well from the accident at the Reform meeting, although it had made him nervous of crowds. Not, he explained earnestly, that he feared another assault upon his person, but his impaired sight was a handicap. Too often, he saw things that weren't there, or failed to see things that were. Also, he thought that perhaps he wasn't really cut out for public speaking.

Madge, who could see that Jermyn was just about to say, 'Amen to that!' intervened hurriedly. 'Perhaps it's just as well. You look far too piratical, with that patch, to make a really convincing social reformer!'

Ian, taking her seriously, said in distress, 'Oh dear, I hope not. There seems to be no alternative. Isa and the girls assure me that a glass eye wouldn't be the thing at all!'

'It's of no importance, anyway,' Vilia remarked. 'Glenbraddan needs you more than the Reformers do, now the Act has gone through at last.'

'Yes, but there remains a great deal to be done. The Act didn't go far enough. Only the urban labourers have benefited, and rural labourers are no better off than they were before. The first priority, however, is to frame the Scottish version of the Act that has just gone through for England and Wales.'

Amy said, 'I am sure that Mr Randall is at a loss, as I am, to know why a separate Act for Scotland is necessary.' Gideon glared at her, but she returned him a look of angelic innocence, and went on, 'Couldn't Parliament simply have incorporated the Scottish provisions in the Act they've just passed?'

Ian gasped in something very near outrage. 'Oh, no! You must understand that when the Treaty of Union between Scotland and England came into effect on May the first, 1707 . . .'

Twenty minutes later, Vilia brought his discourse to an arbitrary end. 'I believe we are all sufficiently enlightened, Ian, thank you. And now that we have finished dinner, Fraser tells me there is a messenger from Glenbraddan to see you. He is in the dungeon.'

Amy, suppressing an almost insuppressible giggle, could see that Madge was in the same straits. Kinveil wasn't exactly homey.

When Ian joined them in the Gallery a little later, it was to say that he was leaving for Glenbraddan almost at once. 'No, nothing wrong,' he assured his wife. 'You know I was expecting the gentlemen from the Reform League soon after the New Year? Well, their arrangements had to be changed at short notice, and it seems they are at Glenbraddan now. They sent a telegram, but apparently Johnson thought it could wait until someone happened to be coming this way.' He shook his head disapprovingly.

'It seems unnecessary to set out tonight,' Vilia said. 'Must you?'

'They have to leave again the day after tomorrow.'

'New Year's Day? Well, really!' She said with some asperity. 'They're English, I suppose?'

'Yes Aunt Vilia.'

Grace said, 'But Ian, it's after eight, now. You can't possibly get back to Glenbraddan tonight!'

'No, mother. But the moon is full, and the snow makes it as bright as day. I should think I might reach Jock Tamson's before the moon goes down, and that will shorten tomorrow's journey considerably, and give us several more hours for our discussions.'

It was the most marvellous night, if, as Theo remarked *sotto voce*, one cared for that sort of thing. There was a blanket of snow over everything, thick enough to muffle sound, but still thin enough for the going not to be difficult. Scarcely an inch of the sky was free from its dusting of stars, and the moon shone brilliantly, striking sparks off the frosted snow, and throwing long black shadows as thick and sharp-edged as woodcuts. It was as if the whole firmament was laid out on display, above and below, for the loch was a perfect mirror of the heavens, with every planet and nebula and star reproduced with pinpoint exactitude on its clear face. The air crackled with cold.

When Ian was no more than a moving silhouette against the landscape, the men went back indoors, rubbing their hands and stamping their feet to restore the circulation.

'My God!' Jermyn said, back in the Gallery. 'Rather Ian than me!' And then, in response to an exasperated glance from his wife, thought to add, 'Don't worry, Isa! He's well wrapped up, and the exercise will keep him warm. Yes – that's true, isn't it? Maybe he's got the right idea, after all.'

'Jermyn!' said his grandmother forbiddingly.

2

Kinveil kept the hours Vilia decreed, and she was by nature a late bird, so it was after midnight before they were allowed to retire. Gideon pulled Amy to him, his teeth chattering, and said, 'Christ, but Lavinia was right! What a freezing barracks of a place this is! And how dared you, madam, invite that tiresome young man to give us a lecture on Scots law!'

She chuckled. 'Because it's the funniest thing watching all the Barbers hang on his words, while everyone else furiously tries to think of a way to stop him!'

He gave a chitter of laughter. 'I suppose it is. Come here, you wicked woman, and let's get warm.'

But the blessed warmth had scarcely begun to seep into their chilled bodies, when there was a violent rapping on the door.

It was Vilia's voice, raw with urgency. 'Gideon, come! Come quickly and bring Theo! Now, this minute!'

With an exclamation, he struggled out of bed and pulled his trousers on, tucking the nightshirt into them, and gathering up as many layers of cardigan and jacket as he could find without wasting time on it. With a hasty instruction to Amy to stay where she was, he picked up the oil lamp and set off downstairs to hammer on Theo's door. There was no response, and he threw it open impatiently, but Theo wasn't there. It didn't look as if he had been, either. Had he gone downstairs already, or . . . Gideon groaned. *Not* the blacksmith in the village! Surely not! Oh, well. Bad luck, Jermyn. He beat a tattoo on his nephew's door, saying, 'You're needed. Be quick.'

When he reached the courtyard, he almost collided with the housekeeper, swaddled in a blanket, and with a plaid over her shoulders and a long, grey pigtail dangling down her back.

'What is it?' he demanded. 'What's wrong?'

'Och, Mr Gideon! Go out to the causeway. Alec Fraser iss out there but he will not be managing on his own, and I am on my way to warm up some water and get the whisky.'

'What *is* it? Is it Mr Barber? Has something happened?'

'Mr Barber? No, no! It iss Sorley McClure. He iss lying out there on the causeway and he iss fast asleep! Mistress Cameron saw him from her window. Chust like a starfish, he iss, flat on his face. It gave her a terrible turn. He hass been overcome by the cold, she says. Och, she iss in an awful state, so she iss! Go on, Mr Gideon. Go and giff Alec Fraser a hand.'

They carried Sorley in to Vilia's carpeted and panelled drawing-room, the warmest room in the place apart from the kitchen, and Gideon and Fraser, with Jermyn's help, stripped him and wrapped him in layer after layer of plaids and shawls. He was ice cold all over, in a state that looked to Gideon more like a last sleep than unconsciousness. He had always been thin, but the muffling clothes he had taken to wearing in recent years had hidden the fact that he had diminished almost to a skeleton.

Vilia and the housekeeper came back, with stone hot water bottles and hot tea and milk and whisky. All Vilia's self-possession was gone. While Gideon and the others chafed Sorley's feet and hands, and slapped the unresponsive face, she hovered, distracted and useless, murmuring, 'Oh, Sorley. Oh, Sorley. What should we do? There was a man in the village – what was his name? The same thing. The doctor said . . . Oh, God! What did he say? Do you remember, Alec? Should we give him whisky, or shouldn't we give him whisky? *I can't remember!*'

One of the footmen came in to pile more logs on the fire, and Gideon said, 'Can you warm up some blankets in the kitchen? Then we can get some direct heat on his flesh. Thank you. Alec, help me move this sofa closer to the fire. That's it. And bring the candle stands nearer; even that might help. Come on, Sorley! Wake up, man. *Come, on!*' He slapped the unresisting face again, and rubbed the hands and forearms with all the energy he had.

This was Sorley, whom he had known all his life, who had looked after them all when they were babies, and then toddlers, and then boys, and taught them so many things. Who had always been there, with his narrow, friendly eyes, and his reassuring sanity, and that funny, amoral realism of his. And the smile that almost made you believe in God. 'Come on, Sorley!' he muttered again. '*Come on!*'

And then Theo appeared. 'Oh-h-h-h, dear,' he said, leaning negligently against the door frame. 'I wondered why all the lights were blazing. Sorley caught cold, has he?'

Gideon could feel his face tighten. 'Don't stand there being so bloody superior,' he said through his teeth. 'Come and help.'

After a minute, Theo did. 'Frozen, isn't he? Where the devil has he been?'

Alec Fraser said, 'He wass saying he wass going up to see Bessie, his cousin, you know? It iss about a mile there, and another back.'

'He shouldn't have got as cold as this in a couple of miles.'

'What the hell does it matter?' Gideon exclaimed, exasperated. 'He's an old man, Theo! He shouldn't have been out at all. Oh, there you are, Jermyn! Have those been warmed? Give them over here, then.'

Sorley's head moved of its own accord. His eyes didn't open, and his face was still slack, but he was trying to say something. It came out as an almost inaudible wheeze. 'Mistress . . . Mistress . . .'

Vilia pushed Gideon violently aside and fell on her knees beside Sorley, both his hands in hers. 'I'm here, Sorley. It's all right. I'm here.

You'll be all right.' Her face was pouring with tears that she didn't seem even to be aware of.

'I wass . . .' And then something Gideon couldn't hear. And then '. . . to help. Always knew what you . . . I knew.'

'I know you did, Sorley. I know you did!' There was a terrible intensity in her face, as if she were trying to will him to stay alive.

'All life . . . This time too . . . But I did . . .' His voice was so dreadfully slurred that Gideon could scarcely make out even the short, obvious words. 'Only one . . . Only one left . . .'

'Oh, Sorley. It's all right, it's all right! Don't leave me, Sorley.' Vilia's voice broke. *'Don't leave me, Sorley!'*

His eyes opened, and he tried to smile. But it was only a glimmer. The freckles were livid against his white face, and his sight was blurred and blank. 'It iss a long time since we wass bairns. I did it, though. Only . . .'

His voice faded, but his breathing resounded through the room. Everyone was still and silent, knowing there was nothing to be done. Then he said very clearly, 'Mistress Vilia. Mistress . . .' And that was all. He gave a shuddering gasp, and then a kind of rictus took him, and then he was gone.

Vilia wouldn't believe it. She went on kneeling there, shaking him, and saying, 'Oh, Sorley! Oh, Sorley!' over and over again until Theo took her by the shoulders and pulled her forcibly to her feet.

In the end, she whispered dully, 'Leave me with him. Go away, all of you. *Go away!'*

Gideon, Theo and Jermyn had a stiff whisky in the ice-cold dining-room and then went shivering to bed. But Gideon couldn't sleep, even with Amy cradling him and wiping away the childish tears that sprang to his eyes, uncontrollably, all through the bleak hours of that bleak night.

Dawn wouldn't come until about nine, but long before that Gideon rose and went downstairs again. The drawing-room fire had gone out, and the candles, and the room had a chill and neglected look in the light of his oil lamp. There were still blankets and plaids scattered around, and the forgotten tray with its burden of cold tea and once-hot milk, the skin thick and wrinkled on it. Sorley lay where they had left him, cold and stiff, the covering plaid turned down to reveal his dead, empty face, and Vilia was sunk on the floor beside him in a billow of

717

dark green dressing robe, her arms on the seat of a chair and her face buried, her hair tumbling over her shoulders like a waterfall. In the oil light, it looked almost golden again.

Gideon, anticipating something of the sort, had wakened her maid on his way down and told her to relight the fire in Vilia's room and warm the bed. Now, bending, he took her by the shoulders and raised her, resistless, to her feet. She seemed scarcely less cold than Sorley, and her tear-drowned face was as empty.

He remembered another night, more than thirty years ago, when a small black cat had died. He didn't understand his mother. He never would. Other women wept for children or lovers, but she took that kind of tragedy in her stride. It was what most people would have considered as insignificant deaths that laid waste her spirit.

He wondered what she had been thinking in all these last dark, lonely hours. He couldn't know that she hadn't been thinking at all. Only repeating again and again, meaninglessly, in her head, 'Oh, Sorley. *Oh, Sorley.*'

'Come along, my dear,' he said softly. 'You need rest.' And then, 'Don't worry. I'll look after him.'

The blank eyes turned up to his for a moment, and then she said, 'Yes,' and, leaning on his arm, allowed him to take her to her room.

3

But the day wasn't over.

The hands of the clock had just struggled as far as noon, and Gideon was in the castle workshop with the carpenter and the woman who did the sewing. She was asking how much cloth would be needed to line Sorley's coffin when the door opened and Theo stood there. At the sight of his brother's face, Gideon's nerves began jangling again. Saying, 'I think it would please my mother if you used the Cameron tartan, Maggie,' he turned and followed Theo in silence to the dining-room, which was deserted.

Theo closed the door carefully, and stood surveying Gideon for a moment before he said, 'Ian Barber.'

'What about Ian Barber?'

'We need another coffin.'

The world began to spin. Heavily, Gideon sat down. 'What's happened?'

Theo shrugged. 'Who knows? Jock Tamson doesn't, and he found him. I thought we'd better hear the whole saga together. I've told Jock to wait in the dungeon, and he's had his dram, so he's contented enough. What I want to know is, who tells Grace and Isa?'

'Not Vilia. It'll have to be Shona.'

'Dear Shona! Yes. She'd better see Tamson with us, I suppose.'

The man stood fidgeting before them, twisting his bonnet in his hands. His kindly, nondescript face with the greyish bristle on cheeks and chin, was high-coloured with embarrassment at Shona's presence.

'What a terrible thing, Mr Tamson!' she said, her eyes distressed. 'Can you tell us just what happened? You think his horse threw him, my brother-in-law says?'

'Aye, mistress. I wass chust taking a last look at the cow, do you see, before I went to bed, and I heard a horse – fair tearing along, it wass, and no one on her back at aal. I wass knowing her at once, but I could not be catching her. She wass wild, ferry wild, and in a terrible lather.'

'What time was this?' Gideon asked.

'Och, it would be about ten, or a bitty after. I knew the chentleman must haff been thrown, so I got my lad Alasdair from his bed, and we took the ponies and came back along the road, do you see. I thought we wass neffer going to find him, but chust where the road comes round from Inverbeg – you will be knowing the place when I show you – there he wass. There iss a ferry sharp elbow in the hill and another wee one close by, so that they make a kind of chimney. Ferry black it iss, and the road iss chust on the edge of the loch, with a nasty chumble of rocks down to the water. Och, they should haff cleared those away years ago! It wass the whinstone they wass digging out when they wass cutting the road, do you see, and it takes a terrible time for whinstone to lose its edge.'

'And?' Gideon prompted him. Highlanders were the worst he had ever come across at telling a story. Either they started in the middle, so that you never discovered what they were talking about, or they started long before the beginning and never reached the end at all. Either way, they took hell's own time about it.

'Och, well. It wass there he wass. Head down over the rocks with his

719

hand trailing in the water. Stiff as a board, so he wass. Och, it wass a cold night. Not a night to be out at aal.'

Shona gave a little gasp, and Gideon put an arm round her shoulder. 'How long had he been dead, do you think?'

'I haff no idea. If he wass killed when he fell, there wass the time it took for the mare to reach my cot, and then Alasdair and I were slow coming back because we wass looking carefully, do you see?'

Theo said, 'From Inverbeg to Jock's place is the devil of a long way for the mare to have kept running. I don't think I've ever known a horse bolt for more than a couple of miles, if that. Have you, Gideon?'

'She may have eased off a bit. And she was on the way back to her stable, so she had no reason to stop.'

Jock Tamson pursed his lips thoughtfully. 'Maybe aye, maybe no. But och, the light was strange last night, ferry strange. Our own ponies are out in the moon, often enough, when we are after deer or vermin, but last night – och, they were shying at every shadow. It wass ferry still, do you see, and the shadows wass as black as I effer remember. With a high-bred beast like Mr Barber's, a fox or a wildcat would have been enough.'

Ian had been a perfectly competent horseman, but the drop to the water – Gideon remembered it now, only about five miles from Kinveil – was on his blind side. Easy enough to misjudge things, trying to steady a rearing horse. Easy enough to pull it too far to the right, when it shied from the left, so that the frightened animal would see the new danger when his master didn't. The animal would lose its trust in him then, and dig its heels in. And that could have been enough.

'Where is Mr Barber's body now?' Theo asked.

Jock Tamson looked shifty. 'Well, it wass like this, Mr Lauriston, do you see. We wass that cold that we took him to Willie Macleod's at Inverbeg, and then we wass talking, you see, and it wass late before we woke. That iss why I wass maybe a wee bitty slow getting here. You know how it iss.'

'I know how it is,' Theo said a little drily.

'But I wass thinking it wass maybe best not to bring the chentleman here chust at once, in case Mistress Barber wass wanting him taken straight back to Glenbraddan.'

Theo and Gideon looked at each other, and then at Shona. She, tears standing in her gentle eyes, said helplessly, 'I don't know.'

Grace, deeply shocked, didn't know, either, and Isa, giving way to something like hysteria, could only moan, 'Whatever you think. Whatever you think,' before Amy led her away and saw her laid down on her bed, with five weeping daughters and one puzzled small son for company.

It was Amy who said, 'You must ask Vilia, you know. Grace and Isa are too distraught. You, Gideon, think it would be simpler if he were buried here at Kinveil, in a double funeral with Sorley, while you, Theo, are sure he should be put to rest at Glenbraddan. You have no choice but to ask Vilia.'

Gideon exclaimed, 'We can't lay another burden on her shoulders, damn it! She's in a bad enough way already!'

'I don't know,' Theo said consideringly after a moment. 'You never can tell, it might divert her mind. I will even take it on myself to go and ask her.'

When he returned, Gideon saw, incredulously, that he was trying to stifle a grin. 'Well?' he said sharply.

'We-e-ell. My trick, dear boy. Prostrate she may have been, but *that* question roused her smartly enough. *On no account* is Ian Barber to be buried at Kinveil! One had the distinct impression that it would be nothing less than a mortal insult to the shade of friend Sorley. If that isn't a contradiction in terms, which I suppose it is. So I win, dear boy. Ian is to be laid to rest where he belongs, at Glenbraddan.'

4

The two funerals followed each other in the same appalling week. There were no painful discussions over Sorley's dispositions. What he possessed – little enough although more than anyone had expected – went to his cousin Bessie, except for one thing that was for Vilia. They found it in the chest where he kept his odds and ends, and there was a note with it. He had found it, years and years ago, in one of the little crevasses in the hills, and he had kept it secretly, because he wanted to be able to leave her something to treasure when he died. Even Theo gasped when he saw it, for, simple though it was, it was anything up to a thousand years old – a spiral silver bracelet, thick and round as a rope, with a rough pattern of antlers impressed into it, and heavy, bevelled ends. 'Viking?' Theo said. But Vilia choked, and repeating, 'Something to treasure when he died', clapped her fingers over her mouth and stumbled from the room.

Ian Barber's affairs, tidy-minded though he had been, were in chaos. He hadn't expected to die in his early thirties, and had made no arrangements beyond the obvious.

It was only too clear that little Jay, fair and nervous, couldn't be left to the undivided attention of a parcel of women.

Gideon was horrified when the family decided that the obvious person to be his guardian was Theo. What could he say? What *could* he say? There wasn't anything. The one argument against Theo's being appointed the boy's guardian was the one argument that couldn't be put into words to his gently bred mother and grandmother, who wouldn't understand it anyway.

Afterwards, Francis Randall was the first to leave. Gideon, having a quiet farewell drink with him, remarked, 'You mustn't think that this New Year has been precisely typical. Mass interment isn't an essential feature of the ritual.'

Francis had eased up a good deal with Gideon and Amy. He grinned. 'I didn't think it was.' But he could see that Gideon wanted to say something else and was having difficulty. He raised his eyebrows inquiringly.

'You're doing a European tour now, are you?'

'Yes. My father had one scheduled for me when I was nineteen, but you may remember that it wasn't just the best time for it.'

'No.' Gideon wrinkled his nose.

Francis could still remember his father saying, 'You'll like Gideon,' and he did. An honest, considerate, humorous man who, unlike so many honest men, was nobody's fool. In some ways, he wasn't unlike Perry Randall, whom Francis still thought of with a deep sense of loss. But he didn't, Francis thought, have either the driving force, or the same ironical, clear-sighted knowledge of himself. One had always sensed that Dad knew himself through and through, and other people, too. Gideon still had illusions.

Gideon said, 'You'll be going to Paris?' and Francis laughed aloud. 'Try and stop me! If I go nowhere else in this whole, wide world, I am going to Paris.'

'I don't know if you – if you remember Shona's dinner party in '51?'

Francis laughed again. 'Don't I just!'

'Do you remember Juliana? Juliana Telfer?'

'Sure I do! Eyes as big and soft as pansies, and the prettiest blonde curls.'

Gideon smiled. 'That's right. She's almost the same age as you. Now, this is in confidence, Francis. You may know that she was – is – married to Theo. She left him a few years ago for very good reasons that I won't explain.'

Francis did know something about the world, and he could guess. But there was something else nagging at his memory. 'But she . . . Oh, yes. I recall. She had a tragic time during the mutiny in India, and lost her first husband and baby as well.'

'That's right. Now she's cut herself off from the family and no one knows what's happened to her. But I do, or some of it at least. I had a very short note from her last year, saying very little more than that I wasn't to worry. She was working her own life out and managing quite well. There was no address but Paris, not even an *arrondissement* number. But I *am* worried, because I know how little money she had, and she's been away three years now. Could you – do you think you might – would you . . .?'

'Keep an eye out for her? Sure, Gideon! What else are family connections for?'

He said gratefully, 'Thank you. And if you should find her . . .'

'I'll let you know, and no one else.'

Gideon smiled in relief. 'I'll tell you this, Francis. I don't know what your brother and sister are like, but your father made a damned good job of *you*!'

Chapter Three

1

Francis Randall spent only a few days in Paris after he left Kinveil, sniffing the strange, characteristic smells, and familiarizing himself with the general layout of the city. He intended to get to know the place better, much better, but he had always been one to keep the best for last, so he postponed the pleasure, and in the meantime set out to 'do' the rest of Europe, Turkey, the Holy Land, and Egypt. He took a long time about it, because he was interested; longer than he had anticipated, especially as it would have been a pity to rush away and miss the grand opening of the Suez Canal. It wasn't, therefore, until early in 1870 that he returned to Paris to stay.

It was everything he had hoped. People told him that the great days had gone, that the Gaslight Empire was dying, but he didn't mind. Humanity was Francis's passion – and when better to study it than when the barque of art and culture and civilization was going down, perhaps for the last time? The death of a civilization was, to him, more exciting than its apogee. He didn't think of it quite in those terms, and he certainly wasn't a vulture; it was just that people under stress were more interesting than when they were content.

There wasn't yet any hint of what form the end would take, nor even any sense of waiting for it, except perhaps in a reckless undercurrent to the gaiety and sensation-seeking that were the hallmark of Parisian society. Never before had Francis experienced the heady delights of that special kind of pleasure that didn't think about yesterday, or tomorrow, or anything but the here and now, and he settled down into it like a born voluptuary.

Rejecting all offers of hospitality, he took an apartment, a splendid place in one of the old houses on the fringes of Montmartre that was being given up by a struggling artist who hadn't struggled hard enough. The decorations, the young man said, had been begun during a brief and all too fleeting period of affluence, and Francis was privately grateful that it *had* been brief. The salon was a nightmare in cretonne, with every available inch, walls and ceiling included, covered with vine leaves and parakeets, while one of the bedrooms was draped, tent-like, in cardinal red, with bed and lamps in the Turkish style, and a terracotta faun for company. The other company – a pet python – the artist took with him.

Then began the months of discovering the city. Francis wasn't after facts but impressions, and he gathered enough to last him a lifetime. Moonlight on the Place Pigalle, and the dark shadows of the streets; student cafés where dinners were paid for in pictures, and others where one rubbed shoulders with thieves and housebreakers; grand restaurants on the boulevards; Hortense Schneider singing Offenbach; night entertainments in gardens, where the foliage under the gaslight was the essence of every green ever known; driving home through the soft, warm night in open carriages; and girls with ostrich feathers and inviting eyes. Francis, sometimes, might err on the side of formality, but he wasn't a prude.

And always Paris's own special smell, a compound of garlic and blue overalls, horses and tobacco, wine, and winds off the Seine. It filtered even into the bistro where Francis soon became a regular, the Nouvelle Athènes, blending with the morning bouquet of coffee and bad cognac and eggs frizzling in butter, with absinthe in the afternoons, and in the evenings with fragrant, steaming soup, and pungent cigarettes, and more coffee, and weak beer. Sometimes Francis sat quietly for hours at his little marble-topped table, his feet on the sanded floor, and a *bock* before him, watching the other habitués – the artist Manet with his square shoulders and his swagger; Degas, small of eye and large of necktie; the voluble novelist Villiers de l'Isle Adam; and Catulle Mendes, the great Parnassian with his high, febrile voice and his phrase-making. In time, they even awarded him a nod and a brief greeting. Francis didn't want any more; he had no desire to talk, only to watch.

But although, in the course of half a dozen months, he found his way on to most levels of society, he found no trace of a pretty *écossaise* with big blue eyes and fair hair. It would have been easy if she had been an American. There weren't more than four or five hundred of them in Paris; but there were five thousand British.

And then, on July fifteenth, war came, and after the first few jubilant weeks the dazzlingly beautiful French army, with its colour, its fanfares, its panache, discovered that Bismarck's drab and stolid infantry and Herr Krupp's cast steel breech-loading cannon were a great deal more than it had bargained for. Francis was there, watching, when Sedan fell and Louis-Napoleon surrendered, and he heard the whole Prussian army sing Luther's 'Old Hundred' in thanksgiving and then begin to pack their gear to accompanying shouts of *'Nach Paris!'*

A sensible man, a man who was more interested in his own skin than in how other people behaved under stress, would have made for the coast. Francis didn't. He went back to Paris to discover that the Third Republic had been declared and the city was preparing for siege.

725

He couldn't decently spend all his time just watching people, so he volunteered to help with the American Ambulance, and since he had been involved with the auxiliary services during the Civil War, he was gratefully welcomed. When the siege began on September twentieth, there were thirteen thousand hospital beds in Paris, which wasn't many in relation to the quarter million regular soldiers and National Guardsmen that the optimists claimed could be mustered to defend the city. But in a besieged city, unable to bring in extra doctors or equipment, there was little that the administration could do except allocate the worst cases to the established hospitals and farm the rest out to private charity, to the makeshift annexes known as *ambulances privées*, some of them located in religious institutions, some in railway stations, some in hotels, and some in the houses of the rich. Paris broke out in a rash of Red Cross flags, and tending the wounded became a fashionable occupation for her *grandes dames*. The only drawback to all this goodwill was that every time there was a battle or skirmish outside the walls the official conveyances of the *Intendance Militaire* became inextricably snarled up with those of the *ambulances privées* in anxious pursuit of customers.

The American Ambulance was something of a phenomenon. A certain Dr Thomas Evans, dentist to the hurriedly departed Empress Eugénie, had been intelligent enough to purchase all the up-to-date medical equipment exhibited by America at the Exposition Universelle of 1867. Further, America had discovered during the Civil War that the most effective way of combating septicaemia, which killed so many amputation cases, was by ensuring perfect ventilation – a concept that to the French, with their inbred horror of *courants d'air*, was entirely foreign. But it soon became noticeable that the Americans were saving four out of five amputation cases, while in the French hospitals the same proportion died. The defenders of Paris began carrying cards around with them saying that, if they were wounded, they would be deeply obliged to be succoured by the American Ambulance.

By the end of November, Francis Randall felt as if he and his ambulance cart, with its roll-up canvas sides and the Red Cross blazoned on it, had covered every inch of the countryside between the walls of Paris and the outlying ring of forts. He had even come to terms with his horses, a pair of ambling, hard-mouthed old nags that he suspected would ruin him forever for driving anything else.

It was on December fifth, when he was urging them, fully loaded, along the last lap of the rue de Rivoli, the canvas sides of the cart stained with blood that was not only today's but yesterday's, and the day before's, because no one had had time to scrub them, that he found Juliana Telfer at last.

2

It was not the coincidence it seemed at first. For days, Paris had pinned its hopes on General Ducrot's plan to break out through the surrounding Prussians and join up with Gambetta's relieving force from Tours. But the Great Sortie had failed. Ducrot's army had been beaten back, and so had Gambetta's. Ducrot had lost twelve thousand officers and men, and Paris all hope of relief.

The wounded streamed back into Paris, some on their own feet, some in the ambulances, some in *bateaux-mouches* that dumped them on the quays of the Seine and sailed away again. The population of Paris rallied to help, and among its number was Juliana.

The salons of the Maison Worth et Bobergh in the rue de la Paix had been converted into an *ambulance privée*, and when the dreadful flood rolled into the city she went down to the nearest quay, at the Tuileries, to see what could be done. She had to leave the cart in one of the cross streets, and go on from there on foot. But she stopped when she saw what lay before her, and for a moment wondered whether she could go on. She had thought that nothing could be worse than Lucknow, and in some ways that was true. Nothing could match those awful, closed, oppressive months, with their sense of personal vindictiveness. But Paris was a great city, and its army was great, and so was the sheer number of its wounded. Not tens, or dozens, or scores, but hundreds. The weather was crisp and clear, so the smells were not too bad; but that was a minor dispensation. So many wounded – and so horribly! Not the clean wounds of rifle and bayonet that were familiar by now, but the damage that could be inflicted by the new Krupp artillery, nominal twenty-four-pounders that threw projectiles weighing half a hundredweight, shells that exploded from their huge charge of black powder and threw great fragments of iron shrapnel to rip and tear through flesh and bone.

It wouldn't have been so bad if the men had all been laid out in neat rows, but those who were capable of it – knowing, perhaps, that unless they moved others would be dumped almost on top of them – had begun to crawl over the splintered old timbers to a safer refuge. There was something obscene about the mangled wrecks of men, some of them half naked, wriggling laboriously on hands and knees between and sometimes over their comrades, leaving a dark, slippery, snail-like trail of blood behind them.

The private ambulances were strictly controlled, and Worth's had been authorized to take only the lightly wounded. It meant that Juliana couldn't help the men who needed help most, except by holding her flask of brandy and water to their mouths, or trying to staunch the bleeding with the bandages she had brought, and, later, strips of muslin torn from her petticoats. Somehow, she kept her senses under control as she tended gaping wounds with gold lace embedded in them, and tattered joints bound with filthy rags, and throats whose tendons glared white through stripped flesh. But after a time, she realized that even to relieve the crush by half a dozen men would be a help. There was one youth with a scalp wound, and another with the flesh sliced off his hip, and a third whose shoulder had been dislocated, and a fourth with a broken leg. All the time, as she helped them drag themselves towards her cart, there were hands clutching at her skirts, and despairing, agonized voices crying, 'Madame! À moi! À moi! Help me. I need you more than they do!'

They were almost at the cart when she found, lying at the side of the avenue, a young National Guardsman, flat on his face, his limbs contorted and his hands clawing helplessly at the ground. None of the people hurrying to or from the jetty was paying any attention. Gently, she bent over him. He must have crawled as far as this, blindly, under some impulse to find his way home. He was only a boy, not more than sixteen or seventeen, and bleeding from a dozen places. Half his jaw had been shot away. Although she was almost fainting by now, Juliana couldn't leave him. The rue de Rivoli was close by. Surely, since the journey was now so short, someone could find space for him in one of the ambulances that were making for the hospitals! She stumbled the few yards to the road, and there blessedly, among the stream of others, was an American Ambulance.

Running into the road, tripping, breathless, she tugged at the coat of the man who was driving. 'Please!' she gasped in English. 'Help me! You must help me!'

Francis Randall looked down, and, perhaps because he was so tired, saw not the distraught expression, or the forgotten face, or the tangled hair, or the thin hands, but only the sapphire-blue eyes he had been looking for for months. With an explosive, 'God almighty!' he hauled on the reins and brought his ambling nags to a precipitate halt.

3

She was shy of him at first, and his intuition told him why. Taking her hand in his over the table at Chez Brébant, he said, 'I won't betray you, you know. I'm not family, only a distant connection. All I want to do is help.'

Looking back into the serene grey eyes, she was reassured. There was something about Francis Randall, something more than charming. Better versed than she had once been in the ways of men, she saw that he had an odd kind of spiritual purity that could have been sickly, but wasn't. It didn't, as it might have done, make him stupid, or naive, or humourless. There was a word to describe what he had, but she couldn't find it at first. And then she did. Integrity.

'Thank you,' she said, coughing a little, and then, in response to the change in his eyes, 'It's only the smoke, no more.'

Lyrically and inevitably, they fell in love. Against the rumble of Prussian guns outside the city, and Arctic cold inside, surrounded during the day by the sick and maimed, haunted at night by hunger and concern over what the next day would bring, they found in each other's company an inexpressible delight. When, after two weeks, he took her in his arms and made love to her, it seemed as if they had been created only for each other. His tenderness was all she wanted in the world, a solace for the heartbreak, the numbness, the tears she had never shed, the loneliness of her adult years, and she warmed her tired soul at it. No one in all her life, except Richard for one brief year when she had been too young to appreciate it, had ever given her love so complete, so committed, so unstinting. Until Francis came, Juliana had thought that, alone with her little daughter, Christian, she had won through to contentment. Now she had more than that. She had happiness.

But Francis was in torment. She was so frail, and sometimes when he saw her with fresh eyes, after an absence of a day, it seemed as if she had lost substance even in the few hours of separation. He was in despair to know what to do. She needed care, and rest, warmth, and food, and all he could give her was love. With pain he looked at little Christy, three years old, pink-cheeked and smooth-skinned despite everything that the last months had done. All Juliana's rations, everything she could afford to buy on the black market, went to the child, and had done ever since rationing began early in October.

He did what he could, but cash was short and everyone nervous of accepting foreign bank drafts, because no one knew how long the siege would continue or how much worse things would become. By the end of December, the ration was an ounce of horsemeat a day. Butter was forty francs a pound, if one could find it, eggs thirty francs a dozen, cheese no more than a memory, and vegetables scarce and unpalatable. Francis didn't know what Juliana was earning, but he did know that the average Parisian wage was five francs a day.

The American embassy was well stocked, and Francis had no compunction about begging, but he couldn't beg to the tune of one square meal a day, or even week. So when he took food to Juliana, he was careful to stay and make sure that she ate some of it herself, instead of giving it all to the child. She smiled a little sadly when he tried to talk about it, and said, 'I'm not hungry, you know, and she needs it so much more than I do.'

It was clear to him that she was remembering her baby son, dead a dozen years ago because, she had said quietly to Francis one evening, she hadn't taken proper care of him. He found her response to the siege infinitely touching, knowing that she must be reminded, every minute of every day, of what she had lived through at Lucknow.

But she said thoughtfully, 'It's not as bad as you might imagine, though when I first heard the word "siege" mentioned, I fainted. Flop! Just like that! I was in the salon at the time, and poor Monsieur Worth was quite put out. If this had been only a village, I couldn't have borne it, because the resemblance would have been too close. But Paris is so big that one doesn't feel closed in, and there are people about, and the guns aren't just a few yards away and aimed personally at *you*.' Incredibly, she giggled. 'Besides, it hasn't even been a hundred days yet! It's scarcely worthy to be called a siege. And not even any cannonballs whisking the roof from over one's head – pooh! siege, indeed!'

He couldn't let it rest at that. 'All that might be true for someone else, but not you. It doesn't go deep enough, my darling.'

'Doesn't it? Perhaps not. Very well, then, I suppose this siege is almost a release for me. Something inside me has come awake again. I was so useless in Lucknow, and afterwards I couldn't feel anything at all, not for years, except a kind of dull shame at always being such a failure, always weak when others needed me. It was that, as much as anything, that made me leave Theo, although I left when I did because everything was so dreadful that I felt as if I were being confined to the depths forever, without any hope of becoming normal and human again. It was no better here, at first. Not until I had my little Christy, and then left Arsène, and began to stand on my own feet.'

She looked at Francis, her eyes almost pleading. 'Can you understand? Every time I look at her, and see her well and healthy and high-spirited, a little more of my numbness drains away, not only because I love her, but because she is a proof that I *can* be strong after all. And working at the ambulance has shown me that it isn't just a small, limited strength. I don't cower any more, and I've begun to *feel* again.' Smiling, she went on, 'Not only for you, you see? But even yet, though only now and again, something does – you're right – bring Lucknow back to me, quite suddenly and horribly. It's usually something small, like the butcher offering me a slice of elephant trunk from the zoo animals, the other day. He must have thought I was mad, for I could feel my face crumpling up like a child's, and I couldn't speak.'

He knew, when the first Prussian shell burst inside Paris itself on January fifth, that this couldn't be other than one of the terrible reminders for her. It was, and for the next few days things were even worse, because the shells began falling at a rate of three or four hundred a day, between the hours of ten at night and two or three in the morning. The guns were trained from the south, so none of them had sufficient range to reach the Right Bank, where Francis had his apartment. But Juliana lived off the rue St Jacques, and that was on the

Left Bank and very much in the danger zone. The strain that had been absent from her face since soon after he had met her, returned, but when at first he begged her to move to the rue de la Tour des Dames, she refused. Savagely, he wondered whether she was trying to put her courage to the final test.

And then, quite suddenly, she gave in. In a kind of useless desperation, he had gathered together the materials for a private banquet, and climbed the stairs to her apartment, just under the attics, bracing himself to make her laugh about it. 'What do you think the butcher offered me? Four parakeets and some donkey sausages for sixty francs. A mere bagatelle! So I began raking the other shops. Rat pie? I rejected it, although the charcutier swore it wasn't a sewer rat but a fine, fat one from the brewery. A cat for eight francs? I said no, again. And then one of the roof hunters offered me three sparrows for six francs, and that was a bargain I couldn't resist! Then I saw a woman with a hen under her apron, and demanded to know how much she would take for it. "Take for what?" I hauled it out by the neck and said, "For this, of course!" I won't tell you what we settled for, but I marched off to Roos's with my three sparrows, my hen, and some butter and a half baguette I'd managed to extract from the embassy, and had it all prepared. So here you are, my darling – an exquisite, if truffleless *salmis de poule et passereaux à la* God-knows-what! Can you heat it up?'

Afterwards, without much hope, he said again, 'Won't you come and share my apartment with me? If it's appearances that trouble you, I'll move out!'

She looked at him, her eyes soft with love and a sadness that ravaged his heart. 'Yes. Why not? I have been a poor mother to keep my child in such danger.' She didn't say that, this afternoon, it had taken her almost three-quarters of an hour to climb the stairs. Always, by the late afternoon, she was as weak as a kitten, although she could still hide it until he left her. Then, the dreadful coughing began, and the burning in her chest, and the feeling that her limbs were about to snap off.

But he knew. He had known long before she said to him, 'No, you mustn't make love to me, just for a while. I'm not very well, and you might catch something.' He had been aware from the start of the danger he was running, but had put it aside as something quite unimportant. And he hadn't argued with her in case she realized that he knew she was never going to be better again.

732

In the second week of December, he had sent a letter out to Gideon by one of the balloons that kept communications open between Paris and the outside world. The limit for private letters was four grammes, which didn't leave much scope for literary refinement, and none at all if one wanted the privacy of an envelope. All he had said then was, 'Don't worry. I have found her and am looking after her.' Now, despairingly, he sent out another. 'When the siege is lifted, for God's sake send us some food if you can. The need is urgent. You know my address. Thanks.'

4

At midnight on January twenty-seventh, the last rumble of guns faded and silence fell on Paris. The city had surrendered, with only a week's food supplies left.

Thirty-six hours later, Gideon himself rode in through the Porte Maillot, with no baggage other than a clean shirt, soap, a razor and a toothbrush, and his saddlebags crammed with tins of milk, jam, tea, cocoa, sugar, butter, a ham, and a dozen tins of boiled beef.

The young man who welcomed him to the apartment in the rue de la Tour des Dames had aged ten years in the three since they had met, and although his expression lightened at the sight of Gideon standing there, his grey eyes remained sombre. Gripping the other man's hand tightly in his own, he said only, 'Gideon! Oh, Gideon. I'm afraid she's dying.'

And then he saw, in Gideon's face, what it would not have occurred to him to look for, and his own face went completely blank for a second before he said, his voice raw, 'I'm sorry. I didn't know.'

Gideon didn't acknowledge it. 'Why?' he asked.

'Exhaustion, and strain, and being cold, and not having enough food, and bottling everything up when she should have screamed, or yelled, or thrown things. I managed to snare a doctor yesterday, and he says it's galloping consumption and there's nothing to be done.'

'Does she know?'

'I believe so. She's been trying to hide it for weeks, for my sake and the child's.'

'The child's?'

733

'Yes. For God's sake, come in, Gideon. Have a glass of wine – that's something we've never been short of. We must talk before you see her.'

When Gideon went in, later, to the exotic best bedroom, he knew most of what there was to know. About Worth's, and Arsène, and little Christian; Richard had chosen the name, years ago, in case little Luke had turned out to be a girl.

Francis hadn't held anything back. He had said, 'You have eyes, and I guess you can see something of what there is between us. I promise you, Gideon, she has been happy these last weeks in spite of everything. I believe you are too wise to let it hurt you.'

Too wise? Gideon thought. Never that. For it did hurt, quite damnably.

She was like a wraith, lying there in the huge, red-tented room. Once before, Gideon remembered seeing her eyes as huge as this, in the pale, peaked little face, but he recognized instantly that Francis was right about one thing. This time there was no anguish, only peace.

She smiled at him, though her voice was little more than a whisper. 'Gideon! Have you ridden to my rescue again? Tea, and butter, and bread, and oranges? And shawls?'

He smiled back. 'No shawls. I couldn't find any palaces to loot.' He sat down and took the almost transparent hand in his. 'No oranges, either. You should have let me know about the baby, you dreadful girl!'

'Have you seen her?'

'Not yet.'

'She's so sweet, my baby. Strong and healthy. Very much alive. I managed it this time, Gideon, dear.'

Lifting her hand, he held it to his lips. 'Couldn't you have managed it without reducing yourself to this state?'

'Oh, no! I couldn't, don't you see? She needed everything. Don't you understand? I didn't dare . . .' She was helplessly anxious to convince him, and hadn't the strength to do it.

'Hush, pet. *Hush!* I do understand.'

Before his smile, she relaxed again, and there was a weak mischief in her defiance. 'I wasn't going to be beaten this time. I was *damned* if I was!'

'Language! That's what comes of all this bourgeois insistence on earning your living.' He knew he was talking down to her, as if she were still the pretty child who had clung to him on the fishing boat all those years ago. But it was an easier note to strike than any adult one.

'I managed that, too. Poor Monsieur Worth. He'll open again soon. I hope he finds someone who can understand my filing system.'

It was an admission, but he wouldn't acknowledge it. 'I don't suppose,' he said reprovingly, 'that you've even rememberd me, slaving away at the family chronicle. Damn the files! What about the diaries?'

'Heavens! Are you still doing that? How funny. I'd forgotten. It's like another world. No, Gideon, dear, no diaries. I'm sorry.'

The small, emaciated hand with its oval, bloodless nails, moved in his. 'Are you tired?' he asked anxiously. 'Should I leave you to sleep?'

'In a minute. Gideon, you've always been so good to me.' She stopped, gathering breath. 'We mightn't have another chance to talk. It will soon be too hard for me, I think. Gideon, I won't be here much longer . . .'

He opened his lips to protest, but she stopped him, her smile a little twisted. 'No, don't be idiotic, Gideon. I *know*. And you must be able to see. I don't mind, really. After all the sad years, Francis has given me so much happiness. It's the best time to go, in the fullness of happiness. Strange, but I've been remembering Vilia. She said something like that to me when my father died, though peace of mind was all she was talking about. I remember it because that kind of softness seemed so unlike her. How is she?'

'Well enough in body. But she hasn't been very – approachable – since Sorley died.'

'Has he gone? What a pity. I liked him. Poor Vilia. There was a time when we didn't get on very well, but it doesn't matter any more.'

Her eyes were distant, and he could see that the world to which she had belonged for most of her life meant nothing to her now. He prompted her gently. 'You wanted to say something.'

'Did I?' Her heavy lids fluttered. 'Oh, yes. It's easy for me to go, but Francis will be hurt. And the baby.'

Gideon put his free hand over his mouth, aware that it was beginning to tremble, but managed to say, somehow, 'You've fought so hard to raise her. You can't just go, now, and leave her.'

When he glanced up, her eyes were open on his and there was a loving mockery in them. 'Silly Gideon! It's not a matter of choice. You can't force me back into the world just with words, you know.'

'No.'

'I wanted to ask you. Will you look after them for me?'

'My dear, I'll try. But Francis is a grown man.'

'We haven't talked about what will happen when I'm gone. He thinks it helps me to pretend, and perhaps he's right. But I can't go on pretending, now. It's too near the end for me. If he wants to take my baby back to America with him – would that be best? He would love her so much.' She gave a little gasp. 'Oh, Gideon, Gideon! Don't look so stricken, my dear. It hurts me more than anything.'

Blinking, he said, 'It's what you want that matters. Christy can go with Francis, or come home with me. Amy and I would love her, too. We have a little boy of almost the same age.'

A light came into her eyes. 'Oh, Gideon, have you? I'm so *glad* for you. Is he a darling?'

Gideon's strangled chuckle helped him to subdue the rising tears. 'That's not quite the word. He's a living terror!'

Her eyes laughed back at him. 'Just what a boy should be, in fact. I don't know, my dear. It's just that, in a way, I feel that Francis and little Christy belong together. The two well-springs of my happiness.'

He left her then, and the next day she was almost too weak to talk.

Four days after that, she died, and it was Francis, not Gideon, who was with her at the end.

Chapter Four

1

'Take your nose out of that book, Steven,' Amy said, 'and come and have your lemonade. There's a biscuit for that idle dog, too, if you'd like to poke him in the ribs.'

It was a summer afternoon in 1879, and the sun cast a sleepy glow over the garden of the house in Clifton Hill, bleaching the colour out of the herbaceous flowers and annuals Amy was so clever with, and whose names Gideon could never remember. It was an English garden, and yet not an English garden, for there was a touch of tidied-up

Chinese wilderness about it, and there was one part that was undiluted Colonial Williamsburg. The lawn was a disgrace. Twelve-year-old Steven was mad about cricket, and Gideon and the dog had worn the grass down to bare earth, the one bowling and the other fielding to the boy's bat, which wasn't as straight as it might have been. It was a friendly, human kind of garden.

The tea table was set out under the old pear tree, and Gideon flopped down in one of the chairs and held out a hand for his cup. He had stopped slaving for the *Times-Graphic* years ago. Fanshawe had died with his boots on – or, to be more precise, sitting at his desk with proofs before him and a pen in his hand – and the paper had been taken over by someone Gideon didn't much care for. So Gideon had retired and begun to write books again. The public had an insatiable appetite for good substantial works of popularization, and Gideon had a talent for those. He was meditating one now, about the Nile, because there was trouble brewing there and it was always good to be first in the field. Writing books was just as hard work as reporting had been, but at least he was master of his own time and could take tea in the garden when he wanted to.

He was just opening his mouth to ask, lazily, what Steven was reading, when the second parlourmaid came tripping across the grass, primly capped and aproned, and said, 'Please sir, there's a gentleman to see you. A messenger from' – she stumbled over the name, and Gideon didn't entirely blame her – 'from Taggart and Meiklejohn. He said I was to tell you it was Taggart and Meiklejohn *WS*.'

WS? Writers to the Signet, which meant a firm of Edinburgh lawyers. He raised his brows. 'Bring him out, Polly, and you'd better bring an extra cup as well.'

But the gentleman who appeared was not the kind to sit in wicker chairs and eat cucumber sandwiches with an inquisitive mongrel sniffing round his trouser legs.

He had come only to deliver, and ask a receipt for a box that had been deposited with his firm fifty years ago. Gideon signed dutifully, and said, 'Who was the depositor?'

'Mr Telfer, sir.'

He didn't have to ask which Mr Telfer. Was it really fifty years since Luke had died?

The man was scarcely out of earshot when Amy exclaimed, 'What is it? I am just dying of curiosity. Fifty years ago! What can it be? Stop teasing me, Gideon!'

'Can't you guess? Luke Telfer's chapters of the family chronicle. Old Mungo wanted to be sure that no cats were let out of bags until – what was the phrase Shona told me he had used? – until everyone involved was either "snibbed in a mortsafe, or past the age of caring". He didn't reckon on Vilia, did he?'

'But surely he can't have known that Vilia would ever be involved? She didn't marry Magnus until years after the old man died, did she?'

Fingering the dark green leather that covered the box, Gideon murmured, 'No, she didn't, of course. I wonder what he'd have thought about that? What a long time ago it all was.'

He didn't open the box until late that evening, when he was alone in his study. He felt a little like Pandora. It was a handsome box – measuring about fifteen inches by ten, and roughly six inches deep, its flat top hinged like the cover of a book – and beautifully bound, the leather scarcely even faded. On the front was a label. 'Confidential', it said, and underneath, in smaller letters, 'In the event of my death, this box is to be consigned, unopened, to the care of Taggart and Meiklejohn WS of Edinburgh, or their successors or assigns, in whose care it is to remain for a period of fifty years.' There was a lock on the side, an old-fashioned coded one, for which the law clerk had supplied Gideon with both code and key. Gideon would have been prepared to bet that the box had been old Mungo's idea; it sounded just like what he knew of the old man. A trifle guiltily, he thought of his own notes, lying about where anyone could read them.

Although he had a sense of expectancy when he began reading, he didn't really expect anything in particular. He thought he knew most of the facts, and Luke, as far as he remembered, hadn't been exactly perceptive.

My father, Magnus Telfer, has no literary inclinations and the most awe-inspiring lack of interest in anyone other than himself, his wife Lucy, and me, his son Luke. And I would hesitate about going to the stake for my belief in the last name on that list.

As a result, when my grandfather took the notion of a family chronicle into his head, he decided to saddle me with the task of writing it. I didn't want it in the least. I thought, in the finical way one does at sixteen, that the prying into people's lives that would be involved would not be quite . . . 'honourable' was the word I think I used at the time. But the old man was set on the idea, and that was that. He was a shrewd and powerful personality and I was terrified of him, even while I was fond of, and admired him. So I would have done as I was bid, even if he had not sweetened the demand with the honest, and very persuasive, bribery of an independent income.

Gideon went on reading into the small hours that night, and on the two nights that followed. There was, after all, a great deal he hadn't known, but he was at a loss to evaluate it. Time after time he stopped reading, striving for a clearer memory of the young man who had died when he himself was only fourteen. He could still catch an impression of the face, and the manner, and the atmosphere of him. He could remember not liking him very much, because he had been so self-centred, and his interest in Vilia's boys had always struck Gideon as false. What had his judgement been like? What the *hell* had his judgement been like? His story struck Gideon as unbalanced, but in a way that it was hard to put a finger on until Gideon reminded himself that this wasn't straight reporting, but reporting complicated by hindsight. He grinned to himself, remembering that this must have been Luke's one and only venture into authorship. He had probably read significance into a great many events that weren't significant at all. Like Vilia's outburst on her first day at St James's Square, and Lucy Telfer's accident with the marbles.

That explained a lot, and Gideon went back to the manuscript in a less critical frame of mind. There was a good deal about people he didn't know, of course, but he was interested to discover the tale of Perry Randall's last few months before he had sailed for the New World. All he had ever heard before was casual references to gambling debts. He hadn't known about Magnus's part in calling them in, or about Perry's months in sanctuary. No wonder Perry had always been reticent about that period of his life, even, Gideon had discovered, with his son Francis.

From Francis, who idolized his father, Gideon had learned a good deal about Perry, and about his affaire with Vilia. None of it would ever have emerged, he thought, if he and Francis hadn't felt the need to grasp at any subject of conversation that would divert their minds from the pale, wasted figure who lay dying in the room across the hall; the shade of the Juliana they both loved. Francis had been asking about Vilia, for he had been quite unable to see in the arrogant old lady of

Christmas 1867 the warm, passionate, loving Vilia Cameron who had possessed his father's heart for fifty bitter-sweet years, and of whom he had spoken so much during his last days. He had been haunted, Francis said, by how beautiful their love had been when it existed in its own crystal bubble, isolated from the world, but sad and almost tragic when he talked of how pride and circumstances and misunderstanding could so easily bring the most perfect love to ruin. Gideon, who had thought he knew, or suspected, all there was to know about Vilia and Perry, had been both astounded and fascinated to discover how lasting and obsessive the relationship had really been. Not just a moment of madness in 1815, and one other meeting and a quarrel twenty years later. He had found himself wondering how much Theo knew, or had guessed, of all this.

That had been eight years ago, and he had never found out. When Juliana died, he had been forced to telegraph Theo, but he had known Theo couldn't reach Paris in time for the funeral. He had no need to search his conscience over what should be done. The moment it was over, he had packed Francis Randall off to the coast with little Christy and a nursemaid, and instructions to sail on the first ship for America. He had said, 'I don't intend to tell Theo anything about the child. He might just insist on taking her home and bringing her up as his own. And that would be an unthinkable betrayal of Juliana's memory. So you must go before he arrives.'

'You'll stay?'

'Of course. I'll convey the impression that this apartment was Juliana's, though I'm damned if I know how I'm going to explain where she found the money for its upkeep. But I'll think of something.'

As it transpired, Theo had been so angry when he arrived that no explanations were necessary. There was ice-cold fury in his eyes when he demanded to know how Gideon had dared to take matters into his own hands when he learned that Juliana was in Paris. And how *had* he learned?

Lying stoutly, Gideon had spoken of the *Times-Graphic*'s man in the besieged city, and an accidental meeting with Juliana, and a message out about her.

'I see. And it didn't occur to you to let me know what had happened to *my wife*? I don't believe you. I believe you have been aiding and abetting her ever since she left me. In fact, I believe you have been cuckolding me, brother dear! Why else were you here so soon after the siege was lifted? Where else did she find the money for a place like this? Why didn't you telegraph me the moment you arrived and discovered what state she was in? Did you want to clutch her death-bed to your lying, cheating, necrophiliac little heart? You disgust me. If this was my wife's apartment, then it is mine now. So take your things and get out.'

Stunned by the viciousness of the attack, Gideon stared at his brother. After fifty-six years of knowing him, he didn't really know him at all. But what was worse than that, what struck him with an almost physical impact, was the recognition that although Theo was wrong on the level of reality, he was right on the level of dreams.

His face like stone, he said, 'Don't be a fool, Theo.'

Then he had walked out and, coming back to London, had told Amy everything. It had hurt and shamed him to discover that she had already guessed most of it, and didn't love him less. He hadn't seen Theo since.

With a sigh, he went back to Luke's manuscript. Where he discovered how his grandfather, Duncan Lauriston, had died. And discovered, too, that Vilia had once thought of marrying Luke Telfer himself.

It was a long time since he had been so surprised by anything. She couldn't have loved him; she hadn't even liked him very much. Could it have been for Kinveil, as early as that? It was only in very recent years that he had become conscious that she was more than just extravagantly fond of the place, despite her talk on that long-ago day about her 'dark and distant shore'. To live with people for so long, to pride oneself on one's understanding, and then to discover how little one knew of them after all!

After a while, he let out a little gust of breath and began putting all the papers back in their box. It didn't matter now. Mungo Telfer had been right, and most of the people Luke had written about were safely underground, even if it was no longer necessary for their coffins to be locked in iron frames to foil the bodysnatchers. Everyone except Vilia, who was eighty-three years old and past the age of caring.

He wondered, again, how much Theo had known or guessed of all this. Inquisitive, perceptive Theo. Perhaps it was time for them to make their peace. Next spring, Gideon thought, he would take Amy and Steven up to Kinveil when Theo would be there.

He snapped the lock on the box, and it sounded like the death knell of a past world. Irrelevant now. So irrelevant, all of it.

2

He was quite wrong about that, although he didn't know until he was told.

In November, Polly brought him a letter that had just been delivered by hand. Fearful of losing track of a rather complicated piece of syntax, he finished his sentence before he opened it. There was a single sheet of paper inside, with a newspaper clipping attached; not from one of the nationals, his practised eye told him. He glanced at the signature on the letter.

It was a moment before he placed the name, but it woke him up abruptly. Dominic Harvey. Lavinia's first husband, and Theo's 'friend'.

Dear Lauriston – Although we have never met, you may recall that I was for some time married to your niece Lavinia, and that I have been acquainted with your brother for many years. I am writing to you now because I have always understood you to have a generous disposition, and I find myself temporarily embarrassed. That sounds misleading. In fact, I ask not for myself, but for a young connection of yours, Jay Barber, who urgently needs assistance. I imagine you may not have seen the enclosed item from one of the suburban papers. The nationals have not yet got hold of it, or else may have been silenced; the latter, possibly, since I understand that a minor member of the royal family is involved. But it is imperative for Jay to leave the country until the fuss dies down. I would, of course, have applied to your brother for funds, if time had permitted. As it is, if you should have fifty pounds about you, that would suffice to see Jay across the Channel. May I say again that the matter is urgent. I imagine that your first instinct might be to come here yourself, but I beg you will not. Jay is in a highly nervous state, and in no condition to face someone whom he is convinced must disapprove unequivocally of the whole unfortunate affair. Yours &c – Dominic Harvey.

Hell, Gideon thought. Oh, *hell!* The newspaper report was littered with words like 'obscene', 'disgusting', 'scandalous', 'indecent', and the usual titillating remarks about things the editor considered too offensive to readers' delicate sensibilities to be stated on the page. But it was perfectly clear that the premises the police had raided the evening before had been a boy brothel. Gideon had visited one once in the course of preparing an exposé of vice in London, when Fanshawe had had a reforming bee in his bonnet. He remembered that the place had been divided into cubicles, with a boy of about fifteen or sixteen in each, his face painted, his mannerisms those of a girl, his 'professional' name a female one, and his voice a high, careful falsetto.

The police, last night, hadn't managed to lay their hands on more than two or three of their quarry. 'Several of these disgusting young perverts, as well as a number of adults about whose motives for being on the premises there can be little doubt, escaped through a secret exit, but the police have been able to issue descriptions of some of them . . . Third on the list is a youth known as "Jane", who is of slender build, fair complexion, and a general delicacy of appearance, if it is possible to use such a word as "delicacy" in connection with such a revolting affair. With all the power of its voice, this newspaper demands of the government that it ceases to conspire in the hushing up of such scandalous offences against public morality . . .' Etcetera, etcetera.

Until 1861, the maximum penalty for what the law termed 'gross indecency' had been death; now it was life imprisonment, with ten years as a minimum. Gideon could understand why young Jay or 'Jane' was anxious to leave the country.

Gideon had always kept a substantial sum of money in the house; more than once it had enabled him to set off on some journalistic mission when he would otherwise have had to wait until the banks were open. Putting a hundred pounds in an envelope, he sent his manservant off with it. Inside, he put a brief note, saying only, 'Bon voyage, Jay, and let us know as soon as you have an address.'

He didn't even know what the boy was like nowadays, except that he had been to a good school and had acquitted himself reasonably well. All he remembered was a pale, fair, nervous child, too much surrounded by women.

'I should have foreseen it!' he exclaimed to Amy. 'I should have foreseen *something* of the sort.'

'Why?' she asked, her eyes on her stitchery.

He knew he shouldn't be talking to her about such a subject, which no well-bred woman was supposed even to be aware of. But when he had told her about Juliana in '71, he had been so anxious to show her in the most sympathetic possible light that he had told Amy about Theo, too, and had been almost shocked to discover that Amy was scarcely shocked at all. She had said, 'I'm not blind, my dear, and it's hardly a new phenomenon. The Chinese, if I remember from my reading, call it *lung-yang*.' She was a remarkable woman.

'Why? Because I've been worried ever since Theo was appointed the boy's guardian. I should have kept an eye on him, on them both.'

'How could you? With Jay at Glenbraddan or at school, and us in London, it wouldn't have been possible.'

'I could have managed it somehow.' Rising, he wandered over to the window and stood looking out at the street. It was dusk, and the lamplighter was plodding along, propping his ladder against each lamp post in turn, climbing two or three rungs, turning the gas on and lighting it so that it burned blue at first and then a cold greenish-yellow, and then climbing down and shouldering his ladder and plodding on to the next lamp on his round. He had to go through the whole procedure again, in reverse, in the morning. What a placid, unsurprising life it must be, Gideon thought enviously.

'Even after you quarrelled with Theo?'

He moved, restlessly. 'Perhaps not.' And then he burst out with more bitterness than she had ever heard in his voice before, '*Damn him!* To take and shape an innocent child, so that it all ends up like this! If I were a violent man, I think I would kill him for it.'

Frowning a little, Amy said, 'Must it be Theo's fault? Surely he wouldn't do such a thing deliberately? What purpose could he have?'

'It's hardly the kind of thing he'd be likely to do by mistake! No, the more I think about it, the surer I am. Even while he was married to Juliana, he had the boy on a leash.' That was something he hadn't told Amy before. 'And you can probably include malice in the equation, too. The boy's father and grandfather were very much holier-than-thou, and I'm sure Theo has derived a good deal of cold-blooded amusement from the whole thing. What I don't understand is what the poor little devil was doing on his own in London – though I suppose he may have been staying with Harvey – and why the *hell* he should have been sitting there soliciting in a cheap brothel!'

Repressing an urgent desire to rush upstairs and make sure that her own son was safe in his room, studying, Amy murmured, 'A boyish trick, probably.'

Her husband turned and stared at her, and she went on, eyebrows raised a little, 'Don't you think so? Schoolboy mischief that went sour? I could see Steven doing just that.'

'God forbid!'

'And amen!' She chuckled. 'You know very well I didn't mean *exactly* that. But if he didn't *have* to be there for – well, for satisfaction, what other reason can there have been?'

'I don't know. I just don't know. Dear Lord, what happens now? I'd better let Theo know, in case Harvey doesn't. He'll have to arrange to transfer funds. It's a filthy world, sometimes. I was going to make my peace with Theo at Kinveil in the spring, but I don't know whether I will even be able to look at him without being sick.'

She said quietly, 'You want to go rushing up there now to have it out with him, don't you? But it's too late, my dear. There's nothing you can do, and it's better to wait until you've cooled off.'

He crossed to her and, taking the embroidery from her hands and putting it aside, pulled her up to her feet and gently into his arms. His lips buried in her hair, he said, 'Oh, Amy, what would I do without you? Never have any doubts, my dearest. For I do love you very much.'

After the dangerous shoals, it was a marriage that had come safe to harbour.

3

The sun was blazing once more out of the blue, and London's gardens were heavy with roses, white and garnet and lax-petalled pink, when Gideon set out in June for Kinveil and arrived to find a luminous grey veil over the whole wide vault of the sky and the rain falling straight and leaden through the still air. Foliage and grass were tropically lush, richly virulently, oppressively green, except where the furious magenta of foxgloves and early heathers screamed defiance at yellow hawksbeard and buttercups, and the lingering blue of speedwell.

Gideon and Theo met like two civilized adults, as if there had never been anything amiss between them. Theo was sixty-six years old now, his long neck stringy and his bony chin standing high above the stiffened collar, with its narrow black four-in-hand tie. His hair was white, smoothed back over his forehead but waving over the ears, and he had grown a cavalry moustache which he twirled affectedly when he talked. His eyes, above it, were bright and bird-like.

'Vilia will join us shortly,' he said. 'She likes her nap in the afternoons, and one doesn't wish to discourage her. It gives everyone an hour or two's rest from dancing attendance. She's very demanding now that she can't get around easily, although since rheumatism is the curse of the glens, she was bound to succumb to it one day. And you will be desolated to know that you won't see dear Shona for a week or so. She has gone to Glenbraddan. One of the girls is being married next month, and you would think from the high state of tension that prevails that no girl had ever been married before. So tell me, dear boy, how are your charming wife and young Steven?'

Amy, considering that her and Steven's presence might hamper Gideon in his dealings with Theo, had cried off, and Gideon hadn't argued. But it was odd how many memories it brought back, finding himself alone with only his mother and brother for company. Odder still to realize that the three of them had never before been alone together at Kinveil, the sturdy little castle on its sea-girt tumble of rocks, that had brooded over all their lives.

He wondered whether Theo was intending to come and live here permanently. 'You're giving up the foundry, I hear?' he said when they were settled in the Long Gallery, with decanters and sandwiches to stay them until dinner.

'Indeed, indeed. We have grown at such dizzying speed since we became a limited company that the place has lost all its charm for me. It's too impersonal now, and it would be quite *infra dig.* for the senior Mr Lauriston to go and poke his nose into the furnaces, the way he used to do. I think I must have more of our paternal grandfather in me than I realized. "A foundry man at heart," as old Moultrie used to say, "with a real feeling for a nice iron bar". But it's Jermyn who's the technical genius now, and Peregrine James is handling the administrative side brilliantly, much though it goes against the grain for me to admit it. They don't need me any more, and, more importantly, I don't *want* them.'

'I see.' He did, too, and better than Theo guessed. Little tin gods never liked having their supremacy whittled away, and with Jermyn's mechanical machine gun making swift headway against competition from the Gatling, the Gardener, the Nordenfelt and the Lowell, Theo had lost not only his godhood but even his acquaintance with revealed truth. He had never mastered the finer details of gun design. 'So what next?' Gideon asked.

'Here, London, and perhaps some of the travelling I've never had time for. Unlike . . .'

He was interrupted by a bustle outside, and then Vilia stood in the doorway, leaning on two sticks, and with a youngish woman whom Gideon took to be her maid behind her.

'Really, Theo!' Her silvery voice was quite unchanged. 'I cannot imagine why you should be up here instead of in my drawing-room. You know how I dislike these stairs.' Her eyes switched forbiddingly towards her second son. 'Ah, Gideon! How very condescending of you to visit me at last. Ten years, I believe?'

He went over and took her by the elbow. 'Which chair, my dear?'

She sniffed. He was much better-looking than Theo now, she thought. Not so scraggy, and his eyes still had that warmth that had always been his downfall – and everyone else's. Infinitely kind; infinitely uncommitted. He had shaved off the moustache and beard he had been sporting when he came back from China, and now wore only sidewhiskers. She was pleased to see that his mouth was still firm. It was a nice mouth, neither too thin nor too full. She had always liked men with nice mouths. But that didn't change the fact that she was annoyed with him. 'Don't fuss!' she exclaimed testily. 'I'm perfectly capable of finding my way to a chair. It's only the stairs that trouble me. Now! Where have you been, and why have you not brought Amy and the boy?'

There wasn't anything wrong with his mother's tongue, Gideon reflected, reluctantly amused, and nothing wrong with her dress sense, either. Unless he was much mistaken, fashion had caught up with her at last, for 1880 had discovered the Aesthetic mode, and his mother was wearing the latest 'Pilgrim gown', a seamless confection in red wool, confined by a cord at the waist, and embellished with a hood that fell, softly draped, over tight-fitting sleeves. She wore no jewellery but the Kinveil ring and, at her throat, Perry Randall's cravat pin. Gideon knew what that meant now, and his eyes softened a little. For eighty-four, she was a marvel, and although she had painted her lined

747

cheeks, and the green of her eyes was arctically pale, she was still beautiful, in her own brittle, rarefied way. He devoted all his attention to placating her, and after a while even succeeded in making her laugh.

He didn't rush to bring up with Theo the subject he wanted to have out with him, but listened smilingly as Vilia talked about the estate and Theo about the foundry. Vilia didn't approve of the armaments business, and neither did Gideon, but Theo said, 'People who want to fight will always find weapons. They might as well find ours.' Gideon didn't argue, because he had long ago resigned himself to the knowledge that there were some things one could do nothing about.

It was four days before he said anything, and then only because Theo gave him the perfect opening. They were standing on the sea wall, looking out over a vista of thick greys and livid greens. The sky was so low that it seemed to be resting on their heads.

'It absorbs you, doesn't it?' Theo said. 'Soaks you into itself, so that you're part of it. Drains you; turns your limbs heavy and atrophies your mind. Nothing exists but you and the landscape – fated, doomed, inseparable, now and for ever more.'

Gideon knew what he meant. After a moment, he said, 'Inseparable? Do you really feel like that about it?'

His brother's eyes turned towards him, malice rekindling. 'Of course. It runs in the blood. You feel it too, surely? After all, there have been Camerons at Kinveil for five hundred years.'

A youthful, silvery voice murmured in Gideon's head, 'And now no more.' He repeated it aloud and then, slowly, said, 'I have to talk to you about Jay.' He wasn't angry any more; he had passed that stage. All that possessed him was a tired humiliation; shame for what his brother had done, and shame for his own indifference. 'Can you tell me how he came to be in that revolting place? How he came to develop such tastes? Because I can't believe you didn't have a hand in it, and I hope you won't try to persuade me otherwise.'

Theo had turned away while Gideon was speaking, so that only his profile was visible, bony but sagging about the jaw, his lower lip pink and protuberant under the white moustache. 'No, dear boy. Why should I? Our young friend is no concern of yours.'

'Of course he is. I'm a human being, and he's related, however distantly. I want to know if he learned his tricks from you.'

Theo's left hand was in his trousers pocket, and with his right he carried his after-dinner cigar to his mouth and drew the smoke in thoughtfully. 'Did I teach him? He didn't need teaching, dear boy. Just – how shall I put it? – encouraging. Even you would have found your enthusiasm for the female sex flagging if you had grown up as one lonely little male swaddled in a blanket of Grace, and Isa, and five sisters, and Aunt Petronella.'

Gideon shook his head. 'It won't do, Theo. The instinct may have been there, but it takes more than that. It takes knowledge he didn't find in his nunnery. Don't play games with me. I want the truth.'

'Yes,' his brother said pensively. 'That prying journalistic nose of yours. You know so much, don't you? But you're soft. You always have been. I'd have liked you more, you know, if you'd thrown a fit that day you found me in Theresa Berkley's brothel in – when was it? – '33? But you didn't. You nobly kept quiet about it. And about friend Hugh in the village, and dear Dominic, and no doubt some of the others. You think you have a charming little dossier on me, don't you?'

Taking a breath of salty air, and wet seaweed, and Havana smoke, Gideon said, 'That wasn't the way I saw it. I was simply leaving you to lead your life, as I led mine.'

'Not quite. You're forgetting Juliana, aren't you?' Turning, Theo hitched himself half up on to the sea wall and sat, one hand resting loosely on his knee, his eyes inimical.

That was something Gideon didn't dare to pursue. 'Perhaps. But what you're doing is evading the issue. You can't just ruin the boy and then shrug it off as if your duty stops with sending funds abroad to him. I want to know what you're going to do to set things right.'

A slow and quite delightful smile spread over Theo's face. 'What am I going to do to set things right?' he repeated.

But before he could say more, Vilia's voice cut in from behind them. 'Why, pray, should he do anything?' She was bundled up against the damp air, shawled and bonneted like some old henwife, and the almost phosphorescent quality of the light made her eyes intensely green. 'After all, if Jay daren't set foot in this country, he can hardly inherit Kinveil, can he? I have written to ask Peregrine James about having Magnus's Will contested. The courts might well agree to pass over Jay in favour of Neil or Callum. Did you know Jermyn and Madge have christened the new baby Callum? I've no idea why.'

All the knowledge, all the suspicions that Gideon had been staving off for months began to fall into place. Because there were great pieces missing, he had tried to persuade himself there wasn't a pattern, although he knew there was. Dully, he said to Theo, 'So it wasn't just casual destructiveness? This was what you were aiming at?'

Tossing the butt of his cigar into the sea, Theo remarked, 'Well, *someone* had to give Vilia some help, dear boy!'

'*Help to do what?* Ruin people's lives?'

'Really, Gideon. There's no need to be melodramatic,' his mother said. 'No one forced Jay to get into trouble.'

'But he's only sixteen!'

'Almost seventeen. Quite old enough to know what he's doing.' She tapped her stick peremptorily on the flagstones. 'I want to sit down. You may bring me that chair from the corner.'

He brought it, and lent her his hand as she lowered herself into it. Then he said, his voice grating, 'What else have you done?' He didn't want to know, but he had to.

After a moment, she replied, 'I've no idea what you mean. Please go and tell Fraser to have some tea sent out to me.' But he didn't move.

Theo, watching Gideon, twirled his moustache and said affectedly, 'I don't think you're going to get away with it as easily as that, Vilia dear.'

She was in a tetchy mood, and Theo's mannerisms irritated her more and more these days. She didn't want him living at Kinveil. 'I don't need your advice,' she snapped.

There was a moment's silence while Theo fought to hold on to the suavity that was the facade he presented to the world. And then it cracked. It was the first time Vilia had seen it happen in all the sixty-six years since she had borne him, and it gave her considerable satisfaction. The prospect of Theo being honest for once had a real, if dubious, charm. It was clear that he was going to be rude to her, and, inside her head, she chuckled. It was quite a while since anything entertaining had happened, and she waited to hear what he had to say with the same morbid fascination she would have brought to reading her own obituary.

But what came was more than she had bargained for.

All his life, Theo had been cleverer than most people at anything he turned his hand to, and that had been enough to justify what his acquaintances regarded as his pose of Olympian superiority, especially as he had enough of the Cameron charm to carry it off. The truth, however, was that it was no pose. It pleased him when some railway baron congratulated him on his mastery of new techniques, or when one of the puddlers remarked, 'There's no doubt you're the best, Mr Theo,' but only because they were acknowledging the obvious. It didn't alter his contempt for them; it didn't even flatter his self-esteem. He simply thought it right and proper that they should recognize that he was second to none.

Unfortunately, over the last ten years or so, they had gradually stopped recognizing it. Not even to himself had Theo ever conceded that his excellence was founded, at least in part, on the fact that what he couldn't do better than anyone else, he didn't attempt. Equally without conscious thought, he had kept the foundry to the type of work over which he had complete mastery. But then had come Jermyn, with the talent that was very near genius for something that Theo at first didn't trouble to, and then found he couldn't, master. And Peregrine James had put his oar in, too, by insisting on having Lauristons' turned into a limited company. Theo hadn't foreseen the disastrous effect that would have on his own authority.

He had always found it satisfying to appear to know everything; even more satisfying, sometimes, really to know and yet remain silent, hugging the knowledge to his exulting heart. But now, still rankling within him, was the memory of an episode that had happened a few days ago. He'd given an order to one of the foundrymen, and turned away; and, too soon, another man had murmured to the first, 'Aye, well, Jock. That's only Mr Theo's view. You'd better see what Mr Jermyn thinks. He'll know better.'

And tonight, Gideon had had the insolence to criticize him, and Vilia was speaking as if he were of no account. Vilia, the only person in the world who had ever made him doubt – just a little – his own supremacy, about whom he had always felt competitive, and who was more secure in herself than he was. It was too much. Everyone thought he was past it, but by God he'd prove that he was still to be reckoned with. 'Omniscient Theo,' Gideon had always called him, and he still was, and knowledge was power. He'd show them. *He'd show them!*

His eyes glittering and his smile fixed, he repeated, 'You – don't – need – my advice? You have no idea, have you, how very tired I am of you underrating me and condescending to me! You never even listen to what I say, because you think you know what it's going to be. You played the same trick with Magnus, I remember. Well, *you know nothing* about me! Whereas I know everything about you. I could undergo a very stiff examination indeed on the details of your insalubrious career, mother dear. You have never told me anything, except when you've been thinking aloud, and let something slip, but it's never mattered. Because I can read you, just like a book.'

It was not what she had been expecting, and she didn't like it. 'That will do, Theo,' she said tightly.

'Oh, no. I've been saving it up for years, what I know about you. And especially I've been saving up the things I know, *and you don't*.'

She would have risen, if she could, and walked away. But her rheumatism was always bad in damp weather, so that she needed help, and she could see from Gideon's face that there was no help to be had from him. And she certainly wasn't going to try – and ingloriously fail – to rise on her own. Gritting her teeth, she waited. Perhaps it was time for the truth to come out. If it had been one of her good days, she might even have enjoyed it.

'You want me to prove it? Well, let's start with Guy, shall we? You didn't just bring him up here hoping that he would put Magnus off him for life. You hoped he might seduce Juliana. He was certainly the type. And then Magnus would have cut *both* of them out of his Will. It didn't work, but at least Guy obliged by seducing Lizzie instead, so you did achieve something.'

Vilia flashed a glance at Gideon, and then put her hand on his arm. 'I was genuinely sorry about that, my dear. I wouldn't have had it happen for the world. Guy was a most unsatisfactory young man, but I'm afraid Lizzie failed to recognize it.'

She didn't realize that she was virtually confirming what Theo had said. Gideon stared at her. Poor, dependent little Lizzie, caught in the toils of Vilia's obsession. 'I see,' he said after a moment. 'I've never understood why you didn't put a stop to it.'

'I tried. I did try. But Lizzie defied me.'

Cuttingly, Theo interrupted. 'It was her chance to escape, don't you see? She knew Vilia didn't care a button for her. Or you, Gideon. That was why she died.'

'Spare us this nonsense,' Vilia said. 'The child simply took an accidental overdose of laudanum.'

Theo crowed, and then, like an obnoxious little boy, chanted, 'I know something *you* don't know! Not accidental, Vilia dear. I found the note she sent Juliana.'

It shocked Vilia more than it did Gideon, who had lived with the suspicion of it for twenty-five years. His mind was more taken up with wondering whether Theo was really right, or whether he had put two and two together and come up with five. It all seemed too devious, too much a bow at a venture. Turning to Vilia, he said, 'You didn't put a stop to Juliana going to India, either.'

She shrugged irritably. 'Don't, for heaven's sake, start talking about the graveyard of the British again. We all had quite enough of that from Magnus.'

'But it was worth a try,' Theo said. 'It could have been a master stroke, except that she survived everything the place could throw at her.'

Gideon remembered Juliana telling him how surprised she had been that Vilia, whom she would have expected to be indifferent, had actively encouraged her in her marriage plans. But he rejected what his brother was saying, because it meant that Vilia had hoped Juliana would die. And that went too far.

Taking another thin cigar from his case, Theo clipped it, and lit it, and blew out a delicate cloud that hung on the muggy air like a halo. 'A pity Juley and I didn't generate any brats to settle the inheritance once and for all. She took a dislike to me; Lavinia's fault, mainly.' He grinned. 'I suppose I deserved it. Something else you don't know, Vilia dear! It was I, sure he'd be impotent, who coaxed Dominic into marrying Lavinia. Pure mischief, I'm afraid. I never liked the girl.'

Gideon could see that his mother was feeling as queasy as he was, but Theo rattled on, impervious. 'Anyway, I told Juley I wouldn't cavil if she wanted to find another father for our child – yes, Vilia, I was past the stage of caring whether it had Cameron blood or not! – but she didn't like the idea. She even finished by cursing me on the rowan tree! It was really quite funny. And considering which of us is still alive and well, I feel it rather blows the gaff on the rowan tree as one of the forces of destiny!'

Somehow, it caught Gideon on the raw in a way nothing else had. Theo was still laughing when he stepped forward and jerked his brother to his feet, twisting his hand savagely in the neat black tie. 'You're

753

mad,' he said, his voice shaking. 'Do you realize it? You're mad, and decadent, and disgusting. Christ, but you make me sick! You're like a child sticking pins in insects. There you sit, lord of creation, looking down on human beings as if they're some inferior form of life to be pricked and prodded as the fancy takes you. I've always known you were spiteful and self-satisfied, but this . . .'

He stopped and, abruptly releasing his grip, took a handkerchief from his pocket and began to wipe his fingers fastidiously. When he looked up again, Theo was still choking, and there was naked hatred in his eyes. Gideon met it levelly. 'It's you,' he said, 'not Vilia, who's the evil genius of this family.'

Half retching, Theo managed to whisper, 'Is it? *Is it?* You think that despising people is worse than murder?'

Vilia sighed theatrically.

But Gideon went on staring at his brother. He was exaggerating to make himself seem important, just like a child. Making mountains out of molehills. That was all. Murder? No. All Gideon's instincts rejected it. Civilized people might manipulate others, play havoc with their lives, even drive them into corners where suicide was the only way out. But they didn't go in for murder. This was Vilia – *this was their mother* Theo was talking about.

Yet still there was the pattern Gideon had sensed; his recognition that nothing connected with Vilia's passion for Kinveil was simple, unassisted coincidence. His mind flew backwards over the years. Ian Barber's death had been accidental; Guy Savarin's unquestionably the result of chloral addiction. Vilia couldn't have had a hand in those. Juliana, Magnus, Lizzie – no, however malign her influence on their lives. Then his mind stumbled for a moment. Juliana's mother, whose death had left the way free for Vilia to marry Magnus?

He looked at her. 'Juliana's mother?'

Exasperated and in pain, she said, 'This is the stupidest conversation! Julia Osmond died in childbirth, poor girl. There was nothing at all sinister about it.'

Theo said nothing.

It had been cholera with Lucy Telfer, and there had been a hundred witnesses to Luke Telfer's accident. Mungo? Impossible. But Duncan Lauriston . . . Vilia, sick and hysterical, pushing; and Sorley trying to save him; and the big man falling and being trampled to death. Was that what Theo meant? Manslaughter at the very worst, unless you were determined to read something into it!

The relief was so great that Gideon almost forgot his quarrel with Theo and spoke to him in the tone he might have used when they were boys. 'Oh, hell, Theo! You mean Grandfather Lauriston? Don't be such a bloody fool!'

And then he saw that Theo didn't know what he was talking about, for after a moment his eyes lit with the old, familiar inquisitiveness and he said slowly, 'Do tell me, dear boy. Have I missed something?'

It had begun to rain very slightly, the thin, fine rain that the English called a mizzle, and the Scots a smirr. It lay like a beaded net over Theo's waving white hair, and dewed the folds of his cheeks.

Vilia interrupted acidly, 'No, you haven't. He was bullying me, and I pushed him and he slipped. Misadventure, pure and simple.'

'Was Sorley there?'

'He tried to save him.'

'*Did* he?'

Her nostrils flared, but she didn't answer.

Gideon, aware of being watched by both of them, still could not prevent his confusion from showing. Nothing made sense. Duncan Lauriston didn't fit, anyway. He wasn't one of the Kinveil heirs who, in retrospect, had vanished as inexorably as snow in summer. Who *had* Theo meant? There wasn't anyone else.

Vilia was studying him with a kind of contemptuous amusement on her face, and at last she said, 'Oh, Gideon! Don't you know your brother by now? He's trying to be clever, that's all. I assure you, I haven't murdered anybody.' She yawned genteelly behind her hand. 'I must go to bed. That new woman of mine is quite Friday-faced if I keep her up. No stamina, these so-called ladies' maids nowadays. I'd like to have seen Berthe complain about late hours!'

'Berthe?'

'Vintage 1812,' Theo said. 'And no, Vilia. Gideon doesn't know me by now, and neither do you.'

Vilia had recognized, as soon as she said it, that she was inviting retribution with that dismissive 'trying to be clever'. But she didn't really care. She was eighty-four, and she was tired, and she wasn't well. Why *should* she care? What did it matter, after all? And Theo couldn't possibly know anything about the things that really counted. She opened her mouth to say, 'Have it your own way, Theo! Just help me out of this chair, one of you, so that I can go indoors. I'm getting wet.'

But before the words were uttered, Theo produced his ace. 'You didn't murder anybody, no. You didn't murder anybody because you didn't have to. Sorley was there to do it for you.'

4

Gideon dragged his eyes away from Theo and looked at his mother. Her face was grey-white, and her lips almost invisible.

She swallowed, and said, 'That will do, Theo!' She had always been able to dominate her sons.

But not this time. Nothing was going to stop Theo. 'Luke Telfer,' he spat. 'There was something going on between you, and you quarrelled with him. Sorley knew. And Sorley killed him. You can't deny it. *I saw it happen.*'

'No!' Gideon exclaimed. 'You're lying, Theo. I was there too, remember!'

'You were there too,' his brother sneered. '*Dear* Gideon, you were standing right outside that damned cottage when the roof tree slipped and crushed Luke's skull, but it never even occurred to you that Sorley had kicked it!'

The cottage had been cut into the slope of the hill, and there had been a fist fight going on above it, the combatants slithering and sliding no more than inches from the edge. Yes, it would have been easy, Gideon thought. A well-placed kick would have been enough to send the heavy beam swinging. But not Sorley! Dear God, not Sorley!

Theo was still talking. 'He took a chance, and it worked. And no one noticed except me. Because I was watching. I *was* clever, not "*trying to be*"!' The venom in his voice made Gideon shudder, but he went on more calmly, 'I've never understood why you allowed Juliana to survive her childhood, although there was that rather mysterious episode at the floating, wasn't there? But you managed without Sorley for quite a long time, until it came to Ian Barber. You couldn't handle him on your own. So Sorley had a go at him with his pocket sling, at the Reform meeting. It must have annoyed him when he missed. He always fancied himself with that sling. But he made no mistake the second time. Except staying out in the cold too long the night he tipped Ian off his horse.' He chuckled, restored almost to humour by the horror on Gideon's face and the frozen blankness on Vilia's.

Over a dozen years, Sorley's dying voice came back to Gideon. 'Only one . . . Only one left. I did it.'

This was something that couldn't be ignored, couldn't be rejected. This time Gideon had to believe what Theo had said, because it supplied the missing pieces of the pattern. It was unthinkable, but it made sense.

He turned to his mother and said, without expression, 'You knew. You must have known.'

They were all wet through now. He could feel the hair clammy against his neck and the trickles beginning to work their way under his collar. Theo's cigar, dropped when Gideon had laid hands on him, still lay on the flags, a sodden, disintegrating exclamation mark, with its head of ash neatly in line.

Theo said, with an opulent smile, 'Of course she knew. They were always close. Too close for decency, if you want my opinion.'

It was then that Vilia raised her stick, and struck him full across the mouth with it. The attack was so sudden that he staggered, and the parapet of the sea wall caught him across the back of the thighs, and he was half over it, backwards, before his scrabbling fingers took hold and he saved himself. After a long moment, he felt for his handkerchief and began dabbing at his lip, where a tooth had caught it. Then he looked at the blood and laughed. Happily. Gideon remembered Mrs Berkley's brothel, forty odd years ago. Theo had laughed then, too.

Incredulously, Gideon heard a faint sound beside him and turned to find that Vilia was giggling and shaking her head. And then she gasped, 'Oh, Mungo! Dear Mungo! If you hadn't been too heavy, and I too wee, how different things would have been!' He had no idea what she was talking about.

But she pulled herself together almost at once, and surveyed her sons, the smile dying from her eyes. 'You make it all sound so tidy! Have you not learned, even yet, what a shambles life is? You scrabble around, looking for bits that fit, and miss most of the things that matter.'

Gideon said, 'The marbles? You mean that Sorley left the marbles on the stairs, hoping Lucy Telfer would come to grief? You were old enough to marry Magnus if she'd died. Perhaps it was a pity he didn't succeed. It would have saved a good many people a good deal of sorrow.'

His mother's lip curled. 'I wasn't talking about that kind of thing.' She eased herself slightly in her chair. 'You both think you're so subtle and perceptive, but you understand nothing at all.'

One hand tucked in the small of her back, she succeeded in straightening up at the cost of a few twinges and a grimace or two. Then she looked at her sons again, and they suddenly realized that she was bitterly angry.

'Sit down,' she said, 'so that I don't have to look up at you all the time. Thank you. Now, you have both had your say, and it's time I had mine. But let us dispose of one little problem first. You choose to believe that Sorley was responsible for the deaths of Luke Telfer and Ian Barber. If he was, it was by no order of mine. You may be right, but I don't *know*, and I have never known. What I do know is that Sorley wanted me to have Kinveil as much as I did, and that morality, for him, began and ended with what I wanted. We knew each other for seventy years, and he was the finest friend I have ever had. Dear Sorley! He was very good to me.'

She paused, and Gideon, choking, said, '*Dear* Sorley!'

'Don't be commonplace.' The arbitrary green eyes turned on him. 'Everything has always been too easy for you. You have no conception of what it means to have to fight, because it's I who have done all the fighting and you who have reaped the benefits. You talk about Theo's Olympian superiority? But what about your own? I remember that marvellous tolerance of yours, that gave you such a delightful feeling of being raised above the common herd. You lost some of it for a while when you saw people bleed, and even bled a little yourself, but now you have your reputation, and your son, and Amy to pamper you, and you can look down your elegant nose again at anything that offends you.' Her voice sharpened. 'Understand me. I said "dear Sorley", and I meant it. You don't know, do you, that he saved my life? Not once, but three times.'

And that puzzled them, she was pleased to see. 'You believe I have never troubled to wonder what my sons were thinking? But my sons have never troubled to wonder about me.' She shook a dismissive hand. 'No, no, Theo. I'm not talking about tantalizing little intellectual puzzles, or vulgar inquisitiveness, I'm talking about agony of spirit, about which you know nothing. Three times in my life I was in so much pain and misery that all I wanted was to put an end to it. It happened twice in a few months when I was carrying Drew, and again in France in '35. On the first two occasions I was so weak that it was easy for Sorley to stop me. But the third time I fought him.' Her voice quivered. 'God, how I fought him! He still had the scar when he died.'

Gideon, appalled, remembered it, the long, white, jagged scar he had noticed when he was wrapping the plaids round the old fellow's shoulders on that last evening.

'So, why shouldn't I say, "dear Sorley?" He gave me more than either of you has ever done. He gave me total love and loyalty all his life. Perhaps it was because he forced me to stay alive when all I wanted to do was die, that he felt he had to make up for it by giving me what I needed more than anything. *I will not have you blame Sorley for anything he did.*'

The passion in her kept them both silent. Fire and ice, Gideon thought. Was this what had enthralled Perry Randall for so long? Was this what had captivated Mungo Telfer? Was this what had chained Sorley to her? The fires were as cold now as the Northern Lights. But they must once have been warm.

In the end, he had to say, 'But it's a specious argument, you know. Nothing justifies what he did.'

Her chin came up again. 'You don't understand even yet, do you? You've blood in your veins, I suppose? Theo has bile. Oh, don't waste your energy contradicting me, Theo! Nothing moves you except your precious vanity and the contempt you have for other people. It amuses you to watch people going to hell in their own way. Just as Gideon is prepared to defend to the death their *right* to go to hell in their own way. Where's the difference? Neither of you knows how to give.' Gideon opened his mouth. '*No*, Gideon! Elinor is dead, and Lizzie is dead, and you could have saved them both. Am I wrong in thinking that, if you had been a different man, you might have saved Juliana, too?'

It silenced him very effectively.

'Yes, well. Nature and nurture, isn't that what they say makes people what they are? I suppose that makes it my fault that you are both such cold fish. My fault that you are both sitting cosily in judgement on your

759

mother, looking down on her for being so crude as to know what she wanted and fight for it. Well, it's an unkind world, my children, and if I hadn't fought, we would all be starving in the gutter. But I don't remember either of you even saying thank you.

'Not that I ever expected it of you. Do you know who first taught me never to expect anything from anyone? My own father. And then *your* father taught me how deceptive appearances could be. And as if that wasn't enough, I fell in love with Perry Randall, and he taught me never to depend on anyone. And Luke Telfer and Magnus taught me all there was to know about people who take and take, and never give.'

Gideon could see that, suddenly, she was exhausted, but she wouldn't give in, although her voice became old and querulous. 'It can't surprise you that I rebelled? Why shouldn't I? I'm human, after all. There have been only three people in my life who have ever given, without reserve. My nurse Meg, who died before you were born. And Mungo Telfer. And Sorley. Everything they ever gave me, I gave back with all the love in my heart. But all anyone else has ever done is take.'

She hesitated, and then resumed more strongly. 'I don't mean Perry Randall. But that is something that *I will not have* pawed over in your frigid little minds! Understand this. I do not have to justify myself to you. It took me a long time to learn to be a realist, and until – until 1851 I was still vulnerable. But after that I taught myself that other people's priorities were not the only ones that counted. Diamond cut diamond. I didn't see why *my* priorities shouldn't matter, too. They've done no more than provide Theo with entertainment, but if they've hurt you, Gideon, I'm sorry. You should have been involved enough to fight back.'

Theo, predictably, was wearing his most irritating smile, but Gideon scarcely noticed. For the first time, he had really seen below the sometimes charming, sometimes autocratic veneer that had, to him, always been the sum and substance of his mother. She was right, of course. He had never really tried to understand her, although – now that they had been shown him – there had been pointers enough that he should have recognized. He had a brief glimpse of the truth Perry Randall had seen – that people and circumstances had conspired to turn her from what she had been into what she was.

And then the veil came down, and he knew that nothing could justify the tragedies that had overtaken his own daughter, Lizzie, and

Juliana, his heart's darling. And Luke, and Guy, and Ian Barber, and even Sorley, in a way. All victims of Vilia's obsession with this rickle of stones and mortar, and these wide, sour, sodden acres.

After a long time, he rose from his perch on the wall and stood before her, looking down into her eyes – 'mermaid's eyes', Luke Telfer had called them. 'You're right,' he said. 'I've never done what I should, and it's time I started. I'm going to try and make some kind of restitution. If it's the last thing I do, I'm going to see that young Jay doesn't fall victim to your obsession. I'm going to see that, somehow, he wins through and comes back here to Kinveil. Because it isn't yours, Vilia, and you have no right to it. Don't you see that? *You can't be allowed to win.*' He turned to go.

And then Theo threw back his head and laughed. 'How I hate to ruin such a splendid exit line, dear boy. But I've been saving my trump till last.'

His eyes brilliant with pleasure, he surveyed them both. 'I know things that you don't know! As Jay's official guardian, I had a communication this afternoon from the police department in Hamburg. Jay, foolish boy, took a young thug into his lodgings and – if you'll forgive me – his bed. A murderous young thug, I'm afraid. Jay is dead.' The rain was dripping from his moustache, but his smile was dazzling. 'And that card, Vilia dear, takes the trick, don't you think?'

5

Vilia had never admitted that it could be cold at Kinveil, but in the February of 1895 she was feeling it. Knowing vaguely that she was slurring her words, she said to the hazy figure by the bed, 'Hot pig', and then giggled. It would be funny if Shona thought she meant a pig from the furnace instead of a stone hot water bottle. Then she'd frizzle rather than freeze to death.

It had never been as cold as this in her childhood, no matter what the astronomers said. They claimed that their registers showed the temperatures had been the same in 1802 as they were now. Such nonsense! She could remember everyone having light summer clothes then, whereas now one wore the same things all the year round, give or take a vest or two. Hazelnuts had ripened then by the bushel, but just try and find one now! On June fourth, the king's birthday, there had always been the first strawberries of the season, whereas today they didn't ripen till July. And as for wild honey! Even thirty years ago there had been so many nests in the grass that the scythers had been forever stopping to raid them, whereas now, if one found a nest, there was no honey in it. Or so young Callum said. It was a long time since Vilia had gone looking for wild bees' nests.

'Uhhh!' she exclaimed, as a hard, hot object was pushed against her feet, and a voice said, 'Is that better?'

'Shona?'

'Yes, Vilia?'

'Nothing. I just wanted to know if it was you.' She curled her toes round the scalding bottle. Shona wasn't a day under eighty, but she hadn't changed since she was eighteen. Probably remembered Drew better than his mother did, for he had always been a shadowy figure to her. He had been handsome – hadn't he? – but his personality had never matched his face. Nature and nurture. Funny.

Vilia knew she was dying and was annoyed. She had set her mind on a hundred. But she wasn't going to last until then, and, if it came to the bit, she didn't really care. Truth to tell, she was bored. It was months – years – since anything interesting had happened. Fifteen years since she had had the pleasure of telling Theo and Gideon what she really thought of them, self-satisfied prigs that they were. How on earth had she produced such sons? Theo had died half a dozen years later, and Gideon in '91. And then Jermyn had gone eighteen months ago, which had been a surprise.

No one interesting had been to visit her for a long time. Jermyn's two girls, spinster schoolteachers, had come, and Petronella Barber, and some of Isa and Ian's girls; she could never remember which of them was which. Dull as ditch-water, all of them. Neil and Callum, Jermyn and Madge's boys had come, too. Vilia hadn't been able to discover how Neil, the heir, felt about Kinveil; too wide a gap between the generations for her to be able to read him.

How long was it, she suddenly wondered, since she had seen Peregrine James? *Sir* Peregrine James! It was gratifying that the business she had built up, almost single-handed, three quarters of a century ago, was now famous throughout the world, if for its military rather than its architectural ironmongery. Young P.J. was as infuriating as he had ever been, and Lady P.J. had produced six sons in a row. Distantly, Vilia remembered saying to someone that P.J. was *just* the kind of young man who would have nothing but sons, and there was a certain satisfaction in knowing that she had been right.

Ah, well. It was almost over now. The end of an old song. She wriggled a little, and kicked, and Shona came to fluff up the blankets and move the pig. Better, much better.

A face from long ago hung just above hers, and a light, vibrant, humorous voice murmured, 'Always, and forever.' Such love as that had been – brilliant, iridescent, beautiful. She remembered, still, how the jewel-bright gate had swung open before her; how she had gazed for a moment down the long, dark, frightening arches of the years, and then, wilfully, turned her eyes back to the loving, lovely threshold. And the years *had* been nightmare-dark, so that often – how often! – she had wished she had been wiser, then. But now, eighty years on, she couldn't quite regret it. Had *he*, she wondered? At least, out of all the agony of life, she had something to remember. The pretty, sprigged room in summer London, and the elegant, fragrant house in France. Now, when it was all over, she could forget the destruction and the instinct for self-destruction that had followed. Now, she could remember only a pure, perfect beauty. It was more than most people had. Such a pity everything had gone wrong. His fault, and hers. And circumstances. And other people. Yet there had been something, and it had been beautiful. Funny how the years changed one's perspective – not once, but again and again.

She yawned cavernously, and Shona began fidgeting with the blankets again. Vilia couldn't be bothered telling her to stop.

In another day, or week, or month, Neil Lauriston would become laird of Kinveil. She had suggested he might change his name to Cameron, but all he had done was smile, the deceptively absent-minded smile he had inherited from his father, and say, 'I can't do that, Great-grandmama.' She couldn't see why not but it didn't matter. It was the principle that counted.

Was there . . . ? She tried to work it out. Was there more Randall in him than Cameron? If Drew was half Cameron and half Randall, and Shona was half Randall and half Telfer, then Jermyn must have been fifty per cent Randall and only twenty-five per cent Cameron. And if that were diluted by Neil's Holman blood . . . Arithmetic was beyond her these days. Irritated, she gave up.

Ironical, though. And nice, in a funny kind of way. Because Perry Randall had always been part of her, whatever had gone wrong. A living part of her. Mungo – dear Mungo! – had known. 'Made for each other . . .'

And whatever Perry had contributed, it was she, Vilia Cameron, who had made sure that her great-grandson – their great-grandson – would inherit Kinveil in the end.

The purpose of so much of her life. She had won, she had won. Smiling, she closed her eyes and drifted towards death.

Epilogue   *August 1914*

Kinveil, when Callum Lauriston left it to return to London in August 1914, looked very much, he thought, as it must have done more than a hundred years before, when Mungo Telfer saw it for the first time. In that immutable landscape, his shiny new Mercer Raceabout looked every bit as out of place as it would have done in Mungo's day.

He stopped at the end of the loch to look back at the castle, perched on its island in the blue water, with blue skies above and a marvellous tapestry of blues and greens and purples around it. As castles went, it wasn't much, and people who expected a Balmoral, a kind of Windsor-in-the-Wilderness, were apt to feel let down. But although it boasted neither gas nor electricity, and although its conveniences were modern only by the standards of the eighteenth century, it still had an undeniable *je ne sais quoi*.

Callum had been innocently fond of the place as a boy, when his brother Neil, fifteen years older, had brought him up to visit their great-grandmother, but reading the family chronicle had changed all that.

What had happened was that Neil had inherited Kinveil when Great-grandmama Vilia died in 1895. And Neil didn't want it. 'Fine for holidays,' he had said. 'But can you see me retiring into that hermit's cave and leaving the world to go to the devil in its own way? No, thank you. There's no fun in that.'

For the next four years he had ignored it, apart from paying an occasional visit and letting it out for the shooting and fishing. Then he had gone off to the Boer War – ostensibly to see how one of Lauristons' new field guns performed in action, but really, his brother thought, because he was a buccaneer at heart – and had got himself killed.

At the age of nineteen, therefore, Callum had found himself laird of

Kinveil, and more than a little overawed by the prospect. Conscientiously going through Neil's papers, he had found an untidy and obviously unlooked-at drawerful that turned out to consist of eighty years of Telfer family chronicle. It seemed that Great-uncle Gideon had decided not to go on with it after 1880, and had arranged for the trust to be wound up. Then he had handed all the material over to Neil, who seemed to have stuffed it in his desk and forgotten all about it.

Callum virtuously resolved that he would do better, and made a note to go through it all carefully – some day. But being the kind of person who chose his reading matter on the basis of the last page of a book rather than the first, before he put it aside he cast a brief glance at Gideon's report of his last visit to Kinveil in 1880. The visit that had seen the final confrontation with Theo – who had died when Callum was six – and Great-grandmama Vilia. It was enough, more than enough, to arouse the liveliest interest in Callum. Soon, he was regretting very deeply that he had been too young and ill-informed to appreciate Vilia properly when he had the chance. What a woman!

In the years that followed, he had spent a good deal of his spare time on sorting out the papers, and the task had a curious effect on him. Most people, he reflected, scarcely even knew the names of their great-grandparents, or their laterals, collaterals, and descendants. But not Callum. By the time he had finished he knew them all personally, and had wept with them, and for them. He went up to Kinveil many times, trying to discover why it should have caused so much anguish and ruined so many lives, but by that day in August 1914 he still hadn't discovered the answer and supposed that, now, he never would.

What he had discovered was that he could never bring himself to make the place his home. His very bones turned cold inside him as soon as he set foot on the causeway. It was as if the shades of Luke Telfer, and Juliana, and her baby son, and Lizzie, and Ian Barber, and all the rest of them, were waiting for him on the other side.

All that old heartbreak, all those old tears, he thought, as he sat in his rakish little two-seater and gazed back at the landscape he might never see again. None of it mattered any more. The world was at war, now, and he was going back to London to enlist.

He had made his Will years ago, when he came into his inheritance. Everything was to go to Gideon's son, Steven, who was Callum's uncle but near enough to him in age and outlook not to feel like it. Callum wasn't sure whether Steven would want Kinveil; it wasn't something they'd ever had occasion to discuss. The assumption had always been that Callum would marry some day and bequeath the place to his children. But nothing was sure any more.

If Steven did want it, well and good. There would still be someone of Cameron blood to carry on the line, and Great-grandmother Vilia would have won in the end, as she died believing she had. And yet . . . It had been irony enough when, after her life-long obsession with bringing Kinveil back into her own family, her great-grandson Neil should have ignored it, though he had still been prepared to keep it. The supreme irony would be if her grandson Steven, knowing from Gideon the human cost of that obsession, chose to reject it completely.

Callum sat frowning at the bright scene, at the sea-girt little castle, that, on such a day, charmed both the eye and the imagination. He would add a codicil, he thought. Steven could sell the land, if he wanted to. But the castle . . . No. That, in justice, must be left to the sun, and the rain, and the ghosts it had created.

He pulled down his goggles, and cranked up the engine, and turned his back on Kinveil for the last time.